I0727866

THE FALLEN WORLD COMPLETE COLLECTION

C.R. JANE

MILA YOUNG

BOUND

BOUND

CONTENTS

DEDICATION

To anyone who ever looked up at the stars and dreamed.

BOUND

They came to Earth. They destroyed my life, took those closest to me, and now they're set on making me their own.

Ella Monroe has only one goal in life. To survive. Trapped in a world that's been taken over, Ella is reminded daily of everything that she has lost because of the Vepar. What was supposed to be a fun night out to celebrate her birthday turns into a nightmare encounter at a Vepar club when she catches the eye of three terrifyingly alluring men.

Powerful and terrifyingly seductive, the three Vepar make clear they will stop at nothing to possess her. Unable to escape, Ella is plunged into their dangerous and secretive world, where everything is more than it seems. Ella doesn't know what the future holds as their prisoner, but one thing is for sure. Their obsession knows no bounds...

They came in the night. There were no gunshots fired. No one's last breath was given for their kingdom or country. It was just over. And they were in charge. They told us that our governments had no choice...that they did what was best for us by giving in. As I watched the President and the First Lady be frog marched out the front gates of the White House by a group of their armed guards, the President and his wife with just one bag in each of their hands, it was clear to see that life as we knew it would never be the same again.

Years later, I would think back on that moment and wonder if that was the first time I had seen them. If they somehow sensed even then that I was out there and that I was something that they would want...something they would obsess over. I wondered if there was anything I could have done, any way that I could have run to ensure a different outcome.

It didn't do any good for me to think about what-ifs. The simple fact of the matter was that I was never given a choice. I belonged to them. I always would.

I

L*iar!*

"I didn't steal the money," I whispered to Greg to avoid the customers in the diner from hearing our conversation. Biting back the fury that danced through me, I curled my hands and stuffed them into the pockets of my skirt, concealing them. How dare he accuse me of theft after I'd worked here for the past year and covered every necessary shift, stayed until midnight to close up most nights, and even cooked the damn food when we were short on staff. I stared at my boss in disbelief. He may only be five foot three and sporting a shaved haircut to cover his receding hairline, but he reminded me of a bulldog with his squished nose, chubby cheeks, and down-turned mouth. His brown eyes squinted in an accusatory manner.

"You were responsible for the register," he barked, not caring that he was raising his voice.

My cheeks burned, and I opened my mouth to respond, but no words formed. I *was* the only waitress on hand today because Sandy called in sick, again, and was most likely having a full day of orgasms with her new boyfriend. *Lucky her.* The cooks couldn't have touched the cash since they never came up front. So that left me...

I exhaled loudly. "I know it looks that way, but it wasn't me. You know me, Greg. You know I wouldn't do that to you." I wished he'd installed cameras as I suggested months ago. Then we wouldn't be having this problem.

Greg huffed, his shoulders rising and falling. "The lost money will come out of your next check."

"No!" I reached out for him, but he batted me away, scrunching his nose as if I were no better than a fly.

"That's a douche move, man," Cherry's voice came behind me, my best friend who often came here for lunch and to bug me. She meant well, but this would only get worse if she tried to interfere.

I turned towards her and shook my head, mouthing the word, *don't*.

She ignored me and climbed out of the nearby booth located right behind the register and strolled toward us in her stilettos. "She's innocent until proven guilty. So, you can't dock Ella's pay without evidence."

Greg stood as tall as he was able, his hands gripping his wide hips, his name badge sitting at an angle across his heart. The corners of his lips twitched in distaste as he looked at my best friend. "My diner. My rules. You don't like it, both of you can leave." His voice rose and I realized that the rest of the diner had fallen silent, listening to our argument.

"Well," Cherry began, but I stepped in front of her.

"It's fine." My heart raced at the thought of losing my job when I was already living paycheck to paycheck. "I'll cover the missing money."

Cherry exhaled loudly behind me, while Greg just grinned.

"That was never a question," he replied snottily before he turned and marched into the back office.

"Fucking ass," Cherry murmured as she snatched my elbow to drag me to sit in the cushioned booth with her. "He can kiss my ass, that dick is lucky to have you working for him." She pushed over her half-eaten vegetable fries and I helped myself, deciding I might as well drown my sorrows in food. But the food didn't sit well in my stomach with all the worry that was churning through me. It also didn't help that I still remembered how real French fries tasted, and this "healthier" version couldn't compare.

I tucked the loose strands of hair behind my ear, but it was a losing battle as it fell right back into my face. "I'm going to lose half my pay, and after paying rent, I'll have nothing left to live off this month," I told her as I gloomily stuck another disgusting vegetable fry into my mouth.

I looked outside the diner window to the blue sky that was growing heavier with clouds. There was supposed to be a storm rolling in tonight and the sky was certainly starting to look foreboding. Just as I had that thought the sound of thunder boomed from outside sending a shiver down my spine. My grandma had always warned me that thunder was an omen, but I'd never given much weight to such supernatural tales. Not when my life was work, earn enough to pay my rent, and save enough for a car.

I sighed again. I was never going to be ahead. I had dreams once upon a time for how my life was going to be. They certainly didn't involve working at the Cinnamon Diner forever. I took the job twelve months ago as a quick fix until I found something that paid better. But this city rarely had opportunities and if they did, they filled up before anyone could think twice. A quick glance over my shoulder, and Greg was back at the till, shaking his head, counting the money again. *Asshole.* As if I'd steal the money. He probably took it and forgot.

I popped two more fries into my mouth and regretted it at once as my stomach riled up.

"Are we still up for tonight?" Cherry said, examining her long red nails nonchalantly that she obsessively wore as a tribute to her name.

My birthday. Right. It was easy to forget about things like that with how my life had been going lately. Or maybe it was how the world seemed to be going lately. Ever since *they* had taken over. Staring out at the sky again, I saw a jet fly by, a long electronic sign shooting out from behind it, reminding us all about registration, as if we could forget.

February 3, 2017 was when the world fell apart. It was done quietly. Everyone went to sleep the night before and woke up to an entirely different world. The churches had declared that they were messengers sent from God to warn us to change before the last days, but I was pretty sure the invaders were the gods themselves.

They told us they had come from a planet called Vepar and that they wished for everything to continue as before...but everything was different. The first thing to change was the required Registration. For some reason, only the women of the world were forced to register every six months. The Vepar wanted to know our names, ages, relationship status, and pregnancy history. Every woman was put on a mandatory special form of birth control that we were told was much healthier than the options we had available to us before. I would never admit it, but there were no terrible side effects with their birth control, and it was no longer a burden to take it. It was the only thing that I could say they had made better for us.

The next change was a mandatory "clean living" mandate. All food that was processed, fried, or had any chemical in it besides healthy oils was removed as an option. No longer could I pick up a hamburger or a pizza anywhere. Instead, I could have lentils or cauliflower pasta, or something equally disgusting. Everyone was required to enter a gym for an hour a day and we were scanned as we arrived to keep track. The bastards of course didn't make anything that was mandatory free so my already thinly stretched budget was now non-existent. I had been pulling double shifts at the diner for a year now, which in my opinion should have covered my hour of exercise, but I was barely surviving.

"Ella?" said Cherry impatiently, annoyed that I wasn't paying attention to her.

"Sorry, just a little tired. Yeah, I'm still on for tonight. You only turn twenty-three once," I told her, the thin thread of exhaustion evident in my voice. She pretended not to notice and stood abruptly. "I've got to hit the gym and then start getting ready," she told me, kissing me on both cheeks like she was some kind of fancy European instead of a girl from Brooklyn. She then walked out the door without another word. As I stood, I realized she forgot to pay for her fries. *There goes my ability to eat at all this week*, I thought wryly to myself, not able to muster annoyance at my best friend due to my exhaustion.

"Your break ended five minutes ago," barked Greg as he emerged from the back. I managed to not roll my eyes as I picked up Cherry's empty fry tray and moved to throw it away. *It wasn't as if the diner was currently empty or that I hadn't taken a break all day,* I thought to myself as I stared around at the restaurant that had cleared out after Greg's fit. My mind conjured up a million different things I would say to Greg if I was a little braver and if I actually had other options for a job. I grabbed a rag and wiped down the already spotless table, my mind full of a million places I would rather be.

I was dragging my feet by the time I finished even though we had hardly had any customers that afternoon. I didn't bother to say goodbye to Greg as I pushed out the front door and into the chilled air. October in New York was a glorious thing but all I could think about was how my heating bill was about to spike. I wondered how long I could survive a New York winter with just blankets. Maybe I could start sleeping in the gym locker rooms on particularly cold nights? My membership was practically as expensive as my one-bedroom loft.

Walking down the sidewalk, I couldn't help but notice all the advertisements featuring various Vepar. Another reason that they were considered gods? Their otherworldly attractiveness. They were built and shaped just like us, but somehow, they were more. Their skin was more perfect, their eye color was more intense, their hair color sparkled in the sun, their bodies were shaped like action heroes. Everything about them screamed that they were the pinnacle of what every human since the beginning of time had yearned to achieve. They were sexy bastards and it was unfair they got to be biologically more advanced on top of all the other ways they had us beat. An ad flashed across a screen and I got caught on the sidewalk, unable to take my eyes off the Vepar showing on the screen in the store window. He was beautiful. Even my hatred for their kind and the havoc they had thrust on my life couldn't prevent me from admitting that.

Just then a woman walked by wearing a perfume that my mother had always worn and whatever spell I was under was broken. Nothing, not even a ridiculously sexy face, could make me forget that the Vepar were responsible for the fact that I had been alone in the world for three years because of them.

So many people, in particular females, disappeared when the Vepar turned up on Earth. The aliens insisted they came in peace, as cliché as that sounded, and had never harmed anyone that we knew of. But the speculations spread that there was more to the Vepar's story, especially after our loved ones continued to vanish. Sometimes it felt like the rest of us were waiting for our number to be picked like a lottery, except this wasn't the kind of prize anyone would want to win. Lots of people insisted they were preparing us to breed with them, which I couldn't dismiss when we knew so little about their race. The majority of speculators insisted they were getting ready for a complete takeover of our planet, a takeover that would eliminate us. Wasn't that what invaders did? As far as I was concerned, I hated them and wanted zero to do with their kind. I wished they would vanish and return to their home planet, leaving us alone. Maybe if they hadn't come here, my parents would still be around, and I wouldn't be so alone.

I hurried along the sidewalk, tucking my handbag under my arm, dodging a young couple who stopped in the middle of the path to kiss. People flowed in and out of stores, chatting, laughing, many of them wearing gym gear. I squeezed in my hourly workout in the mornings because I couldn't think of anything worse than a spin class or doing weights after a long day on my feet at work.

I swung down an alley, leaving behind the hustle and bustle and bright lights of the city. Where I lived was about as opposite of the glitz and glamour of the city as you could get. As I walked, I passed trash cans and puddles that I was pretty sure were filled with urine. I went around the rear of the dilapidated Italian restaurant that filled up my apartment with annoying aromas that only served to remind me how hungry I was all the time. Shadows crowded in around me, and I pushed into a jog, always a little surprised at how much lighter and agile I felt since starting my gym workouts and starting to eat healthier. Didn't make me like the Vepar any more though. I missed my burgers and fries too much.

At the back of my rundown apartment, I grabbed an upside-down milk crate tucked near the wall and set it beneath the metal ladder just out of reach. I got up and seized the base of the fire escape ladder, then pulled it down. I made my way up, and once I reached the metal platform of the winding stairs, I kept going upward to the third floor. A cool breeze fluttered under my ponytail, cooling my neck, and bringing with it a tomato and garlic smell from across the alley, enticing a growl out of my stomach.

I avoided the front entrance since I was behind on my rental payments and the landlord lived on the ground floor. Like a hawk, he watched everyone who came and went, and I hoped to buy myself a few more days before I paid him by avoiding entering from the front.

Once I got to my window, I jiggled the wooden frame at the corner until it gave way. I then dragged the window up and climbed inside. Shutting it behind me, I locked it and switched on the light.

A studio apartment was all I needed, the bed on one end of the room, and the kitchen and a small table on the other side. The walls remained bare as I'd been on an unsuccessful hunt at flea markets since I'd moved in, looking for just the right images to hang. I toed off my shoes, kicking them aside, and walked across my cushioned rug that was one of the few things I had been able to find that I liked. It was the color of the brightest sky and always made me smile when I looked at it. A neighbor had held a sale and he sold it to me for twenty dollars. A bargain for sure.

I made my way to the fridge while unzipping my work uniform and shuffling it down my body as I walked. I tossed the uniform on the table, then reached into the fridge for the spinach and feta quiche and juice that I was rationing for dinner this week. The chef at work snuck me leftovers a few days ago after hours, saving my life this week since I wouldn't be able to afford any groceries with Greg cutting my check.

As part of the healthy living instigation, every morning, free bananas were made available by vendors on the sidewalk, all covered by the Vepar to encourage a healthy breakfast. The fruit went fast, so every morning at six a.m., I was down there, waiting for my small bag of goodies. Bananas and quiche would have to work this week.

By the time I finished my meager dinner, it was almost time for Cherry to arrive. I hurriedly jumped into the shower and got dressed for the night. I spun in front of the mirror in my black dress examining myself. The dress had spaghetti straps and cinched in at my waist. It also had a skirt that flowed in waves, falling about mid-thigh. It was my favorite dress and made me feel pretty which was a hard task with how worn down I always felt nowadays. I dried and styled my hair, a workout in itself since my long dark locks reached half-way down my back. I parted it at the side and sprayed the ends to keep the natural curl I had always liked. I was just picking up my mascara when a knock sounded at the door.

All I could hope was that it wasn't my landlord and instead was Cherry running a few minutes early. *Please don't let it be him.*

The knock came again, and I exhaled the breath I'd been holding onto. I moved to the door, avoiding the wooden floorboards that creaked, and peered through the peep-hole.

Cherry stood there, wearing a grumpy expression, blowing a breath of air upward, flicking at the blonde strands cascading over her eyes.

I unlocked the door quickly and pulled it open.

"About time." She rolled her eyes and strolled inside wearing a red, shiny dress with the deepest neckline I had ever seen. It fell clear to her stomach. The side split on her skirt flashed her thigh with each step, showing off her black knee-high boots. She twirled on the spot. "What do you think? Found it at a new boutique store that specializes in dresses that are supposed to look just like the dresses worn by Hollywood stars."

I closed the door and turned to face my friend. "It's gorgeous. You look so sexy," I said almost wistfully, thinking that I wasn't as excited about my old dress anymore.

"Exactly what I'm going for. And you look so cute, babe. We're going to have a blast for your birthday. Pick up some guys." She winked, her attention falling to my bare feet. She furrowed her brow at the fact that I wasn't ready.

"Give me two secs and I'll be ready," I told her, rushing to the bathroom to finish applying my make-up and then quickly stepping into my black heels. We left my apartment, out the front way, after Cherry's protest on using the fire exit. And it must have been my lucky day when my landlord didn't make an appearance. Cherry called an Uber and by the time we reached the club, I'd forgotten about my crappy day. I was ready to get drunk and party.

We stepped out on to the sidewalk in front of a building that must have once been a warehouse. The brick walls had all been painted black, along with the double doors. Golden words sat over the entrance on a plaque that seemed to glow. *The Garage.*

A bouncer stood outside, decked out in black.

Cherry grabbed me by the elbow and walked me closer. "Everyone's going to this club. It's the hottest ticket in town!"

The bouncer studied us for the longest time. When he finally opened the door, I offered him a smile as I passed by, reaching into my handbag as we walked to put away the ID that he hadn't asked for. An explosion of music poured out of the establishment; a deep, fast beat that made my blood seem to pump faster.

Cherry dragged me inside, giggling and pushing aside the black curtains in the entryway. We entered the nightclub.

The music vibrated around us. The floor beneath my feet bounced with each beat, and my stomach swirled with excitement. The black theme continued inside, a circular bar with blue lights surrounding the dance floor. Overhead there was a second floor, and people were hanging by the railing, looking down at the dance floor and its mass of writhing people. Wall to wall was filled with people dancing, no room for much else. Beaming lights sailed overhead, while the DJ stood in a cage elevated over the dance floor.

"Wow. This is fantastic!" I couldn't stop grinning, and Cherry squeezed my hand at the delight in my voice.

"Told you." She drew me deeper into the crowds. Bodies squished up against me as we walked, and my feet were trampled on a couple of times. It was to be expected in a place this packed.

"We need drinks," I called out, trying to be loud enough to get past the noise, and Cherry glanced back, nodding.

By the time we reached the bar, we found a small open space to breathe. "This place is sick." I glanced around, marveling again at the fact that the place was filled to the brim with what seemed like a million people. I couldn't wait to get out on the dance floor.

Cherry said something, but I didn't hear her because my gaze had settled on three men sitting at the end of the bar, one of them sizing me up. All high cheekbones, he wore a mischievous grin. Except, I'd seen him before. I wracked my brain, thinking for a few moments before it finally hit me. I'd seen him on a billboard in the streets.

I gasped and rocked on my heels, grasping Cherry's arm. Panic dug its claws into my chest. "Did you know, there're Vepar here!"

She wiggled her eyebrows. "Of course. It's a Vepar nightclub."

2

My skin was crawling, and I felt sick to my stomach. I looked at my best friend who was making eyes at a Vepar a few chairs away before turning to scan the rest of the crowded room. Now that I was looking at everyone in the room it was impossible to miss the fact that they were more than just humans. Every single being in the room looked like they had marched off the cover of a high fashion spread of supernaturally gorgeous individuals. Standing among such beautiful beings in the dress that I had thought was so good-looking before, I now felt like a dowdy child that had shown up at the wrong party.

As my gaze skipped across the room, my eyes got caught on three Vepar seated at a booth a few feet away. I pushed my hair behind an ear, nervous as hell. While everyone in the room was beautiful, these three were enough to make me forget how much I hated the Vepar for half a second. While two of them were gazing around the room disinterestedly, the third was staring right at me. His hair was tousled, but not in an artificial way like was the current style. The dark blonde locks were cropped close on the sides, but longer on top, and had enough wave that I suspected they were impossible to tame. Sitting on the far side of the booth, I could see his sexy broad shoulders, emphasized by the perfect cut of his suit. He would have looked almost too perfect if it weren't for the fact that his tie was askew, as if he'd been yanking on it, and the fact that his body seemed to hum with a kind of restless energy like he was looking for something even though he was at a club. His cool blue eyes seemed to see right into my soul and coupled with the hard-as-steel jaw, he was very intimidating. Everything about him was intimidating. And sexy. Really damn sexy.

"Ella, I need twenty dollars," said Cherry, yanking my attention from the blonde predator.

"What?" I asked, my brain a little scrambled from the intense stare down I was just engaging in.

"I ordered us shots. I need to pay," she said in an annoyed voice, gesturing at the Vepar waiter who was impatiently waiting for us.

I looked at her wide-eyed. "Um sure," I said, cringing as I got a twenty out of my wallet. A twenty that I couldn't afford to part with after the debacle at the diner today. She had at least the decency to offer me an apologetic shrug as she grabbed the money.

"I guess I forgot my wallet at home," she said, handing the money to the bartender who then pushed what looked like four candy apple green shots towards us. Alcohol had managed to stay available despite the health restrictions. Apparently the Vepar were just as fond of drinks as us humans were.

I tried to push away my annoyance at the fact that I was paying for my own birthday shots by draining my two shots as quickly as I could. If I was going to get through this night, it was going to be because I was drunk. As I gasped at the burn, I could immediately feel myself relaxing. My muscles unflexed, and my breath slowed down.

"Those were just regular shots, right?" I asked, as the room began to spin a little bit.

"It's a Vepar bar," she said to me haughtily. "Of course, I was going to have us try Vepar liquor."

She slid off her barstool ungracefully, her almost non-existent dress briefly flashing the fact that she wasn't wearing underwear, and I hurriedly averted my eyes as she nonchalantly adjusted herself.

"I think it's time to see if the Vepar men like me as much as human men do," she said, tossing her long blonde hair behind her and doing a shimmy. She scanned the room before homing in on a target, a well-dressed Vepar with slicked black hair who was making eyes in our direction. I couldn't be sure, but it looked like he was looking at me rather than Cherry.

Unperturbed, Cherry grabbed my arm and began to drag me behind her, completely forgetting that this was my birthday and I might have something else that I wanted to do besides be her wingman for the night. Cherry was already getting sloppy from the shots we'd taken at the bar and she narrowly missed running into a waiter who was hustling by with a full tray of glasses. Unfortunately, her narrowly missing the waiter meant that I couldn't swerve out of the way in time and the tray knocked me in the head, sending me falling backwards, the back of my knees hitting something hard. I stumbled into what felt like a rock-solid seat that I realized belatedly was someone's lap.

My cheeks burned from falling into someone, and I sat frozen. I looked up into a shocking green gaze that I immediately recognized as belonging to one of the men that I had noticed earlier, and then I immediately averted my eyes. That wasn't much better as I could see that the Vepar all around me were staring at me, the clumsy human.

I shook my head, telling myself to turn my head and face the situation. Turning, my breath caught a little. He was a damn good-looking man...alien...Vepar...whatever they were called. I could fall into his gaze, and I suddenly found myself picturing us naked with me beneath him. I trembled at the thought, yet I couldn't get his face out of my thoughts. So gorgeous it would stop anyone in their tracks. I'm sure he was used to that kind of attention, based on the little smirk on his face. I'm sure females of both species froze when they crossed his path. He had the greenest eyes I had ever seen. They had a haunting twinkle to them that just added to his allure. He looked like he could see all of my inappropriate thoughts. Heat crawled up my neck, and I prayed that wasn't the case.

Looking around for help, I caught a glance of Cherry walking out the door with what had to be one of the only other human males in the club. Tears gathered in my eyes and my throat thickened at the fact that my so-called best friend was leaving me on my birthday in a Vepar club of all places. And we'd just arrived too. I squirmed to get up, but the arm around my waist held firm.

"What's the hurry, my pet?" he whispered in my ear, his breath sending tremors down my spine.

"I saw someone I know. I should go say hello," I responded weakly, not wanting to let him know that I was now all alone at the club.

"I can hear your heartbeat, pet. I know you are lying." His words carried a light growl, and while they should have scared me, I found myself becoming intrigued. I twisted around, still trapped in his lap, and tumbled into those stunning eyes again that were too pretty to be human. They reaffirmed I wasn't sitting in the lap of a human.

He was most definitely a Vepar.

My breath hitched all the way down to my lungs, and as if sensing my fear, he smiled. His upper lip lifted slightly, a dimple crinkling on his chin. Warmth radiated from his expression, and his gaze fixed on me as if a secret lay between us. Then he gave me a knowing nod.

The blush burning my cheeks was a dead giveaway of the way he affected me. My mouth twitched, and I fought a smile, reminding myself whose lap I sat in.

The monsters who came onto Earth and took over. The ones that were most likely responsible for all the missing people, missing people like my parents.

I'd heard people say to stay hidden when a Vepar made an appearance. *If they don't know you exist, they can't take you.*

And I'd ruined that royally by landing in one's lap. Frantically I looked around again to see if there was any way out of the situation. I needed to run, get away as fast as I could. I needed to forget tonight, forget Cherry, forget my birthday.

I wriggled in his grasp. "You can let me go now."

"What's the rush?" he said, his voice velvety smooth against my ear, and the shivers returned to my skin from his breath on my neck. If my body reacted that quickly from his closeness, I had no hope of saying no to him. He'd somehow get me in bed with him, and before long, I'd vanish from society and probably end up in a prison on another planet. Or so the rumors insisted.

I glanced down at his strong arms, the corded muscles beneath the tanned skin. His shirt was the color of midnight and was rolled to his elbows, giving him a casual look despite the fanciness of the club. Around us a mix of Vepar and human women danced, cheered, and drank. I didn't see any sign of the Vepar's two companions that I had seen him with earlier. Had they separated so they could study the humans and select their prey?

I twisted in his lap to look at him again, and it was a terrible mistake. My heart skipped a beat and I lost my words being this close to someone so incredibly handsome. My fingers tingled with the urgency to reach over and touch his face to see if he was real.

Was this his real form? Was it possible for a whole planet to be full of nothing but genetic perfection? If so, it must have been disappointing to arrive on Earth to find we weren't all spectacular models. I lowered my gaze, curling my shoulders forward, reminding myself I was nothing spectacular. My work uniform hung over my thin frame during the day, and my black dress tonight was nothing special. I wore my dark chestnut hair in a ponytail most days, though I had toyed with the idea of putting purple highlights in it. But just like with most things, I never gained the courage.

I pushed myself out of his grasp, suddenly feeling less scared, but more out of place. I didn't belong here, not with these gorgeous people, not at his club, and definitely not pretending this man would be interested in me. Even as an extraterrestrial being, he'd overlook a simple female like me, unless his goal was to hunt down a slave. Even Cherry had picked up a guy, while every inch of me itched to run back to my apartment.

Quickly, I climbed out of his lap, suddenly appreciating his kindness in showing me interest. I shyly glanced away and turned toward the exit when iron fingers wrapped around my wrist.

"Where are you going, my pet?"

I twisted around to face the man with the devilish eyes, his strong hand wrapped around mine like a shackle.

"I made a mistake in coming here," I answered, not sure if I was talking about coming here without knowing it was a Vepar club or coming here in the first place because I didn't belong. Something about the tenderness in his gaze coaxed me to speak the truth, because I suspected he picked up on small nuances like my nervousness, that I was alone, and how vulnerable I appeared.

I might be vulnerable, but I wasn't about to forget how dangerous the creature was holding on to me.

"Humans have a saying that there's no such thing as coincidences. Do you believe that?" he said randomly, tracing my lips with a whisper soft touch. Somehow the act seemed more intimate than sex. This being was looking at me like he knew all of my secrets or at least felt that my secrets belonged to him. He's touching me so possessively, not even pausing for a moment to ask my permission. I'm suddenly even more aware that the creature in front of me is a predator hidden behind a pretty face. I have to leave.

I shrugged, trying to hide the fact that I felt almost debilitated by fear, and tucked a strand of hair behind an ear nonchalantly. "Haven't given it much thought. Guess if enough strange things keep happening, I'd question the coincidence."

His thumb on the hand that was holding my arm in a vice grip started to rub a circle on the inside of my wrist as he held my gaze, so intent and focused I had no choice but to start shivering. Tremors wiggled south to the pit of my stomach and lower. I'd never had a man stare at me with such depth, not even the boys who'd shown semi-interest in me in the past. This here...this was something else.

"What can I get you to drink?" he asked smoothly, his eyes still on me like I was a shot of single malt whiskey.

The voices, thumping music, and mass crowd in the club floated somewhere behind me. My eyes flitted anywhere besides his face as my mind raced with how to escape. As much as my body responded to his attentiveness, how the heat between my thighs inflamed into an inferno, I was sure I wouldn't survive the night if I stayed any longer.

"Thanks, but maybe next time." I said, trying to draw my hand from his without success.

"Sometimes the hardest thing in life is letting go," he said randomly, finally letting go of my hand.

I should have turned and run at that moment, but something in the way he said that last statement made me hesitate. "What do you mean?"

"Change is never easy."

I blinked against the lights flashing in our direction. "I don't know what you're talking about," I said, the panic starting to bleed into my voice. I regretted my outburst at once as a glimmer of amusement arose in his eyes at my blatant fear.

"You'll find out soon, pet." He released my hand, and I stumbled on the spot. "You better go catch up to your friend."

His riddles made no sense, but considering he knew I came with Cherry meant he'd been watching me before I fell into his lap. I spun and pushed through the crowds, needing to leave, get away, and never visit this club again.

"I'll be seeing you around," he called out, and I glanced over my shoulder one more time. But the seat he lounged in was empty.

Where the hell was he?

I ran from the club like I was being chased by demons, the feeling that someone was watching me settling over my skin like dread.

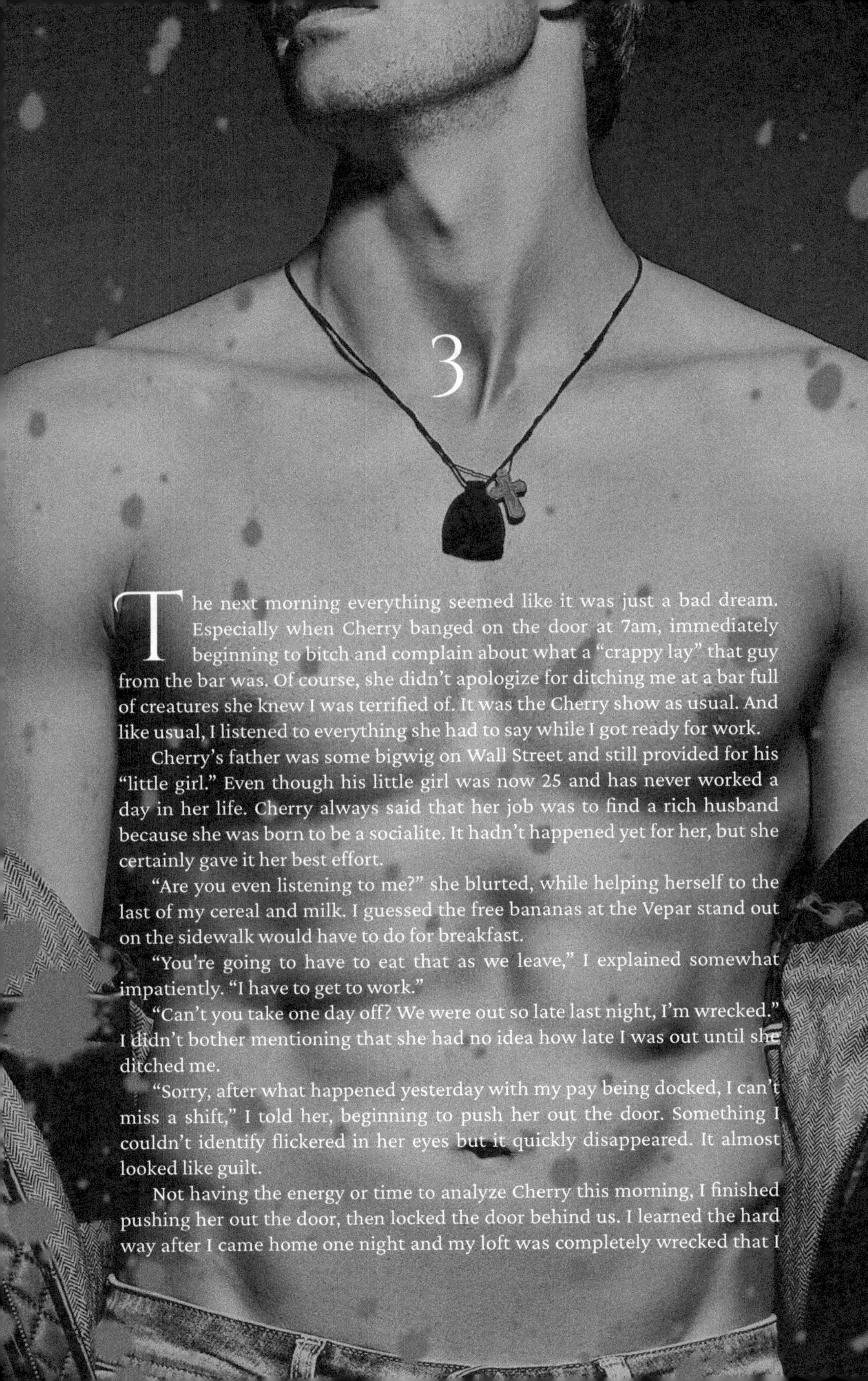

3

The next morning everything seemed like it was just a bad dream. Especially when Cherry banged on the door at 7am, immediately beginning to bitch and complain about what a "crappy lay" that guy from the bar was. Of course, she didn't apologize for ditching me at a bar full of creatures she knew I was terrified of. It was the Cherry show as usual. And like usual, I listened to everything she had to say while I got ready for work.

Cherry's father was some bigwig on Wall Street and still provided for his "little girl." Even though his little girl was now 25 and has never worked a day in her life. Cherry always said that her job was to find a rich husband because she was born to be a socialite. It hadn't happened yet for her, but she certainly gave it her best effort.

"Are you even listening to me?" she blurted, while helping herself to the last of my cereal and milk. I guessed the free bananas at the Vepar stand out on the sidewalk would have to do for breakfast.

"You're going to have to eat that as we leave," I explained somewhat impatiently. "I have to get to work."

"Can't you take one day off? We were out so late last night, I'm wrecked." I didn't bother mentioning that she had no idea how late I was out until she ditched me.

"Sorry, after what happened yesterday with my pay being docked, I can't miss a shift," I told her, beginning to push her out the door. Something I couldn't identify flickered in her eyes but it quickly disappeared. It almost looked like guilt.

Not having the energy or time to analyze Cherry this morning, I finished pushing her out the door, then locked the door behind us. I learned the hard way after I came home one night and my loft was completely wrecked that I could not leave Cherry unattended at my place. I wasn't sure why she came to my place so often in the first place since her father paid for a luxurious apartment by Central Park. There was a lot I didn't understand about that girl.

Cherry and I had just parted ways, and I was about to cross the street to arrive at the diner when a luxurious black town car pulled up in front of me. The back-seat window rolled down slowly. I rubbed the goosebumps out of my arms. A beautiful blue-eyed man with hair so blonde it seemed to sparkle in the sunlight that streamed through the car window was staring at me from inside the car. It was the Vepar that had been watching me last night before I fell in his green-eyed companion's lap.

"Need a ride, Ella?" he asked, his smooth voice sending shivers down my spine.

He knew my name? I tried to remember if I had told his Vepar friend my name last night, but I couldn't remember. My mind felt addled, everything from the night before seemed blurry, like it had all been in my imagination. A terrible dream that had me waking up feeling hot and uncomfortably turned on this morning...

Shaking my head at the direction my thoughts had turned, I turned my attention back to the fact that a Vepar that I had never met was offering me a ride and somehow knew my name. There was no way that this was a coincidence and he had just happened to be driving by and decided to offer me a ride after his friend told him about me. Yeah, right.

Everyone said to stay away from the Vepar, but it appeared I'd gained the attention of multiple ones last night. I'd have to correct that now.

"Thanks, but I'm just going down the block," I told him, my voice trembling as I started to jog away as the crosswalk light turned green, giving me the okay to cross the street. The truth was the diner was quite a bit more than a block away, but I would run twice that distance if it kept me away from the charmingly dangerous stranger. What did he want?

I didn't turn around to see if he was still there as I ran away. It wasn't necessary since I could feel his gaze following me until I made it around the block and was out of sight.

Once I arrived at work, I stored my bag in the locker in the back and put on my apron, then I hurried into the unusually full diner and started my shift. The place was packed. Where had everyone come from today?

The business meant that the day flew by fast. As usual, Sandy had called in sick, so I served all the customers on my own. It was amazing that Sandy could consistently fail to come into work, yet she managed to keep her job. I wondered if her new boyfriend was actually Greg.

Speaking of Greg, he didn't say a word to me all day, not even hello, but he watched me like a hawk, especially each time I used the register for customer payments. Bastard still believed I stole the money the other day, and that annoyed me more than I cared to admit. I knew I shouldn't care what he thought but I worked my ass off, and he was treating me like a criminal. With each passing hour, the walls of the diner seemed to close in around me as my exhaustion and frustration grew. I kept going, in auto mode, taking orders, smiling, delivering food, and cleaning tables. Luckily little thought was needed for those activities because my mind was far too occupied with all of my current problems plus the new Vepar one. Questions like, how was I ever going to get ahead in life? Was I ever going to have enough money to do more than just scrape by?

I finally admitted to myself that I needed to get back to the job hunt. There had to be something, even another waitress job that would pay better and that wouldn't work me to the bone. Not that I had an aversion to working hard, but I needed at least a little bit better quality of life if I was going to live to see my next birthday.

At the end of my shift, I stepped out of the diner with my handbag, pretending not to hear Greg complain to the cook about having to close for the night on his own, and how he needed more reliable staff. Unlike other days, I didn't jump and take the responsibility. If he didn't trust me, then why should I work after hours for almost nothing in return?

Outside, orange and blues streaked across the afternoon sky and a cool breeze cooled the perspiration on my neck. My heels ached with each step from being on my feet all day, but something about the colors overhead reminded me of my parents. A longing swept through my chest at not having them in my life, not having someone to talk to when I felt so alone. We grew up in an apartment, and like me, they lived from one paycheck to the next, but we were happy, and we had each other.

Instead of crossing Bexter Road to head home, I kept strolling straight ahead past storefronts and people shopping, unable to stop remembering my parents. And when I missed them, one location always eased the sorrow somewhat. A little slice of paradise where I could leave society behind and I could think in peace.

It wasn't long before I stood in front of the six-foot-tall gates made of twisted metal rods. The ends were curled in a circular pattern, and while spiders had made the corners of the gate their home with a maze of webs, it still was a beautiful sight to me. Behind me lay the city museum, but it was closed as it was past 4pm, which meant that most of the patrons to the garden had left as well. I had one hour to enjoy Greenwood Botanical Garden before it closed.

The crunch of tires sounded behind me before I could go in, and I turned around, for some reason expecting the black sedan from this morning to be waiting for me. Instead a white hatchback full of laughing teenagers coasted past. I laughed at my jumpiness and proceeded into the garden.

The incident turned my attention from my parents back to the Vepar. He had offered me a ride this morning. Just thinking about it made my earlier goosebumps return. I wanted to believe that it had just been chance that he had found me as he had been passing by. But I knew I was in denial.

I had been unextraordinary my entire life. The most out of the ordinary thing that had ever happened to me was becoming an orphan. Human men didn't pay me any attention. Why would a Vepar?

I hurried into the gardens, tiny pebbles crunching under my worn-out sneakers. I silently chanted to myself that everything would be okay...it had to be.

Lofty trees with bottle green leaves flanked my path, and the blossoming landscape was filled with the fragrance of jasmine. Up ahead, copious flowery beds lay in every direction, segmented by colors. Whites, fuschias, oranges, and violets. I followed the curved path to where the trees grew denser and shadows fell over the land. Birds chirped and the scratching of dried leaves indicated that little critters or lizards were scurrying through the foliage beside me.

There wasn't a person in sight, which on most days I preferred. Today the solitude made the hairs on my arms stand on end. I kept glancing over my shoulder, feeling like someone was watching me. But every time I turned to look, there was no one there. So, I kept walking.

I marched up the hill. I passed the glass greenhouse before crowning the hill which gave the best view of the city. From this height, the city seemed to lay beneath my feet. You could see the way the tall buildings had been so carefully regimented and ordered. The descending sun illuminated the shimmering glow of pollution that lay just above the city.

Up here I could escape it. Getting my fill of the view, I took a seat on a bench overlooking a Koi fish pond several feet away. From here, the water looked opaque green, its surface ruffling from the breeze. There were lily pads in bloom, and I watched as their white petals fluttered in the wind.

I inhaled deeply and slowly savoring the smell of the greenery around me.

Dad had once said that when he died, he wanted his soul bound to the gardens so he could roam our favorite place forever. Maybe it was wishful thinking on my part, but I came here often in the hope that if I didn't sense his spirit, he was somewhere out there still alive.

This had been our place. My parents would bring me to this park for family picnics every week. But that had been before the world changed, before the Vepar took over...before I lost everything.

With a long exhale, I dropped my handbag near my feet and remembered the tales of how he'd proposed to Mom. He had brought her to this very location with takeout burgers from their favorite burger place for them to eat, and a diamond ring in his pocket. He had used his last savings to buy the band, but that was my Dad. He always told me he'd sell the clothes off his back for my mom. He would have done anything for her...anything for us.

They had loved each other with a love that everyone around them had envied.

Mom had admitted to me once after Dad had told that story for the thousandth time that she knew what he had planned all along. But when he fell to his knees in this exact spot, she had still burst out crying from joy even though she expected it.

Something in my chest tightened as I pictured the scene, and then of course my mind inevitably tried to picture my own engagement. Somewhere in the far-off future...if at all. Tears pricked my eyes thinking about the fact that my parents wouldn't be there to see it, or even hear about it.

Heaviness sat in my chest, tearing me apart at not knowing if my parents were still alive. For so long, I told myself they were somewhere, maybe held captive, but it had been years since they vanished. Not a word or note...not anything. They wouldn't have just left me.

Hope.

I held onto it like a lifeline, praying one day I'd see them again, see their smiles, hear their voices. I sighed. I was just kidding myself.

The minutes ticked by as I sat in the park, my mind heavy with sorrow. The shadows surrounding me stretched across the landscape, and the fiery sky darkened. A quick check of my cell showed I only had ten minutes remaining before closing time. My stomach was growling in hunger too, so I collected my bag and headed home.

Outside the gardens, cars filled the road. As I turned down the sidewalk, a black vehicle parked across the road caught my attention. It was the same one from this morning, the same one I had been looking for over my shoulder all day. It sat there with its tinted windows rolled up, and my stomach sunk all the way to my toes.

Please don't let it be him. There were a million black sedans in this city. I told myself it could be anyone. Tucking my chin into my chest, I held my bag tight under my armpit, and walked as quickly as I could away.

Looking back, the car was still parked, and I memorized the number plate. VRA001. When the brake lights came on, a small cry fell from my lips.

I started running, my heart hitting the back of my throat as my unreasonable fear grew. The park stretched out for blocks, so when the cars stopped at the traffic lights, I crossed the road toward the store fronts and apartment buildings. Without pausing, I sprinted as fast as I could, dodging an elderly couple waiting for the bus, and swishing past a group of girls chatting. One quick look back showed me that the black car was driving off in the opposite direction.

I should have breathed easy as its tail lights faded into the distance, but I couldn't stop running and I couldn't remove the fear clinging to my ribs. A sudden gust of wind came out of nowhere, ripping at my hair and clothes, tossing garbage from an overturned trash can across the ground. But still I kept running.

By the time I arrived home, I could barely catch my breath. I didn't bother going around to the back of the building to go up the fire escape. Instead, I ran through the front, not even looking at my landlord who was skulking around the lobby. Once I got to my apartment, I shut the door behind me fast, and then I ran across the apartment and locked the window too.

Once I finished securing the place, I flopped onto the couch in the dimly lit main room, still clutching my bag, and trying to catch my breath.

"Shit!" I started laughing somewhat hysterically at the thought that I had just run across town for no other reason than I had seen one of the million black sedans in the city. I was being ridiculous.

A small voice inside my head reminded me that there *was* a chance it had been him. The notion sat like a boulder in my gut. I had heard the warnings about the Vepars since they had arrived, people saying that you should never gain the attention of the beautiful ones. What if I had?

I sat my bag on the cushion next to me when my phone dinged with a message. I flinched and dug my hand into the bag to grab the phone. Greg. My boss never messaged me, and I frowned, reading the message.

I've changed your shift from day to afternoon. This includes closing up the diner. Starts immediately.

Bastard! Reading the message over and over didn't change the cold hard facts. He was cutting back my hours and wanted me to clean and close up while he left early. He was pissed because I hadn't volunteered my free time, and now I was paying the price with a permanent punishment if I didn't find another job quickly. My chest burned up, feeling as if it might detonate like a supernova.

Who the hell did he think he was?

I tossed my phone onto the couch and leaned forward, hugging my middle. Fewer hours meant less money, so this made my decision to find a new job even easier. First thing in the morning, I'd visit every food joint in the city with my resume.

I glanced across the room at the fridge, thinking about the stale quiche that awaited me for dinner. My eyes raked across my gym bag as I looked around the room. I groaned and sagged into my seat.

"Oh, crap!" I'd forgotten to do my daily gym time, and I didn't need another reason for a Vepar to pay me attention. I dragged myself off the couch and headed to the closet to change into lycra pants and a tank top, hating my life while mapping out the shortest route to the gym that would keep me from prying eyes...or black sedans.

4

The morning winds were ferocious, pulling at the nicer clothes I had put on to apply for jobs. The plastic folder with copies of my resume trembled in my hand from the breeze, threatening to fly away if I didn't hold on tightly. Cars honked as they fought through traffic on their morning commute down the two-lane road. I pressed past the ocean of pedestrians on the sidewalk and made my way toward the Good Morning Café located on the corner of a busy intersection. Once inside the establishment, I pushed the door against the whistling wind. Finally closed, I patted down my hair and straightened my posture before glancing at the half empty diner and catching the eye of a young man in jeans and a freshly pressed white shirt. He studied me with amusement on his face and what seemed like interest. The badge on his chest said his name was Jack.

Then he strode closer. "Hi, there. Seat for one?" he asked with a fake smile I knew too well.

"I'd like to speak to your manager, please."

He shook his head. "Not in, sorry. Can I help you?"

Chewing on my lower lip, I pulled out my one-page resume from the plastic folder and handed it to him. "I'm wondering if you were hiring?"

I handed him my resume, but he didn't take it. "I have several years' experience in waitressing, ordering supplies, and even stepping in as the cook." I said quickly. My voice sounded nervous even to me, and heat crawled up my neck at the thought of another rejection.

"Look," he began, and already my gut clenched. I'd heard the tone he used at the last five diners I visited, and I knew what came next. An excuse of them not hiring at the moment, the place was downsizing, or I wasn't the right fit… whatever that meant.

I lowered my unaccepted resume and turned to leave. I stopped mid-turn when Jack surprised me by saying, "The manager will be in in about a half an hour, so how about you give him your resume then?"

I glanced up at his kind smile and grinned, my mouth tugging into a smile at the first positive response I had received today. "Thank you."

"Follow me." He waved me into the café, and I saw the spark of recognition in his eyes, the understanding of how hard it was to find a job. "I'll get you a coffee on the house until he arrives."

I was already in love with this place, not to mention, having someone treat me like a human and with respect.

The aroma of coffee filled the air, immediately making me feel a bit better. A shiny orange color adorned the corners of the small round tables and the napkins were the same hue. Everything else had a rustic wooden look that seemed like it would make a customer feel right at home. Light jazz music played from the speakers, and customers chatted over their breakfast and coffee. I loved it here. The door opened behind me as someone else walked in, bringing with it a cold breeze. I shivered slightly.

Jack pulled out a chair at a small table near the window, overlooking the hustle and bustle outside. "Won't be long," he said with a gentle smile.

I took a seat, and Jack went to attend to a customer waving him down.

It was about thirty minutes before the bell on the door rang again, signaling that someone had just walked in. Looking up, I expected to see a stranger strolling through the door. Instead I saw *Him*. It was the green-eyed god from the night at the club. The one whose compelling voice had made me want to curl up in his arms forever. The one who called me his "pet."

He wore tailed black pants, and a blue, long-sleeved shirt, looking like he belonged in a boardroom. Except, I'd never seen a man look this good in business attire. I suspected he wore only the best brands considering how perfectly the clothes flowed over his strong form, emphasizing the broadness of his chest and shoulders...the way his waist tapered in. I lifted my gaze before he caught me staring.

What was he doing here, anyway?

He strolled into the café as if he had been here a million times before, except he wasn't looking for the host so he could be sat at a table, he was looking right at me. Almost as if he knew I'd be here.

I was standing up from the table as he sat down across from me.

"Sit down, pet," he told me with a grin. I immediately sat, almost as if I couldn't help but bend to the authority in his voice. That intangible quality that threaded around his words made me want to listen to everything he had to say.

A couple tables down, Jack sent me an inquisitive glance. I averted my gaze so he wouldn't feel like he needed to come over to my rescue.

"Why are you following me?" I finally asked after we had sat there just staring at each other for what seemed like ten minutes.

"Who said I was following you?" he replied with a grin. "Maybe I just felt like an omelet from this charming establishment."

"Look, I'm not interesting, I promise. There are a million other girls who I'm sure would amuse you much more than me. Please, just leave me alone. And tell your friend that he needs to stop following me as well," I added as an afterthought, thinking about the black car. I assumed that they had to be friends of some sort since they had been talking at the club.

"How do you know what I'm looking for?" he asked.

I just stared at him, moving my lips dumbly but not knowing what to say.

"Ella, let me be perfectly clear that you *are* what I'm looking for. And that's not going to change."

Every inch of me froze over. "How do you know my name?"

He glanced down at my resume sitting face up on the table. My name was on full display, along with my address. *Fuck.*

I snatched the file and tucked it under my arm, then finally stood to leave. Even a new job wasn't worth staying here with this creature.

"Where are you going?" he mused, with that grin that both filled me with dread and made my stomach hurt with how attractive it was at the same time. "There's nowhere you can go that we won't find you," he said. And somehow, I knew he spoke the truth. But to hear the words out loud left me shaking. I curled in on myself at the realization that I was trapped.

Stupid, stupid, stupid. Why hadn't I run away that night the second I had realized what he was?

He stood before I could leave. "Stay, enjoy breakfast on me," he said, throwing a few bills on the table that looked like they would cover a dozen meals at this place. "And if you get the job, just know you'll be calling in to give your notice, very, very soon." He stared at me with such intent that I didn't doubt his words, even if they didn't sound menacing. The threat behind them lingered in my mind. Was that how my parents went missing? Vepar decided to target them, and then one day, poof, they simply disappeared? My knees weakened at the thought of that happening to me.

On that ominous note he walked by me, making sure to brush up against my body as he did so. Hard and solid, he smelled of fresh air and a sexy musk. A thought I cursed myself for. I was an idiot for thinking of him as attractive in any way. Especially considering he'd clearly just threatened me. I knew better than most that beauty was only skin deep.

What could I even do? The authorities had all been infiltrated by the Vepar, and what they said went.

I slid shakily back down in my seat once I heard the bell ring on the door signaling he had left. My hands curled in my lap, and I stared outside the window to see him strolling across the road before vanishing into a crowd of people.

What was I going to do? I couldn't stay here. I had to leave, but where would I go with no money? I stared at the notes of $100 on the table more carefully now, noting he'd dropped $500 without a care. I barely came close to making that much in weeks of working lately.

At that moment, Jack came back. "The owner just got here if you still want to talk to him," he said, giving me a concerned look. "Is everything okay?"

I nodded numbly. In another life maybe I could work here, maybe I would even have ended up dating Jack, he was attractive and seemed sweet enough. And he certainly was giving me the look like he was interested. But I couldn't even picture what having a normal life would be like now. My head hurt and fear crowded in my mind like the cobwebs on the front gates of the botanical garden.

I was about to leave without talking to the owner, but a kind looking man in his 60s with salt and pepper streaked hair chose that moment to show up at my table.

"This is the owner, Mr. Kinsley." Jack said as he gestured to the man.

Mr. Kinsley gave me a kind smile that didn't hold any of the menace or sleaziness that my boss, Greg's did.

Within twenty minutes, he'd offered me the job and I was set to start the next day. I bounced on the inside, wanting to scream with excitement. Slipping the money off the table that the Vepar had left for me, I waved goodbye to Jack and Mr. Kinsley, and I walked out of the cafe in a daze. Had that just happened?

I should have been more excited, especially knowing I could now march over and tell Greg to fuck himself. But I couldn't find it in me to fully celebrate. Not after the conversation with the annoyingly attractive Vepar hanging over my head. I still didn't even know his name. Yet he seemed to know everything about me including where I was going to be in a random job search. And now he knew my address. Hell!

Sighing, I found myself heading back to the Botanical Gardens, needing the comfort that only they could provide. As I strolled through the blossoming paths, my mind seemed to clear. Surely this was a short-term fascination for the Vepar. There was no way someone like me could hold his attention. Everything would be fine, it had to be. I was a nobody in a city filled with attractive women.

I had almost talked myself off the ledge when I rounded a corner, and there sitting on a park bench, reading a book, was the third Vepar that had been watching me that night at the club. While the other two had overwhelming beauty, this Vepar's was more understated. With thick hair the color of mahogany, and eyes that reminded me of caramel, he studied me as if I was the most interesting thing that he'd ever seen. He tilted his head to the side, and I could tell instantly he enjoyed observing, studying, analyzing things. Most likely people. In this case... Me.

We both exchanged looks, and the pause should have been awkward, but it wasn't. "So, are you following me then as well?" I finally asked, breaking the tranquility, praying and wishing on everything that he wasn't here for me and that this place could remain a safe space for me.

He cocked his head, still studying me. I might as well be an insect under a microscope. He seemed like he was trying to discover everything about me in that moment. My past, my fear, my loneliness.

"Well, do you actually speak?" I asked, not even recognizing my bravery...or the stupidity I displayed.

At my comment, he smiled, and it was the most devilish grin I'd ever seen. "I like your directness," he said. His eyes lit up, and the corners of his mouth creased into an even wider smile. His smile was somehow so much more though because he smiled with more than his mouth. I could hear it in his voice. I took back whatever I'd been thinking before about his beauty being more understated than the other two. He was glorious. A thought I immediately wanted to punch myself for.

"Did you know that there are around 391,000 different types of plant species that your scientists have discovered on this planet so far?" he asked in a smooth, cultured voice.

I stared at him like he was crazy.

"Um, okay. That didn't really answer my question," I said, beginning to back away slowly, thinking that this Vepar was perhaps a little unhinged.

He grinned bashfully, if a ridiculously good looking Vepar could really be bashful. "Sorry, I've been trying to think of the perfect thing to say to you when I got to talk to you. And obviously that wasn't it."

He patted the empty bench next to him, looking at me expectantly. I should have turned and ran, but then what? Keep bumping into these three Vepar who seemed to be paying me way too much attention? The Vepar in the cafe had warned me to not get comfortable with a new job, so I'd be a fool to ignore this threat and not discover more about their intentions. This creature seemed kinder than the others, almost human with his attempt at finding something interesting to say to me. Thinking it over, I finally took several slow steps forward and joined him on the bench, placing my bag between us as a makeshift barrier.

"Why are you here?" I asked, glancing up at him as he reclined, his arms by his side, his gaze drifting off into the distance toward the city. The morning sun illuminated the golden stubble across his strong jawline, lighter than the hair on top of his head. The corded muscles in his neck lured me in. He was the perfect package just like the others.

Many people had said their beauty came from an illusion they used, a disguise to conceal their real appearance. And if that were true, what did they look like underneath? Scaly with a tail? I laughed internally at myself because I'd obviously watched too many science fiction movies. Where would he even hide his tail?

Never in a million years would I have pictured myself near someone as handsome as him, but then again, who would have guessed Earth would end up invaded by aliens. I almost laughed out loud that time at how ridiculous it sounded, but here I was sitting by a real live alien.

"Did you know there's a Russian village, Oymyakon, which experienced the lowest recorded temperature for a location permanently inhabited by people. -96 degrees."

I met his gaze, unable to understand why he was talking about. "Why do you do that?"

"Do what?" he shrugged nonchalantly.

"Keep ignoring my question."

"Perhaps you're not listening close enough to see I *am* answering your question."

I ran a hand down my face, frustration bubbling in my chest as I recalled the other Vepars' riddled way of talking to me in the club. But these men weren't from our world, so maybe this was their way of communicating. Never directly but hinting at things. So, I'd try to remain patient and follow their logic.

"Okay." I twisted to face him, tucking a bent leg between us. "So, your world is frozen and is no longer inhabitable, and that's why you're here?"

He shook his head. "Look beyond the obvious answer."

I sighed heavily. "Can't you just tell me?"

But he sat there, silence filling the space between us, and he studied me, waiting for my response. Was this part of his experiment? See how the humans' mind worked, what we focused on?

"You asked why I'm here, which could be taken as either why we came to Earth or why I'm in this garden. I answered in a way that best suited both of those questions."

I blinked hard, my head buzzing with trying to make sense of his response. All right, I could do this. "This Russian village has people permanently living there despite the hellish cold, so they've learned to find a life in extreme weather. They've adapted." I met his smiling gaze. "And you're on our planet to acclimate and identify the differences. And for the garden, you want to find out more about me. To adapt." My mouth split into a grin, and I couldn't help it, especially when he nodded and smirked.

"Good girl."

That small gesture made me perversely happy as if I were back at school and I'd just passed the hardest exam. But now half a dozen more questions prodded my mind, and if getting the answer to them required this much work, I'd die of exhaustion.

"Let's start with something simple. What's your name?" I tucked loose strands of hair behind my ear.

"Why do you do *that*?" he asked, studying my hand as I lowered it from my hair.

In all honesty, I hadn't given it much thought or even noticed the habit half the time. "Nerves I guess, and-" But I paused, reminding myself who I spoke with and that this wasn't a casual conversation with a guy I crushed on. This Vepar acted normal and interested and polite, but I still had no clue about his intention. Sure, he wanted to get to know me, but why?

I cleared my throat and straightened my posture before lowering my leg and turning to face the city in the far distance. "Why are you and the other two following me? And be straight with me."

Instead of responding, he stood. "I'd better be leaving. I'll see you soon, Ella." And with those few words, he strolled down the path, leaving me alone with renewed fear bottled in my chest threatening to swallow me whole.

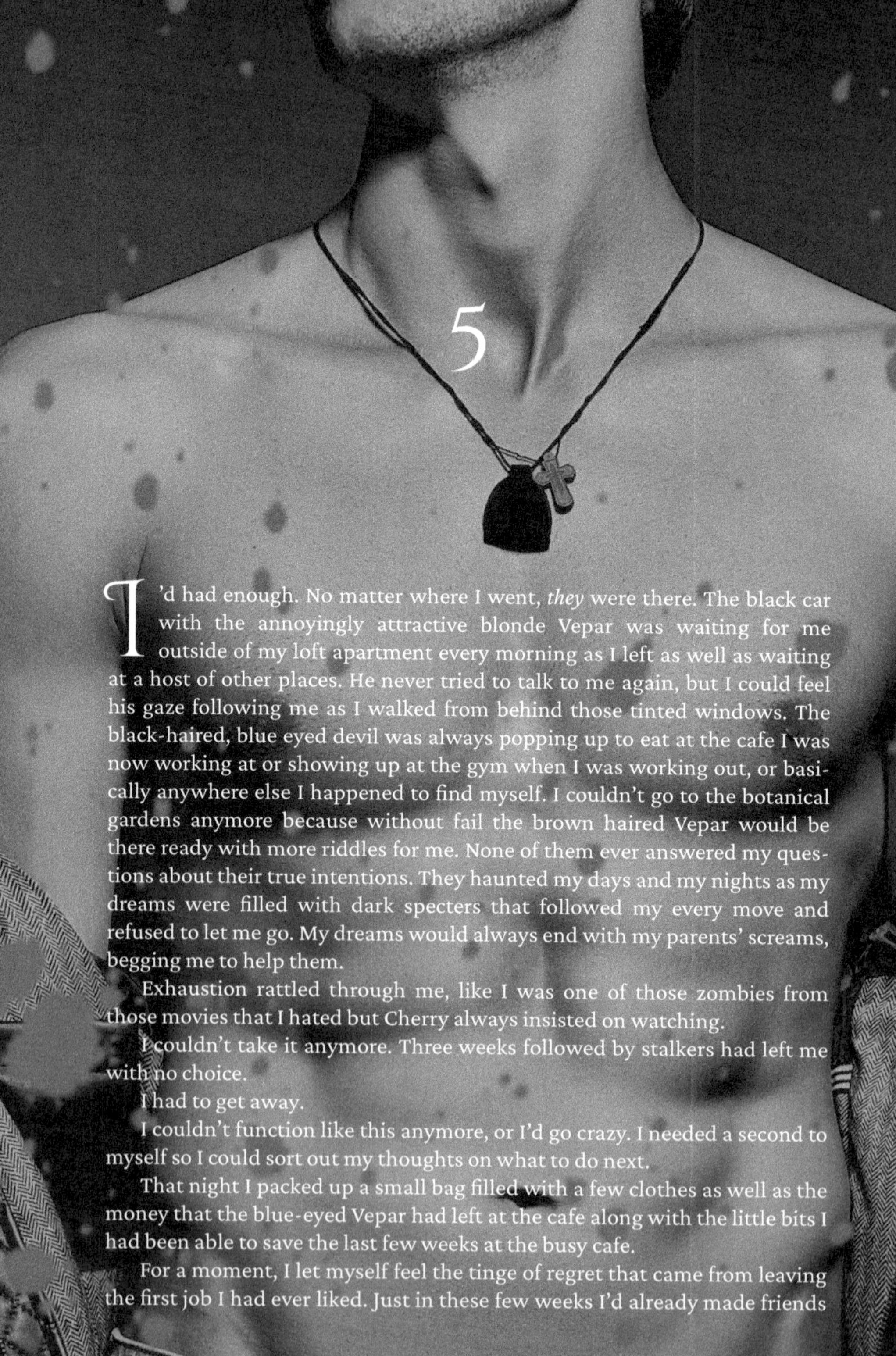

5

’d had enough. No matter where I went, *they* were there. The black car with the annoyingly attractive blonde Vepar was waiting for me outside of my loft apartment every morning as I left as well as waiting at a host of other places. He never tried to talk to me again, but I could feel his gaze following me as I walked from behind those tinted windows. The black-haired, blue eyed devil was always popping up to eat at the cafe I was now working at or showing up at the gym when I was working out, or basically anywhere else I happened to find myself. I couldn't go to the botanical gardens anymore because without fail the brown haired Vepar would be there ready with more riddles for me. None of them ever answered my questions about their true intentions. They haunted my days and my nights as my dreams were filled with dark specters that followed my every move and refused to let me go. My dreams would always end with my parents' screams, begging me to help them.

Exhaustion rattled through me, like I was one of those zombies from those movies that I hated but Cherry always insisted on watching.

I couldn't take it anymore. Three weeks followed by stalkers had left me with no choice.

I had to get away.

I couldn't function like this anymore, or I'd go crazy. I needed a second to myself so I could sort out my thoughts on what to do next.

That night I packed up a small bag filled with a few clothes as well as the money that the blue-eyed Vepar had left at the cafe along with the little bits I had been able to save the last few weeks at the busy cafe.

For a moment, I let myself feel the tinge of regret that came from leaving the first job I had ever liked. Just in these few weeks I'd already made friends and more money than I had in a few months of working at the diner. Jack and Mr. Kinley had fast become some of my favorite people who I'd ever met, and I would miss talking to them. Hopefully they didn't worry too much about me when I abruptly disappeared. Jack knew something had been going on by the way I ignored the Vepar who came into the cafe every day, going so far as to switch sections when he was sitting at my tables.

Opening the window to the fire escape, I steeled myself for what lay ahead. Creeping down the stairs I kept my eyes out for any of them to appear. They seemed to know all of my habits down to what I ate every day and what I wore. It was reasonable to believe that they probably knew I used the fire escape most days because of my landlord. All I could hope was that me leaving in the middle of the night wouldn't be anticipated by them and they wouldn't be around.

I got to the ground without incident. Peering around the corner I looked at the street to see if anyone was around. I gasped when I spied the sleek, black town car, waiting across the street. Did he sleep in the car? Fear sliced across my consciousness as the full reality of the situation struck me.

This was beyond liking someone, this was an obsession.

I backed away from the street, convinced he couldn't have seen me peeking around the building, and I headed down another route. I was going to try Cherry's first. Cherry had been "busy" since my birthday with the guy she had met at the Vepar club. And like usual when she met a new guy, I hadn't seen or heard from her since then.

But she was my best friend. She would take a break from her little love bubble to help me out. She had to.

It took me twice as long to get to her apartment as usual since I had to take the long way, but I was thrilled when I managed to make it to her place without being stopped. About halfway through my trip it had started raining, but as I stood outside Cherry's place, I didn't care that I looked like a drowned rat, I was just happy that I was going to be safe.

I knocked on the door. Music played from inside along with the sound of people laughing. Was she having a party? A party that she didn't invite me to? Hurt filled my stomach, but I continued to knock on the door. *Answer, Answer, Answer,* I chanted in my head as the minutes passed and no one answered. I had no intention of returning home tonight so this had to work. What I craved more than anything was to feel safe for a little while, to laugh with my friend, and have her tell me things would be okay.

Finally, I just tried the door, and to my surprise it was unlocked. Cherry had always been lax about her security even though every human understood to lock their door since the Vepar invasion. You never knew who might be waiting outside and wanting to get in...

I walked into the entryway of her apartment where she had framed photos of the night sky; one pebbled with stars, another of the Milky Way. So many gorgeous images that didn't really fit with Cherry's style. Cherry had no clue about the constellations, nor was she even interested in anything universe related. She had once told me the pieces were conversation starters for when she brought a guy home to make herself look intelligent. While I loved reading about the wonders of the world and beyond, it was just another thing that made me wonder how Cherry and I had ended up staying such close friends over the years.

I knew the answer of course to why we'd become friends... after *They* came to Earth and my parents vanished, I questioned what I had left to fight for after losing everything. The city of New York fell into chaos, everyone stealing and ransacking homes in their panic over the invasion. I found myself trapped in a grocery store one day, while outside, an angry mob of frightened people attacked anyone in their path. They were burning down the stores. And there, in the candy aisle I found Cherry, hiding amid the licorice, crying. I took her hand and together we found a way out through the rear of the store. Guess we'd stuck together ever since out of the pure terror we'd shared. She once told me she'd be my sister and stay by my side always. And I'd been clinging onto that hope ever since, making excuses for all of her shortcomings because I didn't want to be alone. But lately it'd been harder to ignore everything, and I'd found myself questioning her behavior.

Just thinking about those chaotic times sent a chill racing down my spine.

It's the end of the world, everyone had screamed. Panic spread like wildfire across the world, lasting months.

Soon after, the Vepar had broadcasted their rules for our behavior and how everyone who broke them would be punished. No stealing. No killing. Return to our normal lives or else, they insisted. No one knew what the consequences entailed, but when more and more of us went missing, it didn't take long for people to catch on that those who disappeared never came back. Order returned fast to our lives; order born of fear. And then the other rules came into force about females registering regularly, for us to exercise daily, and so on. No explanations, just orders of what to do next like we were being prepared for something big.

I shook my head at the direction my thoughts had taken and took a step forward in Cherry's apartment through the hazy air. There was a thick cloud of smoke that assaulted my senses and it grew thicker as I moved deeper into the apartment, making me cough. There were people everywhere in her living room dancing and drinking. So many people spilled out onto her balcony, overlooking the city. The dance music thumped so loud that it seemed to pound the inside of my skull.

Cherry was sitting on a guy's lap on the couch in her living room, a contraband cigarette in her hand. I noticed that the man she was rubbing herself all over was not the one she'd said she spent the week with or one that I recognized from the club. It was another man she must have picked up. He was tall and lanky with short hair and was pretty ordinary looking. Very unlike the usual dates she picked - all muscles and gorgeous. I just stared at her for a second not believing that while I was having the worst few weeks of my life, she apparently had been partying it up with a crowd of strangers that I had never seen before.

"Cherry," I finally yelled, straining to be heard over the music and the loudness of the party guests.

She looked up at me after I had called out her name a few times. It had to be my imagination but when she first looked up at me it almost looked as if she was annoyed to see me. The expression faded so fast that I couldn't be sure what I had just seen.

"Ella," she said, in the fakest voice I had ever heard from her.

"Can I talk to you?" I asked, letting the desperation I was feeling leak into my voice. She stood slowly, whispering something into her guy's ear, a man that upon closer inspection looked extremely greasy and disgusting. I couldn't imagine where she'd picked him up at.

I started walking towards Cherry's bedroom, looking back every few seconds to make sure she was still following me. There were people everywhere and they all seemed to be closely acquainted with my best friend. One guy we passed even managed to stop Cherry and stick his tongue down her throat before she could follow me again.

I gave a little screech when I walked into her bedroom and there was the guy Cherry had picked up at the Vepar club, balls deep in another girl on Cherry's bed of all places. I expected Cherry to look annoyed, but she just laughed when she saw them. "I need you to move the party somewhere else, baby," she cooed at the couple who seemed to be even more enthusiastically going at it with an audience watching them.

Looking up at Cherry, the creep grinned and pulled out of the girl, not having any problem with the fact that he was butt naked in front of Cherry and me. He took the girl's hand and pulled her out of the room, both still naked, shooting a cheeky grin at Cherry as he passed us.

I eyed the bed and shivered in distaste. It was looking less and less likely that I was going to be able to stay here. And since when was Cherry into swinging?

"What do you need me for?" she snapped at me. "I obviously have stuff going on right now," she continued, not sounding shamed at all over the fact that she was having a giant party that she had failed to tell her best friend about. Not that I'd attend such a sleazy affair, but it was the principle of not being invited.

I let that argument drop just as I did about everything else in our friendship that made me upset.

"I need help," I told her.

Cherry's face remained unchanged at my pronouncement, so I continued. "There are three Vepar that have been following me ever since that night at the club. They're literally everywhere, Cherry. I can't get rid of them and I'm scared about what they're going to do to me. Can I stay here for a little while just until I can come up with a plan?" My breath raced as I waited for her to answer.

Cherry burst out laughing, the kind of laughter that would make anyone cry a little at the fact that someone was laughing so hard at them.

"Three Vepar are following you?" she gasped. "Where do you even come up with this stuff?"

Fire climbed over my neck and cheeks. "I'm telling you the truth!" I snapped

"Oh, honey," she said with a disdainful glance. "If you're jealous that I haven't been talking to you this week, this isn't the way to get my attention back with some made up story. I'm allowed to have other friends." Her voice rose in anger, and she gripped her hips.

I looked at her shocked, my mouth hung open. "You can't honestly believe I'd make this up?" I whispered.

With a raised chin, she began to walk away from me. "I have guests to get back to. You know the way out, don't you?" she asked in a condescending voice as she disappeared from view out the bedroom door.

I sank onto her bed in disbelief before quickly jumping up when I remembered what I'd just witnessed happening on the bed. I slowly made my way back through the party to the front door, taking one last look at my best friend who was now making out with one guy while the one from the club finished his business with his lady friend on the couch next to them - in full view of everyone. Who the hell were these people Cherry was mixing with?

While part of me toyed with the idea of dragging her out here and getting her to open her eyes to what she was doing, I also felt betrayed. An ache curled around my heart, squeezing it tight, reminding me that this wasn't the first time Cherry had let me down.

More than anything though, I felt hopelessness as I stepped out of the building into the night. The rain came pouring down in sheets, drenching me to my bones in seconds and fitting my mood perfectly.

What was I supposed to do next?

I couldn't go home and keep putting up with the Vepar following me. But I also didn't want to sleep on the streets. Looking around, I remembered that there was a small motel a few blocks away that we had stumbled across one night when I was trying to herd a drunk Cherry home. Thinking of the money the Vepar had dumped on the table in the cafe, I decided that wouldn't be a bad option.

A night or two of being alone, hidden, without having to be afraid sounded amazing. Maybe I'd splurge and get myself a big tub of chocolate ice cream and drown myself in it. I hugged my backpack to my chest, trying to keep it as dry as possible, and ran down the sidewalk in the direction of the hotel. The rain fell in chaotic direction, and the violent wind slammed into me making the walk seem ever longer than it really was.

This was turning into quite the night. Not only had my friend turned her back on me, and three Vepar were following me, but now I was stuck in a crazy thunderstorm. I just hoped I wasn't hit by lightning.

The rain fell hard and diagonal as if it meant to wash me away. It pelted into the sidewalk, knocking into buildings, roofs, and cars. Water splashed up to my knees, drenching my sneakers, making each step make a squishy sound. But I kept going past the store fronts and fancy hotels, watching as my surroundings became seedier and seedier. People darted past me, hiding under umbrellas and staring at me with pity, but I kept going, because in that moment, I felt pity for myself too. For my friend letting me down, for the fact that I had to run away at all. I wanted to scream at Cherry, maybe even throttle her. She had been a bitch tonight, and I was right back where I always was...taking care of myself.

After popping into a convenience store to grab a frozen meal and some snacks, I turned right at the next street corner where the storefronts grew sparse and walked towards the neon light of a sign flashing that vacancies were open at the Palace Motel.

This place was anything but regal. A three-story, concrete building was surrounded by a parking area filled with weeds growing out of the cracks in the path. Metal stairs were visible, leading up to the various floors. I somehow doubted the safety inspector had visited this place in years.

A young couple were drunkenly swaying as they ran up the path toward the stairs through the rain. I did the same, targeting the reception door. I burst inside and shut myself in while water dripped down my face and clothes creating a small puddle on the floor beneath me. Even my underwear was soaked.

I turned around to the large reception room. The counter on the right had an older woman picking at her nails, and on the left sat a dusty couch where two men in silky shirts and jeans lounged, legs wide, their eyes all over the newcomer. Me.

Ignoring them, I swung toward the receptionist and made hasty steps toward her.

She glanced up, still cleaning her nails. "How many nights?"

"Umm." I tottered on my feet, unsure how long I planned to stay when I had limited funds and just needed some time to think things through. Check out would be 10am and I wasn't working tomorrow, so I could at least hide here all day. "Two nights please," I finally said.

"$172 for two nights. Towels are in your room." She swiveled on her stool and picked a random key from the wall of hooks behind her before tapping something into the computer on the side.

I dug into my bag, juggling the bag of food, and pulled out two bills. I slid them across the counter holding my breath that she wouldn't ask for a credit card.

The fact that I was paying in cash didn't even faze her. Evidently this was the type of establishment where that was commonplace. She didn't even ask me to show her my license. Once she examined the cash, apparently checking to make sure it wasn't counterfeit, she handed me my change and the key on a ring with a tag for my room number.

"Number 222. Just give the door a jiggle as it gets stuck when it rains. Have a pleasant stay." Her smile was anything but genuine... It belonged to someone bored and exhausted. And who could blame her when this was where she had to spend her time. I could only imagine the type of things she had to deal with here.

"Thanks." I smiled and collected my belongings before turning toward the glass door. Outside, the deluge continued, and I tucked the key and money into my pocket, before reaching for the door. A shadow fell over me from behind.

Thinking I'd forgotten something, I turned, expecting the lady from the counter. Instead it was one of the men from the couch, wearing a purple silky shirt, open half-way to showcase his hairy chest. He smiled with yellowing teeth, even though he looked to be in his late twenties. He really should take better care of himself, but I somehow doubted he'd appreciate me suggesting he brush at least twice a day.

"You got an appointment tonight?" he asked, slouching against the faded wall with his hands in the pockets of his jeans, while he stared at me with a sly grin. His gaze trailed up and down my soaking wet body.

An Appointment? I had no idea what he was talking about.

"I need to get to my room," I said, turning back around as two young girls, maybe eighteen or nineteen, rushed inside with an umbrella they shared. A massive man followed them, clearly some kind of guard for the women.

I stepped back as they splashed water everywhere, including on me.

"Bitches," the guy snapped. "You're getting me fucking wet."

They sneered but never said a word as they rushed over to the other man by the couch, taking a seat on either side of him. They all chatted in whispers, and only then did I realize they most likely were hookers and these guys were pimps.

"So?" The purple shirt guy asked. "You up for a fun night? I'll get you a warm meal." He glanced down at my bag with its microwaveable chicken meal, chips, and tub of ice cream. "And some fresh clothes. We can all do with a fresh start. I'll have your back." He sniffled and rubbed the back of his hand under his nose.

Fresh start. Yes, that was exactly what I needed. I had to stop fooling myself that I'd ever get ahead in my current life, especially with three Vepar on my heels. I knew exactly what I had to do over the next two days. Come up with a plan to leave this city, maybe the state. Relocate to a small town where things were cheaper, where I could keep to myself. Maybe I'd explore getting a job at a school or something better than a cafe. I'd start an online course to get ahead and be able to demand better pay. And a small town would probably have fewer Vepar...or hopefully no Vepar.

I didn't know where a place like that existed, but I had two days to work out a complete rehaul of my life.

"Yo, you're being fucking rude, just ignoring me." His voice climbed, but I didn't have time for him.

"Thanks for your insight," was all I said, gaining myself a confused glare. I ignored his attempt at further conversation, and I darted outside where the ferocious wind and rain once again hammered into me.

Within minutes, I stepped into room 222 and slammed the door shut behind me, quickly locking the two flimsy locks available on it. A new sense of excitement and nerves coaxed my pulse into a race. I was finally doing this... Making the change I'd been pondering for months. Sure, I just earned a new job, but what good was that if the Vepar were planning on kidnapping me, or whatever they had planned? I'd start new. I'd done it before, and I could do it again.

I switched on the light to see a small room with a double-sized bed against the one wall, brown patchy carpet, and a round table with chairs at the back. Nearby stood a small counter with a coffee machine, packets of coffee, filters, and several cups. Looking around I found a microwave on the bathroom counter. Perfect.

It was a crappy room, but somehow it didn't feel as terrible as it could. Here I didn't have to look over my shoulder wondering when the Vepar were going to show up next.

I dumped my bag on the table and prepped my frozen meal, starting the coffee maker up too so that I could help myself warm up. I then stripped off my wet clothes and pulled on the folded robe I found in the bathroom.

Yep, tonight was the start of a new beginning. I giddily picked up the ice cream and plastic spoon that I had gotten from the store and ripped off the lid. For once, I was going to try doing things differently, starting with eating dessert first. I dug into the ice cream and pushed aside the worried thoughts that somehow the Vepar would track me down no matter where I went. If I thought like that, I might as well give up right now.

6

aking up felt like I was treading through a fog, I couldn't quite
get to my destination. I shifted in and out of consciousness for
what felt like days. Strange voices flitted around me, liquid was
slipped down my throat, I could feel someone touching my hair...but still
I slept on.

When I finally emerged from my deep sleep, it felt like I'd been sleeping
for years. There was sunlight streaming in from a large window to my right
that took up almost the whole side of the room...a very unfamiliar room I
might add. This wasn't my place or the seedy motel.

Panicking, I tried to rack my brain for where I was. Had I gone out with
Cherry and gotten drugged? Sleepwalked? Was I still dreaming? A million
different scenarios ran through my head until I fell on one that filled me with
the most dread of all.

They'd taken me.

The Vepar.

The strange three men who'd been following me around for weeks.

Sitting up in bed, I was relieved to see that for the moment, I was at least
by myself in a giant bedroom easily twice the size of my loft. I sat in the
largest bed I'd ever seen, easily able to fit four sleeping adults. Moving my
legs, I noted that the silky sheets were also the nicest I'd ever felt as they slid
against my skin. Wherever I was, the person who owned this place owned
expensive things. And if I was kidnapped, this had to be the strangest prison
I'd ever seen.

Looking down at myself, I found myself wearing a flimsy white nightgown. My brain started to short circuit as I realized I wore nothing under-

neath, meaning that someone had taken off my bra and underwear and had seen everything.

Dread crept over me at the thought of what they'd done to me while I lay unconscious, but as I shuffled out of the bed, I sensed no pain, and especially not the kind I'd expect between my thighs if someone had forced themselves on me. Someone had broken into the motel room, carried me away without anyone noticing, redressed me, then laid me to sleep in a bed that would have belonged in a real palace. Not the run-down motel Palace.

I had to be dreaming.

But if it was the Vepar, and at this point that seemed the most likely scenario, how the hell had they found me at the motel?

Getting out of the bed, I walked on shaky legs to the window to look out and find my location. I gasped at the forest that spread out in front of me for as far as the eye could see. No sign of the skyscrapers that usually graced my eyesight. Wherever I'd been taken, it was a long way from home. My heart beat like it was trying to escape, matching my situation perfectly because I was about to have to try and escape.

A lock clicked behind me, and I backed into the corner, looking around wildly to see if there was anything, I could use to defend myself.

The door cracked open and an older, plump woman opened the door. Her silvery hair fell to her shoulders. "Oh good, you're up," she said cheerfully as if we knew each other. She started bustling around the room, going over to the bed and beginning to straighten the sheets.

Adrenaline flooded my body, and I bolted through the door she'd left open.

I heard her say, "Oh, dear," as I left the room, but no footsteps followed me to signal she was trying to stop me.

A flight of stairs lay a ways down the hallway, and I flew down them not sure what I was going to do if the Vepar were waiting for me down below. I just knew that I couldn't stay still any longer.

I jumped the last few steps, landing on the wooden floorboards with a loud creak. They were cold beneath my feet, icy almost. I glanced around to the open kitchen I'd entered, flooded in bright sunlight that was pouring in from the enormous windows. Everything was sleek lines, white, and very clean. The L-shaped counter was made of white marble, peppered with the latest kitchen gadgets including a mixer, stainless steel coffee machine, juicer, blender, and mini oven. The sweetest aroma of pancakes found me, and my stomach betrayed me, gurgling with hunger as I realized I didn't remember ever getting to my frozen meal last night. I stared at the stack of pancakes on the island counter accompanied by an array of syrups and cream and chopped fruit. I couldn't remember the last time I'd eaten something so decadent. I obviously wasn't going to get to eat it this time either.

Footfalls sounded upstairs, and I spun on the spot, searching for a way out. There on my right, stood a slightly open door with what seemed like sunlight shining out of it. A way out!

Adrenaline coursed through me, and I sprinted forward. When I dragged the door open wider, I ran straight into someone solid as stone. Stumbling backward, I whimpered, staggering over my feet, only to notice someone darting forward from the doorway to capture the mountain of blueberries that had flipped out of the bowl in his hand. Tiny purple balls rained down on me.

I fell on my ass, the tiny fruit tapping the floor around me. I looked up in dismay to see the blond haired Vepar who'd been following me around in the black town car studying me with a raised brow from the doorway.

"Going somewhere?" he asked in an amused tone. He was wearing nothing but a pair of loose pajama bottoms that hung low, showing off that "v" line that every girl seemed to be obsessed with. I hadn't thought that it really existed before now, and I couldn't stop staring. I had to stop.

He glanced down at the blueberry covered floor. "Guess we'll have to have strawberries this morning," he said with a sigh, beginning to walk past me, not bothering to pick up the blueberries or help me off the floor. I stared after him, my mouth hanging open in shock. I stood shakily and turned to bolt again for the door.

"There's nowhere for you to run, my pet," came another voice right as I took my first step. Moving toward the door I was about to run towards was the dark haired Vepar who seemed to be everywhere in my life recently.

"Where am I?" I asked in a trembling voice, suddenly very much aware of how thin my nightgown was. He took a step closer, his gait smooth and predatory. That was a trait of the Vepar that had always scared me, every-thing about their movements were a little too fluid, a little too perfect...a little too inhuman.

The Vepar studied me, not answering my question. He was dressed in jeans and a tight-fitting black t-shirt that went well with the bad boy image he had going for him. I could see the hint of a tattoo peeking out from the top of his shirt.

"Bring her in here," the other Vepar called from the kitchen. As the black haired Vepar in front of me took another step closer, I panicked, my fight or flight instincts taking full effect. I had already tried the flight, apparently now it was time for the fight. I flew at the Vepar, scratching and clawing all the skin I found, shrieking as I did so like I was possessed.

Suddenly his hand encircled my neck in an iron grip, cutting off my air flow so abruptly that I couldn't breathe. I tried to claw at his hands, but I might as well have been a child swatting at him with how little of a differ-ence it made.

Leaning in close to me, he whispered in my ear, "Are you done yet, pet?"

I was just about to pass out, all the fight drained out of me, when he abruptly let me go. I flopped to the floor, squishing several of the blueberries underneath me as I fell. Footsteps sounded behind me.

"Pick her up and bring her here," the blonde haired Vepar snapped. I felt myself being picked up by the waist and something that almost felt like a caress across my hair calmed me as I walked. Had that been in my imagination?

The black haired Vepar set me down in a chair way more gently than I thought he was capable. Still trying to recover from my momentary strangling session, I stared at my surroundings, keeping the two Vepar who were now both watching me in my sights as I did so.

It was clear I was in some sort of home, and not just a house, the nicest place I'd ever been to. There were at least five doors leading from the kitchen alone now that I looked more closely, making it unlikely that I would have been able to find a way out of this place quickly even if the Vepar hadn't appeared. The mansion looked enormous.

"Hungry?" the blonde asked, setting down a giant stack of pancakes with strawberries on top in front of me. I stared at the food, my stomach growling and making me achingly aware once again that it had not had proper food in a while.

"How long have I been out?" I finally asked as I picked up my fork to take a bite, figuring that I needed to keep up my strength if I was going to get out of here. I also figured that it probably wasn't poisoned since they had gone so far out of their way to kidnap me.

That first bite had me letting out an involuntary groan. It was one of the best things I had ever tasted. Looking up at the two Vepar, I dropped my fork with a clatter. Both of their eyes seemed to be glowing as they looked at me in a way that made it seem like they were more interested in eating me than they were the pancakes. I racked my brain trying to think if I had ever heard rumors that they liked to eat humans. I couldn't think of anything I had heard, but their looks didn't seem normal.

"Make that noise again," said the black haired Vepar, and all of a sudden, I realized what that look was. It was hunger all right...hunger for my body.

I began to eat again, pretending not to notice the way their eyes were still glowing. This time I ate quietly.

Laughing as if I'd made a joke, the blonde turned back to the stove where he was flipping pancakes.

"You cook?" I blurted out as he expertly tossed one in the air, catching it on his spatula smoothly like he was a circus performer.

"We got rid of the help before you woke up," he said dryly, turning to look at me. "I didn't want you scaring them with your antics."

I flushed, cold rage seeping into my veins. "My antics," I said in a low voice. "You mean the fact that I acted like any normal human being would when they were being stalked and then kidnapped by aliens," I snapped.

The black haired Vepar threw back his head and started laughing boisterously. Apparently, I amused them. "The little lamb has some bite after all," he said through his laughter, sounding almost proud of me. Even the blonde was looking at me with a different glint in his eyes. I could tell that it took a lot to faze or impress him, and for some reason that glint gave me a warm feeling inside that I did my best to ignore.

I set my fork down after I realized I'd consumed my entire plate. "What are your names?" I asked, trying to continue the brave front I had briefly put on. "I think it's only fair that I know who's been stalking me for the past few weeks."

"I'm Thane and pretty boy here is named Derrial," the black haired Vepar responded, gesturing to the blonde. It was a relief to have names to attach to their faces. I couldn't keep identifying them by their hair color forever. Though the idea of calling them hottie one, hottie two, and hottie three had crossed my thoughts.

"And the brunette guy who liked to stalk me in the gardens...What's his name?" I asked, knowing he had to be around somewhere. Thane looked like he wanted to laugh but he kept himself in check. "Wonder boy's name is Corran," he said.

"Wonder boy?" I asked.

"He's the lead scientist for the Vepar on Earth," said Derrial. "One of the most brilliant scientists to be born in our society in over a millennium."

I had a million more questions to ask based on his statement alone, but I kept myself in check, trying to focus on the essentials. And it also made sense now why Corran had said that weird stuff about plant species and that Russian village. He'd done his research on Earth and knew a hell of a lot more than I did.

"Why have you been following me?" I asked.

Derrial set the spatula down and leaned back against the counter. "A little bet at first. Who could sleep with the scared, beautiful human first...but after we had all watched you for a while...it just became more. And there's something about you that makes us need to find out why you've got us so curious. So, we knew we had to have you."

I pushed my chair back, standing on legs that were once again trembling, pushing a loose strand of hair behind an ear.

"You started to stalk me as a bet?" I asked in a whisper, my pulse racing and my knees weakening. "I've been terrified. I haven't slept in weeks. I left my whole life behind to try and escape you. What kind of monsters are you?"

"I told you that it changed for us eventually," said Derrial in a nonplussed voice. He began to stalk towards me in a way that left me feeling like prey he was about to catch. At the same time, Thane walked out of the room.

"Stay away from me," I whimpered, backing up until I hit the wall and couldn't go anywhere else. I desperately looked around, praying that someone would appear to help me. But there was no one around. Even the lady upstairs had evidently been sent home.

He didn't stop approaching me until he was pressed up against me. I hated myself when heat spread all over my body from his close proximity.

He was tall, so tall that the top of my head only came to his shoulder despite the fact that I'd never been considered a short girl. And his scent... I swallowed hard, burning up at how sexy he smelled. A combination of muskiness and the crisp freshness of the outdoors. It was a pleasant scent that in a strange way calmed me and slowed my racing heart.

"You're safe with us," he murmured as if struggling to find his words while we were pressed together. I was no fool to know what he struggled with. The bulge in his pants nudged against my lower stomach... He was huge. The corners of his mouth tugged upward, well aware of what I felt.

I wasn't sure if I should be scared or turned on as I pictured him naked and what something that size could possibly do to me in the bedroom. An inferno climbed through me, but I pushed the vision away alarmed at my thinking. It was wrong and distracting when I was here as their prisoner, not their lover.

I didn't move. I didn't dare. For all I knew, they had a basement filled with humans in cages they experimented on. The whole Area 51 and aliens came to mind, especially since, as ironic as it sounded, the reporters had said the first alien vessel to make an appearance on Earth was over Area 51. Funny. At least the UFO believers had gotten something right. What they got wrong was everything else...

Derrial studied me as if he could read my thoughts. What exactly had he meant by being curious about me? I was as plain Jane as they came. I led a boring life, followed the rules, end of story. If they wanted interesting, they should look up Cherry.

"I don't think the word, *safe*, has the same meaning to you as it does me," I responded.

Derrial blinked slowly, and I was caught in the perfection of his blue eyes, his lashes were so long and thick any girl would have been jealous. Up close his pupils were a mosaic of blues, like crystalline waters, and for a few moments I wanted to fall into them.

His fingers were like a vise, pressing into my arms as he held me against him, and he stared down at me so intently.

"You're hurting me. Let me go, Derrial." My jaw clenched.

He hauled me toward the enormous window, and I stumbled alongside him before he spun me to look outside. An ocean of pine trees spread out as far as the eye could see, enormous mountains in the distance like sentinels watching over us. Beautiful, but right now it was terrifying as it meant we were alone out here and nowhere near home.

"See that out there?" he said, pointing to the wood covered landscape. I held my breath, preparing for the worst.

"Yeah."

His grip softened and his palms slid down my arms, feather soft. "For miles there's nothing but wilderness, animals, and danger," he whispered in my ear, his breath warm, melting the ice in my veins.

I struggled to concentrate. It was hard to focus on his words when his fingers were skipping across my stomach. The world seemed to be moving in slow motion as he caressed my skin. I couldn't focus on anything but our connection. His rock-hard chest sat flush against my back, his bulge pushing against me, and his hand inched up my stomach ever so slowly.

I gasped for air. "Danger?"

His fingers trailed under my breasts gently, a wisp's touch away from grazing them, only the light fabric of my nightgown between us. Heat pooled between my thighs, and I grew wetter with the anticipation. My breath hitched; my mind focused only on his closeness. My body betrayed me, begging me to turn around and kiss him, discover what a Vepar tasted like. I should have slammed my heel into his foot, instead I stood there, my body thrumming with my racing pulse, my heart in my throat, waiting for him... What was he waiting for?

"There are rumors," he began, his words still hushed, "of escaped *caiks*. Creatures from our world that are akin to your wolves living in these woods. They're carnivores with a sharp beak and tongue, making them ideal for eating creatures. Vicious things that stowed away on a few ships when we arrived." He paused, seemingly for dramatic affect. "So, my advice to you is to not wander out there alone."

"Are you kidding me?" I twisted my head to face him, and his expression remained stoic. "Why would you let them loose on our planet and not round them up? It's your responsibility to not destroy our ecosystem."

Someone cleared their throat, and I glanced over to find it was the Vepar with brown hair, Corran. Clearly the scientist agreed with me.

Derrial's hands disappeared and he backed away, his earlier warmth replaced by a chill from the loss of his body against mine.

Thane broke into a laugh. When had those two come into the room?

I glanced up at Derrial. "You're joking about the *caiks*, right?"

He shrugged, but the edges of his mouth twitched as if he might break into a smile.

Asshole.

"The house is yours to enjoy. We're heading out for a short while." Without another word, the three of them strolled out of the room, and the sound of a door closing reached me.

"What the hell?" I followed them into a hallway containing a chandelier hanging overhead that dripped in crystals and paintings of forests and open land adorning the walls. I rushed to the grand white door that must be the main entrance to the mansion, but it was locked, and I couldn't find any way to unlock it. I felt around thinking there must be some hidden way to open the door, but after half an hour of searching, I gave up. A sinking sensation washed through me. I may not be in a cage, but this was a prison still the same.

If the Vepar were going to lock me up in their home, then they should expect me to do some snooping, not to mention track down a telephone to call for help. Definitely not Cherry after her crap...maybe my new boss at the cafe might help.

I wished I'd spent more time making more friends, socializing, rather than keeping to myself. But I was a fool for too long and believed Cherry was all the friendship I needed as I struggled with losing my parents. I wished I could rely on her, and I kept telling myself maybe she was going through something, struggling with her own things. Maybe I had been the person in the wrong because I hadn't noticed, and I'd never asked her about it. Regardless, her behavior had been horrible, and she really hurt me when I needed her the most. I wasn't sure I was ready to forgive her...or even if it was possible for me to forgive her at all.

Shaking aside my thoughts about Cherry, I returned back to the current pressing need to escape from here. I grabbed one of the stools at the island counter and carried it over to one of the floor-to-ceiling windows. My heart raced; I knew the Vepar would be pissed if they came home to a broken window. But I wasn't staying here if they were going to be stupid enough to leave me alone. With all my strength, I hurled the stool in my hands into the window.

It smacked against the glass with an explosive thud, then bounced backward with such speed that I had to jump out of the way to avoid getting hit. Fear tightened around my chest. The stool rolled and slid across the kitchen floor until it smacked onto the counter and came to a dead stop.

"Shit!"

The window didn't show a single blemish or crack. I walked closer and ran my hand over its smooth surface. They must have some kind of bullet proof glass. This had to be some kind of compound to keep people locked in the house... or something out? Humans hated the Vepar, so they'd have to think there would be someone who'd attack them.

Regardless, unease sat in my stomach because it seemed getting out of here was an impossibility. Still, I spent the next hour checking all the potential exits of the house that I could find.

Finally giving up, I headed back into the kitchen. I opened the fridge, shivering a bit at the chill. The shelves were filled with fruit and vegetables. I grabbed a banana and a bottle of water, then searched every drawer and cupboard. No knives in sight, and I rolled my eyes. No telephone in sight either. I made my way into a room that came off the kitchen. My stomach knotted with anticipation of finding Vepar secrets. In the room I found a King-sized bed perfectly made with black bedding. I padded over to the wardrobe and pulled it open to discover neatly hung clothes. Tailored pants, suits, shirts...This had to be Derrial's room. The room had that tidy, perfectly organized feel to it, and I got the urge to mess something up just to see if he would notice. I controlled myself.

There were no bedside tables or anything else in this room and of course the windows were unopenable, so I took another bite of my banana and rushed into another room, dropping off the peel onto the kitchen counter as I passed through it. I found an in-house gym, filled with weights, and I quickly moved onto the next room as I had no interest in exercising. Another bedroom, simple again with a large bed, tidy once again. The closet held jeans, tees, shirts and a couple of suits only. I fingered the leather jacket, smiling. Okay, someone had taste. The bedside drawers were empty. What the hell... it was as if these men didn't actually live here. Where were their gadgets or anything about their planet... or anything at all? The next room sat empty, and I found no other doors downstairs or even a basement entrance.

Gulping down several mouthfuls of chilled water, I headed upstairs. The bedroom I woke up in lay ahead, the door open, and bright light poured in through the windows. To my right sat two doors. The first one was a bathroom with the largest tub I'd ever seen, possible for three people to share comfortably. The feet were gold just like the small touches on the sink. Opening the cabinets showed nothing but packaged toothbrushes, toothpaste, shampoo and an array of toiletries, plus towels. Everything was expensive, brands that I had only heard of in celebrity magazines but never imagined being able to use on myself. Nothing that could help me to escape or defend myself in any way, however.

The next door sat locked, and I stiffened, then tried the handle a few more times.

"Maybe this is the secret room of mystery." I placed my ear to the door and swore I heard a soft whirring sound as if someone left a fan running. What was in there? Maybe it was where they kept the chocolate and television. I laughed at how unlikely that was, but wishful thinking on my part. I bet they had a telephone in there.

A quick check in the last room had me gasping. Shelves covered three fourths of the room, filled to the brim with books. It was like something out of Beauty and the Beast complete with a window seat that had a cushion, inviting me to sit there and soak in the sun while reading. In the middle sat a round table and three chairs, and I pictured the three Vepar sitting here, discussing new things they found in these books. I hurried inside, forgetting everything else, and ran my hands over the spines of the books, on various topics from governments, inventions, space exploration, and even one on the best slow cooked meals. Interesting. I assumed that belonged to the lady I'd seen earlier making my bed.

Back in the bedroom, I found a pile of clean clothes waiting for me in the closet. Jeans and a frilly blue buttoned-up shirt, which was strange, but they looked about my size. A silky pair of underwear fell out from the shirt and I picked it up, noting how tiny the thong was, and heat crawled up my cheeks, thinking of the men picking this out for me. Had they been planning to bring me here all along, so they bought me clothes? Or was this from another girl who they'd kept a prisoner and she just happened to be my size? If that was the case, what happened to the women once they fell out of favor with these Vepar?

I collected my clothes and marched into the bathroom, needing a shower and non-transparent clothes for when the Vepar returned. One way or another I was going to find out exactly what they wanted from me. And I wasn't taking no for an answer.

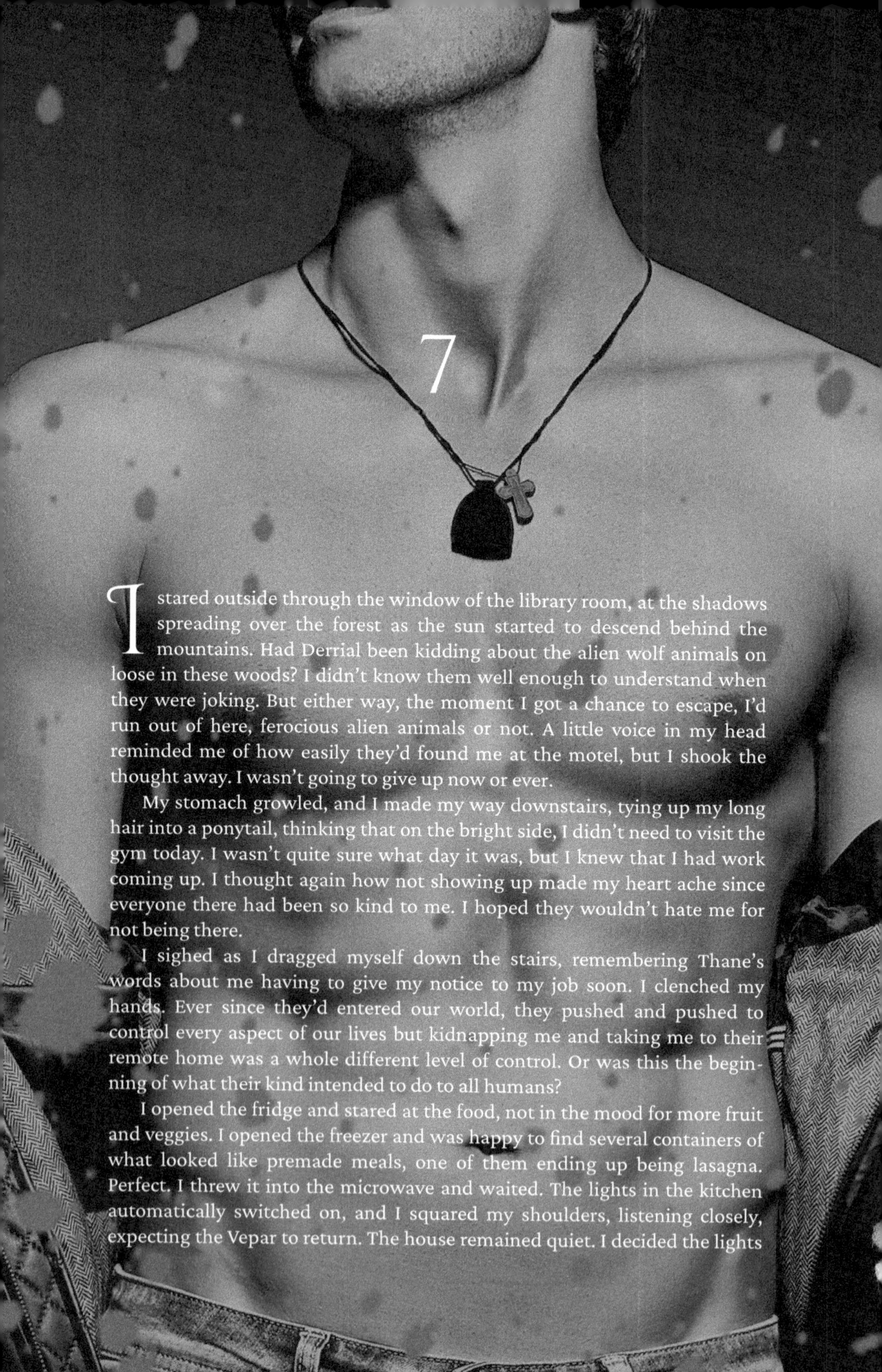

7

I stared outside through the window of the library room, at the shadows spreading over the forest as the sun started to descend behind the mountains. Had Derrial been kidding about the alien wolf animals on loose in these woods? I didn't know them well enough to understand when they were joking. But either way, the moment I got a chance to escape, I'd run out of here, ferocious alien animals or not. A little voice in my head reminded me of how easily they'd found me at the motel, but I shook the thought away. I wasn't going to give up now or ever.

My stomach growled, and I made my way downstairs, tying up my long hair into a ponytail, thinking that on the bright side, I didn't need to visit the gym today. I wasn't quite sure what day it was, but I knew that I had work coming up. I thought again how not showing up made my heart ache since everyone there had been so kind to me. I hoped they wouldn't hate me for not being there.

I sighed as I dragged myself down the stairs, remembering Thane's words about me having to give my notice to my job soon. I clenched my hands. Ever since they'd entered our world, they pushed and pushed to control every aspect of our lives but kidnapping me and taking me to their remote home was a whole different level of control. Or was this the beginning of what their kind intended to do to all humans?

I opened the fridge and stared at the food, not in the mood for more fruit and veggies. I opened the freezer and was happy to find several containers of what looked like premade meals, one of them ending up being lasagna. Perfect. I threw it into the microwave and waited. The lights in the kitchen automatically switched on, and I squared my shoulders, listening closely, expecting the Vepar to return. The house remained quiet. I decided the lights must be automated based on the time of the day, so I swung back around to the microwave which had just beeped, signaling my dinner was ready. The aroma had my stomach growling. A little part of me wondered if Derrial had made the food.

By the time I devoured the entire container of food, I reclined back in my seat and sighed. Maybe I had it all wrong and the Vepar intended to kill me with boredom. No television or music, and my bag wasn't anywhere in the bedroom upstairs. Did that mean they left it back in the motel, along with my house keys and cell phone? I hoped not.

An hour later, the front door unlocked, and voices reached me. I climbed to my feet and moved to stand with my back to the floor to ceiling window, waiting, my stomach twisting with the unexpected.

Thane strode into the kitchen first, his piercing blue eyes finding me in an instant. He smiled. "Missed us, pet?"

I didn't respond, but watched as he sauntered closer, followed by Derrial and Corran who both surprised me by offering me warm smiles. They seemed to behave as if this were normal behavior to have a prisoner in their home.

"Where's my handbag?" I blurted out.

"In a safe place," Corran answered, running a hand through his deep brown hair. It brought attention to his strong facial features and the thought crossed my mind how easily he could grace the cover of any magazine and have women all over the world fawn over him. Crazy how I hadn't thought he was as attractive as the others when I first saw him.

I shook my head in disgust at myself. I shouldn't have had to keep reminding myself that these men weren't human, that they might be wearing a disguise. Despite knowing that, I couldn't stop from staring at them in awe, noticing the small things like how Corran had a dimple in his chin when he smiled, how his breathing picked up when he looked at me.

"When do I get to go home?" I glanced from one man to the next, but none of them said a word. They all just stared at me without expression, giving nothing away.

"That's not how this works," Derrial finally broke the silence. "First, you need to understand you are now ours, that you'll never be free." He glanced outside the window, and I followed his line of sight to the gray storm clouds rolling overhead. Something ominous was coming in... I was beginning to believe my grandma more and more about her superstitions on storms.

I gripped my hips as Thane and Corran headed into the kitchen. One began making coffee, the other pawed at something in the fridge. What exactly did Vepar eat anyway? Humans?

"Fine then," I said. "I'm yours. Now, can I go home?"

Derrial burst into a laughter so powerful and loud, it could have been the thunder booming overhead. I guessed he was mocking me with his chortle once again.

Just sharing the room with these three had me burning up with rage, and I wanted to throw a chair at them. "Why the hell can't you just speak straight and tell me what's going on? Keeping me here is called kidnapping and it's illegal on Earth."

"We have always told you the truth, but you choose not to listen," Corran said, just as he had back in the botanical gardens with his stupid riddles.

I huffed and clenched my teeth, then stormed across the kitchen, my footfalls punching the wooden floorboards. How could I be near these three a second longer when all I wanted was to attack them? I glanced around, needing alone time. I opted for the small library as that place had a similar calming effect on me as the Botanical Gardens. Right now, I needed a bucketload of tranquility to extinguish the inferno in my veins.

I paced back and forth in front of the window, unable to appreciate the gorgeous view outside, unsure if I wanted to cry or scream. What in the world did the Vepar mean by 'understand I was theirs'? Like in a cult? Or was it as simple as starting to show them I accepted their kind in my life, smiled more often, complimented them on their looks and their ideas for the world... I sighed at myself. Clearly, not their looks, but other things. Though I wasn't a fool to believe when they said *ours* it meant simply having them as my friends. I somehow suspected this was far deeper, something to do with the way they lived on their home planet, wherever that was considering they hadn't told anyone, and it was evidently much farther than where humans had been able to travel.

The floorboard creaked behind me, and I spun around to find Derrial walking through the doorway, closing the distance between us in a few steps. Determination seared his features, his golden hair perfectly framing his face, all tanned skin and high cheekbones.

My heart catapulted to my throat, but I stood there, lifting my chin in defiance even if I trembled all over. I refused to show him any fear.

He was on me in seconds, his body pressed against mine, staring down at me, and his hands clasped my arms hard. I backed away, but he followed until my back hit the wall.

"Let me go," I pleaded, my voice cracking.

He paused for a moment, studying me, and a blaze burned behind his blue eyes. But with the bulge nestled against my stomach, I understood exactly his intention. He held me as he'd done downstairs, except now something else crossed his face as if he barely contained himself from attacking me, and that terrified me.

Was that what they meant by being theirs... offering myself to them without hesitation? With our bodies glued together, and the sheer size and strength of him, I stood no chance to push him away. He'd leave when he wanted to, when he was ready.

"Back on our planet," he began, "when we select a female, it's for life."

I swallowed hard, processing his words. They chose me to be theirs for life? Fuck! So many questions circled my mind, but none of those fell from my lips. "Why me?"

He gripped my chin and lifted my head higher to face him. "You remind me of me, desperate for freedom, never giving up the fight, even when you know there's no way out."

"Then please," I begged, ignoring my curiosity about what freedom he needed. "If you understand, release me."

He was shaking his head before I finished the words, his grip easing from my chin, his hand falling to my shoulder. His fingers grazed the tender spot on my neck. "You're not listening again. There's nowhere to escape. You're safer with us." His voice rose, yet he lowered his touch to my collarbone.

I hiccupped a breath. "Yes, there is." Despite my words, desire swept through me as it had downstairs, twisting my thoughts into knots.

"I can smell your arousal."

Heat crawled up my cheeks, and I shoved my hands into his solid chest, but he wouldn't budge.

His body pushed closer, arms locked around me, his chest rising and falling quickly. The expression over his face was of pure ecstasy and urgency, and when he lowered his mouth to my neck, licking me, my sex clenched. It shouldn't have, but something about him set me on fire.

The pressure built within me, and I loathed that I enjoyed the way his mouth tenderly kissed my skin, how the warmth of his quickened breath covered me in goosebumps. Sweeping up and over my chin, he reached my lips, pressing himself against me. He kissed me softly at first as if testing my response, but something about having such a powerful man needing me undid me.

His hands dropped to my hips and he pulled my lower lip into his mouth, sucking on it, tasting me. I squeezed my thighs together, falling beneath his attention, drowning in desire. I shouldn't want him, I shouldn't be inching my hands up his hard chest, looping them behind his neck, or lifting myself on tippy toes. But I did all that. I was losing myself to a Vepar.

As if my behavior gave him the approval he seeked, he kissed me faster, taking my tongue into his mouth, a moan brushing over my throat in response.

I kissed him back, desperate to unleash the building pressure strangling me. He reached up and his fingers snagged into my ponytail before pulling out the elastic. My hair fell around me in waves.

He gripped the back of my thigh and placed it around his hip, nudging himself between my legs, taking me, dominating me while we both remained fully clothed.

Was this how we were meant to be? I parted my lips for him, and when he tapped my other leg to wrap it around him too, I held onto his thick arms while he pinned me between himself and the wall. I hated myself for the way I was embracing him between my thighs. His heavy muscles shifted beneath my palms, and I stroked them, but it wasn't enough when I desired skin to skin, to slide over his naked body.

I moaned with desperation, begging for more. All rational thinking disintegrated when he grabbed my ass, rubbing himself against my sex. I pulsed down there in response. He ground faster, his kisses relentless, and sweat collected across my lower back.

Moisture pooled between my legs, breathing came with difficulty, and my nipples ached painfully against my shirt. I'd never had a man dominate me this way.

He grabbed a handful of my hair and yanked my head back as his teeth nicked the flesh of my lip. A coppery taste flooded my mouth, and I winced.

Derrial licked and sucked my wound ferociously as if tasting my blood drove him wild.

He arched my neck back and found my throat, his teeth raking over my flesh, sinking them into my shoulder but not breaking the skin.

I gasped, the pain sharp, but not excruciating. If anything, it flooded me with an excitement, and I moaned for more. I hadn't been with many men, so I didn't have the chance to explore what I enjoyed sexually, but apparently dominant men turned me on.

Pain and desire blended into an emotion I didn't understand, but I wanted more.

I chewed on my cut lip, tasted the metallic blood as it bubbled, but Derrial returned and captured my mouth. A wave of heat engulfed me, shaking me at the core.

"You want this, you live for this," he whispered. "That's why you're ours."

His words sent a deep shock through my soul.

"Derrial," I breathed. I shouldn't have allowed this, should have fought to take back control, should have hurt him.

But I didn't want to, and I groaned again as he continued to rub against my heat. I was dripping wet and squirming beneath him.

His body curled over mine as he ground so hard he left a wake of vibrations over my sex. One minute I brushed the edge, and then I fell in, all my weight wrapped in his arms. I climaxed, convulsing, and my screams muffled against his mouth.

He grunted too, then finally stopped with an unsteady exhale.

Coming up for air, I gasped, not able to find any words for what had just happened. The silence between us grew unsettled after the noise of our moment, but reality slowly slipped through my mind. What had I just done? A tight knot formed in my stomach, making me feel like I was going to throw up.

I wriggled out of his hold, lowering my legs, and he released me. My knees were jelly beneath me like I walked on a ship deck in a roiling sea, and I had to let the wall hold me up until I found my strength.

Unable to look at the Vepar, I sidestepped past him, wanting to run, to escape, to never see him again as I burned up with embarrassment at how easily I gave myself to him...how my body responded to his. I'd had a freaking orgasm with both of us still dressed.

My body still trembling, I ran toward the parted door from him in shame. And this time, no one came after me.

"Go to your room, little one. Go and tell yourself that I somehow made you like that, that you wouldn't have cum like a bitch in heat if I hadn't forced you," he called after me in a cold, condescending voice.

His words only heightened the shame coursing through my body, and I fled out of the room as fast as I could, not stopping until I got to the room that I had woken up in. I slammed the door behind me, wishing again for some kind of lock on the doorknob.

I backed up until my knees hit the bed behind me, my eyes locked onto the door as I breathlessly waited to see if anyone came after me. Glancing over at my reflection in the window, I stared incredulously at the blood smeared across my chin and neck. Fuck, he'd been tasting my blood... was that what Vepar did? Drink blood?

After five minutes of no one following me, I finally leaned back on the bed, and I cried.

What was wrong with me that I'd let him do that to me? And I actually enjoyed it? What kind of sick person actually delighted in having an alien species that had taken her parents turn her on?

I cried into my pillow for hours, vaguely aware that the fabric beneath my face was a million times softer than the one I slept on in my loft. I cried until I fell asleep. Visions of monsters eating my parents plagued my dreams, and I watched in horror.

When I woke next, night cloaked the room and soft rain pattered against my window. With no clocks in my room and my phone taken from me, I had no way of knowing what time it was. I wasn't going to go downstairs and ask either. I'd rather sit in here forever than face any of the Vepar again.

I felt hopeless as I laid there. This was my life. I had been captured by the same creatures that took my parents, and soon I would disappear just like them. They would either kill me or worse, I would become some sort of human sex slave until I grew too old for them to want me anymore.

Tears threatened again, but I held them in. I would just lay here until they came for me. I wouldn't make it easy on them. They would have to force me to cooperate.

I found myself wishing that they would just kill me.

8

It was two days before they came for me. The door crashed open, startling me out of the hazy dreamland I had been in and out of for hours. I felt weak. It had been too long since I'd eaten or drank anything, and I wasn't surprised that the first thing Derrial did was force water down my throat.

"You need to do it slowly," came a voice that I recognized as Corran's.

"She hasn't had anything for too long," snapped Derrial, cursing as he continued to force me to drink water. Two days. I had no idea it had been that long. No wonder I felt so weak.

"Humans shouldn't go without water this long," chided Corran. "Were you trying to kill her?" he asked.

Derrial cursed again. "Would you fucking shut up and get an IV or something," he snapped. "We've all been distracted with pressing shit."

Corran's footsteps sounded as he hurried out of the room. Derrial continued to have me sip water, a look that almost seemed concerned in his too blue to be human eyes. My stomach rolled, the water too much for my empty stomach. I began to heave, and he hurriedly turned me over on my side as I threw up the water he had just given me.

Corran appeared at that moment holding an IV kit. "Do you know how to do this?" he asked Derrial.

"Get Thane," Derrial snapped, making Corran give him a curious look before he jogged out of the room.

I threw up some more water, soaking the beautiful bed. Derrial softly stroked my hair, pulling it back from my face. "I'm so sorry, beautiful," he whispered, so softly that I could have imagined it.

Thane appeared in the room in what seemed like only a second later. "Is she okay?" he asked in a worried voice.

"I need you to give her this IV," Derrial said in a terse voice that left no room for arguments.

I felt Thane fiddling with my arm, and then a quick prick of pain. "It's in there."

There was silence for a few minutes, then I jumped when there was a crash of glass against the wall.

"She's not to be left alone," cursed Derrial. He then stormed out of the room. I could hear the sound of other pieces of glass breaking somewhere else in the house.

"Stupid, stupid girl," sighed Thane, taking a seat next to me on the bed and absentmindedly stroking my arm. He looked down at me with a pained expression. "Are we really that awful that you would rather give up on life than be with us?"

In all honesty, I didn't know the answer to that because I'd felt so many emotions these past couple of days, I was struggling to wrangle and understand them. How I so easily fell under Derrial's spell, how much I still craved him. I was their prisoner. None of that made sense.

When I didn't answer, he pulled out what looked like a more high-tech version of the iPhone and started to fiddle with it. I already felt more energized from the IV, yet I struggled to sit up.

"Stay there until the IV is done," Thane barked. "You look like you've somehow managed to lose ten pounds in just the few days you've been up here."

Before I could respond, Corran appeared. He hovered by the door as if he wasn't sure what to do with himself. I watched him for a moment before he seemed to come to a decision. He walked over to the bed and took out a small silver device out of his pocket. When he started to move it slowly along my body, I began to struggle to get away, not sure what alien technology he'd use on me.

"Please, no." I found my voice.

"Calm down," said Thane, putting a little pressure on my arm to still me. "It's just a device that makes sure all of your insides are operating normally."

"You should probably run it over her head too to make sure she doesn't have brain damage," he mused to Corran.

I made a sound of displeasure, and Thane grinned at me.

Corran stepped back after he had run the device all over my body. "She appears to be fine besides being starved and still dehydrated. I'll go get her food," he said, practically fleeing the room as if he couldn't stand to be in my presence for any longer. For some absurd reason, my feelings were a bit hurt at his reaction.

Thane must have seen something on my face. "Don't mind Corran," he said in what I considered a soft voice for him. "He's not that great with your kind, or our kind to think of it. He's more of an observe kind of person. It's actually been shocking at how interested he's seemed in you."

For one stupid moment my mind wandered down the path of how far Corran's preference for watching went. I quickly shut down that thought when Derrial entered the room carrying the tray of food that I was certain Corran had gone downstairs to get.

Derrial sat on the bed next to me, the mattress dipping under me, and held out what looked like a grilled cheese sandwich. With the energy that the IV gave me, the full brunt of my hunger struck, and I grabbed the grilled cheese out of his hand, practically stuffing it into my mouth.

"Hey...slow down." Derrial dragged the tray out of my reach since I was already reaching for the other half of the sandwich. "You're going to get sick if you eat too fast."

I nodded, forcing myself to slow down. To my disappointment, Derrial set the tray down where I still couldn't reach it and turned to face me. I was suddenly very aware of just how close in proximity Derrial and Thane sat next to me. I'd never had one guy in my bed let alone two aliens. I was reminded as I watched Derrial's eyes glow just who these two were. They may be sweetly taking care of me at the moment, but I couldn't forget that in this situation they were the predators...and I remained the prey.

"We need to come to an understanding." The glow in Derrial's eyes faded as he spoke, seeming to tame whatever inside of him was causing such a reaction. "We're not going to harm you, but you're not going anywhere either. We've been around for too long not to know that there is something about you that's special. And nothing is going to change until we figure out what that is."

I studied him for a moment while he waited for me to answer. I believed him when he said that they weren't going to harm me. I believed him that they believed that. But what they didn't understand was that by taking away everything familiar in my life and forcing me to bend to their will...they were harming me.

"So, what's next?" I finally asked, watching as something that almost looked like relief flashed across his features, softening them.

"Next, you're going to get better," Derrial said, getting up off the bed and handing me the other half of my sandwich. "We're going to the World Summit, and you'll need to be your best as my date."

With that pronouncement he left the room, leaving Thane shaking with laughter next to me.

What the hell was so funny?

Three days later, Corran pronounced me fully recovered and ready to go. Over those last few days there had been an unspoken truce between the four of us. No talking about the Vepar, or my kidnapping. Nothing about why humans went missing apparently either. And no orgasms... Instead we stuck to safe topics like my favorite foods. I found out Derrial loved to cook human food and after he heard that my favorite dishes were Thai, he cooked up a storm and made the most delicious Pad Thai I'd ever tasted in my entire life. We all ate dinner together that night, and I caught their stolen glances my way like they wanted to each steal me away and carry me alone to a room, so they had me all for themselves. The air grew heavy with their need, but I said nothing and enjoyed my food, admiring their self-control. Maybe it was mean of me, but after they turned my life upside down, I bathed in a bit of payback, anyway I could get it.

The whole set up seemed almost normal...Almost...if having dinner with three of the most gorgeous men in the world constituted as normal.

I stood in front of my walk-in closet, looking through the clothes that continued to appear in there. I wasn't sure how the men were getting access to outfits in the middle of nowhere and how they fitted me perfectly, but at least it had confirmed I wasn't being given clothes from another kidnapped victim since the tags were on every item. Brands that I hadn't imagined I would ever see in real life, let alone get to wear.

Considering I'd been housebound since arriving here I wasn't sure when to wear the ten pairs of Christian Louboutins that were now sitting in my closet. Maybe this trip? Part of me wished I had my phone for the simple reason that I wanted to send a photo of them to Cherry. And that thought made me wonder where she was at. Had she even tried to contact me, and if she had, was she worried at all? What about my new boss? He would have considered me unreliable now and I'm sure my job was long gone. I couldn't go back to working for Greg since I had simply messaged him I was quitting and never showed up again. And I hadn't paid my landlord in weeks, so I'm sure he had started the eviction process for my loft and had probably sold all my belongings. My stomach sunk at the thought, not for my few belongings I had, but for the photos that I had left of my parents that were still at my loft.

Not that I'd accepted my fate here... far from it. But since the Vepar were playing nice, I'd use the opportunity to uncover their real intentions and figure out how to leave in a smarter way.

A knock sounded on my door. After the guys had continued to appear unannounced, I had put my foot down that they had to knock before entering. I was surprised when they actually listened.

"Come in," I called out. It was Derrial, looking so good that it should be a crime in his perfectly fitted grey suit with a black button up and black tie underneath it. His blonde hair had been brushed off his face, falling behind his ears, and I could sit there and stare at him for hours.

"Do you need help packing?" he asked, eyeing the floor with no sign of my bag. I blushed at the thought of this Vepar helping me pack my underwear.

"Maybe just tell me what kind of clothes I'll need, and I can pick them out?" I responded.

"No offense. But I think it's best I select your outfits." He smirked. "In the weeks that we watched you, I don't think I saw you in anything that didn't look like a paper sack. I can tell when a woman is trying to hide herself from the world."

I opened my mouth to object, to say something about my lack of funds, but he was already in my closet tossing things behind him so that they landed on the bed. My eyes widened at the skirt suits and fancy cocktail dresses he picked out.

"What kind of conference did you say this was?" I asked, absentmindedly smoothing out a black, silky dress that I knew was more expensive than six months of the rent for my loft.

"The World Summit," he answered casually, apparently unaware of what effect such an announcement would have on me. When I had heard about the event on the news, I had always imagined the most powerful men in the world sitting around a table in their tailored suits, talking about things I didn't understand. I sighed a heavy exhale at the thought of actually attending the World Summit. Someone like me didn't belong at such a place.

"I can't go with you to that," I squeaked, balling up the aforementioned dress in my hands in distress.

I knew the World Summit was an annual conference held every year in which the leaders of the Vepar and the leaders of various countries in the world met to go over policy and changes that the Vepar wished to implement. Only the most powerful of the Vepar went, making me wonder why Derrial was going to attend. Why would a Vepar powerful enough to represent them at the World Summit have kidnapped a lowly human girl?

When he turned around, holding a glittering gold gown, I took a step back. "What's wrong?" He grinned at me, strolling closer.

"Who exactly are you?" I asked, eyeing him through skeptical lenses. Despite playing happy roommates for the past few days, they hardly revealed anything about themselves, why they were on Earth, why they really took me... nothing to give me some background.

"I guess you'll find out soon." He tossed another blue dress with a flowing skirt onto the bed. "You should have enough clothes right there for the week. Be ready in an hour," he ordered, marching out of the room and closing the door behind him.

I sank to my bed unsteadily. A few days ago, I'd been waiting tables at a small cafe, just trying to make ends meet. Now I was apparently going to wear $20,000 dresses and hobnob with world leaders.

What was happening?

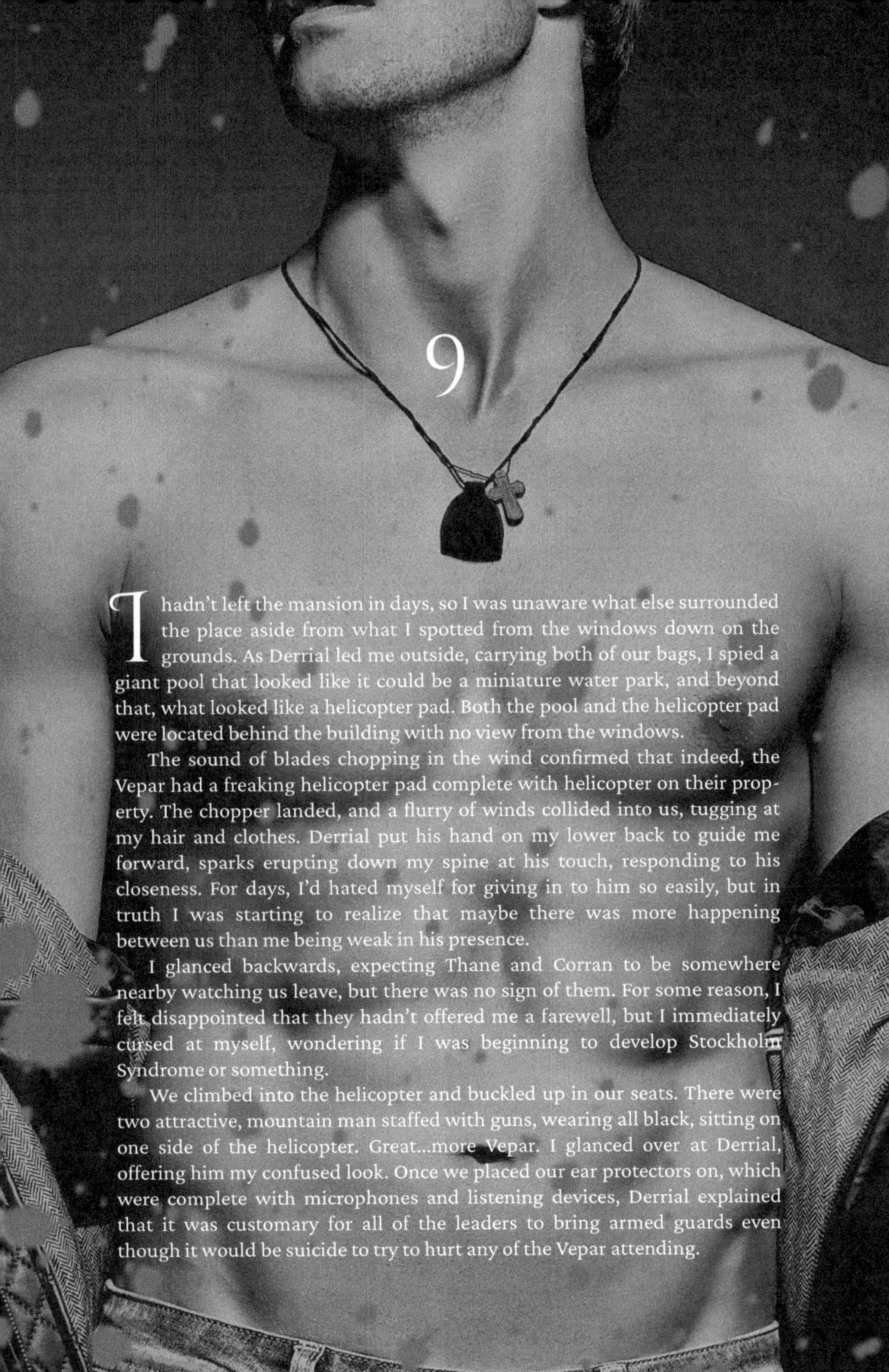

9

I hadn't left the mansion in days, so I was unaware what else surrounded the place aside from what I spotted from the windows down on the grounds. As Derrial led me outside, carrying both of our bags, I spied a giant pool that looked like it could be a miniature water park, and beyond that, what looked like a helicopter pad. Both the pool and the helicopter pad were located behind the building with no view from the windows.

The sound of blades chopping in the wind confirmed that indeed, the Vepar had a freaking helicopter pad complete with helicopter on their property. The chopper landed, and a flurry of winds collided into us, tugging at my hair and clothes. Derrial put his hand on my lower back to guide me forward, sparks erupting down my spine at his touch, responding to his closeness. For days, I'd hated myself for giving in to him so easily, but in truth I was starting to realize that maybe there was more happening between us than me being weak in his presence.

I glanced backwards, expecting Thane and Corran to be somewhere nearby watching us leave, but there was no sign of them. For some reason, I felt disappointed that they hadn't offered me a farewell, but I immediately cursed at myself, wondering if I was beginning to develop Stockholm Syndrome or something.

We climbed into the helicopter and buckled up in our seats. There were two attractive, mountain man staffed with guns, wearing all black, sitting on one side of the helicopter. Great...more Vepar. I glanced over at Derrial, offering him my confused look. Once we placed our ear protectors on, which were complete with microphones and listening devices, Derrial explained that it was customary for all of the leaders to bring armed guards even though it would be suicide to try to hurt any of the Vepar attending.

I stared outside as the country flew underneath, trying to work out where exactly the mansion was located. Derrial's arm was on my thigh and he squeezed my hand to look at him, and he shook his head as if reading my thoughts. I swallowed hard and looked over at the two guards who were studying me. What would they do if I ripped my hand free from Derrial? Probably nothing as I suspected Derrial wouldn't accept it well.

So, I sat there, obediently, still unsure why he insisted on taking me on this trip. An hour into the trip and my ass numb from the vibrating seat, my stomach lurched as we started our descent. I gripped my seat, and Derrial took my hand, holding me.

It wasn't everyday a girl got to travel in a helicopter. Once we landed, jostling us about, the door slid open and the whirring sound of the blades overhead grew deafening. Wind whistled inside, ripping at my ponytail with its invisible hand. The guard stepped out first, followed by Derrial, who turned around and extended his hand to me.

Leaning over, I accepted his help, and once I reached the doorway, he grabbed my waist and helped me down. We hunched low from the spinning blades, Derrial took my hand, and we rushed across the tarmac, buffeted against the gust of air across our backs.

Finally, we slowed down, and I looked at the small building ahead of us, along with noting that this wasn't a major airport, but a private location surrounded by a chained fence. The guards carried our bags and flanked our sides, and up ahead waited a black limousine with two more muscled men in black. One of them had the back-seat door opened for us, everything creating a million more questions about who exactly Derrial was. It was obvious that I had misjudged just who these Vepar were. Again, I wondered what they were doing with me?

Once we were inside the car that smelled strongly of vanilla, a glass of champagne was pushed into my hand and we were off. Across from us sat two of the guards, both of them staring outside at the freeway we'd entered, while Derrial swirled the ice in his whiskey around in his glass.

"Is this normal travel for you?" I asked and took a sip of my bubbly, which was slightly sweet and tickled my nose.

I'd once tasted this stuff, but clearly it wasn't the good stuff, because this drink was incredible. I downed it in two gulps, and Derrial collected my glass before tucking it into a compartment in the door.

"I prefer to travel lighter," he replied, and shifted in his seat, obviously uncomfortable. In a strange way, it made me feel better to know it wasn't just me feeling like a fish out of water. Was this how he felt all the time on Earth? Knowing everyone around him hated his kind?

"You don't like this?" He glanced over at me; his eyebrow cocked as if disappointed.

I shrugged. "Hard to compare when I don't even have a car." The laugh that followed my statement felt forced, and part of that was because being so close to Derrial still left me confused. My emotions were a jumbled mess around him. I couldn't stop thinking of how easily he brought me to climax, how damn much I loved it, and even how I'd experienced a dream with him taking me again and again. I was being a fool.

He was a Vepar. Dangerous. Secretive. Not to mention my freaking kidnapper.

I had to get my head screwed on right and remember what was going on.

I was the victim who would pretend to be content with the current situation while waiting for an opportunity to escape. Sure, I hadn't worked out the finer details of how I'd avoid them once I did run away, but that was my goal now--uncover their weakness, what made them tick, and how to vanish from their lives for good. Until then, I'd bide my time and make them trust me.

"You okay?" he asked, staring at me, trying to read my thoughts, but I smiled widely.

"All good." And I turned toward the window and stared out into the world as we passed it by. A world that seemed so far away from me and out of my grasp that I felt like the alien. I hoped that when I did escape, I would be able to find a place again.

A soft voice sang in my ear. "Wake up, kitten. We're here."

My eyes fluttered open, still in the back seat of the limousine. Sitting up and looking around I saw that we were parked in the front of some kind of building. I rubbed my eyes as someone opened the door and I climbed out onto the sidewalk, Derrial on my heels. A soft breeze swished past, bringing with it a cocktail of smells from the garlic aroma of pizza to the subtle scent of aftershave coming from the concierge standing near me.

"This way ma'am."

I didn't move though because I was captivated, lost in the grandeur of the hotel towering in front of us. Glass doors stood ahead of us with a young man welcoming us with a bow. He opened the door, while two other men in penguin suits rushed to collect our bags from the trunk.

Derrial placed his hand on my lower back, urging me to move, and I let him guide me through the doors into a circular hotel lobby. Visiting hotels wasn't something I did regularly or ever. Reception sat in front of a set of gorgeous steps that curled up around the wall to the next floor. My boots tapped the shiny floor, and I spun on the spot, taking in the glorious surroundings, the loft ceilings, the guests in their expensive clothes, the way everyone whispered when they talked. I'd never even set foot in such a place, let alone even fathomed staying in one.

Derrial was talking to a man in a tailored black suit and moments later he strolled over to me, smiling. "Ready, kitten?" He handed me his hand to take, so I did, and we made our way to the elevator, the guards following us every step of the way.

By the time we reached the top floor, butterflies somersaulted in my stomach. I shouldn't have been excited, but I was so giddy I could scream.

"Is this the penthouse?" I might have squeaked a bit.

Derrial tapped his card to the door lock and opened it for me, staring at me with the widest grin.

I rushed past him and into a room three times the size of my entire apartment. More rooms stretched out in every direction. Sunlight flooded the penthouse through the enormous windows, reminding me of the kind on store-fronts, so high I felt as if I floated on air.

A bird flew past the window almost as a reminder that we were almost in the clouds. Expensive looking beige couches adorned one end of the room, near the biggest television I'd seen. Bowls of fruit and chocolate, along with more champagne filled the tables. I wasn't sure where to look first, but I ran to the window, pressed up against the glass and looked down. The city lay so far away as if it were another world, the people looked like ants on the side-walks below.

"We need to get ready quickly," Derrial said.

I turned to him, noting how he studied me with a grin despite his words. "You'll have time to admire the room later."

"Can't I stay here while you go to the Summit?" I'd watch television and eat everything in sight.

He shook his head. "Get dressed in the skirt and jacket suit you packed and bring the black cocktail dress and heels with you. We leave in ten. And if anyone asks, you're my assistant." Without another word, he marched into one of the other rooms, so well versed in the penthouse's layout that it was obvious he'd been here before.

I nodded, even though only the guards watched me, and headed into the hallway where I found my bag sitting on a queen poster bed. If I needed to play the part of assistant or girlfriend for a few days while living here, well, I'd have to find a way to get through it. Either way I couldn't wipe the smile from my face that I was in a freaking penthouse.

Today would be a day of sitting back and looking pretty, playing eye candy on the Vepar's arm, which I could do if it proved to him I was happy to be theirs. A few days could be enough to get him to let his guard down and give me a chance to escape.

Hours later, and the day dragged. Holding back my yawns grew harder and harder. Here I assumed I'd sit in on the World Summit and learn who exactly Derrial was and what the Vepar were doing on Earth, but instead, Derrial hardly had said a word. He sat in a room amid a large circular table, joined by heads from around the world, listening to their concerns and how they intended to work with the Vepar. I almost choked on laughter as each of them tried to appease Derrial. I sat behind him in a wooden chair that numbed my entire body, attempting to play the role of an assistant by sitting there doing nothing.

Being disappointed was an understatement. Why did he want me to attend the Summit anyway?

Once the event ended, I was on my feet, ready for the cocktail party, but that was an even bigger let down. I spent the night with guards surrounding me, and I ate every hors d'oeuvres that was brought my way as I watched Derrial talk to everyone in the hall decorated with overelaborate vases of flower bouquets. Inconsequential polite conversation, wine, and a light orchestra filled the room. This wasn't what I would call a party.

I stepped toward Derrial but a guard grabbed my arm and shook his head when I turned to face him. Right. My place was to sit. Or stand quietly by myself. To be invisible.

Derrial glanced my way and smiled, raising his glass to me. I raised my brow.

On the inside I was ready to scream. Especially since the black stilettos I wore pinched my toes.

After the party, Derrial led me out to the street, what felt like a thousand eyes watching us as we walked out of the ballroom where the cocktail party was being held. We got to the curb as our driver pulled up in the black town car we were using for the week. Derrial opened the door for me but didn't follow me in.

"You're not coming?" I asked, looking up at him and feeling strangely lonely at the thought.

"I have another meeting to attend. I thought you would want the break," he answered, taking a step back from the car and beginning to close the door. He stopped for a second and leaned back in, an irrational part of me thought he might kiss me goodbye.

"Don't bother trying to get away," he said. "Our driver is highly trained and will be walking you back to our rooms and there will be guards stationed outside." With that ugly pronouncement he closed the door, not bothering to look back as he strode away in that smooth, predatory way of his.

As we drove away, I thought for a second of at least trying to get away, but I was so tired after the day of meetings that I immediately abandoned the idea. Especially when it meant dealing with the muscle heads guarding me. Once we arrived at the hotel, where I was indeed marched up to my room by the driver whose name I found out was Dan, I found myself on the news channels watching their interpretation of the Summit proceedings. There was a lot that I had apparently missed. One thing was for sure, all eyes were on Derrial. His face flashed across the screen repeatedly and I wondered how I had stuck my head in the sand so much these past years to not realize he was someone big for the Vepar. I fell asleep watching the news, barely realizing when a strong pair of arms that I vaguely recognized as belonging to Derrial, picked me up and took me to bed.

I woke to someone nuzzling my hair. I sat up in bed with a start, looking around frantically for who had been touching me. Looking behind me, I saw Derrial lounging near me in nothing but a pair of tight fitting briefs that left little to the imagination. He had a sleepy look on his face that still somehow managed to make him insanely gorgeous.

"Did you sleep in here last night?" I asked, quickly taking a peek at my body to be sure I remained dressed.

"Do you really care if I did?" he asked, an insolent grin on his face. For a brief moment I allowed myself to remember that minute before I had fully woken up, what it had felt like to be enveloped in his arms. And then I quickly pushed the thought away.

"I didn't give you permission to do that," I snapped, getting out of bed. His grin only grew wider.

"I'm pretty sure we've established I never ask for permission," he replied, also getting out of bed. I averted my eyes from all of his perfect golden skin and rushed out of the room. "Be ready in twenty minutes," he called after me. "I have an important meeting this morning."

Twenty minutes later we were in the car driving back to the Summit. Today I was dressed in a sleek black sheath dress with shiny black shoes. I couldn't help but feel a little bit like Audrey Hepburn, and the fact that the soles of my heels were red made me feel even classier. Who would have thought wearing such expensive clothes would make me feel different? Not in an arrogant kind of way, but with my confidence. Most of the time, I wore baggy clothes, putting comfort first, but I'd never experienced this feeling of satisfaction as I did now.

Derrial was dressed to intimidate today. He wore a dark suit with a shiny black shirt underneath and no tie. As we approached the venue of the Summit, the softness in his features faded, replaced by a man who looked ready to rule the universe. My stomach tightened, and the car seemed to close in around me almost as if a menacing, black cloud had descended. Maybe it was the Vepar's version of a "game face" but his serious expression was extremely intimidating even though I had watched the change happen.

Derrial didn't say a word as we strolled into the enormous building. Guards stood everywhere, along with paparazzi.

Inside, Vepar and humans stood clumped in groups, but everyone seemed to take a collective breath as we entered the room. Derrial didn't stop to say hello to anyone, instead he strode in the room where the meeting was to be held, not looking back to see if I followed.

I found myself wanting to watch his face during this meeting, so I sat in a chair across the room from his designated table. He shot me a quizzical glance but said nothing about my move.

Only a few minutes passed, and the room filled. An air of expectancy flooded the space with everyone intently watching Derrial, expecting, waiting. After a few more minutes of him looking over some papers as if he didn't have the eyes of the whole world on him, he stood.

"As you know one of our main initiatives since coming to this planet has been to improve the quality of women's lives. On our planet, females are revered, they are worshipped. One of the first things we noticed about your planet during our first visits was the utter lack of care that is given to women on this planet. That's why we mandated the use of a new birth control and that's why we instituted higher penalties for crimes against women. Whether Earth wants it or not, things are going to improve. That's why today we'll be announcing a new mandate. All women will now submit to new health screenings, to be conducted every six months. Any medical concerns discovered will be automatically addressed at the cost of governments of each respective country represented at this Summit."

Silence.

Not a word.

Then as if someone had unleashed a typhoon, a rising sound of gasps and groans escalated, followed by loud whispers because this was huge. It was fucking goliath in terms of the impact it would have on our society.

Holy shit!

Derrial was forcing governments to cover medical bills for females! Who the hell was he again to sway such power?

I stared at him in shock. All of this came from a creature that literally had stalked me for a week and abducted me in the middle of the night. And now he claimed that women were important to him? Had I misread his intentions? Where I called it kidnapping, did he call it protection on his planet?

I studied the faces around the room. Shocked expressions, a few women nodding, and some men scowling.

But I didn't miss how Derrial's eyes focused on me for the entire speech. Even in a room full of people and the distance between us, I thrummed with a feeling deep in my gut for him. There was no way for me to escape his pure magnetism, for me not to want him. Not after he'd just showed part of his plan, and it wasn't horrific or the end of the world stuff. But simple things, like ensuring all females received the medical treatment they deserved for thousands who couldn't afford it. So many were too afraid to visit a doctor. This would change so many lives.

When I met Derrial's gaze, the sparkle in his blue eyes glinted, my knees weakened and damn him on how he affected me, how he touched me so deeply with his mandate. I wanted to keep hating him because I understood those emotions. The itch I felt for him now made me see him in a different light, but underneath the surface I couldn't forget what he was... Along with why he was so protective of human females.

I sensed his stare over me like a lover's caress. Maybe if I itched this persistent scratch, we'd both move on from one another. Maybe that was the answer right there to finally end his obsession with me. And mine with him.

We were on our way back to the hotel from yet another dull cocktail event that night, and I was glad for it, as I'd had enough of watching the most attractive women on Earth paw at Derrial all night, trying to get his attention. For some reason it had bothered me. I scanned the traffic quietly as it passed by, trying to understand why I felt this way.

"The traffic. I never appreciated it before tonight." Derrial moved closer to me, taking my face in his free hand. Derrial's other hand softly stroked the skin that was showing from my short cocktail dress. "This skin has been torturing me," he murmured. My breathing shifted to panting as he slid a finger along the hem of my dress. He began to lift the hem higher, ignoring my startled gasp at the fact that he was doing that in the backseat of a car with a driver in the seat in front of us.

He brought my face closer to him but stopped short of kissing me. Instead, he lingered for a moment, and I breathed him in, losing myself momentarily to his touch, his scent, his nearness. When he finally crushed his lips to mine, my hand flew up and caught his, shocking both of us as I held him to me, greedy for the taste of him. As he kissed me, Derrial's hands urged my legs apart and he slipped his hand up so high that his fingers brushed against the silk of my underwear. I wrenched myself away from him, gasping for air. When his fingers moved to pull my underwear to the side, I locked my legs on his hand.

"No," I mouthed to him.

I could see the driver struggling to keep his eyes on the road as it was impossible for him to miss what was going on in the backseat.

Derrial took pity on me and withdrew his hand, giving me a smirk as he did so.

"I can smell you," he said, inhaling deeply and closing his eyes as if he was in ecstasy and the car was somehow full of my scent. I blushed and turned so I was staring out at the traffic and the historic buildings instead of looking at him. My lips burned from his efforts and it was a struggle to sit still in the car as we made our way to the hotel. I could see him in the reflection of my window, silently watching me with that infuriating look he always had that told me he could see right through me.

We couldn't get to the hotel fast enough.

By the time we had made our way to the Mandarin Oriental, I had almost convinced myself to go through with it. Sex with Derrial. It was clearly what he wanted. And maybe once the whole mystique of what having sex would be like with me was over, he would be over me and I would be left alone.

I ignored the part of me that balked at the idea of him leaving me alone.

He seemed in no hurry as we got out of the car. All of his motions were smooth...and slow. It took him what felt like a year to come and open my door, and then he chatted with the driver for another five minutes before we moved to go inside. The only thing that signaled that he still wanted me was his hand placement on the small of my back. It burned through my dress and into my skin and I was halfway certain that there would be an imprint in my skin when I took my dress off.

We walked slowly through the hotel lobby, Derrial stopping to chat with other Vepar staying there as we did so. They stared at me curiously, but Derrial never introduced me. Which was probably a good thing since his hand that was on my back had started to slowly trail lower, rendering me speechless.

We finally made it to the elevator, and he continued my torture by taking out and typing on the little silver device that I had seen him playing with occasionally.

"Is that a cell phone?" I asked, wanting to break the silence. He looked up at me, a slow grin on his face. "It's a computer," he said. "I'm going over the recordings from today so I can look more closely at who was in the audience and what their reaction was to it. It will help me know better what leaders we have to lean on, or what Vepar are thinking of going against my plans."

I looked at him shocked.

"How did it record all of that? Wasn't it in your pocket the whole time?"

He looked at me with what resembled an almost pitying expression. "We're watching you all the time, surely your news media told you that?"

I looked at him baffled; my thoughts momentarily sidetracked by what he had just told me. The elevator made it to our floor at that moment, the bell ringing to signal we were at our destination. We walked down the hallway to our suite, a million questions running around my mind. All of the questions disappeared when the doors opened.

Evidently Derrial had the same thing in mind as I did this evening.

The room was dimly lit with candles flickering in the breeze coming in from the open balcony doors. There were two bottles of Crystal in an ice bucket on the grand piano along with two flutes. Soft classical music was streaming in from the sound system that was wired throughout the suite. It was the most romantic setting that I had ever seen.

And the exact opposite mood I was trying to set. One and done was my goal tonight and I didn't need to be distracted by whatever he was trying to create here. Yes, he and his friends were the most gorgeous creatures I had ever seen. But if he thought I could forget that they were aliens who had taken over the world and ruined my life, he had another thing coming.

I blew out the candles as I passed by them. I could see him frown as I did so.

His hand flew out and caught my arm, pulling me against him roughly. "Kitten, did I read you wrong and you aren't the romantic type?" He asked in a raspy voice as he trailed his lips down my throat. He bit down softly, and I stiffened, remembering the other day and his reaction to my blood.

I pulled away from him, taking a few steps away so I could keep my wits about me. I would need them if I was going to keep control of the situation. Facing him, I slowly unzipped the side of my dress, sliding the dress off so that it pooled at my feet.

At first, Derrial's eyes widened, and I could see him thinking as he tried to understand my sudden willingness to play. He quickly recovered however and flashed me a wicked smile, walking up to me and tracing my lips with his fingers. The move sent shivers down my spine.

"I've thought about your lips all day. I've pictured you on your knees with that pretty little mouth wrapped around me sucking me off," he said, a growl rumbling in his throat as he spoke.

I melted at his words, desire pooling low in my stomach. The sensible side of me held on though. "What are you waiting for?" I asked, trying to give him the same smirk he always gave me.

His finger dropped from my face, trailing along my collarbone and leaving a trail of fire in its wake. "Your body was meant to be mine," he murmured, his eyes beginning to glow as he took another deep breath that looked like he was smelling me. Maybe that was a Vepar thing. "Has anyone ever told you that you had a body that was made to be fucked," he said, continuing his slow trail down my body.

I was standing in nothing but a strapless bra and thong and despite my best efforts he was beginning to cast a spell of seduction on me that I wasn't sure I could control. I shook my head at his question, thinking about the trail of boyfriends I had left that had all been terrible to boring in bed.

"It is. In fact, I've never seen something I wanted so much before," he continued. I couldn't force a reply out of my mouth. I couldn't think clearly with his hand touching me like that.

"I need to taste you, kitten. It's all I've been thinking about for days. Will you let me do that?"

I moaned a yes. Derrial didn't wait for more encouragement. His fingers caught the waistband of my thong and ripped them away. He dropped to his knees and urged my legs apart.

"Wider," he ordered, and I shocked us both by immediately widening my stance. "Perfect." His hands moved along my thighs and when he reached his destination, he spread it wide and studied it for a moment, a look of appreciation on his face, before his fingers found my cleft. My eyes snapped back shut as he pushed two fingers inside of me.

"Are you always this wet?" he asked.

I shook my head again. "Do I do this to you?" he asked, fucking me slowly with his fingers. I nodded. "Say it, kitten."

"Yes."

"Yes, what? What do I do to you?"

"You make me wet," I moaned.

"Good girl," he murmured with approval. He continued to tease me with his fingers for a few seconds and then the warm rasp of his tongue sent a series of shivers trembling through my body. He licked across me leisurely as his fingers continued to plunge into me. I began to shake as I neared the edge. He pulled away; the effect similar to being doused with ice.

"Not until I say, kitten."

I whimpered at the command, but it gave me the resolve I needed to try and take back control. I didn't need to enjoy tonight, I just needed to get through it. Taking his hand, I pulled him towards one of the bedrooms. I could feel his frustration trailing behind me as we walked.

Despite the fact that his ministrations thus far had lit my entire body on fire, I aimed for a look of nonchalance as I crawled across the bed and laid down on my back looking at him.

I was acutely aware of his eyes on my naked skin as I laid there, but I pretended to ignore the effect he had on me. If he didn't think I liked it, he wouldn't want it again, right? No one wanted a disinterested lover. I was just hopeful that my momentary lapses where he was concerned would be forgotten if the overall package was disappointing.

Derrial slowly took off his jacket and undid his tie. It was amazing that after everything that had happened already this evening that he could still look perfect. He undid his shirt, showcasing a perfect tapestry of golden skin that defied all logic. I had somehow forgotten how good he looked without a shirt over the past few days. He was unreal.

I wondered again if this was his real form or if the Vepar could somehow change their forms to look pleasing to the human eye. If that was the case, he had nailed it. My thoughts flickered over to thinking of what Thane and Corran looked like without a shirt, but Derrial quickly got my attention back by unbuttoning the top of his dress pants and pulling out the most impressive cock I had ever seen. He began to stroke it while looking at me through a hooded gaze. I couldn't keep my eyes off of it. If they did change their appearances, he had gone a little too big. He must have seen my look of panic because he chuckled darkly and took a few steps closer to the bed until he was standing right on the edge of it.

"Don't worry, kitten. It will fit," he said.

"Spread your legs," he ordered, and somehow, I found myself dropping my legs open as he finished dropping his pants so that he was completely naked standing in front of me. He started to crawl across the king bed towards me, so blatantly seductive that I could feel myself becoming wetter just by watching him.

He moved on top of me, hovering there with those strange glowing eyes staring at me as if he was looking for something in my eyes. I gulped. This was actually happening. "Aren't you forgetting a condom?" I asked, suddenly thinking of getting a strange alien disease or worse, a strange alien baby. They had us on mandatory birth control, but I had never seen a discussion if it worked on the Vepar.

Something flickered in his eyes again, but it was gone before I could tell what it was. "Your birth control protects against pregnancy by any species. It's infallible unlike the birth control your human doctors were giving you before. As for diseases, it's impossible for us to carry diseases as our bodies have evolved past that. You'll probably be healthier after this," he said wryly.

I hesitated, not sure if this was a trick. What would he have to gain by getting his hapless human prisoner pregnant? Surely that would be the last thing he wanted. "Ok," I told him, hesitantly.

His eyes glowed up even more before he suddenly struck, sheathing himself inside of me at the same time as he bit into my neck, causing me to cry out as a wave of euphoria like nothing I had experienced before passed over me. I came immediately, tightening around him in what already felt like a vice grip.

He drove into me in relentless strokes, moving to my mouth after his initial taste of my blood. I could feel it running down from my wound. I could taste the coppery flavor as he attacked my lips.

I found myself crying his name as another orgasm splintered through me in violent waves. He continued his thrusts as he raced towards his own, not taking his eyes from me as he did so. There was blood all over his face. He looked more heathen than man in that moment, his eyes glowing so brightly that it almost hurt to look at them.

The moment felt too intimate and I turned my head away from him. "No," he growled, in a voice that was so dark and deep that I didn't recognize it in the moment. My gaze flew back to his. It was as if something inside of him had taken over and it was no longer Derrial in the body above me.

His hands clenched my hips tightly, and I was sure there would be marks there in the morning. He continued to thrust until I could tell the moment that he came undone. Just as I felt him tighten inside of me, he reared back and struck at my neck again. This time the pleasure was so powerful that I passed out, the last thing I saw were those glowing eyes of his looking at me possessively. Everything was dark after that.

When I woke the next morning, my body felt like I did right before the flu hit; achy and feverish. I laid in bed for a moment with my eyes closed, getting my bearings, wondering how a sickness could have struck so quick when I'd been feeling fine before. I shifted and an ache bit between my legs and on my neck. Instantly, I sat up with a start, my eyes flying open as I remembered what happened last night. I scanned the room for Derrial, but I was alone. He'd gone and left me here? We'd scratched our insatiable itch, so was I now free? I ignored the part of my heart that flickered with what felt like pain at the thought.

This was what I had hoped for, so now I could go home. Thinking of my hovel of a loft and my job that gave me just enough for bare essentials and not anything else didn't fill me with the happiness it had in the past. But it was still freedom in a way.

No sooner had those thoughts passed through my mind then the front door of the suite opened with a click, and a second later Derrial came into view. I tugged the blanket up to my neck, suddenly very much aware of the fact I remained naked. Of course, I shouldn't have been shy or had my cheeks on fire after our time together last night, but in truth, those memories of letting myself go made the embarrassment worse. I'd wanted him like I needed air, and just remembering our time together sent a shiver of excitement down through me.

He looked somehow brighter this morning, a huge smile on his face, the corners of his eyes crinkling. He seemed to carry a vibrant sexiness this morning. Plus, his skin seemed to have a sun-kissed glow. He wore a perfect suit as usual, today's was a black pinstripe one with a light blue shirt underneath. In a word, I couldn't believe I slept with a specimen that looked that perfect. An alien who for years I'd detested. Now, my emotions left me lost and confused.

I glanced at myself in the mirror hanging on the side wall and saw how tired I looked, dark circles under my eyes, and my hair sat limp, in desperate need of a wash. My skin appeared abnormally pale. I glanced back at Derrial who stared at me with a speculative gaze. I tried to remember if I'd ever heard of health repercussions for humans who had sex with Vepar, but all I could think of were the stories I'd read about women, and men, who became addicted to whatever the Vepar did in bed. How they spent every moment trying to get the Vepar to notice them and "keep" them. Those people had become obsessive, and I prayed that didn't happen to me, especially with the way I admired Derrial.

So, if the Vepar weren't hazardous to your health, then why did I look and feel like an extra in the Night from the Living Dead?

"How are you feeling this morning, kitten?" Derrial asked in a nonchalant tone.

I scowled at him, now even more suspicious. "What did you do to me?" I asked, my body shaking from the flu like symptoms that seemed to be growing worse. "

"You mean besides the best sex of your life?" he stated in that same casual tone that was beginning to drive me crazy as my anxiety escalated.

I gestured between the two of us with a flick of my hand. "Why do you look like you just got off a yearlong vacation whereas I look and feel like I'm hovering on death's door?"

He stared at his nails as if there was something on them before answering. "Oh, are you feeling the effect of the incomplete bond? I've heard that can be painful to experience," he explained nonchalantly as if we were discussing the latest score of the Lakers.

Bond.

What the fuck.

My heart slammed into my ribcage. What was he talking about? Granted I hadn't done my best to learn as much about the Vepar after my parents vanished as I could, but I'd think if there was such a thing as bonding between humans and Vepar, surely someone would have mentioned it by now?

"What do you mean? What bond?" I whispered in a hoarse voice, curling forward as I clutched the blanket to my chest tighter.

"I'm sure you remember my bites from last night?" he asked with a smirk as if proud of himself. "The bite is something that dates back to Vepar ancestors, it was a way to claim property...or claim their mate. It made it so that the intended creature was bound to males because of the enzymes that are deposited in their skin. The symptoms you're feeling are withdrawal symptoms. They'll only be evened out by either me biting you again...or you drinking my blood."

I padded over on bare feet into the kitchen admiring how the floorboards in this hotel were shiny and so clean. I pictured myself living somewhere like this, with such luxury, and I doubted I'd ever leave to go outside. Not when I had everything I needed right here.

Like the previous days, I swiftly scanned the tables and couches in case Derrial or one of the guards had left behind their cells considering all the phones had been removed from this penthouse. Maybe I was being foolish in even believing I had anyone to call for help. After witnessing Derrial's influence over world leaders, what exactly would authorities do if I called, insisting he'd kidnapped me? I wasn't a fool not to know how badly that could go for me. I would need a different tactic. Sure, I loved it here, but this was me floating high on an alien's blood and daydreaming of living in a fairytale.

Stomping over to the fridge, I pulled it open, expecting food, but instead I stared at bottles of water. I sighed before having a bright idea. I grabbed some water and headed over to the couch. I flopped down and collected the menu from the hotel's restaurant. This would all be under Derrial's name, which meant I could order anything.

Once I made my choice, I headed to the front door and cranked it open. In a flash, a guard stepped in my path, broad shouldered and enormous.

"You can't leave," he snorted.

"Fine by me." I shrugged and handed him a piece of paper.

He stared at it, his brow furrowing in a dozen lines, then glanced up at me quizzically without accepting the note.

I pushed it to his hand once again. "I'm hungry and I need you to go order this food for me."

He cocked an eyebrow, stiffening as if getting me food was below his pay rank. The other guard farther down the corridor chuckled, and I noted only two of them guarded my door.

I slouched a hip into the door frame and huffed. "Do you really want me to tell Derrial I've been starving all day, close to fainting, because you refused to get me a bit of food?"

He made a grunting sound deep in his chest, glaring at me from hooded eyes, and snatched the paper from my hand before studying it. He snorted. "A bit of food? Where are you going to put all this?" Looking my way, he scanned me head to toe. "And there's no salad or vegetable in sight?"

I gritted my teeth, refusing to show him how much I wanted to hit him in the nose, even if it required me to get on tippy toes to do so. If I was trapped in a penthouse, then I was spoiling myself, and right now I was so hungry, it made me impatient and my pulse raced with a desperation to eat something.

"Don't forget the sundae." I stepped back inside and slammed the door shut.

Where had my feistiness come from, all in the name of food? Hell hath no fury when my stomach rumbled. I smirked, grabbed an apple from the complimentary hotel fruit basket, and crashed onto my bed while switching on the television.

Half an hour later and still no food, I was about to check with the guards where my order was, when the click of the front door sounded.

Yes!

I hurried out of my bedroom, calling out over my shoulder, "Give me a sec, I'll be right out."

With my mouth already salivating and deciding I'd devour the sundae first, I rushed down the hallway and into the living room.

But instead of food waiting for me, I found Derrial, his back to me, staring out the window. He wore jeans and a black dress shirt. When did he get changed? Peering at him closer, I realized that he stood wrong. One shoulder sat slightly lower than the other, he looked somehow smaller, deflated. Strange since he was a man who towered over others, never backing down. Maybe something had happened at the Summit?

"Derrial? Is everything okay?"

He didn't respond at first, but he cracked his neck, and a shiver slithered up my back. Unease crept over me when he didn't answer.

"What's going on?" I asked.

The space around him seemed to quiver or was I seeing things?

When he started to turn around, the room dimmed...

Something was very wrong.

The energy around him darkened and now flowed off his body like waves. And when he faced me, I gasped.

My stomach sunk through me, rattling me at the core.

"Who are you?" I recoiled, hugging myself, noting he stood in my way to escape.

A different Vepar I'd never seen before stood before me, and in a heartbeat, he lunged towards me. Eyes wide and dark, hands reaching out for me.

I screamed when my world tilted under me.

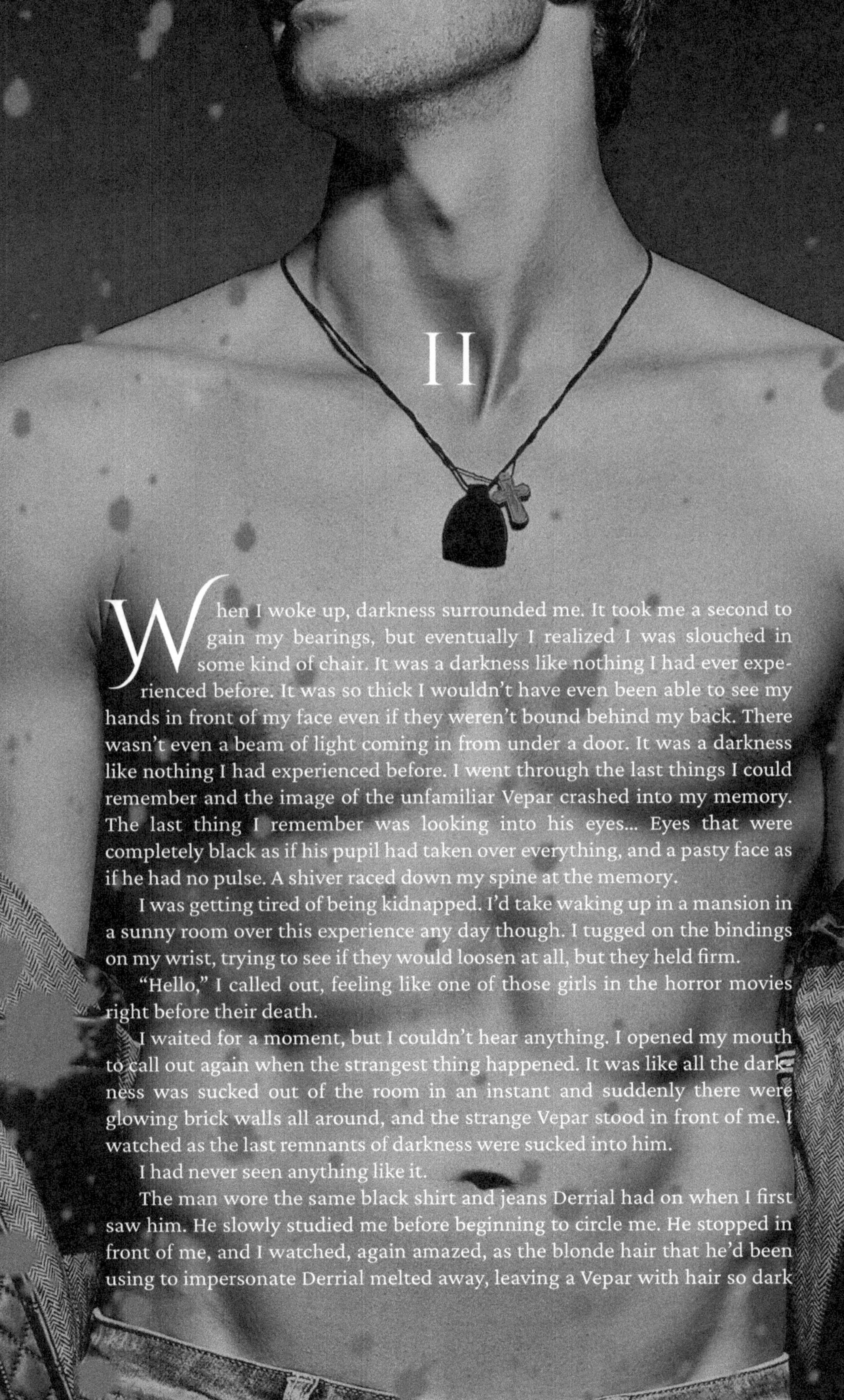

II

When I woke up, darkness surrounded me. It took me a second to gain my bearings, but eventually I realized I was slouched in some kind of chair. It was a darkness like nothing I had ever experienced before. It was so thick I wouldn't have even been able to see my hands in front of my face even if they weren't bound behind my back. There wasn't even a beam of light coming in from under a door. It was a darkness like nothing I had experienced before. I went through the last things I could remember and the image of the unfamiliar Vepar crashed into my memory. The last thing I remember was looking into his eyes... Eyes that were completely black as if his pupil had taken over everything, and a pasty face as if he had no pulse. A shiver raced down my spine at the memory.

I was getting tired of being kidnapped. I'd take waking up in a mansion in a sunny room over this experience any day though. I tugged on the bindings on my wrist, trying to see if they would loosen at all, but they held firm.

"Hello," I called out, feeling like one of those girls in the horror movies right before their death.

I waited for a moment, but I couldn't hear anything. I opened my mouth to call out again when the strangest thing happened. It was like all the darkness was sucked out of the room in an instant and suddenly there were glowing brick walls all around, and the strange Vepar stood in front of me. I watched as the last remnants of darkness were sucked into him.

I had never seen anything like it.

The man wore the same black shirt and jeans Derrial had on when I first saw him. He slowly studied me before beginning to circle me. He stopped in front of me, and I watched, again amazed, as the blonde hair that he'd been using to impersonate Derrial melted away, leaving a Vepar with hair so dark that it matched his strange black eyes. I gasped. That was the most alien thing I'd seen so far.

Staying on the theme of horror movies, he looked like a character from one of those movies that portrayed people who were possessed by demons. Except I was pretty sure the creature standing in front of me was far scarier than a demon would be. For one, I'd seen enough flicks and read enough to know what a demon was. But this thing in front of me... I had zero clue and that terrified me. I shook in my chair, desperate to run. Except, I was stuck inside a room.

Another prison.

And this time I was with a monster.

"So fascinating," he whispered in a voice that was as smooth and slick as oil. The voice seemed to emanate from inside my brain, and I shook my head at the strange feeling.

I knew I shouldn't say something, but my curiosity won out. "What's fascinating?" I asked.

The creature grinned. Unlike the other Vepar I'd seen who all seemed to have perfect movie star smiles, this one carried a mouth filled with razor sharp teeth, kind of like a shark. I had been thinking that this creature was a Vepar, but now that I had seen the strange teeth, I wasn't so sure. All I knew was that this being made Derrial and the others look as friendly as a teddy bear compared to him.

"It's something I'm sure they weren't anticipating," the creature muttered to himself, still staring at me avidly. He must have seen the look of confusion on my pale face because he smiled again, flashing those horrid teeth that had me pressing back into my chair. "The bond, little human. You're the first successful human/Vepar bond to be completed since they started trying. And by completing the bond, you also became the target for every Vepar enemy in the vicinity." He chuckled and the sound was like knives down my arms.

Nope, nothing good would come from this thing in front of me.

I must have still been staring at him with a dumb look on my face because he continued. "Humans normally don't even appear on our radar. Your species are like ants scurrying about with no idea of anything that's going on around them. Only higher-level beings garner any interest." He raised his chin, his shoulders back.

He went on, "Vepar and all the rest are almost like glowing figures in night vision goggles, they're easy to spot. While they appear as a faint glow, you my dear are like the fireworks. You light up the darkness like nothing I've ever seen before. Every creature within a hundred galaxies will want you. And I got to you first." His voice darkened and he almost drooled at saying those last few words.

I was trying to absorb his words and their meaning. "If what you're saying is true, how did you get to me so fast. The bond only just happened."

He smiled again, his teeth sending sharp shivers of dread throughout my body, and I decided right then I loathed his smile. Better he grimaced.

"We had something planned for the Summit. But when I saw you, everything changed. You were too good to pass up," he answered with a shrug.

"What are you?" I demanded.

The room started to darken, black mists erupted from his skin until it started to envelop everything, creating that same all-encompassing blackness as before.

"We are the Khonsu," his voice whispered, seeming to be coming from all around me. I could feel something stroking my face, almost like a hand. It was as if the dark mists were an extension of him.

Suddenly the faint touches changed from a soft sensation to what felt like a whip lashing across my face. A jolting pain shuddered across my cheek, and I screamed as the lashes spread all over my body, ripping at my skin.

I screamed and tucked my chin low, but my hands tied at my back kept me locked to the chair.

A piercing pain seared across my body worse than a branding iron.

It was impossible to tell where the next lash would hit next since I couldn't even see an inch from my face. All my mind could comprehend was pain. I lost all thoughts; all I could do was burrow my head into my chest. Away from the pain radiating me, burning me alive.

The assault never relented, never stopped, never gave me a chance.

Blood soaked my torn clothes, each new strike a sharp bite to my flesh, ripping me to shreds. My throat grew raw from cries, but they went unheard.

In those moments, I prayed for my death, to be taken because I couldn't take another second.

As if sensing my end, the whips paused, granting me a brief reprieve. Tears tracked my cheeks and fell over my jawline, every inch of me drowning with agony.

I glanced up from the curtain of my hair covering my face, looking for the creature, hoping for an end. But as before, only darkness surrounded me.

Still, I sensed the bastard. Felt him in my head because just when I would recover enough to stay conscious, the whips returned.

Over and over he tortured me, and his laughter echoed in my head.

Please god, kill me.

My whole life I'd fought for survival, battled through depression after losing my parents, struggled to keep a job and keep myself going every day for the simple reason that my mom and dad would have wanted me to, that one day I might see them again.

But now... Now I had enough of everything. The exhaustion tore through me, and I no longer wanted to face the shitstorm of my life. This was it.

Just like most things in my life, I was taken, forced, and shoved aside. And I went along each time, believing in hope. But I'd been fooling myself, and now I had enough. I needed the exit button because I wanted to tap out.

I hiccupped a strangled cry and ached as a deep strike raked down my back. I floated back and forth out of consciousness.

In that moment, I would have done anything to escape.

The agony faded once again, easing the darkness that was consuming me. I watched through barely open eyes as my tormenter appeared in front of me. He smirked and heaved each breath as if my bloody state and agony delighted him. But he looked different, gone was his pasty complexion, and now he carried a shiny, healthy glow like Derrial had earlier that morning. Was this creature somehow feeding on my blood too?

The fear in my veins melted under the inferno of rage drumming through me. I had enough of being used and abused by this monster.

As I slouched in the seat, my quickened breaths grew raspy during the small reprieve, and an idle thought floated through my mind. I'd been told of vampires around campfires as a little girl. And now meeting these aliens, I questioned if the tales didn't have it wrong. They romanticized vampires, others had them as misunderstood, or starved undead. But what if they were creatures who came from space to use humans? If I had known that as a little girl, I wouldn't have ever been able to sleep another wink.

"Such a strong, brave, little human," the creature cooed as he stepped closer. He reached out, catching a little of the blood that dripped from the side of my face. He licked the droplet he'd caught on his finger, almost sounding like he was having an orgasm when he tasted it, his eyes rolling back into his head, groaning. The sound disgusted me, bile climbing to my throat.

"You're beautiful painted in red," he declared, his eyes snapping open. Before he even started to let the darkness out once again, I was prepared for my life to end at that point, so nothing shocked me more than when the walls started to dissolve around us. The creature jerked around, his face twisting into a disfigured beast.

What was going on?

"I'll just take some for the road," he snarled, his upper lip creased with a look of disappointment. In haste, he swiped his palm across my bloody arm. I screamed in agony as white-hot pain raced over my skin as if his touch was barbed wire, shutting my eyes.

"See you shortly," he whispered in my ear and licked my neck, the sound turning my stomach.

When the pain had subsided enough for me to open my eyes, he was gone, and the walls had almost completely disintegrated with only a puff of dust in their place.

I couldn't imagine what creature was waiting for me now, I couldn't comprehend what could be scary enough to get the black-eyed devil to flee but whatever came next would end up killing me.

Shaking all over and my vision blurring in and out, I sat there with what felt like hundreds of open wounds, blood dripping on the concrete floor around the seat, and tried to prepare myself for death.

I was ready...Ready to face my maker. To end the horrendous pain.

Tears rolled down my face, stinging the cuts they fell into and continuing their journey down to the corner of my mouth. A hooded vale of death hung over me, and in that moment in time when I wasn't sure how I could ever recover, I welcomed the easy way out. As gutless as it sounded, I couldn't keep this up.

When a figure appeared where a wall had been minutes earlier, I blinked hard to clear my vision. Was I seeing right? A familiar, gorgeous, tatted Vepar appeared in front of me, my brain evidently having enough. I was hallucinating. Thane's penetrating gaze was the last thing that I saw before I finally let the effects of my wounds carry me away.

"Pet, wake up," were the words I woke to. I really would like to stop losing consciousness I decided as I struggled for what felt like the millionth time to open my eyes. I sighed as I felt a soft, wet cloth gently being moved over my burning wounds. The coolness helped ease away the pain somewhat but considering I felt as if I'd just climbed out of a pool it was clear that I was still bleeding profusely.

My muscles hurt as I tried to move them. When I finally wrenched my eyes open wide enough to see anything, I stared up into Thane's worried, blue gaze. I'm sure I looked like hell.

"Stay with me, pet," he murmured, continuing to move the cool cloth over my aching wounds. "We just need to get the bleeding to stop and you'll be better in a flash." He held a device similar to the one that corran had used on me at the mansion and started to run it over my injuries.

"Fuck."

His sudden outburst had me flinching, and I regretted the sudden movement as a searing pain shuddered through me.

He threw the device down beside him, his brow pinching, and he must have seen the questioning look in my eyes. "We use that device to heal skin lesions. That bastard must have used his darkness to inflict these wounds because I can't heal cuts this way."

It was like I could actually feel the life leaking out of my body. Thane had gently laid me down on the concrete floor in the torture room, and despite the ugliness of the location, I soaked up his beauty as he tended to my injuries. At least I'd have something gorgeous to look at as I died, I thought amusedly. There could be worse ways to die.

"So, we may have to do this the old-fashioned way." He offered me a soft smile and I wasn't sure if that was meant to be a joke.

"You could always take me to the hospital," I suggested in a whisper, well aware of what his answer would be, but figuring it was worth trying.

"That's not what I was talking about, pet." He brushed a strand of hair caught on my lashes out of my face. "The quickest way to remove your pain and heal you is with a blood exchange." He stared at me with a smirk as if he knew what Derrial and I had done.

"Do you mean a bond?" I asked, sounding snappier than I'd intended, or maybe I had meant it that way because no one had even explained what such a connection entailed. "You need to explain what a bond means first," I gasped even as a wave of pain shot up my leg and I convulsed as the pain rolled through me, faster and harder. Shutting my eyes, I let it pass and stayed statue still until the thrumming eased.

Soft fingers stroked my hand. "My blood will run in your veins and yours in mine. I will share with you some of my healing ability, but it also means…"

He wiped his mouth, almost nervous, and I looked at him, sensing something big was coming. "It means what?"

"The fact you didn't die when you were bound with Derrial means your blood is compatible with ours, and we were right to sense there was something special about you."

"What does…" My words trailed off from the burning pain, feeling as if someone jammed blades into my open injuries. "Why does it hurt so much?" I cried out, gripping Thane's hand, squeezing it as the deadening sensation crashed through me over and over.

His breath was on my cheek. "Pet, I can help you, but you have to willingly agree to bond with me. The darkness he used to cut you up has a toxin in it, made to bring you unbearable pain for weeks after the infliction."

Sweat slid down the side of my face, or maybe it was blood. I had no clue. I still stared at Thane incredulous though. Was he fucking kidding? He was staring at me with compassion and he had offered me a way out. Earlier I was willing to die to stop the torture, and now I was ready to be set free from the pain.

"Yes," I cried. "Please, make it stop."

"I will," was all he said, then took out a small blade from his belt. "I need to make a small incisor on fresh skin as your cuts have poison that sits on the wound."

"Do it. Hurry," I cried as another stream of pain rushed over me, making me feel like someone was raking nails across my body. The pain was so bad that I couldn't even tell Thane had finished cutting me until I glanced over and saw him pressing my finger into his mouth. His eyelids fluttered as if the taste did something to him, taking him to another realm.

When he finally lowered my hand and licked his bloody teeth, he sliced his thumb and pressed it to my parted lips. Drops rushed over my tongue, and I lapped the blood, its coppery, sweet taste flooding my mouth. Already, the sharpness of my wounds was retreating.

He must have cut himself deep, because I was taking in more than I had with Derrial. As my pain eased, I gripped his hand, holding on. I needed more until the pain was completely stopped. As I drank his blood, I found myself forgetting the day, forgetting that I had ever been hurt.

Thane ripped his hand from my grip, his thumb tugged out of my mouth, making a popping sound.

I licked my lips feverishly, in those seconds believing he might try to take the blood back.

"Enough," he growled. "Blood sharing can become an addiction, so we need to be careful."

As I lay there, feeling the calmness spread over me, I remembered the monster's words. How I shone so bright they'd find me, how I was special, and how his kind, the Khonsu, would hunt me down. A different fear strangled me now, and it became hard to breathe once again as the truth of my reality slammed into me.

No matter where I ran or hid, I'd never be safe.

12

Who are the Khonsu?" I shuffled in my bed in the mansion, pulling the blanket to my chest. Thane had flown us both back to their place in the helicopter after exchanging blood with me. Derrial needed to attend an urgent matter in another country so he hadn't returned home yet after he had been assured by Thane that I was safe. I suspected Derrial was an ambassador for his home planet, even though he had refused to tell me what his position was while I was with him. But it would explain why he seemed to be so damn important. I wished he would hurry home so that I could ask him more questions. Despite how my relationship had changed with the Vepar, I still wanted to know all about them and how the hell I could avoid them and the Khonsu for eternity.

"You need to get some sleep for the blood to fully heal you," Thane insisted, staring down at me, his strong arms folded over his chest. I couldn't help but stare at where his biceps bulged. With his short, dark hair, he could easily pass for a god. He looked like he was almost built of stone, and ready to battle any monster.

I lifted my arm and wiggled it. My wounds had healed to thin marks on my skin. "Looks pretty good to me. Your blood is like magic. You could help so many humans with it, you know."

He studied me, and I wasn't sure if he intended to burst out laughing or scold me. "My blood is toxic to anyone who isn't compatible with our kind."

There was that word again. *Compatible.* The way he said it made it sound so robotic. But why was I special to the Vepar? I gained healing from them, but what did they get from me? I tried not to think too hard about the fact that Derrial took the chance to exchange our blood, knowing if I wasn't compatible, I'd die. We would be talking about that later. I'm just glad their hunch that I was "special" from the beginning had been true.

"Khonsu," he began, and I shoved all other thoughts aside, focused on his words. "They're a race that inhabit my home planet, Veon." He paused for a moment, the wheels of thinking spinning behind his gaze. He sat on the bed's edge, facing me. "I'll try to explain using Earth terms. There are over 400 billion stars in the Milky Way, and all kinds of races exist there. But Veon circles a sun that is the closest to your Solar System. Your scientists call it Proxima Centauri."

I nodded, wishing I had my phone to Google all of this. I tried to lock it in my memory for later.

"The Khonsu aren't originally from Veon. They arrived after the sun near their home planet died. They apparently came from one of the rings of stars that circled the Milky Way. Their kind had to either escape or die, and we accepted them onto our land."

I nodded, wondering if there was more to these Khonsu then what had first appeared. I couldn't imagine what it would have been like to get up one morning and leave a planet forever.

"At first, they settled on the isolated side of Veon, but soon, Vepar started going missing, and we later discovered the Khonsu were hunting our kind, killing us in masses, to take the planet for themselves. We also found out we weren't the first race to have them attack in this manner. And now we hunt one another on Veon, and it's unsafe for anyone."

Engrossed, I almost forgot to breathe. "Holy shit! So, what the hell are they doing on Earth?"

He exhaled loudly, his shoulders sagging forward. "Some stowed away on our ships when we came to Earth."

I recalled Derrial's threat about the dog-like creatures escaping from the vessel. I still didn't know if those creatures were real, but the creature that I knew for sure had escaped was a million times scarier.

"You should get some sleep now." He pulled the blanket to my chin, but I didn't want to sleep. I had so many questions, so many things I had to understand.

As he turned to leave, I grabbed his wrist. "Please, don't leave."

He stared at our connection, at my hand so pale and small against his tanned skin, his strong arm. When he met my eyes, an expression I didn't understand fluttered across his face, and his breathing quickened. His reaction made my pulse start to race as the heat from where our skin touched spread over to me.

I released my hold, and he sank onto the edge of the bed, pulling a bent leg between us as he faced me.

"Nothing will harm you in this home. It's reinforced, and you're safe."

"Why did the Khonsu come after me?"

With a deep inhale, he sighed. "We never should have let you go to the

Summit, but we didn't know the Khonsu had infiltrated the meeting. Or maybe they didn't infiltrate it, and they just happened to see you while you were outside."

I swallowed hard. "That doesn't answer my question."

"Just like we sensed there was something different about you, so can they."

"Is that why you brought me to your house in the first place? That Khonsu said I glowed and that I was easy to detect to your kind."

The corners of his mouth tightened. "He's not our kind," he snapped, then inhaled sharply. "We are different races, but share some abilities, like blood bonding. For us, it's about finding our forever mate, but for them, it's a feeding frenzy as others' blood heightens their energy. It makes them stronger, feeds their adrenaline, and not even one of your human bullets would stop them. They have one purpose. Take over worlds and hunt down as many compatible females to feed from."

"Crap." I paused for a moment. "Wait! Why wouldn't they attack men for their blood?" I pulled my knees up under the blanket and hugged them.

"Only females carry the pheromone."

I swallowed the boulder in my throat because this told me the women on their planet were in danger, and the men would have had to step up to protect them, save them.

"What's stopping them from going out there and finding another compatible woman to drink their blood?"

"You're the only one we've found so far on Earth, and we've been watching your planet for years."

I studied him for a long pause. "So, you came to search for compatible females?"

He paused and the way the features on his face morphed into an expressionless one, I suspected there were more reasons for their interest in Earth, and not something he'd just offer up.

"You're special, Ella," he said.

I choked on a forced laugh. "If being special means attracting the attention of a blood-sucking monster, then count me out. I don't want any of this."

He looked at me with pity in his gaze, but that wouldn't help me. What was I going to do? Hide out in this mansion forever?

"How do I stop them from coming after me?" I pleaded, my voice coming out barely a whisper.

This time, he took my hand in his. "If we knew that answer, we would have eradicated them from our planet long ago."

His confession sat in my gut like concrete, spreading, dragging me into a sea of fear because it meant I was stuck. These things that snuck onto Earth now saw me as a means to make themselves stronger, and I wasn't a fool to ignore what that entailed.

Me imprisoned.

For life.

Tortured and whipped.

Drained of blood but kept alive so they could keep taking and taking.

I could barely take a breath as I pictured myself locked up for life by these things.

Thane's thumb caressed the back of my hand in small circles. The move was slow and tender, and it made me glance over at him. He must have seen the fright on my face because he leaned closer, his arms reaching out and looping around my back. He pulled me against him. Embraced by his strength, I let myself melt against the rock wall that was his chest, my ear just above his heart.

Bang. Bang. Bang. It thumped.

"We'll be by your side always."

But my mind refused to make sense of his words because all I heard was forever, and that terrified me. How could they stay with me so long? And then they mentioned the whole being bonded to me forever. What the hell did that mean? Forever until I died of old age? I couldn't live a life without freedom, without the chance to make more friends, to maybe even get married and have kids. Not that I wanted that now but wasn't that what people did? Maybe that wasn't possible in our world now with the Vepar here.

On one bright side, if the Khonsu couldn't find another compatible person, they wouldn't have to kill anyone. Maybe they'd leave this planet, or perhaps the Vepar had already put into motion a means to eradicate them from our planet. I didn't know the answer to anything, I just wanted to survive. To not be miserable, or be dragged down with fear, and definitely to not be tortured.

This was a new world we all had ventured into and the unknown was like an ominous cloud over all our heads.

Were the Vepar really here as a potential backup home in case they couldn't remove the Khonsu on their planet or before all their females were killed by the Khonsu? But then why would they bother bonding to me? Or did I have it all wrong and they bonded to many females, which begged the question of what they got out of the connection? Dozens of questions circled my mind, my head buzzed, and didn't want to face any of this because things seemed so much more complicated than I anticipated.

Thane rubbed my back, his breath washing through my hair, his arms were like lifebelts wrapped around me.

"Will I ever have my normal life back?" I finally broke the silence and glanced up.

He stared down at me, his blue eyes glinting. "You will always be safe with us," he said again.

I couldn't find any words to say to him as he had basically just admitted I would never be returning home. I pressed my cheek back against his chest, seeking comfort even though he was partially the cause of all my problems. The dreaded answer I knew all along was now confirmed. Normality was gone for me, and only uncertainty lay ahead. While so many other questions poured through my mind about where I'd live such an existence, and if they intended to stay on Earth forever, I didn't ask them. I couldn't bear to hear the answers because holding myself together now was hard enough as I trembled in his arms and tears pricked my eyes.

Everything I knew would change.

Any dreams I had were gone forever.

I curled further into Thane.

He nudged me slightly as he shuffled further onto the bed and climbed in under the blanket with me. Taking me into his arms once again, we lay together, tears sliding out of the corners of my eyes. Everything was happening so fast, and now I couldn't even be angry at the three Vepar. If they found me glowing, then the Khonsu would have done so sooner or later and I would much rather be with the Vepar than the Khonsu.

"Everything will be alright," Thane whispered softly, his voice as light as a caress. He kissed the top of my head and I couldn't help the warmth that spread over me.

I'd be lost without their protection, because nothing would ever be all right again. Not a single thing.

I woke with a start, my pulse jumping beneath my skin, my heart banging in my ears. A droplet of sweat rolled down the side of my face, while the room spun around me. I could have sworn I had just experienced the worst nightmare of my life, but somehow, I couldn't remember a single thing that had happened in the dream. Only the darkness lingered in my chest, that ominous feeling that told me danger lay near.

When I pushed myself up in bed, I shuddered at the sight in front of me.

This *was* my bedroom in the mansion, except it wasn't. Instead of the walls and ceiling, lofty trees crowded together, grand ones with busy branches covered in the greenest leaves. They swayed and the rustling flooded the room, yet I felt no wind.

What the hell was going on? I rubbed my eyes, but the trees remained.

In slow motion, I crept out of bed, almost tripping from the sheets tangled around my legs. Tugging on the blanket, I finally freed myself and stumbled, teetering on my feet and falling against a tree.

I glanced up into the canopy covering the ceiling. Everything seemed so real, but I didn't understand how it could be. I felt a nearby tree and pulled back immediately in surprise. The bark was rough and bumpy under my hand.

A fogginess clung to my mind as I tried to think straight, work out what exactly was going on. From across the bedroom, a shadow shifted in the far corner, and my heart hit the back of my throat. Sliding across the wall of trees behind me, a scream pushed through my lungs as the darkness flitted across the opposite wall as if mimicking my actions.

Was this some kind of Vepar thing, or had the Khonsu found me? Thane said I'd be safe here, that the mansion was protected. But then where the freak did the trees come from? My head felt like it was swimming in fog.

I reached for the door handle and opened it in slow motion. Barely able to breath, I turned and sprinted out of the bedroom.

The hallway blurred around me, everything fuzzy and jumpy, but I didn't care. Not when dread crept up the back of my legs and there was a monster in the house.

More trees flanked the passage as I ran faster than possible toward the stairs.

A quick glance back, and the shadow emerged, a lofty figure with piercing red eyes.

My earlier scream tore past my throat, and I darted down the steps, moving too fast. Everything felt strange, like I was moving in slow motion and I couldn't run faster. It was going to catch me, just like the Khonsu. And I doubted I'd survive this time.

A thundering sounded around me, getting louder, closer.

Panic gripped me, and my feet tangled over one another. I tripped, the world racing up toward me. Everything was happening too fast, and my sight was blurring in and out.

Something huge raced up toward me from the kitchen. There were more of those creatures?

I cried out louder as I fell, my arms fluttering outward for something to grab onto.

I hit the ground; except I didn't hit the wooden floorboards like I was expecting. I landed in someone's arms, soft and strong at the same time. It had gotten me. I wasn't going to go down easily, so I started to kick and punch, digging my nails into whatever I could.

"Ella!" Thane's voice found me.

"Help," I shouted, thrashing, my vision still a wash of blurs and shapes.

Someone grasped my hands and legs, carrying me as if I were a sacrifice. Two figures hovered over me. I kept blinking, shaking my head to clear the fuzziness, the tears making it worse.

Finally, I was laid on something soft, the hands releasing me.

I scrambled backward into a corner, rubbing my eyes, and slowly the view in front of me cleared. It seemed to still be blurry, but as I stared up, I could see well enough to realize that Thane and corran were in front of me, both wearing worried expressions.

"There is something upstairs," I blurted frantically, pointing to the stairs.

Corran stared up, following my pointed finger, while Thane suddenly had a glass of liquid in his hand. He pushed it into my grasp.

"Drink."

I did. It had a sweet fruity flavor that I didn't recognize. But I was so thirsty that I gulped down the whole glass, drenching the heat consuming me. "Why are there trees upstairs? Is that some weird Vepar technology?"

They exchanged glances before looking down at me once more, Thane's mouth spreading into a grin.

"Pet, there are no trees upstairs, no monsters either. You're safe."

I stared at him for the longest moment, then glanced up to see the branches of a tree sticking out from the hallway. Looking back at the men, I couldn't remember if I had responded to them. They were staring at me as if I'd lost my mind. We continued to stare at each other. I wasn't sure how much time was passing without words, but I couldn't seem to form any. It felt like fifteen minutes had passed, maybe more before I could finally find my voice. I said, "It's up there, go and see."

Running a hand over his face, Corran collected the empty glass from my grip while Thane headed upstairs, right past the trees without giving them a glance.

Was I imagining this? I kept shaking my head, unable to dislodge the feeling I was floating on air. Was I still dreaming? Staring at my hand, it seemed to shine. Wow, this was new.

"Ella?" Someone touched my hand and I looked down to find it was Thane, crouching in front of me.

When had he come back downstairs? "You're hallucinating, pet. It's a normal reaction from the poison on your wounds from the Khonsu."

I shook my head, and the room tilted around me. "Whoa, did you feel that?"

"You just need to sit here and let that drink get through your system." Corran flopped down next to me. He looped an arm around my back and brought me closer. I lay on my side, with my head on his lap. His hand stroked my hair so gently, it lulled me into a calmness, my raging pulse easing.

My eyelids closed and I let myself fall under his touch.

I had no idea how much time had passed, but when I opened my eyes, the sunlight had dimmed and now Thane shared the sofa with me. We were alone, and he looked down at me, caring for me, holding me tight. But something felt different inside of me, an emptiness and barren feeling I hadn't had before. I was lost in a world that was meant to be my home, or was it that I felt trapped?

"I think something's wrong," I murmured. "I feel wrong."

He smiled and pushed a lock of hair out of my face. "What can I do to aid you?" And with those words, a mischievous grin split his lips.

I3

"Make me feel something, Thane. Please..." I begged, the words so easily falling from my lips. I was never needy, I hadn't ever been allowed to be. But right now, I longed to feel his touch. I needed to feel his skin on mine, to wrap my arms tightly around him, to feel him consume me. To feel he was real, that they all were real. To remind myself I wasn't all alone in the world even though it felt like it in that moment.

He scooped me up in his arms, carrying me to the room upstairs where I was glad to see there actually were no trees, setting me down on my feet beside the bed. He took my face in his hands, his beautiful blue eyes penetrating deep into my soul. I moaned in response to his feverish kiss, my body pulsing from the onslaught, my hands taking him in thankful ownership, working their way around his waist, up the sculpted form of his back and shoulders.

His fingers slid into the hair at my nape and pulled tight, cocking my head back roughly to force my gaze. "You're not alone, Ella." He paused, his eyes searching mine. "Don't. Ever. Fucking. Leave us. We'll find you every time. Do you understand?"

"Yes. Please..."

His mouth crashed back to mine, desperate orders spewed into our kiss... "You'll stay. You'll never leave. You're mine, Ella."

His large body overtook me, forcing me onto the bed. The sight of him crawling over the top of me sent my pulse racing in anticipation. The feel of his weight was intoxicating as he lowered his lips passionately to mine. I relished in the strength of his body, running my hands along his form, needing to feel all of him. My fingers squeezed and clawed at every perfectly defined muscle. My head screamed to push him away, to hate him, but at the same time, I longed for him. I yearned to forget the shitstorm I'd found myself in, or maybe something was really wrong with me since I couldn't help myself around these Vepar.

Our kiss was hectic, intense. We consumed each other, reaching to the deepest recesses of our mouths, the need to brand each other mutual. Heated, our fingers working in a desperate urgency to touch. Our clothes came off in a whirlwind of hands, tugging and ripping each other's shirts off, before moving to discard our pants. I gasped as he slowly, teasingly slid his hands up my legs, tearing my underwear from my body, eliciting my slight scream.

My gaze darted back to his, and I whimpered at the burning heat emanating from his stare as he slid his muscled form over the top of me, resuming his passionate kisses. Kisses that worked their way down my trembling body, pausing at my chest, my belly button, to tantalize every inch of my skin with savoring licks of his devouring lips and tongue.

"Thane," I moaned as he spread my legs with a firm pull, my whole body clenching in anticipation of his sinful mouth, but desperate for him to fill it at the same time.

"You're so beautiful," he whispered, kissing my thighs, teasing me with his tongue. "It's like you were made for us. Such a delicate, perfect little human," he sighed out. His words only heightened the sensations that I already drowned in. I needed to hear words like this.

My body bowed to his delicious mercy, and I panted as he continued his ministrations. I grabbed his hair, moaning with every touch. I pulled and urged the return of his lips to mine, missing the feel of them against mine. Everything he did felt out of this world, different but just as good as my night with Derrial. I wondered if it could be like this with any experienced men or were the Vepar just particularly good in bed?

Kissing was incredible, but I needed him inside of me. I pulled him closer to me, trying to signal what I wanted without breaking contact with him. Finally he moved to settle between my legs, his heat scorching hot against my sex.

"You're sure about this?" he asked me, sounding almost like he was in pain as he paused above me.

"Isn't it obvious?" I clasped his face and resumed our frenzied kiss. When he finally thrusted inside of me, our simultaneous moans echoed through the tangle of our lips. He felt euphoric, like he was always meant to be a part of me. Like I've been missing him my entire life.

He glided in and out with precision, his gaze never straying from mine. I was mesmerized by the intensity of the moment. I'd been so full of anger when I was with Derrial. Would it have been like this if I had let myself feel something?

"Is this real?" I whispered as an unwelcome tear slid down my face.

He thrust inside me one more time before responding, watching the tear's descent. "This is the realest thing I've ever felt," he finally answered in a gruff voice that almost sounded as if he was choked up. His words consumed me, and he continued to move in and out of me.

The strength of our connection was to die for, every nerve inside of me awakened at his touch. I bowed uncontrollably, moving in helpless abandonment as the pleasure heightened. Seated fully, he stilled, and lifted his head to stare into my eyes. His blue gaze searched mine. I was speechless. Breathless. The pure emotion reflected in his stare had me sucking in air. There was something there between us, something I couldn't put into words, but I realized I wanted to hear it desperately. We stared at one another for what felt like an eternity until he finally closed his eyes, breaking the moment. When he opened them again, the words were gone.

He brushed his fingers along my forehead, pushing the strands of hair away. His lips started to move, and I pulled his lips back to mine before he could speak. Our bodies said what our lips couldn't. I mewled into his kiss as his thrusts grew faster. My hips met his thrusts, measure for measure, needing him so deep inside me I wasn't sure I'd survive otherwise. We were frenetic in our need for each other, desperate, unable to pull away.

He drew his lips from mine, and instead, he took mock bites out of my flesh across my collarbone. His hand slid beneath my back, pulling me closer. I arched my body towards him, my head falling backward as his lips continued to move down my body.

"Fall for me," he whispered, and his words are my undoing. The sexy timber of his voice combined with the steady tempo of his thrusts sent me plummeting over the precipice. Screaming his name, I slid my hands in his hair, gripping hard, riding the overwhelming waves of pleasure, convulsing uncontrollably. His thrusts pounded relentlessly as I rode the ebbs and flows, in and out, deeper and deeper into my clutching depths, before he finally stilled above me. He gave a delicious groan as he peppered my face and neck with kisses.

Harsh breaths amid the grasp of each other's arms, we awaited the slowing of our rapid heartbeats in euphoric silence. Sliding out of me, he chuckled at my elicited whimper, turning to his side on the mattress, pulling me with him.

"I'm not done with you yet, sweetheart," he warned playfully, running his fingers gently along my sweat-slickened back.

"I hope you'll never be," I admitted shyly.

His eyes widened at my admission, and I worried for a second, I'd said too much.

"Good," he replied, giving me a sexy grin. He wrapped me in his arms, lifting me up with ease, moving to stand. "Time for a shower." He smirked, as he carried me to the bathroom, holding me in one strong arm, and leaning in to turn it on.

"Thank you for saving me," I whispered to him as the steam from the hot water began to envelop us, making me feel as if we were in our own little world and the outside world and all of its problems didn't exist.

"Always," he answered.

It was a long, long time before we said anything else.

I was alone when I woke up, the house perfectly still around me. I shuddered at the feeling of being alone, my feelings unreasonably hurt at the fact that Thane had left me after the night we'd shared.

Getting out of bed, I wandered to the window. It was a dreary day, so cloudy that it looked later than it actually was. With my stomach rumbling, I pulled on the only pair of sweats in my closet and wandered downstairs, and through the rooms on my way to the kitchen.

I searched for a sign of Thane or of corran but they weren't around. I finally made it to the kitchen, also deserted. Opening the fridge, the first thing I noticed was the bowl of blueberries. It had only been a few days since I fell in a pile of blueberries, getting choked by Thane. My how things had changed. Maybe something was wrong with me? I'd adjusted so quickly to everything...had even slept with two of them after being terrorized by them for weeks. Thane had literally choked me right outside this kitchen. And here I was, casually eating breakfast instead of trying to get away like any normal girl. Was I so desperate for affection of any kind that I had latched on to the first sign of it? This was literally the species that I believed was responsible for my parent's disappearance.

My appetite had disappeared with my morose thoughts, so I closed the refrigerator and wandered into the other rooms in the house. I decided to explore the house a bit more to get my mind off things. I could wonder if I was sick in the head at some other point. After yesterday I needed a day off.

I walked through the rooms, stopping to admire the expensive artwork on the walls. I'd been in a hurry to find an exit the last time I had explored the house and I hadn't had time to admire the fact that there was a movie theater and workout room that was the size of the gym that I attended near home.

I was strolling through the library filled with more books than I had ever seen in one place, and was about to leave, when I noticed a section of the wall that looked like it stuck out farther than everywhere else.

Walking over I realized that the wall seemed to be sticking out farther because it was some kind of disguised door, and it had been left open. Peeking through the crack I spied a steep staircase leading to an open area. I opened the door a little wider and listened for a moment, trying to see if I could hear any voices coming from down below. I couldn't hear anything. Ignoring the voice in my head that said I should leave it alone; I opened the door wider and started to descend. I paused every couple of steps to see if I could hear anything, and then would continue on when everything remained silent. I had been searching for a reason for their arrival, so maybe I'd finally stumbled across the answer. Excitement tangled in my gut, layered with fear over getting caught.

When I reached the bottom of the steps, I stared around in amazement. Out of everything that I had seen related to the Vepar, this room was the most "out of this world" yet. Sleek, silver tables were set up with hologram images projecting out of them. There was one table that displayed what looked like about 100 different screens showing different parts of the world. Another table had a hologram screen with thousands of numbers scrolling down. I examined the 100 plus images for a moment trying to see if there was anything familiar looking, but I couldn't recognize anything.

Skipping the numbers for now I walked over to the left wall which was made up of an enclosed glass bookcase showcasing various specimens in every chamber. I gasped in amazement at some of the creatures that must have been from their planet. A black, spider with twelve legs instead of eight. It was easily three times the size of a tarantula, and I shivered as I watched it eat a mouse whole. There was some kind of purple creature with four eyes, reminding me of the embodiment of the Furby toy that had been popular when I was a child.

There were also things that were recognizable and left me shivering. In one chamber sat a human heart... Still beating. In another one was an organ that I was pretty sure were female ovaries. And in another one was a human embryo.

Sickness rose through me, so I finally backed away and headed over to the hologram with all the numbers. There were thousands of digits on the screen, but only two columns fully caught my attention. One said Vepar Female and one said Human Female. The numbers were changing rapidly on the human column. What was it counting? Deaths? Or women attending gyms. I almost laughed at how stupid that sounded. What if it was somehow tracking every birth and death? The Vepar column was barely changing with almost no deaths and no births at all.

I tried to think what they would need such information for. Looking through the other columns I found no columns for males.

"What are you doing in here?" barked an angry sounding Corran from behind me.

My heart skipped in my chest, and I twirled around to see him at the base of the stairs, a red tinge to his very handsome cheeks.

"I was just exploring the house and the door was open," I tried to explain, my voice shaking.

"You shouldn't be down here," he snapped. "Did you touch anything?"

"No, I just looked," I answered, my hands trembling at how angry he sounded. Corran had always only sounded interested or mild-mannered. I hardly recognized the seething Vepar in front of me.

"I'm sorry," I started to say, but he was already pointing to the stairs.

"Get out of here," he yelled, and I didn't waste a second more trying to apologize. I flew up the stairs with tears in my eyes.

I ran into Thane at the top of the stairs. "What were you doing down there?" he demanded.

"I've already been yelled at enough; I don't need you to chime in. I'd almost forgotten I was a prisoner in this place, but I won't be forgetting again," I told him, flying by before he could grab my arm. I ran to my bedroom and slammed the door, wishing there was a way to lock the door from the inside.

Ten minutes ticked by as I pouted on the bed, my mind racing with what had been in that room and the look in Corran's eyes when he'd seen me down there. Why didn't they want me to see whatever those things were measuring?

A knock sounded on my door, startling me from my musings since I hadn't heard anyone climbing the stairs. "Can I come in?" asked Corran through the door.

"No," I belligerently said, knowing that I was acting like a two-year-old even as I said it. He opened the door anyway. I didn't expect anything less because from the beginning the Vepar had done whatever they wanted.

"I'm pretty sure I told you not to come in," I said as he stood at the foot of my bed. I was pleased to see he looked a bit scared of me...and slightly ashamed.

"I came to apologize," he said, fiddling with the bottom of his shirt in a decidedly human gesture.

I continued my childish behavior by not saying anything and just staring at him stonily.

"I'm sort of a rarity on Vepar," he continued, when he saw that I wasn't going to say anything. "Our scientists have for the most part been able to eradicate any abnormalities or disorders that used to be present in the Vepar genetic line. My parents were Vepar that were a part of the last nomadic clan though, so they hadn't been subject to any of the genetic cleansing like the rest of the population. I have a disorder most similar to your human Obsessive-Compulsive Disorder. When I saw you down there, all I could think about was that you had touched something, and it was out of the order I kept it in." He took a deep breath and looked at me beseechingly, "I had no intention of scaring you, Ella."

Sorrow flooded his gaze as he stood there, and my anger ebbed. I remembered a classmate in high school who'd suffered from OCD. He couldn't walk out of a room without tapping the side of the door three times and he had to walk three steps behind someone at all times if he was walking in the hallway. He'd been the nicest guy, and I remember how much it bothered him to have all these things to do to stay sane. If Corran's mental issues were anything similar to that, I wasn't surprised he grew so mad when he found me down there.

"I really am sorry for going into the room. My parents always used to tell me I was too curious for my own good." I smiled, feeling a momentary pang at the thought of my parents. For a second, I was tempted to ask if he knew anything about their disappearance, but I pushed the thought away. I hadn't seen any sign that they were in the business of kidnapping older humans...only ones they seemed to be sexually attracted to.

Anyway, I did feel like I had the right to ask what was going on in that room. Everything about the gadgets was strange...including the fact that they might be tracking human and Vepar females.

"So, the hologram that I was looking at down there... It looked like it was recording births and deaths of human females," I asked hesitantly, watching Corran carefully to gauge his reaction.

He sighed and sat down on the bed, turning his face away from me as he gazed out the window. "We came to this planet because our planet is dying and killing off our females in the process. Doesn't help that Khonsu have killed so many of our females as well. We've spent hundreds of years searching space to find a planet that would be similar enough to Vepar for us to relocate. We'd heard about Earth, but we also learned that females were in danger here. Part of my job on the planet was to monitor Earth to ensure the same thing happening to our females is not replicated here."

"How does the planet dying affect your females?" I asked, my eyes widened with everything he was saying.

He sighed. It was a heavy sigh filled with frustration. "We're not quite sure. But since the only connection we have to the Vepar woman dying is our planet also dying, we decided that we needed to find other options."

"Other options like finding new planets to inhabit?" I asked, dread growing inside of me.

He nodded.

I looked at him amazed that he'd so casually told me their plan. Up to now they'd been firm with the message that they were here in peace. But obviously that was all a lie.

He must have seen the growing panic in my face because his eyes widened, and he threw up his hands as if to calm me down. "We're not planning to takeover. We want to share the planet. All of the rules that have been put in place have been to help sustain the planet and make life better in preparation for the Vepar arrival."

I studied his face. He seemed to be telling the truth but Corran had always seemed to have that air of trustworthiness about him from the beginning. For all I knew, he could have been the best liar out of all of them.

"You had no problem taking me without my permission, and you've pretty much taken over Earth," I said bitterly. "Why should I believe that you wouldn't do something else?"

He pursed his lips in frustration before checking his watch. "I have to leave right now on a short expedition I've had planned for months, and I'd like you to come with me. We can talk more on the trip. I'm sure you'd like to get out of the house too."

Corran and I hadn't had the time together that I had experienced with the others. It still felt awkward between us, and the thought of going somewhere with him made me feel more awkward than anything. But I did want to find out more about the Vepar's plans and he seemed to be much more willing to provide me with information than Derrial or Thane were. So, I might be able to uncover more secrets, maybe even if my parents' disappearance had anything to do with them. I decided to go.

Corran was already pulling me behind him before I had even said yes. Evidently the scientist was just as pushy as the others. Before I knew it, I'd found myself standing next to the helicopter pad that had housed the helicopter I'd flown in with Derrial. The helicopter evidently was being used however as the pad stood empty. I looked at Corran quizzically, wondering what we were waiting for, but he was oblivious to my look. He took out a silver contraption that looked like a car fob and pressed a button.

Suddenly, the pad seemed to dissolve and a sleek silver machine that resembled a cross between a car and a small airplane came up on a pedestal like a scene out of Batman. I gasped in amazement, but Corran, unperturbed as always, gave me no explanation as he began pulling me towards the machine. As we approached the contraption, an entryway appeared in the side of the machine and a set of stairs appeared out of nowhere. I stopped abruptly.

"What is this thing?" I asked, needing answers before I got into the machine.

Corran looked at me confused. "Isn't it obvious? This is how we travel. I guess you could say it's our version of an airplane if you had to label it, but the term really doesn't do it justice since it can travel through any terrain including water."

I stared at him incredulously, then the machine. "Wow."

He began to ascend the steps, and then looked at me with a raised eyebrow when I didn't follow him. I was still in shock about the fact that I was about to travel in an alien spacecraft.

"We're on a schedule," he said impatiently, jarring me from my thoughts. I tentatively followed him up the steps, stopping on each one to make sure that they didn't disappear. Once inside I couldn't help but freeze again.

Everything was black as if I'd crawled inside a licorice jelly bean. The walls, ceiling, seats, and even the controls. Light drenched the inside of the shuttle, and the sleek walls glimmered under the right illumination. No other windows lined the rectangular ship.

Corran took the single seat in the front with the controls, and I slid into one of two available in the back. Buckling up, I couldn't believe where I was, and what I'd give right now to have my phone to snap photos. I was pretty sure if I shared them, my social followers would leap from a measly thirty to millions.

Anyone who shared images revealing anything about the Vepar went viral because they were so secretive. If only people knew something more dangerous lingered amid them. The Khonsu. Then again, maybe that would just cause unnecessary panic because everyone would be safe unless they were compatible like me. Lucky me.

My thoughts turned to the bomb Corran had dropped on me about their race looking for a new home. That information was massive and could easily end up with us going to war with them because the rest of the planet coming here would be construed as a complete take over. I didn't know what to do with such knowledge as it was still processing in my head on what it meant. I mean I knew what it meant, but the situation seemed delicate and I could sympathize with them wanting to save their race. Plus, I didn't want to cause a universal war when I didn't understand all the facts myself, especially when I was pretty sure that humans didn't have a chance against the Vepar technology.

I sucked in a deep breath to calm myself.

"You ready?" Corran glanced over his shoulder at me, his eyes alive, clear he was in his element right here.

"Let's do this before I change my mind." I laughed, but it wasn't a lie either.

A light vibration buzzed under my feet, followed by a brittle silence, but we lifted into the air with such ease and swiftness that I barely felt it. When we finally took off, the vessel moved as if there was no sound, no wind, and it didn't even disturb the air. We glided seamlessly through the air, and my earlier worries faded, replaced by a tingling excitement. My knees bounced and I gawked outside, wanting to stand near Corran to see everything, but I didn't dare move.

Unlike Derrial, who'd talked my ear off during the whole flight on the helicopter, Corran didn't say a word. Instead, he spent the entire time on a tablet that would have looked like an iPad if it weren't for the fact that it projected holographic, 3D images much like the tables in that secret room. Numbers and charts all detecting what looked like other aircrafts.

We traveled for twenty minutes before the machine started to drop smoothly out of the sky. My stomach lurched to my throat, and I clutched my seat belt, surprised how fast we'd arrived, but then again, I suspected we traveled quicker than planes.

When we landed, all I could see out the front window was darkness and the bright starry sky as far as the eye could see. Where in the world were we?

The front door opened with a rush of hot air, hissing in the process. And before us stood a mountain covered with tropical looking trees. This didn't look like anywhere near home.

I hopped out and Corran followed behind me.

"Where are we?"

He took my hand and drew me closer to the mountain. "We're at the edge of a crater."

"Wait!" I pulled against his hand. "Like in a volcano?" It did feel hotter here, the heat so intense it was singeing my skin.

He smiled and moved closer, cupping my face. With a kiss that shocked me, he whispered, "Would you have preferred if I took you to a beach?"

I shrugged and nodded. "Actually yes."

"Well, we might have time after this. We are in Honolulu."

My feet froze, eyes growing. "Are you kidding me? I've always wanted to go to Hawaii. I could have brought my swimsuit."

He broke into a laugh, the sound so soft and sweet that I ate it up. I adored the way he laughed. "Then we better hurry up and get this job done."

14

The grainy sand was almost white, speckled with tiny rocks along the shore. It may be close to midnight in Honolulu, but the moon hung low and was heavy with silver light, beaming off the silent sea like a jewel. Corran had finished collecting samples from the volcano crater, and true to his word, he took me swimming.

"You look spectacular," he said, and I glanced over at him, still in his jeans and buttoned up shirt looking proper as always. At least he'd removed his shoes.

I looked down at myself in a swimsuit we'd found at one of a handful of stores still open. A skinny black bikini, barely covering the sides of my breasts and so skimpy that I might as well have been naked in the back. Corran had surprised me by insisting I wear it. I tried to tell myself that I didn't adore the way his eyes glinted when he stared at me, eating me up with his gaze.

"Why do you enjoy dunking yourself in cold, salty water?" he asked.

"Stop analyzing everything." I grabbed his hand and drew him toward the water lapping across the shore. "It's such a hot night, and it's refreshing to go swimming, especially with someone else." I winked his way. "Especially when the two of us combined should be wearing a lot less clothes than you are right now." I eyed him head to toe.

"If you're implying sex, the friction is painful in water."

I sighed and hauled him closer to the water. "Just follow my direction, okay?"

And to my surprise he nodded.

The water rushed toward us, running up and over my feet. I giggled and latched onto Corran's arm, while he stood there, the hems of his jeans getting wet. He didn't seem to notice as he kept staring at me.

"What?"

"Something in your face looks different when you smile today." He watched me closely, or more like studied me. Corran was always trying to work me out, while me... I just wanted to laugh for a change, stop being afraid.

"It's called freedom." And the moment the words fell from my mouth, an awkwardness fell over me because he was my captor and I wasn't really free. After our time together with him carefully explaining all the data he was collecting on the volcano, I'd foolishly let myself imagine that our situation had changed. All because he'd made me feel incredible in his company, trusting me to help him, taking me to the beach, spoiling me. The hard facts remained however that I remained under his control.

I turned away from him and faced the ocean, my hand slipping out of his grasp. Out in front of me, the dark waters came in gentle waves, proving that nothing would ever tame the ocean.

Corran placed a hand on my shoulder, his touch sizzling hot. "Did I do something wrong?"

When I met his gaze over my shoulder, his lips curled upward, and he reached over cupping the side of my face so tenderly I almost let myself believe he truly cared.

"On my home planet, women are worshipped and adored. We protect them above all else, and we keep them close at all times to ensure they are safe. But you say freedom like claiming you is wrong."

"Are you listening to what you're saying?" I said, my mouth hanging open from his response.

"Earth is no longer the place you once experienced," he retorted. "And it will never be the same. We've offered you freedom from what is coming," he growled, his expression darkening, and in a heartbeat his features schooled, and his words faded as if he'd said too much. "Go, have your swim, we have to leave soon," he snapped.

I turned and headed into the waters feeling less than a person because the Vepar had this way of giving, then taking away any good they did. Always reminding me of my place. If they revered females so much, why dominate them? My stomach churned with his last words about Earth never being the same again. Something was happening, and it had to do with the test results I found in their secret lab, I felt it in my bones. Regardless of what Corran told me, I wasn't sure how much I could believe. After all, they'd arrived here, shrouded in secrets, so why would he so easily divulge their information? Nope... more secrets lay hidden, and I had every intention to find them out. If I was stuck with them, hidden from another monster, then I'd at least uncover the truth.

The cool water lapped around my thighs and I pushed deeper into the water, dunking myself into the sea's embrace, the iciness refreshing. There was an eeriness about floating in water so dark I couldn't see my hand just below the surface. Who knew what swam around me... but was that any different to being in the company of Vepar?

I stared back to Corran. He leaned against a palm tree, arms folded over his broad chest, watching me. What would he do if I dove under and never resurfaced? Probably drain the ocean to find me. I would laugh if I didn't believe he'd do exactly that.

I left the water behind, my skin pricked with the cold. Corran hadn't moved from his position even though the towel he'd purchased lay right by his feet. Instead, he drank me in from my head to toes, his sights fastened on my breasts in the skimpy bikini, at my pebbled nipples. When I reached his side, he picked up the towel and dusted it of sand before wrapping it around my shoulders. He rubbed the fabric over my arms and back to dry me. His moves were smooth and unaffected, but his eyes held a hunger that showed how he truly was feeling.

He leaned down and kissed me, his lips on fire. His breathing escalated and he held onto my shoulder while another hand cupped my breast. With deft fingers, he peeled back the material, revealing one of my breasts. Then he bent over further, collecting it into his mouth.

I gasped, glancing around to see if anyone was around. Finding we were alone I relaxed although the knowledge that we could get caught still filled me with a nervous thrill. His hands fell to my backside and he kneaded my cheeks. The way he sucked on my chest had me swooning, arousal escalating quickly through me, my head fogged with heat. And he wasn't letting me go either, plucking at my flesh with his lips.

"Corran," I breathed, fire scorching hot between my thighs. As if sensing my need, his fingers found the edge of my bikini bottoms and slid inside. Caressing me softly, he slowly slid into me. I parted my legs slightly for easier access, only the towel sitting on my back like a cape concealing what was going on if anyone watched. My cheeks sizzled, but nothing compared to the heat I felt that he was touching me so intimately in public.

I groaned, grasping his shoulders, needing him with every fiber of my being. I ought to be pissed at his treatment of me earlier, but as always, his attentiveness won me over, taking all my anger away.

When he turned me around, driving my back to the palm tree, he ripped the bikini top the rest of the way off. I could barely breathe from need. His mouth latched onto my other breast, eliciting another gasp out of me. His fingers pushed back into my bikini bottoms, and his knee nudged my legs wider.

"We shouldn't do this here," I moaned, staring around us, but when his fingers slipped inside of me again, I lost myself. Gone were all my thoughts, the only thing remaining was a desperate desire to float on the clouds. His tongue flicked me and holding out seemed an impossibility. His teeth bit down softly on my flesh, and it all become too much, too fast. I fell over the edge, and a cry of pleasure fell from my mouth, my body shuddering.

Diving into my mouth in a deep kiss, Corran's tongue slayed me, erasing every thought of the outside world until I was breathless, and we had to break away to drag in air. I writhed, soaking, every last inch of desire throttling through me. It took me a few minutes to settle down. Corran kissed me softly before moving away and pulling the towel tightly around my chest. Embracing me once again, I melted into him.

"Come, you must be starved." We began to walk along the sandy beach of Honolulu. As I stared up at the stars, I knew I would never forget my brief time in Hawaii.

Corran hadn't touched his Wagyu ribeye, only the vegetables, but even those he only picked at. He seemed miles away as we sat in a restaurant fit for royalty. Embroidered curtains, dark oak tables, sandstone tile floor, and meals were served from silver trays. The restaurant was full, each table bustling, voices buzzing, and a delicate piano played throughout the dimly lit room. I was worried if Corran regretted what had just happened when he finally looked over at me with a smile, the worry he had carried moments earlier vanished.

"You look beautiful." His attention fell to my low v-neck dress, the one he'd bought me once we arrived in New York for a meal. The trip itself was another testament to Vepar technology since Hawaii to New York had only taken thirty minutes. I blushed all over, the earlier fire from the beach surging through me once again, and I grew hot and bothered as I clenched my thighs. It didn't take long for him to affect me, for any of them to affect me, just a simple look did the trick. Something had to be wrong with me to react to the Vepar so fast.

I looked down at the blue gown I wore, it was the color of the night sky with tiny sparkles all over it when the light caught it in the right direction.

I blushed when I looked up and he was still watching me with admiration.

"I'm sure this dress could make even you look handsome," I told him, laughing at myself trying to downplay the fact that he and his friends were the most gorgeous males I had ever seen. Looking around at my surroundings, this place was the most posh and uppity place I had been to in my life. I'd never be able to afford to visit such a place, and if I stepped foot in here without Corran, I'd be marched out. I suspected that the way we had been treated while we were here, like we were royalty, had everything to do with being on the arm of a Vepar.

"I didn't mean to upset you back by the ocean. I've got a few things on my mind," he explained and reached over to take my hand in his. His thumb stroked the back of my wrist in slow, gentle circles. His hair, the color of mahogany, framed his strong face and his eyes reminding me of milky caramel. Despite being the quieter of the three Vepar, the one who analyzed things first and who seemed to calculate everything before he acted, Corran was incredibly handsome in his own way. But unlike the others, he didn't seem to know it.

Despite all the logic in my mind and everything that had happened, I couldn't help but fall under his spell each time we exchanged glances. What would it be like to really date someone who looked this perfect...Someone normal. Not an alien with so many secrets it gave him a Dr Jekyll and Mr. Hyde personality. I wanted to look past that, to believe Corran meant well.

"Feel like talking about it?"

He sighed heavily. "Some things are better left unsaid."

I wasn't sure if that was one of his riddles I had to decipher, or he was speaking directly this time.

He flinched and reached for his pocket, before pulling out a ringing cell. "Give me a moment." He was on his feet and marching outside with the phone pressed to his ear before I could respond.

Glancing down at my half-eaten gnocchi, I pierced one with my fork and ate it, loving the buttery taste. Why hadn't I tried these before?

Eating could only distract me for so long and I couldn't prevent my thoughts from thinking about the complicated situation I had found myself in. For so long my life has been about living to get through the day and into the next. With these three Vepar, my life had become so much more in such a short time. The deep-seated emotion they awakened in me was enticing, and it makes me want to feel even more. The opportunity to taste any level of the type of intensity they brought into my life was becoming a necessity.

When someone flopped into Corran's seat, I sat up, expecting him, ready to say that was fast, but it wasn't his face I met.

Across from me sat the Devil, and I shuddered in my shoes.

He wore a black jacket, hair oily and slicked off his face, and he had regained that haunting gauntness in his cheeks of the monster who'd tortured me with whips.

I pushed back in an instant, my seat's feet scraping the ground in a terrifying screech, drawing attention from those at nearby tables. My heart pounded in my chest, and I shook, unable to stop remembering the way this bastard had hurt me, took my blood, and threatened to come for me. And here he was, trying it in public.

Shit!

"Don't go," the Khonsu whispered, glancing toward the door where Corran had left moments earlier. I mentally counted the space between me and the exit. Fifteen, maybe sixteen steps.

I jolted to my feet, but he grasped my wrist before I could get anywhere, also standing, his grip as cold and solid as iron.

"Sit!" he growled beneath his breath, hauling me back to my seat with such force, I stumbled into it, almost sliding off.

Fear pressed down on my chest, squeezing my lungs as he held onto my wrist, not letting go.

I was never going to be left alone. I would always be hunted. I hated this. I loathed the constant terror.

"What do you want?" I snapped, wrestling to free my hand, but he didn't budge.

"Tonight, you're not my prey," he murmured, his gaze flipping back and forth from the door to me, and I prayed Corran returned fast.

"What do you mean?" I asked.

"I have some information I think you would be interested in," he replied, picking up Corran's dinner knife and casually inspecting it as if it held interesting information.

"I can't think of anything you could tell me that would interest me except why you're stalking me." My words came out brave, but inside I was trembling. I set my napkin purposely on my knife and slipped both off the table. I gripped the knife hard under the table determined that when he did try to take me, I would fight back.

"Little human, what have they told you about why the Vepar are on Earth?" he asked.

I studied him wondering why it mattered. "The Vepar are here because their planet is dying and it's making their females sick."

"Ever wondered why they seem to care so much about the health of human females?" he said with a sly grin. His question dug in deep to the issues that I had tried to push from my mind.

I said nothing and his grin widened. "The Vepar women are barren," he stated in a matter of fact tone. "And even though the Vepar have long lives, so long that some would consider them immortal, their numbers are still dwindling without any hope of replacement." My eyes widened. It had been something that I suspected ever since seeing the graphs in their basement room, but the way Corran had talked to me so earnestly had made me want to not question him. Corran seemed the most trustworthy of the three of them, but what if he was the best liar of them all?

I shook my head. Why was I even deigning to listen to anything that this creature was saying? A creature who had cruelly tortured me for no reason other than I existed.

"Trying to convince yourself that I'm lying?" he asked with a chuckle. "Your three males are three of the most powerful Vepar in their society. To get in that position, don't you think there has to be something a little bit more special to make them stand out in a race that prides itself on superiority?"

My trembling grew. I didn't know what was coming next, but I knew I was going to hate it.

"They're going to breed you," he whispered to me. "Corran discovered how to make a Vepar embryo be accepted into a human female. Thanks to you."

"Thanks to me?" I said, my voice sounding horrified even to me. "Your blood had the magic touch," he said with a shrug. "There's a whole list of you with the same special chromosome that will allow for you to birth little Vepar."

"You mean hybrids, right? Half human, half Vepar?" I asked, thinking that it wouldn't be so bad if the three of them loved me and we wanted to have children someday.

He laughed. It was a dark laugh filled with glee over my ignorance. "No, little human. They plan on knocking you out and putting in embryos just like you humans do with surrogates. Then they're going to keep you hooked on machines like true breeders until the birth of the Vepars. And then, when you've done your job and continued their race, you're going to die."

I stared at him, dread threatening to choke me. My mind was having trouble trying to fathom how what he was saying could even be real. An image came to my mind of me strapped with a pregnant belly on a gurney in a tank with tubes coming out of me. I wanted to throw up.

A shadow fell over our table, and I jumped in my seat, so on edge, I was ready to scream.

Corran towered over us, and relief crashed through me. But before I could take another breath, he grabbed the Khonsu by the throat and hurled him across the room. Our table lifted from the alien's feet kicking in resistance and flew sideways.

And then, panic broke out.

Screams. People running toward the exit, fear gripping their expressions. Chairs and food flying across the room from where the two aliens fought. And this wasn't just punches and fists, but a battle between two animals. They charged for one another, headbutting, throwing one another against the walls.

Each time Corran fell, I curled over, hugged myself, the idea of him in pain feeling like a blade to my heart.

Every inch of me trembled, and I sat in my chair, frozen with the chaos erupting in the restaurant.

Get out, my mind yelled. I finally leaped to my feet, my muscles high on pure adrenaline. I felt nothing but the urgency to escape drumming through my veins. The grip of panic pushed me, my brain synapses fired away scenario after scenario on how I could die here tonight, but it also came with the idea that this might be my chance to escape.

I felt horrible leaving Corran this way, drowning in a scuffle of grunts and snarls, of blood and aggression, but what could I do? I didn't even have a phone to call the other two Vepar for backup.

So, I ran. It was something I was good at.

I pushed past the overturned tables and chairs, pushing myself into the bottleneck of people squeezing out the door. Cries of terror surrounded me, and my heart beat faster and harder listening to everyone panic.

I burst out onto the sidewalk with the horde, and I swung right, away from the direction of the shuttle. While I had no idea where I was going, I just knew I had to run. I shoved past people, my mind racing with the need to find a place to hide.

"Ella?" A female's voice cried out, but I didn't look back, I didn't dare.

When someone grabbed my arm, I flinched around, hands fisted, ready to fight. But when I saw Cherry standing there, holding onto me, wearing a strapless dress, her hair curled, and dark makeup around her cerulean eyes, I let out a light cry.

My mouth gaped open at bumping into her.

"Shit, girl, where the hell have you been, and what are you wearing?"

My throat thickened, and despite our past, I leaped into her arms, not caring about anything as it felt incredible to see a familiar face, to feel some connection to the life I thought I'd lost.

She pushed me off her. "What's going on? I've called you for days, and when I went to visit you, the landlord said he'd kicked you out and was selling your stuff to pay for your unpaid rent." Gripping her hips, she glared at me, waiting for an explanation.

My heart sunk through me, but I didn't have time for this. "Listen, can we go to your place now? I have so much to tell you, but I'm in danger."

Her brow pinched. "I'm here with friends. But you can make it up to me tomorrow by taking me out to brunch."

I shook my head and glanced up the sidewalk behind her where the mass of people hovered near the restaurant. "Please, Cherry. For me, do this for me. I never ask you for anything."

She rolled her eyes. It seemed she hadn't changed much. In that moment I finally realized how stupid I had been to ever consider her my real friend.

"Forget it," I snapped and whipped around to run.

Instead, I crashed into a wall of stone muscle. And when I looked up into Corren's bloody and furious face, I winced.

Oh, fuck.

"Who's this guy?" Cherry purred behind me, and was she really flirting?

But I couldn't move. My feet were glued to the sidewalk with dread.

"I told you you're ours!" And he leaned over, snatching me up before tossing me over his shoulder as if I were a sack.

I screamed and slapped my hands across his back, but people just stared at us, doing nothing.

Corran's large hands held down my legs, one hand on my ass, and he hiked it back toward the ship.

Cherry stared at me in shock.

"I've been kidnapped, help!" I yelled at her. But she simply stared after me, a shocked and jealous look on her face. The last thing I saw before we turned the corner was her making a call on her phone.

What the fuck!

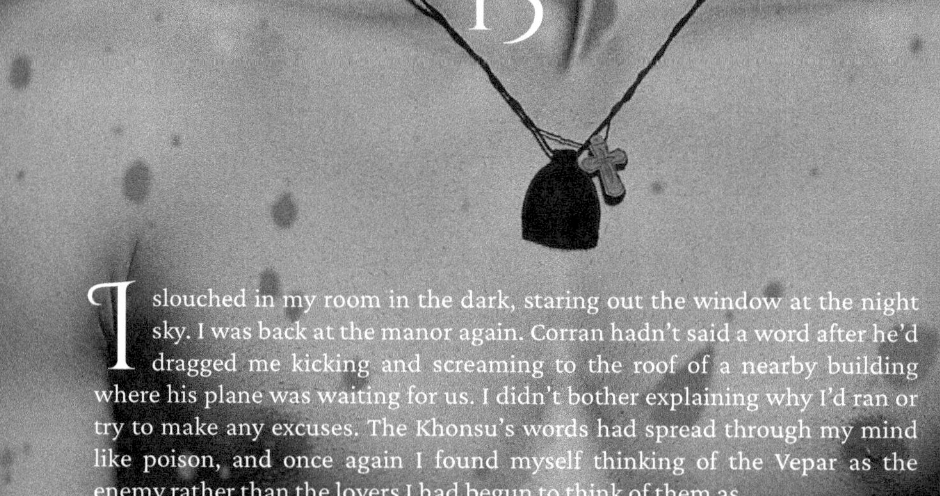

15

I slouched in my room in the dark, staring out the window at the night sky. I was back at the manor again. Corran hadn't said a word after he'd dragged me kicking and screaming to the roof of a nearby building where his plane was waiting for us. I didn't bother explaining why I'd ran or try to make any excuses. The Khonsu's words had spread through my mind like poison, and once again I found myself thinking of the Vepar as the enemy rather than the lovers I had begun to think of them as.

We landed and Corran had grabbed my arm roughly before practically dragging me into the house and up the stairs to my room. He threw me onto the bed and turned to leave the room.

"So, I'm a prisoner again?" I asked, my feelings irrationally hurt at his treatment of me even though I never should have expected anything else.

"You ran, again. That doesn't earn you any privileges."

"So everything that's happened wasn't real?" I asked, my voice clogged with the tears that I was desperately trying to keep at bay.

His eyes closed for a second as if my question pained him, but when they opened again, they were as cold as ever.

"Just stay put," he said exasperatedly, storming out and slamming the door behind him. Surprisingly, I didn't hear the lock engage. After his footsteps faded, signaling he'd gone down the stairs, I walked to the door to check it. Sure enough, it wasn't locked.

Feeling slightly mollified, I went back to my bed and laid down, the intensity of the day suddenly catching up to me and making me realize how exhausted I felt. Every inch of me ached.

And that's what I had been doing for the last few hours.

As I laid on the bed, my mind continued to obsess over what the Khonsu had said. I had to know for myself if it was true. Asking the Vepar obviously wasn't going to work since they had already told me the story, they wanted me to believe. No, if I was going to find out, I was going to have to do it myself. And I was pretty sure that the answers to my questions lay in that secret room.

I waited until the middle of the night. I still wasn't sure about Vepar sleeping habits, but I knew that they at least slept for a few hours based on my experience with Derrial in the D.C. hotel room.

Once the clock struck two a.m., I carefully tiptoed to the door and slowly opened it, pausing every couple of inches to listen. When the house remained quiet, I opened the door all the way and slipped out into the hallway. My heartbeat felt unnaturally loud as I crept through the hallways. The journey seemed to take forever since my entire body was on hyper alert sure that one of the Vepar was going to appear at any moment.

I finally made it into the library, and I fumbled with the bookshelf where the hidden door was located for a few minutes, trying to figure out how to open it since it had already been opened last time. My hand finally slipped across a book towards the bottom of the bookshelf that when pulled, released the door. The door creaked as it slid open and my heart stopped as I listened, nervously expecting to hear the sound of feet coming down the hallway.

Five minutes passed and then ten and I finally got the nerve to continue. I slipped down the stairs, the lights automatically coming on as I entered the room.

Everything looked as it did the other day. The holograms still glowed from where they were suspended in the air above the tables. There were still creepy creatures on the side wall. Yes, everything looked the same, but I was sure that somewhere in here was the answer to my questions.

I ran my hand over all the surfaces thinking that there had to be some hidden button that would show me something. When that didn't work, I searched every nook and cranny in the room to try and find another hidden passageway.

After thirty minutes of searching, I wandered over to the table with the birth and death graphs, frustrated at the fact that I hadn't been able to find anything and would have to leave soon so that they didn't find me. I waved my hand in frustration at the hologram...and to my surprise, the screen changed.

No longer was I staring at changing graphs. Instead I studied what looked to be a medical file.

My medical file in fact, and my stomach dropped. It listed everything about me on the screen. Where I'd gone to school, who was my first kiss, my blood type. I waved the screen again and to my horror a mockup appeared of a chamber that looked similar to the images that had filled my head when the Khonsu had been talking.

The chamber rotated in the air, all the specifications listed in a paragraph below. It was labeled as an "incubator." But I knew that it wasn't going to be hatching eggs...it was going to be growing Vepar.

My stomach ached with each passing second.

I kept scrolling through the various screens. There was more information about my chromosomes. Pictures of Vepar embryos. And on the last screen was a list of names labeled, "Probable Subjects." I was the very last name on the list.

It was one thing to hear about such a scenario, but to actually see evidence of a plan to make human women into Vepar surrogates was almost more than I could comprehend. And here I let myself have feelings for these aliens, and I was nothing more than a lab experiment.

Stumbling backwards away from the hologram screen, barely able to take breath into my lungs, I spun to get out of the room.

Much to my horror, Thane was standing in the doorway, a menacing look capturing his expression. Narrowing eyes and a pinched nose, he grunted. And with his curled shoulders, he was beyond pissed.

Dread squeezed around my chest, and I could barely take a breath.

"Find something interesting, pet?" he growled.

I looked widely around the room, my mind desperately trying to come up with scenarios of how I could escape...what excuse I could use.

Thane was upon me in a flash, and I screamed. The last thing I saw was him raising a small black device up to my neck as I struggled to get away.

Then, everything went black.

Author's Note

C.R. Jane

It was such a great experience working with Mila on my first co-write ever. It's come at the best time since sharing the writing load helps a lot during my pregnancy right now. I'm so grateful for all our readers. This was a departure from what I normally write but as we came up with the story, I knew it was going to be fantastic. I love sci-fi. I grew up on Star Trek and even though this one is set on earth; I loved the idea of working with aliens. We have an amazing series planned, and I can't wait to show you what's in our crazy brains!

Mila Young

Thank you to all the incredible and inspirational readers who've joined me on my writing journey from the beginning and for spending time with my imagination. Bound was an incredibly fun and rewarding tale to write with C.R. Jane, our creativities blending to bring you a sci-fi romantic tale about what could happen should Earth ever be visited by another race of beings. You will love what we have planned for this series, so join us on this voyage to experience the unimaginable, the beautiful, and how love can be found in the most unlikeliest of places.

BROKEN

CONTENTS

BROKEN

Their obsession will destroy her...

Ella Monroe is broken and betrayed. After the discovery of the Vepar's secret, Ella would like nothing better than to get away from her three Vepar lovers and hide from them forever.
Unfortunately, the Vepar have other ideas for Ella.
Imprisoned and taken away to a place that defies imagination, Ella must fight for her life and discover the truth about the Vepar's agenda.
One thing is for sure though...the Vepar are never going to let her go.

I

I woke up with a gasp, my body drenched in sweat, and I looked around trying to get my bearings. As soon as I did, I wished to return to sleep. They had put me in what resembled a metal room with no visible entry point anywhere. Only smooth, metal-looking walls.

My heart raced, and glancing down at myself, I found myself sitting in nothing but my bra and underwear. Cold fury rushed over me. That bastard stripped me.

Everything had been a lie. The closeness I'd been feeling with them wasn't real. They manufactured it to gain my trust. All so I could become their little test subject.

Impregnating humans. It was almost hard to fathom. From what I had seen, they carried little respect for humans. Why in the world would they want them to carry their babies?

I thought about what Corran had said, about the issues with their Vepar women struggling to fall pregnant. Despite that, I couldn't believe that the Vepar would lower themselves to such depths as to have humans be their incubators.

A sense of hopelessness rushed over me. I had imagined at various points in my life what it would be like to be a mother. Having a family similar to the one I had grown up with. A loving husband who adored my child and I.

Instead, I was facing motherhood as a surrogate for an alien species.

It was a disappointment to say the least.

The hours dragged, and I needed to pee. And a glass of water would be nice.

Maybe they had given up their plan to make me their baby incubator. Maybe they were now just gonna starve me to death in punishment for discovering their secret. I was sure it would have been easy if they just kept me their little sex toy until they were ready to perform the experiment. I ruined everything for them.

I looked around the tiny room once more for anything I could use as a weapon for when they finally came to visit. But it was useless as there was nothing. The guys were too smart for that. I tried to remember how long a human could go without water. Was it three days? Or was it longer than that? I couldn't remember. I hadn't really had to think about something like that in my life.

I wouldn't admit to myself that I'd been falling in love. I wouldn't admit to myself that I had imagined a future with them. I wouldn't admit anything to myself.

The hours continued to tick by. Sickness stirred in my stomach, an ache that I was all too aware wasn't due to being dehydrated or needing to pee. I recognized the pain... my body craved for the exchange of blood with them. It seemed melodramatic. But in that moment I wanted to die rather than depend on them for the rest of my life. They'd told me so many lies, what if the whole blood exchange was a lie too? And like a fool I'd gone along with it. I guess some girls just never learned.

A scraping noise sounded from the wall in front of me, and a barrier seemed to dissolve before my eyes. Thane came into form and he strutted inside.

I seethed, hating my treacherous body in that moment. Heck, he looked delicious. A part of me craved him, desired him to want me. *Stupid, stupid girl,* I mumbled to myself.

"What was that, pet?" Thane asked cockily, leaning against the wall that had once again regained its shape.

Stubbornly, I said nothing. Instead I stared off at a spot just to his right, so I wouldn't be forced to look at him. His eyes called to me, made me want him, but I had to remember who he was... who he'd been this whole time I let my defenses down.

A Vepar.

The outsiders.

And I was their captive.

"You know we didn't want to do this," Thane murmured as he walked towards me and crouched down so we were at eye level. I kept my gaze averted.

"Are you starting to feel sick? Starting to need anything? Do you need to pee, a drink?" he asked insidiously.

My body trembled as I sat there. I couldn't believe he was mocking me.

"You should have just trusted us," he said before standing and walking back to the wall. He waved his hand and to my surprise a toilet slid out, complete with a toilet paper roll. I sighed in relief, even as I tried to keep my face blank. He looked back at me.

"No thank you?" he mocked.

My hands curled, and how I'd love to punch him in the face. *Thank you.* Thank him for the mess I was in? I may not have been happy before I met them. I may have been a scared girl that let her friends walk all over her. But at least I had been free.

He looked at me for another long pause before sighing. The door once again dissolved in front of him and he walked out. I wondered where we were. There had been nothing but a grey hallway when the door opened, giving me no clue where we were. It was obvious that I had just seen a small taste of all the technology that the Vepar had.

As soon as the door closed behind him, I was up, practically running to the bathroom to pee. I emptied my full bladder hastily. After finishing, I stood a little bit too quickly and the room tilted under me. I leaned against the wall for a second before returning to the floor. I leaned my back against the wall, groaning softly as my sickness heightened. All of a sudden, a glass of water slid out from a compartment that opened in the wall. I salivated, suddenly parched, my mouth dry. I could drink about five glasses of water.

But I wasn't sure if I could trust it. What if they were drugging me? Drugs that either put me in a deep sleep, or got me ready for the procedure? I picked up the water glass and sniffed it. It smelled like water. Bile rose up inside of me, and I decided that in this case I just needed to take the risk. I gulped down the water, not caring that I was pretty sure that I was supposed to sip the water slow since I hadn't had it for a while.

It helped the sickness slightly, but it didn't stop the shaking and the feeling like I was suddenly catching the flu. There had to be something they could give me to prevent these kind of symptoms.

I was just about to slide down to the floor to lay down when a cot appeared through another compartment in the wall, making me jump. Damn aliens and their technology. I wanted to avoid sleeping on the thing just on the principle. But as the coldness of the floor seeped into my bones, I reluctantly shuffled over to the cot and laid down. Its softness cocooned me, and already my eyelids felt heavy.

A yawn pressed through me, but it was hard to sleep knowing that at any moment they could come in.

I stared up at the ceiling, going through everything that I'd seen in that room, obsessing over it. A part of me was still trying to find a way to make it better, to try and remember anything I had seen that would point to a different motive.

But I came up blank. And I was beginning to feel so sick at this point that it was impossible to think coherently in the first place. Sweat dripped down my forehead and pooled around my chest, collecting under my breasts. I was afraid that I was going to start hallucinating or something at any minute. Even if I had been given a chance to escape at that minute, I couldn't have gone anywhere.

My eyes were growing heavy when a sudden, blaring alarm broke the stillness inside the room. It screeched and moaned and a flickering red light accompanied it from the ceiling. My pulse was on fire, and I scrambled upright despite my muscles screaming in agony at the effort. *What's going on? Was there a fire? Was I going to be burned alive because I was trapped in this room?*

An opening appeared in the wall and there stood Derrial in all of his glory. I chewed on my lower lip when I saw him, my body betraying me and burning up with a wanton desire, I suppose knowing that the remedy to my pain was just a few steps away.

He wore a wrinkled suit with his black tie loosened around his neck. His hair sat shaggy around his face and a part of me couldn't help but clench up in jealousy at the fact that it had a "just fucked" look about it.

There was something really wrong with me, obviously.

"What's the alarm for?" I croaked in a weak voice, as he began to stride towards me.

'We've been compromised," he snapped as he scooped me up off the cot and carried me out the entrance.

I was too weak to put up a fight, not that I wanted to battle. "What do you mean we've been compromised?" I mumbled as he carried me through hallways that I didn't recognize.

"Our enemies have found the house," he said. "We have to get you out of here, before they arrive."

Panic crawled through my chest, and I struggled in his arms at that pronouncement. If by "enemies" he meant the Khonsu, I wanted out of there as fast as possible. A shiver skitted down my arms as I remembered the torture session that I had been apart of the last time I had some alone time with the Khonsu.

"Calm down, kitten," he murmured to me distractedly as he sprinted through the hallway, and I bounced in his arms.

My heart clenched at his sweet endearment, while my brain raged against him.

How dare he call me that. How dare he pretend to care after all the lies that he's told. I struggled further, but it was a half-hearted effort at best since I was so sick and getting sicker by the second.

"What about everyone else on Earth? Will they be safe from the Khonsu? They attacked your race." I gasped for air, my pulse on fire.

"They're looking for special women like you, not a home as they have those already around the universe."

A strange rattling sound came out of my chest as I breathed and Derrial looked down at me worriedly.

"What is that?" My words shook.

"Fuck," he muttered under his breath. "When was the last time you had blood?"

I struggled to remember, my will to fight him almost completely zapped as it was taking everything inside of me to keep breathing.

"We've been trying to hold off as long as possible in hopes that whatever happened to your body to make you basically a homing beacon for everyone on the planet would fade some. Obviously that's not going to work," he said with a curse as another shaky rattle came out of me.

He bit into his wrist and pressed the wound to my mouth. "Take some," he insisted.

I moaned in response, the blood trickling into my mouth with the movement.

I hated that it was the best thing I'd ever tasted. I hated that I had become an addict, needing their blood to survive. Piece by piece they were slowly chipping away at my humanity and I wasn't sure that I would ever be able to get it back.

If only my parents could see me now, I thought darkly.

I could feel myself rejuvenating as the blood slid down my throat. After a minute, Derrial ripped his wrist away from my mouth with a small moan that sounded way too sexual for the situation. I'd been sucking on the wound like a freaking vampire.

But I was feeling much better, as twisted as that sounded. I craved his blood like a lifeline. God, what had they done to me?

We reached a metal door and Derrial stood in front of it as a purple light started streaming out of the door and scanning him.

"Access granted," came a robotic voice and a second later I found myself in a room that looked straight out of a scene from Independence Day.

I had no idea where we were, but now... my mouth dropped open... now, we stood inside a room the size of an airplane hanger. And in front of me...was a freaking real-life spaceship.

It was a marvel of design. Utterly seamless, smooth matte charcoal colored metal with no visible means of propulsion or weaponry. No windows or doors. And no wings either. The vessel just sat there like an oversized crouched wolf, waiting for instructions to leap. A sense of claustrophobia started rushing over me, tightening around my chest at the idea of getting inside that thing. Unlike the vessel that Corran had used to take us to Hawaii where you could see through the walls to the outside, this ship was different. Sleaker. Powerful. Intimidating.

The alarm heightened, and Derrial sped up as we headed towards the spacecraft.

I squirmed against him, not ready to go in there.

An opening appeared in the side of the ship, pulling sideways into itself. Thane waited for us there, grasping a menacing black gun... or maybe a laser. "What took you so long?" he barked at us as we took a step inside.

"You apparently were trying to starve her," Derrial replied back in an accusing voice.

"It was what we agreed," Thane growled, running his gaze over my body as if he was checking to make sure everything was intact. But it wasn't... my mind was haywire with fear.

"I don't want to go in here," I mumbled but no one heard me.

"How close are they?" Derrial demanded as we rushed down a hallway inside the ship. It was the same licorice color inside as the ship Corran had created. We moved through passages with sharp corners at the vertexes, and there was minimal light, shadows in every corner.

"What are we doing?" My words quaked, and I hated showing my fear, but right now, the two Vepar were on high alert, stiff and focused on anything but listening to me.

We hurried through another opening wall, and I found myself in some sort of control center room. Gadgets and darkened windows lay across the front of the ship. I had either stepped into the set of Star Trek or I was hallucinating because I had never seen anything like it.

There were gadgets and screens all over it, but what caught my eye the most was Corran, standing in front of a screen, pushing his hand on various buttons frantically.

He turned when he heard us, his eyes widening a fraction. He looked frazzled, his hair all over the place, his sexy glasses askew.

"Took you long enough," he barked in a very un-Corran like tone.

Derrial rolled his eyes, evidently not feeling like sharing again that he had to stop and give me his blood.

"How close are they?" Thane strode to the screen and peered closely at it.

"Five miles out." Corran tapped his fingers anxiously on the side of the screen. "They're locked in on her."

"Why don't you just let them have me?" I said petulantly.

Thane just shot me an amused smirk at my outburst.

"Want a repeat of last time, pet?" he warned, and I recoiled back against Derrial.

"That's what I thought," Thane said.

"Three miles," Corran added, scrolling through another screen that showed an incoming convoy of trucks going down a road.

"It's time to go to sleep now," Derrial said to me as he stroked the side of my face almost lovingly. I stared up at him, trying to read his eyes until I spotted Corran approaching with a silver device in his hands. It was one that I knew would make me pass out.

"No," I begged as I began to thrash. Derrial just made a shhhing sound and held me tight. Only a second passed before I felt the small sting on the side of my neck signaling that Corran's device had arrived.

"I hate you," I whispered as my eyes immediately started to droop.

The last thing I saw were Derrial's piercing blue eyes, full of what looked strangely like regret.

I woke with a scream on my lips and I jolted upright. Squinting against the bright yellow light, a strange room with four barren walls came into view. No furniture, no windows, no door. Panic clawed at my chest as I shoved off the floor and recoiled until I hit a wall. I didn't recognize this room. Breaths didn't come quick enough. Left and right, I scanned for a way out, for anything that looked familiar, for lines in the walls for a door.

The last thing I remembered was being carried into the black spacecraft, enemies closing in, and Corran jabbing me with something, then I passed out. So where was I now?

My stomach tightened, and all I could think was that the Vepar had played me, and I foolishly believed them after everyone had warned me about catching their attention. Well, I'd done that royally. And now look at me? I was stuck in hell.

"Hello!" My voice seemed to echo, but it went nowhere. "Thane, Corran, Derrial, where am I? Can I come out now?"

The scream in my lungs rushed past my lips, a desperate call for them to hear me, to come for me.

Still nothing.

You're special, Ella. Thane's earlier words circled in my mind. They hounded me.

Being special in the eyes of the Vepar came with consequences, and I could see them now, clearer than I had before. They were monsters who tricked me.

I frantically checked the walls, running my hands over their smooth surface for a way out. But I knew the truth. They'd covered all potential escape routes, perfected the art of capture and like before, they had no plans on letting me escape. The reality crashed through me... I was trapped. Locked somewhere.

Under their control.

And I hated them for it...

Stumbling away, dread ripped across my chest. My knees hit the ground, and I dropped my face into my hands. A heady blackness swallowed me, and fear choked me. I cried, letting the despair rip through me. I cried for losing my home, for being lied to, for the past I could never take back.

I couldn't remember how long I wept or waited in that room, but when a mechanical beep chimed, I tilted my head up and wiped my eyes.

The wall in front of me shimmered, and with a small popping sound, two doors slid open in the middle of the wall with a swooshing sound.

Corran strode inside, dressed in black pants and a matching long-sleeve top.

My gaze swept to my escape, to the dark room behind him which vanished in seconds as the doors shut. How long had I been closed up for?

"Is this your spaceship?" I asked, hating the pleading in my voice. Dread spiked in my chest, and I fought against every instinct to run to him and beg him to release me.

The lead scientist studied me, his eyes always reminding me of warm caramel. His thick hair, the color of mahogany, was tucked behind his ears. The black-framed glasses he wore gave him a sexy teacher look, and I shouldn't have admired him, but I had already stepped forward like his very presence controlled me.

I tried to shake those feelings away because I couldn't... wouldn't keep falling for them while they had just stolen my life from me. So I stood my ground and tilted my head up to meet his deep, captivating gaze.

"Tell me where I am," I demanded, my voice stronger this time.

"You're safe," he murmured, stepping closer, studying me like he always did... Me as the experiment that intrigued him.

"I doubt that. Since you three came into my life, I've been anything but safe. The Khonsu never would have tortured me or put me on their radar if it wasn't for you. I would still have my new job at--"

"They would have found you eventually. We saved you." He moved closer, and I recoiled from his reach.

"Huh, you call it saving, I call it kidnapping."

"On our planet, Veon, you'd be honored to have us claim you because there are many females who'd kill to take your place." He said arrogantly, his voice darkened like I should be thanking him... On Earth, Corran would be runway-model material, the hunk on the cover of magazines, and the man every woman fantasized about. Except, many people said their beauty came from the disguises they used to conceal their real appearances, and it intrigued me what they hid behind their masks.

"Well, we're not on your planet, we're on Earth," I snapped. "Without your interference, I could have had a normal, simple, safe life."

He closed the distance between us in three long steps, shadows dancing under his eyes, the wrinkle across his nose having nothing to do with an oncoming sneeze.

I moved backward, and my spine pressed against the wall.

"You don't listen," he growled, hard muscles flexing with his every move.

I should have been terrified, screamed for help, except my body was alive and on fire around him.

"I'm special, I get it. The Khonsu aliens want me so they can continue draining me for themselves, rather than you and your friends doing it, right?" I held my chin high, trying to show him I wouldn't be pushed around, finding confidence I never knew I had.

He braced a hand on the wall over my shoulder, his body pinning me in place, not saying a word but staring at me.

Something about their presence affected me when I stood too close to them. I loathed that their dominance and controlling ways turned me on when it never should.

"I...is t...that all I am to you," I asked, lowering my voice, remembering the times I'd spent with him and enjoyed, believing he cared for me... truly cared. But I'd been mistaken. "Someone to please you?"

He leaned down and his lips brushed the skin beneath my earlobe. Soft and tender, the opposite of the way he held me in place. "I'll never hurt you."

His words left me shaking, a moan pushing on the back of my throat, and all I could focus on was his body against mine, the swell of his chest, the inferno raging inside me.

"You need to trust me," he murmured and leaned closer, his lips grazing mine. His mouth pressed harder against mine, kissing me with a fever I never imagined. A light pinch pierced my lower lip, and I pulled back.

"Ouch."

Corran was licking the drop of red blood... the blood he'd drawn from my lips.

His kiss had been electric, and I almost believed him... almost fell for his hypnotizing words... almost let myself feel something other than fear. But *he* wanted me to lower my defenses.

When darkness curled behind his eyes, alarm bells blared in my head. I pulled away from him, jerking free from his grasp, and recoiled.

He turned on me so fast, I didn't see him take the syringe from his pocket until it was too late.

A firm hand caught my wrist in a flash, and I was wrenched toward him. I dug my heels as I twisted to pull away. Intensity rippled over my flesh, and I screamed, struggling against him...but it was useless. I shot a leg out to strike him but missed him.

"Corran, please don't do this. Please," I cried, fighting to wrench my arm from his grip, but I might as well have been trying to break free from a mountain.

My heart was pounding and dread was closing in. "Don't do this. I don't want to be a baby incubator. Please." My voice quivered, and I drove my fist into his chest, over and over. Hitting with all my might.

"Ella, please trust me. I don't want to hurt you," he kept saying those damn words but I couldn't think of anything else but escape, my eyes gliding up to the syringe in his left hand.

My breaths grew ragged and rash, and I kicked him again, this time in the shin. His grip softened, and I ripped free before running to the wall where the doors had been earlier.

A cry fell from my lips, and my hands searched for the door, hitting the wall for an escape.

Come on, come on, damn you.

A sudden gush of pain pierced the side of my neck and agony shuddered through me. It hit me so fast, I didn't remember falling back or landing in Corran's arms.

"W-what d-did y-you do?" I whimpered.

Heaviness darkened his eyes... but I saw something else behind his gaze... sorrow. "I'm sorry, little bird. We can't lose you."

Shadows crowded the corners of my eyes, and the next thing I knew, I was falling into an endless pit of darkness, my world vanishing.

3

his seemed to be a habit, waking up in an unfamiliar place. I groggily came out of whatever Corran had done to me, whatever he'd jabbed into me. I stretched, and I was pleasantly surprised I could move freely. They hadn't chained me up. But instead of the floor, I lay in bed. The only piece of furniture in the room.

I stood up on shaky legs, my head swimming from whatever ran through my body. Looking around the room, I was shocked to see that there was an opening in the wall, unattended.

It felt like a trick. But I was done being stuck in small rooms and needed air and open space to shake this claustrophobic feeling gripping me.

I clung to that thread of hope I'd find a way out of this mess and pressed forward in hurried steps out of the room. Light illuminated my passage along a long hallway, walls made of black like the previous ship I'd been in with Corran. But this was different. Loftier and wider, and I had no doubt I was in over my head because this had to be their main vessel they'd used to come to Earth. But why were we hiding in here?

My steps quickened as panic clawed across my chest with the notion that we weren't hiding in here at all, and I couldn't... wouldn't even think about that possibility.

No windows graced the walls, and at the end of the corridor, two doors slid open upon my approach.

I flinched in response, but when my gaze swept inside, I shuddered on the spot, my mouth dropping open.

A long room spread out before me... the room that I had seen when I was first brought on. Now that I was lucid, I could see that it was a Bridge room on a spaceship to be precise. A darkened window stretched over the far wall with two seats facing the window, reminding me of the captain's chair in science fiction movies. A four seater bench lined the long side of the area, while monitors and numerous controls covered the opposite wall.

Corran stepped out from the shadowy corner, holding some kind of tool that resembled a wrench and looked up to find me. He smiled.

"How are you feeling?" He set the metal tool on a seat and strode toward me. Dressed in black pants and a V-neck shirt with long sleeves, I noted the golden insignia over his heart of two golden circles overlapping... the middle section was black and reminded me of an eclipse.

"What did you inject in me? Where are we?"

A corner of his mouth curled upward as he pushed his glasses to sit on top of his head. His caramel eyes smiled at me with a cheekiness I wasn't expecting. "A little something to help you breathe outside of The Brig. Our environmental systems are down, and oxygen was only available in the holding room."

"That's why you locked me in there?" I raised my voice. "Then why the hell didn't you just tell me, and why did you jam a needle in my neck?"

"Because you would have panicked." He remained so calm, still smirking, while I burned up on the inside, tangled in a mix of anger and frustration.

"I did panic! You came at me with a syringe."

"Oxygen levels were running low and I needed more time to fix up the regulators. Plus it gave me the perfect chance to trial the throat ring." He studied me like a specimen. "How are you feeling?"

My hand instinctively reached for my neck, half expecting to find a collar. "What are you talking about?"

"It's a small device that looks like a ring and sits in your throat esophagus. The ring gives you oxygen and eliminates other gases you inhale. Now, you can walk around the ship freely."

I blinked hard, and my brain stuttered for a while. "Y-you operated on me?"

He took a gulp of his coffee before setting it aside like it tasted bad. "It's a non intrusive quick implant. Either that or you would have died."

He reached out and took my hand in his, his face softening, but I pulled free from his grasp. I kept swallowing, convinced I felt the ring in my throat now. My lungs seemed to close up and I couldn't take enough air into them.

"I don't want your alien technology inside me."

His lips pursed. "Come with me." He marched past me and down the short hallway, then turned right through a set of doors that slid open at his approach.

I stood in the doorway, scanning the white room, the long table and chairs located in the middle, and eyed the panel of buttons on the rear wall. Everything looked pristine and almost too clinical.

"Take a seat," he commanded.

"No thanks. I don't want another injection."

"Sit!" he boomed and crossed the room before jabbing the control panel.

Seconds later, the whole wall seemed to vibrate, and I held my breath, unsure what was going on. But in a heartbeat the bottom half jutted out of the wall and a whole kitchen counter with cabinets and appliances appeared.

Corran pressed a button on the coffee machine and reached for the ground beans.

"This is a kitchen? And why do you have human stuff in here?" I stepped into the room and slid into a chair, watching him make two cups of coffee.

When he returned and placed a cup in front of me, he sat across from me. "I ordered them and set up this whole kitchen for you with foods you enjoy."

"Why would you think I'd ever come into your spaceship?" I picked up my mug and inhaled the nutty aroma before sipping it.

"You ask a lot of questions. And Reaver SC is a space cruiser."

I didn't know where to begin because my head spun with everything of late.

"You're safe now," he murmured. "That's what matters."

"Stop saying that."

Something behind his eyes shifted. Gone was the smile and patience.

But I'd had enough of being shoved here and there without explanation.

"Our compound on Earth was compromised and the Khonsu found you. They were coming to take you as theirs, so we left in our ship."

"And where are we now? I want to see my friends."

He was on his feet, shaking his head. "You know that's not possible."

Just hearing the words left me shaking, and my throat thickened, but then I fingered my neck, wondering if I'd choke on the ring inside me.

"Let me show you something that might answer your questions."

I climbed to my feet and took my cup of coffee with me, cradling it in my hands because each time I inhaled it's aroma, it reminded me of home.

In the narrow hallway, we passed several doors, and he stopped outside one. He tapped something into the keypad and the door zipped upward, vanishing into the wall.

"This is your cabin."

I peered inside to find a bed that looked like mine back home along with a bedside table, lamp, and even a bookshelf filled with books.

"The Mess Hall is stocked with all kinds of food for you, but come, I need to show you something in the Bridge."

I tracked after him into the main control room, closer to the enormous black window. Corran pointed to it. "What do you see?"

"Blackness," I retorted.

"Look again and closer," he insisted.

So I turned and stared into the eerie darkness, when I caught something blinking in the distance... tiny and far, but I leaned closer, squinting.

"This might help." Corran suggested and hit a button, the lights in the room fading.

The view outside of me changed, came to life, became so much more than I first thought. Outside the window, a pitch-black curtain draped over the sky all around us. No, not the sky... couldn't be when the blinking stars around us made shapes against the dark backdrop.

"Are..." Oh, shit. "Are we..." I glanced at him as he nodded, a tight smile pulling at his lips.

I should have known better than to think I could trust them in any way, but this... Fuck. "We're in space!"

Even before Corran answered, my knees wobbled and I collapsed into one of the seats looking out at the endless world ahead of us.

"It's beautiful isn't it?"

Words left me, and all I could do was gape at the expanse of the universe, caught up in the breadth of it, the sheer explosion of... space. I couldn't move my mouth to speak, instead I felt trapped as if I was frozen underwater, my world moving in slow motion.

"Are you okay?" he asked.

"Space. I'm in freaking space in a spaceship."

"Cruiser," he corrected me.

"Reaver SC is small and only has energy shields if we encounter enemy ships, but since we're on an exploration mission, we don't have weapons. We're also lacking entertainment on board such as a biosphere to replicate your botanical gardens, or a bar, but we're fast."

"What?" I couldn't comprehend what he was saying and I rubbed my eyes but it was useless. "Where are we going?"

"Veon. We have to return home."

I jerked toward him, a shiver slithering down my flesh. "Are you kidding me? You just kidnapped me from Earth and now you are taking me to your home planet?"

"We told you before. You're already ours."

I was on my feet pacing and didn't recall getting off the chair, but I wrapped my arms around my middle, barely able to breath. I kept prodding my throat with my tongue to feel for the ring. How could they have done this?

"You didn't even ask me," I mumbled.

"We had no time," he explained.

Fury raged through my veins that these three Vepar pushed and pulled me in every direction at their own accord, never what I wanted. "So what now?" I began. "You put me to sleep for years until we arrive there, and I'll wake up an old woman because I wasted my life here. I might as well have died at the hands of the enemies." I gasped for air, and the walls seemed to close in around me.

"It'll take us just under a month to reach home. We use a rift in space-time," Corran explained as if I ought to understand what he was talking about.

I blinked fast and glanced back outside the window. "I don't know much about science, but I'm pretty sure no one can move faster than the speed of light."

"Our technology might challenge that theory. Long ago we discovered two entangled black holes. Our scientists found an anomaly and..." He tapped his chin as if finding the easiest way to explain what I already didn't quite understand. "They found a way to separate these two black holes, and that space in between turned out to be a wormhole, which allows anyone with the right vessel to take a shortcut through the universe."

"Shortcut?"

"Space and time can be bent. One of Earth's great geniuses, Albert Einstein was correct," Corran's words sped up in his excitement to tell me this explanation. "A wormhole is a tunnel that joins distant locations in space or even two universes through space time curvature. And one of our scientists discovered one that goes from our world to your universe."

"So, that's how you've watched us for so long before you invaded."

"Invaded is a very harsh word." He picked up his black framed glasses and slipped them back on his face.

"Where's Thane and Derrial?"

"Sleeping. We've been traveling nonstop for the past two weeks and are nearing the wormhole. If you'd like, I could put you to sleep for the next two weeks?"

I slumped back into the seat, my head hurting from the influx of information, and yet I couldn't stop staring out into space, both terrified and lost.

At least this time he asked me if I wanted something done to me. Maybe sleeping wasn't such a bad idea as it would stop me from stressing constantly, but what if I woke up with something else operated on me?

"No sleep. I prefer to experience the next two weeks on the ship."

No matter what Corran said, him and the other two had indeed kidnapped me and now I was about to be taken to an alien planet, so I needed my eyes wide and to be alert.

Terror washed over me, sending another chill down my back. I looked outside once more into the endless universe.

Would I ever see Earth again?

4

Today was the day, we would finally be getting to Veon. I stood in front of the window Corran had designed for me after I had complained a million times about feeling like I was locked in a metal box. From space it looked completely different than Earth. It had a smoky red complexion that seemed to swirl before my eyes. Corran had explained that it was part of their defense system to look as inhabitable as possible and it was nothing but a complicated hologram that Corran had designed himself. Underneath the hologram lay a world that looked very similar to Earth. There were oceans, purple in color instead of blue because of an algae that provided unique nutrients, and land masses with forests, jungles, and mountains.

The similarities between the two planets had been almost too good to be true when Corran had first stumbled upon Earth and it had been months of performing positive tests before he had alerted leadership. Leadership that included Derrial. Corran had told me that Derrial had been furious that Corran hadn't told the Vepar leadership about Earth and it had actually taken them a few years for Derrial to forgive him and trust him again.

It was a crack in the trio's friendship that I had filed away for later, to be used if I needed it.

Looking at the red swirling mists, it was almost incomprehensible to think that a planet similar to Earth was waiting beneath its depths. I watched as we drew closer and closer, a sense of apprehension filling me at the thought of entering them. I suddenly regretted having asked for a seat as close as possible to the huge window. It would be much easier to go through the mists blindly.

"We need to go over a few things before we land," came Derrial's voice from seemingly nowhere. I hadn't gotten used to the invisible technology on the ship and every time one of their voices spoke to me through the sound system I either jumped or I looked around, expecting one of them to be standing right behind me.

"Yes master," I said sarcastically, heading to the Bridge to talk to my three captors. We had entered an uneasy truce over the past couple of weeks. I still hated them, but I also didn't particularly relish the idea of being captured by the Khonsu so I was being their good little pet for the moment, just until I could figure out a way to escape them forever and somehow keep myself safe from the Khonsu.

"You only need to call me "Master" in bed," came Derrial's voice from the sound system.

"You wish," I muttered back, but my mind couldn't help but fill with images of the time when I had been in his bed, how good his body had felt against me, in me...like we were a perfect match. The images were distorted in my head now that I knew their true motives, but I couldn't help but crave that feeling again. That feeling of finding what I had always been looking for.

I mentally berated myself all the way to the Bridge. I couldn't afford to let my lust get my guard down around them. Nothing but pain and misery...and possibly little alien babies that I would fall in love with but wouldn't get to keep lay in a future that involved them.

Despite my mental admonitions, the sight of all three of them in one room still threatened to leave me a quivering mess. I hated my body's reaction to them, how they had made me crave both their bodies and their blood. Corran had promised that he was working on some kind of antidote to help with the blood cravings but I trusted he'd come through with something about as little as I trusted myself to navigate this ship back to Earth on my own.

"Glad you made it, pet." Thane smirked my way as he leaned against one of the chairs in the center of the room that seemed to be suspended in the air.

I rolled my eyes. Thane in particular had loved to antagonize me over the last couple of weeks and I was trying my best to ignore him in hopes that he would get tired of his games and go away.

"Well? You called?" I asked sharply, venom in my voice. I saw something flash in Derrial's eyes. Out of the three of them, he seemed to be the most affected by the fact that I wanted nothing to do with them and regarded them as Public Enemy No. 1. I'm sure there was a story out there to explain his reaction but I couldn't find it in myself enough to care.

"We need to talk about what Veon will be like," Corran explained, fixing me with those intense, caramel colored eyes. "The culture is quite different from Earth and there will be a lot of things that don't make sense to your earthly sensibilities."

I opened my mouth to offer a retort but Corran cut me off. "Could you just get off your fucking high horse for one minute, Ella. I'm not trying to be offensive for fuck's sake. These are just things you need to know."

My mouth opened in shock. In all the time that I had seen Corran, he had never appeared so angry, not even when he thought that I was running away after he fought the Khonsu (which I was by the way). The heat in his voice burned through my body and I found myself strangely turned on.

"Okay," I said meekly, thinking that I should probably listen if he deemed it important enough to crack his usually emotionless shield.

Corran took a deep breath and his expression morphed into his usual stoic one, where he revealed no emotions. A moment later he was back to the cool and collected Vepar that I was used to. "First things first, the Vepar don't like the humans. They think that they are a lesser culture and I don't see that changing any time soon," Corran added, matter of factly.

Once again I got the urge to say something sarcastic, like how he'd just made an obvious statement. But I held back the words.

Thane was watching me, an amused twinkle in his eyes because he knew how hard it was to keep my mouth in check. I shot him a look and then turned my attention back to Corran who was waiting impatiently for me to pay attention to him again.

"As I was saying," he said. "The only way that a human would be accepted onto Veon is if the leadership thinks that we need you to continue with the fertility experiments. The way that the program has been explained to them, our human subjects will be nothing more than vessels and prisoners of Veon during their time here."

I couldn't stop myself this time. "Isn't that the truth though. It's not that the leadership has to think that, it's how it is. As far as all of you are concerned I'm nothing but livestock for you to do whatever you want with." Frustrated tears filled my eyes as the realization of what I was facing once again rolled over me.

Derrial was in my face suddenly, his hands gripping my arms so hard that I was sure he was going to leave a bruise.

"Stupid girl. If you would just let us have a second to explain it, it wouldn't need to be like this. Why do you have to be so fucking prideful? We've been trying to get you to let us have a second to explain what you saw for the past few weeks."

"There's nothing you could say that could make this better," I snapped at him childishly.

Derrial let me go with a growl, throwing up his hands in frustration. "I can't deal with this right now," he practically screamed as he angrily strode out of the room.

I trembled in the aftermath of his rage. There was a piece of me that did want to listen to what they had to say about their secret basement room and their planned fertility experiments, but he was right, my pride wouldn't allow me to give them the chance to explain. I was still too hurt by everything that had happened.

"You'll have to listen to us eventually," said Corran, watching me as if I was a particularly vexing science problem.

"Can you please continue with what you were saying?" I responded stiffly, keeping my eyes glued to the floor.

"Yes, as I was saying...because of the Vepar attitude, we will have to walk you off the ship in cuffs...as our prisoner."

"How perfect. I wouldn't expect anything less," I said in a dull voice. This time I saw Thane flinch at my tone out of the corner of my eye.

"You'll be kept in a prison until we can talk to the rest of the counsel and convince them of your suitability in the project," Corran continued.

Their words were like punches to my gut, and they kept coming, kept taking and taking from me. A tear slid down my face as I watched my life disintegrate into ruins.

Silence, but I felt both Thane and Corran's piercing stares as they watched my tears continue to fall.

"We're just here to keep you safe. The experiment is a front," came Derrial's voice from behind me.

I freeze and then slowly turn around to look at him. We stared at each other. There was a muscle twitching in Derrial's cheek and his eyes seemed glossier than usual. "That's all we want to do is to keep you safe. This might have started out as something else. But it's not that way anymore. It hasn't been that way since the first time I held you in my arms...since I tasted you."

His voice was choked with emotion, and I felt like I couldn't breathe. There was a part of me, the stupid girl who wanted to believe in fairy tales...even if they were the science fiction version, that wanted to believe him. But I promised myself I wouldn't be that girl anymore. I refused to be sucked in again. It hurt too much.

My heart couldn't handle it again.

"I know you don't believe us, pet. But we have so much to tell you. You'll see. We'll gain back your trust," Thane murmured from behind me. He walked towards me and I sensed the heat emanating from his body against mine at my back.

I took a step away from him and walked to a nearby chair, settling in so I could control the trembling in my body.

"It's very important that you don't talk back in front of others. The Vepar are looking for any chance to cut you down, to punish you, to take you from us. Please don't make our jobs any harder than they will be already."

I nodded stiffly, feeling like there really wasn't another option but for me to cooperate.

"The air on Veon has a higher concentration of nitrogen than what you are used to and that's why I implanted that ring in your throat. But now I need to inject you with a chip that will allow your body to adapt quicker in these conditions compared to the ship," Corran explained, his voice softening.

"Is that all the chip does? Not sure I want all these things inside me." I stared him straight in the eyes, daring him to lie to me. He gulped.

"It also has a tracking device in it," he replied hesitantly. "It's important just in case anyone tries to take you."

"Tries to take me?" I asked, my voice quivering. "Why would they want to take me?"

Corran opened his mouth to answer but Derrial replied instead. "We aren't sure that our reaction to you and your blood isn't something that other males on the planet will be attracted to as well. The Vepar are an extremely competitive and territorial race and there's a chance that some of the males will be tempted to steal you for themselves."

I tried to comprehend a whole planet full of overbearing, chauvinist pigs like the three of them. It sounded like a nightmare.

"And what about the Vepar women? Are you worried about them?" I finally asked, my mind filled with images of packs of men running after me with spears. I wasn't sure why they were all dressed in loincloths, but it was still an intimidating sight.

The three of them looked at each other grimly and suddenly I was afraid of what they were going to say next.

"Our females don't take kindly to competition for the attention of their males," Thane added grimly. "There's a chance that they will try to take you out if they find out about fertility experiments and calculations that Corran has come up with. As of right now they don't know that one of the main reasons that we were sent to Earth was to try and find a solution to our planet's fertility problems using humans. If they do find out...well we don't think they will take it well."

I gulped, the images in my mind changing to women in loincloths chasing after me with spears.

"So you're saying I'm not going to be welcomed with open arms," I finally retorted, and Thane let out a snort.

"She's a lunatic," he said to Derrial and Corran, waving his arms at me. "She's going to get herself killed."

"I do have some kind of self preservation mechanism," I retorted. "I'll do what I'm told, because I don't feel like dying on this trip. But I need answers."

Derrial gazed at me, an almost proud look in his eyes. "A worthy mate indeed," he muttered as he walked out of the room.

I blushed, not believing what I had just heard. A mate? Please say that wasn't what he just said.

I ignored the part of me that swelled up with happiness at the thought of being his...of being all of theirs.

I turned back to Corran, the intensity in Derrial's voice too much to take.

Corran brought over a pair of silver handcuffs. He looked genuinely contrite as he put my hands behind my back and fastened them. "I just wanted you to get a feel for them so you don't panic when they're on your wrists for a long period of time. Hopefully Derrial will be able to convince the council to release you quickly."

He unhooked them, and I shook my wrists out. It was going to be torture to have those on for a long period of time.

"It's very important that you don't struggle while you're in the cuffs. I was feeling particularly malicious the day that I designed them, and they are programmed to release spikes into your wrists if it believes you are trying to get them off without the key," Corran said nonchalantly.

I gaped at him. "We can't use a friendlier version of the cuffs?" Indignation burned inside of me.

He shook his head. "The Council would notice something was amiss if we tried to do that. We use them for all of our prisoners and they would expect them to be used especially for a human prisoner. No one has ever been able to escape them. They're basically foolproof," he said, almost sounding proud.

I glared at him. "You don't have to sound so happy about the fact that I'm going to be stuck in something that could impale me at any minute!" I said dramatically.

"I don't know...I for one like you in cuffs," Thane pipped in, a hungry glimmer in his eyes.

Despite my anger at the both of them, tears started dripping down my face. I guess I was becoming a crier in all situations. When I was afraid, when I was angry, when I was sad. It wasn't ideal.

Just like before when I had cried, Corran and Thane seemed to be enthralled at the tear streaks on my face. After a moment, Corran shook his head as if he was trying to shake himself out of something.

"When we get off the ship, you need to keep your head down. Don't look anyone in the eye. I don't trust that you're going to play the complacent human very well so it's best if you don't even look up," said Corran.

I snorted. He was right about that. Although if complacent and meek was going to save my life, I could probably try it.

"I put your language translator in you already obviously, but I want you to pretend that you don't understand anything that they're saying. I'll tell them that I haven't done it yet. It might raise suspicion with the Council if they know we did it early."

"Language translator?" I ask.

"Yes," said Corran, looking at me as if I was an idiot. "We speak a different language on Veon. I'm speaking Veon right now," he explains. "We've been using our language since we got on the ship."

I stiffened.

"How long have I had the translator in?" I said, feeling a coldness start to creep over me. "What else have you implanted in me?"

Corran had the sense to look a little ashamed at my question.

"Since you came to us," he said quietly.

"Where is it?" I asked.

"Behind your right ear," Corran murmured, clearing his throat.

I brushed my fingers along the skin behind my ear, but I couldn't feel anything laying underneath the surface. I was afraid to ask my next question.

"Has anything else been put into my body without my permission?" I finally asked.

Corran's face fell blank. "Just something that allows me to track your body's vitals better. It was put in when we were going to use you as the main specimen in my experiments. But now it just helps us to make sure that you're healthy."

I felt my annoying tears dripping again because with everything they did, I was losing control more and more. I was so sick of crying. "And where's that one?" I asked in a quivering voice.

"That one is in your left arm," Corran said in a nonchalant voice.

I brushed my hand over my arm, all the while knowing that I wouldn't be able to feel anything.

"Anything else?" I asked coldly.

Corran shook his head. "That's it."

"Is it even worth me asking that you get permission before you put things into my body from now on?" I asked, trying to keep my voice steady.

Corran sighed. "I can't promise you that. If you refuse to do something that we feel can help you, I can't say that we won't do it anyway. You belong to us. That means that we're responsible for your health, your safety, and everything else that comes with that."

In this moment, I truly felt exhausted. I had always assumed that they felt like I was their property. But the thought of them putting whatever they wanted into my body, it left me feeling desperate, and out of control. I took a few deep breaths, trying to tamp down my emotions that were threatening to spiral. That's all I needed was to have a panic attack right before I met an entire alien race that hated me on principle.

Derrial returned to the room at that moment. "I have to go meet with the Council and prepare them for you," he said.

I couldn't find the words to respond, so I just stared at the floor.

Derrial sighed. "What's wrong with you now?" he muttered in an annoyed tone.

"She's not very happy with some of the devices that I have been using on her," Corran said calmly.

Derrial barked out a laugh. "Unbelievable." He stalked back out of the room without another word.

"You're going to need to pull yourself together for this," Thane spoke sternly. "The Council would love to see you lose control and confirm all their thoughts about humans."

I wanted to respond that they were the reason I was feeling out of control in the first place, but it didn't even seem worth it.

As we waited, Thane began to explain further what would happen when we walked off the ship. "As Corran said, you're going to be marched through a line of Vepar. They're going to say things, things to make you angry. You need to ignore them. Once we get through the line, you'll be taken to a new building where prisoners are kept. Derrial will have arranged for you to be in your own cell thanks to your status as part of Corran's fertility experiments. The prisoners that will be in the cells next to you are very dangerous. Don't engage them, don't look at them, don't even acknowledge their presence." Thane pulled up my chin, forcing me to look at him. "You understand me?" he said in a serious voice.

I nodded, fear churning in my gut at what I was about to face.

"Hopefully Derrial will succeed in having you in different quarters quickly under the guise that Corran needs to start performing tests. It should only be a few hours that you have to stay there, but if you do have to spend the night, the same rules apply. One of us will try to be stationed in the jail if that happens." He tapped his ear, seeming to be listening to something, almost as if he had a phone hidden in there.

"Derrial is ready for us." He looked at me, his penetrating green eyes seeming to see right through me. "You can't mess up with this," he said seriously. "If there ever was a time for you to listen to us, it's now."

I just nodded, unable to utter actual words as I tried to pump myself up for what I was about to experience.

"We need to change first," Thane suggested.

I watched as he walked to a plastic tube that stretched from floor to ceiling on the side of the room. He stepped inside and pressed a button. I watched in amazement as his clothes changed right before my eyes without him even moving a muscle, fabric vacuumed off him, and new ones wrapped around him, seeming to sew shut right before my eyes. Thane's usual outfit of jeans and a V-neck were gone. He now stood in what looked like a cross between an outfit you would see in a Star Wars film, and an outfit from a Victorian byopic. The entire outfit was made up of different shades of brown. He wore a tan silk blouse I'd seen on the cover of a Harlequin novel. The front was cut low, showing a great deal of his ridiculously perfect chest. On top of that was a darker brown fitted jacket and matching pants, so tight it had me gawking. Every muscle on his legs showed. I had never thought that breeches could look good on anyone, but like with a baseball uniform on a major leaguer, the pants managed to make his lower half look very tantalizing. Tall brown boots that resembled riding boots completed the look.

Thane came to stand by me as Corran took his turn in the device. He pressed the button and his usual all-black outfit that looked similar to nursing scrubs, changed into a grey version of what Thane was wearing.

I looked down at what I was dressed in. The guys had continued with their habit of wanting me in dresses. My current skater style dress was sure to stand out.

"Am I going out in this?" I asked, finally finding my voice again. They scrutinized my outfit, Corran rubbing his chin. My body heated up as their eyes lazily made their way down my body. Thane looked over at Corran.

"Do you think it's better for her to stand out or look like she's trying to assimilate into the culture?" he asked.

Corran thought for a moment. "Maybe she should change," he said. "It might help to make the differences less obvious."

I wondered about his use of the word differences. From what I could tell, the Vepar looked just like humans, albeit perfectly formed godlike humans. What would make me stand out so much? The fact that I looked as plain as could be next to them? I didn't know that clothes were going to fix that.

Thane walked me over to the cylinder. I experienced a brief moment of panic when I stepped in, my newly developed claustrophobia surfacing. Thane pressed a button and without me feeling anything, my clothes were replaced by a completely different outfit, down to my underthings. I was going to have to get Corran to explain how this device worked.

I looked down at myself. My dress definitely looked old-fashioned. The gown fell down to the floor and was made of a beautiful cerulean blue fabric. A torture-like corset constricted my breathing, threatening to make me pass out from lack of oxygen. The front of the dress was cut low, displaying my ample cleavage. I didn't have a bra on anymore, but the top of the dress fit so tightly that my breasts couldn't move even if they wanted to. The sleeves were long and form fitting. I lifted up the dress to examine my footwear. They looked like simple ballet slippers, slightly lighter blue than my dress.

Although it felt like there was a lot of fabric to the dress, it was dreamily lightweight. All in all, I didn't hate the look.

I lifted my head up and caught Corran and Thane gaping at me. It set my cheeks on fire the way they were studying me. My other dress had been much shorter than this one, but it had covered a lot more of my chest. Evidently they liked that about this one.

"We should've kept her in the other outfit," Thane moaned.

Corran nodded in agreement.

Whatever communication device Thane had in his ear must have alerted him, because he put his hand to it, seeming to be listening to something.

"We're coming," Thane said in an annoyed voice. He listened to whoever was on the other line, saying nothing in response. Thane then grabbed my arm, and we started walking out of the bridge, and through the never ending hallways.

5

We stopped in front of a wall and Corran fastened my handcuffs again. I winced as the metal dug into my skin. I was scared to even walk for fear that it would trigger the spikes that Corran had mentioned. Hopefully they weren't that sensitive.

"Remember what we said," Thane said softly, a hint of trepidation in his voice for the first time. I looked up at him worried. He always seemed so confident. It didn't seem like a good sign that he was beginning to freak out now.

The wall dissolved in front of us, and I felt a cool breeze across my face for the first time in a month. Corran had explained earlier that scientists had been able to manipulate the environment to keep the temperature ideal for Veon's citizens year-round. In places that they needed crops to grow the atoms in the atmosphere had been altered to produce wetter conditions, similar to the tropics. For the Vepar who worked in those types of climates, a sort of force field had been created that allowed personal ozones to be created keeping them cool and comfortable while they worked. I was amazed at how advanced the Vepar were compared to humans. The ability to manipulate nature had seemed impossible to me before Corran had explained it.

Despite their admonition that I needed to keep my head down, I couldn't help but try to get a look at the new world I found myself in before I was locked away, perhaps permanently.

It was so colorful, and not what I expected.

A simple observation, but I had never seen such a lush looking place before, especially considering the air felt perfectly cool, somewhere in the upper 60s or lower 70s Fahrenheit.

We were in a large grassy clearing that looked like it could fit a few dozen spacecrafts. Large mountains surrounded the clearing. There was a variety of tree species spanning the mountains in all different colors. I had never seen a purple tree before but here I was seeing hundreds of them. Flowers bloomed all over the clearing in every color imaginable. I felt like I had walked onto the set of Wizard of Oz. Everything was so bright and beautiful that it hurt my eyes. I couldn't imagine the guys wanting to stay on Earth over this.

Overhead, two suns hung in the sky, and Corran leaned close, whispering, "We have a binary star system. The suns revolve around each other as our planet circles them."

I'd never heard of a solar system having two suns before.

As soon as I had that thought I spotted two lines of Vepar standing in front of a brown structure that had a roof that curled into the sky. My mouth dropped. I had never seen so many beautiful creatures in one place. I said creatures because they were human-like with legs and arms, but at the same time...they were distinctly alien.

Once I got past their first flash of beauty, I noticed what set them apart. Some of them had horns... horns of all shapes, sizes, and colors. Some were short and pointy reminding me of ears, while others were curled like those of mountain goats, the colors varying from creams to blues and blacks. Others had thin tails coming out of their rear ends that seemed to have pincers at the very end. I watched in amazement as a particularly attractive male picked something up off the ground that he had dropped with his tail. Others looked normal with the exception of their eye colors. I had never seen orange eyes before, let alone some of the other colors that caught my attention. All I could do was gape at them, the very opposite thing that Corran and Thane had told me to do.

"What are you doing?" Thane growled.

"It's all so amazing," I exclaimed, finally averting my eyes to the ground where they were supposed to be.

Suddenly something struck me. If the Vepar here had all of these different characteristics, why didn't my Vepar?

Everyone on Earth said they used disguises to cover their real appearances.... And they were right.

"Do you have horns or a tail?" I asked. I'd never imagined that such features and strange eyes were something that I'd be attracted to. But seeing them on all of these beautiful Vepar had me thinking differently. It was so exotic...so exciting.

Thane stared at me for a moment, seeming to be thinking over his answer before he spoke. "We'll talk about it later," he finally said gruffly. "Now keep your head down before we look even more suspicious."

Well that wasn't a no, I thought somewhat excitedly. Then I finally remembered that I was supposed to be hating them, and I was about to walk through a line of Vepar that thought I was lower than the dirt at their feet.

Fear started to stamp its way up my spine as we began to walk, tramping the wildflowers under our feet. I watched as they sprung up as we moved, none the worse for wear. Even their flowers were superior to the ones on Earth...

The air thickened with hostility as we got closer and I shivered. The line consisted of all men, their glares skating all over my body, and I felt wrong and uncomfortable. I had never encountered such hatred before. Thane and Corran must have felt it too because they both inched imperceptibly closer. Thane gave a small nod to Corran, who took over holding my arm tightly. Thane fidgeted with his belt where he was keeping the silver stun gun that I had seen him use before. Did they think we were going to be attacked?

I made the mistake of lifting my head when a large neon purple bug landed on my face. I put my head down again quickly, and blew a breath up my face to get it off my nose. A quick shake of my head and it flew away. But the damage had been done. I'd looked them in the face and seen them up close. The Vepar no longer looked beautiful. Their faces were scrunched in hatred and twisted with disgust. I couldn't help but wonder what they had heard about humans to give them so many strong emotions.

From what I understood, I was one of the first humans to ever be brought to Veon. At least on Earth we had reason to hate the Vepar. After all they had come over and taken control of everything. As far as I knew, the humans hadn't done anything to Veon. In fact, the Vepar needed humans to keep their population going. It seemed a little ungrateful to me.

"Vadiah," one of the Vepar hissed at me. I didn't need my language translator to understand that whatever he had said was not a good thing.

Corran and Thane both stiffened next to me and I heard Thane give a growl that made the Vepar step back. I had been under the impression that all three of my Vepar were higher ups in the Veon society.

My Vepar...why did I say that.

More angry voices spat out hatred and curses as we walked through the line. Thane stiffened, his hands curled into fists, like he itched to shoot them all. I expected Thane and Corran to stand up for me, but I guess that would go against the impression they were trying to present me as their prisoner. I wondered what the Vepar would think if they knew that I had slept and made blood bonds with all three of them.

The thought made me absurdly want to laugh. And then I wanted to cry again.

Maybe I was going crazy.

We finally made it through the line and were about to enter the building when I was hit in the back of my head with something sticky and horrible smelling. It slid through my hair, down my neck, and into the back of my pretty dress.

It took a second and then my skin started to burn. I let out a small scream and started to claw at my neck and hair, which then made the skin on my hands start to burn as well.

"It hurts," I moaned, fear sticking to my ribs like tar.

Corran cursed and started to drag me inside. I suddenly heard Thane's gun go off.

Bang. Bang.

Despite the pain, I looked back and was shocked to see one of the Vepar lying dead on the ground, Thane standing over him with a ferocious look on his face.

I couldn't worry about any repercussions for Thane at that moment because the burning started to increase until I felt like I was being burned alive. Was I going to die?

"What's happening to me?" I cried out as I stopped in my tracks, unable to move any longer due to the immense agony I was feeling. Corran picked me up in his arms, murmuring softly in my ear about how I was going to be alright, how they would never let anything hurt me again.

He hauled me into a room that looked like Corran's secret basement lab. Or at least I think it did. The pain was making everything seem distorted.

Corran laid me face down on a table that was much softer than the other medical exam tables I'd encountered in my life. I sobbed as the burning continued to spread throughout my body. He picked up a knife and quickly slit the back of my dress open so that the fabric slid off of me.

I stiffened when Corran sprinkled something wet all over my skin. Immediately my pain faded, replaced by a cooling sensation. Corran continued with the liquid for a few more minutes before stopping. His footsteps quickened around me, drawers shutting and closing. I was so exhausted from the pain that I didn't even bother to open my eyes to look where he was going.

A second later, his footsteps approached and he applied a soft gel all over my neck and shoulders under my dress. I moaned with how good the coolness felt.

Corran stiffened at the noise, then cleared his throat. "How are you feeling?" he asked hoarsely.

"Better," I croaked, my voice faint from screaming so much. "What was that?"

"A creature most similar to the barnacles you have in your oceans. Except ours contain one of the most toxic poisons on the planet."

"So I could have died?" I asked, starting to cry again at the memory of how much it had hurt.

He was silent for a moment. "I never would have let that happen," he said, rubbing in some more of the gel. "I'm so sorry this happened to you," Corran whispered softly, gently continuing to stroke my skin. There was such remorse in his voice, the kind that I rarely got from them after everything they had done to me. It did something to my insides.

His gentle hand trailed down my skin almost sensually even though this wasn't the place for any of that to happen.

Thane walked into the room, rage still written across his face. "How is she doing?" he asked, his hands trembling with adrenaline.

"I applied the antidote. She should be completely back to normal in a few more minutes," Corran explained. "Did you take care of him?"

Thane nodded, his cheek twitching as he tried to control himself. "Evidently we're going to have to remind everyone just who we are. I guess we've been gone a little too long."

Corran nodded. "If we're going to keep her safe, we'll have to do that fast."

Once again I felt conflicting emotions. They were so protective of me. Yet they didn't respect anything in regards to my free agency. I didn't know how those two things worked together.

After a couple more minutes I did indeed feel back to normal, better than normal in fact. Corran helped me off the table and led me over to a cylinder clothes changer that was also in this room. I was immediately changed into a new dress, this one a crimson color. The cylinder even somehow took care of my dirty hair and skin, leaving my hair looking more shiny than it did after I went to a hair appointment. I was kind of bummed that they didn't introduce me to this technology earlier. It would've saved me a lot of time.

"How come you didn't use this at your house on earth?" I asked, thinking that if I had this at my disposal I would have never chosen to go without it.

Thane smirked. "There's something to be said for the shower," he stated, giving me a wink. It took me a second, and then I was blushing furiously.

Thane's communicator device must have sent him an alert, because his hand went to his ear. After listening for a moment, he looked at me regretfully. "I'm sorry, but we need to get the cuffs back on you and get you to the prison. You already drew enough attention just walking through the line. It will get even worse if they sense that we're giving you special treatment."

"You mean like killing someone who hurt me?" I asked, raising an eyebrow.

Thane growled. "That's expected in our society. That Vepar disrespected us by harming something that belonged to us. It would have looked stranger if I hadn't done anything."

I filed that away for later. The Vepar were obviously a very aggressive society, but I had already known that, hadn't I?

Sighing, I obediently put my arms behind my back. I grimaced as the cold metal once again clicked around my wrists.

Thane and Corran walked me out of the lab and down another long hallway. I looked around with interest. Like the space cruiser, the Vepar seemed to like simplicity. The walls were a stark gray gunmetal color. There were no pictures or ornamentation decorating any of them. I guess when you lived on a planet as beautiful as Veon, you didn't need elaborate decorations.

We turned right, arriving at what I assumed was my new home for the time being. We were in a large, long room, with doorways on either side.

As we began to walk, I realized that Thane hadn't been lying when he said that the prisoners who were about to be my neighbors were dangerous. The prisoners were all beautiful, yes, but they were all distorted in a way that sent fear spiraling down my spine. Some of the prisoners we walked by had fangs that they flashed at me when I looked at them. There was another prisoner that had shiny black scales that flickered across his skin before disappearing. Another cell held a dark figure in the center of the room with black mist swirling all around it.

I gasped. It was all I could do to suppress the urge to try and run away.

"You didn't tell me that there were Khonsu imprisoned here," I said coldly to Thane and Corran, my voice quivering with fear.

"We told you that our most dangerous prisoners were kept here. Khonsu would be included in that of course," Corran said mildly.

I trembled, thinking about having to be near them. What if that thing escaped and came after me? I didn't think I could take that kind of torture again.

I felt the tip of Thane's finger brush against my arm soothingly. When I looked up at him, his face looked as blank as ever, and he continued to stare straight ahead as we walked. My heart couldn't help but warm at the thought that he was attempting to offer comfort despite the fact that he needed to keep up appearances that I was his prisoner.

Just as soon as I had that thought, I shut it down. They were the reason I was here to begin with. They were the reason the Khonsu came after me. They were the reason for everything bad that had happened in my life.

We stopped in front of an empty cell that was right across from a Vepar that looked to be missing half of his appendages. There was another unidentifiable creature in the cell next to the empty one that looked to be gnawing on some kind of bird carcass. He leered at me manically, and I jumped back as his smile revealed rows and rows of sharp teeth that resembled the mouth of a shark.

Corran waved a small device over the glass of the empty cell and it disappeared. They then led me inside. The room was practically bare. There was a small cot against the back wall that held a threadbare blanket, no pillow. Corran showed me how to press a button on the wall to get the toilet and a small sink to appear. Other than that there was nothing in the room. Nothing to pass the time with either.

Suddenly, I couldn't stand the thought of being trapped in this room.

"Please don't leave me here," I begged. Corran looked at Thane anxiously. Thane reached out and brushed my hair softly.

"It should only be for a few hours," he said. "We'll be back for you soon."

Looking around to see if anyone was watching us, which all of the prisoners on the opposite wall were, Corran stood closely next to me and pulled out what looked like a small tablet.

"This will have things on it to keep you busy. I downloaded some Earth movies and books for you to use on the ship. But obviously you never used it. I'll turn off the cameras on half of your room. As long as you're laying on your cot when you look at it, the cameras won't pick up that you have the device.

I nodded gratefully, even as tears continued to humiliatingly stream down my face at the thought of being left alone surrounded by all of these dangerous creatures.

Thane's communication device must have popped on because he started to talk to someone. "We're just loading her into the cell right now," he instructed. "We'll be there in a minute to talk to the Council." He rolled his eyes before tapping his ear again, assumedly to shut off the device. "We have to go," Thane said.

I couldn't seem to control my body as it continued to shake. Corran unhooked the handcuffs, and I gratefully shook my wrists out. At least I hadn't managed to engage the spikes. That would have been the cherry on top of a craptastic day.

Thane and Corran stared at me. "I really want to kiss you," Thane murmured in a growly, worried voice.

I wanted that too. But I wasn't going to tell them that. "I'll be fine," I said, wiping away my tears.

Corran took my hand. "It won't be long. I promise." I nodded, not really believing that would be the case. Something told me the Council wasn't going to love the idea of me wandering around Veon.

They finally turned to go. Stepping out of the cell, Corran once again waved a device in front of where the glass was supposed to be and it instantly reappeared.

I wanted to run and beat on the glass wall, but I knew that it wouldn't make a difference. I collapsed face down on the cot, listening to the screams and moans of the prisoners around me.

How did I get here?

6

Time inched along. After laying there feeling sorry for myself for what seemed like hours, I finally picked up the tablet that Corran had given me and started to search through it. "Some" was not an accurate description for the amount of movies and books Corran had uploaded. There were literally millions of movies and books on here. I could read and watch movies every day for the rest of my life and still not even come close to making a dent in the content. It must be nice to be practically immortal like the Vepar, they could actually take advantage of everything that life offered.

Tired of the pity party I was throwing myself, I finally settled on Sweet Home Alabama, a movie guaranteed to make me feel better. There was nothing like a little Patrick Dempsey to soothe the soul.

It was impossible to get comfortable on the cot so I ended up just sitting on it and leaning against the wall. It seemed a bit inhumane that they didn't provide pillows for the prisoners. I'm sure most of the prisoners here were lifers.

Of course I glanced over to my cellmate across the aisle who was currently flicking pieces of what looked like ash off his burned body...maybe the least of my concerns were pillows.

I clicked start on the movie, but there was something offsetting about trying to watch a romantic comedy with all of the terrifying noises that surrounded me. The cells were definitely not soundproof. I jumped when a scream that sounded more dinosaur-like than intelligent creature sounded from my next door neighbor.

Please hurry back to me, I thought to myself, wondering how the guys were faring in front of the Council.

My stomach gurgled just then. I wondered what they fed the prisoners.

Hopefully it was something humans could eat. Thane and Corran probably should have mentioned something about that.

I tried to concentrate on the movie but my mind was just too full. Full of them, full of what had happened, full of my fear for the future.

I had to get out of here. I had to get off this planet. And I had to get away from them.

There had to be a place where they couldn't find me.

I thought about my recent bloodlust and felt a momentary flash of panic. That was a problem I would have to deal with before I escaped. Hopefully Corran would give me some sort of solution sooner rather than later. I didn't want to return to Earth as some kind of vampire.

Maybe I could somehow take some of their blood with me to hold me over?

As soon as I had that thought I felt sick. Just a little bit ago I was a normal girl, poor...but normal. Now I was thinking about blood.

They really had ruined me.

I was lost in my musings so I didn't hear the footsteps walking down the hall until there was someone staring at me through my cell glass.

I almost peed myself when I heard the throaty peal of laughter come out of her.

It was my first sighting of what had to be a Vepar female. And just by looking at her, I knew she would bring me nothing but trouble.

She was stunning, so gorgeous that I didn't think I had ever seen another female so beautiful before. Deep, auburn hair tumbled to her waist. A perfect, petite nose, doe-like emerald eyes, and bow-shaped lips made up her face. Her skin was a perfect creamy color that looked like it had been airbrushed. Her waist tapped in, and her boobs were big. Essentially she was everything I was not. Not even the two small ivory horns sticking out of her head could detract from her beauty. Not when they had silver threads curled around them in a decorative manner.

She stared at me, a small smirk stretching on her face.

It broke me to admit. But this was the kind of girl that fit with the guys. I couldn't believe that Thane, Derrial, and Corran could actually deign to sleep with humans when they had females walking around who looked like that. They must really want to procreate.

I remembered some of the details of the plan I had seen in the guys' basement lab. From what I'd seen, I would just be an incubator for an embryo made up of all Vepar DNA.

Something burned inside of me at the thought of Thane, Derrial, and Corran's DNA being combined with this beautiful creature. I felt dark just thinking about it.

I wasn't sure what to say to her. From what I had been told, Vepar women held an even greater distaste for humans than their male counterparts did. And a male counterpart had already tried to kill me.

What was this one going to try and do to me?

"Hello little human," she said in a voice that literally sounded like music to my ears. I had never heard a voice so melodic before.

I remained silent, watching her carefully.

"I just had to see what all the fuss was about. What would make my mates leave Veon. I can't say that I'm impressed."

I tried to understand what she was saying. Mates? Please don't be talking about the guys...

"I'm sure you know all about me. But I must say, I know very little about you," she said, her gaze shrewd and cold.

I wasn't sure what the right move was here. I had a million questions, but I was deeply afraid of the danger that was emanating from this Vepar. There was a cruel glint in her eyes that terrified me. All I could pray was that she wasn't able to open this cell. I didn't think I would survive, and I knew that the Vepar women were close to as strong as the males. And we all know how well I'd fared against them...

"I'm sorry, I'm afraid that there's been a mistake. Who are you?" I finally asked, feeling like I was antagonizing her more by not saying anything.

Obviously I should have stayed silent. The smirk she had been sporting transformed into a look of unadulterated rage.

"Don't lie," she seethed. My eyes widened as she hit the glass crazily.

I guess the old adage that the craziest things came in the prettiest packages was correct.

I tried to sink into the wall behind me, my eyes flickering into the hallway behind her, hoping that someone would appear soon to help me.

"I'm going to make sure that your time here is an absolute nightmare. No one touches what's mine," she spat the threat, finally stalking away.

I couldn't relax until the sound of her footsteps disappeared.

What did she mean about someone touching what was hers? And the whole mates' thing? As much as I wanted to tell myself it wasn't about my three Vepar, who else could she be talking about? And my stomach dropped through me... what else hadn't the men told me?

I shouldn't care though. If she had been talking about Thane, Derrial, and Corran, than that was a good thing that they had someone like her to take their interest away. Right...?

It didn't bode well though as far as the fertility experiments went. If they didn't care about me than there didn't seem to be anything that would stop them from using me in them.

It was all such a clusterfuck.

I turned on the movie again, desperate to quiet my mind and calm my shaking.

Thirty minutes passed and more footsteps headed down the hall. I climbed to my feet and moved to the front of my cell, not wanting to be surprised again. There was a Vepar male in a grey outfit similar to the one that Corran had changed into, pushing a cart down the hallway. He stopped in front of every cell and somehow passed a bowl full of something that was steaming to the prisoner waiting behind the glass.

I was in awe of the Vepar technology. My stomach was growling.

The Vepar handed food to the prisoner in the cell to my right and rolled his cart towards me. I waited anxiously by the glass, afraid that I was going to drop the bowl during the handoff.

Apparently I didn't need to worry, because he didn't even look at me as he passed right by my cell before stopping in front of the prisoner to my left.

I stared at him, not understanding what had just happened. Maybe I couldn't eat the food as a human? So, I banged on the glass, trying to get his attention. But it was like he didn't hear me.

Several prisoners laughed at me around me, and I realized that it wasn't that he hadn't heard me, it was that he was ignoring me.

Just another way to torture the unwelcome human apparently.

7

I wasn't sure how much time had passed. I watched at least four movies and the meal cart had passed by three times, so it had been at least a whole day. I guessed the Vepar running the meal cart decided he better not kill me and on his last pass through he reluctantly pushed a small pitcher of water through the glass. I gratefully accepted it and gulped down the whole thing immediately. I was glad not to have to resort to the sink water since I wasn't sure if it was normal water or not. I had seen Derrial, Thane, and Corran drink water before, but there was so much I didn't know about the Vepar that I didn't want to run the risk.

My thirst quenched, I settled back onto the cot, picking up the tablet to figure out another movie to watch. Just then the lights in the hallway outside the cells dimmed. I looked around, wondering what was going on. I gave a small scream when a blurred figure suddenly appeared in my cell. Was it a Khonsu?

I shrunk against my wall, convinced this was the end. Suddenly, Derrial's face briefly appeared. He held up a finger to signal for me to be quiet. His face disappeared after a moment, returning to the near invisible blurred form.

What was going on? That Khonsu had impersonated Derrial the first time I had met him. Was this something like that? Could the Khonsu infiltrate the prison? When Derrial's face appeared again, looking frustrated, I decided to just go for it. Maybe he was breaking me out?

I held out my hand and the blurred form seemed to absorb it. I all of a sudden felt like I was weightless. I tried to look at my body and it was like I had disappeared. Something flickered out of the corner of my eye and I looked in amazement at an image that looked like me, that was lounging on the cot I had just abandoned. The fake me laid down on the pillowless cot and pulled the blanket up to her neck.

I felt arms wrap around my waist just then and all of a sudden I was moving, carried along by the blurred figure that I hoped was Derrial. I watched in amazement as we floated through the cell glass, down the hallway, and out of the room holding the cells.

We continued to move down more and more hallways until we left the building all together through what I assumed was the back entrance. I gaped in amazement as we passed through another large field of gorgeous flowers, this time all of them purple in color. They seemed to sparkle in the sunlight and I was only able to take my eyes away from them when we entered a forest. A forest that looked far different from the forests I was used to on Earth.

For one thing, all of the trees were different colors like I had seen when I exited the ship. I gasped when some of the trees started changing color right before my eyes. What was once a patch of bright, yellow-colored trees, there stood trees in a vibrant red color.

We continued blurring through the forest. I had lost all sense of fear as there were so many things to see. Small animals skittered around the forest floor. While some of them had resemblances to animals on Earth, they all had something different that set them apart. What looked like a squirrel from the back, actually only had one giant eyeball on its head. Somehow it made it even cuter.

We suddenly came to a stop in what looked like just another portion of the forest. I felt gravity again and found myself leaning over to throw up from the sensation. Hands held back my hair and softly rubbed my back until I was done. Looking up at my travel companion, I was pleased to see that it did still look like Derrial standing in front of me.

Nevertheless I took a step back from him. "What did you cook for me the morning I woke up at your house?" I asked, wanting to make sure that it really was him.

He grinned. "Pancakes with strawberries. I would have made you blueberries but I believe there was a little accident," he said with a wink.

I gave a sigh of relief, convinced it was him. "You got me out!" I exclaimed, spinning around and enjoying the feel of fresh air after spending the last day surrounded by the stale air of my cell.

"We told you we would," he said softly, staring at me rather intensely.

"What are we doing out here?" I asked, looking around. "It's amazing by the way," I couldn't help but add.

Derrial gave me a smirk and reached into his pocket, pulling out what looked like a tiny black disk the size of a silver dollar. He threw it on the ground and stepped back, pulling me with him. We both stared at the disk for a second until I started to feel foolish.

I turned my head to ask Derrial what exactly we were waiting for when I heard a small popping sound. Turning my head to see what had happened, I stumbled backwards in shock. Right where the disk has been sitting, now stood a black, dome like structure.

I was speechless, and didn't even say anything when Derrial pulled me with him to the front of the structure. Just like with the Vepar spacecraft, an opening appeared in front of us and Derrial guided me inside.

I looked around in wonder. We were in a room the size of a hotel room. There was a king size bed directly in front of us. On another wall was a table with two stools in front of it. Next to the table was a machine that resembled a refrigerator with the exception there was a touchpad in the front of it. There was an opaque glass wall to the left of us set up in front of the other wall. Through the glass I could see a toilet and a sink.

Vepar technology was amazing.

I twirled around, taking it all in. "I can't believe everything you've been holding out on me," I finally said to Derrial.

He was leaning against the now doorless wall we had just come through, staring at me in that amused way of his, like he was watching a child discover something new. "It does all seem pretty amazing through your eyes," he finally said.

I stopped gaping and looked at him closely for the first time. He looked...exhausted. There were dark circles under his eyes and his skin was paler than normal. "Is everything okay?" I finally asked.

He pushed away from the wall and started to prowl towards me until he was standing right in front of me. I backed away until my legs ran into the bed.

"What are we doing here? Why did we have to sneak out?" I asked, feeling heat start to spread all over my body.

"Are you feeling hungry?" he asked. At first I thought he meant food, but then I realized he was talking about my unfortunate newfound bloodlust. I realized that I was starting to experience the initial signs of that; the shakiness, the feeling that I was going to faint.

But I didn't want to admit that. I was still so angry at the three of them, still so confused about what was going on, what their plans for me were.

"I'm fine," I said in a breathier voice than I would have liked.

"Are you sure?" he said, getting even closer. His lips hovered right above mine, and it was taking all of my self-control to prevent myself from making up the distance.

"Tell me what's going on," I said, my voice a whisper now.

"I don't think I feel like talking," he said.

Reaching for my neck, he pulled me up to his lips in a forceful kiss, his tongue taking ownership of my desire. My body lost all sense of control as I gave in to him, my tongue dueling his in mimicked want. Grabbing my torso in a sexy, dominant motion, he pulled me swiftly under him. My arms instinctively wrapped around his neck, pulling and clawing at his shoulders in wanton need. I scratched down his back, making my way to his perfect ass. His sheer size prevented my reach and I struggled to adjust our position, squirming for a better vantage point beneath his large form. My attempts to maneuver were fruitless though as he pinned my arms down at my sides. Pulling his lips from mine, they brushed along my jaw and neck, his tongue leaving a tingling wetness on my overheated skin. My body arched at the sensual feel of him devouring my neck, his licks catching my skin on fire.

The wet burning trail continued along my chest, stopping suddenly at my neckline. Pushing me back on the bed, he pondered the obstruction for a second before reaching for the front of my dress, tearing it off in one strong fluid motion, before absently tossing it to the floor. My heated skin perked against the sudden cool air, my breathless gasp turning his lustful, burning gaze molten as his lips quirked back into a sexy smirk. With a deftness I'd become quite familiar with, he undressed quickly, standing in front of me and letting me admire the view.

Holy shit. I felt the blush staining my burning cheeks as I got the view of him I had been obsessed with since the last time I had seen it.

He seemed to be in a hurry, but all of a sudden I wanted to take my time. I promised myself right before I reached out for him that this would be the last time, a goodbye of sorts. After this brief moment of comfort I could go back to being furious at them. I just needed one last break from it right now.

I sat up and took his face in my hands, pulling him up towards me for a soft kiss. Nuzzling his nose against mine, we stared at each other for a long moment in silence. I could see his eyes asking me questions about what I was doing. With a gentle squeeze at my waist, he shifted me back onto the bed before coming over top of me, resting his weight on his arms to stare deep into my eyes.

"Is this okay?" he asked. There was a depth of genuine concern in his question that was so different from how he normally was. This was the first time that I actually felt like I had a choice in the matter.

I could read his unease clearly as he awaited my reply. I couldn't seem to make my voice work, so I just nodded.

"Make me forget everything," I finally whispered after a long moment. I didn't want to think about the world waiting outside of our little room. I just wanted the here and now. I didn't want to think about my cell and the gorgeous, perfect Vepar female who seemed to want them. I just wanted him...right now.

I found myself feeling rather possessive at that moment. Perhaps territorial was the most apt description, the words *he's mine* floating through my head. A sudden uncontrollable urge to imprint myself on this Vepar flowed through my body like a tidal wave. To remind him exactly why I should be satisfying his needs. Not that beautiful Vepar. Not anyone else.

If this was going to be the last time, I wanted to make it a lasting one.

I pulled him down to my lips, needing to express my passionate insight through touch, putting every ounce of myself into my kiss. Sliding my tongue along his, I nipped his bottom lip, eliciting his released moan. It ignited my ardor and I tugged hard on the hair at his nape. He growled in response to my aggressiveness, rolling onto his back as if sensing my unspoken need for control, pulling me to lay atop his lean body.

Bracing myself on his chest, I pushed up to straddle him. Staring down into his stunning face, my mouth curled into an enticing smile, taking in his wet, swollen lips as a result of my fueled kiss. "This is different," he said with an awestruck look.

"Don't misunderstand this," I said, biting my lip seductively, brushing my palm across his glorious pecs.

"Oh?" The feel of him under my fingertips was intoxicating. My hands devoured his chest, thumbing his hardened nipples before feeling my way down along his happy trail. His intensified exhale of breath exhilarated my senses all the more.

"I'm simply hungry...."

"Hungry?" he questioned, his eyebrow tantalizing me, testing my restraint for control.

"Mmhmm," I nodded as I teasingly licked my lips.

"Is that right?" he managed, as he glided his fingers up my thighs, resting his hands on my hips, his palms scorching my skin. The feel of his hardness between my legs enticed me. Rolling my hips, my head fell back in a moan at the feel of him sliding along my sensitive skin, assailing me with shooting darts of pleasure.

I steeled myself above him, desperate to maintain some level of equanimity. His eyes were molten, beginning to glow in that telling way, fueling my desire to take charge. Placing my hands over his on my hips, I proceeded to move, a slow, measured gyration over him.

"Yes, that's right. I want you buried so deep inside me you'll never forget how it feels. I want you to crave it as much as I'm craving you."

His lust-filled expression at my declaration, combined with the image my words evoked, shot my arousal sky high. I throbbed in time with my accelerated heartbeat as my need to feel him overtook me. I shifted backwards until I could touch him, the solid feel of him in my palm sent tingles through me as I stroked up and down. His eyes closed on a guttural moan.

"Crave you? I'm already there, kitten. I'm already there." Witnessing my effect on him was empowering. Thrilling. I wanted more.

Pushing myself up, I surprised him with my instant drop, taking him all the way in. The fullness was overwhelming, exquisite. The pleasure escaped from my lips in a breathless cry, echoed by his husky groan. I lifted without hesitation, eager to feel him, rising slowly to savor the sensation. Pausing, I was lost in exhilaration, the tip tantalizing my entrance. He gripped my thighs, tempting my teasing power. I felt brazen with command.

Reaching down between us, I grabbed him, and stroked him with gentle dominance before taking him to the hilt once more.

"Fuck, Ella," his throaty release filled me with sexual authority. I created a rhythm above him, sliding up once more before dropping back down.

"Ella . . . " his emission urged my increase in speed, wanting to continue pleasing him, needing to elicit such reactions. Every moan, every delicious squeeze of his fingers at my hips spiked my fervor as I rode him relentlessly, spurring my body to an exploding peak.

I fell over the edge, screaming his name, right as he lifted his head up and sank his teeth in my neck.

"Fuck . . . " the delightful edge of pain brought me back to earth. Wrapping his hands firmly around my waist, he swiftly flipped me onto my back, still savoring the blood dripping from my neck. He moved with an almost out of control enthusiasm.

I wrapped my legs tightly around him. My control was gone, stolen in his dominant display as he thrust into me over and over again.

"Yes!" I screamed, eagerly relenting to him. I pulled his head from my neck and bit his lip hard until I could taste the salty sweetness of his blood.

My body immediately began to feel stronger, more alive. My bite was his undoing. He buried his face in my neck, groaning as he came. Minutes passed before he stirred, lifting his gaze to mine. I moaned in contentment.

"I'm not done with you yet," he offered with the seductive smirk I realized I was beginning to crave. He gave me another soul-deep kiss, my toes curling in renewed lust as we began to move again.

I knew that hours had passed when he finally collapsed to the bed next to me, both of us sated beyond belief.

I was already regretting my vow that this would be the last time as his fingers traced my skin as we both laid their contentedly.

I wanted to stay in this little room forever. I had never felt so pacified or safe.

Right as I had that thought, the wall in front of us opened and Thane and Corran stepped through. I sat upright in the bed, pulling the covers up to my chin, surprised by their sudden appearance.

Derrial was slower to get up. He was like a cat who had just drank his fill of cream...he even had the same satisfied look.

"Really?" said Corran, lifting an eyebrow that displayed his obvious annoyance.

"What, mad you couldn't watch?" said Derrial smugly.

A sudden heat filled Corran's eyes, igniting my skin again. Evidently my little scientist was a voyeur.

Who would have thought?

"We need to get her back. I figured you would have lost track of time," said Thane in a bored voice that didn't match the way his eyes were dancing all over me possessively. "I didn't think when you said that you were going to give her a break that it was going to include playtime."

Derrial just shrugged, not looking apologetic in the least bit.

"I have to go back?" I asked, a hint of panic in my voice.

Corran looked at me apologetically. "Things are...complicated."

I looked at Derrial now, feeling like I had every right to demand answers after what had just happened. "What's complicated? Do they not believe you about me being the right subject for the tests?"

Derrial looked guilty all of a sudden.

"The Council hasn't been as accepting as we hoped," said Derrial reluctantly.

"Were we expecting them to be accepting?"

"We were hoping that they would let Corran do his experiments on his timetable so that we could figure out a plan," said Thane.

"What kind of timetable do they want?" I asked, feeling a sense of dread washing away all the endorphins Derrial and I had just created.

"Their insistent that the experiments start immediately. While we were gone, there were no Vepar children born," said Corran, sounding like he was almost trying to make excuses for the Council who didn't seem to care if I was willing to be a surrogate or not.

"By experiments, you mean implanting me with a Vepar embryo," I said softly, a knot forming in my chest.

Everyone in the room was silent. "How soon is "immediately," I asked, wanting to gauge how much time I had to make my escape.

"Next week," said Corran.

I sunk lower in the bed.

I felt Thane come and sit next to me.

"We're going to figure it out," he said. "No one is going to make you do something you don't want to do."

His statement had the opposite effect in comforting me. Instead, I just felt angry.

"You're going to figure it out. Just like you figured out how to make me not need your blood. Just like how you took me from Earth because you couldn't figure out how to keep me safe from the Khonsu when you were the ones who brought me to their attention in the first place. You figured out that I must have been unhappy in my life on Earth, and that I needed to be in your life. Just like you figured out the fact that I was the special human who could birth Vepar humans in the first place. You guys have really done a good job of figuring things out...," I was almost screaming by the end, and the guys all looked shell shocked. It was the most emotion that I had shown to them.

Corran sank to his knees in front of the bed, crossing an arm across his heart. "I swear to you Ella, we will make this right. We'll protect you even if it costs us everything."

Thane and Derrial slid off the bed and sank down to their knees next to Corran, making the same arm motion.

I refused to let their vow mean anything to me. They had already let me down. They had already ruined my life. There was nothing they could do to make up for it.

"I'd like to go back now," I said, even as my stomach sunk at the thought of being back in the cell. It said a lot for how upset I was that I would rather be back in a cell surrounded by monsters, starving, than be around the three of them.

The guys exchanged looks after they got off their knees. I was handed a new dress to put on. I guess the hut didn't include the nifty changing cylinder. Corran and Thane left the room. Derrial and I were quiet as we both got dressed. There was no trace of the affection and ease that had been present between us earlier.

We walked out to where Thane and Corran were waiting solemnly. Derrial swiped his hand across the wall of the structure and it shrank before my eyes, disappearing into the black disk once again. Derrial pocketed the disk and turned back to us.

I felt a touch on my shoulder. "Talk to us," said Thane, his voice sounding almost desperate.

"I have nothing to say. There's nothing you can do to make this better."

Thane sighed and ran a hand through his hair frustratedly. He looked at Derrial. "Did anyone see you getting her out of there?"

Derrial scoffed, his arrogance showing itself. "Is that even a real question?" he asked.

Thane rolled his eyes. "Let's go," he said to Corran. They both looked at me. "I guess it's too much to ask for a goodbye?" Thane said.

I turned my attention to the ground resolutely, my emotions feeling ravaged at the moment.

"Just let her be," said Corran. There was a faint buzzing sound that made me look up. To my surprise Corran and Thane were gone.

More cool Vepar technology.

"Let's get you back," said Derrial stiffly. I knew his feelings were probably feeling a bit hurt at my cold shoulder, but what did he expect?

"I'm going to have to touch you to get you back without anyone noticing. Try not to bite my head off," he said sarcastically.

I humphed and reluctantly moved closer to him. I watched as Derrial turned into nothing but a blur. He wrapped his arms around me like he had before and I felt that sense of weightlessness.

We set off the way we had come. Nothing held quite the same wonder as it had before. All I could think was that this was probably the end. This would be the last time that I felt real air, the last time that I would see daylight.

I wondered how many times I would have to get pregnant if the fertility procedures worked. Enough that my body would probably be too tired and worn out to have my own kids.

Not that I would even have that opportunity. Even if somehow I was let go eventually, I was confident I would be so used and abused that I wouldn't even be like a human anymore.

I literally had nothing to look forward to in life. It was all over.

We were back to my cell before I knew it. Derrial disabled the fake me who had still been on the cot, pretending to sleep, and then he let me go. I sank down gratefully on my cot, the nausea hitting me hard. I leaned over, trying to stop myself from throwing up again. After a minute, the nausea passed. I looked up wearily and saw that the blurred Derrial was still floating in front of me.

"You can leave now," I hissed, keeping my voice down so I didn't attract attention. His face appeared. "I promise we'll make this right," he said. I just shook my head, a tear escaping from my eye. I laid down on the cot. I felt Derrial's hand stroke my cheek briefly, but when my eyes opened, he was gone.

I stared up at the ceiling, listening to the screams and moans of the prisoners around me. Their noises were the perfect soundtrack to my shitty life.

I closed my eyes. It was time to await my fate.

8

The thud of footsteps approaching me tore me from my broken sleep. I opened my eyes to see a Vepar with completely black eyes staring down at me. I widened my stare, my heart suddenly pounding against my ribcage. In a flash, I scrambled backwards in my cot, dragging the blanket with me as I hit the wall with my back.

"W-what do you want?" Had a prisoner broken into my cell?

"You've been summoned," he snarled as if being in my presence disgusted him.

"Summoned?" Was this the day that I was to be taken in for Corran's procedure? Could the guys not even face me?

"I think you're mistaken. I'm meant to stay here."

One of his bushy eyebrows climbed up his forehead, while the tip of his horns seemed to shimmer. "You think you have rights?" He broke into laughter, sounding more like someone screeching for help, and I cringed, reminding myself to never make this guy laugh again.

He reached over and grabbed my arm, then hauled me off the bed and across the room. I stumbled after him, barely catching my balance, the smooth floor cold under my bare feet. "Please can I get my shoes?"

"You don't need them." With a wave of his hand, the glass wall dissolved and we were in the corridor.

Other prisoners glared at me, their faces and hands pressed up against the glass, twisted faces judging me.

"Where are we going?"

But the guard didn't answer, only dragged me by my arm, his fingers like an iron grip around my wrist.

"Does Derrial know about this?" I demanded and as much as my mind screamed with a warning that I shouldn't have said that, I was on a freaking foreign planet. It was hard to be reasonable.

"He's waiting for you."

His words were a blade to my chest. Derrial allowed this guard to manhandle me this way, to collect me in the middle of the night? Or was this part of the plan to make my capture appear authentic?

With the latter in mind, I hurried along beside the guard to show my compliance and not appear like I had been dragged in like a prisoner. It was all about confidence, my mom used to tell me. So I lifted my chin and power walked to keep up with the Vepar. The door at the end of the corridor swung open of its own accord and we entered another hallway, then another, followed by stepping into an elevator where the doors shut and opened within a heartbeat and we were on a different ground. I'd stopped asking questions and accepted it might take me years before I'd comprehend this planet's technology.

We raced toward two enormous doors, colored like the brightest sky, engraved with swirls. My stomach was locked up tight, but I kept moving. The doors opened on their own and we strolled into a circular room.

Bright lights flooded the tiny arena-like center with a raised platform of circular seatings. At one end stood four Vepars, each inside a circular cylinder, and only when the guard ushered me close did I see their bodies were slightly transparent. They were only projections and not physically present. Each of them were older men, wrinkles, and silvering hair, but their horns had me gaping. They were long and curled, falling over their shoulders.

So they grew longer with age....interesting.

With their deep blue uniforms and the double moon insignia on their jackets, I could only assume these were the Council.

With a shove at my back, I stumbled forward toward the Vepar. I glanced up to the first row and found Thane, Corran, and Derrial sitting there, staring down at me with blank expressions. But their eyes gave them away... the worry slithering behind them.

I swallowed hard and turned to the four who'd summoned me.

"Human," the tallest began. His white hair was parted down the middle and one of his horns curled over the top of his head like a halo. "In Veon, mating is a life or death situation and is not entered lightly which is why we have rituals to find the perfect life partners. Something I'm sure humans wouldn't understand. Three of our most respectable Vepar have approached us, asking to be granted a waiver. Do you know what that means, child?"

I shook my head, though my mind was whirling like a spinning top with what my Vepar could have asked the Council. My words refused to come.

The Vepar with bright golden eyes tilted his head high. "Derrial and his team have requested to bypass the mating ritual and for the human, Ella, to be deemed their mate for life."

Their words sliced through me, but I knew... at least I thought I knew, why Derrial had put that request through. The social rules to finding the one you loved differed on Veon and they intended to bypass it to simply get approval to choose me as their mate. And I couldn't deny the joy blooming inside me at hearing this. This was their way to save me.

I fought to hold back my smile.

It seemed romantic. But I wasn't a fool. They did it to save me... except if they had to get approval for who to mate with for life, this wasn't a light decision to make.

"What is your decision?" Derrial and the men stood from their seats, their fists tapping their chests twice before lowering them.

I wobbled on my bare feet, praying this worked as it would mean freedom from prison and avoiding the need to juggle social protocols.

"Denied!" All four announced in unison.

My legs weakened beneath me. A quick glance showed that my three Vepar showed no emotions or reactions.

"This is new territory for us," the man with a devil's tail spoke up, his voice gravelly and harsh. "You brought a human to our home under the pretense that she could be the key to our fertility issues, then you announce she's your mate and want to disregard rituals in our race since the beginning of time. This isn't going to work."

Words pressed to the front of my mind about how I'd be their perfect mate... anything to convince them to approve this.

The first Council member stole my moment. "We cannot let you disregard our ceremonial customs. So, we decree this human will join the other suitors to win you three over during the mating ritual."

I stood there, unsure what exactly they were saying. What in the world was a mating ritual? But when I glanced up at Derrial, he smiled and nodded. "Agree."

The fourth Council member with only one horn the color of mahogany cleared his throat. "This isn't your decision to make," he snapped, and the harshness of his voice had me trembling.

"Procreation is an uncharted area with a human, but..." He sighed heavily. "With the current state of our race, maybe this is something we need to explore. So, Ella, you will join the other suitable females, undergo compatibility tests, and then the right female will be selected to bond with the three Vepar."

Dread washed over me. "Tests," I mumbled, my mind conjuring up me having to fight someone to win the hand of these Vepar, or maybe they meant laboratory tests? If that was the case, I'd run and take my chance in space as I'd had enough of being poked and prodded and things inserted into me.

"Thank you," Derrial stated, his voice loud. The three of them now had grins on their faces. I guessed this was a favorable outcome.

"Not so fast," One-horn retorted. "As these are unusual circumstances, there are three new conditions you must adhere to. You will complete all mating ritual tests within two weeks. The final decision of compatible female will no longer rest with the males, but us as the Council."

Thane groaned loudly, while Corran shifted on his feet, both disagreeing with the decision. Derrial just stood silent, but if his gaze could hurl daggers at the Council Vepar, he'd have stabbed them several times over.

"Is that--"

"Silence," the Vepar snarled. "You have not been permitted to speak." He turned to the three men. "And thirdly, should this human fail in the compatibility tests, she will no longer be under your guard, but fall under our command. And we will do with her as we find most suitable." Their stares lingered over my body, and I felt them studying me for purposes other than someone willing to help me. I shivered under their gazes.

"You can't change the rules," Thane barked, but Derrial stuck his hand out in front of his friend to prevent him from taking another step forward.

"Boy, we are the Council and what isn't right is you trying to circumvent the rules we'd put into place."

"My sincerest apology." Derrial gave a slight deferential nod of his head.

"The new rules *will* be applied," One horn declared and turned his attention to the guard. "Put her back into prison until Derrial arranges the commencement of their mating ritual." All four council members clapped at once, and their projected images faded.

"Fuck! That went shit," Thane thundered.

I reached out to them, worry biting along my flesh, needing them to really explain this to me in layman's terms, but the guard snatched my arm and yanked me toward the door. "Hey stop," I yelled, pulling against his hold, crying out and driving my fist into his arm.

"You heard the Council," he barked.

Corran jumped into the make-shift arena, landing with a thud, and stormed after us. His gaze drilling into the guard who shoved me behind him.

The two Vepar faced off, both staring, neither backing down.

"Nothing you can say or do will change what's about to happen. I'm following the Council's directions. Obstruct me and you'll be the one locked up."

"All I ask is a few minutes with Ella. And then she'll go with you."

I stared at Corran, pleading with my eyes that he whisk me away that very moment, away from the cell, from Veon, from everything.

The guard's eyes narrowed, having no intention of relenting.

Thump. Thump. Thump.

I glanced over my shoulder to see Derrial and Thane strolling toward us, also in the middle of the room.

"I can make your life very easy," Derrial addressed him. "A new job with double the pay, for you to leave us alone with Ella for a few moments."

That got the guard's interest and he scratched his chin, releasing his hold on me. Corran scooped me toward him, folding me into his arms, his lips on my brow. I let myself melt against him, yearning for more than anything to have them by my side.

The guard finally nodded and he and Derrial walked to the door, lost in whispers I couldn't decipher.

When he returned, Derrial and Thane closed in on me while I remained in Corran's arms.

"Plan has changed." Derrial's voice sounded deflated. He ran a hand through his golden hair, worry etched on his face. "I assumed the Council would approve our request but that was foolish on my part. So, now we need to make sure you win them over in the mating ritual."

"And what exactly are these mating rituals?"

Thane took my hand and placed it on his chest. "On our planet, the only way to select your true mate is for several females who accept the call of mating to undergo three compatibility tests. Then the Vepar chooses the one who made the biggest impact on them, who survived the three tests."

I blinked hard and stared at him with bewilderment. "Survive? Why can't it just be something easy like I don't know... falling in love with someone."

"Because our race has always believed finding the most compatible mate will produce the strongest offspring and ensure a lifetime of mating bliss."

"So, I am fucked then. The Council will select your best mate, so how in the world am I meant to survive something that is foreign to me? And if I fail, I become their property?" My voice sounded hysterical.

Derrial nodded, his expression grim. He looked away like he couldn't hold my gaze.

How did I end up in this mess? "You've got to end this. Tell the Council you've changed your mind and all three of you aren't ready to settle down yet."

Corran hugged me tighter. "Once the Council makes a decree, it must be completed or it comes with a punishment of death."

I rubbed a hand down my face. "So, what am I meant to do?"

Just then, the guard re-entered the room. "Time's up." He stood there, hands crossing his broad chest.

Panic curled in my chest, and I grasped onto Corran's arm. He kissed my head and whispered, "Go. We'll be in contact shortly as we have a mating ritual to prepare."

My gaze swept each of the Vepar who each offered me a confident smile, a promise all would be all right. I prayed they were right.

9

Day three and still stuck in the cell with no sign of any of my Vepar. The Council had said we had two weeks to complete this and while I didn't want to rush into some survival test on an alien planet, I also didn't want to belong to the Council.

I had been passing my days by sleeping as much as possible, my dreams filled with images of Corran, Derrial, and Thane. I wondered what they were thinking, why they had done this?

Did they really want me as a mate? It didn't seem possible. Was this some kind of misguided attempt to make amends with me after everything they had done?

I somehow felt angrier at their efforts than before when I thought I was going to become a Vepar surrogate. First I was being forced to be a mother, and now I was being forced to be a wife.

My anger was mostly directed at the fact that over the past few years, when the loneliness felt like it was going to overwhelm me, I had dreamed about meeting the love of my life. Someone who would sweep me off my feet and save me. My dreams had been dashed into a million pieces and my dream guys had ended up being the villains in my story.

I guess I should have dreamed about saving myself.

I was dozing off again when suddenly I was startled awake by the Vepar who ran the food cart. It made me uneasy about how silent the Vepar all were. I never noticed they were coming until they were practically standing on top of me. Who knows who else was going to come into my cell.

"Let's go," the Vepar said without any explanation.

My stomach erupted in butterflies. Was this finally it? Were we starting the mating trials today?

I was tempted to ask, but I knew it would be a fruitless endeavor. This guy hated my guts. Over the past three days he had given me lukewarm water and something that resembled stale bread.

At least I was hoping it was something related to bread.

To be honest, I wasn't feeling ready for any kind of trial. I wasn't even feeling ready to get out of bed. I could also sense that a withdrawal was coming on.

I thought it cruel that Derrial, Thane, and Corran had left me to fend for myself and get progressively weaker when I was supposed to be getting ready for tests that were supposed to help me to save my life.

Or maybe that was their plan all along, make sure that I didn't have a chance so they didn't have to follow through with something they didn't want to do.

"Why would you come here?" asked the Vepar walking beside me in a gruff voice. I looked at him, surprised that he was even deigning to speak with me. He was beyond good looking as all the Vepar were, with ashy blonde hair and grey eyes flecked with gold, but there was a sort of melancholy air around him, like he had been beat down by his life.

"I didn't have a choice," I said, too tired to not tell the truth.

"What do you mean?" he asked, sounding confused about my answer.

"You've heard of the Khonsu right?"

He nodded, his grey eyes darkening at my mention of them.

"The Khonsu were after me. Apparently the only way that I could come here was to be saved."

"And they saved you from the Khonsu?" he asked incredulously.

"They as in Derrial, Corran, and Thane?" I clarified.

"It's very strange," he said, instead of answering me.

"What's strange?"

"How casually you can say their name. Their practically celebrities on Veon. Each of them celebrated in their fields almost above all others. No one can figure out how they got tied up with you." He scanned his eyes over me, like he was trying to figure out what they could possibly see in me.

It was the same question that had been plaguing me since I met them.

"They're threatening everything about Veon by whatever game their playing with you pretending to do the mating ritual. There's rumors that their using the games as a front before they stage a coup and take over the Counsel." He laughed, as if that was the craziest thing he had ever heard. "We've long known that the Vepar on Earth had dalliances with the human females. But bringing them back here...It's the craziest thing that I've ever heard of."

I didn't feel the need to answer him. It seemed like he was more talking to himself than me. His observations were very interesting though. I wondered about the coup idea. With how displeased Derrial, Thane, and Corran had been lately with how the Council was handling my situation, I could see them trying to take over. I didn't think I should probably say that to this Vepar though.

We walked down a hallway that seemed dimmer than the rest. The Vepar furtively looked around, and I started to get a bad feeling. What was he doing? Where were we going?

Suddenly, he pushed me against the wall. I could feel every ridge of his body and my stomach lurched when I realized that he was aroused.

"What are you doing?" I whimpered, struggling to get away. It was no use though. The Vepar were genetically superior in their strength and my struggling only seemed to amuse him.

"I want to see what all the fuss is about. If you somehow have managed to spark their interest, there has to be something more to you. Are you a good fuck? Because I think I need to try human out. If it's good enough for them, it's good enough for me," he said with a sick smile.

I tried to knee him in the balls, but he easily avoided me. He forced his lips on mine, sticking a long tongue down my throat that seemed twice as long as normal. It went so far back that it awakened my gag reflex and a rush of bile came up and went straight into his mouth.

He broke away from me coughing bitterly. "You skitch," he said, and I could only assume it was some alien insult. He raised his hand to strike me. I flinched and prepared myself for the impact. But before his hand could touch me, it was caught in a crushing grip. The grip of a furious looking Thane.

"Arrrgghhh," the Vepar screamed as Thane's hand tightened. I heard the bone crunching together and I knew that the Vepar wouldn't be using that hand for a long time, if ever without some serious help.

"How dare you touch what you knew was mine, Simeon," Thane growled.

He looked at me. "Where did he touch you?" he snarled.

I stared at him, shaking in fear from his wrath.

"Where?" Thane roared. I finally managed to move. I touched my mouth and began to drag my hand down my body where the Vepar had pushed against me.

"Your mouth. We'll start there," he said. Faster than I could blink, he reached inside the whimpering Vepar's mouth and ripped out his tongue with such swiftness and strength that I shuddered. It flopped to the ground like a slug, turning black with decay immediately. I wanted to throw up again. I had been right about the Vepar's tongue seeming long. The tongue laying on the ground looked as long as a snake. It was terrifyingly disgusting.

The Vepar was gagging and shooting a deep blackish red blood every-where. All I could do was stare as Thane next grabbed a knife from around his belt and proceeded to carve a deep line from the Vepar's mouth all the way down his stomach. He didn't sink the knife in enough to cut him open, but it was enough for blood to seep out and make the Vepar's garbled screams even louder.

If I thought the Vepar's screams were bad before, it was nothing to how it sounded now. I pitied him for half a second before a sense of dark satisfaction passed over me. For one of the first times in my life, someone had avenged me. If Thane hadn't shown up, the Vepar would have raped me. He would have raped me after days of trying to starve me. He had deserved this and I was glad that I had seen it.

"You liked that, didn't you pet?" Thane asked with a smirk, wiping off the blood on his knife on the Vepar's pants as he huddled on the ground, an intermix of moaning and screaming coming out of his mouth.

My eyes must have shown just how much I had liked it because Thane suddenly swept me off my feet and began to carry me bridal style down the hallway.

"What are you doing?" I said in an annoyed voice. I was getting tired of Vepar men deciding they could do whatever they wanted with me.

"Giving us something that we both need," he said in a rough, gravelly voice that sent sparks along my synapses.

He stopped at a door and after waving his hand in front of it to open it, walked us both in.

"What is this place?" I asked, looking around. It reminded me of the hospital rooms in Grey's Anatomy where the doctors' slept when they were on call, except instead of bunks there were rows of full size beds along the long wall.

"Just a room for staff to get some rest during their shift," Thane answered. "Workers on Veon usually work for fifty hours straight before getting a day off. This allows them to sleep."

"Won't someone come in?" I asked.

Thane took a step towards me. "Not if they know what's good for them."

I rolled my eyes at his arrogance. "I thought I was supposed to be starting the trials today. At least that's what I assumed I was being taken to before that Vepar decided to take a detour."

"We have enough time for this." Thane took another step towards me.

I summoned as much bravery as I could, despite the fact that all I wanted to do was weep, and I glared at him. I glared at him, trying to channel all the hatred and betrayal rattling through me.

"If you think for one fucking second that you can touch me you've got another---"

He cut me off before I could say another word by lunging towards me from several feet away. His hand snaked out, fingers grasping my neck. He shoved me up against a wall, towering over me. The bastard just stared down at me, breathing heavily, his lips an inch from my temple, his hand still against my throat, not squeezing but possessive, making a point.

"I like it when you get fiery," he murmured slowly in a low and terrifying voice, his eyes burning into me. His body pressed flush against mine, and his hardness nestled against my stomach. "I've been dreaming about how good you tasted...how perfect you felt."

I forgot how to breathe for a second. I finally gulped against his hand and tried to regain my bearings. I was breathless, totally surprised, pretty much petrified, and unfortunately very turned on. When I tried to slink away from him, he tightened the grip on my throat just a little. My hands came up and I tried to pull on his wrist to get him to let go. He wasn't cutting off my air supply, but it was firm and scary. His jaw tightened. My nails dug into his wrist.

"I would be careful if I were you," he growled. "I wouldn't want you to draw blood."

But it was too late. My nails sunk into his hand until droplets of blood started to roll.

The smell got to me almost immediately. It smelled...like the most delicious thing I had ever come across.

He watched as a drop of blood trailed down his arm. Then he looked at me triumphantly. "Hungry?" he asked in a sing-song voice. I started trembling, my mouth watering. Evidently the guys had no problem taking advantage of my new blood lust to get what they wanted from me.

He let go of my throat and in a flash he tossed me toward the bed and I laid out on my back on his bed like a buffet. He climbed onto me and pinned my arms above my head. I tried to struggle but all it succeeded in doing was rubbing me against him, which immediately set my body on fire. I was starving, and I didn't know which one I wanted more. His body...or his blood.

He caught both of my wrists in one hand, re-pinning them to the bed over my head. His free hand ripped my dress off my body until I was bare to him except for my bra and my miniscule thong.

"Look at this..." He palmed the side of my rear end and snapped the thong quickly against my hip.

"Don't touch me!" I ordered half-heartedly, letting out a soft moan at the heat of his hand as it traveled softly across my skin.

"You're a very naughty girl," he said, wedging a hand under my hips as he cupped me between the legs. I gasped. I felt a finger dip under the elastic of the panties and sliding toward my heat, his greedy finger sliding over my silkiness, teasing me. I let out another groan. His hands were magic.

"Hmmm...seems like you're enjoying this," he teased as he let out a sexy laugh that only turned me on further. "Could it be? Do you enjoy playing games?"

I squeezed my eyes shut tight and held my breath. His finger circled leisurely and then I felt him gyrate ever so slightly against my behind. "You do. Fuck. You're perfect."

His tongue traced from my earlobe down to the crook of my shoulder. "How did I get this lucky?"

"Not by your personality, that's for sure," I muttered as I found myself moving against him.

Why did I say that? Why was I provoking him? There had to be something wrong with me because Thane had lied to me. They all lied to me. And here I was practically begging to be under his body.

I was so screwed up. I hated that it felt good. Was I just as sick and twisted as him? He kept going and then he started to rub circles around my clit, eliciting an "ah" from me. He leaned into my ear and announced, "Guess you don't hate me as much as you thought."

I guessed I didn't hate him. Or at least I didn't hate what he could do for my body. He wasn't pinning my arms any longer and yet I was obeying him.

"Please, Thane," I begged, not even sure what I was begging for, and I opened my legs for him.

His weight fell between my thighs, and without ceremony, he slid into me. A groan of relief sounded out of both of us. He started pounding into me, grunting a myriad of nonsensical words as he did so. I did catch one sentence. "Your body was fucking made for me."

I wholeheartedly agreed.

Goose bumps popped up all over me. Thane laughed low in his throat, a knowing laugh, knowing that he owned me, reveling in the fact that my body was doing just what he wanted it to do. He leaned back, rotated his hips, and smacked me across the top of my ass with his hand, as he drove in. My eyes rolled back into my head and I let out a loud "ah." He hit again with his hand, making me scream out not only in pain, but also in pleasure because inside, he was hitting that spot. He touched me then, forcing my body to explode.

He leaned forward and grabbed my throat, mid-climax and lifted me back up to my knees, grinding out a husky, "Perfect, baby." He kept going, hand covering my throat possessively, as he used me like a ragdoll. He went on for what felt like forever. Just when I thought that it was going to last forever, his mouth moved to my neck. He glided over sensitive places inside of me, making me feel so good that I didn't even realize it was happening until his teeth had sunk into my shoulder. I let out a scream that was a mix of pain and pleasure.

A husky groan fell from his mouth as he licked the blood that trickled down my shoulder. I knew I should hate it, but I didn't. I just wanted his in return.

I didn't even have a frame of mind to judge myself.

I flipped suddenly, surprising him with the movement and allowing me to be on top. I kissed him, biting his lip hard as I did so until drops of blood started to fall onto my tongue. We both let out low groans of pleasure.

Time seemed to stop after that as we kept going and going until I couldn't even remember my name, or why I was mad. There was only Thane. There was only this moment.

When it was all over, I was limp on top of him, totally spent. I could do nothing but just lie there. I wasn't sure what to think about what I had just discovered about myself. I had never thought I would get turned on by being dominated.

But I had been more than turned on. I had fucking loved it.

Something was so wrong with me. I didn't know if it had always been lurking there, or if I had been conditioned to act like this by them.

I rolled off of him and lay on my back, staring up at the ceiling.

"Stop it," Thane said, pulling me back onto him.

"Stop what?" I asked in a frustrated voice.

"Thinking."

I barked out a laugh. "You don't even know what I'm thinking."

"I do know what you're thinking. This is what you always do. We fuck up, then we fuck, then you hate yourself because we fucked."

I looked over at him, hating that he was right. "That's not what I was thinking," I said half-heartedly.

He snorted and ran his hand gently down my naked back. "It was what you were thinking, pet. And you need to stop it. How can we ever move forward when you are always forcing us back?"

"I don't trust you," I whispered softly, staring into his eyes.

"We get that. And we're going to keep proving ourselves to you. But you have to help us out. Hell, I've killed five Vepar since we've been here, all because they dared to look at you wrong."

"Five?" I squeaked.

He grinned. "Don't get squeamish on me now. You barely even flinched when I almost gutted Simeon like a fish earlier."

"Something is wrong with you," I replied.

His smile grew even wider at my words.

"Probably. But I know it does something for you when you see me go all crazy on anyone who is giving you a hard time."

"Why did you three set me up for these tests?" I asked, ignoring his last statement because it was the truth.

"Because it's what we want."

"You want me to be your mate?" I asked.

Suddenly all the earlier levity disappeared.

"You can't even comprehend how much. You think we made you our prisoner but it's been the opposite all along. You've captured us. And the funny thing is...none of us want you to let us go."

I couldn't say anything in response. His words did something to me, they gave me hope that I'd been trying desperately to get rid of.

I laid back, unwilling to look at him anymore. I was too afraid of what he would see in my eyes.

"So how will this all work?" I asked, thinking about the trials and how a part of me actually wanted to win now.

"You mean being the mate of three Vepar?" Thane asked slyly.

I ignored him. "You know what I mean."

"The trials used to be the opposite. It was the men who would compete for the woman's attention that they were interested in mating with. When most Vepar women lost the ability to conceive the Council changed it. The thinking was that the strongest and most cunning women might have the best ability to have a child. It became a sort of culling strategy as the Council tried to fix the fertility issues."

"How did they know that it wasn't the men who were having the issues?" I said, feeling defensive for some reason for all the Vepar women.

Thane gave me a look. "Do you really think Corran wouldn't have ruled out everything before going to drastic measures like thinking about mating with a human?"

I reluctantly couldn't argue with that. I had never met anyone as brilliant as Corran, as obsessed with detail, and determined to get everything right. It still bit my insides however at the thought of the female Vepar having to prove their worth.

"You're thinking about this the wrong way," he said with a wry grin. "This goes back to our beginnings when both males and females did everything they could to show their ability to provide and complete the other person. This is no different."

"I don't see you and the others having to go through anything to show me you're the best," I remarked saucily, sparking hunger in Thane's eyes. "Maybe there are other Vepar more suitable for me, more likely to produce strong offspring," I taunted him.

Thane growled, his eyes began doing that glowing thing and suddenly I was a little bit afraid. When he spoke, it was like he had been possessed, like there were other voices mixing in with his own.

I couldn't help but shiver.

"You're never going to know any other male's touch again, human or Vepar. Do we understand each other?" he insisted.

I nodded, breathless at what I was seeing and hearing.

"And if any other male does decide to touch you...well you've seen what will happen to them," he said, referencing the now tongueless cart Vepar.

I opened my mouth to say something stupid like ask what would happen if I actually wanted another's touch, but Thane quickly cut me off.

"You can lie to yourself all you want but we've ruined you. We've made sure that there won't be another who could satisfy you the way we do, could make you burn the way we do. Oh.." he said, a sly smile on his face. "There's also the matter of our little blood bond. You wouldn't be able to find pleasure with another now that we've done that."

"So you've ruined me," I said woodenly. "Meaning if I lose these trials than I'll never find someone to be with that could make me happy. You've literally ensured that I will be miserable for the rest of my life." I could feel tears gathering in my eyes at the prospect.

Thane's eyes stopped glowing and I could feel the intensity lessen.

"You're going to be happy, pet," he said, taking my hand in his and putting it over his heart. "And you're going to win."

I looked up at him forlornly. "Have you seen the other Vepar women?" I asked. "It's not even a contest."

"The tests aren't just for physical strength, they're also about someone's mental toughness...their inner strength. And you Ella, have more of that than anyone I know."

I looked at him gratefully. Everything he had been saying was shocking to me. It added a whole new depth to this thing going on between us, and I didn't know how to handle it.

But one thing was for sure...I actually wanted to win the trials now.

10

"I can't do the mating ritual," I murmured, staring outside into a manicured garden that belonged to a castle. It resembled an over-sized courtyard with statues of various miniature spaceships. If it wasn't for the tree canopies shaped into strange looking birds, or the hundreds of Vepar mingling out there, drinking from silver goblets, dressed in gowns, or their horns glimmering in the sunlight (not to mention the two suns in the heavens), I might have said this was Earth. Maybe.

"You only need to cross the woods and reach the destination on the map in two days. You said you've gone hiking back on your planet, so this is the same."

I turned to face Thane, barely able to breath as fear shook me from the inside out. He wore a black uniform with the double sun emblem on his chest, and looked strong and so damn sexy, but my heart was pounding too hard with dread. "Then why are all those people out there? And what are those drone-like things flying outside? Cameras?"

He sighed a heavy exhale. "Mating rituals that receive applications from more than fifty potential females end up being broadcast to the public."

"Fifty?" I breathed, a surge of jealousy swirling in my chest that so many wanted to be with these three Vepar. Not that I could blame them because if these three bachelors were seeking a mate, I'd be inclined to put up my hand too if I wasn't being forced to.

I gaped at him. "So, fifty women are going to be traipsing through the woods? That tells me it's gotta be a process of elimination so this hike you mentioned is more than a hike, isn't it? How am I going to win against that many?"

"Your only competitor in this challenge is yourself. The council has selected nine females from the submission, plus you." He stretched a hand toward me and cupped the side of my face. I softened against his touch, except his comfort did little to chase away the worry drumming on my mind.

I saw the resolve in his gaze, the admittance that his hands were tied, all of ours were, and he was trying to soften the blow of the upcoming test.

"We never meant for this to happen," he added as if he could read my mind. "Or for everything to get out of hand so fast. We are doing everything we can to help you. Follow our lead, and trust us."

I wanted to protest, wanted to yell with frustration, wanted to beg him to just sneak me into a ship and take me back home. Except then what? I prayed the enemies roaming on earth didn't find me and make me their personal snack machine? And I'd grow weaker without taking the Vepar's blood because I'd become a vampire now apparently. Or whatever the bond exchange between me and these Vepar had done to me.

"I don't have much of an option," I muttered. "Looks like I have to succeed."

He dragged me into his arms, and I pressed myself against him, inhaling his timber and musky scent that drove me crazy. Except now, it gave me the confidence to keep going, to know I wasn't alone. It was more than I had on Earth.

Someone cleared their throats and Thane broke away from me. Derrial and Corran stood at the entrance to the waiting room, both dressed the same, and between the three of them, I let myself fall under their trance.

"They're about to start."

The Councilmen appeared in the hallway and Thane's posture stiffened.

Offering me a smile, he mouthed, *good luck,* and strode out of the room. Derrial winked at me while Corran blew me a kiss, and within seconds they were all gone. I returned to the window to watch them emerge from the Council's building, and the crowd broke into a cheer as if they were celebrities.

I kept running my hands over the simple, straight dress that hung off my shoulders and fell to my feet like a sack. Nothing like the gowns the women outside wore. A requirement for the challenge apparently.

I turned to the empty room and paced to an oversized TV screen and back, unable to quiet my brain as I waited to be called. Half an hour later, the shrill sound of a siren shattered through the room, and I flinched. It blew three times in short sequences. After which the mass of Vepar outside broke into a cheer.

A man appeared at my door, his hair white and tumbling to his waist. With small horns the color of snow, he reminded me of an elf. He had a softness in his eyes.

"This way, little one." He waved me to leave the room, and I quickened my steps, my stomach doing somersaults.

In the hallway nine women lined up in front of the rear door, all dressed in similar clothing to me, their hair plaited, or tied up, and I hurried to collect mine into a ponytail, before curling it in on itself. I joined the end of the line, so nervous that perspiration dripped down my spine.

Each of the women were stunningly beautiful, and I didn't belong here, not with them. A few of them looked my way, their noses wrinkled at the sight of me. They wore wry smirks as if I were nothing but a bug they stepped on.

I held their stares, refusing to look away as a sense of wanting to prove them wrong collided into me. Show weakness and they'd treat me that way, but when the girl standing in front of me turned a bit to face me. I lost my breath as I recognized her. Her auburn hair was plaited and wrapped around her horns,

Hell, just great. She'd visited me in the cell the other night, sprouting threats.

Her bow-shaped lips thinned, and the same cruel glint passed behind her eyes... I remembered her earlier warning about making my life here an absolute nightmare. Well fuck... I was spending two days in the woods with her, and if I said I wasn't afraid, I'd be lying.

"Do you remember me now?" she whispered, her tone mocking, clearly still upset I didn't know who she was.

"Face the front," the elf man called out, and she sneered before snapping back around.

Wonderful, so not only was I having to carry out a challenge on an alien planet, but a jealous psycho was joining me. Why did nothing ever go easy for me?

At once, the doors to the outside opened wide, and a fluttering of cool air rushed inside, grabbing for my dress.

And we were moving, one at a time. We emerged from the house, receiving applause. The Vepar females waved, strolling with a swing in their hips, while me... I just wanted this over with.

I stepped outside, the clapping subsiding with my presence, and my breath caught in my lungs. It was one thing to walk out in a line on parade, but to be singled out and stared at like a freak was terrible. Following the others, I stood on the lawn facing the four Councilman. My three Vepar joined them. I did a double take, my eyes widening.

Derrial sported blood red horns like traditional devil one's, a contrast against his light golden hair, and a tail that curled around his leg. Thane's horns were black but merely stubs like they'd been snapped off, while iridescent looking scales ran down the sides of his face and neck. Black, cork-screw horns adorned Corran's head, his caramel eyes glowing. Several months ago I might have been repelled by their Vepar appearances, now... there was something so sexy and masculine about their true forms. Unlike what everyone thought, the beauty of Vepar were their own but they simply concealed their additional features.

All three studied me, watched for my reaction, and my gaze swept from one to the other, with a smile stretching my lips. In response, Derrial's tale unfurled from his leg, and slithered on the ground in my direction.. only a couple of feet forward.

"Welcome," the one-horned Council Vepar announced, rising to his feet from his seat, tearing me away from Derrial's stare.

"Today, we are blessed with a mating ritual to leave the heavenly gods envious. Three highly outstanding Vepar have come together and requested a mate to share. For the first time ever, we've received over eight-hundred entries." Everyone broke out into oohs and ahhs while the crazy brunette next to me groaned under her breath.

But I was still stuck on the number of applicants. Holy crap! I thought Thane had said 50.

"Let's give Derrial, Thane, and Corran recognition."

The cheers rose into a deafening boom of applause and a weird clucking of their tongues.

I caught Derrial's gaze, and his wink softened the nerves racing up my spine. No denying, he was hypnotizingly handsome... as were the other two.

"As is customary, the selected will now undergo three compatibility tests," the Council Vepar stated. "First up is the Endurance challenge. Over two days, each participant must cross difficult terrain. This will reveal the strong from the weak, those who persevere when times grow hard, and we can evaluate their decision making skills."

His words ran through my mind, and I fought the urge to roll my eyes because they were deciding who was good enough for mating based on being a freaking warrior, which I wasn't.

"We live in a hostile world, and three powerful Vepar deserve only the best woman by their side." He looked upward and I followed suit, spotting a small space vessel, not too different to the one Corran had used to fly us to Hawaii.

Everyone parted and the ship descended before landing on the lawn so gracefully and smoothly, no one batted an eye.

The side door opened and a set of steps slid out.

"Aery from house of Teaxer, do you accept this challenge?" The first in the line stepped closer to the Council member and stretched out her hand to him. He clasped her wrist, and she offered my Vepar her pearly whites. Then she spun and strolled toward the ship before climbing inside.

The rest were called in the same manner.

"Zeni from house of Julthorn, do you accept this challenge?"

The crazy one next to me sauntered over, her eyes glued to Derrial, even as she offered her arm to the Councilman. She blew him a kiss and twirled on the spot before lightly running to the ship.

"Ella from house of Monroe, will you accept this challenge?"

My legs wouldn't move at first, but I pushed myself, to stop everyone from staring, to get out of the limelight. I lacked the enthusiasm the others carried.

"This will help us track your vitals," the Councilman whispered.

He snapped my bracelet, and I turned away from him.

A quick look at my Vepar and their grins were filled with encouragement, I needed every inch of it. Without a word, I tracked my way to the vessel, keeping my head down to avoid the glares. Their snide remarks still found me though.

"She's a human. Such a primitive race."

"Disgraceful to be allowed in this ritual."

I sped up and scrambled onto the plane to find a line of seats lining both sides of the ship. I slid into the last one available toward the rear. On a bright note, Zeni sat across from me and closer to the front.

The door shut and we lifted with barely a shudder or sound. I curled in on my seat.

Just two days of hiking. I'd keep to myself and get this done fast. How hard could it be to trek through the woods?

The brunette next to me with the whitest eyes I'd ever seen smiled at me and leaned closer. "So you came from your planet with Derrial, Thane and Corran. What are they like?"

A few of the others looked my way, interested in me for the first time.

"You don't know them?"

She shook her head. "We've only read about them, seen them on our monitors. And I barely held it together at seeing them in the flesh and up close. It would be a dream to be selected by them." Her eyes smiled with so much excitement, except she'd never get that chance. I'd make sure of that.

"Why would a human know anything about them?" Zeni spat. "I dated them, you should be asking me questions."

The women all gushed and turned to Zeni, asking her dozens of questions, which was fine. Most days I toggled between hate and lust and a growing attraction for them.

It wasn't long before we landed, the ship giving a slight jump, and I glanced outside the front window to find greenery everywhere, mountains in the distance.

This was happening.

Once the door opened, we all filed out into a small clearing. Lofty trees with enormous umbrella style branches surrounded us. The trunks were patterned as if carved by a rainbow. They streaked the bark in random strokes, the colors muted but so varied and beautiful.

The elf Vepar stood there, hands on hips, his horns glistening beneath the sunlight.

"Please drop your clothing where you are, then come and collect your survival bag."

"Wait, what?" I rocked on my heels, convinced I'd heard wrong. Except the females around me were pulling their dresses up and over their heads. Boobs everywhere I looked, their nipples glistened different colors to match their horns. Then they dragged down their underwear and each went to collect their bag. I shouldn't have stared, but I'd never seen female aliens and curiosity got the better of me. The hair between their legs was a thin line only, and each of them was the same. Maybe it was a trend of styling? And they were colored in all kinds of shades from gold to white to vibrant blues. I didn't know where to look but one thing was certain, Vepar females had all the same bits I did.

"Hurry up, Ella," he said.

"No one said anything about doing this naked."

Zeni glanced at me, smirking, proud of herself. "Why would anyone have told you? You're not one of us. Drop out now, head back." She turned and hurried into the woods, vanishing like the rest of the females.

"You can do just as well as the rest of them," the elf Vepar stated. "Don't let clothing come in the way of those you love."

I met his pale eyes. "Thank you for being nice to me. It's hard to find many here who are." I pulled up my dress and tugged it over my head, finding myself in just my underwear. The coldness brushed past my skin, rippling it. I cupped my breasts at first, but then dropped my hands, remembering his words. I pushed down my underwear, feeling vulnerable and fought the urge to cover myself back up. Stepping out of my shoes, I hurried forward and collected the white bag with a long strap, clutching it against me like a lifeline.

"Inside you'll find a map of where you need to go." He glanced over his shoulder at two mountains at his back, to the valley and back at me, a brow raised. No words, but I understood that was where I had to go. "As well as a blade, firestarter, and pot." He leaned closer, and up close I saw tiny white scales running across the tops of his eyelids. "I checked with Corran and you can drink the water and eat the vegetation out here."

I nodded, memorizing everything. "Now go show them what you can do."

"Thank you." I slid the strap over my head and lay it diagonally across my body before making my way into the woods. Foliage and dead twigs stabbed my soles, but I kept going, needing to catch up with everyone. A quick look behind and the ship was in the air, zipping out of sight. In its place several of the drones lingered in the air. Right, we'd be watched.

I stopped in a small clearing and opened my bag to find my supplies, then pulled out the map, showing a great expanse of woodland, rivers, and mountains. Start was marked where we were and a big cross sat over the mountains for my target. Except, it lay further to my right, compared to where the elf Vepar pointed. The mountains ahead offered three valleys.

So which way would I go? What if the Vepar lied to me so I'd lose since everyone else seemed to hate me? I swallowed the rock in my throat, knowing I'd have to make a decision soon as I didn't have much time, plus I'd have to find somewhere safe to hide for the night.

I stuffed the map into the bag and headed off, part of me wanting to believe that there were nice Vepar on this planet amid the hatred. Plus Corran had mentioned that the water was safe for me to drink as well, so I raised my head and steered right, away from the direction of the target and to where he'd guided me. I prayed I wasn't making a horrible mistake.

II

Most of the day had passed by uneventfully, my shoulders were sun kissed, and I hadn't crossed paths with anyone. The farther I traveled through the woods, the more I doubted my decision to follow the elf Vepar's suggestion. The only sign of life were the insects that kept chewing on my skin, and I swatted another one on my arm.

Jitters lingered in my gut as I contemplated backtracking, taking the other path, except I'd come too far and going back meant I'd never reach the destination in time. So, I had to believe this was the right direction. *Please let it be the case.*

Mountains soared overhead like giants. Shadows already stretched over the landscape from the two suns dropping behind the hills. My stomach growled, but I checked my map for the tenth time for a river that should be around here. Finally, I emerged from the woods to an open cleared land, overshadowed by a sheer cliff where the most stunning crystal waterfall tumbled into a river.

A brilliant tranquility fell over the place despite the roar of the water.

Dying of thirst, I rushed forward, dumped my bag on the bank, and quickly scanned the crystalline purplish water for any creatures, finding it all clear.

Maybe I underestimated how easy this test might be. I stepped into the cool water, the pebbles under my feet were slippery. I dove in at once, the water crisp against my skin, a refreshing sharpness awakening me.

I swam toward the edge of the fall, water splashing everywhere and I found my footing soon enough. I cupped my hands to collect the chilled drink and sipped it at first, then gulped it feverously. I'd watched enough survival shows to know a waterfall was safe to drink.

A sudden explosive cry came from behind me, and I jerked around, choking down the mouthful of water.

Out of instinct, I dipped under the water, just my eyes and top part of my head visible, and I stared at a massive boar trotting toward the river's edge. The animal had three eyes, the center on the bridge of the nose. And he was purple. If it wasn't for the four inch tusks and razor teeth, I might have found it cute.

High pitched battle cries burst out from the forest. Four of the female Vepars charged into the area, brandishing blades, targeting the pig.

The animal unleashed a sound that sounded more like someone plucking the strings on a guitar on the same note, over and over, merging together into a weird sound that confused me. The boar spun and scratched the ground, the back of its neck frizzing.

I watched in horror as the animal charged after them, kicking dirt in his wake.

The women, suddenly realizing this may not work out so well, yelped and darted in three different directions, the boar chasing after them.

I laughed quietly to myself.

But this meant I wasn't so alone in this area after all, and maybe this was the right direction in the first place. When no one returned after a long wait, I rushed out of the water and grabbed my stuff, noting a dead red fish on the shore. I ran past it. As much as I'd love to eat something, I wouldn't starve for a couple of days and refused to make myself sick by eating something that had been rotting for who knows how long.

The cold settled in fast, and being wet, the chill had me shivering.

Another snarl came from up ahead, and I skidded to a stop, clutching my bag to my chest. I gasped for air, glancing left and right. I jolted sideways, deeper in the woods, the ground stabbing my feet with each step.

Another growl came from that direction too.

Panic strangled my chest, and with instinct taking charge, I rushed to a nearby tree with a low hanging branch. Threading the bag's strap over my head, I threw myself upward and snatched the branch. I climbed the tree with my feet, then drew myself up and swung onto the branch, my heart pounding. But I was too close to the ground, so I scaled higher, finally taking a seat fifteen or so feet off the ground and trying to catch my breath.

I scanned the grounds only to see the purple boar dart past the tree, making his musical notes, which seemed so wrong. No signs of the other females.

Another growl sliced through the afternoon, and I shuffled closer to the trunk, clutching it, convinced whatever made that sound wasn't the boar.

Night crawled over the sky, and howls continued along with numerous other animal cries and noises. I made the decision to spend the night in the tree, even if I had to stay awake to avoid falling out. Better to take my chances up here then down below.

Settled with my back to the trunk, I shifted until I found the most comfortable position and slouched back, my legs straddling a thick branch. The bark pinched my ass and here I was spread and naked out in the open. I ought to be mortified, but my only worry was that no bugs found me.

Staring up through the canopy, I found three moons, two of them so close, it felt like I could reach up and touch them.

Despite the beauty of this place, a sense of emptiness swept through me. Here I was on an alien planet, so far from my home, but the irony was that I never felt at home on Earth either. Not since losing my parents. With the Vepar's reaction to my presence on their planet, it told me all the missing people from Earth couldn't have been brought here, so where were they? Were Mom and Dad still alive somewhere?

Please be alive.

A half snort, half musical sound shuddered me awake, and the first thing I saw was the ground swinging toward me as I was falling out of the tree.

Panic gripped my heart as I frantically grasped for the branch, my body lurching sideways. Adrenaline soared through my veins and I let my legs swing outward while I gripped the tree, dangling there, my body swinging back and forth.

I stretched my legs down to find leverage on the next branch down. I shuffled toward the trunk, and quickly let go of the branch to wrap my arms around the tree. In slow motion, I climbed down, my breaths rushing in and out of my lungs so hard, I must have sounded like a grunting beast.

Morning streaked the sky in purples and oranges. I dropped to the forest ground. With my back pressed to the trunk, I checked my surroundings when the terrified cry came again and from my right. I flinched, not daring to move, except the cries weren't of an attacking animal, but despair.

Without hesitation, I went to investigate because to hear any animal in distress killed me on the inside. Or what if it was one of the other women in trouble? Around an oversized shrub with golden berries, I spotted a tiny purple piglet with the tiniest tusks tangled up in vines and tree roots. All three eyes were wide and the little thing was thrashing for escape, shaking with terror.

"How did you get caught up in there?" I bent at the waist and leaned down to help him.

He pulled from me, his back legs wrapped up on the vines, so I made busy work of tearing them off him, one bit at a time.

"Is this a trap?" I asked, but he just made small crying sounds that broke my heart. With him free, I picked him up, his little belly round like he'd just eaten. Thrashing in my hands, I set him down away from the shrubs and freed him. He stood there and squeaked once more.

"You're welcome. Now you better get out of here."

I took my own advice, needing to reach the target by the end of today, and marched toward the mountains. My stomach growled but I could live without food for one more day.

Twigs snapped under my feet, stabbing my soles, and if I could have anything right now, it was shoes.

The snap of foliage came from behind, and I jerked around, my heart hitting the back of my throat. My gaze fell on the small piggy tracking after me.

"You can't come with me. Go back and find your family."

He halted and stared at me, all three eyes blinking, so I turned and kept going. Looking over my shoulder frequently, I saw that he kept following me.

I kept wondering if his mom was alright after being chased by the women yesterday.

From beyond the fluttering of the wind and rustling leaves came another sound. Heavy and guttural, it was distinct and I couldn't place it to anything I'd recognize. I froze on the spot, the piglet rushing to my feet and hiding behind me, and I listened, willing the sound to fade and vanish.

But it grew louder, closer from the direction we came. The piglet cried, and I backed away because whatever made the terrifying sound wasn't a boar and it was coming this way.

The shrubs and trees swayed wildly ahead. The crunch of gravel suggested it might be a deer or even a rabbit, except I wasn't on earth. And when the snarling growl came again, I doubted with every inch of my being that it belonged to anything cute and fluffy.

Fear cut through me, so I swung around, swiped the piglet off the ground and ran. I couldn't leave him behind. My sights set on the mountains close now, and I kept running, not stopping. Distance was all that mattered.

Someone screamed behind me, high pitched and terrifying. I flinched, fear choking me. I looked back, but a shadow flitted through the woods, and I couldn't stop now.

Not when my own scream rose through me. My feet ached and pinched, the woodland jabbing me, snagging on my hair, scratching my body.

But no stopping.

Glancing behind me, I saw it and my scream rushed out.

Running on two feet, a monster the same color as a muddied lawn with yellow eyes was hunched forward, sprinting towards me. What sort of animal was this?

Eyes glued on me, it unleashed a wailing screech, and I stumbled over a tree root almost losing my footing, but I caught myself.

I set the piglet on the ground and jammed my hand into my bag, grabbing my blade. I spun to face the oncoming fiend. I couldn't outrun him and I'd rather face an enemy than let him jump me from behind.

A sign of desperation had him coming for me, arms stiff by his body, leaping over dead logs, his mouth open like a ravenous tiger. The string of gravelly snarls that fell from his mouth escalated, and with every rushed step he took, the muscles shifted beneath his skin.

I trembled, barely able to grasp the knife because I'd never fought before, but I had no choice. So, I stood my ground.

Four other figures flanked the monster in the woods, but I couldn't look away. Couldn't deal with more of these things coming for me. Each movement of theirs was fluid and rapid.

Suddenly I felt foolish for thinking I could take this thing on.

He lunged at me, clawed hands first, mouth gaping open, and all I saw were eyes like sallow lamplight, yet they looked familiar...

Adrenaline pumped and beat through me.

Legs apart, knees bent, I grasped the blade, trembling. He was too fast, too strong.

Within striking range, I swung out my blade to strike his heart, but he dodged my attack.

He slammed into me, his hand snatching my wrist with the weapon before I could swing it at him again. Feet tangled under me, I cried out as I fell backward, hitting the dirt.

He leaped onto me, his weight pressing down on my body, hissing, his words inaudible. Teeth dug into my shoulder, nails digging into my sides.

I thrashed and screamed, kicked and convulsed against him. My yells rang in my ears as a piercing pain sliced my flesh. I pressed my spine into the dirt, the heat from the scorching bite marks across my collarbone rising, and my heart pounded to a climbing temp.

I couldn't die here.

Wouldn't.

My legs and arms exploded in violent motion, and I fought with everything I had for my life.

The monster suddenly arched backward, barking a cry of agony.

He rolled off me, wailing, his arms reaching for something in his back.

I scrambled backward and rushed to my feet, barely able to breath and my eyes pricked with tears. I stared at him, frozen and terrified. Four knives were jammed into his back, and black goo slid out from the wounds. He kept convulsing, but his jerky movements slowed until he slumped on the ground, his bright eyes fading to black coals and the wisp of mist around his body disappeared with the breeze.

A pungent stench like rotten eggs struck my senses, and I groaned, placing a hand over my nose and mouth.

Four of the women from the challenge stood around the monster, including Zeni who eyed me with curiosity. Their chests rose and fell, hands fisted. Blood smeared across their faces and chests, three of them were the same women who'd hunted down the boar. Warrior women, they were the opposite of who they portrayed themselves to be back in the city.

"They always stink when they die," the one with bull-like green horns said. She had matching tiny scales running along her temples...also matching her nipples.

I could barely find my voice, let alone speak.

The monster's body seemed to morph into a dark fog, wisping away from his body, and that was when the truth hit me and I knew exactly who this was.

Khonsu," I hissed.

"You got that right," the brunette added.

"Thank you." I looked up at them, my teeth chattering, and I clenched my jaw to stop.

"He attacked our camp this morning," the blue haired female with round hips added. "There aren't supposed to be any Khonsu in these woods. It's a protected sanctuary."

I nodded, remembering the stories from the Vepar about the Khonsu hunting females on their planet, how a large portion of their world was now uninhabitable.

"We better move," the woman who sat next to me in the ship instructed. "There could be more."

I turned and reached down for my bag, when my shoulder screamed with pain. Deep teeth marks, puffy and bloody sat over my shoulder, more peppered toward my collarbone under my mouth. Searing pain tore over my skin like someone marked me with a branding iron. The urge to fall to my knees and curl in on myself grew as something primeval settled inside me. All I felt was the scolding ache. I used my hand to wipe the blood dripping down my arm, but it was useless. What I needed were stitches and a bandage.

In slow motion, I crouched down and reached for my bag, only to find the little pig curled underneath, so I snatched him up as well and stuffed him in my bag before turning to the women.

They stared at me expectantly, no one moving.

"What's wrong?" I asked, praying they wouldn't have an issue with my little hitchhiker.

"Which direction do we need to go?" the Brunette asked, while her two friends collected their blades from the creature.

"Don't you know?" I shifted the strap to my uninjured shoulder.

"We've been following you," Zeni spoke up. "You're close to the three Vepar and they gave you the answer, didn't they?" Sarcasm lined her accusation.

I shook my head. "They've told me nothing. But I've been following the valley, figuring it would be a faster walk than the other." I didn't dare tell them the elf Vepar's hint and swallowed hard as they all started marching past me, deeper into the woods. I had no idea if they believed me or not.

When Zeni strolled past me, she halted and sniffed the air. "Come, let's go. There's a plant I can find to help cleanse your injuries."

Stumped, I wasn't sure whether to trust her or not, but I joined her on our fast walk through the woods, and I cringed on the inside each time I stepped on something sharp. She never made a sound. No one did, they just all kept moving.

Zeni fell behind me, but I kept moving. It wasn't long before she caught up with me. "Let me put this on your wounds."

I nodded, needing anything to stop the sting from the bite, and I sure didn't want to catch any alien virus from his saliva. There was also the matter of whether he had infected me with his poison. The last thing I needed was to start hallucinating out here in the middle of nowhere.

Zeni had several small leaves she'd crunched in her fist and small droplets of green juice rolled over their surface. She reached over and placed it over the bite mark.

The sting felt like she'd dabbed vinegar on my open wound. I bit down on my lower lip until that hurt and shut my eyes as she rubbed the leaves across my lesions.

When she finished, I opened my eyes to see she had hers shut, almost swaying on the spot and licking her lower lip.

"Are you alright?" I asked, and her eyes snapped open, something dark swirling behind them.

Her mouth pulled into a grin so wide, it scared me a bit. "Absolutely." Her voice dripped with honey, and my breath hitched all the way down to my lungs because I shouldn't have trusted her or believed she wanted to help me.

"What did you put on my injuries?"

"Healing potion and you're welcome. More than you deserve for stealing my Vepar." She strolled through the woods to catch up with the other women.

Goosebumps slid over my flesh, and a chaotic onslaught of panic crawled through me. I made a mistake and let down my guard. The wounds burned but was that the leaves doing their job or was she just being a bitch?

I had to believe I'd be okay or I wouldn't take another step, and I hurried after the women, ready to reach the destination and get out of this forsaken forest.

The rest of the day dragged by. My feet ached, but the pain across my bite marks had subsided. The bleeding had stopped and I couldn't feel the skin around the wounds, but I kept going, holding my bag and the little pig close to me. I checked the bag again and he'd fallen asleep with his head inside the pot. At least someone was content.

With the sun starting to lower, our pace picked up as we now traveled along the valley, where pebbles covered the forest floor and few trees grew. The wind grew cold, and I crossed my arms for warmth.

"Do you think the other women have made it to the final target?" I asked, breaking the silence we'd shared for the last few hours.

"Maybe," the brunette spoke with her back to me, everyone just breathing hard and marching onward.

Hours later with night starting to creep over the sky, my body burning with exhaustion, and fear pricking my chest that we'd miss our target, we emerged into an open field, past the mountains. And up ahead, a circular set of lights beamed, bringing our attention to the ship parked a couple of yards away.

I small whimper of relief fell from my lips, and I suddenly breathed easier and moved faster. All five of us ran toward it, laughing, and I never thought I'd be so happy to see a spaceship. Holding my bag with the little piggy, I smiled and laughed for the first time since arriving on Veon.

The elf Vepar was waiting for us, and he handed clothes and water to each of us as we passed him, congratulating each woman. When I reached him, he winked and pressed clean clothes into my hands and water. "Knew you could do it." He leaned closer. "But you weren't supposed to bring any of the girls with you."

I realized then that he must have been working with Derrial and the men to ensure only I won, but Zeni and the others were too suspicious. It never occurred to me, and I felt foolish for being so blind sighted.

"What about the other women?"

He shook his head. "They're trackers show them still heading to the other valley. They won't make it. Get in the ship, we're about to take off."

Only five women passed the first test, so better than ten. I set my bag down and got dressed rapidly, before collecting my little stowaway and cradling him inside the bag in my arms. He squirmed and let out a small musical note. When I looked inside, he yawned. "Almost there."

I hurried on the ship and took a seat as far from the others as possible. If I intended to survive, I'd have to be savvier in my approach.

When we landed back in the city, each girl was escorted out to a holding place until the next mission. No outside influencers.

When I entered my room, they shut the door behind me and the familiar sound of a lock clicked in place. Yep, it wasn't a prison but it might as well be.

The lights flicked on, and I flinched to find three figures in my room. My back hit the door, only to find friendly, sexy smiles and my three Vepar waiting for me.

"Are you allowed to be here?" I stepped deeper into a large room, and I figured most other things were tucked into the walls.

"We can't stay long." Derrial reached out for my hand and pressed my knuckles to his mouth. "But we had to check on you after we heard you arrived in time."

The piglet's head popped out of my bag and made a singsong sound, grabbing everyone's attention.

"Why do you have a Raxu in your bag?" Derrial asked, sounding amused. "Those things are super territorial and aggressive."

I glanced down and scratched his head as he made a cute chirping sound. "Thane Junior won't hurt anyone. I'm calling him TJ."

Corran burst out laughing and clapped a hand to Thane's back. "She named a Raxu after you."

Derrial couldn't stop chuckling, while Thane eyed me and the piglet with narrowed eyes.

"He's cute just like you, and super persistent," I added.

He strolled closer, those emerald green eyes calling to me, framed by the darkest lashes and thickest eyebrows. My attention fell to his lips, slightly parted. Would he kiss me?

Instead, he reached down and lifted the little piglet into his arms, holding him against his chest. "I'll take TJ with me. Pets aren't allowed here." He leaned over, his lips grazing mine, and I should have pushed him aside but I craved his touch, all of their touches. My mind filled with images of him taking me the other day, and I'd been craving those moments, desperately holding onto the memories. Our mouths merged and his tongue danced with me, while TJ sang his tune between us.

"Is that the new thing?" Corran asked. "Whoever holds the Raxu gets to kiss Ella?"

"We need to leave," Derrial's words ruined the moment, and I broke free from Thane.

I'd spent the last two days alone and now I wanted company. "Don't go, please."

"If we're caught here," Corran explained, "You could be disqualified from the trials."

I breathed heavy until Corran cupped my face with both hands, and he kissed me gently. I softened against him, picturing myself in all their arms and naked. Yep, I had no control around these Vepar, but the more time I spent with them, the more I questioned why it couldn't be.

Corran pulled back, smiling and joined Thane, both of them stroking TJ. I looked up at Derrial who stood in front of me now, and for those few moments, I didn't expect him to kiss me, but in a swift move, he grabbed my arms and drew me to him. His touch fell to my waist, and without missing a beat, he lifted me off my feet and walked me to the wall.

Pinned beneath him, he guided my legs around his waist as his mouth sank against mine. Fire soared through me like a volcano. He set his hands on the wall over my head, his body pressed against mine, and he kissed with a fever I'd never experienced from him before.

His hips gyrated against me, the erection in his pants rubbing the sensitive spot between my legs. Only a few layers of fabric lay between us. His mouth fell to my neck, his tongue stroking and licking me. His breath on my ear was hot and delicious. "I've missed your smile, your taste, your pussy squeezing my dick."

I shuddered at the words, and already I grew hot and wet. He lowered me to my feet and I stood there, letting the wall hold me up as I breathed hard. When I squeezed my thighs together, a euphoria of tingles spread over me.

The three Vepar just stared at me with hungry eyes, desire locked on their faces. If they asked me to strip for them at that moment, I know I'd be naked in a heartbeat.

Derrial cleared his throat and knocked on the door.

"Pet, we'll see you soon." Thane blew me a kiss and when the door opened, the three stalked out before I was locked up in the room alone. Just me and a spiking storm of heat that needed releasing before I exploded.

12

The next two few days passed in a blur of waking up, breakfast, exercise, lunch and dinner with more activities like training to fight. Each meal consisted of vegetables, grains and fruit with small portions of protein. No dessert or breads, and most of the dishes were minimally cooked, so raw foods evidently were a thing here. I understood now why the Vepar insisted on healthy eating back on Earth. They believed in clean living.

The second test had commenced and a different girl went out each night, dressed gloriously for a date with the Vepar. I'd watched a few of them get ready, waiting for my turn, making themselves perfect, revealing a lot of skin, and even practicing their dainty laugh. It made me want to hurl. Thank god they weren't going to win... or I hoped they wouldn't, and then I could put all this crap behind me. If I attended this mating ritual as a real contender, unsure who the men would pick, I'd be so high strung and stressed.

To clear the constant thoughts hammering into me, I sat crossed legged on the lawn in the small yard filled with benches and gorgeous flower laden trees with the dual suns burning brightly overhead. There was a tranquility and peacefulness to Veon. Unlike Earth, most here rarely complained about their jobs and loved whatever it was they did. This place felt safe, though I also heard the maids talking about more attacks outside the city. How guards patrolling the perimeter were becoming more effective against the Khonsu.

A shadow fell over me, and I flinched, glancing up, squinting to see Zeni staring down at me, her hands gripping the loose orange dress she wore. It flowed to her ankles and with her hair loose and dangling over her shoulder, she was beautiful. Then again, who wasn't gorgeous on Veon?

"I have something to show you," she murmured and offered me her hand to stand up. I shouldn't have accepted, but if I did end up becoming the Vepars' mate, I didn't want enemies but friends.

I accepted her offer and stood. The wind brushed past, pushing the hair out of her face. Her smile was bright today, and she almost bounced on her toes as we walked as if she was excited.

She looped her arm around mine like we were BFFs and strolled across the lawn, around the side of the house and through an opening in the gate.

"I've been thinking about you lately," she began, while I glanced back remembering being told we weren't to leave the house or grounds. But I was also curious what she had to show me. In reality, I was bored on my own. No books were written in english and the big monitor TV inside the communal room only showed news. The room was empty for a reason.

"It must be so hard being away from home, from those you love, and your family. I bet you had a boy or two who was interested in you too."

I cut her a hard stare, and I saw right through her words. She played on my emotions, and sure, it worked a little because I missed things from Earth, mostly my freedom and mocha vanilla coffee, but what was she going to show me?

"Where are we going?"

"It won't be long." We strolled down a back alley flanked by towering fences backing onto numerous mansions. No one was around and Zeni sped up her walk.

"When I was young, my parents sent me to Journey, our nearest moon, to the best boarding school in our universe. While there, I missed them everyday and hated how everything seemed so foreign. So I understand what you're going through."

"Not sure you do." Ever since losing my parents, I struggled to feel comfortable on Earth again and always felt like an outsider.

When she looked at me, something shifted behind her expression... doubt, but that was quickly chased away by her fake smile.

"What happened between you and Derrial, Corran, and Thane?" I asked. Yeah a low blow, but I wasn't liking the way she mocked me as if she understood my life. I'd lost so much and barely kept it together most days.

She didn't even warrant looking my way or responding, but pointed to something in the distance to a warehouse. "That's where we're going." There was no heat in her voice, and her heart thumped steadily, but her smile sat crooked on her face.

Guilt skated over my mind because maybe here she was trying to do something nice in her own way and I brought up a hurtful past. Though she also threatened me in the cell... But she healed my bite marks in the first test and she didn't need to. My arm didn't drop off.

"I once read a quote that said, *yesterday is gone.* It's a little something I try to tell myself everyday when I think of everything I've lost."

"So, you're happy to move on from the past because you can't do anything about it? That's very defeatist," she retorted.

"Not really. I don't want to live with regret and always wishing I did something differently. I can only change my future." As the words fell from my mouth, I wondered how much I truly followed this path since my parents were always on my mind, and I still drowned in the sorrow of what my supposed best friend, Cherry, did to me.

Zeni shrugged, not saying anything but hurrying her steps until we reached the side door of the steel gray building. She punched in a code into the security system on the wall, and the door slid open.

She grabbed my hand and dragged me inside, laughing. "You're going to love this."

We ran through an open space, our shoes thumping on the hard floor like gunshots, and we headed straight for a small spaceship. Black and slick, it was about the size of Corran's first ship back on Earth.

Once we arrived, Zeni hit the controllers near the door and it slid upward before a set of stairs unfurled before us. She rushed inside and looked back at me, her face beaming with joy.

"Come on in."

"What's going on?" Nerves danced over my skin.

"Get in here, stop being so scared. I'm not going to kidnap you." She laughed hysterically, except I wouldn't put it past her.

Reluctantly I stepped inside, curious and needing to know what made her so excited and if I'd feel the same way once I found out.

Black interiors and the lights across the front dash threw light across the small ship that contained a small bed and table in the back but loads of buttons which I assumed were all about revealing stored items.

Zeni was in the driver's seat, swiveling around to face me, her horns throwing shadows on the walls that looked demonic. "What do you think?"

I shrugged, unsure what she referred to. "It's a nice spaceship."

She jumped to her feet. "Well this small cruiser is yours. I called in a lot of favors to make it happen. Isn't that exciting?"

"What? How can this be mine?"

She snatched my hand and dragged me to the front, pushing me into the driver's seat, and I flopped down.

"It's all programmed and it practically flies itself."

I stared at her blankly, trying to work out what was really going on? Was this a friendly thing to do in Veon? Give people spaceships?

"You have no clue, do you?"

I shook my head.

"Ella, you're so slow sometimes. This ship can take you back home to your planet, Earth. You can leave right now and no one will stop you as I've got a few guards ready to turn a blind eye."

Her words swirled in my mind, over and over, still not sinking in. "I can leave now?"

"Yes!" she boomed and danced over to me, taking my hand. "Isn't that exciting? You can be home in under one human month, and put everything here behind you."

My brain numbed for a moment, and my heart should have leapt at the chance, yet something in my chest sank through me. A sorrow for leaving behind what I'd found.

"What do you think?" she was jumping up and down in front of me like an excited child.

"I...I need to think about it."

"Well, you only have a short window to make that decision. And you don't want to miss this one time opportunity." She paced toward the rear and back again, letting me think.

Thoughts shot through my head like a ping pong ball. How I'd dreamed of nothing more than going home, how it might give me a chance to put distance and hide from the Vepar once and for all... but did I really want that? We had the blood bond, but maybe such distance between us would break it. I could find another job.

But they wouldn't let me go. They'd return and hunt me down... and what about the Khonsu roaming on Earth? What if they found me.. Who would come to my rescue?

Trying to organize the chaos of my life seemed useless because every time I thought of never seeing Corran's smile again, feeling Thane against me, smelling Derrial's sexy scent, I felt sick to my stomach and tears pricked my eyes. Uncertainty spreads across my mind like running ink.

The feelings roaming inside me told me everything, even if my brain screamed the opposite, telling me to accept the offer, to head home. But then what?

Freaking hell. This should be an easy decision, yet I slumped in my seat, my chest aching. Had I really fallen this deep for the Vepar? And if I left now, they'd be forced to select one of those five females as their mate. Then they'd hate me, and my heart would be ripped to shreds to imagine them with another woman.

Struggling to breath from the sheer stress pressing down on my chest, I got to my feet, needing to follow my instinct. Right now, it was yelling at me to get out of the ship as fast as possible.

"Zeni, thank you for the chance, but I'll pass."

Her mouth gaped open. "Are you crazy? I'm giving you a free ride home and you want to stay here where most people want to see you imprisoned and everyone else would love to see you experimented on so we understand why you don't have horns or a tail."

I shuddered at either of those options, noting that she didn't seem to know about the fertility procedures yet. "You don't need to understand why, but I am doing this for me." Without waiting for her response, I climbed out of the cruiser and walked away, my knees knocking together, my throat choking with tears falling down my face.

I just walked away from returning to Earth.

Hell!

What was I thinking?

I3

I was officially going crazy. That was the only explanation for the reason why I wanted to throw all of the beautiful Vepar women vying for the guys' attention off a cliff. I had chosen to stay, to try and fight for the Vepar that I had come to care for. But the current trial was making me second guess my decision.

After the first trial we had all been put into a huge structure that I assumed was considered a mansion on Veon. I thought at first it would be better than the cell I had called home, but it was infinitely worse.

It was like I was in high school again, except all the girls I went to school with were a million times prettier and a million times bitchier than the ones I was used to.

I had been put in my own room, while the four remaining participants shared rooms. I quickly realized that this was for my own protection when I hadn't been able to figure out how to make sure no one else could get in the room and I had made the mistake of exploring the house. When I had made it back to my room, all of my meager belongings were in shreds like someone had dragged sharp knives through everything. That night I had been accosted in the hall by a gorgeous blonde Vepar whose nails I found out could transform into claws. She had been about to impale me when a Vepar guard happened to pass by and stop her.

One of the few girls who didn't seem like her goal in life was to kill me, the girl I had first sat next to during Trial 1, happened to see me shaking in the hallways afterwards and showed me how to successfully lock my room. She claimed that she was only involved in the trials because of the pressure her family had put on her to apply due to the prestige having Derrial, Thane, and Corran for mates would bring.

She seemed nice enough, but I had learned not to trust anyone on Vepar with the exception of the guys. After that incident, and the whole Zeni trying to get me to leave the planet one, I had decided to spend all of my time in my room when I wasn't training or being forced to participate in group meals with the other females.

I hadn't anticipated how much it would affect me though. Each of the girls was getting alone time with the guys for this trial. I had never been a jealous person, but just imagining what was happening on the dates had me going crazy.

I had been tempted to leave the safety of my room to find out how the dates had been going, but I hadn't had the nerve. It was enough seeing them getting ready for them. Plus, I was sure that the girls would exaggerate anything that did happen.

Still a part of me worried. What if one of these girls caught their eye and they decided that I wasn't worth the hassle?

I hated how these trials and my time with the guys had reduced me into such an insecure woman. I wished I was in a place where I felt more confident about my place with them.

They had been saying all the right things, and my heart wanted to believe them. My head just couldn't get on board.

Tonight was my turn to spend time with the guys. While some of the girls had been on activities with them, I was going on a dinner date with them. I didn't have a dress or any makeup or hair tools to get ready in my room however, so I needed to venture out into one of the common rooms to use one of the cylinders.

I headed out of my room when I couldn't delay any longer, sealing the door shut behind me. I tiptoed down the hallway, a useless endeavor since I knew the Vepar had extremely good hearing. I had just about made it to the common room with the cylinder when I overheard some of the contestants having a conversation in the room next door.

"It's only a matter of time before we're back together," Zeni was saying to someone else. "It was like no time had passed when I saw them. There was always something between us, something that defied logic. We've loved each other since we were young, that wasn't going to change because of a little time on Earth."

"But what about their relationship with the human?" another girl asked. I recognized her voice as Aery, another of the contestants.

Zeni scoffed. "They needed something to do while they were on Earth. Granted, I didn't expect them to bring the little brat with them back home but Thane told me all about how she threatened to kill herself if they didn't bring her with them. You know how Corran is, such a bleeding heart. He reluctantly convinced the others to bring her along. That's why we're doing this stupid thing in the first place, to get rid of her."

"So, you're saying that the rest of us have no chance at all?" Aery asked, her voice growing angrier.

"I don't recall you coming home two nights ago and telling me that you fucked them," Zeni gloated in an amused voice.

"You didn't...last night?" Aery said in an astonished voice.

"Of course we did. They couldn't keep their hands off of me. I'm telling you, this will be all over soon and things will be back to how they were always supposed to be," bragged Zeni, making my heart burn with her confident attitude.

"I may be wasting my time, but I intend to see this through to the end," said Aery, her voice low and broken. I heard her getting up and walking towards the entrance so I hurried into the other common room where the wardrobe cylinder was waiting.

I leaned against the wall, rubbing at my chest. It hurt, kind of like I was having a heart attack.

She couldn't be telling the truth. There was no way. She'd been trying so hard to get rid of me. It had to be because she was jealous. Just the thought of the guys wrapped around her gorgeous body made me want to scream. In that moment, I could understand how territorial they sometimes got. I felt like I was capable of murder.

I had to talk to them about Zeni tonight. I had to know what their relationship and their history was with her.

After taking another moment to recover, I dashed into the cylinder, desperate to get back to the safety of my room before the date. I pressed a button and couldn't help but smile when my clothes changed right before my eyes. I was now wearing a gorgeous sapphire colored dress that reminded me of Derrial's eyes. This one was short sleeved and more form fitting in the bodice area, something that my lungs hadn't thought was possible based on how tight the corsets usually felt. The fabric also seemed to have sparkles built into it. This must be one of the outfits they used to dress up. It was beautiful, but I couldn't help but wish I had a dress with a little less fabric to wear on a date tonight. I wanted to look so good they couldn't help but want me.

My hair had been done in soft waves down my back and the machine had even managed to apply a light dusting of makeup across my face.

I decided this was my favorite Vepar technology. Nothing could beat it.

I rushed back to my room, wanting to make sure that I didn't run across any of the other contestants and risk them messing up my look. Making it back without interference, I paced my room, anxious for the date to start and anxious for answers.

It was start time and an intercom in my room alerted me that I needed to head to the front to meet the guys as they weren't supposed to enter the mansion...apparently whoever was watching the place had missed the guys sneaking in after the first trial.

I felt sick to my stomach as I headed to meet them. My mind had gone crazy after I had gotten back to my room, continuing to dissect everything that Zeni had said.

It had affected me enough that I had to pause before leaving the house to try and get myself under control.

"Something wrong?" came a voice from down the hall. It was Zeni of course.

"Nope, everything's great," I said, knowing that she could see right through me.

"Tell Thane I liked his new tattoo," she said with a wink, disappearing from sight.

Now I really felt like I was about to fall apart. I definitely hadn't seen a new tattoo the last time I had seen Thane undressed, meaning it had to be new this week. I really needed to take classes in how to psych out my enemies. Because Zeni was a professional at it.

My worries were dampened when I caught sight of the guys. They were standing in front of the mansion, one of Corran's small planes behind them. They were back to their usual human forms and I made a mental note to ask them to go back to their natural forms. I didn't want them to hide anything from me. If I was really going to make this relationship work I would need to love all of them. Horns and all.

It wasn't like it was hard. The three of them were enough to set the mansion on fire. They were dressed in traditional Vepar clothing, but the clothing had some kind of silvery threading this time that made it seem dressier than their usual clothes. They looked perfect.

"Fuck pet, you look stunning," said Thane. "I had always pictured you in Veon clothing and it looks better every time I see you in it."

I blushed.

"Hi," I said softly, feeling shy all of a sudden.

I realized we had never really gone on a date. Hawaii was the closest that I had come to a date with one of them, and I had only been brought along because they needed me to be watched at all times and Corran needed to do his experiments.

This felt different. And it was making me feel nervous.

"Ready to go?" asked Derrial as he slowly took me in. I nodded.

Corran came up beside me and put his arm around my waist, pulling me in close to him. He buried his face in my neck. "You smell delicious. I just might take a bite."

They were being so playful. I wasn't used to it. The thought hit me that maybe they had been like this with the others. It made me see red.

I shrugged Corran's arm off of me.

"Tell me what the other dates were like," I told them, looking at each of them in the eyes.

"What do you mean?" asked Thane, taking a step towards me. I held up my hand to stop him. I couldn't seem to think when they touched me and I wanted a clear head for this.

"Some of the other girls..." I started to say before my voice broke. I cleared my throat and started again. "Some of the other girls mentioned that their dates had gone rather well," I finally was able to get out.

Derrial looked at me with something that resembled pity. I hated it. "They went fine," he said slowly as if I was a feral animal that he was trying to calm down.

I kind of felt like one.

"What does fine mean?" I spit out.

"It almost sounds like you're jealous," said Thane in an amused tone.

I was silent for a moment and all three of their eyes started to do that glowing thing. "You are jealous," said Corran delightedly. "I didn't think it was possible. Does that mean...?"

"That I care about you?" I asked exasperatedly. "Yes asshole, it does."

Their grins were the widest that I had seen.

Suddenly I found myself being shuttled towards the plane. "Time to go, green eyed monster. That's a human saying, right?" Thane laughed at his own joke since we knew the only green eyed monster in the area was him.

Derrial scooped me up and began carrying me before I could put up much of a fight.

"You still haven't answered my question," I screeched, trying to get loose.

"Kitten, don't you know by now that there's no one that compares to you? I don't even see anyone else," he said, before licking the side of my face.

I looked at him, my anger rapidly dwindling in the face of his sweet words. "Why exactly did you just lick me?" I asked. Derrial shot me a grin.

"I thought that was the thing on Earth, if you lick it, it's yours," he said innocently. I rolled my eyes, not so secretly loving his playfulness.

We stepped onto the plane where Corran and Thane were impatiently waiting for us. Corran immediately scooped me up and sat down, placing me in his lap. They were all acting like they couldn't keep their hands off of me. I kind of loved it.

Derrial and Thane took the controls since it was obvious that Corran wasn't going to let me go.

"So where are we going?" I asked as the ship took flight. They had made the walls around us completely opaque so that you could see everything as we flew. Once again, Veon took my breath away with its beauty.

"It's a surprise," said Corran, placing a gentle kiss on my neck that gave me goosebumps. He gently caressed my arm, continuing to place soft kisses from the nape of my neck down my shoulder as we watched the landscape pass by.

I gave a little gasp when the plane went over a mountain and a sparkling lavender sea was laid out before us.

"It's gorgeous," I gushed as we began to fly over it. The suns were just setting on the horizon and the water seemed like it was sparkling as it reflected its fading light.

"Not as beautiful as you," whispered Corran. I rolled my eyes at the corniness of the line even as I blushed. What could I say...I liked a good corny line.

Evidently this was just a lake as we reached the opposite shore rather quickly. There were more mountains on the other side and as we scaled them, I couldn't help but gasp.

There was a city, right out of a fairytale, laid out in front of us. There were white dome like structures all over the valley, going up the mountains. They had brightly colored flowers all over them. Explosions of color were everywhere you looked. Planes similar to the one we were in were flying all around. Lanterns were hovering in the air. I couldn't see anything keeping them afloat so it resembled the floating lantern festivals that I had been to a few times before. The effect was stunning.

"What is this place?" I gushed, my eyes going everywhere as more amazing things caught my attention.

"This is the capital of Veon. It's called Valin," said Derrial in an almost reverent voice. This city is a millennia old. It's where all of our history is. It's where Thane and I were born."

"It's the most beautiful city that I've ever seen," I said, not knowing how to adequately describe the splendor of what I was seeing.

"Yes, it is," Thane said as we began to make our descent.

Derrial and Thane landed us expertly beside one of the white structures.

Instead of letting me walk off the plane, Corran carried me.

"Is this the way that it's going to be all night?" I asked, enjoying being carried around much more than I should.

"Yep," said Corran. "And it's probably going to be me doing it. The other two have gotten your attention too much lately," he said it matter of fact but I wondered if Corran was feeling a little left out. I had formed a bond with him after the other two, but it didn't mean that what I felt for him wasn't as strong as the others. There were so many things special about him, so many things that set him apart from the other two. If I ended up winning these trials I vowed that I would make sure he never felt left out again and always knew where he stood with me.

I placed a kiss on his lips and he looked down at me, a storm of emotions in his golden eyes. "You can carry me all you want," I said softly and he rewarded me with one of those rare Corran grins that never failed to light up my world.

The four of us stopped outside the structure. Derrial waved his arm in front of the door and like with most of the other Vepar structures I had been to, an entrance opened up to allow us inside.

"We thought we would do a little meet the parents night before we got to the next portion of the evening," Thane threw out casually over his shoulder as if he hadn't just dropped a bomb on me. Corran set me down and I wobbled on my feet as anxiety threatened to overtake me.

"Meet the parents? Why didn't you warn me? I would have brought a gift or something," I started blubbering, even though I didn't have access to a gift.

"You didn't need to bring a gift," said Derrial, suddenly pulling me towards him and gifting me with a mind-blowing kiss. He pulled away from me and looked at me with satisfaction. "Perfect. You've got color in your cheeks again. I was afraid you were going to faint on us you were so pale," he said as he brushed a piece of his hair out of his face.

I tried to punch him but Thane caught my hands and put them behind me. With Thane behind me, Derrial in front of me, and Corran watching aptly beside me...I felt like I was going to combust.

"Get your paws off the poor girl," came a sweet voice from the hallway. The guys reluctantly stepped away, but I knew my face was as red as a tomato. Of course their moms had to catch us in a compromising position. What a way to make a first impression.

Once they stepped far enough away, I was able to see a gorgeous blonde headed Vepar that I knew right away had to be Derrial's mom. She had the same color of hair as him and the same sapphire eyes stared back at me that I had started to love so much.

"Hi darling," she said, looking me over not in the disdainful way that I had grown used to, but in a curious, friendly way. She had two small ivory horns that barely peaked out of her hair. She was shorter than the other Vepar women that I had seen, closer to my height, but no less beautiful than any of them. There was an intrinsic goodness about her that I could sense already that made her even more beautiful in my eyes.

"I can see why my boys are taken with you," she said, stepping towards us and pulling me in for a tight hug. "You're absolutely stunning."

"Your boys?" I asked, looking at the guys confused. I had been under the impression that they weren't related.

She laughed, and I immediately fell in love with the sound of it. It sounded almost like a bell chiming.

"They're not all my sons, but they might as well be," she said lovingly. "They've been apart of my life for so long I can't remember what life was like before them."

"So you can give me all the dirt on them," I joked even as Thane let out a half hearted growl next to me. She must have liked that joke because she laughed again, throwing her head back as if it was the funniest thing she had ever heard.

I loved her already.

"I'm Koria," she said, beginning to lead me deeper into the home. "And I'm so happy that you're here."

I could hear other voices as we walked down a white wall, devoid of any decorations as the other Veon structures had been. The room we walked into however, was very different from what I had seen.

It felt like home.

There were five Vepar in the room, lounging in various cozy looking pieces of furniture. The flowers that had adorned the outside of the structure had also somehow blossomed on the inside of the indoor walls as well, making it feel like I had stepped into paradise.

"You're home is beautiful," I told Koria, who to my surprise blushed.

"I've been working for the past month to make it perfect for you," she said, surprising me.

"A month?" I asked, perplexed.

"Oh yes, as soon as I knew my boys were coming home, I knew that it had to be for a special reason, that they had met someone. And I was right!" she said, practically jumping in excitement.

"Don't hog the girl, Koria," said a deep voice affectionately.

Koria led me to one of the male Vepar who I immediately guessed was Derrial's father. While Derrial had Koria's eyes and hair, the rest of his features were all this Vepar. "Welcome to our home lovely girl, my name is Canton," he said, surprising me when he hugged me too.

"Okay Dad, that's long enough," joked Derrial. Canton gave me a wink as he let me go and I immediately liked him too.

The other three Vepar stepped forward, friendly welcoming looks on their faces as well. All of them looked the same age as my Vepar, once again reminding me how different their life cycles were from humans.

I met Corran's parents next. They both had golden eyes and chestnut colored hair, resembling siblings they looked so much alike. Corran must have seen the questions in my face because he explained that he and his family were from a different province of Veon where most of the population carried the same signature golden eye color.

"None of them are as handsome as our son though," bragged Tenly, Corran's mother. I was amused when the tips of his ears turned pink at the praise. Corran's father was named Kenroe, and while the two of them were much more reserved than Derrial's parents, I liked them both immediately as well.

The last parent I met was Thane's father, Lanton. He was alone, making me wonder why Thane's mother wasn't around. He was built like a truck, the biggest Vepar in the room and he reminded me of a bodybuilder. Contrary to his intimidating form however, his voice and personality were tranquil. More Buddah than The Rock. I felt more calm just hearing his voice.

"We're so glad you're here," he said, placing a soft kiss on my cheek.

"Thank you," I said, trying to keep my voice from quivering. I had never really thought about meeting the guys' parents. Our lives had been too chaotic to even think about doing something normal like that. But if I had thought about it, I would have feared it, convinced that they would hate me on sight the way the rest of the Vepar did that I had met.

I was so glad to seemingly be wrong about that.

We sat down, and just like he had warned me, Corran immediately scooted me onto his lap while the other two sat on either side of us holding my hands. It felt awkward to be showing so much affection in front of their parents that I had just met, but none of them even batted an eye. Derrial's parents even looked proud about it.

Koria brought us a liquid that tasted a bit like green tea as we all chatted. Corran's father wanted to know all about Earth, asking me question after question until Corran let out an exasperated sigh.

Corran's father blushed the exact same way that Corran had earlier at his mother's compliment, making the family resemblance even more obvious.

"Oops," said Corran's dad self deprecatingly. "I get carried away whenever your planet is involved. I've been obsessed with learning all about it since Corran left to stay there. It made me feel close to him I guess."

My heart melted. I would never have guessed that my three guys came from such loving families. I was pleasantly surprised and it made me like them even more. It also made me realize that I had so much I still needed to learn about them and that they needed to learn about me.

Hopefully we would have the chance.

"We're all so happy to have them back home," said Koria softly, looking like she was about to cry. "Thank you for getting our boys back to us."

Hmmm, wonder what she would say if she knew that her "boys" had forced me to come here...

Thane pinched my side, seemingly reading my mind as usual. I shot him a grin.

"Would you like anything to eat?" asked Lanton, gesturing to a tray next to the tea that was laden with food that I couldn't identify.

"Thanks dad, but we've got a full night planned for her," said Thane, standing up. "We'd actually better get going."

All of their parents looked so disappointed. "We'll visit again soon," I promised. "There's so much I need to learn about the three of them that they won't be able to keep me away."

Derrial groaned in jest, but it seemed to do the trick of raising all of their spirits.

More hugs were exchanged and we exited the dwelling, all of their parents walking out after us to wave goodbye as we took off again.

"I loved them," I said, cuddling into Corran's lap.

"They loved you too, kitten," said Derrial happily.

"Where was your mom Thane? I would have loved to meet her," I said.

Silence descended on the ship. I knew immediately that I had said something wrong.

Thane cleared his throat as if he was trying to give himself more time to figure out what to say. "My mother is in a special facility," he said quietly.

"A special facility?" I asked hesitantly, feeling terrible for bringing it up.

"She was captured by the Khonsu when I was nine. They tortured her until she lost her mind. She's been in the facility ever since we rescued her."

I sat there shocked, not knowing what to say.

"I should have brought it up before we got there," said Thane. "But as I'm sure you can imagine, it's hard to talk about. Dad brought me up with Corran and Derrial's parents helping out."

"I'm so sorry, honey," I said, tapping Corran to let me down. He reluctantly did so and I walked over to Thane, wrapping my arms around him.

"It happened a long time ago," Thane said gruffly, but he pulled me towards him tighter and buried his head in my neck.

I had a million questions but I didn't want to pressure him to tell me anything he didn't want to. He would tell me eventually, and I could accept that.

Corran walked over and grabbed me after a few minutes, bringing me back to his chair to sit in his lap again. Derrial and Thane both snorted, and it lifted the somber mood that had descended on the ship.

"Where are we off to now?" I asked as Corran started kissing down my neck again. I laughed and snuggled in deeper to him.

"Dinner," said Derrial. "We figured that it was time to show you Vepar food. So far you've gotten trial food and cell food. Not the greatest stuff."

I had always been an adventurous eater so I was excited about the prospect of trying something new.

"Can I eat everything that you eat?" I asked, thinking that their altered forms hid how different they actually were to humans.

Corran frowned. "You should be able to eat most things, but I haven't tested everything so we'll just have you try things that I know for sure are alright."

Thane snorted again. "I think she'll be okay no matter what, lover boy."

Corran pulled me in closer to him. "We're not taking that chance."

"Um guys," I asked Thane and Derrial. "What is going on with Corran?"

Thane and Derrial both looked at each other with amused looks on their faces.

"Have you ever heard of blue balls, kitten?" Derrial asked.

"Um...yes?" I asked, confused.

"He has the equivalent of Vepar blue balls, right now," Derrial said with a smirk as Corran growled into my neck.

"What does that mean?"

"You've just fed on the two of us recently, right?" asked Thane. I nodded.

"Well he's starting to feel a blood craving. His body is pushing him to be with his mate. You."

"Oh," I said, startled. I craned my neck so Corran had access to it more. "Go ahead," I asked.

Corran growled again, but this one sounded more like a moan.

"I think you better wait until you can do everything," said Derrial with a chuckle.

"Everything?"

"Sex, pet," said Thane. "Exchanging blood with your mate is practically a sacred act. You don't just go biting each other. It's almost always shared with sex unless the circumstances demand otherwise."

"Like when we escaped from the house on Earth," I said, shivering just remembering how terrible it was.

"Exactly."

"You said mate," I said slowly to the guys. "You've said that before, that we have a bond. What will happen if I don't win?"

All three of the guys growled. "That won't happen," said Derrial darkly.

I said nothing, just continued to look out at Veon through the window.

The mood had lightened a little bit by the time we landed by the lavender sea that I had seen earlier. Thane and Corran both held my hands while Derrial walked behind me as we headed towards a glittering gold structure that was right on the shore.

"This is gorgeous," I said, letting go of Thane's hand and reaching my hand out to touch the outside of the structure. It literally looked like it was built out of gold.

"This is one of our nicest restaurants," said Derrial, letting out a laugh when an entrance opened right where I had been reaching out to touch and I almost fell through.

"Welcome to Lankardia," said a as usual, beautiful Vepar woman dressed all in black. "We're delighted to have you here this evening," she said, beckoning us forward. I walked inside, gaping like a fish, and wishing that I had worn a more glamorous outfit.

While all the other Vepar structures I had been too had been relatively the same with the exception of the flower colored ones in the capital city, this one could only be described as opulent.

The walls inside were the same sparkling gold material as the outside. There were crystal orbs hanging from the ceiling. Tables seemed to be floating in the air covered by glittering white tablecloths. It was incredible.

"You can close your mouth now," whispered Corran, nuzzling against me as he had been doing all evening.

"It's just all so incredible," I said in an awed voice. I noticed that the other Vepar in the room were staring at us as we walked by. "I wish they would stop staring," I muttered.

"I don't," said Derrial in a proud voice. "We purposely picked this place. It's where all the elite of Veon dine. We wanted to show off our mate."

My heart fluttered at that word again...mate. And at the fact that they were proud to be seen with me.

We were led to a different room that only had one table and privacy from the rest of the patrons. The back wall of the room was made up of a glass balcony that overlooked the lavender sea. It was perfection.

The hostess sat us at our table and left, leaving one last longing glance at the three guys who hadn't paid her any attention. The jealous bitch inside of me was glad about that.

We talked for a little while about little facts about Veon until a male Vepar with black hair and black horns came into the room. "Good evening everyone. Welcome to Lankardia. My name is Rodolphus and I'll be your server for the evening. The chef has arranged a special tasting menu for you tonight if that is agreeable to you."

The men nodded, all of them looking pleased.

"Can I start you out with drinks? We have anything you could want available."

"We'd like four of the house wines," said Derrial.

"Of course. I'll have that right out," said Rodolphus, leaving the room.

"If he gives her one more look I'm going to cut his head off," said Corran mildly, scooting his chair so close to me that our sides were practically glued together.

"He didn't do anything!" I scoffed, shooting him a glare.

"He couldn't keep his eyes off of you," said Thane with a menacing glare.

"It was probably because I'm the token human in the restaurant. I'm sure that he hasn't seen very much of my kind."

"Doubtful," growled Derrial.

Rodolphus returned to the room with four glasses filled with a smoky blue drink. "Our house wine," he said, looking right at me and this time giving me a wink. I held onto Corran's hand for dear life as he was twitching like he was going to jump across the table and gut him.

There was a deadly silence in the room and Rodolphus finally caught on. He looked at the three angry Vepar warily and left without saying another word.

I took a sip of the wine before they could say anything. To my surprise, it was sweet. More like fruit juice than any wine I had ever tasted. I took another big sip.

"I'd be careful with that if I were you," Corran said with a smile on his face. "That has five times the alcohol content as Earth wines."

I gulped the sip I had in my mouth and then set the drink down carefully. I could barely handle a glass of Earth wine without starting to feel tipsy. I would need to be very slow in enjoying this.

Rodolphus seemed to have learned his lesson because the next time he came in carrying our first course, he didn't even look at me.

After he left, I eyed the dish he had set down. It was a dish covered in flowers. I wasn't sure how I was supposed to eat that.

"Here, like this," said Derrial, scooping up a handful of the flowers and beginning to squeeze them into the bowl that was in front of him. To my surprise a honey colored liquid began to fall from the flowers until the flowers completely disappeared in Derrial's hands.

I gasped and then quickly scooped up some flowers and started to squeeze just like Derrial had. To my delight, I was able to get the same liquid to appear. I tentatively took a sip and moaned as the flavors exploded across my tongue. The liquid had a nutty, rich flavor like nothing I had tasted before. It was officially my favorite food.

"What did he call this? Lankardia's specialty?" I said with a mouth full of the dish.

Corran snickered next to me. "It's actually the Veon national flower. It's called a Vetri. It's delicious properties were discovered by a group of Vepar who got lost while camping and had to try and eat plants to survive."

"I could eat fifteen bowls of this!"

"I wouldn't do that, kitten. The flower has certain properties if consumed too much. Certain hallucinogenic properties."

I put my spoon down immediately remembering how awful it had been after the Khonsu had injected me with its venom.

"There's no problem eating the bowl," said Corran gently, pushing the bowl towards me. "It takes several bowls to even start the effect."

I nodded, but took small sips after that. Evidently Vepar food packed a punch in all of its forms.

Speaking of dangerous things. I needed to ask about Zeni. I had to know or I was going to go crazy. I took a deep breath, trying to draw in some courage.

"So…about Zeni," I began.

The men all immediately set down their spoons and looked at me tensely. Rodolphus chose that moment to come in. He was immediately sent away with curses. Poor thing. He probably was going to quit after tonight.

"What do you want to know?" asked Derrial tersely.

"So it's been pretty clear that she at one point was someone important to you…what happened to stop that?"

Corran sighed next to me, clutching my hand even tighter that he had been holding all evening as if he needed comfort for what was about to come.

"We grew up with Zeni. She was younger than us and had a crush on us for years and we never noticed her. Zeni would tag along with us whenever we went out with friends but we never thought of her as anything more. We all dated a lot back then. Zeni would always bother everyone to find out how our dates went. She was our little stalker. We went on a five year mission to explore nearby planets when the fertility issues started to become a problem. When we came back, Zeni was all grown up and she caught our eye."

I looked down at that comment. The inferiority over how beautiful Zeni was compared to me hitting me all over again.

"Hey," said Derrial, reaching over to grab my chin. "Stop that. You're the most gorgeous woman that we've ever seen," he said. I scoffed as I looked into his eyes. But I couldn't see any sign that he didn't believe that. They were delusional.

"Keep going," I said with a sigh.

Corran eyed me before he continued talking. "Zeni wanted all of us and for a time we were fine with that. But pieces of her personality that we hadn't seen before started to come out. There were strange things that happened to some of our exes and our female colleagues began to be changed to different departments. She was always checking up on us randomly as if she thought she would catch us with another female at any moment. It finally became too much and we all decided this wasn't going to work for us..." Corran's voice trailed off.

"And that's when she told us she was pregnant," said Thane.

I gasped. They had a child with her?

"Oh don't worry," Thane said sarcastically. "That viper was lying. She had fake tests and everything since she knew that we would be doubtful because of the issues going on. She fooled us for months, even going so far as to gain weight so it looked like she was getting a bump. We decided to try and stick it out for the sake of the child, thinking that we would get a paternity test and only the real father would have to be stuck to her. She finally faked one thing too many and Corran began to get suspicious, going to visit the doctor she said she was going to. Imagine our surprise when it turned out that the doctor was in on the plan and had been giving her special pills so that her labs made it look like she was pregnant whenever Corran made her run tests. The doctor was quick to tell us everything when the three of us confronted her. We broke up with Zeni immediately. She's been on the warpath ever since trying to get us back."

We were all quiet. That was a lot to take in. I was tempted to tell them about her offering me her ship to leave the planet but I was afraid they would go off the handle after everything they had just told me. I decided to tell them later, when they were calmer.

"Can we please not talk about her anymore," said Corran in a frustrated voice, pulling me into his lap. "This is supposed to be a date...not to mention your second trial. I think we should start the festivities now."

"Festivities?" I asked in a breathless voice as Corran's hands started to stroke farther down my body.

"Yes," he said, his voice almost a whisper as he picked me up and laid me down on the table. "And festivities usually start with dessert first."

I looked at Thane and Derrial to see how they were reacting, but they seemed content to let Corran take the lead.

Cupping my jaw, he angled me for his kiss. I was immediately consumed by him. His intoxicating taste seeped into my mouth, his tongue dueling with mine. Sliding my fingers through his hair, I luxuriated in the soft feel of it, painfully aware of the other two's heated gazes on me.

Corran's body devoured me. I felt wholly protected in his arms. Cherished. I moaned into his kiss as the sparks of lust fueled through me, scratching my nails along his skin. As if sensing my complete desperation, he pulled back slightly, flashing me a sexy, knowing smile. His eyes glazed over with desire, staring down at my chest, my hardened nipples clearly visible through my dress. His smirk transformed into deep wanting, his eyes turning a darker shade of gold, more like caramel than anything else, his lips parted on a needy breath.

His need for me was thrilling. To see him standing before me, wanting me like this. I lost my breath. Staring up into his face, watching him take in my highlighted form, I quivered in need.

"Corran . . . touch me . . . " I gasped out.

Gripping the bottom of my dress, he lifted it, surprising me. I tensed, waiting to be touched. "Please," I begged.

Just as Corran was about to touch me, a speaker came on. "A reminder to the contestant that erotic touching is not allowed in Trial 2. Further action will result in disqualification."

Corran immediately stopped touching me and bowed his head. "I'm going to die," he said dramatically. Thane stood up and slapped him on the back.

"Better luck next time, buddy," he teased, sounding so human at the moment that it made me giggle.

"Laugh now. But when I finally get my hands on you..." said Corran threateningly.

I laughed, excited for the prospect of a pent up Corran being unleashed.

As I sat back down I noticed all three Vepar adjusting themselves. Maybe they would all get a case of "Vepar blue balls," I thought smugly, loving how much they wanted me.

There was a knock on the door and a timid looking Rodolphus popped his head in. "Are you ready for the next course?" he asked.

"Come in," Corran confirmed, in a very unwelcoming voice.

Corran was a bit sullen and touchy the rest of the night, but it was still the most fun I had experienced with them.

Plate after plate was brought to the table, filled with the most exotic looking food that I had ever seen. I was passed from lap to lap as they all wanted to feed me. I had never thought that I would like that but it was kind of fun to feed each other. It also helped me be brave with some of the more interesting looking items like a plate full of sauteed Danter eyes. It wasn't one of my favorite dishes.

When we were finally done eating, I was a little worried that I wouldn't be able to walk out of the restaurant I was so full.

"We need to get you back," Derrial admitted, regretfully. "We've already kept you out hours longer than the others."

"Don't mention the others," I said, a bit drunkenly.

"There's my jealous girl again." Thane wrapped his arms around my waist and walked out on the balcony.

"We should have a house here," I said sleepily, too tipsy to monitor my words.

"You can have whatever you want," he replied.

Corran and Derrial strolled out just as our ship landed on the shore below us. Thane helped me down the stairs since I wasn't moving very steadily and we climbed on the ship.

I stayed cuddled up in Thane's arms for the trip back to the mansion, feeling better about our relationship than I ever had before.

"Tonight was perfect," I whispered as I hugged each of them in front of the mansion. "One of the best nights of my life."

Corran pulled me in for a kiss that left me breathless. The tension was bubbling at the surface for us. I wanted him badly and I didn't know how much longer we could hold out. I was just contemplating how we could possibly sneak him in when lights all of a sudden shone down on us. They were bright, like spotlights, and they blinded me for a minute.

"What the hell is going on?" Thane looked like he was going to break the neck of whoever was responsible for this. To my surprise, three members of the Council appeared.

"Say your goodbye's boys, this one is disqualified," one of them said, grinning.

The three of them stood in front of me protectively. "On what grounds? Corran stopped before anything happened tonight," Derrial said.

"One of the Councilmembers stepped forward with a device that started projecting a holographic image. I gasped in horror, feeling very sober all of a sudden. It was a picture of me sitting in Zeni's ship.

"She tried to escape earlier and was stopped by one of the other contestants. Her attempt counts as a forfeiture."

I could see the guys' bodies stiffen upon seeing the picture. I could only imagine how disappointed they were in me thinking that I had tried to leave. I should have just told them what happened at dinner.

I guess this was it.

"And I suppose the other contestant who stopped her was Zeni, was it?

Doesn't it seem suspicious that Zeni bothered to take a photograph of an escape attempt instead of letting Ella go and immediately reporting it. We know for a fact that Zeni was the one who offered Ella the ship and she refused it," said Derrial, shocking me with his defense of me and the fact that they seemed to already know exactly what had happened.

Thane stepped forward and pressed a band on his wrist, his own holographic image popping up, but this one a video. I watched in a mixture of amazement and horror as the exact scene that had transpired with Zeni played out on the video.

After it was done there was a grim silence. "There's obviously been a mistake," one of the Councilmen said stiffly before all three of them walked away.

I watched numbly as the ship the Councilmen had flown in on disappeared into the sky.

All three of them turned to look at me. There was an awkward silence.

"I should have told you what happened, but how did you get that video?" I asked, not knowing whether I should feel angry or grateful they had been spying on me.

Corran shifted guiltily. "I had a tracker activated in you after what happened with that prison worker who attacked you. We wanted to be able to check in on you in case something happened."

"You put something else in me without my permission?" I asked, my voice climbing. I reached up to brush against the skin where I knew at least one of the devices resided.

"No," Corran responded fast. "It was just a feature that hadn't been activated yet in the sensor that monitors your health."

"Does that make it any better?" I snapped. "You never told me it had that capability. What else have you recorded of me?"

"Calm down," barked Derrial. "You're not being rational. We obviously needed that video to prevent you from getting kicked out. It's not like you bothered to tell us about that happening."

I immediately backed down, feeling chagrined. "You sounded so mad earlier that I didn't want to upset you any more," I explained lamely.

"How about we all just forgive each other. I told you that I would never let someone mess with you," said Thane. "That applies to women as well."

I was suddenly very tired. "I'd better go inside now," I said wearily. They nodded grimly, each of them hugging me in turn.

"I hate this," Derrial whispered in my ear. "Someday soon there won't be goodbyes."

I laid my head on his chest and listened to his heart. "I hope that day comes," I said, reluctantly pulling away.

I could feel their eyes on me as I walked inside.

What a night.

14

"You're still not ready?" Giny exclaimed from my doorway, dressed in a black gown that fell to her ankles, her fabric glimmering from the lights overhead. The thin belt around her waist matched her tiny pink horns, while glitter sparkled from her trimmed black hair.

She was one of a couple of women from the house who smiled at me, said hello, and even sat next to me during meals. Her family, I learned, lived on a nearby moon and were both scientists, and she admitted to have a major fangirl moment over Corran, but like me, she was alone on the planet.

"Is everyone going fancy for dinner tonight?" I slipped out of my tennis shoes and rushed toward the cylindrical wardrobe as I'd spend most of the day training, while my mind had been floating on clouds from my date with the Vepar last night. If that was an indication of what my future with them would bring, I was ready and had no doubts about my decision to not take Zeni up on her offer to fly back to Earth. Though part of me kept hoping I hadn't made the wrong decision.

"Yeah, it's a big feast and Corran, Thane, and Derrial will be attending. Everyone's getting dressed up."

"Really?" The idea of seeing my men again so soon had me rushing into the wardrobe cylinder, needing to look perfect for them.

"Oh, one of the girls dropped out of the ritual last night. Did you hear about it?"

"Who? Why?"

"Jexie. Her father insisted he found another mate for her and ordered her to return home."

"That's horrible. Do females not get to choose their own partners here?"

"It's more of a family event." She lifted her wrist and stabbed something on the screen, making the monitor in the common room switch on.

Three columns of print appeared on the screen, and it was slowly scrolling down to show more and more and more.

I stepped close and read a few of the titles.

Xeorian Estate Heir Searching for Mates.

Galaxy Engineer Seeks Union with Three Vepar.

Underneath were a list of traits like this were a job interview with details on education and wealth and even a description of her appearance and size of horns. Apparently the smaller the better on a female.

"Are these ads for husbands?"

"If by husbands you mean mates for life, yes. It's all orchestrated by families to find the best mate for the best possible chances of conception."

"Wow. It's very different on Earth. We select who we want... well maybe not in all cultures."

"The mate selection process means we're united with the best possible suitor. Makes sense to me."

I could see the benefit of both sides, and with the way my Vepar selected me, I didn't quite get a choice either.

"Alright, hurry up, Ella. We're going to be late."

I turned to the small panel and selected the type of gown I was after, down to the color, and even a hairstyle. Several minutes later, I emerged.

Giny's mouth gaped open. "What style did you just select? I need to change my dress."

I laughed and glanced down at myself, but my eyes widened. "Whoa!" A white dress studded with miniature diamonds dropped to my feet with a split racing up the side all the way to my bikini line. The dress cinched in at my waist with the corset lifting my breasts. I twirled on the spot, revealing stilettos that were clear as glass.

"I look like freaking Cinderella." My dark hair fell in curls past my shoulders and when I glanced in the mirror, I wore a simple diamond tiara.

"Cinderella?" she asked. "Is that a really famous celebrity on Earth?"

"Yeah, sort of I guess." I spun in the mirror, still in awe. "You think this might be a bit too much."

"No. You want to look the best you can. Anyway, I'll see you in the dining room." She whisked away, unable to leave quick enough.

With another quick look in the mirror, I couldn't believe I had an hourglass figure this insane. Sure, the corset made it a bit hard to breath, but... my three Vepar were going to die when they saw me.

"Dinner," Luren, the elf Vepar called out as he rushed past, herding all the girls.

I pouted my ruby lips at the mirror and strolled out, struggling to remain steady on such high heels.

"Ella, you look gorgeous tonight." Luren joined me. "Just watch the other girls tonight because this dress will take everyone's breath away."

I looked over to his brilliant smile. "Why do all these beautiful clothes resemble the ones we have on Earth? It's like I am back home but on steroids."

"Our scientists have been studying your planet for centuries, along with the culture and history and fashion. Some of the elements it seems have slipped into our world. Some Vepar embrace it, while others resist and stick to the old ways."

He smirked and nodded. "Now, let's move fast, you don't want to be late."

We moved through the corridor and stepped into a lift. Seconds later the doors slid open, and we walked out into a ballroom. We no longer were in the plain rooms they were keeping us in. This clearly was where all the opulence was.

Floors of marble, floor to ceiling windows, and golden pillars lined the walls along with mahogany framed paintings of the galaxy. They reminded me of the ones in Cherry's home. My life had changed so much since we were friends. The last I saw her was in the streets when I begged her for help and she refused to lift a finger. I'd come a long way to realize the only reason I was her friend was fear. I didn't want to be alone, so I excused her using me. But those times felt like a lifetime away.

I walked into the grand room with at least six chandeliers dripping in crystals. To the right lay a dressed table with gold cutlery and goblets and so many flowers of every possible color. There were even balloons in the corners. Things didn't quite match in this room, looking like a mash of various styles.

Everyone was gathered on one side of the room, chatting. I scanned the small crowd and found no sign of the men.

I spotted Giny and strolled over to her. She no longer wore her black dress, but was in a golden, strapless dress, straight and body hugging.

"You look gorgeous," I mentioned to her.

She turned and shrugged. "Couldn't let you be the only one to steal the limelight." She broke into a laugh, while the two women she spoke to earlier sneered my way and walked away.

"What's up with them?" I asked, swallowing hard as I noticed everyone's eyes on me.

Giny shrugged, but avoided looking at me. "What would you like to drink?" She walked off before I could respond.

I tried to smile when all I wanted was to run out of there. I shouldn't have worn this dress, and hated how everyone glared at me, judged me. Except I had to remind myself this was a competition to them, and despite their jealousy, I also knew my three Vepar wanted me over them.

Luren was at my side, taking my elbow and guiding me to the table. He wore a steel gray outfit with a red crevet. "Do you like the room?"

"It's beautiful."

"Derrial insisted we dress it up to resemble a human party."

I turned to him, unable to stop smiling so widely. "Really? It looks gorgeous. I've never been to a ball this fancy before, but always wanted to."

His smile brightened my evening and he walked me to a seat at the table, others joining too. He pulled the chair out and I sat down, but before he left, he leaned down and whispered, "Don't drink or eat anything one of the other contestants give you."

He pulled back and broke into laughter with someone else, all fake of course.

Giny sat down next to me and set down a flute glass with blue bubbly inside. "We call it, Shooting Star."

"Thank you."

"Try it."

I swallowed hard. "Maybe a bit later. I can't drink on an empty stomach without it going straight to my head."

She studied me with a strange look. "Not sure what that means, but okay." With her own drink in hand, she sipped the blue beverage.

Everyone else joined us at the table, most chatting to each other, and I felt left out. I fiddled with the golden cutlery that had tiny engravings at the end of the dual sun emblem. I sat tense amid bubbly conversation and smiles, my gaze kept shifting to the door. Listening to the conversations, everyone was fake, complimenting each other, but you could see in their eyes, they tossed daggers at their enemy. The first round of food came out, and still no sign of my Vepar. A jelly-like sausage was placed in front of me, the color of a cucumber. Was this a sea cucumber...or a slug? Did they even have those here?

Everyone around me cut into their dish, slurping the pieces into their mouth, and I gagged. I poked mine with a fork and it wobbled.

"Our food isn't good enough for you?" Zeni blurted out, grabbing every-one's attention and turning it towards me.

"Umm it's fine."

"Then eat the sea sausage."

I almost vomited in my mouth at the sound of that. Eyes... so many on me, expectant. What if it's a major faux pas to not try something at a Vepar party?

I sliced a tiny bit off the end, and stabbed it with my fork. Swallowing hard, I slid it into my mouth.

They watched me, studied me, ready to judge me.

I smiled while I chewed the most disgusting thing in the world. It tasted like I had just eaten a dirty sock.

"Announcing Derrial, Corran, and Thane," Luren called out from the doorway.

The women all cheered and turned their attention away. Swiftly I grabbed the napkin and put it into my mouth, spitting out the sea sausage. I reached for the blue drink, anything to get the bitter taste out of my mouth, but stopped, remembering the warning. I pushed the glass away from my section of the table.

The three Vepar took seats at the table, several spots away from me, but I caught Corran's attention from further across the table.

They were served the starter, and all three didn't touch the sea sausage. Smart idea.

Music played overhead, a high beat, and at once I almost burst out laughing. It was the Macarena, and everyone was bopping away at the table to a song that was a fad back on Earth so long ago. I wondered what exact history they referenced for their ball information.

Two of the females moved to sit closer to the men, chatting their ears off, and I'd be a nun if I said I wasn't jealous to see them laughing and placing their hands on their arms and touching their hair. They were even sticking their chests out when they spoke with them.

The second meal came, a round dish with what looked like lasagne. I poked the top and pulled out a forkful. There were layers of what looked like vegetables amid something green. Seaweed sheets? I tasted it, rolling it over my tongue. It tasted like an explosion of sweet and savory flavors, much better than the sea sausage. I dug in, trying to ignore the giggles or the men's voices, sounding honestly interested. Fire raged in my veins, but I sat quietly, pretending to smile and remain calm when I wanted to scream for them to stop touching my men. Yep, clearly I was the green eyed monster today.

Zeni slid into the empty seat next to me, staring at me, touching my cutlery. "Are you having fun?" she mocked.

"Absolutely," I responded, my voice dripping with honey.

"Good. The party's just getting started so be ready." She reached out and grabbed my drink before guzzling it down in one go, then left.

I should have stopped her, but then again, it might be interesting to see if Giny had indeed spiked the drink.

When the waiter came around, I ordered myself water, catching Zeni practically sitting on Corran's lap. I clenched my jaw. When Giny returned to her seat, she leaned in closer to me. "She'd do anything to win them over. It must be burning you up to see her all over them."

I nodded, unable to pull my attention from them. Zeni caught me looking and broke into a fake laugh. "Oh Corran, I have something you'll want to see," she cooed and slid her fingers down the front of her heart-shaped dress, pulling the fabric purposefully down to show lots of boob.

I dropped my gaze, crossed and recrossed my legs, and tapped my fingernails on the table. Derrial and Thane were hard to see from the heads between us. And it scorched me alive to sit at a table with three men who captured my heart, who drove me insane, and ignore all the women who were pouring themselves all over them.

My mind filled with revenge. Tampering with their wardrobe cylinder, having Zeni wake up and find fifty sea sausages in bed with her, a threat. They sounded reasonable to me.

A gasp caught my attention and I looked for the source. Zeni and Corran were so close their heads touched, both of them staring at something that looked like a photo. Did they have old fashioned cameras here?

Corran shot to his feet, his chair scraping across the marble floor, Zeni flailing as she almost fell face first to the ground before she caught herself. He rounded the table to show Derrial and Thane the photo or whatever it was.

I swept my gaze back to Zeni who reclined in her seat smiling like a Cheshire cat, staring at me, proud of herself. What did she do?

The desserts came around as Corran took his seat, and none of them looked my way, seeing to be ignoring me on purpose. I felt sick to my stomach, and despite the fact that the pyramid green desert intrigued me, I couldn't stomach a thing. My knees bounced under the table, and I had to know what was going on.

Fire scorched my insides. I needed water, fresh air, something before I combusted.

When Zeni made her way to the bathroom, I excused myself, climbed on my feet, and marched after her.

I didn't remember ever feeling so furious, but I left the room and saw her slipping into the bathroom.

Quickening my pace, my fists clenched, I was about to shove myself into the bathroom when someone looped an arm around my waist and swooped me backward and off the ground.

I kicked and wrestled, looking back to find Corran. "Put me down," I roared.

"Not until you calm down." He said, as he carried me farther down the hallway and into a lift. We stepped out into what looked like a hotel room. No people were around.

"What did she show you? What lies is she spreading now?"

He grabbed my wrist and hauled me into a bedroom, my legs wobbling on my too tall heels. Once inside an empty room, he released me and locked the door.

"Are you going to talk to me?" I demanded, the fiery anger still surging through my veins.

He pulled out the paper from his pocket and held it by his side. "It's nothing, seriously."

He lifted the photo and flipped it over. I blinked hard at seeing a photo of me completely naked in a full frontal straddling a tree branch while I slept.

"I don't get it?" Sure, it wasn't my best side and hell, I could do with a brazillian, but what was I missing?

"Zeni is very competitive, and everything to her must be perfect."

I glanced down at myself in the photo. "And I'm not perfect?"

He smiled and tucked the photo into his back pocket. "You're more than perfect, which is why I took the photo so I always have you with me."

I stared at him bewildered.

"On Veon, women never let their hair grow too long." And it took me several seconds to realize exactly what hair he was referring to.

My mouth dropped open, and I felt violated to have Zeni laugh at my private area and show it to the Vepar like I was a monkey on display. "She's sick. And besides, when was I supposed to get waxed? When I was locked in my prison cell?"

"Told you. Nothing to worry about."

"I doubt that. So with all your technology, why do you still have printed photographs."

"Nostalgia mostly."

Walking predatorily in my direction, he stopped in front of me, lowering his head in a flash to capture my mouth, stopping any further discussion of Zeni. I moaned as our lips connected. His kiss was remarkably soft as he cupped my jaw in his hands, tilting my head slightly to deepen it. I wasn't sure how he was managing to control himself so well when I felt like I was about to combust.

As was always my reaction to him, I was lost, completely swept up in him and his ability to render me speechless. I absolutely loved that he made me lose all thought with his kisses, all my insecurities of being here completely obliterated once more, every kiss feeling like the first.

He walked me backwards towards the bed, through the embrace of our lips and tongues. Pulling away, he lifted me gently, searching my eyes before laying me down softly on the bed. I reached for him in unspoken need, his body molding over me as he searched my lips for another passionate kiss.

I needed him to show me how much he wanted me after days of watching other Vepar females do everything they could to get his attention. I needed to know that he needed me as much as I craved him.

A visceral feeling passed over me. Our eyes met and I saw enthrallment in his gaze, in the sensations of our kisses as our coming together imparted. Feeling his hardened erection pushing against me, I moaned into his kiss, sliding my legs along his length. My desire and need clear in my pursuit to speed things up. It was all for naught, as he took his sweet time, gently nipping along my jaw and down my neck. I remained still, taking my cue from him as he proceeded to undress me in slow measures. Unzipping my dress, he peeled it up and over my head, then rained gentle kisses along my stomach before worshipping my breasts through the thin layer of my strapless lace bra that I had finally figured out how to get the dressing cylinder to give me.

"I don't want any barriers between us," he whispered, slowly removing every layer of my clothing, my overheated skin relishing the coolness of the room. Leaning forward, I dragged up his shirt, pulling it over his tight stomach, across his strong arms, like unwrapping the most cherished and wanted present. Lost in our silent fantasy, he stared lovingly into my eyes as we unfastened and removed his pants, dropping them and his briefs to the floor. Completely naked, no barriers between us, as he'd wanted.

The anticipation of feeling him on me, in me, overtook my body, and I shuddered in his arms. He lowered himself over me. His strength and weight felt absolutely delicious, warming my blood with desire. In unspoken understanding, our undeniable mutual need declared the undressing experience as foreplay enough. I thrummed with so much kindled desire, that I already floated on the edge of an orgasm from his touch. My silent pleas signaled I was more than ready to welcome him inside me. He spread my legs with a gentle push of his knee. With slow, measured movements, he slid into me before leisurely thrusting deeper. I moaned, my back arching, captured by his unwavering stare.

"Yes, that's it, baby. So perfect," he whispered, pulling himself all the way out, before pushing back in slowly, forcing me to open. I pulled his face down to mine to devour his mouth, gently nipping his lower lip. I was lost to the sensations of his steady rhythm, the slow sensual gliding in and out, as though he had all the time in the world.

I wished we had that kind of time. This was a stolen moment. We'd escaped from the party and everyone would ask questions soon, then it was back to the games. I memorized this moment inside of me for when it got too hard...for when it felt impossible to keep going.

But I realized at that moment that I want a lifetime of this. Of these Vepar men.

"I want you to fight for me...fight for us, because I'll never stop fighting for you," he whispered, not breaking eye contact for one moment.

Maintaining his languid strokes, he brushed his hand down my body, pushing it between us to gently stroke me, skating his thumb along the bundle of nerves in succession with his thrusts. Euphoria soared within me, growing, escalating. He drove me wild, pushing me over the edge.

I writhed uncontrollably in his grip as he dangled me closer to the plunge of ecstasy. My body trembled in desire, achingly empty in the need for more, begging for release.

"Corran . . . please . . . "

"Shhh, baby," he whispered.

Fisting his hand roughly in my hair, he held my hip securely in place, refusing to let me speed up our movements.

"It's too much," I pleaded in desperation.

I quaked in his arms, screaming in pleasure, my body pulsating and tightening around him. Pulling my lips from his, I screamed, "Corran!" Slowing the gentle glides of his fingers on my sensitized clit, he pulled his hand away, entwining his fingers in mine, our hands held firmly as he drove into me with final thrusts. He'd taken his time until I exploded, and now this was for him to take me, to bring himself to the edge with me. He hissed as he slammed into me harder. Our mesmerized gazes locked and he whispered my name, before coming deep inside me.

15

Close to a week had passed without any news from the council on the third test or my Vepar, and I missed them terribly. Worry bubbled in my gut at the delay. Everyone gossiped about what it meant, along with talking about me. Most now completely ignored me, well except out in public. There they pretended to be my friend, and I played the game. Maybe too well because they squirmed when I hugged them, and I made sure to do it every time. Ever since the team dinner where I vanished with Corran, they accused me of cheating and treated me even worse than before at the mansion.

A bitter breeze washed past, and the trees in the backyard swayed, their fruit swung back and forth like globes on a Christmas tree. This was the only place that the others left me alone most days and it gave me time to think--if I made the right decision to stay here.

Someone rushed across the yard, and I perked up.

"Luren," I called out as I caught the elf Vepar crossing the mansion yard, waving to him.

He glanced over, squinting beneath the glare of the two suns.

I stood from the bench near the mansion and ran toward him.

"Haven't seen you in days. Or the others. What's going on?" Nerves danced down my spine as I watched Luren's brow furrowed. He glanced back and forth before leaning in closer.

"I shouldn't be telling you this, but the council is selecting the mate today."

"What? But we haven't done the third test."

He turned away and continued his march across the yard, leaving me alone, not looking back. Dread sank through me.

Something happened...something bad. Why else had the Vepar disappeared and now suddenly there's a selection without the completion of the last ritual test.

My heart beat like it intended to stop, and sickness churned in my stomach. I rushed back to my room and shut the door, then paced when a message popped up on the monitor.

"Ella. Council have called you to the front yard."

I paced some more, not sure I wanted to find out who they selected. I couldn't stand it if it wasn't me. Except the Council picked their mate, not my men. My focus was scattered and I hurried into the common room's cylinder wardrobe, changing into a simple yellow, summer dress with short sleeves.

Despite the new clothes, I sweated, and couldn't bring myself to move. I hadn't expected the selection to happen this fast and had kept telling myself there was one more test and then I'd worry about the outcome. And now that it was here, panic strangled me because all I could think about were the what ifs.

What if they picked another girl?

What if I had to live with the Council?

What if my Vepar couldn't do anything about it?

What if I became a slave or they experimented on me?

But I had to finally get this done. I hurried my steps out of the room and toward the front entrance where the remaining women joined me. They all wore pale faces and worry crammed behind their eyes. They knew... We all knew something wasn't right.

Four of us lined up in front of the three Council members. At the side near a bubbling fountain of purple water, my three Vepar stood stoic, their emotions barren.

Terror consumed me. I remembered the Council's threat. If I didn't win, they would take me as their own.

A few staff were present, including Luren, but where were the media crew needing to publicize the event?

The one-horned Council member stepped forward, the blue cape he wore fluttered in the wind around his legs. "Thank you for your patience while we deliberated. This was a hard decision. The four of you who remain showed exceptional strength and bravery during the first test. The devotion and dedication were extraordinary in the social dates and confirmed you're each well suited to our matches." He paused for a moment, his gaze skimming over all of us, pausing on me a bit too long. "The third test... is complete."

Everyone murmured, and my mind was on fire. Had I missed a test?

"What third test?" Zeni called out.

"The dinner you were all called to was a test of keeping your emotions in check."

My mouth dropped open because I spent the whole time keeping to myself, never showing interest in the men, then I disappeared with Corran. Crap.

Everyone else cooed like birds... their fakeness made me sick.

The Council member raised his chin. "We've made our decision on who we believe is best suited for these three Vepar and our decision is final. The winner is Ella Monroe from Earth."

I rocked on my heels, convinced I hadn't heard right. I won?

The females around me gasped and cried out in protest. But the Council members didn't even congratulate me. They looked away and spun on their heels, then were ushered toward a small spacecraft sitting on the front lawn that took off almost instantly after they boarded.

"What just happened? This is a joke," Zeni cried.

My three Vepar watched everyone until they finally moved forward. Derrial collected my hands in his and drew me closer. Corran and Thane stood at my back, my protectors.

"This isn't fair!" Zeni wailed, and she glared at me, so much hatred projecting from her stare. She spun and rushed back into the mansion, while the other women stood there, lost and confused.

Derrial drew me with him into the house and the four of us marched to my bedroom. He shut the door behind us and stated, "Pack your belongings, we need to leave now. We're going home."

I turned to face my three men. "What just happened? I mean, it's my first mating ritual, but that seemed rather sorrowful."

Thane stepped alongside me. "You weren't going to be selected by the Council, so we had to... what do you say on Earth? Pull some strings."

"And we need to leave quickly," Corran murmured.

Worry rattled me. "Am I safe?"

"Of course, pet," Thane added. "It's just not safe here anymore."

I had so many questions, and I wanted to celebrate the win, knowing that I'd just gained myself three mates, which in itself was scary and exciting, but something felt wrong about today.

I glanced around to what had been my home for the past couple of weeks. "I don't have anything to pack."

"Good, you'll have everything you need at your new home." Derrial hauled me outside, and their speediness, their dread leeched into me. What were they so afraid of?

"What strings exactly did you have to pull?"

But no one answered as we rushed into the space vessel parked in the backyard. We climbed on, and without looking back, the door shut. We lifted into the air.

Suddenly, I felt like I'd somehow landed in the wolf's den. Thane sidled up next to me on the seats and drew me into his arms. His lips were on my cheek, my neck, my ear. "Don't worry, pet. We'll never let anything happen. But most importantly, you are officially ours by Veon law."

Then why did my instinct scream that something worse was waiting for me around the next corner?

16

(DERRIAL)

We were called to meet with the Council the next morning. We left Ella sleeping soundly in bed in the secure room we had created secretly in our home. We didn't know who to trust when it came to Ella, so we took all precautions. I fucking hated to leave her, but the Council would only get suspicious if we didn't show up.

As soon as we arrived it was clear that something was wrong. Zeni was standing next to one of the Councilmen, a triumphant grin on her face as we walked in.

"Why the hell is she here?" Thane snarled. He had wanted to break up with Zeni before any of us and had been the most resentful when we found out that she had lied. His feelings had obviously gotten stronger with time.

"Why were we not informed that Ella Monroe had a blood type almost guaranteed to be a success in Corran's trials?" asked one of the old fuckers.

I froze. How in the world did they find out? We had been holding them off claiming we had more tests to do.

"Zeni was able to procure some of the human's blood during the first Trial. She brought it to us and the test results just came back. She's a perfect match for genetic suitability."

None of us seemed to be able to speak. After everything we had done to try and protect Ella, we were watching it all crumble before our eyes.

"What tests did you run?" Corran demanded, trying to make it sound like they'd made a mistake.

"All the ones we needed," said Chloped, my least favorite of the Councilmen. "With the data we had already received from the first team about her parents, you should have known we would look into her," he continued happily.

"She belongs to us," Thane growled, looking like he was ready to destroy them all.

Vepar guards began to file into the room. The Council had clearly been expecting us to be angry, to retaliate and not take this lightly.

"The human is currently being escorted to a secure lab where we will begin the procedures," said Chloped. He pulled up a holographic image of a shell-shocked Ella being led out of our supposedly iron clad hiding place.

How the fuck did they find her?

"You surrendered your hold on her once you had her enter the Trials under false pretenses. She is now the property of Veon." Gunter smirked, pleased with himself.

I trembled with rage, not sure who I hated more, the Council or Zeni.

"You can leave now," Chloped ordered. "You are all currently suspended from your duties as we investigate your deception further."

Thane took a step forward and Corran and I both grabbed his arms before he could do anything to make matters worse.

It would take all three of us to save Ella.

BETRAYED

CONTENTS

BETRAYED

Survival is just the beginning. Ella must fight for love and freedom on the rim of the galaxy...

Years ago, the skies blackened with the arrival of the Vepar to Earth. Dominant and secretive, they changed the world, ruling over Earth with fear.

Ella's always been a survivor, a fighter. But now kidnapped, she finds herself on a foreign planet and running for her life.

The three men she fell for made a mistake. A grave mistake, and now their blood-mate, Ella must pay the price.

Fear drives them to keep Ella safe from the monsters who are determined to hunt her down and use the power in her blood for their own deadly purposes.

But what happens when Ella finds out that Thane, Derrial, and Corran might be the monsters she needs to fear the most....

I

Beeeeeep....

It felt like someone was trying to drill a hole through my head. Something tugged on my arm and pain sliced down my skin.

My eyes grew heavy like they had been glued shut.

What happened? I tried to retrace my steps. I had won the competition. The guys were mine. We were going to go somewhere...and then?

Fuck.

I tore my eyes open when I suddenly remembered what had happened. I say tore because that's what it actually felt like. Maybe those psycho scientists had glued my eyes shut. I wouldn't put it past them.

The room was white and sterile and there were beeps coming from everywhere. I wanted to go back to sleep just so I didn't have to hear their screeching anymore. It was hard to move like my body had been paralyzed. I started to take stock of all my body parts one by one.

I wiggled my toes first, giving a huge sigh of relief when they moved. I wouldn't put it past the Vepar to decide that baby incubators didn't need to have use of their limbs. I tried to move my legs next but all I could do was twitch them briefly. They must have given me some heavy meds because it felt like the hardest thing I had ever done to move my legs an inch. Giving up on my legs for a moment, I moved to my arms. I wiggled my fingers first and gave another sigh of relief when they moved. As soon as I tried to move my arms though, piercing pain shot through me. Glancing down, a scream gurgled from my throat.

There were at least ten wires or IVs or something sticking out of my arms. Panic curled in my chest, a scream building in my lungs. I pulled at them even though the movement made me want to throw up from the pain. I was faintly aware of an alarm sounding, mixing in with all the other beeps in the room, creating a cacophony of torture for my ears.

I heard frantic footsteps, and then I was surrounded by what seemed like twenty Vepar in white coats. They were yelling and gesturing and grabbing at me, but my mind was in such a state of panic that it was hard to comprehend what they were trying to say. Finally, one of them pulled out a sharp-looking needle and stabbed it into my upper arm.

I was so sick of being knocked out.

When I woke next, I saw the same scene. Except this time when I tried to move, I realized that I had been bound to the table underneath me with thick fabric around my hands and with leg cuffs. Before I could scream, a gorgeous Vepar with ebony hair pulled back severely from her face stepped into my field of vision. She wore a stark white lab coat and carried a calm expression on her face as if it was perfectly normal to chain humans to a lab table and stick things in them without their permission. Maybe it was on their planet, but back on Earth, it was called kidnapping. Veon needed to get with the times.

"How are you feeling today, Ella?" she asked kindly.

I stared at her shocked that she could even ask that with a straight face. "Let me out of here and I'll let you know," I ordered, struggling with my restraints.

"Now, Ella," she began, while typing in notes on her tablet as she observed me. "We really need you to calm down. It's very important your body is stress-free right now."

Was this Vepar for real?

"Are you having any cramps? Do you feel bloated?" she asked.

Why was she asking that?

She must have seen the confusion on my face because she smiled and patted my shoulder. I flinched, but she pretended not to notice. "We've been giving you a steady dose of fertility drugs and they often cause cramping and bloating. We just want to make sure that you're comfortable," she explained.

Sick dread spread all over my body. It was happening. My worst fear was being realized.

Where were the guys?

I started gagging as I tried to trace back my steps. What if the Trials had been a trick to get me to lower my guard? What if the guys were behind this?

I took a breath, trying to calm myself down. They wouldn't do this. Not after everything that had just happened. It would be like playing with your food before you ate it... making me do the Trials while they intended to use me as a baby-making machine the whole time.

Someone else was behind this... because they wouldn't do this, would they?

"Who are you?" I asked, my voice sounding scratchy from disuse. How long had I been out, and what had they done to my body?

She laughed self-deprecatingly. "Forgive me for being so rude. My name is Dr. Cryon. I'm one of the head researchers in this lab."

When I didn't respond to her introduction, she turned her attention to her tablet and started scrolling through something on it.

"Looks like it's time for your Bromocriptine," she remarked, setting her tablet down and grabbing an angry-looking syringe from off a stainless-steel table next to her.

The sight of the needle sent me into hysteria, and I began to thrash like a madwoman.

"Oh, dear," she said calmly before setting down the needle in her hand and picking up another one. "It looks like you need to spend a little bit more time relaxing before you're willing to cooperate."

I continued to pull at my restraints as she inserted the new syringe into my I.V. Her amused eyes were the last thing that I saw.

Coming out of whatever drug-induced sleep the doctor had put me in was a bitch. I lay there for what seemed like an hour, awake, but unable to open my eyes. It ended up coming in handy when some of the scientists started talking near me.

"We've searched every one of his databases, the entire file is missing."

"It's one piece of the puzzle, surely we can come up with it ourselves," barked a voice I recognized as Dr. Cryon's.

"It's a little more complicated than that," another voice said. "It took Corran years to find the right compound that made up for the genetic differences between the Vepar and the humans. Without that information, I just don't see how the subject can have a successful pregnancy. The genetic differences will just be too much," he continued worriedly.

"There hasn't been any sign of him has there?" Dr. Cryon asked.

"They've all disappeared. And a member of the Council's disappeared as well. They think it has to do with them."

"Are the risks just to the fetus?" the doctor asked suddenly, her voice contemplative.

"No. Unfortunately, there's a good chance that the subject would pass as well. In the tests that were initially run on subjects the genetic differences would always lead to the host body attacking the fetus."

"Attack? What did that consist of? Is there a way for us to control that?"

"In every experiment, the host body would get confused because the fetus's blood and host's blood would somehow mix. That would lead to an all-out assault on all of the host's internal organs. Their death was usually very messy. If I remember correctly, there was a lot of blood involved coming out of every orifice."

His words terrified me. All of this was said with total objectivity as if they were discussing the weather rather than whether someone lived or died. It was terrifying how little the Vepar seemed to care about what happened with the human race considering they were depending on said human race for *their* race's continued existence.

I made myself stay still as they continued to talk even though the urge to pull at my restraints was strong.

Just then a voice interrupted the conversation, a voice that simultaneously made me furious and filled me with dread.

"I would stop talking if I were you," said Zeni. "She's awake."

I heard footsteps and then there was a sharp poke in my arm that made my eyes fly open as I gasped in pain.

"Told you," Zeni said viciously.

I realized that the sharp pain I had felt was from her nails, nails that had been sharpened into talons. They fit her perfectly.

The doctors looked annoyed to have her there, but they didn't say anything when Zeni began fiddling with various objects on the table behind her.

Whatever deal she made with the Council in order to get me away from the guys obviously had come with a change in her title.

"So has the deed been done yet?" Zeni asked, playing with a wicked-looking needle.

"There have been some delays," Dr. Cryon said stiffly.

"What does that mean?" Zeni seethed.

"It means that my boyfriends weren't entirely pleased with your plan to get me pregnant without them, and they took some of the information with them," I said triumphantly, even though I was in no position to be triumphant in any form.

The doctor shot me an exasperated look.

"Corran was somehow able to take his research with him and we're missing a key part of the treatment," the doctor explained.

Zeni's face scrunched up in displeasure. "I believe the Council gave you specific instructions to deal with this creature," she said, gesturing to me. "She's to be fertilized immediately."

Dr. Cryon immediately objected. "Considering the risk and that this human is our best possible chance for a successful Vepar surrogacy, it would be unwise to attempt to do the embryo transfer without Corran's missing research."

"The Council is not going to wait. You need to do the transfer now, and then I suggest you start working your asses off to make sure that you uncover the missing information," Zeni ordered.

Dr. Cryon opened her mouth to object once more.

"Have you heard about the new law passed by the Council?" Zeni asked with a very satisfied look on her face.

"No, I haven't," Dr. Cryon explained stiffly. "But I'm sure that you're about to tell me."

Zeni's face flushed scarlet at the doctor's impotence. "Anyone found to be disobeying the Council's direct orders will be immediately imprisoned with the potential for further discipline if needed."

She looked over at me. "You can thank your mates for that," she said with a smirk.

The doctor and her companion both looked ill at the possibility of imprisonment. I could tell them it wasn't a walk in the park from first-hand experience.

Tears burned in my eyes. There was no way they weren't going to do the procedure now.

"You know it really is a pity," said Zeni. "This all could have been avoided if you had just taken me up on my offer and left when you had the chance."

I seriously doubted that I would've been allowed to leave the planet. Zeni would probably have arranged to have me shot down and killed or something like that.

"At least you can take comfort that if you die, absolutely no one will miss you," said Zeni sweetly.

"Are you meaning to talk about yourself?" I responded snidely. "Because we both know that the males around you have a habit of picking me over you."

"Let's get this started," Zeni barked at the doctor, her face turning red with fury at my words.

A resigned look passed over the doctor's face. She placed a hand over her ear. "Get the team in here," she ordered through the communicator device I knew that most of the Vepar had stored in their ear.

A team of at least ten Vepar began to flood the room.

This was really happening, my panic-filled stomach clenched. I tugged against the restraints frantically.

"A big congrats to the mother-to-be," cooed Zeni.

I had never hated someone more.

"I'm sorry about this," Dr. Cryon whispered to me, actually looking sorry.

I guess it was one thing to force someone to get pregnant. It was another thing to knowingly kill that person.

I didn't accept her apology.

"See you soon...or maybe never," Zeni crowed delightedly.

It was really too bad that the last thing I was going to remember was her disgusting face.

Dr. Cryon approached me with a needle that I knew would put me to sleep again.

All I could think as the room started to fade around me was that I wished I could have seen *their* faces one last time.

2

(DERRIAL)

"They'll never find out," I growled, sick of this shit and tired of looking at the Councilman's slackened body. Gritting my teeth, I ripped my gaze away. "Just shove him inside already and be done." Thane's lips twisted into a frown, but he knew I was right. He knew there was no other way. This Councilman, Chloped, ordered the blood tests on Ella and tricked us into surrendering our hold of her once she signed to enter the trials. Now, she was in a lab being experimented on.

My blood boiled at the thought.

I looked down at his security pass in my hand. This was our key to saving Ella. Torturing him to get information had been easy, he broke instantly. And once we learned the names of the scientists involved, we'd hunt them down to make them pay for their deceit. The Council was on that list too... they wanted us removed from power for gaining too much attention, too much popularity. My arms tightened at my side at the betrayal.

Not wasting a moment, Thane scooped his arms under the Councilman's armpits and dragged him into the space cruiser before dropping him. He landed on his back, his head hitting the floor with a thump, and laid there unconscious.

"Corran, everything's ready to go?" I looked over to him as he jabbed his finger onto the control monitor in his hand. Shadows crowded under his eyes, his posture curled forward, his black cork-screw horns now a deep gray... he always responded this way when he was angry. We all were angry; we weren't playing games anymore. We had Ella to rescue and nothing would stand in our way.

Corran nodded. "He won't wake up for the next month. His nutrients patches are inserted. All comms and navigation systems will disable by the time he wakes up. By then, he'll be on the outer edges of our galaxy, right into Nebian territory. Then he'll be their problem."

Thane dusted his hands and climbed out of the ship. "Those bastards will imprison anyone who steps foot in their territory."

"That's what I'm counting on."

He deserved so much worse but getting him off the planet didn't make him or his disappearance our problem. I gave Corran a nod and the door to the cruiser slid shut as he returned to his monitor to get the cruiser into space.

Thane and I marched across the hanger, my thoughts darkening each time I remembered the Councilman's words. *The human is currently being escorted to a secure lab where we will begin the procedures.*

With the information I'd dragged out of him, we'd found the location where they held Ella.

"Our ship's ready," Thane stated. "We won't be detectable on entry, but once we land, we'll have about ten minutes to get in and out of the place with Ella before they sense the vessel."

"That's tight, but we'll make it work." I shoved open the door to my small hideout I had built long ago once I realized that the Council pried into everyone's business. I had never truly trusted their agenda. Of course, my instinct had been right, and this place had come in handy. It wouldn't be safe for long though... not after we got Ella.

"We pack with no plans of returning," I ordered.

"Corran and I already have the coordinates set for our escape with Ella." Thane's words were clipped and short, all business. It was how he dealt with the fear that we'd somehow be too late, somehow find her gone or worse... dead.

My gut knotted; I couldn't think like that. "Perfect." I turned away and prepared to leave.

I was going to spill blood and break spines.

3

I hadn't expected to wake up, so when my eyes opened and the procedure room was visible around me, I immediately began to cry.

Looking around, there was no sign of Zeni or the doctor. There were just a few of the doctor's team huddled around a tablet, discussing something with each other.

I tried to move quietly, taking inventory of how my body was feeling. They hadn't explained the procedure to me, so I wasn't sure how they put the Vepar fetus in, if it was like how humans did IVF, or if it was put in another way.

Besides my head hurting, I didn't feel too different. Maybe they experienced a change of heart?

Remembering the look on Zeni's face and the fervor in her voice when she had ordered them to start the procedure, I didn't think that they would have been able to get around it with her in the room.

Dr. Cryon suddenly walked into the room with her male companion that had been introduced to me.

She looked very focused on me, and I expected her to start asking questions about how I was feeling. Instead, she turned to the two Vepar that had been talking on the other side of the room.

"You're needed in the east building," she said to them.

They immediately nodded and left the room, not even glancing over to where I was strapped in.

The doctor waited for a long minute. She seemed to be listening to their footsteps as they faded down the hall. I wondered what was going on.

Suddenly her companion was by the table, unbuckling the straps that had me trapped to the table.

I looked over at them confused. "What's going on?" I asked, wondering if I would now be allowed more freedom because the procedure had been done.

They didn't answer any of my questions, not even when all of the straps had been released, and I was sitting up. Dr. Cryon carefully helped me off the table since I was feeling weak after laying down for who knows how long.

"Can you walk?" she asked, a hint of urgency in her voice.

"I think so," I croaked, my voice groggy from my latest blackout session. Hopefully, there wouldn't be long term damage from being knocked out so many times. I wondered how much the effect of Vepar medicine on the human system had been studied. I was doubting very much based on their attitude towards the human race as a whole.

I wasn't sure why I was thinking of that at the moment. I really should just be excited that I seemed to be alive. Unless this was the afterlife and I had been doomed to hell, the hell where I was the Vepar puppet for eternity.

Now I was just being dramatic.

"We need to go," the doctor's male companion said fiercely to her.

I was so confused.

Dr. Cryon began to quickly walk towards the door. Her companion nudged me to follow them. I began to walk, my gait unsteady as we went along.

The doctor looked back. "We're going to need to go quicker than this," she ordered.

Nodding, the male Vepar picked me up in his arms and began trotting behind the doctor who had left the room.

"What's going on? What's the rush?" I asked, but he kept his focus dead ahead. "Please just tell me where you're taking me." Fear slid down my spine, and I began to jerk in his arms, trying to get away.

"Keep still," he muttered under his breath. "We're helping you."

I stopped struggling immediately. Helping me? "How?"

All of a sudden, one of the doctor's team members came out into the hall. A younger woman with short cropped orange hair and matching irises. She stopped short, looking at us confused. "Isn't she supposed to remain laying down for at least a few hours after the procedure? What's going on?" she asked him.

Dr. Cryon stepped forward. "It's okay, Teky, We're transferring her to the lab. We received instructions for additional tests."

Teky's wide nostrils flared, her fierce gaze meeting mine, and I could have sworn somewhere behind that gaze, she held pity for me. My head spun with confusion and I wanted to scream, to run. But the man's arms tightened against me like he sensed me panicking. I had to believe him and the doctor were helping me, had to trust these strangers who experimented on me at Zeni's command. I had no plan B to escape aside from my three Vepar coming to rescue me.

Teky stepped aside, and I was rushed forward, bouncing in the man's arms. I let myself cradle against him, my head resting on his shoulder as I prayed for once that something was going to go in my favor.

It wasn't long before we stepped outside, bright sunlight beaming down on us. I lifted my head, squinting my eyes to find that we stood behind a building made of a kind of plexiglass... or maybe it was glass, minus the transparency. Wide open land spread out before us... all green grass and trees of varied colors in the distance.

A small gray space cruiser sat a few feet away.

The man set me on my feet. I wobbled at first before I caught my balance. "You're free," his rushed words whispered as he pointed to the ship. "That ship will take you from here and back to Corran."

"You're letting me go?" I faced him and the doctor. I knew the looks on their faces. Something terrible was going to happen to me and they wanted no part of it.

"Is Corran on that ship?" I asked as I stared at the vessel.

"It's a friend. He'll help take you to Corran. Now go, stop wasting time." Dr. Cryon gave a shove to my back, and I stumbled forward.

My heart sank to my feet as I stared at them over my shoulder, tears pooling in my eyes. "Thank you." Both of them met my gaze for a sliver of time, worry pulling their expressions taut, then they turned and rushed back into the building.

They risked too much to release me, to not follow Zeni's orders, and I didn't blame them. She was a massive bitch and I was sure there would be repercussions.

Wasting no time, I burst across the field, moving as fast as my exhaustion allowed, my sights set on the ship. Each step shot pain through my body, but I wouldn't stop. Not when it meant seeing my guys again and stopping the experiments. Corran would help me, he'd fix whatever they did in that lab.

Vibrations suddenly traveled up my legs from the ground, and I glanced down and around me, seeing nothing. I turned to stare at the building, expecting to find guards chasing me down.

Except, a long ship with upward bent wings hovered in the air between me and the lab. My breaths were barreling out of me as panic lashed over my chest.

They'd found me!

I spun and ran, my feet punching the ground.

My teeth chattered, and I sprinted madly. Adrenaline pushed me, numbing all pain. But the closer I got to the gray cruiser, the more something looked wrong.

The side of the vessel came into view and it had a gaping hole across the back half, its edges charred black. Someone had shot the vessel. My brain wasn't catching up with the sight fast enough or I might have burst out crying.

Ice-cold fingers gripped my arm, and I jumped at the touch, but they swung me around with such force, I tripped over my own feet.

Stumbling, I fell to my knees and looked up to an alien wearing a black body-hugging suit that glinted in the sun. Dark oily hair was slicked off his face, and his cheeks were hauntingly gaunt. Black eyes blinked down at me.

"Khonsu!" I whimpered, punching his grip with my free hand, trying to scramble backward. "Leave me alone!"

"So, this one can talk. She'll be popular." He wrenched me to my feet and tossed me over his shoulder like I weighed nothing, and in two flashes, the darkness stole the sunlight.

I glanced up to find myself inside a ship... the enemy's ship. He tossed me onto the floor, and I landed so hard, all the air was knocked out of my lungs. I gasped for air, when the forcefield shot up in front of me, trapping me inside a confined corner of the ship.

Jolting to my feet, I cried out, "Release me now."

But the two Khonsu settled into the seats at the front of the vessel and the shuttle trembled before we lurched forward. Unlike Corran's ship, this thing shook like a rust bucket.

"Let me go!" I continued to scream while searching the area for any weapons, but the place was barren. Just black walls closing me in.

4

I was in a corral, that was the only way to describe it. Inside were what seemed like hundreds of beautiful women around me, in various states of dress or undress as it may be. A girl next to me was wearing what looked like an outfit from Xena, Warrior Princess, that TV show that had been popular when I was young.

The ground was covered in a thick lush green grass, and there was a metal fence around the outside of us. A faint buzzing filled the air, and I suspected that the fence was electric. The women were trying to stay as far from it as possible.

I let out a small shriek when a creature passed outside the fence in front of me. It looked similar to the monster that we'd encountered and killed during the trials. Like that one, it was standing on two feet, the color of its skin a muddy green. It looked over at me, and its piercing yellow eyes had my heart beating faster. It opened its mouth and smiled at me, if you could call it a smile with its sharp teeth that looked to be leaking a fluorescent green saliva. Where in the world had I found myself now?

The leather bikini girl, as I'd been calling her in my head, put her hand gently on my shoulder.

"Are you all right?" she asked. I could tell she was a Vepar because of her vibrant, almost glowing, blue eyes. That and the horn that was extending out of the middle of her forehead. It didn't take away from the fact that she was beyond attractive though.

"What is this place?" I asked, choking in the delirious screams that were threatening to erupt out of me as another creature walked by outside the enclosure.

It seemed like they were acting as guards of some sort. Looking beyond them, I could make out brown domes dotting the landscape around the corral. They were similar to the Vepar structures, just a little rougher looking as if there hadn't been as much time or technology put into creating them.

"You don't recognize this place?" she said with a broken laugh.

I shook my head. "Those are Khonsu though, I recognize them at least," I said, taking a deep breath to try and relax. I obviously wasn't going anywhere at the moment.

"This is their capital city," she explained, brushing off a piece of dirt on her arm.

Corran, Derrial, Thane. I suddenly thought, everything coming back to me.

Constantly being knocked out couldn't be good for my brain, it was clear that I was beginning to forget things. If this kept happening there was going to be permanent damage.

Fear and regret darted through me. The doctor had said that Corran was in that grey ship. What had happened to him? Where were the others?

I began to look around for them frantically, just on the off chance they were here somehow. The female Vepar put another comforting hand on my shoulder. "You need to calm down. You'll only attract their attention by acting like this. I'm pretty sure they can sense fear and they feed off of it," she said.

I glanced over at her. She appeared perfectly calm. As if she wasn't in the camp of the Vepar's worst enemy, or at least what I thought was the Vepar's worst enemy. I still knew next to nothing about these people.

"How are you not freaking out right now?" I asked as my body began to tremble. "And what are we doing here? Why are we in a corral?" As I was talking, my gaze continued to scan the landscape for my men. I had been suspicious of them since the beginning. I thought we had finally gotten to a good place. I should be more trusting than this. There was no way they had been working with Dr. Cryon. Right?

"You're the human, aren't you?" she asked understandingly.

I nodded hesitantly.

"I thought that you were just hiding your Vepar features so as not to attract attention. But this is how you look, isn't it?" she asked, eyeing me head to toe.

"Yep, no horns for me," I said jokingly, not even sure how I was able to joke right now about anything.

"You would look good with horns," she said with a serious tone. That hysterical edge of laughter threatened to erupt again, and I had to use all my effort to tamp it down.

"So, you know what we're doing here?" I asked, redirecting her to the issue at hand.

Her face sobered. "I've only been told about it, but I believe that we're here for the Tangazi, or Mating hunt in your language," she said softly.

The word "hunt" made my blood freeze. I knew all about being hunted by the Khonsu. First by the one who had come after me on earth, and second by the monster in the woods.

"Can the Khonsu take different forms?" I asked, realizing that no one had explained this to me.

"They have many different forms. What you see walking around this area is their real form. It's my understanding that they can look however they want, although I haven't seen that myself."

I nodded, that explained a lot. I had to admit that I much preferred their other forms to the monsters currently patrolling the area. I shivered, thinking of how that first Khonsu had tortured me, flaying off pieces of my skin while I shrieked in agony. Maybe I did prefer this form actually, at least it didn't look like they had whips on their person, if it were even capable of carrying whips in its clawed hands.

"What does this mating hunt consist of?"

She threw me a look of sympathy.

"Just what it implies. They let us loose, and then go hunt us. And whoever catches you is your new mate," she said in a haunted voice.

True terror surged through me. "It sounds so barbaric. Why wouldn't they just mate with their own kind?" I asked.

"Now what fun would that be?" she asked sarcastically. "They wouldn't be the Khonsu if even their mating rituals didn't involve fear and destruction."

I saw a flash of blonde hair, or at least I thought I did. And I looked hopefully to see if it was Derrial. But whatever I'd seen had disappeared.

"Why are you here? Did you venture too far from the Vepar cities?" I asked.

A look of rage briefly passed over her face before she smoothed it out. "I'm here because many of the Vepars are just as bad as the Khonsu, if not worse."

A wave of pity passed over me. It was obvious that this poor woman had a dark story.

"I'm Ella," I offered with a small smile. I was grateful that this Vepar woman wasn't treating me as the rest had and was taking the time to at least explain things to me. I knew if Zeni were here, she would probably be throwing me up against the electrical fence at my audacity to ask any questions.

"My name is Bruda," she answered with her own small smile.

"Bruda," I repeated, thinking that the tough sounding name perfectly fit this Vepar who resembled a warrior Princess.

"Do you know when the hunt is supposed to start?" I asked, still desperately looking around for help.

It was interesting to watch the women around us. Some of the others were Vepars, but most were definitely of different alien races. They all were distinctly feminine, but also distinctly alien looking.

A woman off to my right was a dark, inky blue color. She had tubes coming out of her head instead of hair. The tubes were held back in some kind of elaborate headband. Her eyes were completely black, no white showing, and I jumped when they briefly turned to me, before losing interest quickly.

I was guessing it would be helpful in this situation that I resembled a form that the Vepar could take.

There were three gorgeous women off to my left, who were all a bottle green color. I gasped in amazement when I realized that there was a tube connecting the three of them. Literally, they were all one entity. It was like our conjoined twins back on earth, except in this case they had three distinct bodies.

Bruda must've seen me staring, because she made a small coughing sound to get my attention. They're from the Dacasi," she explained.

"Many of the women there are born into groups of threes like that."

"What do they do about dating, having sex, or anything else?" I asked.

She laughed. "Women on that planet who are born to a pairing like that, which is almost all of them really, all marry the same man. That takes care of all of those issues."

For a second, I wondered if my guys felt like that, like they were connected for life, since they were all dating me. What a strange life I had ended up having.

"Do they not have different species on your earth?" she asked.

We had gotten off topic, I needed to know about a million more things about this "hunt" before it started, but it was probably good for both of us to have some sort of distraction right now. It wouldn't hurt for me to answer a few questions.

"There are a lot of different species on Earth," I explained. "But before the Vepar invaded, we weren't aware that there were any other species from different planets on Earth."

Her eyes widened. "Really, there weren't any? So you thought..."

"So we thought we were all alone in the universe?" I asked self-deprecatingly. "Yes. As stupid as that sounds, we did think we were alone on the planet. That obviously has changed now."

She shivered. "Surely your leaders must have known. I can't imagine living in such a state of ignorance."

"We really didn't know any other way," I told her honestly. Thinking of the phrase 'ignorance is bliss.' I think I missed being able to be ignorant.

"I really don't think that our leaders knew either. But maybe I'm wrong about that. Our leaders are a bit lock lipped about state secrets to the common people."

She nodded.

"Bruda, I would love to answer whatever questions you have about Earth and the humans, but I need to know about this situation we're in before I can do that."

She nodded again, and I was once more glad that I had landed myself next to her. "Stories of the mating hunt are told to all Vepar children growing up. It's a story that our parents tell us to try and keep us in line. "Be nice to your brother, Bruda, wouldn't want to have to send you to the Vepar for the hunt," my parents would tell us. "The stories could never compare to the real thing though," she said looking around us in disgust. "Obviously everything that I've heard is rumor. But how I've been told that it works is that sometime soon, sometime this week at least, the Khonsu men who are looking for mates will gather in an arena and we will be brought in to be inspected. They examine our looks, the strength of our teeth, use their technology to look at our fertility probability... Basically take stock of our assets," she explained.

My terror at this point was so thick that it was hard to breathe. They would know I was human. What if their technology could pick out what was special about my blood? What if I was already pregnant, what would they do? Horror like I'd never felt before swept through me.

"You're not fainting on me, are you? You've got to stay strong," Bruda ordered.

I took a deep breath, unwilling to tell her exactly why I was so afraid. A few more deep breaths seemed to calm me down.

"Continue," I said, proud of myself for keeping my voice calm.

"After they've showcased us to the hunters, they take us into the woods on their mountain."

"Their mountain?" I asked perplexed.

She nodded. "The Khonsu have a mountain that they consider sacred. All of their important rituals are done within their woods or at the peak of the mountain. It's called Velati."

She turned me around and I saw where the giant mountain was located in the distance.

"And what happens on that mountain?" I asked, dread trickling down my spine because I knew what she was going to say next.

"There, we are hunted," she said matter-of-factly. "Each Khonsu male who is participating in the hunt would've located their favorite based on the exhibition in the arena. They let us out into the woods under the guise that there's a chance we could escape. But obviously that never happens," she said with a whisper. "Once the Khonsu male catches their desired mate, the woman is then taken to the top of the mountain. And there she is raped on their sacred stone or in the woods or wherever they please." Bruda delivered this news in a voice void of any emotion.

My body felt like it was going to collapse. Raped. There had actually been quite a few times in my life where I had been touched without my permission, and there had definitely been situations that could've led to rape if I hadn't been saved. I thought of the prison guard in the hallway where Thane had saved me.

Who was going to save me this time though? A wave of loneliness passed over me. I had just gotten to the point where I had felt safe for the first time in my life, and then it had been ripped away.

A thought hit me just then. What if the guys were dead? What if they had been found out after I had been captured?

"I'd been expecting that when I learned it was called a 'mating hunt'" I said softly, trying to distract myself from the terrifying images that had filled my mind of the guys each being tortured and killed in various ways.

At that moment Bruda reached over and squeezed my hand, an act of solidarity and compassion that brought tears to my eyes.

"And then after the hunt, is there a marriage ceremony?" I asked with a faint laugh.

"According to what I've heard, by performing the..." she hesitated before continuing. "By performing the ritual, on their sacred mountain, that acts as the marriage ceremony."

I looked around and examined all of the women in the corral, all women that at least to me didn't look like they were Khonsu.

"Why don't they take their own women for their mates?" I asked.

"I've heard through gossip that the Khonsu women have the same fertility problems as the Vepar women. Unlike the Vepar, the Khonsu have no problem going outside of their race. From what I've heard, the Khonsu gene is dominant to all but the Vepar and any characteristics of other species are thus not carried over during the mating process. The child is born a Khonsu then for all intents and purposes."

I was immediately outraged upon hearing that. "If the Vepar genes are so strong, why was it so important to them then to take over Earth where the humans there have similar characteristics to them? Why couldn't they just go with another species and let the Vepar genes dominate whatever child was born?" I asked, furious at the idea that Earth could've been taken over for no reason.

Bruda was already shaking her head before I had finished ranting.

"Unfortunately, the Vepar genes do not work that way. The Vepar can only mate with compatible bloodlines, and your Earth is the only planet that's been found to have beings that are compatible to us." She cocked her head, staring at me intently. "That is the reason that you are here, is it not? Even on Earth you were the only one found to be compatible."

I looked at her suspiciously. How would she know that? I knew it was common knowledge for the Council and Corran's scientists, but I didn't think that the regular Vepar population would've heard about me.

She sighed. It was starting to get dark, and the last rays of Veon's two suns cast her in a haunting orange glow. "As I'm sure you're aware now, the Council's become corrupt. Your men were gone for too long. After they were gone, the Council decided that although they could not mate, they could still play."

I inhaled a shaky breath. The pain she had endured was so tangible, I could taste it on my tongue. Bruda had suffered immensely.

Her voice faded to a whisper, and I had to lean in closer to her to be able to hear her as she continued to haltingly speak.

"I was stolen from my parents and used as a slave for their pleasure."

"How did you end up here?" I asked gently, thinking that she was a beautiful woman. Whatever horrors she had been through had not affected her beauty.

"When I was first taken as the Council's pet, I complied with whatever they wanted thinking that it would make things easier if I just went along with it. But as time passed, I couldn't keep going. I started to fight back, making it so that every interaction was a battle. Although some of the Council members were into that sort of thing, the others didn't think that I was worth it. After all, there are a million women on Veon with the same looks as me. I was sent here as punishment, a gift to the Khonsu by the corrupt Council."

I didn't know what to say. I was shocked. I obviously had hated the Council for my own reasons but knowing the depths of their depravity took my hatred to a whole other level.

I suddenly remembered what she had said, that the Khonsu didn't mate with the Vepar because of the gene domination issues. Plus, the Vepar women were infertile so that wouldn't work to begin with. I looked at her confused.

"You're wondering why I'm here if I can't have children?" she asked, a resigned look on her face.

I nodded, feeling bad that I was having her answer all of these difficult questions. "I'm here to continue what I was doing for the Council. But there's not a Khonsu male alive that won't enjoy my noncompliance."

I didn't know what was worse. If they thought I was a Vepar, or if they realized I was the evidently amazing alien baby breeding machine that I actually was.

Big ugly tears streamed down my face, garnering stares from the surrounding women. I didn't know how they were all handling this so well. If only they weren't, maybe we could all storm the walls or something and get out of here.

I laughed a little bit hysterically. That obviously wouldn't work. Not with the Khonsu in their beast forms patrolling the area. One swipe with their claws and we would be goners.

Then Bruda did something I would never forget. She gathered me in her arms and began to softly sing a haunting melody. Thanks to Corran's language chip, I was able to understand it even though it was in Vepar.

I didn't understand all the terms. Even translated some of the Vepar words were too alien for my mind to comprehend.

But it filled me with peace. The fact that someone like Bruda, who had been through a life that was a literal nightmare for who knows how long, could offer comfort to me...Well, the world...or worlds as it was couldn't be that bad of a place.

I stayed in her arms as the sun set. Too scared to go to sleep, we spent the night talking about Earth.

"I would like to visit it one day," she said wistfully. "It sounds beautiful."

I thought of Veon and how beautiful it was, even compared to Earth. I thought of the poverty I had experienced on my planet, the loss of my parents. "Beautiful things sometimes hide the most terrible things," I told her.

She stared off into the distance as a pack of Khonsu in their beast forms ran by. "I know all about that."

We both somehow drifted off to sleep, but we were awakened savagely by loud horns and laughing and roaring crowds that had gathered outside of the corral.

I sat up in alarm as did Bruda. "It must be time," she said sadly.

I couldn't answer her. I finally saw that the other women in the pen were starting to look nervous. They looked even more nervous when at least a hundred of the Khonsu in their beast forms surrounded the pen and started to chant loud savage sounds that shook the ground. It was terrifying to see so many of them in one place, gnashing their teeth. I noticed that the ground sizzled where their green saliva fell on it.

"Do they hunt us in those forms?" I asked in a horrified voice.

"I don't know," Bruda said in a worried tone. "I don't know how we would make it to the top of the mountain if they did though, so let's hold off panicking about that."

I had become accustomed to the slight buzzing of the electrical fence, so I noticed right away when it stopped. Suddenly, a section of the fence started to slide by, creating an opening. Several of the Khonsu guards came to the opening and grunted at us to start moving. Apparently, they weren't able to communicate in their beast forms.

One by one we started to file out. I could feel the Khonsu's leering gazes as we walked by, and it reminded me of that first Khonsu who had looked at me like I was more food than a person.

I couldn't help but look in the crowd for any of the guys. Despite my initial doubts, I was sure that they hadn't betrayed me. If they had wanted to use me for a certain purpose, they would've given me to the Council to begin with. As it was, they had sacrificed everything to try and make me safe. I was pretty positive that they loved me.

Although Bruda had said that the exhibition happened in their arena, there were so many Khonsu both in beast and man forms gathered around us, that it seemed like the exhibition had already started.

I was sure the view of the women as we walked resembled a kaleidoscope of colors. It seemed like almost every female there had to be from a different planet.

A Khonsu near me made strange moans as I walked by. Just like some of the more despicable men on earth, the Khonsu grabbed themselves and started rutting their hips like animals as we walked by.

I was going to be sick.

There were females sprinkled among the crowd, and I assumed they were the Khonsu women. They looked worn down, unhappy, and resigned with their lives. I didn't think that bade well for any of the women marching in this line.

I was still dressed in the hospital gown that I had been put in, and I was sure that my hair was all over the place. It didn't seem to matter though as the Khonsu's eyes seemed to always find me. And it looked like they liked what they saw.

It became easier to try and ignore their looks, and I concentrated on studying the Khonsu city. It seemed like unlike the Vepar, who preferred to have space between their dwellings, the Khonsu didn't mind living close to one another.

They didn't seem to have the technology that the Vepar did to cook food, as I could see smoke coming out of the tops of some of the dwellings. Most of the buildings were plain, but occasionally we would pass by some that had silvery markings all around the entrance.

Bruda leaned closer as we passed by an especially elaborate one. "Those markings denote the elite of the Khonsu culture. The ink used to make the markings is very expensive, and only certain families possess it."

I nodded; thankful she knew so much about the Khonsu.

I came to a screeching halt a moment later when we passed by what looked like a courtyard. There were five very human looking Khonsu playing with the black whips that had been used to torture me. My mouth opened in a silent scream as I saw that they were using the whips on a dozen tiny creatures that possessed shiny white fur. The little creatures were emitting shrieks of pain that threatened to burst my eardrums.

Losing my head momentarily, I took a step forward to go to them. I was only stopped by Bruda grabbing my arm tightly. "You cannot intervene. Do you want them to use those whips on you?" she hissed urgently.

Resuming my slow walk in line, I shivered as we left the screams behind us.

Bruda was silent for a moment as we marched. "What was that back there? Do you have no sense of self-preservation?" she asked.

"I know exactly what those whips feel like. Forgive me if it was hard to see them using them on such innocent creatures," I said softly.

"You're going to need to toughen up if you are going to survive this next part," Bruda said matter-of-factly.

I could see what had to be the arena rising in front of us in the distance. Unlike the dome like structures that made up their dwellings, the arena looked to be a perfectly square copper colored box. I had never seen anything like it.

"From what I've been told, the Khonsu will do whatever to get their prey in the hunt," Bruda continued urgently. "If you're going to fight, be prepared to have those whips used on you again."

The thought of those whips touching me again almost made me want to just give in. "Almost" being the important word.

We arrived at the arena. Unlike the crudeness of their dwellings, the arena's outside walls were perfectly smooth. A few of the guards at the front of the line made some grunting noises, and the wall in front of us began to slide open.

I gasped as we walked inside. There had to be thousands of Khonsu in both beast and their human looking forms sitting on stands that appeared to be floating in the air. The bottom two rows of the stands held only human looking Khonsu, however. They were all dressed in dark purple tunics. The fact that their eyes were lit up in anticipation let me know that these were the Khonsu who would be taking part in the hunt.

"I bet their dicks are small," I muttered to Bruda, who let out a surprised snort.

The guard ahead of us looked backwards to make sure we were following him and must've seen the smirks on both of our faces. He rolled his eyes. "Pay attention," he barked at us. We immediately sobered up.

In the center of the arena was a large open space with packed dirt that was so smooth it almost looked like a giant basketball court. A pedestal stood in the very middle, where I presumed we would be put on display one by one for observation by the crowd.

The beastly guards at the head of our line made a roaring sound and the women in front of me all stopped. A Khonsu with oily black hair that reminded me of the first Khonsu that I had met, dressed in crimson robes, appeared from behind us and walked towards the pedestal, paying no attention to the prisoners he passed by.

He stood up on the pedestal and tapped his throat three times. The arena immediately went silent.

"Let the Tangazi begin," he said in a voice that reminded me of a hissing snake. The crowd immediately began to roar again. The Khonsu dressed in the purple robes stood in unison as if they had practiced the movement. They began to beat their fists over their hearts. The loud thumping sound echoed across the arena, sending shivers down my spine.

The Khonsu on the pedestal stepped down and impatiently signaled the first female prisoner to step up on the pedestal. Another Khonsu male stepped forward with some kind of device in his hand. He waved it in front of the terrified looking female, a beautiful alien with gold looking skin and green hair that shimmered down her back. A series of numbers appeared above her head.

I leaned toward Bruda. "What are those?" I asked, gesturing to the numbers.

She looked at me wide-eyed. "I have no idea. But it can't be good," she admitted, and her response terrified me.

The Khonsu with the device said something to the female and she opened her mouth, displaying her teeth.

I again leaned towards Bruda. "What's their obsession with teeth?" I asked. I must have said something humorous because a smile crossed her face despite our dire circumstances.

"Are good teeth not important on your planet?" she asked.

"I mean I guess they are, but not to this extent," I replied, listening as the crowd cheered at the beautiful alien's display of her shiny, shark-like teeth.

I suddenly regretted all of the dentist visits I had been forced to attend growing up. Maybe if my teeth weren't so straight and shiny the Khonsu wouldn't want me.

The Khonsu must've been pleased with her exhibition, because she was led off the pedestal much more gently then she had been put on it.

Dread curdled in my stomach as female after female was displayed. Some of them garnered appreciation so loud that my eardrums threatened to burst while others had much quieter receptions. I somehow thought that those prisoners were the luckier ones as they were more likely to have less Khonsu after them once the hunt began.

Bruda had been standing behind me, but when there were only three females in front of us, she stepped in front of me. I wasn't sure why she was so intent on protecting me, but I was grateful for it. She grabbed my hand behind her back and squeezed it in solidarity. Her strength gave me strength. Whatever happened, I could get through it. I would live through it. If Bruda could do it, so could I.

Bruda was finally called. She stepped up onto the stone pedestal, her head held high. Shrieks, hisses, and loud cheers from the crowd filled the air. They obviously could tell that there was their enemy, a Vepar, standing in front of them. And they loved that she was their prisoner.

Bruda clasped her hands behind her back, the only sign of nerves a slight trembling of her hands. She kept her head held high, her brown hair floating in the soft breeze. She really did look like the picture of a warrior princess standing there.

The crowd grew louder and louder, and I could see the anticipation in the purple clad Khonsu's eyes as they stared at her. They would be well aware that she couldn't provide them children, so the glimmer of excitement in their eyes could only mean one thing-that they were excited at the prospect of torturing her. I couldn't think of anything I could do to help her.

The Khonsu were yelling strange words at Bruda, words that my translator once again couldn't pick up. I could tell by their connotation though they weren't anything good. Still Bruda kept her chin held high, refusing to let them know that they were affecting her.

Numbers appeared in the air over her head. I still hadn't figured out quite what they meant, but I saw that the bottom score was a zero. Perhaps that was her fertility score? That would make sense it was a zero and none of the others had been a zero if the Vepar was the only race that the Khonsu couldn't have children with.

Bruda's teeth were checked, and then she was finished, and it was my turn.

I took a deep breath, determined to put on as brave a face as Bruda had just done. I stepped onto the pedestal and the same hissing and cheers filled the air as they had with Bruda. They thought I was another Vepar so of course it made sense for them to act that way. I kept my chin held high, holding onto the sides of my hospital gown. I was well aware of how naked I was underneath it and wished so badly that I had some form of undergarments on. I had never imagined myself in a position like this.

I could tell when the numbers appeared above my head, because the crowd all of a sudden descended into silence. I took a peek upwards, and was terrified to see that the bottom number, the one that I suspected was a measure of fertility, read one million.

It was like the crowd took a collective breath, and then all hell broke loose. Khonsu, even the ones not dressed in purple tunics, were trying to clamber off their benches to get onto the field to get to me.

The two that had been in charge of the exhibition started screaming and yelling to try to gain order, but there was nothing they could do.

It was pure pandemonium, and I was pretty sure that my worst fears were about to be realized a little bit earlier than I had anticipated.

Evidently, I was never going to make it to the sacred rock.

I was going to die out here.

When an especially fierce looking Khonsu, who was halfway transformed between his beast form and his normal form was just about to touch me with a long clawed hand, a sudden bolt of electricity burst out of the ground, covering the entire field with an electrical shock save the stone pedestal I was standing on. All of the Khonsu who had rushed the field had been struck down with the blast. I watched as they convulsed in agony, some of them still attempting to move towards me despite their obvious pain.

At this point, all semblance of me remaining calm was gone. I was shaking as I watched them all writhe on the ground. Some of them looked like parts of them had been charred. It was a gruesome sight.

Looking behind me was even worse. I cried out when I saw what had happened. There had been three captives left in line behind me. They had been roasted to a crisp in the blast and were almost unrecognizable. Obviously whatever electrical waves went out catered towards the Khonsu and was deadly towards other races.

The beautiful blue alien that I had first caught sight of in the corral was one of the fallen. I only could tell it was her because her headband had been bejeweled, and somehow it had survived the blast and was lying near her body. A deep sense of loathing passed over me. This had happened because of me. Whatever mutation was in my blood that caused the alien male species to absolutely lose their minds, had also caused these females' deaths. It was bad enough that they had been prisoners to begin with, but there could've been a chance that maybe the Khonsu who caught them would've been a good mate for them. Not a large chance, but still a chance. Or maybe they would've even escaped or been saved by their planets. Now they would never get that chance.

I was yanked out of my mourning by the Khonsu who must've set off the blast, the one who had been in charge of the ceremony, with the crimson robes. He pulled me away without saying a word.

A path had been cleared to where the other prisoners had been taken. I could see them huddled in the tunnel we were walking towards, their faces alight with fear. Bruda was at the head of them, her face twisted in horror and relief at the sight of me.

She rushed toward me. "Are you all right?" she cried.

I was shaking so much I could barely respond. "I can't believe that happened," I said.

I didn't get a chance to speak with her further. The crimson robed Khonsu dragged me by an arm past the long line of frightened prisoners.

"Where are you taking me?" I cried.

"Somewhere safe," he growled. "You'll be in isolation until it's time for the hunt to begin." He looked back at me, his eyes dragging from my head all the way to my toes, making me feel like I was naked and dirty. "It would be to the benefit of our race if I let all of them have you though," he said with a smirk. "You're so fertile, who knows how many Khonsu children you could give us."

I threw up right then and there. There was nothing but bile since I hadn't been fed in twenty-four hours, but it was enough to make me not look as palatable.

"Let's go," he ordered with a disgusted look on his face.

I was thrown into a concrete cell. Two guards were set up outside of the entrance to my cell. They didn't even look at me, and I wondered what special orders they had been given concerning me. At least it didn't seem like they were going to jump me.

I was alone and freezing, but a tray full of food that resembled vegetables was pushed into the room eventually along with a faded, threadbare blanket. I guess they figured that it wouldn't be good for my fertility for me not to eat at all.

I picked at the food despite the fact that I was starving. It was hard to muster up a willingness to eat when I couldn't get the scene from the field out of my head.

The night was long. Without Bruda to help me pass it, it felt like it stretched on forever. Like I had actually lived several nights instead of just one.

I was exhausted when one of the guards finally opened the cell door.

"Get up," he barked.

My joints felt frozen with the cold, and I stumbled a bit trying to get up. He led me down a long hallway. When we finally got outside of the arena, I was relieved to see the rest of the female prisoners waiting outside of a small spaceship that I assumed would be transporting us to where the hunt began. It reminded me of the ship we had been taken on during the Vepar trials.

That had seemed a lot less foreboding then the situation now did, however.

Looking around, I realized that I didn't see Bruda anywhere. Were their multiple ships? Had some of the female prisoners already been taken? I hadn't counted how many of us there were, but it looked like all the other prisoners were here based on the ones I had remembered. What had happened to her?

I felt a sense of panic. Once I was released by the guard to mingle with the rest of the prisoners, I turned to the alien closest to me. "Excuse me, have you seen the Vepar that I was with yesterday? The one dressed in a leather outfit with dark brown hair?" I asked her. The alien I spoke to was gorgeous, just like all the others, with shiny orange skin and hair that was a flaming red color. Her eyes matched her hair.

She scanned the crowd around us. "I haven't seen her. Not since last night. I didn't notice anyone being taken away though, so she must be around here somewhere."

"So there hasn't been another ship that's left for the mountain?" I asked.

She shook her head at me sympathetically. "No, as far as I know, with the exception of the ones who died yesterday, the rest of us are still here."

I nodded despondently. There wasn't anything I could do about Bruda's disappearance at the moment. I just hoped that she was okay. It was a stupid thing to hope since how any of us could be okay in a situation like this as a prisoner of the Khonsu. But I still sent up a silent prayer that something good had happened to her. She deserved it.

If I ever got a chance, I would try to find out what happened to her.

The golden skinned alien had asked me a question, but I'd been so lost in my thoughts that I didn't hear her until she was almost done speaking.

She tapped me on the shoulder to get my attention. "What planet are you from?" she asked curiously. "You look like you could be a Vepar, but with that performance yesterday, there's no way that you are," she continued, studying me closely.

"I'm from Earth," I responded absentmindedly, my thoughts still on Bruda's whereabouts.

"I've heard of that place. It is one of the Vepar colonies, isn't it?" she asked innocently. Earth being called a Vepar colony filled me with a hate so strong that I could barely answer.

"I suppose you could call it that," I said stiffly. "Colony does denote that the planet was taken over. Which is what happened," I continued.

She nodded uncomfortably. Obviously, I wasn't doing a great job of keeping my emotions in check when it came to that subject.

"I'm sorry, as you can imagine by my presence here, it's a little bit of a sore subject," I said conciliatorily.

"My planet was taken over by another as well. You don't have to apologize to me about having anger over such a thing."

I opened my mouth to respond, but just then a horn sounded, and we were surrounded by a horde of Khonsu guards who began to push us towards the spacecraft. A long plank descended from the opening of the craft and we walked on it into the ship single file. The inside of the ship was set up somewhat like the aircraft I had seen in military movies on Earth. There was a long row of seats on each wall with harnesses attached to each seat. Staying in line, we all took a seat and strapped ourselves in the harnesses under the careful watch of the guards.

There was still a part of me that expected one of my guys to appear at any moment to save the day. But as everyone filed in, and the doors were closed, it looked less and less like that was going to occur.

I was truly on my own.

The ship took off, and I felt my stomach heave at the sudden movement. There were no windows inside the craft, and that didn't help my motion sickness. Obviously the Khonsu hadn't bothered installing the technology or didn't possess the Vepar technology that allowed you to travel without sickness.

I couldn't decide whether it was a good thing or not that we landed so quickly. On the one hand, I didn't feel like I had to throw up anymore, but on the other hand, this meant that the hunt was about to start.

I guess there was no sense in delaying the inevitable.

We unhooked the harnesses and again left the ship single file. Stepping out, I could see that we had landed at the base of the Khonsu's sacred mountain. The mountain was covered with an assortment of trees. The trees all had different colored leaves, kind of like how fall had looked back home. Things were different here than where the Vepar lived, however. The colors weren't nearly as vibrant. It actually reminded me a lot more of Earth in general than the Vepar side had.

When I was younger, my parents took me on a trip to Utah during my school's fall break and we had hiked Mount Timpanogas. This mountain reminded me of that, and a sudden bout of homesickness hit me.

Looking around to distract myself from the feeling, I realized I didn't see any of the purple tunic clad Khonsu anywhere in sight. Where were they? Were they hiding in the mountains, intent on pouncing on us as we tried to run for our lives?

My question was answered when a more decadent ship that was obviously superior to the ones that they had put us in (it had windows at least) landed a little ways away from ours.

The Khonsu filed out of the ship eagerly, looking immediately to where their prey was standing. Most of their eyes were centered on me, and I had the feeling that this was going to be the hardest experience of my life.

We were led to the edge of the forest at that point. The Khonsu didn't seem to have any intentions of giving us instructions. Looking around at my fellow prisoners, they all looked terrified, but also resigned. They must've grown up with stories of the hunt as well.

The Khonsu warriors stayed close to the ship. Evidently, we were going to be given a head start...how kind of them.

Just then a loud blast went off. The females in front of me started to run into the woods.

It was starting.

I took off after them, and then took a hard left after a few minutes. If I was going to have to go through this, at least I could take some of the pressure off of the rest of the prisoners since I knew most of the Khonsu would be after me.

The woods were like a whole other world. Large trees blocked the sun, making it cool and dim. Dead leaves crunched under my bare feet. I was lucky that my feet had toughened up during the trials or I would be limping right now.

There were strange noises all around me, and occasionally I got a glimpse of the end of a tail or the feathers on a wing as whatever creatures I was disturbing as I ran through the woods tried to hide.

Another blast sounded. I could tell it was for the Khonsu warriors because despite the fact that I'd probably made it at least a mile away from where we had first started, the ground shook a bit as the warriors entered the forest.

It only took a few minutes for me to hear the screams start as the Khonsu found some of the prisoners.

A burst of adrenaline sent me pushing forward. There had to be a way out of this, there just had to be.

I was so caught up on running as fast as I could, that I didn't even hear the first Khonsu when he reached me. I wasn't aware that he was there until a thin, silver colored rope was suddenly wrapped around my neck, choking me.

Stupidly, I still tried to lurch forward, desperate to get away. This only served to choke me even further. Maybe I would die before the rape happened, I thought to myself as the world started to fade to black.

Suddenly the rope was cut behind me, and I fell to the ground, heaving huge gulps of air. The sound of flesh hitting bone had me turning around to see the scene behind me.

Two purple clad Khonsu were wrestling on the ground. I gasped at the scene, shocked as one of them pulled out a razor-sharp knife the color of black obsidian. He raised the knife high above the Khonsu he had forced to the ground, a Khonsu who had the remnants of a broken rope in his hand, and he slashed the knife down. I watched in horror as the other warrior's flesh was split open, his blood seeping into the ground below him.

Only at that point did I get the wits about me to begin to run again. As much as I didn't want to be caught by the first one, this other Khonsu seemed like he would be even worse judging by the delighted look on his face as he had stabbed his fellow warrior.

Just as that Khonsu was about to get up from the ground, another Khonsu warrior tackled him to the ground. This time I didn't stop to watch what happened.

I just ran.

A fierce grunt came from behind me, and then the gurgle of blood as one of them killed the other.

I continued to run.

I was almost captured at least five more times. Each time I thought that it was the end until another Khonsu warrior would erupt from the woods to stop my current assailant and try to claim me.

There was a trail of Khonsu corpses littered behind me on the path that I was traveling.

I was exhausted, but still I kept running.

5

Excitement roared through the crowd of Khonsu behind me, while terror choked me. I panted for air, legs and arms pumping as I ran up the mountain. Sharp twigs and rocks tore at my skin and embedded themselves in my feet. I was sure I was leaving a trail of blood behind me making it easy for them to track me.

A shadow fell over me. I glanced back swiftly, and a whimper spilled from my lips. A Khonsu, in his purple tunic, rushed up after me so fast, my knees wobbled with fear. He might as well have been as big as a bear! Huge arms, a broad chest, and he carried such savageness in his eyes. Determination on his face screamed he was ready to take me, and nothing would stand in his way.

I burst onward with sheer adrenaline.

Another woman screamed somewhere on the mountain, while a man howled like a monster, probably claiming her.

I searched the land for a weapon, for anything to beat them back. A branch or rock? Both would work.

The beast pounded the ground with rapid steps, his breaths on my neck, coming for me... to claim me. To rape me. This wasn't okay, and I hated everything about these aliens. From the tests to being hunted down, I was put through hell and back only to still be in mortal danger. I wasn't okay with any of this at all.

My heart ached. I was going to die on this planet, never to see Earth again.

An iron-grip hand grasped my shoulder, the other my hair, drawing me backward.

I let out a terrifying shriek and pivoted on the balls of my feet, swiveling around, hurling my fist, connecting it with the monster's face.

He emitted a piercing guttural sound that had my skin shivering. Was it a battle cry, a sound these things made before they took a female?

He grabbed both my shoulders and wrenched me sideways, while my feet tangled and barely touched the ground.

"Let me go," I chided and slammed my balled hands into his gut with everything I had, but he didn't so much as flinch. "I don't want you. I'll hate you for eternity and never stop trying to escape."

A sudden gust of air battered into us, tossing his messy black hair over his shoulders, bringing with it a delicious musky scent. Except, that was wrong... I'd never admire a single thing of these brutes. He had the kind of look I imagined on a barbarian. All strong and muscular, his face square and brutish, and when he'd speak, he'd made just incomprehensible sounds.

He growled, wrenching me into a cluster of trees. He was picking a location to rape me.

I screamed and hit and kicked. I'd die before I let him do anything to me.

Blue eyes pierced through me, but I fought and bucked against him.

"Silence, kitten."

His words wove through my mind, but my brain cogs weren't working today. *Kitten.* Why would a Khonsu call me that?

The answer smacked me in the face when the savage hauled me against him, our bodies pressed close, his lips mashed to mine. I gritted my teeth and winced, hands splayed against his chest, pushing him away. But I might as well try to move a mountain.

Kitten!

I glanced up into those now deep blue eyes. "Thane?"

His smirk lit up his gaze, and even if he didn't look like my Thane, I saw him in his eyes.

"Surprised to see me?" he whispered.

"Oh, shit." I threw myself into his arms, and tears of joy spilled down my cheeks before I pulled back. "You terrified the hell out of me. You could have given me a clue or something it was you. I almost had a heart attack out there." I cupped the side of his face, his skin feeling so real. "What kind of mask are you wearing? You look like the real deal."

He took my hand and pressed my fingers to the back of his ear. "It's a disguise, a glamor to everyone else. An effect Corran designed."

"Like magic?"

He tilted his head to the side like he didn't quite comprehend the word, *magic.*

A sudden loud exhaling sound of someone running up the mountain nearby had us both frozen and turning toward the open mountain to my left. The trees around us provided a small, temporary cover.

"Hush." His hand was on my mouth as he glanced out to a woman sprinting up the hill, two men charging after her.

She tripped over a tree root, and both men leapt into a fight over who'd claim her. "Get up," I mumbled. "Run." And she did.

I turned to Thane. "I hate this hunt. We need to get out of here."

But Thane's hands clasped my hips and hauled me against him, his lips on my neck. "We're being watched." His words were but a ghostly whisper in my ear. "We need to go through with the claiming ceremony."

My stomach dropped, and I was fully aware of what that meant, and if anyone found Thane disguised, they'd kill him. So drawing as little attention to ourselves as possible was the goal.

He lifted me off my feet so fast, I lost my breath. "Fight me," he murmured.

His earlier smile faded, replaced with a hunger I knew had nothing to do with play-acting, but everything to do with his attraction toward me.

I shoved my hands against him. "Put me down," I yelled, wriggling out of his grasp.

The Khonsu wanted a show.

They expected Thane to mount me, to claim me like a savage.

I stumbled backward across the foliage covered floor.

"You're not going anywhere," he growled, his voice menacing, drowning in desire and hunger.

His mouth was on my neck, teeth raking over flesh, causing me to cry out in shock.

In an instant, he snatched the hospital gown I still wore and ripped it off me so fast, I stumbled on my feet from the motion.

Standing completely naked, I lashed my arms over my body, my mouth dropping open. I wanted to scream at him, but he just grinned at me.

Asshole. He was enjoying this show and tell a bit too much.

His gaze trailed up and down on my body, showing me his pleasure in his parted mouth, in the hardness in his pants.

He reached out for me, but I pulled away and spun from him.

The Khonsu in the audience wanted to be entertained, enjoy this show of dominance, of women taken against their will.

Bastards. The whole lot of them.

Greedy hands clasped me by the waist, stopping me in my tracks, his touch sending my body into a devilish buzz. I spun to strike him, hating that I was naked out in public and he still wore his clothes. But his grip tightened, and he forced his chest flush against my back. His hand clasped my chin and turned my head to face him.

Lips on mine, he kissed me hard, his tongue slid inside my mouth, making me taste his sweetness. My body responded to his touch and lips instantaneously, heat coiling deep in my gut. Nipples hardened, and my body betrayed me when it came to my three Vepar.

Except, this wasn't about falling, but resisting him. I ripped out of his grasp and swung around with a fist aimed at his face.

He caught my wrist. "Not so fast, kitten."

I kicked him in the shin, and he winced. I smirked and wrenched to leave and grab my hospital gown off the ground. But he held onto me and squeezed my forearm so hard, a sharpness shot up my arm. "Ow."

"I'm in charge here, not you. You're mine, and now I'm going to fuck that sweet cunt of yours."

Raising my head, I was startled by this response, heat already burning through me to hear him talk so dirty. But it was all an act, right?

"Don't touch me." I chewed on my lower lip, while liquid fire burned between my thighs.

"I can smell your arousal." One step closer, and he towered over me. His hand pressed to my back, holding me in place while he nuzzled my neck. "I missed you," he breathed heavily, and when he looked at me, primal desire darkened his gaze.

He licked his lips, staring at me with such heat. I felt trapped right then... caught between the inferno inside me demanding I throw myself at him, but I couldn't.

His hands grabbed my shoulders and he spun me around, then pressed a hand to my back, forcing me to bend over.

I placed my hands on the tree in front of me, quivering as my ass stuck into the air. His hand slid down my back, feather soft, and over my cheeks. I released a noise of protest, but his hand connected the flesh of my ass with a smack. Crying out, I pushed upright, but he shoved me back down.

Somehow, I was caught between this strange exhilaration that already soaked my thighs, and a searing pain that stung but quickly faded and left me eager for more.

He pushed his hand to the apex between my thighs, running his thumb gently along the sensitive skin of my seam, and my nipples pebbled in response. His other hand wove into my hair before fisting it, holding me.

"You're mine," he growled.

Something about his possessiveness sent a shiver of delight through my body. It shouldn't have, but it did. Another slap to my ass, and I cried out with pleasure. Was it possible to orgasm so quickly?

"Spread your legs," he demanded, and humiliation spiraled through.

But someone watched us, someone perverted, and our lives were on the line.

I shuffled my legs wider, when his hand slapped between my legs. A moan slipped from my lips, and I arched my back. He just slapped my pussy. Was that even a thing?

I loved it even if it left me feeling a bit dirty. I needed him like never before.

"You're so wet for me." A finger plunged into me.

I took a sharp breath, pushing myself backward to take more of him, needing so much more. And he understood, fingering me rapidly, pumping. But it wasn't enough.

Pushing two fingers into me, in and out, I rode him, groaning, so close to the edge already. He pulled out, and I whined in protest, looking over my shoulder at him.

He unzipped his pants, his hard cock bopped out, and I reached over to touch him, but he nudged me back around. "I didn't say you could move."

My mouth opened with a protest, when the tip of his cock lined up with my entrance. Desire stirred inside me, and I breathed hard, waiting, needing him. The rest of the world fell away in those moments. Just us two existed.

He thrust deep into me so fast and sudden, I gasped, not from pain but from that slick, hot cock filling me, hitting just the right spot. I grasped onto the tree, holding tight, Thane pumping into me.

My moans intensified, and the storm inside me rose quickly. And just then Thane withdrew from me, leaving me boiling hot and so wet.

I lifted myself up and turned to argue, but he grabbed my waist and lifted me off my feet against him. Automatically, I grasped his shoulders and wrapped my legs around him. The tip of his cock found me as if we were made for one another, and he lowered me onto him, stretching me, and I gasped for breath.

The edge of pleasure drew closer. His hands cupped my ass and his mouth latched onto my neck as he rode me. I closed my eyes, my groans intensifying.

A sharpness pierced into the side of my neck, and shock froze over me when I realized he had bit me and was feeding off me.

I welcomed the familiar feel of him as he began to drink down my blood. All of a sudden, he pushed himself away from me, clenching his throat. He let out a garbled roar as he tore at his neck. It was almost as if his throat was being burned from the inside.

I was aware of the confused stares of the Khonsu that were watching us just past the trees around us.

Thane began to spit out the blood he had just taken from me. He took a few frenzied breaths after spitting out more of my blood before looking at me.

"What did those bastards do to you?" he roared.

"What's wrong?" I whispered, not understanding what had just happened. Thane seemed to become aware of the many eyes that were watching us.

"We'll talk about it later," he said through clenched teeth. Thane stared at the blood on my neck and collarbone from his bite, an infuriated look on his face.

He wiped his mouth with the back of his hand, his gaze darkening, and I caught him taking a sharp side glance at movement from farther up the mountain. A Khonsu with no partner watched us, and I shivered. He was looking to see if he could claim me as his own.

Thane snatched my arm and kicked my legs out from under me with such force, I cried out. Strong hands caught me before I hit the ground and laid me gently on my back. But to an onlooker, it would seem like he had just readied me for the taking.

Hands on my knees, he pried my legs open, his attention falling between my thighs. He grinned.

"So fucking sexy." Kneeling in front of me, hands gripping my hips and wrenched them up to meet him. As if on cue, the tip of his hardness found my entrance with such ease like he was practiced in finding the right spot in a heartbeat.

His hands slid up my legs and grasped my ankles, placing them over his shoulders before he slid into me, stretching me. I moaned so loud, despite the twigs digging into my back, all I could focus on was our point of contact. Him sliding in and out of me, picking up pace, his friction igniting a blaze inside me.

Despite the confusion about his bite, the terror of being watched, Thane managed to push ahead and make love to me like it was just the two of us in this world.

Going faster, I writhed, needing him so desperately, so much, I cried out in pure bliss.

In a sudden movement, he spread my legs on either side of him and collected me into his arms while he remained imbedded inside me. I now straddled him while he kneeled on the ground, and I wrapped myself around him, staring into his eyes. They belonged to my Thane, not the disguise he wore.

Hands on my hips, he moved me up and down with haste over his cock, the sound and smells delicious. I gripped his shoulders, riding him, my body shuddering as he thrust over and over. When I couldn't take it any longer, euphoria snapped within me and tore through my body. I convulsed against Thane, and as if sensing my own climax, he grunted and stilled, his cock pulsing inside me with his orgasm.

Pressing me tight against his body, he held me, his mouth on my ear. "I meant what I said earlier. You're mine and I'll never let you go."

I wanted to stay in his arms like this forever, to never face reality, to not be running for our lives constantly. But when the siren went off somewhere in the distance, the horror of where we were punched me in the gut.

He lifted me to my feet as he climbed up, and hot liquid dampened the inside of my thighs. What I wouldn't give for a bathroom break right now.

The savages were now headed down the mountain, their women over a shoulder, and I grimaced. Before Thane grabbed me and did the same, I hurriedly snatched the hospital gown and slid it over my head.

"Let's go," he snarled as he did up his pants. He then swept me off my feet and threw me over his shoulder. His hand sat perfectly positioned over my ass so I wouldn't flash the whole world. Thank goodness for small gestures.

I jostled over his shoulder, the world upside down, my stomach churning with sickness at being shaken about.

By the time he slid me down to my feet, my world spun, and it took me several moments to find my bearings.

Thane walked over to a table strewn with pieces of clothing and came back with a midnight blue dress. He pushed it into my hands. "Put that on."

I glanced around to the other couples in the small field, the spectators watching us from farther away. The other females were naked and were just pulling on their new garments, so I quickly took off my hospital gown that was splattered in blood from my neck, dirt, and bits of leaves.

I quickly dragged the blue dress over my head and down my body. It hung like a sack over me, falling to my knees, sleeves loose to my wrists. I looked like some cult mistress but at least every other woman was dressed the same way.

Thane grabbed my hand and hauled me after him and the rest of the couples. We walked quickly over the grounds and headed for an oversized building up ahead. Black as the night, the one-story building had a flat roof with windows peppered all along the walls.

What in the world now?

By the time we stepped inside, my heart was pounding. I wasn't sure how many more surprises I could take. Being taken by Thane in public was pushing me to my limits. We needed to escape and get as far from the Khonsu as freaking possible.

Behind others, we headed inside hand in hand to find an enormous hall set up with rows and rows of wooden tables layered with platters of food and drinks. Down the middle of each long table was a roasted animal. I didn't recognize any of the species. The walls were lined with large wooden wine barrels and taps on each one, surprising me they looked so human like. On the far-right hand side, an enormous fireplace roared and crackled, warming up the room. Yellow lanterns dangled from the ceiling, giving the place a magical kind of feel, which was so wrong. This was a celebrational feast for savages who had just hunted down and raped their new wives.

Everyone moved with haste to a table, and Thane took me to one closest to the door. He pulled out the long bench that was lined with fur pelts and I sat down. In front of each place setting stood a hollowed-out horn sitting inside a metal bracket that was evidently meant to be used to hold the wine according to Thane.

Thane collected both our horns and headed to the barrels on the wall. He filled them up and then returned. He handed me the horn and I sniffed it. It certainly smelled like wine, and a quick taste confirmed it. I needed to drink a whole barrel to forget what I went through today.

In front of me, I stared at the flowing cuts of meats, fruits and strange vegetables. There were also piles of nuts and breads strewn around the table.

"Eat," Thane commanded. "Fit in."

A quick look around to the rest of the room showed that the women were smiling and eating, while the Khonsu drank and laughed with their friends. This was a wedding festival I realized. It was amazing to me that the women seemed to have recovered so quickly.

I piled my plate with roasted root vegetables and something that resembled grilled fish.

Two Khonsu came and sat at our table on my free side, one of them so close that I gave him a death glare to try and get him to move. Two beefy looking brutes, both with short hair, one cleanly shaven, the other with a scruffy beard. They stared at me like I might be their meal.

I trembled and shuffled closer to Thane who wrapped an arm around my shoulders.

When the newcomer's hand reached for my thigh, I slapped him away. "I'm taken."

Please don't let there be another rule about mate sharing.

"You don't need to be scared of me," he said, and I recognized that voice in an instant. "Derrial?" I gasped.

He gave a small nod and smirked, then I glanced over at the bearded one. "Corran?"

"Holy shit, what are you doing here?"

Corran leaned forward, his disguise had a scar running down the side of his face, and it pained me to look at the scab. Then again, it matched the rest of the ferocious Neanderthals in this room.

A sudden stomping of feet had me lifting my gaze to several Khonsu who walked into the room wearing crimson robes that fell to their ankles and hoods over their heads. They held chains that were tied to several women behind them. Beautifully stunning women, some were Vepar by their horns, wearing corset type blood-red dresses that flowed to their feet. Furs warmed their shoulders, while the chains around their throats reminded them, they were nothing but eye candy. A possession. A slave.

My insides tightened to see women treated this way.

There was no sign of Bruda though. I didn't know if that was good or bad.

With the females' arrival, a band started playing music on a string instrument, not too different from a violin, the music building up to a crescendo. Everyone broke into chatter and dug into their foods. Thane nudged me as he got up to fill his horn and mine, even though I hadn't drunk any yet.

Derrial and Corran reached for the food, and I picked at my plate, not sure I could stomach too much right now. "So, what's the plan?" I whispered to Derrial.

"We eat and wait for everyone to have their fill of what you call pumpkin wine."

My eyes widened. "We don't have pumpkin wine."

"Those grape things. Just the Khonsu use pumpkin. It's probably the best thing to come from these vermin invading our planet." His words were barely a whisper, and I looked up to see the elite were sitting on the table next to us with their new women. I was surprised the women were allowed to even sit at the table with them.

Thane returned, already drinking from one of the horns.

"Take it easy with the pumpkin wine," I murmured, but he didn't hear me as he flopped back down next to me and set to eating. Food was probably good, so he didn't get drunk. Though could you get drunk on fermented pumpkin juice?

A conversation at the next table caught my attention. One of them mentioned the word "humans." All of my attention immediately gravitated towards the two Khonsu speaking. They were both dressed in crimson robes I'd seen the elite wear, so I assumed that whatever they were talking about was probably important.

"Why have the other humans showed no signs of possessing the same traits as this one," one of them said, gesturing over to where I was sitting. The other one looked over at me and I immediately averted my eyes, trying my best to pretend like I wasn't listening.

I elbowed Derrial, who was paying attention to another conversation between another group of crimson robed Khonsu.

"Just a minute," he said as he tried to listen. I elbowed him again.

He looked over at me impatiently. "What is it?" he asked. I blanched for a moment at how fierce he looked in his Khonsu form. It was only his eyes that looked anything like my Derrial.

"They're talking about other humans. Do you think that it's possible that there's other humans that were taken to this planet?" I asked, my voice a mixture of eagerness and concern.

A look passed over his face, one that I couldn't read very well.

"They're talking about other humans on Veon?" he asked, sounding concerned.

"Yes," I responded, this time more eagerly as I continued to listen to the conversation taking place between the Khonsu's. I was only faintly aware of the looks being exchanged between Derrial, Thane, and Corran.

"You have to do more testing, especially after those numbers that she displayed," one of them said. The other one nodded, a look of pure excitement all over his features.

I shivered at the thought of what tests they had in mind. I'm sure they were even worse than the ones used by the Vepar during their fertility treatments.

"We have to find out where they are keeping them," I said urgently, pulling on the side of Derrial's tunic.

I immediately dropped my hand and adopted a demure expression when I saw a few of the other Khonsu at the banquet table watching me suspiciously. I knew in their culture that the women were extremely subservient to the males, so it probably looked bad how I was behaving towards Derrial.

Corran reached out and touched me gently. "Of course we will do everything we can if there are other humans on this planet," he said. Thane nodded beside him. "Anything we can," Thane repeated.

I was surprised that they were being so agreeable about this. I'd expected them to say something about how my safety was more important than any other humans or other crap like that, but they seemed to agree with me.

Maybe our short separation had gotten through their thick skulls that the rest of the human race wasn't completely worthless.

I doubted that was actually the case, but I took the victory where I could.

At that moment the two Khonsu that I had been listening to got up from the table and began to walk away together.

I looked at Derrial frantically. "They didn't say where they're keeping them. How are we going to find them?" I asked urgently.

Derrial had a determined look on his face as he looked after them. A quick look at Thane and Corran's faces showed that they were on the same wavelength as him. What were they going to do?

Derrial and Thane got up from the table, and Thane took one last drink of his wine before leaving Corran with me, I supposed as my guard. I watched as they followed the two Khonsu, keeping their distance from them so that they wouldn't suspect that they were being followed.

I thought I remembered them saying it was rare for a human to be on their planet, yet these Khonsu spoke about them as if it was common practice. How many of us had these savages kidnapped and brought back here?

I prodded Corran in the arm. "Hey, did you know the Khonsu were bringing humans on this planet?"

He looked at me for a long pause and gave me a small shake of his head, and kept eating, so I did the same.

Several servants came to our table to collect empty plates, while others delivered more food, and when I looked up at the young man with short blond hair, he smiled. "Thank you," I said.

He leaned over to pick up an empty platter and murmured, "Did you just arrive on this planet?"

His question threw me off at first, and I tried to make sense of it. "I've been here a bit, but I really wanna go home."

"Me too," he sighed, and something shifted behind his eyes, something that had my heart clenching. I knew the look... it was someone who had been ripped from their home.

"I miss pepperoni pizza so much," he said. "You'd think I would miss my family, and I do, but it's normal food I crave."

I bristled in my seat. "You're human? How long have you been here?"

"I think five years. I lost track, but there are others who've been here longer."

"More drinks," a male Khonsu yelled nearby, and the servant stiffened and rushed away, leaving me drowning in his admittance.

I looked over at Corran who hadn't even paid attention as he leaned away, listening to another conversation from other Khonsu. I got it, this was time to gain intelligence on the enemy, but these monsters built their empire by stealing humans and who knows what other aliens as their slaves.

"Corran," I mumbled, poking him in the arm, and he turned toward me with concern behind his eyes.

"Is everything okay?"

"There are humans at this party. They're working as slaves, taken from home. We need to save them."

He swallowed loudly and lifted his gaze as if searching for the other two. "Let's wait for Derrial."

My knees were bouncing under the table and all I could do to distract myself was stare at the others in the huge room. Drinking, laughing, groping women. I could have sworn I stepped into an ancient world of barbarians, and I wanted to get out of here... get off this planet if possible.

By the time the other two returned, I was jumping out of my skin.

"Derrial, there are humans here, kept as prisoners."

He stared at me just as Corran had.

"I want to free them, please. This world is terrifying, and they've been here for years." I reached out, my fingers curling over his arms, my whole body trembling with fury. I couldn't stand how they treated females and other species and wished there was so much more I could do to help those in need.

"Once the dance starts, we go and scour the place, then leave. Alright?"

I turned to Thane, who looked a bit pale around the face. "Are you feeling okay?"

It wasn't long before the music changed to something upbeat, and most of the Khonsu got to their feet, heading for the open floor near the fireplace. Thane climbed to his feet, and I joined him. His hand clasped around my forearm in a possessive manner, and I followed him around the tables, keeping my gaze low.

Thane wobbled into a table, sending the whole thing, food and plates, into a tremendous wobble. My heart soared with fear.

Luckily its occupants were dancing, and I grabbed his arm, trying to hold him up. "You're drunk," I whispered, and we hurried out a back door into a hallway. I assumed this was used by the servants.

Thane erupted into laughter, and his face seemed to grow fuzzy, almost like static on TV. Was this disguise playing up?

"Shit," Corran blurted. "How much did he have to drink?"

I shrugged. "Three, maybe four horns. Maybe more. What's going on with him?"

"Pumpkin wine has an enzyme in it that interferes with our technology. It's my fault. I should have told him, and I didn't even notice him drinking."

"Don't worry about that now. We need to leave," Derrial snapped.

"No." I dug my heels into the stone floor. "I want to free the humans, then we can go. Please."

They stared at me for so long, and all I could do was give them my best pleading look. They had to understand how I felt about being taken against my will, how it hurt me to see others who had lost their families and lives also stuck here.

"Fine," Derrial answered. "We do a quick look around and help those who are willing to leave. Then we leave." He exhaled loudly and spun around. We all followed him down the narrow corridor, where the waft of food was strong. At the end lay an open door and we rushed outside, coming out at the back of the building where I assumed they had landed their ship and covered it with invisibility.

Derrial took my hand and we ran, Corran aiding Thane who stumbled about, his eyes glazed over. How had that wine hit him so fast?

Farther on the property stood several sheds, and I hoped we had stumbled upon one of their holding facilities. "Let's check there." I pointed to the sheds.

"Good, as our ship is just behind them," Derrial snarled.

Clearly, he wasn't happy with my idea, but I didn't care. We moved quickly, but luckily no one was around, probably partying too much.

In the first shed, Derrial stepped toward the door and looked inside. "Empty," he called over his shoulder. I had already moved with Corran to the next one.

Up on tippy toes, I peered in through the glass window in the door but found only wooden crates.

"Shit." I looked back to the main building. "Maybe there are none being held captive since they're all being forced to work. I want to free them as well."

Corran took my hand in his. "You can't risk your own life. Not like this. We'll come back when we're ready and with ammunition."

"Let's go," Derrial whispered loudly. "There's nothing here."

My stomach churned and my blood ran cold at the idea of leaving them behind.

"Hey," Thane slurred. "There are little humans in here."

We all snapped around, and I burst toward him into another small metal shack that had been hidden behind the others.

I pushed past him and ripped open the door to find a huge cage inside. A dozen males sat there, wearing torn clothes, dirt on their faces and arms. They looked human to me. No horns or strange horns or eyes. I closed the distance and reached for the lock, then throttled the door. All three Vepar stepped alongside me.

The men in the cage stared at us with terror behind their eyes, a couple standing up, backing away. It killed me to see their fear, recognizing it all too well. "We're going to get you out," I said, my words coming out croaky.

"What are you doing here?" A raspy male's voice came from behind, and I flinched around.

A bear of a guard hovered in the doorway, heaving breaths like a grunting beast. Before I could respond, Derrial and Thane lunged at the Khonsu, throwing him off his feet. An explosion of groans, fists and punches burst out into the night. I turned to Thane.

"Get them out, now!"

He grabbed the lock and yanked, but the metal held tight. He rushed outside, and my heart pounded against my ribcage.

"Ella," a soft male's voice came from within the cage, and I looked up to find who belonged to it.

A man with graying, messy hair stepped forward.

I didn't trust what I was seeing. There was no way it could be him...

"Ella," he said again, in that same soft voice he had always used with me growing up.

I walked towards him as if in a trance, my hand outstretched. His hand reached through the bars of the cage, trying to reach me.

I tentatively touched his hand. He wasn't a mirage. It really was him.

It was my father.

A siren blared, and I flinched. Shouts and voices rang from outside, but I couldn't move.

"Dad." My voice squeaked, but heavy footfalls rushed in behind me.

"We've been found!" Derrial barked. Strong hands wrapped around my waist and ripped me from my dad, our hands slipped apart.

"No," I cried. "Put me down. Dad." I bucked and fought.

"Silence," Corran snarled in my ear. He spun me around and we were out of the room. My heart splintered and tears drenched my eyes as he forced me away.

"My dad was in there; we have to get him out."

But no one listened to me. Corran ran through the woods, holding me tight against his side, and in seconds his black space cruiser shimmered into sight. The door slid open and we rushed inside. I glanced back to see Derrial and Thane running toward us with a horde of Khonsu charging after them like a pack of animals.

Fear shackled through me when Corran hauled me deeper into the ship and pushed me into a tiny room before the door slid shut.

I burst forward and slammed my fists into the door. "Let me out. We can't leave my dad behind. Can you hear me? Please, Corran. My dad."

Tears fell and I slid to my knees. When the tiny vibrations beneath me started, I knew it was too late. We were taking off and we'd left my father behind.

I wanted to die knowing we'd left him behind with those savages.

6

I had never been so angry. Not when they stalked me, not when they kidnapped me from Earth, not anything else they had done had left me feeling this level of rage.

We had actually left him. My father who I had thought was dead. The man who I had mourned for, who I had missed with every breath in my body.

They had left him there.

I had left him there, and my heart felt broken.

How could I get over this?

They had locked me in a room on the spaceship again. I had learned this was their way of dealing with me when they weren't sure what to do, just lock me out of sight where I couldn't cause trouble.

I guess at least they hadn't knocked me out this time. Although I'm sure they were regretting that since I had spent the last hour screaming and crying against the door, trying to convince them to turn the ship around so that we could go and save him.

As usual, my cries fell on deaf ears.

Corran had tried to reason with me. He tried to tell me it was too dangerous and that we could go back when it was safe. He tried to tell me that my life was too important for them to risk it by trying to save those humans, by trying to save my father.

My resentment grew with every word that he spoke. What had happened to them that they held such little compassion inside of them? How could we have just left them all there? How did they even live with themselves right now?

I had screamed that question at them through the door and Thane had yelled back that he was feeling great about himself in the moment seeing as how he had just "saved my ass" from the Khonsu hunt.

When my voice grew too hoarse to function, I sank to the ground and sobbed. I was so done with feeling like I had no control over my life. When was that going to change? How could I change that?

How could this even count as any semblance of a relationship when they were the ones who made all the decisions. I had no voice in anything. They always did what they thought was best.

I'll admit that at times I had found their bossy ways to be attractive. But this...leaving my father...it was on a whole other level.

I didn't know how I could forgive them for this.

I felt exhausted, more exhausted than I could remember ever feeling. Right then it was too much. Finding my father after all these years. Being hunted by an alien race whose end goal was to rape me. Thinking that I was about to be raped before Thane revealed himself, and then having to have sex in front of the Khonsu.

It was too much.

Before I had met Derrial, Thane, and Corran, I had just been a regular girl, a nobody. Sure I was poor and basically a doormat for everyone around me, but at least I knew what to expect out of life.

Now everything was up in the air. It seemed that just when I found the answer to one thing, another problem would pop right up, more often than not worse than the problem before it.

And I hadn't even let myself think about the fact that I could be pregnant right now, scientifically knocked up with an alien baby. I mean how was this my life?

The image of Bruda passed through my mind at that moment. I thought about the fact that she had literally been a sex slave for the Vepar Council for years, yet she still somehow managed to keep her spirit alive.

Just thinking about everything she had been through made me feel guilty at my current freak out. Despite the fact that I had been through a lot, I hadn't been through that.

I resolved right then and there that I was going to find a way to go back to my father. I wasn't going to leave him with the Khonsu. I could be a hero in my own story for once.

And what if my mother was still alive? I hadn't seen her in the cell, but that didn't mean she wasn't there. I hadn't seen any females in that cell so maybe she was being held somewhere else.

Just the thought of feeling my parents' arms around me again gave me a strength that I didn't know that I still possessed.

I dragged myself off the ground and walked into the bathroom. Washing my face, I stared at myself in the mirror.

I had scratches and cuts all over my body from the Hunt. Corran hadn't had a chance to use his little machine to fix me up yet. I almost didn't want him to heal me. I wanted to make sure that I never forgot what had happened, that I never forgot this sense of resolve that I had.

Faint voices caught my attention. Looking around the room for where they were coming from, I walked over to the wall where I saw a small speaker. The guys' voices were coming through it. Evidently, they had forgotten to turn it off with the craziness of what had happened. There was no way that they would have intentionally left it on. They did their best to keep me out of everything.

I guess they weren't going to get what they wanted this time.

Corran was talking frantically to the other two. "What if she finds out we knew?" he asked, his voice soft like it pained him.

What if I find out they knew what?

Thane answered him sternly, "She's never going to find out. There would be no coming back from that," he explained.

"It would be better for us to be upfront about it," argued Corran. "We should just explain our reasoning, how we've changed since then," he continued. "I'm sure she would understand if we just explain."

Derrial laughed. "When has she ever been reasonable?" he asked sarcastically.

I bristled at his tone. I felt like I'd been very reasonable about everything considering the circumstances. They were the ones that were completely unreasonable about everything.

Now I was even more suspicious about what they were talking about.

"It's not like we knew for sure that her parents had been taken, at least not at first," Derrial continued.

I sank to my knees. My heart felt like it was being squeezed to death. Were they talking about what I thought they were talking about? Had they known this entire time where my parents were?

And they had done nothing.

Just let them go through who knows what with the Khonsu?

Thane was right, there really was no coming back from this.

"That's the least of our concerns right now," Thane finally said after a lengthy pause when all of them seemed to be thinking.

"You're worried that the procedure was successful?" Derrial asked.

They were talking about me getting pregnant in the lab, and my heart shuddered.

"You're not?" Thane barked.

"Corran, what do you think the chances are that they were able to get it figured out? Is there a way to tell," Derrial asked, ignoring Thane's question.

"Not this early," Corran replied. "It will take at least two weeks for the hCG to be strong enough to be detected," he explained.

"Do you really think that they were able to work it out, how to do the implementation successfully without you?" Thane pressed.

"My team was very capable, and they had all of my work. So they should have been able to do it."

He sighed.

"I had hoped that it would have dissuaded them when they found out that I had taken the compound before I left. But now I'm not sure that any of them would even have cared."

This was so much to deal with. Not only could I be pregnant, but I also apparently could still die because of said pregnancy. And my parents had been captured by the Khonsu and had been here the entire time. Once again, how was this my life?

"We need to give her the compound just in case," said Derrial sternly.

"The compound had to be administered at the time of the implementation," Corran added. "It would be too late for that. But she should be fine with our blood sustaining her. That acts the same as the compound because we're her mates."

"Then we have a fucking problem since our blood is no longer compatible with hers," roared Thane. He was so loud that the walls shook.

"What the hell do you mean?" said Derrial. "How is that possible?"

"Up on the mountain, when I was saving her..."

"You mean when you were fucking her brains out in front of the Khonsu?" interrupted Derrial dryly, making me blush at the memory because it was a pretty apt description.

"Fuck you," Thane snapped, annoyed. "This is serious. I bit her while we were having sex...and it made me really sick."

"What do you mean it made you sick?" asked Corran, I'm sure his brain already thinking of a million scientific reasons why that would have happened.

"I mean it made my throat burn, like it was eating my insides. I had to cough it up before I could even continue."

As furious as I was at the guys, it felt like I had lost something important knowing that our blood bond had been severed.

"Corran, how does that happen?" asked Derrial. "I've never heard of that occurring."

"Kella," Corran answered, scornfully.

"What does Kella have to do with anything?" asked Thane.

"Kella was heading up another team. The Council said that he was working on different farm techniques when I asked. I didn't bother to inquire further because I was busy with my own stuff and I've never been particularly impressed with anything Kella has ever done. But this had to be something he was working on..." Corran explained, the end of his sentence trailing off.

"Blood transfer is an integral part of the Vepar's life," said Derrial. "Why would he be working on something that disrupts that?"

"What's that phrase that Ella always uses, oh yes, that's the million-dollar question," Corran said.

"How long do we have to give her our blood before she starts suffering?" Thane asked, sounding a little bit frantic.

There was a silence, and then a roar and bang as one of them smashed something against a wall. Evidently the answer wasn't good.

I noted that they hadn't talked about what they would do with the baby if I was pregnant, and they hadn't talked about any preventative pills. Maybe they didn't have that in the Vepar culture because of their fertility issues. I had a sense that even bringing something like that up would cause issues that I didn't want to get into at the moment.

I did need to know the differences between caring for a Vepar fetus and a human fetus though. I couldn't help but think of what happened to poor Bella in those Twilight books when she got pregnant with a vampire baby. What if this Vepar baby implanted its little horns into my uterus or something, or maybe it required blood to grow. I didn't even know if Vepar fetuses required a shorter or longer pregnancy than human babies.

Corran hadn't said anything about any of it in our discussions.

I didn't know if I was pregnant, or if the doctor had a change of heart in the end. I needed to stop worrying for now though. I guess I would cross all of those bridges when I came to them, if I survived to that point that is.

"If they've created something that breaks the blood bond, surely they have something to fix it," Derrial muttered. I was sure his mind already came up with possible solutions. They took turns being the leader, but I had noticed that Derrial took the lead more often than not.

"I wonder..." said Corran.

"Wonder what?" Thane snarled, obviously annoyed with Corran's analytical mind at the moment.

"I wonder if Kella's experiments have anything to do with the rumors that we've heard," Corran expounded slowly.

"The rumors that an unusual amount of our people have seemed to be going crazy lately?" Derrial asked.

"Yes. We've never really studied everything that the blood bond provides our people. I wonder if the blood bond experiments and the fertility issues are somehow connected."

"I don't care about any of that. I'm only concerned about the fact that our mate might die because of it. Do you think you can come up with something that fixes it?" Thane asked. "If she is pregnant, there's no way for us to reverse it. You know this."

Despite how furious I was, I felt a twinge of sympathy for how upset Thane seemed to be.

"I'm sure I can figure it out, but again, I would assume that they have an antidote for the blood bond issues already created. We just need to get to Kella's lab."

"We're heading to his lab then," Derrial said. "Thane, come with me. We'll need to look at what routes we need to avoid to the capital city. Corran, go check on Ella and see if you can calm her."

I couldn't hear anything after that, signaling the end of their conversation.

I sat there, unable to really move with everything I just learned. Vepar pregnancies weren't reversible. The guys had possibly known that my parents had been here all along. If I was pregnant, I was definitely going to die without the blood bond being fixed. Some of the Vepar were going crazy.

There was so much that they kept from me. I hated this feeling that we were always unequal in our power.

We were now heading to the capital city, where I assumed the lab was. That meant it would be who knows how long until we would have a chance to save my father. I couldn't let that happen. If I did die, then no one would ever save him. It was the least I could do to take care of him. And I still needed to find my Mom.

I wandered back into the bedroom and sat on the bed, thinking of a plan as I did so. I had no idea how to fly a ship, but I was pretty sure that there were smaller emergency cruisers located on all of Corran's spaceships, if we were on one of Corran's spaceships to begin with.

I would assume that they would have coordinates already plugged in for places they had been, like the Khonsu settlement. Zeni had offered me a spaceship to return to Earth. That meant that Vepar ships could basically fly themselves since she would have known I had no experience.

I would just have to watch them as we flew to see if I could figure it out.

Just then footsteps sounded outside the door. A second later, a door opened up in the wall and Corran walked inside.

He looked a bit hesitant. "How are you feeling?" he asked gently.

I had to make this look real, that I wasn't actually that mad at them. But I couldn't be too calm, or they would get suspicious.

"I guess I did need this time to think," I told Corran. "I'm still upset, but I somewhat understand. I wouldn't hesitate to save one of you if it were between your life and someone else's."

Corran's face visibly brightened. It was as if I had taken a huge weight off his shoulders. He came to sit next to me on the bed. "That's exactly it! We can't stand for anything else to happen to you, Ella." He reached out and softly stroked the side of my face. A tinge of pleasure flashed down my spine. He leaned in to kiss me, and it took everything I had to let him. The fury I felt against them was so hot that I could practically taste it on my tongue. The last thing I wanted to do was kiss him.

He must've sensed my hesitance, because he softly brushed his lips across my mouth before pulling away. "It would kill me if anything happened to you," he said softly.

I ignored the look in his eyes. I knew he meant every word. But what they all needed to understand was that true love didn't come with stipulations. From the beginning, everything had been based on what they wanted and that was the only way the relationship worked. That wasn't love.

My stomach chose that moment to growl. Corran looked excited at the fact that I had a problem he could fix. "Let's go get you some food," he said eagerly.

I nodded, allowing him to take my hand as he led me out of the room and down to the mess hall. He grabbed a tray from a cabinet, pressed a few buttons on his admittedly useful invention that allowed for basically whatever food you wanted to appear, and then loaded up the tray.

He led me out to the hallway again, and my heart leaped. Was he taking me to the Bridge?

It was just my luck that Thane and Derrial were busy planning the best route to avoid the Council's army that was on the lookout for us and get to the Capital...because that meant that Corran needed to watch over the ship's controls.

We walked into the Bridge, and I was relieved to see that it looked similar to the past ships that I had been on with them. This had to be one of Corran's fleet.

I watched him as he fiddled with the controls, absentmindedly putting food in my mouth just because I knew I would need energy for what lay ahead.

"You're having to press a lot of buttons over there," I told him. "I was under the impression that these things practically flew themselves," I continued disingenuously.

Corran laughed, a rosy hue appearing on his cheeks. I had caught him doing something. "They can fly by themselves, but there's something about the thrill of doing it myself. I only put it on what you humans call "cruise control" when I'm out of the room."

"So how does that work? I've been in Earth's planes' cockpits before, but this looks nothing like that," I asked him.

I felt a little bad. I was praying on Corran's love for all things tech. Corran had from the beginning loved to show me how his creations worked. Evidently, showing me how to fly the ship wasn't any different.

He began to show me exactly how everything worked. If I managed to get away, I know he would be kicking himself. I put my emotions to the side. I would think about my complicated relationship with all of them later.

Corran had just finished explaining how to input in the coordinates when the entrance to the Bridge opened and Thane and Derrial walked in.

They looked as nervous as Corran had looked when he had first come to talk to me.

"On a scale of 1 to 100 how mad are you right now, pet?" asked Derrial, peering at me intently.

Try a billion, I thought to myself.

"I'm still angry, but I understand more why you felt the need to get me out of there as fast as possible," I said, shooting Corran a look. "I would have a problem with all of you being in danger as well," I explained.

And it was the truth.

A part of me understood their need to keep me safe. The problem I had with them was their inability to consult with me about anything and all the secrets that they continually hid from me. They had known how devastating it was for me to think all these years that I had lost my parents. Now to know that they had been here all along, and that the guys had potentially known that they were with the Khonsu...It just was incomprehensible that they would have kept that from me. Maybe in the beginning before there were any real feelings between us, I could see them keeping it quiet. But they claimed I was supposed to be their mate now.

How could they have continued to keep my parents' existence from me?

"Ella?" asked Thane suspiciously.

Shit. Going off into lala land wasn't how I needed to be acting right now. I smiled weakly. "Sorry, it's just all been a lot. I can't believe that my parents are alive," I said, the threat of emotion tickling my throat.

Corran moved over to me and softly touched my back, trying to comfort me. "We promise as soon as we get settled, and can come up with a plan, we will go back for your father," he said meaningfully.

It was funny, but I didn't believe a single word that was coming out of his mouth, even though I think he meant them. Something would always inevitably come up that would make them feel the need to try to keep me safe rather than do what I wanted.

Continuing with my plan, I kissed Corran softly on the cheek. "Thank you. That means so much to me," I told him.

"What's the plan?" I asked. "Where are we going to right now?" I said pretending that I was unaware of anything.

I watched as the guys exchanged wary glances. "We haven't talked very much about what happened back in the lab," Corran began.

"You mean the fact that I'm possibly pregnant with an unknown Vepar embryo?" I asked sarcastically.

He nodded somberly. "As a safeguard, to protect my experiments, I had taken one of the key compounds with me whenever I left the lab. The compound was integral to the success of the viability of both the embryo and the host."

I interrupted him. "Can't I just start taking it once I find out if I'm even pregnant," I said.

Corran shook his head. "It's too late already. It had to be administered at the time of implantation," Corran explained seriously.

I let the fear that I'd been trying to block from my mind briefly show through on my face.

Thane stepped forward. "But it will be okay," he said quickly. "Because we've all blood bonded with you, if we just continue to share blood with you, everything will be alright," he said, trying to comfort me.

"I'm sensing a but...," I told him, annoyed at how long it was taking them to get the information out that I already knew.

The guys exchanged another glance. They had been around each other for so long that they could have whole conversations without even saying anything. Or maybe there was a telekinetic aspect to it all that they hadn't bothered telling me about. I wouldn't put it past them.

"Something's wrong with our blood bond," Thane answered reluctantly. "We're on our way to another of the Council's labs to try and see if they have the fix for it."

"And if they don't have the fix?" I said, trying to calm the hysteria I felt every time I thought about it.

"Then I'll figure it out," Corran said resolutely.

"Right," I said with a nod knowing how important it was to Corran that I believed him. "I think I'm going to go lay down," I told them. "How long until we get to our destination?" I asked.

Corran looked at some of his controls. "Another three hours I believe," he said.

Veon was a lot bigger than Earth, I thought to myself. It had seemed like we were able to travel extremely long distances within just a few minutes on Earth. I would have to ask Corran how all of that worked. Just not right now.

"You want one of us to go with you?" Derrial asked, even though I could tell that he was itching to get back to his planning.

"I'll be fine," I said with a smile that hopefully looked convincing. Everything depended on me being alone obviously. They all nodded, and I forced myself to kiss them on the cheek before leaving the room.

My next stop was the medical room. I needed to find whatever Corran had used to knock me out the last time we were on one of his ships. I would need at least a little bit of a head start to get out of here, and that would depend on all three of them being out for the count.

I walked along the corridor of the ship as calmly as possible. I knew that there were various cameras all over the ship, I just didn't know where they were located. Hopefully they wouldn't be paying attention to my whereabouts since they had so much to do. I kept myself at a steady pace just in case they were. If they saw me walking naturally, maybe they would think I was just going to grab a headache tablet or more food or something since I wasn't in my bedroom yet.

I got to the medical room and walked in. I felt a wave of desperation as I looked at the rows of silver cabinets. There was no way I was going to be able to tell which of the medicines here worked to knock you out. What if I picked the wrong one and I accidentally killed them?

Something shiny on the counter to my left caught my attention. There were two syringes full of shimmery liquid laid out on a tray. I knew the medicine that Corran had used on me had looked like that. I'd gotten a good look right before he knocked me out. Had they pulled the syringes out just in case they needed me to "cooperate" again.

Just the thought made me even more furious. They were willing to do anything required to get me to do what they wanted; I knew this already.

It wasn't a far stretch to think that these syringes had most likely been meant for me.

But I still felt like I needed some way to confirm. I wasn't comfortable giving them something when I wasn't positive what it was.

Maybe I could just hit them over the top of the head with a pan, I thought to myself, beginning to giggle a little crazily. Just then voices sounded in the hallway. It was Thane and Derrial, apparently walking to wherever they were monitoring the position of the Council's forces.

"At least we didn't have to knock her out again," said Derrial mildly. Thane laughed. The sound of it made me want to kick him in the nuts.

"Corran had the syringes ready just in case," said Derrial casually, like he was talking about the weather rather than drugging his mate.

That comment made up my mind for me. I didn't care if these were the right syringes, I was so upset that maybe I didn't care at that moment if the syringes were filled with something dangerous.

No, I didn't mean that.

But what they had just said cleared the way for me to use this medicine on them. As far as I was concerned, if it wasn't the right one, it was their fault.

I carefully emptied both syringes into a cup and took them back to the room where I had first been held.

My next order of business was figuring out if there were, in fact, the smaller safety ships on this ship. If not, I was going to have to knock them all out and take the ship back to the Khonsu's city.

I made my way down the various corridors of the ship. It was a lot larger than it appeared from the outside and I wondered if that was another invention of Corran. After 30 minutes of searching, I was starting to get nervous. What if I didn't find where they were kept in time and we traveled all the way back to the Capitol?

I guess I could hijack the ship after they got off to find the fix for the blood bond. I didn't want to wait that long though. That meant I would be traveling the entire distance back to the Khonsu city by myself. I wasn't sure I was ready for that. Somehow it didn't seem so bad to only have to retrace our steps halfway.

I finally got to an entrance that looked more industrial than the others. I felt around the outside, trying to figure out how Corran operated the entrance. When he walked through, they seemed to just appear, but other times when Thane and Derrial passed through the entrances, it had opened like a regular door.

I waved my hand in front of the door just in case it had a motion sensor, probably looking like a lunatic. When that didn't work, I then started to feel around the edge of the door, hoping there was some kind of invisible button or something I had to press that would open it. I had gotten all the way around the other side of the door when it suddenly opened.

Lo and behold, two, small, one-to-two person-sized ships were sitting there.

Perfect, I whispered to myself.

I retraced my steps back to the mess hall. I had Corran's machine create a small meal for all of us. I included some of the guys' favorites. Then I incorporated the liquid from the syringes, hoping that they were tasteless and that they worked when taken orally.

Taking the tray, I walked to the Bridge, butterflies filling my stomach. I couldn't believe I was about to do this. I almost talked myself out of it several times. It was only the memory of Thane and Derrial talking so casually about knocking me out that kept my feet moving forward.

I walked into the Bridge. Thane and Derrial hadn't come back yet. Corran looked at me in surprise as I walked in, his face flushed with pleasure as he saw my loaded tray.

"What's all of this?" he asked, walking towards me and taking the tray from me so that he could set it down on the table.

"I just wanted to do something nice for you. You guys are always taking care of me," I responded, the words feeling dirty as they left my mouth.

Corran brushed another of his gentle kisses across my lips. "Thank you," he said.

He put his hand to his ear, speaking into the communicator that they all seemed to have. "Come eat," he said, his voice definitely not as sweet as when he was talking to me.

A few minutes later, Thane and Derrial walked into the room. Their faces held the same pleasure as Corran's had as they saw the food spread out. "Did you do this?" Thane asked.

"Just wanted to say thank you," I repeated, forcing a smile on my face. I wasn't sure why this was making them so happy. Maybe I hadn't done as many nice things for them as I should have.

Our lives were always so up in the air, that I couldn't remember a time since our stay together on Earth where I had actually had time to do something like bring them dinner.

If we ever got back together after this, I was probably going to have to make a lot of dinners to make up for what I was about to do. But then again, I wasn't sure if there was anything they could do to make up for what they had done to me.

I nibbled on my food, trying not to stare at them too closely as I waited for the medicine to kick in. It happened to Corran first, I assumed because he was the smallest of the three. He began to look drowsy, his eyes opening and closing slowly as he tried to fight it. He looked over at me questioningly, but before he could say anything he passed out.

Thane was next, following Corran into slumber just a couple of seconds later.

Derrial was the last one. He stood up in his chair to walk towards me, a look of betrayal written across his face. I got up as well and started to back away from him. He only lasted a couple of steps until he sank to his knees and passed out.

It was time to go.

I was sure I didn't have a lot of time. I sprinted down the corridor, running as fast as I could until I got to the room where the ships were kept. I jumped into the closest one. Looking around at the controls, I tried to figure out where everything was located. Despite its size, it still had most of the same controls that Corran had showed me earlier.

I went through in my head what Corran had shown me and then started pressing buttons. Once I got the ship turned on and it seemed like I had inputted for the ship to return to the last destination inputted, I turned my attention to opening up the main door of the spacecraft to let my smaller ship out.

I looked around in a panic, trying to see which button looked correct. I just knew that they would wake up at any time now and run in to stop me.

Finally, I saw a green button on the left side of the ship that wasn't a part of any of the controls that Corran had shown me earlier.

Taking a deep breath and sending a silent prayer that it wasn't a blaster or something, I pressed it.

A few seconds later the doors of the main ship opened. Pressing the control I knew moved the ship forward, I flew out away from Corran's spacecraft.

I never in a million years dreamed that I would be flying in an alien spacecraft on an alien planet.

It was as terrifying as it was invigorating.

7

(THANE)

My head was still groggy from being drugged, and my blood boiled that she had knocked us out. I scrubbed a hand down my face, remembering us all waking up on the floor, and it didn't take long to work out what she'd done.

Ella's flight path had been easy to follow as well since all our ships shared the same database. With a few taps to select her coordinates, her journey flicked up on my screen. But I didn't need it to know exactly where she'd gone. To understand why she'd stooped so fucking low.

My heart had shattered at hearing her cries, and I felt like the worst person in the universe when we tore her away from her dad. It broke me, but her running from us like we were monsters wanting to hurt her, fucking hurt me.

Taking a deep breath, I recentered myself. I clenched my jawline but reminded myself why she did it.

Desperation to get her dad.

Instead of talking to us, she did the unthinkable.

Guilt chewed on my insides because I should have guessed she'd do something stupid.

"How in the hell's galaxies does she know how to fly a ship?" Derrial hissed, his words clipped and sharp. He flopped in the front passenger seat near me.

"Give her credit. She's been watching everything we do, teaching herself, learning. And desperation does funny things to people. Thing is..." Corran said from the back where he attempted to make contact with her ship, apparently, not only had she learned to fly a space cruiser, but she had also learned how to switch off the comms. "The ship practically flies itself if she selects the last destination we flew to. I told her so myself when she suddenly seemed interested in how to fly the ship. I should have suspected something then."

"Yeah well, hurry up and get us there already," Derrial growled my way. Fuck, he had a temper on him, but we were all just as tense.

The faint vibration of the ship thrummed under us, and we lifted off. I wasted no time and hurled us forward.

"Well, I can't get ahold of her," Corran hissed. "I've initiated the comms destabilizer. Better no one detects us since we have everyone after us."

Derrial ran a hand down his face and huffed loudly, his knees bouncing.

All I could do was focus on flying, avoid heavily populated air space, and pray to the universe Ella hadn't been captured by the Council or the Khonsu.

Flashes of Ella filled my mind, her bending over in the forest, me ravishing her, seeing her naked out in public had me burning up. I wanted so much more time to really show her pleasure, and how I could make her scream with arousal. The memories in my mind were uncontrollable, repeating over and over until they drove me insane.

Her scent still clung in my nose, and her moans echoed in my ears as I thrust into her over and over.

Life taught me to never get too close to anyone, to not believe in deep relationships that lasted. My past partners never worked out. We ended up in arguments, with differences, and it was easier to walk away. Always easier to walk away. But this was different with Ella. She'd somehow crawled under my skin and now I'd lost myself with a human woman when so many odds were stacked against us. I refused to let myself think of the future when we'd be lucky to survive today.

Focus on the here and now.

Save her.

Get to a safe place for all of us.

Everything else could wait for later.

"What if she's captured?" Corran asked, his voice pensive.

"Then we go and rescue her, we do whatever the fuck we need to until she's with us and safe. That's what we'll do." Derrial didn't move but kept his attention out the front window as he spoke.

"How far are we from reaching her?" Derrial barked.

"Five minutes tops."

"Make it two."

Silence suffocated us, and we cut through the sky, the reflective shields up, masking us, meaning to anyone looking toward us, they'd only see the sky, the charcoal clouds promising a storm.

As we finally cruised over the landscape of the Khonsu's territory, I spotted our other black cruiser down amid the woods, finding no sign of Ella.

To our right sat the compound and sheds, while on the far left, the mountain sat where Ella had run up.

I commenced our descent in a small clearing not far from hers. The surrounding trees would cover us hopefully from detection. At least until we rescued her stubborn ass and ran.

Derrial cleared his throat, while my gut clenched with dread. Was she okay?

With a small lurch, we landed. Unbuckling myself, I shot to my feet and raced into the main cabin. I dragged open the weapon compartment latch and my mouth dropped. "Why the fuck is this container empty?"

"We haven't really had the chance to load weapons," Corran growled.

"Fine. We do this the old-fashioned way. Corran, you check the other ship for any weapons."

I shook my head and did a double check of our surroundings through the heat sensor monitor. Once I saw that it revealed no one in near proximity, I hit the door button and it slid open.

We rushed outside, my muscles tense, my senses alert.

I ran through the woods toward her ship. *Please don't be dead.* Derrial and I surveyed the perimeter, keeping watch while Corran entered the cruiser.

Moments later, he emerged. "She's not here. No sign of struggle."

Good. That meant she may not have been found yet.

Stalking the grounds, we pressed on, targeting the shed where Ella had found her dad, knowing it was exactly where she would have gone.

"You know the protocol," Derrial muttered. "Get Ella out of here the moment you see her. Leave without the rest of us if needed, just evacuate her. Understood."

Corran and I nodded.

I'd never leave without her.

A high-pitched scream came, violently ripping through the air.

Moving faster, we burst out from the treeline, emerging into an open field. Up ahead lay those three sheds.

Ella emerged from around the corner of a shed with a man I recognized from the cell, the man we'd torn her from...her father, and together they ran in our direction, their faces fear-stricken. Behind her, four Khonsu guards charged after her. Big sons of bitches, pounding the ground with long strides, moving with greater speed than I expected for someone their size.

My heart slammed into my throat.

She glanced toward us, her eyes widening with hope, silent words falling from her lips.

That's right, keep running, kitten.

We ran toward them.

The monsters were almost upon Ella and her father. They were moving too fast.

I darted forward, a war cry bursting from my lungs. My fists curled, feeling nothing but raw adrenaline. A Khonsu with a shaved head and the reddest eyes I'd ever seen was within arms' reach of Ella.

I propelled myself forward and launched past Ella and up at him. My fist connected with the side of his head so hard, the crack shuttered up my arm. But he fell.

Stumbling to my feet, I ducked a swinging punch from another Khonsu and rolled out of reach. I shot to my feet and attacked the brute, my fist connecting perfectly with the roaring Khonsu's face. He stumbled backward from my strike, and I threw a curved kick into his gut to help him along. His feet caught on a patch of grass, and he fell head over heels. Fuck yeah, that was what I liked seeing.

I spun around as the guards started to climb to their feet. Up ahead, Derrial lunged onto the back of another guard who had Corran pinned to the ground.

Ella and her dad kept running past them, and all I could think was that I had to get her out of here.

Priority.

A roar sounded behind me, and I jerked around to see a horde of savages pouring out of the main building. They were coming in our direction like a fetid wave of sewage. Some kept their humanoid form, others morphed into four-legged monsters with black leather hides. They were damn fast. Bastards.

I spun on my heels and ran. This wasn't a fight we'd win. There was no shame in running away.

My feet punched the ground as I sprinted after Ella and sucked in air rapidly. Veon was becoming a dangerous and ugly planet, no longer feeling like my home. Things had changed so much in the last couple of decades, all because of the Khonsu invasion and our Council's response to hide in the cities while these monsters slowly grew in numbers, kidnapping women from around the galaxy to breed with.

I burst into the woods, following her and her father. She was swinging left and right through the woods like she'd lost her way to the ship.

But I didn't have time to chase down a lost girl. Our time was almost out.

Closing in on her, I swept an arm around her side and swooped her against me. "Faster," I shouted toward her father noting that his clothes were ragged, his flesh bruised and covered in healed wounds. The Khonsu had tortured him for fun, for blood, for anything they needed. Fucking vile things.

"Run faster or we die," I barked the order, needing to get them both to safety.

"Thane," she cried with relief in her voice, her breath racing, eyes wide and terrified.

I dashed toward her ship as it sat closer. Slapping my palm over the sensor, the door slid open with a swooshing sound, and we rushed inside. A sudden surge of exhaustion rattled through me and I stumbled on my feet. I dropped Ella on her feet and darted to the controls as the door shut closed.

"Don't hurt us," the man's shaky voice pleaded, his body so frail and thin.

"Dad." She scrambled to her feet and threw herself into her father's arms, crying uncontrollably. An ache settled under my heart to hear the sorrow in her whispers, to finally find her father after he'd gone missing so long. Once she settled down, she'd ask questions... so many questions about how her dad ended up here...like if we knew anything about it. I swallowed down the boulder in my throat and my head spun, but I couldn't collapse now. Not fucking now. I refocused on getting us out of here.

The cruiser hummed beneath me, and we started to ascend.

"What are you doing?" Ella's footsteps padded toward me in a rush. "What about Corran and Derrial? You can't leave them." Panic strangled her voice.

"They have the other ship." I'd find out as soon as they escaped in their ship. We soared higher, and I glanced down to the ground.

Ella was crying and her sorrow sent a spear into my heart. "You can't leave them behind. We just found out that my dad was alive and rescued him, we can't now lose Derrial and Corran."

"You should have thought of that before you drugged us. Now come here." I leaned over and grabbed her arm, bringing her closer to the window. "Look down below. What do you see?"

She leaned over, staring at the field, at the army of Khonsu running toward the woods. "Where are Derrial and Corran?"

"Exactly, they got away. We're trained warriors, kitten. You don't need to worry about us, but you scared the hell out of us. What were you thinking running off like that?"

She faced me and fresh tears tracked down her cheeks, her chin quivering, and my heart melted.

"I'm sorry."

"Kitten, please don't cry. Take your father into the back room as he looks ready to pass out. We have food rations filled with vitamins his body will need and it will help him sleep."

She didn't move at first, but as if my suggestion took a second to sink into her thoughts, she rushed into the back to her father, and I focused on flying us out of here.

I rapidly punched in our coordinates and flicked on the masking shield over the space cruiser. A small green flash in the bottom of my screen told me the other ship was engaged and ascending. I breathed a sigh of relief.

I hated seeing Ella this broken, but what her actions taught me was that she was a danger to all of us because she was reckless. And that was something we needed to rein in if she intended to survive on Veon.

Already exhaustion swept through me, and the energy I used to fight had diluted my last reserves. There was only one way to address that... something I hated but I had no choice. Return to the Council lab for an antidote.

If I didn't pass out first.

8

(ELLA)

"You sure you can fly this thing?" I asked, emerging from the back compartment where Dad had fallen asleep. My pulse was thudding too loudly for me to take stock of my emotions, but amid the darkness, happiness swept over me at finding my father. I never thought I would and had given up hope so many years ago. Even held my own farewell ceremony for him and mom... but I should have known he was kidnapped by the aliens on Earth along with so many others that went missing for years. So many had vanished, but where were they all now? I don't think anyone on Earth knew that the Khonsu had invaded Earth along with the Vepar.

Through all these dangers and impossible foe, to have my father here with me, to know I wasn't alone on this strange planet...it lifted the weight off my shoulders.

Thane was swaying in his seat. He shook his head and blinked to keep his eyes open. Except his gaze looked hazed over like he might pass out at any moment, and my stomach clenched.

I moved closer and stared outside through the front window to the acrid and dried land where we'd landed. Desert and dunes in every direction, the dual suns burning strong.

In front of us, the other ship with Corran and Derrial landed. Thane looked so close to passing out... he was really sick. He couldn't take my blood and he was fading so fast, it terrified me.

I rushed to the door and hit the button. The door slid open just as Corran and Derrial emerged from their ship, walking like drunk friends leaving a bar. Their faces were pasty white, eyes half closed, and the same sickness consumed them.

"Hurry up," I called out and shut the door once they stumbled into our ship. I threw myself into their arms for risking so much. Despite everything, I worried for them as well, and now as their arms wrapped around me, I was lost to the emotions they always stirred within me. It seemed we always ran from something or someone, but just having small pockets of time so close reminded me why I kept fighting and why I wasn't alone in this huge mess I'd landed in. If we ever survived somehow, I wanted to live somewhere peaceful, where the only concern was what to wear that day and what the weather would be like. I'd had my share of danger and adventure to last a lifetime.

"Don't ever do that again," Derrial growled his threat in my ear, while Corran seemed to lose his balance and stumbled free from us before hitting the wall with his back.

I charged after him, a hand grabbing his. "Steady there."

Looking over at Derrial, his brow furrowed in a dozen lines, and with his blood red horns, and the shadows under his eyes, he reminded me of the devil.

"I wouldn't leave my father there. And now he's back there sleeping, and as far as I'm concerned, it was worth it."

"What you could have done was talk to us, not drug us," Derrial spat. "You don't go off on your own ever again, understand?" his voice boomed, his lips twisted with fury.

I gritted my teeth and held his stare. Anger pushed through me as he reprimanded me when I had never asked for any of this. The words flew past my lips before I could tame them.

"Your kind invaded Earth and drew us into this huge mess. All I ever wanted was to have my parents back and have a normal life."

Nothing would ever be normal for me again. Never.

The three of them watched me, and my arms trembled by my side. Derrial's mouth twitched, and I swallowed hard.

"You three can't even stand, let alone fly us out of here. I'm taking the helm, so where are we going?"

"No," Derrial chided. "Thane will take us to the Council, then we'll get our blood connection corrected." He stared at me with intensity, and I clenched my fists. I'd been through so much lately, I was moving on pure adrenaline, and patience wasn't something I had right now.

"Does that even make logical sense to you?"

He ran the back of his hand over his mouth, pulling against the pouty flesh of his lips like he could barely control himself from drawing me to him, sinking his teeth into my veins.

"Pet, once we make a blood bond, our bodies change and rejects any other blood. So, we're getting this corrected, and then..." He paused, staring into my soul it seemed. "Then, we'll address this properly."

The warning behind his words pressed in around me like an invisible vice around my chest.

Thump.

I flinched around to find Thane had fallen out of his driver's seat and was on his knees, pulling himself up, groaning in pain.

"Yeah, he's going to get us killed, flying this thing," I blurted, meeting Derrial's glare. "Tell me where we're going and I'll take us there, okay?" I wasn't taking no for an answer. Technically the space ship was easier to fly than driving a car, so I had this in the bag.

"She has a point," Corran added. "We reserve our energy for once we arrive at the Council quarters. We'll need it."

Derrial huffed, staring at me with uncertainty. He didn't trust his life in my hands, I saw it in his shifting expression, but I'd prove him wrong.

"What have you got to lose?" I pivoted on the balls of my feet and headed to the front where Derrial stepped aside from the driver's seat.

"Get buckled in and I'll set the coordinates," he said. "It should be pretty straightforward, but I'll give you a crash course on flying on our planet and how to avoid detection."

He strained to smile, and his voice was low and tired. He looked like death, his face so pasty and pale. But he was trying, and I knew time wasn't on their side.

"Okay, I'm ready." I tried my best to focus while my brain synapses were snapping with panic, with the urgency to get moving already, with the terror of where the Khonsu had taken my mom. I couldn't stop trembling, but each time Thane looked at me, I smiled and nodded.

Focus.

By the time we were in the air, I pushed us forward with such speed, we all lurched backward, and Corran cried out as he tumbled about back there.

"Oops," I called out and slowed the ship with Derrial's assistance.

"You'll burn the engines if you use them at full power. You ease into it and slowly build up, all right?"

I nodded and concentrated on the empty space out in front of the ship.

"Look here." Thane pointed to a screen with a green line shooting outward. "You want to keep the ship following this path. Fly too high or low, or change trajectory, and it will change to red. Always keep it green."

"Okay, green it is." One hand on what looked like a gear stick, I sat back in the captain's seat and pushed everything else out of my mind. For those few moments, I let the smile pinching at the corners of my mouth spread, feeling like for once, I was doing something to help rather than just being protected.

"What's so funny?" Thane asked from the seat next to me.

"I feel like I'm in Guardians Of The Galaxy."

"What's that?" Derrial asked from somewhere behind me. "I'm not aware of the Council appointing guardians."

I laughed, surprising myself that I found anything funny right then. "They are a band of misfit aliens and a human guarding the galaxy you could say. And they have a sassy talking, adorable raccoon, but he hates being called that. They go on adventures in a way."

Thane queried. "This band of warriors sound a bit like us."

I laughed at his comment. "Guess I can see the similarities. Always getting in deep trouble and trying to find a way to escape."

"Fantastic," Thane announced loudly. "We'll call ourselves, Guardians Of Veon, and you can be the cute raccoon. We'll be the guardians."

I cut him a stare. "Hold off on that. If we get out of this and somehow back to Earth, we are watching that movie."

"Of course," he continued, not listening to me. "I will be the strongest of the guardians of course," Thane went on, and all I could picture was him as Drax the Destroyer from the movie. He always made me laugh. What I wouldn't give to be home, on the couch with a bag of chips, and movie binging.

The thought brought with it a sinking feeling that somehow, I'd end up stuck on Veon forever, running for my life, and never able to watch another new movie again.

I glanced over to Thane who slouched in his seat, eyes closed, his breaths heavy. Refocused on the flight path, I made sure to get us safely to the Council's compound.

An hour later, the city down below came into view, along with the familiar park in the distance--our destination. My senses went on full alert, danger shivering down my spine.

"Umm guys, we're here."

Only snores responded. I reached over and nudged him in the arm. Thane snapped awake, sitting upright in his seat, eyes glued to the front window. "What's wrong?"

"Nothing, but we're here."

Scrubbing a hand down his face, he started hitting the buttons on the dashboard, then pointed to a tight open area behind a curtain of trees. "Can you land us in there?"

I nodded before really seeing what a tight spot it was, but I'd done this before. Hovering over the spot, I glanced out the side window and lowered the lever in slow motion, unlike the last time when I dropped so fast, I screamed and was surprised the ship didn't fall apart around me.

We landed with a small shake, eliciting grumbles from the back.

"You did incredible," Thane said. "Now, you stay in the ship while we go and find out how to reverse the blood incompatibility."

I glared at him, but he already had risen from his seat, shoulders squared like he drew on his last reserves of strength.

Twisting around in my seat, I watched the three of them get to their feet, shaking off the sleep. Derrial looked my way. "When you see us returning, have the ship running and ready to take off. If guards or anyone spot you, leave. You can pick us up later." He closed the distance between us, cupping my cheeks and staring at me like he wanted to say so much more but struggled.

I nodded and held onto his hand, leaning into his touch. "Part of me doesn't want to let you go."

The corner of his mouth twitched, but he never smiled, just held onto his hard veneer. "I'll see you soon." Yep, he was still pissed.

He turned and Corran was standing behind him. He crouched near my seat and plucked free a strand of hair caught in my eyelashes. "You're so brave, Ella, and I want nothing more than to keep you safe." He wasn't wearing his glasses much in Veon, and I missed them. He looked nerdy and kind of cute in them. Kissing the back of my hand, my insides melted, and he left my side as well.

Thane gave me his cheeky grin and leaned over, his lips grazing mine. His musky scent washed over me, and my body responded, nipples tightening.

"I'll be back."

Goosebumps pricked down my arms, and not even his sexy words could put at ease the unrest in my gut. All three guys stared at me, and I wanted to say so much more, tell them despite everything, they'd grown on me, gotten under my skin, crawled into my heart. I was terrified that something would happen to them and I'd lose them.

"We won't be long," Derrial promised, but how did he know that? He just said it to make me feel better, but my stomach churned. It ached at seeing them leave.

I watched them traveling through the woods like shadows before vanishing out of sight. Then I slouched in my seat and scanned the grounds while I waited.

And waited.

And waited...

The sun descended and over two hours passed. The food I gave my dad had knocked him out, and he slept like a baby. I worried for him, but I also knew that now that we were together, I'd do anything to help him get better.

I waited some more.

Still no sign of the men.

My knees bounced, and I jumped to my feet, tired of sitting back. I paced to the rear of the ship and back. What if they didn't return? What then? I would sit in the ship until someone found me? I doubted this was a shuttle I could fly back to Earth, or even then, how could I leave without my mom and knowing if the three Vepar were alive?

Panic rose through me like an exploding volcano, and all I pictured were the three of them dead, bleeding out as I sat here waiting when I could have done something. Anything to help.

I searched the compartments in the ship for a weapon, for anything to defend myself because I had enough of sitting here.

Manuals and tools were all I found, so I collected a screwdriver, gripping it in my hand. If anyone got too close, I'd jam it into their throat. A glint caught my attention from deeper in the drawer and I pushed things aside to pull out a knife that looked a bit worn. It was probably used to cut cords, but it was perfect for me. I tucked it into the deep pocket of the dress and headed outside.

The wind had picked up and it buffeted into me, shaking trees with pink and orange and green leaves around me. For a world that looked so beautiful, everything here was deadly and wanted to kill me.

Steeling myself, I hurried forward, hiding in the shadows, until I emerged from the tree line and stared out at the familiar building. The same one I'd run away from after being used as a lab rat. My breath raced, and I trembled hard. I surveyed the open land between me and the compound. No one around... and no sign of my three Vepar. I had to cross the open ground and pray no one saw me. My heart squeezed painfully.

I had to do this.

Nothing but silence surrounded me, so I lowered my head and ran for my life across the yard. I targeted the rear of the building, figuring there was less chance of being seen. My pulse was thudding in my veins, and I kept expecting an alarm to sound.

Bursting to the back door, I stopped and pressed my back to the wall, gasping for air. When no one rushed out after me, I scrambled toward the door only to find it slightly ajar. I pressed a hand to the handle and pushed it open, my other hand falling to my pocket with the knife.

Inside, a guard lay sprawled on the ground, his nose bloody and lip busted. He wasn't moving. Yep, the guys had definitely come this way, and they must have switched off any sensors since no one had detected this guy. This looked like a delivery and storage room, so I stepped around him and cut across the room filled with shelves and boxes. I grabbed a white coat hanging on the wall and pushed my arms into the sleeves, then pulled the coat tight around me, noting it said "janitor" in Vepar on the pocket. I pushed my long dark hair over the title, and figured I looked close enough to pass as a doctor if anyone took a quick glance my way.

With my heart running a marathon in my chest, I pushed past another door and entered a white hospital like corridor, the antiseptic smells strong. I looked left and right and headed to where the location looked familiar from when the doctors rushed me out of here. The men would have had to go this way too. Hardly anyone was around which left me unnerved.

A voice came out from up ahead, and panic strangled me. I rushed into the closest room and shut the door in silence. The room was empty with nothing but a metal frame for a bed and light pouring in from the window. My skin pricked, unable to shake that horror movie feeling.

Footsteps faded outside, and I crept back into the hall, finding a man in a similar white coat as me. He was marching to where I'd come from seconds earlier.

I slipped out and ran in the opposite direction, my breath ragged and rushed.

"Hey, stop!" A male's voice yelled from behind me. My insides froze. I shot a glance over my shoulder, to see a guard, tall and broad, with a spiky black horn.

I burst into a sprint away from him, my hand diving into my pocket. I gripped the blade, my body shuddering.

"Shit, shit, shit," I mumbled under my breath.

Up ahead, the path divided into three, and I knew this location by the bright green light overhead I'd seen, so I swung to the left and ran like the devil himself chased me.

I passed only a few doors, but I followed the curved path and slipped into a passage and waited. Listening for anyone to follow me.

Sweat trickled down my back, and my heart was beating so hard, it rang in my ears.

When no sounds came, I peered out only to see Zeni emerge backward from a room several feet away, pointing a silver laser gun at someone back in the room. But I couldn't see who it was.

Hot lashes of hatred whipped through at seeing her, remembering the vengefulness in her voice when she had ordered the doctors to start the procedure on me. How she'd wanted nothing more than to ensure I was dead.

Frozen in place, I watched.

"I tried so hard to do the right thing," she blabbered. "All I wanted was for you to accept me, take me as your mate. And then you disappeared. Leaving me without even an explanation." The ache in her voice did nothing to garner sympathy from me.

"Zeni, look at what you've become," Derrial snarled. "You don't want to do this. Let us pass and... and we'll come to some arrangement."

She snorted a laugh. "An arrangement? Like killing the filthy human and admitting publicly you made a mistake, then pledging your loyalty to me. All three of you. Then... only then will I maybe convince my father to speak to the Council about dropping the warrants out on all of you."

"You know we did nothing wrong," Thane snapped. "Put down the gun and give me your hand. Let's talk about this properly."

She was shaking her head. "No! We are doing things my way. You've done everything wrong," she yelled. "Get on your knees. I've had enough of looking at you three, reminded of your betrayal. I just wanted to be with you, be happy. That's all I asked for."

Her threat rang loud in my ears. She was going to kill them. My chin began to tremble, and I held back the cries, the terror choking me.

"Zeni, please," Corran began, but the bitch fired her gun.

I shuddered and died on the inside.

Then everything happened so fast. I didn't remember moving, but I was lunging at her, blade raised just as a guard rounded the corner.

My heart hurt so bad, it felt like I'd shatter into a million pieces. Anger fueled my actions, and all I wanted was to make her pay.

Her head turned in my direction, eyes wide, but it was too late. I sunk the blade into her back, the slurpy sound disgusting and blood spurting from the wound like syrup.

I stumbled backward, releasing my grip on the knife, barely able to breath.

Zeni fell to her knees.

I stumbled backward, releasing my grip on the knife, barely able to breathe.

A whimper fell from her lips, an expelled breath, and I clasped my chest.

What had I done?

Derrial emerged from the room, along with the other two, all three turning on the guard roaring down the hall. Grunts and punches sounded, while I stumbled into a wall, staring down at Zeni who fell onto her side, shuddering.

So much red blood poured from her wound, spreading outward around her. I must have hit a major artery or something for her to bleed so heavily.

I wasn't a killer, and tears pooled in my eyes. I'd done this to her, stabbed her.

Someone took my arm, and I flinched backward, their face blurry from my tears, my heart aching.

"Ella." Corran said softly while fear threaded behind his voice. "We need to leave."

But I couldn't pull my gaze from Zeni who'd fallen silent and stopped twitching. She lay on the floor, still bleeding.

"I-I killed her." The words burst from my lips along with my cries. I shouldn't feel anything, but I did. Killing someone wasn't who I was. This wasn't me. I didn't do this.

Corran seized my hand in his, fingers tight around mine, and we were running in the opposite direction. I glanced back to find the guard also on the ground. Derrial and Thane ran after us. Derrial's sleeve was blackened from where Zeni must have missed her shot, and their faces were white with terror.

All I could do was push one leg in front of the other, drive myself to keep moving, to not think about what I'd done.

Since coming to Veon, I had become many things, experienced more situations than I'd ever wanted to, and even tracked down my father. But never in a million years did I expect to become a murderer.

9

"What are you doing here?" Derrial tossed the angry words toward us as we ran down the white stark hall.

"I was worried, and--" The rest of my words were stolen by the alarm bell that boomed overhead. An explosion of voices and foot-falls suddenly engulfed the building that was silent moments earlier.

Corran's hand squeezed tighter as he hauled me with speed into the rear storage room I'd entered from, and we flew to the exit. The unconscious guard was no longer there.

My head was a cyclone of emotions, of terror, or remorse. I never should have left the ship. Should have just stayed there.

Running across the open field, the four of us never stopped. I breathed hard, pushing on pure adrenaline.

The sirens blared from the building behind us, they rang through the air.

Panic tightened around my chest. We were going to get caught. And this time they'd kill us, no sympathy whatsoever. I couldn't stop trembling. I didn't want to die, couldn't let my dad die after we'd just found him.

The black ship came into view amid the trees as we darted into the forest and didn't stop until we all scrambled onto the ship.

Derrial shut the door, and I heaved for breath. I sprinted into the back room to check on my dad, who still slept unaware of what had just happened. Thank goodness he was okay.

Back in the main area of the ship, Thane lunged into the driver's seat getting us lifted off the ground. Derrial marched back and forth, while Corran headed into the back room where my dad slept.

I glanced outside to the throbbing lights from approaching authorities already flying toward the building. My pulse spiked, and panic squeezed my chest. We rose higher and turned away before flying in the opposite direction.

Unmoving, we all stood in silence, and I prayed no one followed us, that Corran's invisibility cloak device actually made us virtually undetectable.

When no one followed, I collapsed down on a seat against the wall of the ship, my mind whirring.

I looked up at Derrial who now stared out through the front window, and he looked different.

Tall, full of strength, and breathing hard. His face was no longer gaunt. Same with Thane and Corran's. They looked healthy and full of energy like they'd fed.

"You found a cure to the blood connection?" I asked, my fingers interlaced in my lap.

No one responded, and Derrial kept his back to me. Corran answered, "My science team had actually created an antidote, but I just had to combine the ingredients to activate it. It's in our system now, giving us a temporary boost of energy. For the bond between us to stick however, we need a blood exchange."

I nodded. "Okay, let's do it now."

Corran was shaking his head. "It's not that simple. We needed another ingredient for you to take before the exchange, but I couldn't find it in the lab. I was sure it was somewhere in that building, but then we got caught before we could look further."

Zeni had been going to kill my Vepar, and I loathed her for trying to ruin everything. That wouldn't be a problem any longer, and I pushed away the guilt. She would have murdered the men if I didn't stop her.

Derrial turned to face me, shadows darkening under his eyes, lips tight. He was furious. "You disobeyed me."

I bristled at his words, stiffening in my seat. "You were gone for two hours, and I was terrified something happened to you. Sorry for worrying."

He closed the distance between us in three long strides, his hand lashing out, grabbing my chin. Pushing my head back, he stared down at me. "You could have died. Jeopardized our mission."

I bit down hard on my lower lip and spat out the words. "I saved you. Zeni could have shot again and struck you in the heart if I didn't stop her, but you're welcome."

His grip tightened on my chin, and he stared down at me, fury burning behind those green eyes.

He released me and whipped around, walking away.

I didn't know what to expect but holding onto any kind of composure and schooling my emotions was impossible in that moment.

"That's not the point," he snapped. "It's that I can't trust you. You drugged us then stole one of our ships and endangered yourself. Then I asked you to stay in the ship, so we all knew where you are at all times. So, we didn't compromise the mission and worry that you'd run off again. But you didn't listen."

"Run off? I went to save my dad before." I pointed to the room in the back. "If I didn't go, he wouldn't be here, he would be who knows where."

"Then you talk to one of us. Tell us and we'll work as a team."

I huffed, clenching my fists. "You wouldn't have gone back with me; you would have made me wait. And I'd return for my dad again in a heartbeat if given the chance. He'd been tortured, did you see how he looked?" My words quivered, and I held my chin up, hating Derrial for looking at me like I was the monster in this scenario.

I didn't know what he expected. That I'd sit obediently while those I cared for faced danger. Hell no!

"We just want you safe," Corran added.

I blink.

"Then why bring me to this psychotic planet?" I snapped, and I regretted the words as they fell from my lips.

I tore my gaze from him and Derrial and swallowed the thick ball of dread sitting in my throat. Tears rolled down my cheeks, my insides tearing apart because everything was too much, and I wasn't sure how much more I could take. Anger raged inside me, but it was tapered by the fear I had for me, my men, my parents.

This was the version of Derrial from back on Earth, when he was dominating and in control, when his words were blades piercing my heart. I'd fallen for him since arriving on Veon, given myself to him, believed he wanted the same. Now all I could remember were his kisses that tasted like the best chocolate cake in the world, the strength of his arms around me, and yet fury bubbled under my skin that I'd made a mistake.

His disappointment made me feel like utter crap.

I shot to my feet and crossed the room before heading into the back room where I shut the door. There, the tears flowed like an untamable rapid. With my spine pressed to the wall, I slid to my ass and cupped my face as I cried quietly.

I cried for killing someone who deserved it. For rescuing my father and still not knowing where my mom was. For Derrial being such a dick. For the frustration surging through me. Since arriving here I'd been pushed and pulled in every direction, and I'd had enough.

I didn't remember how long I stayed in the room, but it was my father's groaning that had me stirring and climbing to my feet.

His eyes were wide open, and he pushed himself to sit up, panic in his gaze.

"Dad." I rushed over to the side of the bed and hugged him. I closed my eyes tight and couldn't stop crying. My stomach tightened.

"I thought you were dead." His voice was strangled, and I held him tighter. I'd found my dad, after he'd gone missing, after I buried an empty coffin. I found him.

His arms were strong around me despite his fragile state, and he needed this embrace as much as me, to remember we somehow survived this far.

"I thought I'd lost you forever." He pulled back and wiped my tears. "I can't believe you found me. I was resigned to dying in this barbaric planet with these aliens." Sleep clung to his eyes, but there was hatred on his face.

But when he looked at me, the fury faded, replaced with a genuine smile filled with devotion and utter love. I was transported back to my younger days when our lives didn't include aliens and invasions. When all I worried about was convincing my parents to take us back to the beach on sunny days because my friends were all there.

"Where's Mom?" I finally asked and pulled back.

He was shaking his head, the agony on his face shattering my heart. "We were separated years ago. Women were taken to be sorted for training to become servants or for mating." His ache deepened his frown and he lowered his gaze, my insides shattering like shards of glass.

"Mom's strong," I added. "She'll fight against that; you know she would."

"You take after her." His voice broke, and my whole body wracked with despair, but I blinked hard and swallowed back the hurricane of sorrow pushing forward to engulf me.

"Tell me how you got here, who those Vepar with you are?"

I held onto his hand, feeling like I was a kid again, except this time, I was the strong one. I explained what happened on Earth after him and mom vanished, how the Vepar instilled new rules, stepped into the seats of power, tried to make us healthy. Dad laughed at that part.

Then how I ended up on Veon and a summarized version of what I'd been through. But I didn't mention my feelings for the men or the blood connection. Did Dad even know such a thing existed...and how would he react? I'd tell him soon, but I wasn't ready yet.

"You like these three Vepar?" he asked.

My mouth dropped open. "I never... wait, where did that come from?"

"It's not the words you used, but how you say them when you spoke about the men. Your eyes lit up like they used to do when I snuck you a chocolate cookie when your mom wasn't looking."

I was lost for words because after all these years, Dad didn't miss a beat. "They are arrogant, rude, and super bossy, but..." I combed a hand through my hair. "But I do like them. Maybe more than like. All three in fact." I raised my eyes to his. "Is that wrong?"

He laughed like everything would be okay in the world, and twice in as few minutes he surprised me.

When he stood, his legs gave out and he stumbled back onto the bed.

I reached for him. "Dad."

He pushed to a sitting position on the edge of the bed. "I'll be alright. Just need food and rest I think."

A knock came at the door before it swished open. Corran entered and approached us.

"Nice to meet you, son," my father said, his hand jutting out for a shake, but Corran went straight for a hug, taking Dad back for a moment. But he went with the flow. They hugged each other, patted each other's back, and if it felt awkward to me, it looked double awkward to Dad who stared at me over Corran's shoulder.

"In Vepar tradition," he began. "You always greet a family member of anyone close to you with a strong hug."

Dad's smile brought me endless joy. Here I thought I'd lost him, and that he'd never get a chance to be part of my future, but not anymore.

"Back on Earth, we do strong manly handshakes." Dad said, offering his hand to Corran who accepted and wasn't sure what to do. So, Dad shook it up and down, leaving Corran to over exaggerate his attempt.

I laughed at them, wishing this was our life. Dealing with simple cultural differences not that I might be pregnant from who knows what alien.

"How are you feeling?" Corran asked, staring into Dad's eyes as if trying to see into his soul. "Still dehydrated I see, and your body needs a lot of rest."

"Feeling tired and keep having dizzy spells."

"Your blood sugar is most likely very low. Let me grab something and then stay lying down and you'll just need a few weeks rest."

"A few weeks?" I exclaimed. "We can't even return to your homes."

"We have it sorted. I need to get a hold of the herb that will help with the blood connection, and we may have a solution for where your dad could heal."

"Blood connection?" Dad asked.

I cringed on the inside, not ready to tell him anything about my tie to the three Vepar, how without us feeding on each other's blood, we could get really sick. Yep, he might really freak out and right now I needed him to just get better.

"I'll explain later." I reached for Dad's hand and turned to Corran. "What's the solution?"

"We are going to Derrial's parents' home. They're expecting us."

The last time we went there, his parents accepted me, and I adored them, so going back there came with an excited anticipation as if I might be going back home to visit my family.

"Derrial!" Koria, his mom opened the door with the widest smile, and she embraced her son, holding him so tightly, I knew she was worried for him.

Her blonde hair sat off her face with several hair pins, her floral print dress cascading to her feet. She turned to me and hugged me without a second thought like meeting me once was enough to make me officially part of the family.

"Ella, dear," she gasped. "I've been so worried about all of you. Your faces have been all over the broadcasted news."

"Thank you. It's been an ordeal all right."

She pulled back, staring at me with sympathy and so much agony behind her eyes. "Quickly, in the house. All of you."

We moved indoors to the house that reminded me of a gorgeous botanical garden. Flowery wallpaper lined the walls, flowers in thin metal vases filled every corner, and it smelled like a bouquet in here.

"Koria, this is my dad." I held onto his arm close to me. "I thought I'd lost him, but he'd been taken by the Khonsu." Just saying the words flooded me with so many emotions and already my eyes teared up.

"It's wonderful to meet you," Dad said. "It's a miracle Ella somehow found me and was able to get me out of that slave camp. I wasn't expecting to ever be rescued in all honesty." There was a deflated tone to his voice, and I squeezed his arm tight by my side.

"That's in the past," I added. "We've got each other now." I wanted to say more about finding Mom, but the words wouldn't form. They wouldn't come when fear shuddered through me. It locked me up to acknowledge that we may not find her. Now that I had Dad, the possibility of hope dangled over my head, and I clung onto it for dear life.

"Come sit down," Koria added. "My husband is at work right now, but Derrial has already told me everything. We would love to have you stay with us for as long as needed." She stared at my dad.

"Thank you."

I hugged Koria again because Veon needed more beautiful people like her who loved and not hated.

Corran stepped into the room and shut the door behind them. "Do you mind if I raid your garden? I have a few things I need to prepare downstairs in Derrial's old lab."

"Of course." She was nodding and waving him away as she would do her own child, and I loved how comfortable everyone was here. Taking Dad's arm, she guided him down the hallway. "Come, let me show you your room."

I stared at them, seeing the lighter step in Dad's walk like his determination to fight resurfaced, and I couldn't even begin to imagine what it would have been like for him in the prisons under the Khonsu's ruthlessness.

I shook off the shivers, refusing to let myself go there or I'd drown in sorrow.

Thane hugged me from behind while Corran left the room and Derrial called out from the kitchen, "Take a seat, while I help Corran."

I softened against Thane's embrace. So much had happened lately, and I knew the guys were still upset with me. But to have Dad here with me was everything to me, so they'd just have to understand and accept my decisions.

"You think everything will work out?" I asked, holding onto Thane's arms looped around me.

He kissed the top of my head. "Our enemies could set this world on fire, kitten, but I'd never allow a single flame to touch you."

My heart gave a skip at his words and I looked up at him, at the sincerity behind those ocean blue eyes. My heart started racing at his intensity, at the captivation in his gaze. He wanted me as much as I desired him. And I let myself fall... let myself believe that maybe in this insane world of war and hatred, in a place that wouldn't accept us easily, I could find a way to have a future with these men. Maybe I was being foolish...

"Any chance of having a quick shower?" I asked, and Thane walked me to the bathroom. Inside I noticed the plastic large tube that stretched from floor to ceiling in the corner of the room. Just like the cylinder clothes changer wardrobe I'd used in the house during the trials. My heart soared at the sight because I needed one of these in my home badly.

"Want me to join you?" Thane teased, and as much as I'd love to get all soapy with him, I couldn't do it with my dad in the house.

I pushed a palm against his chest and drove him backward and out into the corridor. "Not here, but you can picture me running my hands all over my body." I winked, and the sexual glaze lashing over his gaze came so instantly, I knew he would do exactly that.

"See you soon." I shut the door and couldn't wait to wash myself and feel semi-normal.

Half an hour later, I stood in front of the mirror dressed in a teal skirt that tumbled to my knees and a body-fitting, white buttoned-up shirt with three-quarter sleeves. I straightened the collar and the top sat open around my throat, showing just a smidgen of cleavage. Running my fingers through my towel-dried hair, I pushed the dark strands off my face and stared at how much thinner I looked since first arriving here. There was a glow in my cheeks, a wildness in my eyes, and despite running around, I couldn't help but feel like this was the prettiest I'd ever looked and felt. Maybe running for my life constantly was good for my health in a weird ironic way.

I returned to the main room where everyone but Corran sat around chatting. They glanced up at my arrival, everyone smiling, and I gaited over to sit between my men, feeling lighter after that wash.

"You look delicious by the way," Thane whispered in my ear.

Just then, Corran returned, carrying a glass of a deep purple juice like this was the world's salvation. The rest of us were sitting around the main room talking about donuts. Trying to explain to Derrial's mom what they were and her insistence she'd attempt to make them.

"Drink this." Corran handed me the glass that was surprisingly warm to the touch. "It needs to be in your system warm, then we need to go."

"Go?" I looked up at him.

Derrial was already on his feet as was Thane, standing tall like sentinels.

"This will awaken your immune system to a state that will allow our blood connection to merge once again. But it'll only stay active in your system for a short time. Maybe an hour or two."

"Hell, then let's bottle it and I'll take it a bit later when we're ready." My cheeks blushed at trying to hint the need for exchanging blood with each other came in the form of sexual contact. And I was not going to sneak into one of the bedrooms here with all three guys while our parents were out here. I died a little on the inside at the thought.

"Drink it while it's warm and fresh or it won't work," Corran said.

Steeling myself, I pressed the glass to my lips and gulped it all back, the concoction tasting gritty and sour with a hint of lemon.

Corran collected the glass which he placed on the coffee table, while Derrial drew me to my feet by my arms, and I kept licking grit on my teeth, feeling like I'd just drank a glass of muddy water. "That didn't taste great."

"We gotta go," he explained to his mom. "I'll be in contact soon."

I turned to my father and rushed over to him as he climbed out of his seat with care. Without a word, I embraced him. "I'm going to miss you, but you'll be safe here. And I'll be back as soon as I can."

"You won't get hurt with this blood connection, will you?"

I was shaking my head, but not really knowing the answer to that but I hoped and prayed and trusted the men knew what they were doing. "We need this, so we don't get sick. I promise to explain so much once I return. Love you."

He hugged me tighter. "Love you too, Ella. Thank you for finding me."

"We need to go," Derrial added.

I broke from my dad, feeling an urgency flooding my veins like I didn't know anything about what I'd just drank, and I needed to know what I'd gotten myself into. "We'll be back when we can. You'll be safe here."

I turned and left my dad behind just as a strange tingling wormed through the pit of my stomach.

Thane took my hand in his, and we rushed outside and toward the ship in the large back yard, hidden from sight with the reflective shields.

That earlier tingling spread through me faster and warmed me up so fast, I was breathing faster. "I feel strange."

Looking over at Derrial, at the corded muscles of his arms, the strength in his body, I was suddenly engulfed with heat, my nipples puckering, and all I could think about was his mouth on me... on all of me.

I shook my head. "What was in that drink?"

"The herb we used can have some side effects when used fresh, which is why in the lab we always used the dried version," Corran explained.

"What sort of side effects?" I demanded.

Derrial's fingers holding my wrist twitched, and that slight movement sent my body into a shudder so deep and arousing, a moan slipped past my lips, and I squeezed my thighs so tight, I was convinced I was about to orgasm from a simple touch.

All three men stared at me with desire flaring in their eyes, and I couldn't help but love the way they looked at me right then. Even if my body felt like it might self-combust.

"What's happening to me?"

"The herb can heighten your arousal significantly."

"Significantly?" That idea terrified me. "How long will this last? Oh my god, you gave me Viagra!"

"Get inside the ship," Derrial commanded and dragged me through the open door, my feet stumbling after me.

"What's Viagra?" Corran studied me intently.

I leaned against the cool inside wall of the shuttle, needing to stop burning up. "A tablet taken by men usually to help them stay... erect for longer." I rolled my back across the wall. "Can someone die from being so horny they might explode?"

Thane laughed, and the sound was so damn sexy, my skin pricked with excitement. All I could think about was taking off his clothes.

He strode to the driver's seat, and I chewed on my lower lip as I stared at his tight ass in those black pants.

"Why's it so hot in here? Switch the air con on to max."

Derrial stared at me like he had no clue what I was talking about, but I was already pulling at the buttons of my shirt, tugging the collar away, needing to cool down.

The small vibrations of the ship started, and we ascended into the air.

"Come, take a seat." Corran's hand slid to my lower back, and his touch ignited a spark of shivers jolting through me. I turned on him so fast, I scared myself. But just having his hands on me felt incredible. Pinpricks coated my bare skin with anticipation. That drink had my body reacting so quickly, it spun my head.

I looked over at him as he sat, and I did the same. His eyes hazed over like he saw nothing else but me. He leaned in closer, his lips capturing mine, and I softened against him, thrumming like a leaf in a storm.

"I need you," I breathed desperately into his mouth.

His lips left a trail of kisses down my cheek and found the tender spot right between my neck and collarbone. I moaned louder, and the apex between my thighs pulsed wildly.

I was on fire.

Fingers pulled at my shirt ferociously, buttons ripped free, popping around us, but I didn't care. Not when Corran's hand claimed my shoulder and dragged the strap of my bra down my arm, not when I pushed myself up and over to straddle Corran's lap.

My breast slipped free, gaining Corran's attention and eliciting a smirk.

Large palms clasped my ass, hauling me against him, and he drew my hardened nipple into his mouth. I kissed him with the fever that took me, rubbing myself against the hard cock in his pants.

I needed this.

I needed him.

I needed all of them.

My fingers flexed against his shoulders. His teeth dragged over the flesh of my breast, leaving me trembling.

He suddenly jolted himself to his feet, taking me with him still wrapped around him. Strong arms held my thighs, and I kissed him endlessly, grasping his shoulders, holding on.

Turning us around, he pinned me to the cool wall, grinding the hard bulge in his pants against my fire. He worked against me, and my hips bucked to meet his thrust, only thin layers of fabric between us kept us completely apart.

He was strong and his moans were filled with desperation, frustration of needing to get to me.

His mouth nipped at my flesh of my breast, his hand pushing up and under my skirt.

I looked up to see Derrial standing feet away, his shirt off and his hand on his thick cock, the tip already glistening with his excitement.

"I need you all," I murmured.

Thane already leapt over his seat and joined us, pulling his shirt up and over his head, revealing spectacular ripped abs. My fingers tingled with an urgency to touch him.

Derrial pushed his shirt off and removed his shoes as he dragged his pants off. He stepped closer completely naked, breathing heavily. His red horns seemed to almost vibrate, and his long devilish tail curled forward, reaching for me. He was so beautiful, so handsome, I could orgasm from just staring at him naked.

As if sensing him, Corran lifted his head from my breasts, his canines seeming longer as if they'd extended. He turned me around and Derrial's greedy hands pulled my shirt off my back in one fast move before unclasping the bra at my back. He tossed the clothes aside and left me topless. Rugged hands pushed aside my long hair and his mouth found my neck, hands sliding around my body, clasping both breasts, pinching my nipples to the point of pain... delicious pain and I moaned loudly. He drew me backward, lowering my back against his chest, my head cradled against his shoulder. Thane was there now too, his large palms sliding under my lower back, holding me as Corran wrenched my skirt off, still holding me in their arms, like I was a feast they were about to devour. And I welcomed it.

Thane's hand slid to the waistband of my thong, his fingers curling around it before he snapped it off me so aggressively my whole body shook. Fingers reached down and trailed down my heat, a guttural sound rolling from his chest at finding me already so wet. So ready. And I pushed my hips toward him, needing more, but his fingers slid down my inner thighs, teasing me.

"Please, no teasing. I can't take it," I begged.

In unison, they set me down on the floor where a thick blanket waited, and I had no idea when they'd laid it down.

The whisper of a zipper sounded as Corran undressed himself before dropping to his knees and with rough hands on my knees, spread my legs. He glanced down at me, smiling wickedly.

Derrial's hands sailed over my breasts, pulling at my nipples and I writhed, driven closer and closer to the edge.

Thane knelt next to me, his mouth on my stomach, licking me as he went lower.

Corran spread me wider for Thane who licked over my small mound, then slid deeper, his tongue aggressively lashing over my clit.

An explosive groan rolled through my chest as I arched my back.

The slurping sounds he made were intoxicating with his mouth clamped over me, and I floated away on the heady desire carrying me away.

I was gushing with euphoria, moaning, unable to work out here I started and ended. "Yes, yes, right there."

"Fuck, you smell so delicious," he growled and pulled back, while I groaned in protest for more.

Just then, Corran pushed a finger into me, and I met his stare, those brilliant caramel eyes enthralling me. He pushed another finger inside me, and I raised my hips to meet him as he fingered me so fast, I exploded into a scream.

My thighs fell wider, and he leaned down, his mouth on my inner thigh, taking small mock bites of flesh. I felt his teeth, and he nicked skin, rough and painful... just what I wanted. When his fingers slid out of me, I was left needy and starved.

Thane's attention shifted to a breast, his mouth opening wide and sucking me hard.

Derrial lifted my shoulders against him as he kneeled behind me, his tongue on my neck.

All three kissed and nibbled on me, hands all over my body, reaching, touching every part of me. And I gave myself to them, needing them endlessly. My body felt heavy with arousal yet light enough that I could be floating. I couldn't explain it, but the desire intensified.

"Fuck," I yelled out.

"That's nothing compared to what you're about to feel," Corran stated, his breath on my flesh burning me up, his mouth dragging lower over my bikini line, driving me insane with his teasing.

Lust and buzzing seared through my veins, and I was so close to coming.

Corran's mouth slid over me, taking me, his tongue sinking into me, his nose pressed to my clit.

I screamed as the orgasm tore over me.

Sharp fangs pierced my neck.

My breasts.

The inside of my thigh.

I convulsed, seizing Thane's shoulder with one hand, Derrial's hair fisted in another and my thighs clenched around Corran's head. My body rocked with lust, liquid hot fire, and I was so wet, dripping. All three men drank from me in that exquisite moment of lust.

The sensation stretched out, the men drinking my blood, taking and taking while I burned with a desire I'd never experienced before.

Thane released his hold first, blood dripping from his lush lips, and he bit down onto his wrist before pressing it to my mouth.

"Drink, my kitten."

I clasped his arm, taking his life force. The metallic taste smeared my lips and tongue, sliding out the corners of my mouth, and I gulped the coppery blood down....it tasted so sweet.

Corran's head moved from my thigh, and his face was suddenly buried against my pussy again, licking and tasting me feverishly.

I moaned and sucked on Thane's blood while the men devoured me. Thane plucked his hand from me, and I lurched after him, needing more, licking my lips with hunger, but it was Derrial who drew me to him next, giving me his forearm, the gash bubbling with fresh blood.

I ran a tongue over the cut and latched my mouth to him, starved for the taste that was now a part of me.

Already, my body responded, awakened, stronger and I craved so much more.

"That's enough," Derrial ordered, also taking his arm from me, and I winced.

The men pulled back from me, sitting on their heels, their mouths and chins and chests coated in blood, their horns vibrating, and I'd never seen anyone this sexy in my life. I wanted us smothered in our bloods, rolling in it, fucking in it.

"On your knees," Derrial ordered. "And turn to face Corran."

My aroused induced brain kicked in and I rolled over onto my stomach before sticking my ass into the air and pushing myself to hands and knees. Like a prowling cat, I turned around in slow motion on hands and knees, blood dripping from my wounds, the men staring at me like predators about to strike.

Derrial's large hands grabbed my hips and hauled me against him so hard and fast, I cried out.

Thane lay on his back and shuffled in underneath me, taking a breast into his mouth, his sharp teeth marking me, bleeding me, while Corran walked on his knees closer. With a sharp fingernail, he sliced himself just above his groin. I pressed my lips to him, licking and tasting him, taking him into me.

The tip of Derrial's cock pressed against my entrance, and he nudged my thighs wider with a hand. Then he pushed into me without ceremony, inch by inch he pressed deeper, slowly and gently, making room for himself inside me. He was so big. And he kept pushing, filling me further even when I was full.

With a slap to my ass, he pulled out and thrust back in, harder, faster.

Then he fucked me hard. Rode me, never letting up. Burst of arousal engulfed me, and I wanted more and more and more. I gasped for air, sweat and blood coated me, and I drank from my lovers.

All the while, Derrial dominated me, and wanted me to know it. Wanted me to remember my place.

And there was no doubt in my mind who I belonged to.

To three intoxicating Vepars.

Three men who owned me, body, soul, and mind.

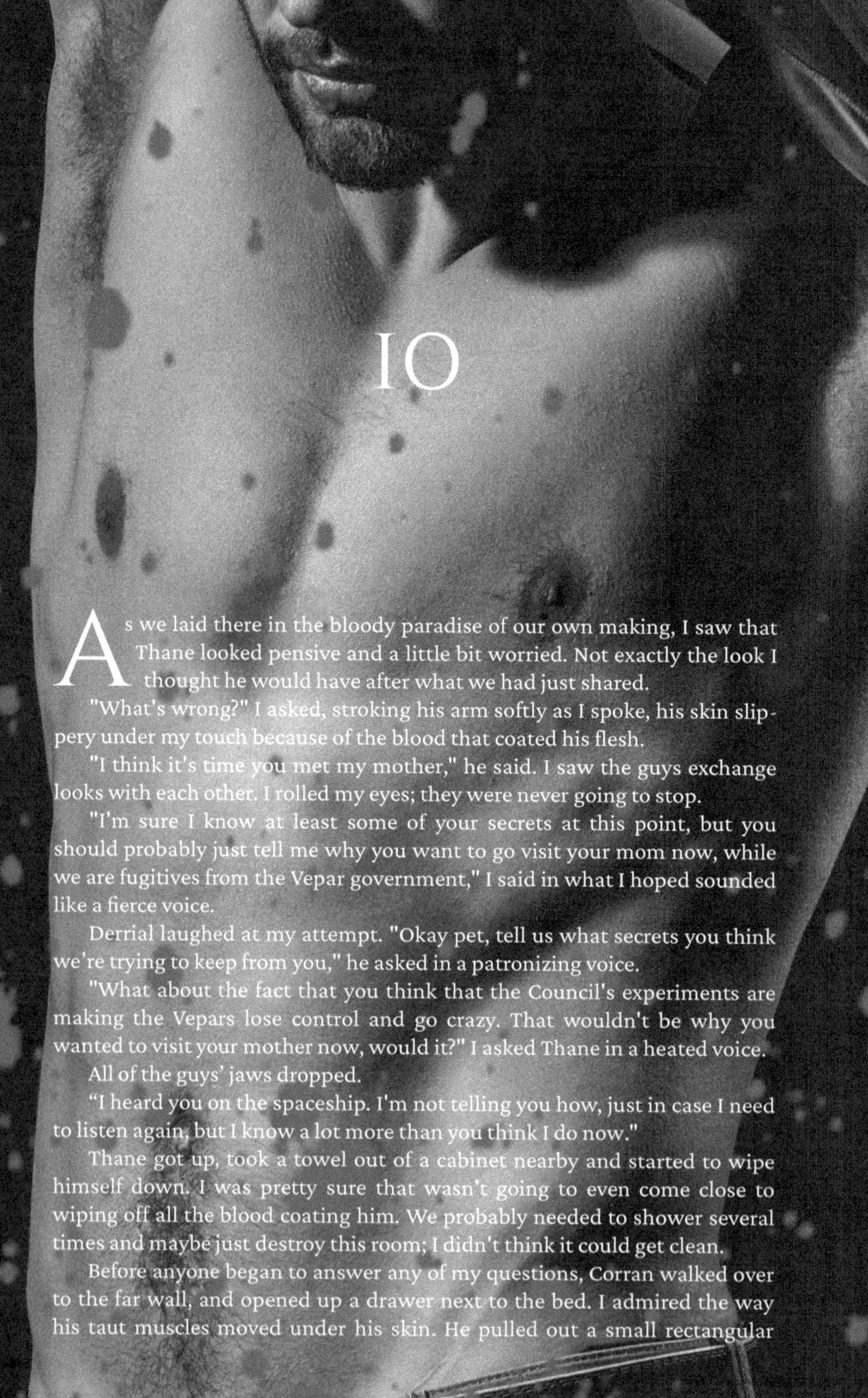

As we laid there in the bloody paradise of our own making, I saw that Thane looked pensive and a little bit worried. Not exactly the look I thought he would have after what we had just shared.

"What's wrong?" I asked, stroking his arm softly as I spoke, his skin slippery under my touch because of the blood that coated his flesh.

"I think it's time you met my mother," he said. I saw the guys exchange looks with each other. I rolled my eyes; they were never going to stop.

"I'm sure I know at least some of your secrets at this point, but you should probably just tell me why you want to go visit your mom now, while we are fugitives from the Vepar government," I said in what I hoped sounded like a fierce voice.

Derrial laughed at my attempt. "Okay pet, tell us what secrets you think we're trying to keep from you," he asked in a patronizing voice.

"What about the fact that you think that the Council's experiments are making the Vepars lose control and go crazy. That wouldn't be why you wanted to visit your mother now, would it?" I asked Thane in a heated voice.

All of the guys' jaws dropped.

"I heard you on the spaceship. I'm not telling you how, just in case I need to listen again, but I know a lot more than you think I do now."

Thane got up, took a towel out of a cabinet nearby and started to wipe himself down. I was pretty sure that wasn't going to even come close to wiping off all the blood coating him. We probably needed to shower several times and maybe just destroy this room; I didn't think it could get clean.

Before anyone began to answer any of my questions, Corran walked over to the far wall, and opened up a drawer next to the bed. I admired the way his taut muscles moved under his skin. He pulled out a small rectangular device that looked similar to a cigarette lighter. He opened up the top and pressed a button.

I watched in amazement as beads of blood started to rise up in the air from where they had been plastered all over the sheets, floor, our bodies, and the walls. The blood droplets gathered and zoomed towards the machine, disappearing into it somehow even though it was way too small to hold all the carnage of the room. After just a few minutes, the room, our clothes, and everything else was perfectly clean, like I had just imagined the mess we had just made.

"Better close your mouth, kitten. You wouldn't want a Daygar to get in," advised Corran with a laugh.

"What the hell is a Daygar?" I asked. "We say flies usually when we're talking about closing your mouth, is a Daygar similar to that," I asked, confused.

The guys were all openly laughing at me at this point. "The Daygars are monsters that eat your tongue while you are sleeping. They're not real, but we tell children that in order to get them to behave," answered Derrial.

I thought about Bruda's similar tale about parents telling the children about the Khonsu to keep them in line. Clearly these people had a different idea of appropriate stories to tell their children than humans did.

"I'm going to be closely monitoring any stories we tell our children," I announced to all of them.

Immediately there was a soft look in all of their eyes, you would've thought that I had just given them one million dollars or something like that. "What?" I asked suspiciously.

"That's just the first time you've really talked about actually having children with us," said Corran softly.

I stared at him. "I thought that was a foregone conclusion considering I could possibly be pregnant already. Although, I guess there's no chance the child would be one of yours though, is there?" I asked, a wave of sadness and frustration welling over me.

It was bad enough to be forced to be pregnant. But then to not even know who the father was? What if he was a monster? What if I was growing a monster's baby? What would we do then?

"We can't worry about that right now. And there's always the chance that it could be one of ours. Our sperm was used in the experiments since I was in charge of them," Corran explained.

He must've seen the confused look on my face, because he answered before I could voice my question. "That whole God complex that us scientists have. If we were going to create new life, I wanted that life to be because of me," he said, not sounding a little bit embarrassed about it.

A thin tendril of hope rose up in me, even though I knew that I should tamp it down.

"But I'm sure everything was labeled. There's no way that the Council would've allowed one of your sperm to be used in an experiment with me after everything that's happened," I said, my hopes dashing into pieces at those thoughts.

"That's probably true," said Corran. "But there's still a chance that it could be one of ours if you are even pregnant."

I nodded. If I believed that enough, maybe it would come true...right?

"Now that Corran has managed to clean us all up, let's get out of here," Thane commanded, breaking the suddenly heavy silence.

"To see your mother?" I asked.

Thane nodded. "I want you to meet her. But... I also want to check in on her. I usually visit her once a month when I'm on Veon. I know that they've taken a lot of the affected Vepar to her facility, so I want to check on the security precautions to make sure that she's safe."

My heart melted at how worried he sounded. All of them were so layered. It felt like I was always discovering new things about them. Thane's concern over his mother's safety was just another layer. It had been a very long time since she had been any form of a parent to him, but I could tell that she still meant so much to him.

"Let's go," I said.

Thane and Derrial spent a few minutes mapping out a route to the facility. It was obviously a risk going there since it was a risk going anywhere public right now. They didn't think that the Council would put resources toward scoping out the facility, but you never knew. It was apparently common knowledge among the higher ups where Thane's mom was kept.

We would have to don disguises when we went into the building though, just in case the staff had been alerted to our "most wanted" status.

Finally, we were off. Zipping through the Vepar sky, I watched the myriad of colors underneath us, I once again marveled at how I'd ended up on this crazy planet.

The trip was short. Only an hour passed before we were there. We stopped about a mile away so that the ship's sensors could detect the area for any of the Council or its army. When none appeared, except one in one of the facilities' buildings upstairs who had gone crazy, we flew in closer and landed in a patch of woods outside the facility.

Corran disguised me as a blonde with two Vepar horns the color of ebony coming out of my head. The guys disguised themselves as well and we left the ship. There was no way that anyone would recognize us in these getups.

I wasn't sure what to expect as we got closer to the building. We were about to walk into what basically amounted to a Vepar insane asylum. I wasn't sure what insanity looked like here considering I was pretty sure Zeni had been insane and she had still been allowed to roam free. Their standards for what counted as crazy must have been a little different from Earth's.

From the outside the facility looked similar to other Vepar dwellings I had seen, except it was a lot larger. In fact, it was almost as large as the

Khonsu arena had been. Except this was in the familiar dome-shape of most of the Vepar dwellings.

It was perfectly white on the outside, a light dusting of silver sparkles peeking out from the pristine whiteness. It was impossible to tell what the front of the building was and what was the back since there were no visible doors or windows.

I followed the guys to the building. We stood there in front of the blank wall, which I assumed had to be the front, and we waited. After what felt like ten minutes, I jumped back in surprise when a holographic image of a beautiful Vepar woman appeared in front of us.

"Please state your name," she said in a perfectly calm voice. The tone of her voice was so calm that it evoked images of meadows and rippling streams just by listening to it. It was the perfect voice for a place like this whose inhabitants were probably the opposite of calm.

"Aeryn," Thane said, not giving a last name. Corran had hacked into the facilities database when Thane's mother had been first admitted and inputted several aliases for them all into the system. They now had several names with security clearances to be used with their different disguises. I guess the guys had always believed in being prepared.

"I'm here to see, Lania," Thane continued, cutting off my thoughts. The hologram nodded.

"Please wait," she stated before disappearing.

Lania, that was a pretty name. I wondered if she and Thane looked alike.

I was nervous when a door appeared in the previously smooth wall and we walked in. Even though by the sound of it, Thane's mother wouldn't talk to me very much, I still had an innate need for her to like me.

The inside of the facility was the same stark white as the outside. Apparently the Vepar had come to the same decision as facilities on Earth, that the mentally ill needed the serenity of white rather than the chaos of the other colors.

We went down a long hallway with no windows or doors. There was no sign of anyone else although I thought I could hear faint yells and screams from beyond the walls. I started to feel claustrophobic. Corran must've sensed my distress because he grabbed my hand in his and squeezed it reassuringly.

After a time, we came to another wall and stopped in front of it. The hologram appeared again.

"Lania is having a good day today. Please be advised that she continues to suffer from intense hallucinations and is prone to outbursts of anger that can lead to physical violence. Today she has been allowed to freely move around her room. Please make sure that you are not carrying any sharp objects or other items that could be used as weapons," the hologram told us.

Thane's body had stiffened at the robotic way that the hologram spit out his mother's medical information, like she wasn't a living being, just another statistic in a computer. I felt a rush of pity that I knew Thane wouldn't appreciate. What had his life been like, having a mother who suffered from issues like that?

It made me think of my own mother and the fact that she was still missing. Soft was what I thought of when I thought of my mother. Her voice, her mannerisms, the feeling of her skin. Everything about her had been soft and loving. I wondered if years of torture under the Khonsu had knocked that out of her. If she was alive, would she be joining Thane's mother at a place like this?

I shivered just thinking about it. After Thane nodded his understanding and the rest of us all nodded as well, a door appeared in the wall. It slid open, and we walked into another white room. There was a white metal bed in one corner of the room. It looked like it had been wrapped in some kind of padding. I supposed so that she wouldn't be able to hurt herself on it. The room was empty of any furnishings besides a large screen that was embedded into one of the walls. On the screen played a slideshow of various images that I recognized as different places around Veon. Soft smooth music played from hidden speakers in the walls. And there, sitting on a white pillow on the floor in front of the screen, was who I assumed was Thane's mother.

She turned to look at us as we came in and her face lit up with a stunning smile. She was gorgeous, as were all the Vepar, but she had a certain look about her that was different from the other Vepar that I'd seen. There were deep lines around her eyes and her forehead unlike other Vepars. She also had a certain sadness in her stunning blue eyes, the same blue eyes that I stared into whenever I gazed at Thane's face.

"Visitors," she said delightedly in a raspy voice that sounded more like it was a result of screaming than how her natural tone was. "I don't have visitors often," she said self-consciously, running a hand through her hair. "Don't mind the mess. I told Thane to pick up his toys, but you know how little boys are," she continued.

No one had mentioned to me that Thane's mother was so far gone that she wouldn't recognize him. I watched the devastation flicker in Thane's eyes and saw how it turned into resignation. I suspected that he always held out hope that his visits would go differently than this and that she would actually recognize him.

"Little boys are mischievous," Thane told her softly. He approached her slowly, as if he were approaching a wild animal. He crouched down in front of her. She watched him; eyes wide. "How are you today, Lania. My name is Aeryn," he said in that same calm, gentle voice that sounded more like Corran than it did him.

"It's been an excellent day. I tended my flowers, I picked some food from the garden, Thane and I skipped rocks on the pond out back. My husband should be here soon. I'm sure you and him will get along wonderfully," she said.

Thane nodded. He continued to ask her questions, inquiring after her health and trying to get her to tell him how she was being treated at the facility. It was hard to do since she was stuck in an alternate reality. Not once did she ask him why he was visiting her. I wondered why that was.

After a while, she took her attention off of Thane and looked at us.

"And who have you brought with you?" she asked, giving me a big smile as she spoke. Thane stood up and walked over to my side. "Mot- I mean Lania, I'd like you to meet my mate, Ella," he said, wrapping his arm around my waist and walking me towards his mother. She stood up off her pillow and held out her hand. "It's so wonderful to meet you, Ella. My, you are a lovely girl. Just the kind of girl I could see my Thane marrying someday."

It took me a moment to remember that I looked nothing like myself, and a pang of sadness hit me that I may never get the chance to have Thane introduce me as myself.

I clasped her hand in both of mine. "Lania, it's a pleasure to meet you. Your Thane sounds like a lovely boy."

That must've been the right thing to say, because Lania launched into a million stories about Thane as a young boy. I listened in rapt fascination, hoping that they were real stories and I was getting more clues into my mysterious mate's past. I knew he would never tell me these stories himself.

She was in the middle of a story about when Thane had tried to capture a Khonsu by himself at five years old, then she suddenly stopped talking. She began staring off into the distance as if she could see something else in the room other than us.

With a high-pitched scream, she began to thrash and moan. Her words were garbled and nonsensical, and she leapt at Thane with her hands outstretched like claws as if she was going to tear him apart with her bare hands.

"Lania," Thane said soothingly as he grabbed her, holding her hands to her sides as she thrashed and screamed in his arms. Tears streamed down my face as I watched Thane. His hands were trembling, and there was pure agony on his face as he held down his mother. The door behind us suddenly opened and a stream of Vepar clad in white doctor's coats rushed into the room. One of the staff, a Vepar male close to the same size as Thane, with dirty blonde hair and two small, lime green horns on his head, pulled a syringe filled needle out of his pocket as he approached Lania.

"Is that necessary?" Thane asked brokenly.

"Her episodes have been getting worse as of late. The only way to calm her down is to knock her out," he answered stiffly.

I hated seeing them administer the injection. It reminded me of all the times that a syringe had been used on me.

The medicine worked instantly, and soon she went limp in Thane's arms.

He helped the staff move her back to bed and tenderly pulled the blankets up to her chin. The staff left as quickly as they had come in. Alone again, Thane patted his mother's shoulder gently, pressing a kiss to her forehead softly. "Sweet dreams, mama," he whispered, and his pain was so tangible it was like I could see his heart breaking.

I wanted to give Thane a hug, but I could tell it wouldn't be welcome at the moment. Thane liked to grieve privately, and he probably hated that we were in the room to watch him right now.

"Should we go?" asked Derrial calmly, as if nothing had happened.

Thane nodded and stepped away from his mother, taking one last look back at her as we left the room. I finally couldn't help myself, and I grabbed his hand in both of mine. I brought them to my lips to give them a gentle kiss in an attempt to provide some comfort.

His sad eyes looked at me, and I watched as they briefly warmed at my touch.

We had just taken a few steps down the hall when a door to the left of us opened. A Vepar with a yellow stump on his salt-and-pepper flecked hair walked out of the room accompanied by a staff member. Looking closer at him, I realized that it looked like his horn had been sawed off.

When he saw us, immediate recognition lit across his features. I didn't know how this was possible since we were disguised. From the stiffening shoulders of my mates, it was clear that they recognized him as well. Derrial suddenly grabbed me around the waist, as if we were going to have to run at any moment.

"Still using the same disguises, are we?" the Vepar sneered at us. I looked at him in shock. How would he have seen these disguises before? He didn't look at me, he only had eyes for the guys.

"Nice to see you all walking around free, while I'm stuck in this hellhole," he spat at us. We had all stopped in the hallway, facing each other. The staff member was looking back and forth between us confused.

The Vepar finally glanced at me. "And who do we have here? Is this the human bitch that you betrayed me for? It's a nice Vepar mask she has on. I would love to see what she really looks like," he snarled.

My eyes widened and I rubbed a hand across my face, making sure that my disguise was still in place and you couldn't see it pulling away from my skin or something.

Derrial started to pull me down the hallway, away from the altercation taking place.

"I did everything I was supposed to for you," he yelled angrily. "Did you find her and decide that you wanted to keep her from the Council? Is that why I'm stuck in here?" he asked.

I stopped and pulled away from Derrial, who had still been trying to urge me forward. What was this man talking about?

He saw my confusion and began to laugh, an eerily crazed laugh that fit in with this place perfectly.

"You must be something special." He leered at me. "The other girls we harvested for the Council didn't make any of these assholes so much as blink."

At that statement, the staff member gripped his arm firmly. "That's enough now," he barked, beginning to drag him away from all of us.

"Did you ever find out what the Council was doing with all those human women, or do you still not care?" he cackled. "Because I did," he said, beginning to laugh uproariously. The laugh echoed down the hallway until he was out of sight, leaving us alone.

I stood still for a moment, struggling to put together everything he had just said with what I had been told and learned before this. I finally looked at them. "Were you the ones that brought women like Bruda to the Council to be their slaves?" I asked, horror freezing my insides.

"I don't think we should talk about that here," Thane said warily. "There's more to this than you can understand right now."

Derrial tried to grab me again to lead me out of the facility, but my feet refused to move. It was like I had been encased in ice.

It was bad enough when I had thought that they had known about the existence of my parents and possibly other human beings on this planet. But to find out that they'd actually been the ones harvesting humans to bring them back to Veon for the Council's use. And that the Council had then used the human women as sex slaves...

Everything just kept getting worse. It had been awful to think that I was the special human that they had brought back for the first time to try and solve the Vepar's fertility issues. But I was just one person. The idea of them stealing human women on a mass scale...it was just incomprehensible.

They were monsters. There was no way around it.

I felt something break inside of me at that moment. It was like something snapped, and I was left with an emptiness in its wake that felt irreparable.

"Stop looking at us like that," Derrial groaned, rubbing his heart like I had mortally wounded him.

"You make me sick," I spat at them. "How can you even deign to call me your mate when I'm human. What made me different than all of those poor people that you sentenced to a life of unending torment?"

"Just let us..." started Corran.

"There's nothing you can say to make this better," I screeched, probably causing a scene to whoever was listening behind closed doors. I expected the facility's security staff to arrive at any moment, but I didn't care.

"We've changed, you have to admit that," Thane answered desperately.

I began to back away from them, not sure where I was going to go. I knew I wasn't safe to be away from them, but in this moment...I wasn't sure how I could stay.

Just then an alarm started blaring, practically bursting my eardrums with how loud it rang. The guys looked around, immediately trying to analyze where the danger was coming from.

Derrial grabbed me, this time not letting me go as he began to drag me down the hallway. I didn't fight him this time, I wasn't a fool.

I noticed that Thane hadn't moved from where he was standing. He looked torn.

"What are you doing? We need to go!" barked Derrial.

"My mother," he said. And that was all he needed to say. Whatever this alarm was, it sounded serious.

"Fuck," said Derrial. "Let's go." He turned around and started to move back in the direction we'd come from. He was walking so fast that I couldn't keep up, so he had to hoist me into his arms as the guys started to run.

His touch made my skin crawl, but what could I do?

We had just reached the wall where I thought his mom's room lay beyond, when a sudden trampling of hurried footsteps came from the left of us.

I looked up and immediately felt Derrial shudder with panic beneath me.

"Grab her," he barked, but Thane was already blasting through the wall to escape. Evidently, we didn't have enough time for him to try and activate the door.

Derrial must have decided he needed to get me out of there because he turned to run back outside.

But it was too late.

Vepar after Vepar came streaming towards us. But they weren't regular Vepar. Something was wrong with them. The sounds coming out of their mouths didn't resemble any language I had ever heard.

They lurched like they'd lost control of their functioning body and now it just moved like someone controlled them. Faces pale, clothes torn, limbs inflicted with wounds and bloody cuts. What happened to these people?

An unsuspecting nurse headed out of a nearby room when three of the Vepar lunged at her, dragging her to the ground. She screamed, and Thane charged. He hurled a fist into one man, then lunged for the two other attackers. He flipped one off the men in an incredible wrestling match to the ground. Shoving the last man off the nurse, he dragged the woman back to her feet by the back of her uniform, the poor thing crying, blood pouring from her bites and scratches. She darted back into the office.

I whimpered and recoiled into Derrial. My heart shuddered as I watched them scratch and bite her. They were like zombies.

Please don't let it be zombies. I can't handle that on top of everything else.

Derrial pushed me behind him. "Corran take the few at our rear," he commanded, his voice tense and strained. "I'll take the rest with Thane."

"Pet," he said to me without looking back. "Please stay low and hidden."

Then he burst forward at the onslaught of Vepars.

Behind me, Corran had fought and knocked to the ground a man with a single punch, while two others lunged onto his back.

I cried out and trembled insanely. But instinct punched me in the gut, and I scanned the hallway, finding only a metal table on wheels for a weapon. I ran and grabbed the damn table and shoved it toward one of the demons, driving it right into the hip of a man about to pile on top of Corran as well.

He groaned with shock and stumbled over his own feet, hitting the ground hard.

Corran kicked a man in front of him, while I grabbed the arm of the woman clinging to his back like a monkey, her mouth gaping open, readying to bite him. Drool seeped from her mouth and I gagged, but I wrenched her backward.

"Get off him," I cried.

Corran whipped around, his expression startled, but he flashed me a grin. "Thanks." A fast kiss on my lips, and he threw himself back against the three encroaching Vepar. If I wasn't so terrified, I might swoon.

Someone slapped a hand to my shoulder.

I flinched around, my heart racing, and shoved the hand off me.

A young man with stubby white horns and a square head snarled, lips peeled over sharp canines. His shirt had been half torn and hung off low on one shoulder. His flesh was dotted in bite marks.

My feet slipped backward.

My stomach clenched.

Hands raised; grubby fingers reached for me as he rushed forward.

I screamed, backing away.

Corran whirled toward me in an instant, grabbed the attacker by the throat, and hurled him into a wall.

I stared in awe, in complete and utter amazement at his strength.

More of the infected or whatever they were, staggered down the hallway, and I looked left and right, unsure where to go, where it'd be safe.

I reached for a nearby door, pushing on the handle, but it was locked. I snapped around, my heart in my throat. No other doors to try, so I slid down near the metal table, my back to the wall, and tucked my knees against my chest. I tried to curl myself tight, too scared to move. A scream bubbled on my throat. After everything, I didn't want us to die here. Not like this.

The fights grew vicious, and I remained low, watching every blow... every bite and punch. I lost concept of time, but when I saw Derrial fall, I couldn't help but run to him. I didn't even register what was going on around me. All I could see was Derrial lying on the ground motionless, blood seeping from his body.

I sank to my knees beside him. My hands immediately went to his chest in a desperate attempt to stop the bleeding. Not that that ever worked... even in the movies. But I still had to try.

"It's okay, it's okay," I said desperately. Derrial opened his eyes and took a deep, rattling breath. Even with my nonexistent medical knowledge, I knew that rattling wasn't a good thing.

I looked around desperately for Corran. Surely, he would have his device with him to help heal these injuries. He was in the middle of a fight with two rabid Vepar however, and it didn't look like he was winning. Looking around next for Thane, his situation was even more dire. He was on his knees, bloody slashes all over his body as he tried to fend off at least five of the crazed Vepar who were attacking him from all angles.

Looking down at a dying Derrial, I realized we weren't going to make it.

Derrial slid his trembling hand to mine and took it in a weak grasp. "I'm so sorry, Ella," he wheezed out.

I didn't know what he was saying sorry for, was it for kidnapping me in the first place or transporting humans to Veon for years... Did it really matter? At that moment, honestly, I didn't care.

Maybe that made me a terrible person that I could forgive all of that but seeing the being that I'd fallen irreversibly in love with dying in my arms...that made forgiveness a lot more possible.

"I'm so sorry for all of it," he repeated, his eyes glistening. "At least now you will be free."

This wasn't happening. This wasn't real life. After everything we'd been through, this was really the end.

I heard a pained grunt and my eyes flashed over to Thane. Piles of Vepar surrounded him, but he was on his hands and knees on the floor, covered in blood. My eyes flashed over to Corran, still expecting somehow that one of them was going to be able to save the day. Corran was passed out on the ground, the two Vepar he had been battling on the ground alongside him.

I stood up and ran over to Corran's body. He was still breathing, but barely. I started patting him down, looking for the device. I couldn't find it.

"Where is it?" I cried out in an anguished voice.

His eyes fluttered open. "I left it on the ship. I don't know why I did that. This is my fault," he rasped. "All my fault."

"Shhh," I soothingly told him, stroking his face and brushing his lips with a gentle kiss. The ship was too far away for me to make it there and back in time, if I could even find the device in the first place. We were out of time.

I was aware that there were still some crazed Vepar stumbling in the hallway around me, but at the moment, I didn't care if they killed me. What was my life going to be like anyway alone on this forsaken planet without these three men?

I wished at that moment it was possible for me to be in three places at once. I wanted to touch Thane one more time.

"I love you, kitten," I heard him call out softly. My crying intensified.

I was trying to be strong, but the tears were falling so rapidly that they were soaking Corran's shirt.

Looking at his face, I realized that I wasn't even going to get to look at them as they really were because they were still wearing their disguises. We were all going to die looking like other people.

I began to hear a loud buzzing sound.

It grew louder and louder until the whole building began to shake. What was that? Had the Council arrived to blow the building up?

The buzzing seemed to really affect the surviving crazed Vepar still milling around. They sank to the ground, screaming in agony with their hands over their ears.

I didn't understand what was going on. The buzzing was loud, but not loud enough to cause physical pain. They were acting like they were being tortured.

The buzzing finally stopped. There was an intense silence, it almost sounded louder than the buzzing had been. It was funny how that worked.

The wall down the hallway opened up and a group of male and female Vepar dressed in battle gear came running in from the outside. Was this the Council's army? I looked around for a weapon that I could use against them, but the group was upon us before I could grab anything.

I took a deep breath, prepared for whatever came next and the inevitability of my enslavement or death.

I was shocked when a familiar face made his way from the back of the group. It was Lanton, Thane's father. I had never been so happy to see someone.

"Ella," he said, looking relieved. That relief immediately disappeared as soon as he saw the carnage around us and the fact that his son was one of the fallen. Pulling a device out of his pocket that looked achingly similar to Corran's healing device, he ran over to Thane and started running it over him. Within a minute Thane's cuts were sealing up, and his breathing was improving. Once Thane had opened his eyes, looking so much better than before, Lanton next ran to Derrial. "Shit," he muttered to himself. "It might be too late."

Thane's father started running the device all over Derrial frantically. "Come on, son," he barked frantically.

I was distracted by Thane sitting up. A wave of relief so potent that it almost succeeded in knocking me to the ground rushed over me. I looked down at Corran. We didn't have much time left with him though. What if he and Derrial didn't make it?

Thane walked over to me, and I had never been so intensely grateful for Corran's brilliant mind that had created such amazing technology. Thane looked almost completely healed.

Thane gathered me in his arms, burying his face into my neck. "I love you," he whispered fiercely. That emptiness that had built inside of me since the earlier revelations, and which had only gotten larger in the aftermath of seeing their broken bodies... it started to fill.

I heard a sigh and my attention leaped back to where Lanton had been furiously working over Derrial's broken body. To my relief, Derrial's breathing had started to steady as well, the rattling sound disappearing, although he hadn't woken up yet. Lanton kept moving the machine over him for another minute before he stood up and made his way quickly to Corran.

Corran's eyes blinked open, but his gaze was hazy. "It's okay, son," Lanton said soothingly to him as he started to run the machine over Corran's body.

At that moment I was so grateful for the men's bond that had extended to their parents as well.

Corran recovered before Derrial even opened his eyes. We had been so close to losing him. It was going to be a long time before I would be able to let any of them out of my sight.

While Lanton had been saving my men's life, the rest of the Vepar that he had brought with him had disposed of the remaining infected Vepar. Derrial, Thane, and Corran had taken care of a lot of them, but the sheer number of them had made it impossible for warriors even of their caliber to win.

Everyone still standing looked around the hallway with a little bit of shock. The amount of infected Vepar they had been holding in this facility was almost unbelievable. It didn't surprise any of us that they had been able to escape and get past the staff.

Thane put a hand on his father's shoulder and bowed his head in respect. "Thank you, father," he said, his voice choked with emotion. "That was almost the end for us."

Lanton seemed equally choked up. Coming so close to death definitely brought everything into perspective, even for two gruff and powerful men like Thane and his father.

"But how did you know to come here?" Thane asked after a moment, looking puzzled.

"I knew you would try to see your mother when I heard about all of the crazed Vepar that the Council had started to put into this facility. A large group of them tried to invade the Council building this morning," Lanton continued. "As soon as I heard that, and none of you had checked in with any of us, I knew I needed to make sure you were all right for myself."

He pulled Thane in for a tight hug. "I don't know what I would do if I lost you," he said, his voice swelling with emotion. "I've never recovered from what happened to your mother. But losing you would be my final breaking point."

Thane looked up suddenly. "We need to check on her," he said worriedly.

"I already sent in some of my men to make sure she was safe. She didn't even know anything was happening."

Thane nodded, looking relieved.

"Let's get out of here," Lanton said, looking around in disgust at the carnage around us.

"We need to bring her with us," said Thane, moving to walk to his mother's room.

"I'll be taking her with me. You aren't really in a position to be moving her around with you right now," Lanton said.

That made sense to me, but by the look on Thane's face, what Lanton had just said surprised him.

"You're taking her with you?" he asked, sounding concerned. "Are you going to be alright seeing her every day?"

Lanton cleared his throat, resolve shining from his face.

"She's still my wife," he said in a gravelly voice. "I can still picture her as she was, every memory that we shared runs on a loop in my head. I guess I've just been a coward since everything happened. It just felt too hard to see her as she is now when I can remember so clearly how it was in the past. But I still love her, I'll love her until my dying breath. And maybe someday she'll come back to me."

He cleared his throat. "Until then I'll keep her safe." He clapped Thane on the shoulder and walked away. Thane looked like he was holding back tears. He had shown more emotion today than I had seen from him ever.

I suddenly felt exhausted. I knew it would probably take a very long time before the images from today left my own head. I just hoped that we would get the chance to replace them with the good memories that Lanton at least had of him and his wife.

A pair of arms encircled my waist, and I whirled around, knowing who they belonged to immediately. Derrial was up. He looked tired but healed. I wrapped my arms around his neck and began to sob. It seemed like all I did nowadays was cry.

"Shhh, it's alright, pet," he whispered in my ear. The sound of his voice only made me cry harder.

"You almost dieeeed," I whimpered. "You all almost did."

He didn't say anything, just continued to hold me in his strong grip.

"Let's get out of here," he said after a few minutes. I pulled away, trying to wipe his shirt discreetly as I was sure there was a bucket of snot and tears covering his shoulder after the cryfest I had just engaged in.

Derrial surprised me by picking me up in his arms.

"Are you sure you're strong enough to hold me?" I asked, trying to get out of his grasp.

He looked offended at my question. "I feel better than ever," he said. I looked over his shoulder at Corran. "Have I told you how much I love your big, beautiful brain?" I asked him.

The guys threw back their heads and laughed at me. The sound of their laughter was a balm for my soul.

"What?" I asked, pretending to be affronted.

"You like my brain, do you?" Corran asked with a smirk that set off way more fireworks inside of me than was appropriate in this situation. "Are you sure there isn't something else on my body you like better?"

"I happen to find your brain the sexiest part of you," I replied haughtily, my cheeks flushing under their teasing. The fact that they could tease me at all, however, had my soul soaring.

I pressed a firm kiss against Derrial's cheek, and they laughed again.

"Looks like we need to have more near-death experiences so that kitten can retract her claws for a minute or two," joked Thane. I stuck my tongue out at him but squeezed Derrial tighter. I didn't want to experience anything like what we had experienced today ever again.

"Let them joke," Derrial whispered in my ear. "It's the only way that we'll get past the fact that we almost lost you forever." I pulled back away from him.

"Haven't you heard that it's always the living that are left behind when someone dies?" I asked him, stroking his face gently. "You would've been rolling around in heaven while I was left behind to mourn you,"

"The Vepar don't believe in heaven. And even if we did, the three of us are never going to make it there. We'd be fighting our way out of hell to get back to you," he swore softly.

I didn't say anything to that. I had already come to the conclusion that they were monsters.

And maybe it was wrong to love a monster, but they were my monsters, and I was never going to feel guilty about that ever again.

We finally followed Lanton's men outside of the facility, and I had never been more grateful to be in the fresh air as I was right now.

Derrial set me down long enough for me to give Lanton a huge hug, although he didn't stray more than an arm's length away from me. "I'm forever in your debt," I told Lanton, starting to cry again, which was getting really frustrating.

Lanton held my face between his hands and looked at me fondly. "I would do anything for my children," he said. "And now that includes you."

I didn't have any response to that, so I just threw my arms around him, I was sure, shocking the gruff Vepar. I would find some way to show my appreciation to him, even if it took the rest of my life.

After Thane, Corran, and Derrial all gave their thanks and said goodbye to Lanton, we walked back to Corran's ship. As we stepped inside, I couldn't help but feel like I had lived an entire life between the last time I had been on the ship and now. And even though we had made it through, I didn't let my guard down until we were up in the air pulling away from the facility. I never wanted to see that place again.

If our lives kept up this way, there wouldn't be any place on Veon that wouldn't give me terrible memories when I visited it.

"So where do we go now?" I asked my mates as we sat in the Bridge, all exhaustively pondering what we had just been through.

Corran looked back at me as he fiddled with the controls. "Let's go home."

II

Home happened to be another one of the guys' safe houses. I had never been happier than I was as I walked into what I hoped would be our home for at least a while.

Considering this was a safe house, it actually was my favorite place that I'd seen on Veon. And that wasn't just because of the experience we had just had.

The house was located on the edge of Veon's lavender ocean. There wasn't another soul around for miles. The colorful trees went all the way up to the shoreline, and the dwelling was situated in the midst of the trees, hidden from sight just in case a Council ship flew over. But the men weren't too worried about that, this area was so remote that the Council had never paid attention very much to it in the past.

The outside of the dome structure was a soft brown color, and I was grateful that it wasn't white like the facility had been. The trees around us held a multitude of colors and combined with the lavender sea, I felt like I had fallen into a beautiful dream world.

Corran had designed the inside so that you could see through the walls, so it felt like you were living amidst the trees, even though no one could see in.

It was perfect.

Corran must've used the same technology as he had on his ship because the inside of the house seemed to stretch on forever despite the fact that it looked like a very humble dwelling from the outside. We each had separate rooms complete with our own bathrooms. There was a large living area, an office that resembled the inside of a computer it had so much technology in it, a gym, and a gourmet kitchen that contained the same machine as Corran's ships, meaning that I could get ice cream whenever I wanted it.

I collapsed on my bed as soon as I walked in, immediately knowing which bedroom mine was since it had the largest closet. The closet was of course filled with more clothing than I could wear in a lifetime, but it made me feel normal to see it, like we were back in our house on Earth and we were just living a normal life.

I stared through the wall at the candy-colored trees as they blew gently in the breeze. Derrial had said it was safe to go out into the ocean, but for now, I was content to stay hidden in the house. It felt like for the first time in a long time, I didn't have to look over my shoulder.

Thane walked in with his hands behind his back. The guys had been hovering just outside my door for the last hour. I guess they felt as needy as I did at the moment.

"I have a surprise for you," he said with a big grin.

I sat up. "What is it?" I asked, so sleepy it was hard to muster up any excitement.

Thane pulled a tiny purple piglet out from behind his back, and I immediately started squealing.

"Thane," I said excitedly, jumping off the bed to grab him. "I mean Thane Jr.," I amended laughingly, looking up at Thane's annoyed face.

"But how did you get him here?" I asked, lovingly petting the tiny purple creature. I felt like a terrible alien pet parent considering I hadn't really thought about him with everything that was going on. Although really do most people think about their pet piglets when they're being forcibly impregnated, hunted by an evil alien race, or fighting for their mates' lives?

I didn't think so.

Thane Jr. snuggled into me, squeaking excitedly. I'd forgotten how cute the noises were that he made. Now, this really felt like home.

"We had left him with Corran's parents before everything happened. My father actually brought him on his ship to meet up with us." Thane explained. "I think he was happy to hand him off," he said with a laugh. "Evidently our little piggy caused a lot of messes."

I was barely listening in my excitement at having my pet back. "Oh...you are so cute. Did you miss mommy?" I cooed at Thane Jr.

Thane's arms went around me, and he snuggled into my neck, petting Thane Jr. as he held me. "I'd love for you to talk that sweetly to me," he said, licking the side of my neck. His touch sent delicious shivers down my whole body. I was exhausted, but he was making me think about how much energy I could muster up for some extracurricular activities.

I turned around and tried to kiss him. But Thane only let our lips touch for a second before he pulled away.

"What's wrong?" I asked, confused at his reaction.

Thane knelt down and put our foreheads together. "You need to rest, and then we need to talk about everything before I can have the privilege of being back in your bed," he said softly.

Everything he had just said made sense. I might have decided that I loved them too much to leave them, but we still had a lot to talk about.

I looked back at my bed, holding Thane Jr. close. "How about if you get in my bed just to nap?" I asked as I yawned.

He gave me a little smile. "I think that's within my rules," he said.

"Oh good," I answered, already climbing back into my bed. "But Thane Jr. is joining us," I warned him.

Thane got in the bed with me, spooning me from behind. "I wouldn't expect anything less. Just as long as he doesn't cock block me later," he replied. I fell asleep before I could answer him.

I woke up screaming, rabid Vepar had chased me through my dreams, not stopping until I was standing in front of the corpses of my lovers.

"Ella," Thane said frantically, shaking me. "Are you alright?"

My piglet was squealing in a panic on my other side.

"It's just stuck in my head. The attack, your bodies lying on the ground," I said with hiccupping breaths. "I don't think I'm ever going to get those images out of my mind," I said, as tears started to streak down my face.

Thane lovingly caressed my cheek, his eyes speaking a multitude of words that his lips never would say. "Then I guess we'll need to make it our mission to build a life full of memories good enough to replace yesterday," he said tenderly.

I smiled at him through the tears. "I would like that."

"You need to sleep for a couple more hours," he said to me as he pulled me back into his arms. With Thane's warm body sheltering me from behind and my piglet's warm body in front of me, I drifted into a surprisingly dreamless sleep.

When I first woke up the next morning, my mind was blissfully clear. It took me a minute before the previous day's events floated over me. Thane's presence behind me was gone, and I knew he had probably been up for several hours as the Vepar didn't need to sleep nearly as long as humans.

Despite the fact that I had to have slept for at least twelve hours, my body felt sluggish and tired.

Thane Junior nuzzled my face as I laid there. "I guess I better get up," I told him as he snorted excitedly. I was not looking forward to the hard conversations that we had to have today.

After getting dressed in a simple purple sheath dress, I walked out of the room. I found the guys gathered around a table, pouring over tablets and other documents. "Is everything okay?" I asked, my voice rising a bit frantically at the thought that they were already having to plan evasive maneuvers to escape from the Council or the Vepar zombie hordes.

Derrial got up and walked over to me, "Everything's fine, pet," he reassured me, brushing a kiss firmly across my lips. I took a moment to lean into his chest, soaking up his warmth. He was here. They were all here. Everything was alright.

Corran came over with my favorite smoothie from his kitchen machine. I took a moment to savor the coconut-chocolate taste before I moved over to the table to sit down with everyone. They were all looking at me with concern and a little trepidation, I'm sure wondering how the conversation was going to go.

"Why don't we start from the beginning," I said softly, looking at all three of them while I spoke. "Explain what you did know, and what you didn't know...and maybe that will help me to understand." I took a deep breath. "Whatever you say though, it won't change the fact that I'm irrevocably, forever in love with all of you. I just want the truth."

My words seemed to soothe them because they settled back into their chairs. Or at least Corran and Thane did. Derrial scooped me up and sat me down in his lap. "I need to have you in my arms for this conversation," he explained as he ran his hands nervously up and down my arms.

I settled back into his arms, and I waited.

"We told you the truth that we were originally sent to Earth to look for humans that would be compatible with the Vepar genes enough to carry a Vepar child. But we never told you that we had a whole team there," began Corran. "And one of those team members was a member of the Council, Edipe. He's dead now apparently, killed by another member of the Council quite a while ago over some kind of dispute. But he was a piece of work. He struck up a relationship with a human woman almost as soon as we got there. The first of our kind to do so. When he wanted to go back to Veon not long after, we didn't think much of it. It only became an issue when he wanted to bring his human with him. But he was on the Council, so no one argued even though we had tested the girl and she was not compatible in the least bit for our fertility efforts."

It was shocking to me that a member of the Council had been the first to form a relationship with a human woman. But maybe it shouldn't have been shocking considering all that we had found out about them having certain secret proclivities for human women all this time.

Corran continued. "We didn't think much of it when we didn't hear anything about the human woman causing a stir among her people, we were busy with our mission on Earth. But when the Council issued orders that we were to send one human female back to them once a year, we got a bit suspicious as we knew they weren't related to the fertility experiments..." Corran grimaced and stopped speaking.

Thane continued for him as it was evident Corran had trouble with the next part of the story. I braced myself for what I was going to hear next. Derrial's arms were like a vice around me as if he was afraid that I was going to bolt at any minute.

"We were busy searching for someone like you, and we didn't want to be bothered with the Council trying to make things difficult for us. So we had members of our team periodically send women to the Council."

I opened my mouth to respond to that, but Thane hurried on before I could speak. "In our defense, the women were all obsessed with everything Vepar. They had already started to participate in the clubs on Earth that facilitated sexual relationships between the Vepar and humans, and they were eager to get to Veon. None of us knew what the Council was doing with them. And honestly, we didn't ask," Thane said in a shamed voice.

There was silence for a moment as I thought about what he had just said. It made it a little bit better that the women wanted to go. But I'm sure if they knew they were going to be forced into sexual slavery for the alien Council, they probably wouldn't have volunteered.

"Continue," I said, not trusting myself to say anything soothing at the moment.

"The Council wasn't satisfied with just one woman a year after a while though. They sent another team to Earth to start bringing them back at a more frequent rate. We were told they were performing other studies on humans and Earth for use in further population of the planet. And again...we didn't look any further into it."

"That all explains a lot, but it doesn't explain about my parents," I said in a terse angry voice. I was obviously a bad person because I could get over the women...but my parents' imprisonment was another story.

"We didn't bring your parents to Veon," said Derrial, squeezing me even tighter. I flinched at how tightly he was holding me, and he immediately loosened up.

"Then who did?" I asked, feeling an immediate rush of relief that they weren't directly responsible.

"Your mother was originally chosen to be taken by the Council's other team. Your father fought so hard when they came to get her that they brought him with them, thinking that they would let the Khonsu take care of him since there was a mandate in place against the Vepar killing humans at the time."

I snorted. "They were alright with taking humans as sex slaves but they drew the line at killing?"

"It was a line they didn't follow for very long," inserted Thane sarcastically.

"But you did know that they had taken my parents when you met me?" I asked sadly.

"When we met you, we did research on you until we knew everything there was to know about you. And we thought that your parents would just be another detriment to you accepting your place with us. If you were all alone, you were more likely to want to stay with us," explained Corran softly.

There it was. The truth stood there tall and foreboding between us, threatening everything. I had promised them that nothing they would say could change how I felt about them. But was that the truth?

"You told me you had changed. Have you really? Or was that just something you told me to try and save us?" I asked them, staring at the table, too afraid to hear what their answer really would be.

Derrial gently took me off his lap and stood up. I watched as the other two stood up as well. They all towered over me, staring at me intently before they got down on their knees. My heart began to flutter at the sight.

"We're sorry, Ella. So fucking sorry for how everything has happened. If you'll give us a chance, we'll show you that we've changed...even if it takes the rest of our lives," said Derrial in a broken voice that was far from the confident Vepar that I was so familiar with.

I looked at all three of them, knowing that they were giving me a choice for the first time since they had kidnapped me. I could forgive them, and we could move on and hopefully have a chance at happiness, or I could choose to hate them and maybe still be forced to be with them regardless. But all of our lives would be terrible.

I knew looking at them, that it actually wasn't a choice at all. I was theirs. There was no choice but to love them, to forgive them. Despite everything that had happened, they had saved me. Saved me from a life where I had been literally fading away.

Now looking at them, I could see how much they had changed, how much they had softened and melded to resemble a love that I had been looking for my whole life and just hadn't known it.

Maybe they had saved me. But I had also saved them.

"I forgive you," I told them, sinking to my own knees in front of them.

There were no sounds but the rustle of clothes being taken off, and the intake of soft breaths and groans as we lost ourselves in each other.

I would get my happily ever after one way or another.

12

"Where did you get this?" I asked with shaking hands as I stared at the picture of my parents on their wedding day. It had been with my things at my old apartment in New York. I had figured that all that was long gone.

Derrial ran a hand over his face. "Nothing with you has gone as planned. We got all your things from your apartment when we took you. But everything was so messed up, and so many things happened, we kind of forgot to give it to you."

My hands trembled as I held the portrait in my hands. I knew my father had been changed forever, and even if we found my mother, it was unlikely that she would bear any resemblance to the way that she used to be. Looking at this picture reminded me of who they had been when I was a child, so full of life and in love.

I looked up at Derrial. He was staring at the picture with a funny look on his face. "What is it?" I asked.

"Why do humans get married?" he asked, not taking his eyes from the picture.

I pondered his question. "Isn't that similar to what you do on Veon? I mean, isn't being someone's mate considered the same thing as being husband and wife?"

He thought about it for a second and then shook his head. "They are similar. But I'm wondering why they exchange such elaborate vows. Mates on Veon are for forever. But there's no exchanging of vows or any other sort of ceremony," he explained.

My heart sank a little bit after hearing that. I'd still kind of hoped there was some kind of ceremony we were going to have to solidify our bond. I dreamed about my wedding day for as long as I could remember. Guess that wasn't going to happen. "Well if mates last forever, that's quite a bit different than with human marriages," I said with an annoyed laugh. "Humans exchange vows to each other, promising each other the world, but a lot of the times those promises get broken. But I guess as humans we want to try and start our lives together as best we can." I traced the image of my mom's ecstatic face in the picture. "A lot of people say that the day they get married is the happiest day of their lives. I guess they just forget how happy they were."

Derrial touched my face softly, looking into my eyes as if I was the answer he had spent his whole life searching for. "I won't break my promises to you," he said quietly.

"I don't think we've made many promises to each other yet," I whispered back, unable to take my eyes from his.

"Then I guess we should do that," he responded. We stared at each other for a minute more before he moved away from me. I missed his touch as soon as it was gone.

He walked out of the room without another word, leaving me with a million unanswered questions.

A few boxes on the side of the room caught my attention though. Walking towards them I lifted up one of the flaps and gasped in delighted shock as I saw that Derrial had been telling the truth. These were boxes filled with my possessions. I forgot all about my strange interaction with Derrial as I spent the rest of the afternoon going through everything. It felt like another life when these things belonged to me.

And as I looked at the pictures and some of my photo albums, I couldn't help but feel like I was looking at a stranger.

"It's been two weeks," Corran said as he strode into the room.

My stomach dropped. I turned to look outside the window. It was dark out, and I could barely see anything beneath the faint touch of moonlight peeking through the dense trees, but it was better than facing what he was reminding me of.

"I-I d-don't think it's been enough time, we don't want a false positive," I stuttered.

Corran came up behind me and pulled his arms around me, holding me tight. "You can do this," he told me reassuringly, even as I could feel the tension in his hold.

"What if it is positive?" I whispered; my head buried in his chest.

"Then we'll have a child," he said matter of factly.

"And what if it isn't yours?" I asked, not daring to look at him.

"There was always a chance it wasn't going to be mine to begin with.

This just expanded the pool a bit," he said wryly. "Even if it's someone else's, it's still yours. And how could we not love something that had a part of you."

I melted at his words. I could feel the truth behind him. I could feel the love he had for this child.

"How do we do this?" I asked, wondering if the Vepar also peed on a stick to find out if they were pregnant.

"Just a tiny drop of blood from your finger is all I need," said Corran, releasing me and pulling a small white device out of his pocket no bigger than my pinky.

"I'm surprised you didn't do this while I was sleeping," I teased him, even as my hands shook at my sides.

"I guess you've changed me," he said with a wink. I laughed weakly but held out my finger.

"How long will it take to find out," I asked, my voice fading to a whisper as he brought the machine closer to my hand.

"It's instant," he said, right before I felt a small pinprick.

"What does it say?" I asked. But it was obvious as Corran's eyes started to fill up with awestruck emotion what the test had shown.

I was having a baby.

I once believed monsters were born. But I was young and an idiot because after everything I'd seen in the past few years on Veon, there was no doubt in my mind that they were made. Formed by the ugliness around them, by society, by hatred. This wasn't the kind of world I wanted to bring up our baby with Ella... so that meant change was needed. Massive change, starting from the top.

"I can hear your brain cogs working from over here." Thane tossed a snapple at me from across the room, and I caught the purple fruit with one hand before biting into its sweet flesh. I wiped my mouth from the juices dripping down my chin.

Thane lounged on the sofa, reading from his monitor while picking at the bowl of fruit in his lap.

"Our Council is broken," I stated.

"What's new."

"They need to go. Get replaced with fresh blood and no corruption."

Thane snorted a laugh. "Fuck yeah they need to go, but corruption is close to impossible to eradicate. I vote for finding a new planet to live on."

I ignored his suggestion. Leaving our families here wasn't an option, and neither was running away. "We start at the top because everything has a trickle-down effect. Just need a plan to overturn the Council. End their corruption."

"And then the next in line step in, who are just as corrupt."

"No, that's the thing. We show evidence to the public, let the civilians see the truth, and we push for a forcible removal of the Council."

"That could lead to rebellions in the streets, which brings a lot of attention. We would need strong evidence."

Right then, Derrial emerged from the bedroom and shut the door behind him.

"How's she doing?" I asked.

"Tired. I didn't have the heart to tell her that Vepar pregnancies are usually half the length of human ones. She's panicked enough as it is."

"We'll tell her later, and that once she hits two months, we should be able to test for the baby's father."

Thane groaned and placed the bowl on the table in front of him. "I really hope the baby's one of ours."

Neither of us replied. In truth, I wanted that too, we all did, but we'd have to deal with whatever happened.

"Ella and the babe are ours, regardless," Derrial murmured, his shoulders rising and falling with each rapid breath. "What was this corruption you were talking about?"

"Corran plans on finding evidence to overthrow the Council finally."

Derrial turned in my direction. "Do we have evidence?"

"We might, but it stays between us for now."

Both of them stared at me strangely, like my words didn't make sense. But they'd understand soon enough.

I headed to the side table near the window and pulled open the drawer. "When we were in the testing facility recently, I discovered some files and I took them." I turned around, holding in my hand several papers folded up to easily fit into a pocket.

"And?" Derrial asked.

I unfolded the pages and handed them to Derrial. Thane was on his feet, walking over and reading them over Derrial's shoulder.

"The Council are purchasing kidnapped females from the Khonsu to conduct fertility experiments on. Those papers are the receipts. Which is why they've turned a blind eye to the Khonsu living on our planet, building communities on our planet, hunting down Vepar females. They allowed this to happen." My blood was boiling at all the lies we had been fed, all the Vepar slayed and forced to live in tight cities while the Khonsu took over our world.

"Fucking bastards," Thane spat.

"But the document shows something else," I continued, pointing to the papers in Derrial's grip. "It shows that the Khonsu have a separate camp just for females."

Thane's gaze met mine, his response flying out. "Ella's mom could be there."

He stole my words right from my mouth, and I nodded. "We need to find out urgently."

Derrial was pacing. "This changes everything. We need to let all the people know about the Council's corruption."

"Agreed," I answered, ready to do whatever it would take.

A beep came from the main monitor sitting on the wall. A new incoming announcement.

Thane switched it on a tap on the remote, and the screen flicked to life. A message in big white letters ran across the black screen.

Virus outbreak.

Emergency declared.

Everyone must remain indoors.

Anyone bitten by an inflicted should be quarantined.

It is believed to have originated at a Council laboratory. Investigation underway.

BELONG

CONTENTS

DEDICATION

To you, our readers. For always looking at the sky and seeing possibility. Thanks for supporting Ella and her aliens. We love you.

BELONG

My love for you has no regrets...

Ella has made her choice, and Derrial, Thane, and Corran belong to her. Desperately in love and with a baby on the way, they want nothing more than to ride off into the sunset together.

But Veon is on the brink of destruction and the Council's infection continues to spread. Veon will fall if something isn't done.

All Ella wants is her happy ending, but things keep getting in the way of that...like the fate of a fallen world.

Ella and her men will never be the same...

I

Pregnant.

I stared out through the window, past the multicolored trees at the lavender ocean that stretched out before me.

A baby.

I still couldn't wrap my mind around it.

I stroked my stomach absentmindedly as I watched the lavender waves roll gently onto the shore, so alien but so beautiful at the same time.

A strange cerulean blue serpent-looking sea creature jumped in and out of the water. It moved smoothly along until a giant blood-red fish creature with five eyes burst out of the water and snapped it up, causing me to jump back a step despite the fact that I was on the shore and safely encased in our safe house.

It was amazing that a place could be so gorgeous, yet so dangerous at the same time. Every creature on this planet - including the Vepar that I was desperately in love with - was designed to lure you in and then destroy you.

I rubbed my stomach again, a wave of nausea hitting me as I thought about the immense task it would be to keep this baby safe if we were to stay on a place like Veon. My baby needed three fathers just to have a chance.

Except I didn't know if they were really the fathers though, did I? They had said all the right things...about how they would love my baby, whoever it belonged to, as if it were their own...but was that true? Two of them would always have been left out regardless, but at least they would know that the baby belonged to one of them.

In this situation. I rubbed my stomach again...I couldn't think about it. Parents on Earth who adopted kids claimed to love those kids as much as the kids they birthed. They couldn't all be lying about that.

My nausea only intensified. Which reminded me how lucky I was that one of my lovers happened to be the most brilliant scientist on Veon, and perhaps anywhere, as he'd been creating things to try and make my pregnancy easier since before I'd even gotten pregnant. That fact alone should have eased my worries. They had wanted a baby so badly, they'd been planning for it, despite how against it I'd been since they met me.

I wasn't against it now...that was for sure.

My mom had told me stories about how she'd loved me from the moment she'd found out that I existed. And I remember wondering how that was possible. How could you love someone you'd never met?

And now, I knew.

Since the moment I saw Corran's elated reaction, signaling that my pregnancy test was positive, I had been irrevocably in love with my baby. It could come out with green tentacles and one eyeball, and I knew that I would still love it forever and ever.

"*Little darling,*" I whispered to it softly. The Veon did have better than average hearing, so there was a chance I guess that it could actually hear me, even inside of me.

Although I was being silly, since there was no way that the baby had ears yet. The little flutter that I kept thinking I was feeling since Corran gave me the news was just my imagination.

I wondered what kind of mother I would be. Would I be able to keep my temper? Would the long nights be hard or easy? Would I know all the right things to say when they were sad, or when I needed to teach them something?

Thoughts of being a mother inevitably made me think of my own mother and how very good she had been at it. She would have been the best grandmother. The very best.

She will be the best grandmother, I thought fiercely, trying to stay positive. I'd found my father somehow, despite the fact that he hadn't even been on Earth. I could find my mother if she was out there. The guys had already promised to help me, and one thing I'd learned about them was that when they sought out to do something, it happened.

We would find her.

Random memories flitted through my mind as I thought about the kind of mother she was.

There was this one time when she had to go into surgery on Valentine's Day, and she felt so bad that she couldn't be with me that she stayed up all night getting surprises ready for me to wake up to. I remember I'd wandered out into the living room and there had been pink, red, and white balloons everywhere-on the ceiling and on the floor. There had been special presents and a special Valentine's cake. She'd been exhausted for her surgery, but she'd never put herself first. My father and I were always top of her mind.

I wondered if I could be even close to that good of a mom.

"Where are you, mom?" I whispered through the window, focusing on that strange lavender-colored sea once again.

I'd once been scared of the ocean. The sheer vastness and emptiness of it had made me feel alone and terrified.

The emptiness of the skyline in front of me was comforting now. After months of being on the run, I savored feeling alone. I would stay here forever it if was possible and the whole world wasn't falling apart around us.

That made me think of the guys, and the whispered conversations they'd been having since we'd been here. I frowned, thinking of how protective they still were...would probably always be. I would be grateful for that trait when our child was born, but it still drove me crazy when they overdid it with me.

Speaking of the guys...where were they?

Since the news of my pregnancy broke, one of them had always been close by.

I tore myself away from the view and set off down the hallway to track them down. We needed to get a plan together for how we were going to find my mother before I got too pregnant to do anything. We still had at least 6-7 months before that happened, but the less cumbersome my belly was, the better off we all would be.

As I approached the main room where the Veon version of a living room was, I heard raised voices. I sped up, trepidation tingling down my spine. All the stakes felt higher since finding out about the baby. And whatever they were yelling about...it just sounded like more bad news.

"I know I can fix this if we can find the source," Corran was saying to Derrial and Thane as I stepped into the room. They were standing around a table watching a hologram display a scene of mass chaos. I shivered as I realized what it was.

It was more of the infected Vepar that we'd encountered when we went to visit Thane's mother. Except what was being shown on the hologram looked like it was a thousand times the amount of infected that had been in that mental health facility. It reminded me of that one movie I'd seen back on Earth, *World War Z* I think it was called.

Except this apparently was real life.

"Is that happening right now?" I squeaked out, causing all three of the guys to turn their attention immediately towards me, various looks of concern and dismay on their faces. They obviously hadn't wanted me to see that. But I was glad that I did.

"Ella, you should be resting," Corran said as he approached me, his eyes dipping to my stomach, even though it was much too early for me to be showing. "You look pale and exhausted."

"Thanks," I said wryly, causing Corran to give me a very uncharacteristic eye roll. "I just need one of those magic shot thingies. I've thrown up three times so far this morning." Corran was already pulling one of the syringes out of a drawer before I could finish my sentence. I shivered just looking at the needle. I'd been on the wrong side of a shot like that too many times since meeting the guys.

It's not like that anymore, I scolded myself. Corran gave me a questioning look at the nervousness bleeding out onto my face, but I answered him with a reassuring grin. Old habits died hard for me apparently, but I was working on it.

The prick of the needle was gone in an instant, and then I began to feel blessed relief as the nausea instantly started to fade. The Vepar really needed to share technology like this with Earth. There were a million expectant mothers that would kill for relief from morning sickness.

"Feel better?" Corran asked, brushing a kiss across my forehead. I pulled him towards me before he could step away, burying my face into his chest and inhaling his delicious scent.

"Love you," I whispered, and felt his chest rumble with pleasure.

I had fought this thing between the four of us for a really long time, and it felt so freeing to give in to the feeling of love that had been beating to get out from almost the very beginning.

Finding out that I was pregnant had finally pushed me to stop being so wishy-washy with everything in my life, including my relationships.

Taking one more second to savor Corran's embrace, I stepped away, expectantly looking at the other two, who were looking at the two of us with a mixture of jealousy and warmth. The hologram had been shut off.

"How many are they saying have been infected now?" I asked, striding to the table and picking up the hologram device, trying to figure out how to get it working again.

"Give that to me," Thane grumbled, taking the device from me and flicking it on once again. We all watched in rapt silence at the footage of the crazed Vepar trashing cities and towns. The horns and different colors of their skin only added to the surrealness of the video.

"They're saying it's only a couple of thousand right now, but knowing the council, I'm sure it's three times that number," murmured Derrial as he watched a group of the infected demolish a government building in just a few minutes.

"Do you have any guesses about what's happening?" I asked, biting a nail nervously. I cringed when two infected Vepar tore into a Vepar man who had been trying to run away from them.

I saw the guys exchange glances with each other. "Alright, what are you hiding?" I growled, putting my hands on both hips and giving them what I hoped looked like a stern glare.

Derrial sighed. "I liked it much better when I didn't ever listen to you," he chided, but the complaint only came out half-hearted. "We think it has to do with the fertility experiments they were doing on the side. The medicine mixtures involved in that sort of thing are highly sensitive, it's why Corran was supposed to be the one in charge and monitoring everything, one wrong mixture and anything could happen. And it looks like something did happen," he said, gesturing to the screen where what easily looked like a thousand of the infected were running at breakneck speed towards a group of Vepar soldiers.

"Okay, you can turn it off," I said with a shiver, looking away before the soldiers were destroyed.

"Do you think there's a cure?" I asked, wondering if my father and the guys' families were safe or if they needed help.

"I think I could figure it out. But I need to find the source first, and since the council had hundreds of these secret labs based on those files I stole, it's not an easy task figuring out which lab is the culprit. And I can't even think right now if its multiple labs that are contributing to what's going on. Different strains of this infection could be the end of Veon," Corran explained, his eyes focused far off, likely already mapping out a plan for if that occurred.

"Have you heard from our families?" I asked, walking to the machine in the wall and punching in a request for a soup that I'd come to love. I wouldn't have normally had an appetite...but pregnancy problems.

"Lanton's been communicating here and there. So far, their city hasn't been attacked," Thane answered.

I stopped perusing for food and glanced back at him. "How's your mom?" I asked quietly.

He just shrugged. "Dad hasn't given many details. She obviously wasn't going to get better just because she left that place and was back with him. But he's determined to take responsibility for her this time. That's all I can ask of him."

I nodded, wanting to go over to him and hug him, but knowing that he didn't want the pity that came with mention of his mother.

The hologram started up behind me and more reports came in of new attacks on cities. My hunger dimmed. I began to think about the infected finding and attacking our safehouse, hurting our child. The room all of a sudden became stifling.

I turned to face the guys, who were once again hunched around the table watching the hologram aptly and making plans. "Is it safe for me to walk outside?" I asked, feeling like I was going to suffocate if I didn't get out of here.

Corran looked over at me concerned, I'm sure seeing how pale I looked. "Yes, of course. Just stay within the trees and where we can see you out there," he said, gesturing to the transparency of the dwelling's walls.

I quickly walked over to one of the walls and waited as an entrance appeared, allowing me to go outside. The breeze coming off the water immediately helped to calm me down. Our safe house was meant to be as open as possible, both the walls and the ceiling allowed you to see outside, but there wasn't anything that could replace the feel of the breeze against your skin and the sound of the leaves rustling on the trees.

It was at least half an hour before I sensed that they were behind me, watching me. I turned around and saw my three lovers, standing right outside of the domed structure, watching me pensively.

"What is it?" I asked worriedly, striding towards them, expecting to hear more terrible news.

"It doesn't usually happen like this," said Derrial. "Once you're mated, there's a ceremony that you do right away, but it doesn't really matter, because the expectation is already there that you belong to each other forever."

"What are you talking about?" I asked, confused, even as a nervous tickling sensation started in my stomach at the intense way he was looking at me. Like I was the only thing that existed in the world.

"He means that it's still your choice whether you are going to be ours. It took us a while to get there, but now the only way this can happen is if you choose to be with us forever."

"Are you asking me..." I began.

One by one, they got down on one knee, similar to when they had asked for forgiveness. But this time, I knew this was for something completely different.

I hadn't really been the kind of girl that dreamed about her wedding day. Once my parents disappeared and all I'd had was Cherry, I'd stopped thinking about happily-ever-afters and walks down an aisle in a pretty white dress. And I'd certainly never dreamed that I'd end up with three Vepar as husbands.

But seeing the three of them all down on one knee I realized that somehow my reality had become much more romantic than any scene I could have created in my head.

"I love you," began Corran. "I love you in a way that's illogical to me, someone who's only cared about numbers and cold hard facts his entire existence. You are my dream. You are the only thing I could ever not live without. Marry me. Love me. Choose me," he said in quiet voice threaded with more emotion than I'd ever heard from him, even when he found out that I was pregnant.

Before I could answer, Thane began to speak. "I didn't realize that I was looking for you, until I found you. And then we fucked it all up, over and over again. But somehow you're still here, and somehow you still love us. And I just want the chance to show you how much you've changed my life, how much I love you, how I would do anything for you, forever and ever. Marry me."

I turned to Derrial next, knowing that it wouldn't be my turn until all of them had spoken first.

"I saw you first, you know. I'd never had such an immediate reaction to another being before. I knew that I wanted you, that I had to have you, that there was no other option. It was obsession at first, but maybe it was always love too. There is no one else in all of the galaxies that could ever complete me the way you do. You are my moon, my stars, my end, and my beginning. I will never love another the way I love you. I will never put another above you. You will always be my everything. Marry me," Derrial almost whispered, his voice also heavy with emotion like the other two.

I was crying. How could I not? Somehow, since the moment I saw them in that nightclub, our paths had always been leading to this. And maybe I didn't see that at first. Maybe at one point, all I'd seen were monsters. But now, all I could see were my saviors, my loves, my future.

I would always love them. That was never going to change. I'd never felt more confident about anything than the fact that they would always love me, they would always want me, and they would always do everything in their power to be there for me.

There was no other answer that I could give.

"Yes," I told them, my voice so hoarse from my tears that it was difficult for the words to be heard.

But of course, with their superior Vepar hearing, them not hearing me wasn't an issue.

The three of them were all around me. They devoured me as they showered me with love.

Derrial pulled me towards him and started to brush kisses down the side of my neck.

"Tomorrow, you'll be ours. We won't wait any longer," he growled as he bit down on my shoulder roughly, sending shivers across my skin.

"Tomorrow?" I asked breathlessly, finding it hard to concentrate as Thane started down the other side of my neck and Corran's lips met mine.

Corran pulled away for a second, and my lips immediately tried to follow his. He laughed deliciously. "We're done waiting. Tomorrow, we'll have the ceremony. We'll take care of everything."

For a moment, I thought about walking down the aisle in a white dress, my father on my arm as he gave me away. And then I let that thought go.

I didn't care if we got married in the middle of a swamp surrounded by wild creatures and swarms of mosquitos, I would marry them anywhere.

Tomorrow.

2

one of the guys were in bed with me when I woke up the next morning. Thane Jr. was still curled up on the pillow next to me, tiny musical sounding snores coming out of him as he slept. It took me a moment for the consciousness to fully hit me, and when it did, I sat up in bed in a flash, waking up Thane Jr. and sending him running into my arms, his little body trembling.

It was my wedding day.

A gliding sound caught my attention, and I turned towards the bedroom's entrance and watched as a cart with a table and a tablet rolled towards me, stopping right beside the bed. I stared at it for a moment, not sure what I was supposed to do with it, before I finally grabbed the tablet. As soon as I touched it, all three of the guys appeared on the screen.

I watched, confused, as they began to speak through the screen.

"We've been studying up on human weddings, and we know that it's a tradition on your planet not to see the groom until the wedding ceremony," Corran began.

"That's a stupid tradition by the way," Thane growled grumpily next to him, and I laughed at the disgruntled look on his face. I thought it was a stupid tradition too.

Corran elbowed him and continued. "We wanted this day to be everything you've ever dreamed, so we set up some surprises. First up, breakfast in bed. Eat up, sweetheart, today's going to be the best day of our lives."

I looked around, wondering where breakfast was, when suddenly I saw a plate piled with food on top of the tray that had just been empty moments before when I grabbed the tablet.

And it was filled with all Earth food - eggs, bacon, pancakes - all food that I hadn't eaten since coming to Veon.

Luckily, Corran had given me my nausea medicine the night before, and I was still feeling perfect. I attacked the food with gusto, savoring a little taste from home. I was a little salty that the guys had been holding back from me about the ability to get Earth food. I'd eaten so many strange things over the last few months that I deserved a freaking medal.

Once I devoured everything on my plate, I got up to get out of bed. Suddenly, the tablet came on again, and once again, I saw all three of my men.

"It's time to start getting ready, pet," said Thane. "If you walk into the bathroom, I think you will find a few surprises. I can't wait to marry you," he continued before the tablet once again shut off.

I walked to the bathroom eagerly, thinking that whatever it was probably wasn't going to rival the pancakes I'd just eaten, but it was still going to be good.

I was wrong, it did rival the pancakes.

I loved Veon technology.

Somehow, the guys had transformed the bathroom into an area that now resembled a fancy day spa, those ones on Earth that I never could afford. There were two hologram attendants waiting patiently for me, which was a little creepy, but the bath that they'd drawn filled with flower petals and scented oils along with the massage table that was set up in the middle of the room promised good things.

The attendants disappeared momentarily while I slipped off my clothes and settled myself on the massage table, covering myself up with the white folded sheet on the bed. The bed was set up for a prenatal massage, complete with a donut hole looking pillow for my stomach, even though I didn't have anything resembling a bump at the moment. I still appreciated the gesture and hoped that whichever of the guys had created this could recreate it again and again throughout my pregnancy.

What followed next was the most amazing experience I'd ever had. I was pretty sure that I would marry my hologram masseuse if given the chance. I'd never felt so relaxed. All of the stress I'd been holding in my muscles disappeared, and as I slipped off the bed into the bath that was still perfectly warm, I'd never felt better. I wasn't sure how they were doing it in their holographic state, but I once again chalked it up to a Veon technology win.

One of the hologram attendants appeared next to the tub and began to wash my hair, putting an assortment of different creams and serums in it as she did so. The service, of course, came with a head massage, and I was practically purring by the time she finished. The oils in the tub were jasmine and orange-scented, heightening the entire experience.

I stepped out of the tub, drying myself off with a warm towel that one of the attendants had set up near the tub. I knew that I could have cleaned myself instantly in one of those machines that I loved so much, but I was grateful to do it the old-fashioned way - that is, if the old-fashioned way came complete with more luxury than I'd ever dreamed.

I was led to a chair where they began to buff and polish my skin and nails. My nails were painted a soft pink color, and my skin was softer than it had ever been in my life. My hair was next.

Using a machine that looked like a more high-tech version of a hairdryer, my hair was dried and then curled, pulled up into a half-up, half-down hairstyle with soft tendrils framing my face.

I was turned away from the mirror for makeup. That process took forever, and I was a little afraid that I was going to look like Mimi Bobeck from *The Drew Carey Show* when she was done.

They didn't let me look at the final result, instead, leading me to a room off the spa-bathroom that I was sure hadn't existed before today.

A long rack was set up in the middle of the room, and three rows of shoeboxes were set up in a line in front of the rack.

The tablet had made its way into the room, and it blinked on as soon as I looked at it.

"I saw that show once on your human television. *Say Yes to the Dress* or something like that," said Derrial, making a face. "I know we can't give you that same experience, but hopefully, we've created something a little like that. I've been assured by our computers that these dresses are all the right style. I love you, baby," he said before the tablet clicked off.

Hesitantly, I walked over to the rows of dresses. I knew they didn't wear things like this at Veon weddings. I'd heard the girls talking about what a Veon mating ceremony was like during the trials, and it made my heart explode with how they were trying to mimic a human wedding, even though it was so different than what they were used to.

I shuffled through the dresses, my eyes getting larger and larger with each one. They were gorgeous, the kind of dresses you could imagine a princess wearing, not a poor girl who'd never worn brand named clothing in her life before meeting the guys.

It was the second to last one that stopped my heart. It was almost an exact replica of Kate Middleton's wedding dress, with the exception that it had what looked like pink diamonds all over it.

I teared up just looking at it, suddenly wishing more than anything that my mom could be here today to see this.

Unfortunately, that wasn't something that the guys could deliver on today.

The attendants had disappeared when I'd come into the room, but they reappeared once again as soon as I'd chosen my dress.

There were a few sets of lacy undergarments set up beside the rack, and my skin heated just thinking about them taking it off of me.

I chose a bright white pair that seemed perfect for a bride, and slipped them on before allowing the attendants to help me put on my dress.

I really needed to ask the guys about the technology that they were using for these attendants, because I still couldn't believe that I could feel them despite the fact they appeared to be holograms and appeared and reappeared in an instant.

Although the back of the dress appeared to have a row of hundreds of buttons holding it together, the designer of the dress had hidden a zipper underneath the buttons that made putting it on much easier than I'm sure it had been for Kate Middleton.

The dress fit perfectly, better than anything I'd ever worn before. I'd expected the dress to feel heavy since there were so many layers, but the dress must have been made out of a special kind of cloth, because it almost felt like I wasn't wearing anything, as it was so light.

I was finally led over to a giant mirror that had appeared on the wall, and I gasped as I looked at the stranger staring back at me. It was me, but it was a much better version of myself. I'd never imagined that I could look so good. The attendant who had done my makeup had managed to accentuate all of my features perfectly so that I still looked like myself, but as myself if I was a magical fairy princess.

A wave of longing once again passed over me as I imagined what my mother would have said to me at this moment, how there would have been tears in her eyes. I thought of my father's reaction when he would have first seen me. The pain at their absence was almost crippling, and I had to take a few deep breaths in order to calm myself down.

"Are there any changes you would like made?" the hologram attendant asked in a worried sounding voice. Obviously, my reaction was not what they were programmed to be going for.

I gave the woman a tremulous smile. "I look perfect. Thank you so much," I told her, not knowing the proper procedure for thanking a fake person.

She smiled and gave a small bow before disappearing from sight.

I began to be nervous as I looked at myself in the mirror more. It was really happening. This was really my wedding day, and I was about to marry three aliens. How did this become my life?

Looking at my side profile, I squinted because it almost seemed like I suddenly had a small bump...which was impossible. There was no way I would be showing already. I guess I'd just eaten too big of a breakfast.

I didn't have any regrets.

The tablet began buzzing behind me to get my attention, and I stopped staring at my new bump and walked over to grab it.

My three men once again appeared on the screen as soon as I picked up the tablet.

"There's a little present for you lying on the bed," Derrial told me. "I'm sure you look more beautiful than I can even imagine. And I can't wait to marry you. Come out to the main room after you find your surprise," he said before their images disappeared from view.

I walked out to the bedroom and found a blue velvet colored jewelry box waiting for me on the bed. With trembling hands, I picked up the box and opened it. Inside was a pink diamond necklace and matching earrings that perfectly matched the pink diamonds on my dress. They were more gorgeous than words could describe. I slipped them on and then hurried out of the room, ready to make this wedding happen.

I stopped short when I saw the back of a man talking to Corran's parents in the living room.

It was my father. He was here.

Corran's parents let out little sounds of surprise when they saw me and then my father turned around to see what they were looking at. His eyes immediately welled up with tears at the sight of me and he rushed towards me. He looked so much better than he had when we'd dropped him off and I knew I would feel eternally in debt to Derrial's parents for taking such good care of him.

He looked like he'd just finished with a tropical vacation instead of imprisonment.

"You're here," I gushed emotionally as my father gave me a careful hug, not wanting to muss my dress and makeup.

"And you're beautiful," he told me, the same emotion threaded throughout his voice.

He pulled back to look at me. "You look like a dream, my angel," he told me. "If only your mom was here to see you like this." Great wracking sobs started to come out of him, and I soon followed him, giving him a giant hug that I'm sure wreaked havoc on everything the attendants had just spent hours doing.

After a few minutes, my father pulled away, wiping his eyes. "I'm sorry. This is a happy day. Forgive your old man for getting so emotional," he said with a sniffle. I saw that both Derrial and Corran's parents were standing by the door looking at us sympathetically. I gave them a tremulous smile.

Suddenly, my holographic ladies appeared and started buzzing all over me, trying to fix the destruction I'd just caused. They stepped away after a few minutes, looking satisfied with their handiwork.

"Let's get you married before I mess up your makeup again," my dad said with a wink, looking recovered now. Corran and Derrial's mothers both came up to me, cooing over my dress and accessories.

"We couldn't have picked a better mate for our sons," Tenly, Corran's mother, whispered to me after giving me a gentle hug. Koria, Derrial's mother, just beamed at me with watery eyes after she pulled away from our hug.

All of a sudden, Lanton walked in from outside, stopping as soon as he saw me and giving me a loud whistle that sounded very human. "The boys are getting restless, darling," he told me. "We'd better get this show started."

I nodded and blew him a kiss, glad that he could be here. I'm sure that Thane's mother was somewhere close as well.

They were all here.

Everyone I loved, except for my mother.

I chose not to dwell on that, giving them all a smile I hoped looked grateful.

Koria went over to the counter and grabbed a bouquet of light pink Veon flowers that I'd never seen before. I inhaled the soft, almost tropical scent of them. Koria gave my shoulder a light squeeze and then led everyone out besides my father.

"You ready for this, my darling girl?" he asked me, his voice still gruff from the emotion he was trying to control.

"Ready," I said, marveling for a moment at how much I meant those words, despite how everything had started with Derrial, Thane, and Corran.

"Let's do this then," he said as he led me towards the door.

My jaw dropped as I saw what had been set-up. The guys must have messed with the transparency of the walls and programmed them to keep showing the outside of our house as it usually worked...because what I was seeing now was nothing like what I had seen through the walls all morning as I was getting ready.

Instead of the colorful forest that had resembled a cotton-candy colored fall backdrop, there were now flowers blooming everywhere, so colorful and numerous that it was almost too bright for my eyes. The flowers framed a small path that led to a white wooden arch that was also covered with an explosion of flowers.

The flowers faded from view though when I saw my three Vepar standing up there, dressed in their usual tight uniform looking outfits with the exception that these were white.

I belatedly noticed that white stool looking seats were set up in front of the arch and were occupied by our families.

My dad patted my hand and began to lead me down the aisle as a soft harp sounding melody began to play a tune that I'd never heard but was so beautiful that it made me want to cry.

The walk seemed to go on forever as I resisted the urge to run towards my beautiful men. The three of them were staring at me as if I was everything good in the world. Thane, my usually stoic warrior, had tears in his eyes. Derrial looked like he was having to hold himself back from coming towards me. And Corran looked like he couldn't believe how lucky he'd somehow gotten.

The three of their gazes on me at once left me feeling heady.

After what seemed like half a lifetime, we made it to the arch where my men were waiting for me.

"You take care of my girl, you hear me?" my father ordered, his voice hitching as he spoke.

Derrial took my hand from my father's. "Forever," he vowed, the intensity in his eyes sending a blush over my cheeks.

My father gave me one more kiss on the cheek before walking over and joining the other parents on the stools that I realized were hovering a few inches in the air.

Butterflies erupted in my stomach as I continued to stare into my lovers' eyes.

Derrial opened his mouth and began to speak, a cacophony of strange words in a language that didn't resemble the Veon language that I'd been around for months. Somehow, I knew the words he was uttering were older than the Veon language. They sounded sacred...they sounded binding.

Thane and Corran began to join him, following along with him word for word. The words rushed over me, and even though I had no idea what they were saying, I could feel their almost magic quality spreading through my veins. As I listened, it was like the bond between the four of us became a tangible thing, brightening and strengthening until it was so strong that it could never break.

They finally stopped speaking and the three of them just looked at me proudly. Derrial leaned forward to kiss me, but I held up a hand to gently stop him. They had just given me their vow, and I wanted to do the same.

I'd had the attendants give me three simple gold-colored bands. It had taken a bit since I don't think wedding bands had been programmed into their abilities. I pulled them out of the binding at the bottom of my bouquet where I had been keeping them.

My hands were shaking, but I managed to slide a band on each of their left hands.

"I am my beloved's and my beloved is mine," I whispered, recalling my mother's stories of her Jewish heritage and my parent's wedding vows. "I, Ella, take you Derrial, to be my husband, and these things I promise you. I will be faithful to you and honest with you. I will respect, trust, help, and care for you. I will share my life with you. I will forgive you as we have been forgiven, and I will try with you to better understand ourselves, through the best and worst of what is to come, for eternity," I vowed to him.

I then moved to Thane and Corran and said the same vows.

All four of us were crying by the time we were finished, and my three men each took their time kissing me, each kiss so hot and deep that my body was on fire when the three of them finished.

Of course, the Vepar being the bloodthirsty people that they were, there was one more part to the ceremony. Corran took out a small knife and cut a cross-looking incision into all of our hands.

He then picked up a small gold bowl that had been sitting on the ground behind us and squeezed his hand until a drop of blood fell into the bowl. He then handed it to Thane, who did the same thing, followed by Derrial. Derrial then wrapped his hand around mine and helped me to squeeze one drop of blood into the bowl. As soon as my blood touched theirs in the bowl, a purple mist began to rise from the bowl. The mist collected and spread, suddenly surrounding the four of us, so thick that I could no longer see the flower colored meadow we were standing in. Images began to appear in the mist. There was a little girl, with Derrial's green eyes and my hair, being tossed up in the air by Thane. Corran and I were curled up on a porch watching a sunset with two suns instead of one fading into the distance. Derrial was making love to me by a lavender-colored waterfall. The four of us were eating dinner along with a little girl and three little boys, all perfect combinations of myself and my four men. On and on the images appeared until my heart felt like it was going to beat out of its chest at this glimpse into what must be our future. It was a future more beautiful than anything I could ever have imagined for myself, and I craved it with every fiber in my being.

The mist eventually faded, and I realized that the four of us had at some point during the montage of images sunk to our knees. All four of us were steadily weeping, more love reflected in their eyes than I'd thought possible.

We were then joined by our family members as they all rushed around us, sinking to their own knees as they embraced us, doing a lot of weeping of their own.

I had never felt such happiness, such completeness...such hope. At this moment, anything sounded possible.

At this moment, I felt more love than I could have ever dreamed.

We'd just said goodbye to our families, and I watched as the ship that they'd flown in on disappeared from sight as the invisibility shields that Corran had installed to keep our location secret engaged. Even the sound of the ship's engines was muted as they took off. I didn't get the burst of homesickness that I thought I would get saying goodbye to my father again. As I stood there on the porch, Thane's body wrapped around mine, and with my two other new husbands on either side of me, I felt home.

There had been a short reception after the ceremony, a combination of Veon and Earth traditions that managed to somehow meld perfectly together. There had been a five-tier wedding cake that resembled any celebrity's wedding cake back on Earth. But there had also been a purple slug type dish at the wedding dinner that the guys had somehow managed to get me to try. I wouldn't be repeating that mistake any time soon.

Regardless of the purple slug incident, it was a time spent with lots of laughter, and lots of love.

Our families hadn't been able to see the images in the purple mist, but there was a lot of reminiscing about what had happened in all of their wedding ceremonies. I was grateful that my dad hadn't gotten a glimpse of me rolling around in bed with my three new husbands.

I felt so much peace as I stood there in front of our home and the sound of the engines faded off into the distance...peace, but also a greater awareness that I'd just gotten married and how much my body was ready to seal the deal with my lovers.

Taking things into my own hands, I pulled away from Thane and grabbed each one of their hands as I began to lead them back into our home.

They quickly caught on to what I wanted. In their eagerness, Thane swept me into his arms and the four of us practically flew into our bedroom.

I wasn't nervous at all I stood in front of them, the three of them staring at me hungrily. I turned around and throatily asked Corran to unzip me. He quickly complied, and my gorgeous dress was soon pooled at my feet, leaving me in nothing but the white lingerie I had put on earlier. I heard their quick intake of breath, and it only made my own lust spiral higher.

Unsurprisingly, Derrial stepped up first, spinning me around so I was facing him. His lips brushed mine, gently at first, sending tantalizing shivers down my spine. He deepened the kiss, his firm mouth nibbling and caressing. Heat quickly rose between us, and he began to devour me.

The rest of the world faded around me, until all that existed was his lips against mine and the sensations building up inside of me. His tongue flicked teasingly at my lips, until I parted them to admit him.

He broke the kiss long enough to lay me back on the bed. Before I could blink, he'd ripped my underwear off. "Open your legs for me," he ordered. Despite how many times I'd been with them, my face heated and my heart began to pound. I obeyed him though.

"Wider," he urged me. His hand moved to my knees, pushing them apart. "Beautiful," he murmured as he began to softly tease my swollen lips.

He bowed his head over my lap, and I gasped as he blew a teasing puff of air across my folds. An instant later, I cried out in surprise and jerked as he began to stroke me more insistently, his caress making me wild.

He chuckled, a low, satisfied sound, and touched my clit. I cried out with surprised pleasure and unconsciously thrust my hips upwards, spreading her legs further apart.

"Just like that," said Thane from somewhere around us. His voice brought the room back into focus, and I saw that Thane and Corran were both lounging in chairs, in different states of undress, their eyes sparking as they touched themselves as they watched Derrial and I.

Derrial brought my attention back to him as his fingers hit the perfect spot, again and again, teasing and circling with just the right pressure. I moaned against his mouth and clung to him.

Pleasure gathered like a thunderstorm on the horizon, but Derrial didn't seem in a hurry to push me over the edge.

"Derrial...please..." I begged in a ragged whisper. He cradled me with one arm as his finger slid in and out, meeting little resistance from my slick, throbbing flesh.

"Sweet Ella," he said hoarsely. "You're so perfect." He returned to kissing me, his mouth devouring mine, his tongue ravishing me as he quickly penetrated me with a second finger, then added a third. A soft, pleading moan escaped me, muffled by his mouth as he continued to caress me, winding my arousal ever higher. My tension continued to gather like a storm in the pit of my stomach, and I burned with need. He gave me one last punishing kiss, and then sweet, hot lightning struck across my senses in an explosion of pleasure. I cried out and writhed against his fingers, the pleasure almost unbearable.

"Derrial," I breathed, pulling on his arm. "I want to feel you inside me," I begged.

Placing his elbows on either side of my head, Derrial rocked his hips, sliding his cock back and forth along my folds. A tingle began again where he was rubbing me. As the tension mounted, I closed my eyes. He lowered his mouth to mine, and after another deep kiss, slid his lips over to my ear and nibbled. Wave after wave of sensation flashed over me, through me. It felt like I would die if he didn't bury himself inside me soon. I reached down between our bodies to palm him. He was hard steel encased in smooth silk. Chills ran up my spine in anticipation of having him fill me completely. He wrapped his hand around mine and guided his cock to my opening. I released him and wound my arms tightly around his neck, tilting my hips to ease his entry. He covered my mouth and slid his tongue between my lips, even as he pushed himself home. I arched my back, moaning as the slow glide triggered every nerve ending in its path. Moisture blurred my vision. Balancing on his elbows, he cradled my head in his hands while keeping his hips still. "I love you," he whispered. I shivered as the husky tones of his voice washed over me.

"I love you too." I ran my hands down the ropes of muscle on his back, until I could curl my fingers around the tight globes of his butt. There was a reverence in his eyes as he began to move. A tightening feeling began to build up in my core as he withdrew one inch at a time, until only the head of his cock remained inside me. When I could stand it no more, he plunged. He repeated this over and over until I cried out.

With a knowing look, he grinned at me. "What do you want, baby?"

"More," I begged. Lowering himself completely on me, he gripped my ass, tilting my hips up, and began pounding into me with short hard strokes. With his face in the crook of my neck, he kissed and nipped at my shoulder.

Suddenly, I was desperate to feel his bite. I gripped his head and tried to push him lower. When he didn't understand, I made a mewling sound of displeasure. He lifted his head, and I knew by the sexy look on his face that he was teasing. With a seemingly innate understanding of my needs, he raised himself to his knees, pulling me tightly against him so my bottom rested on his thighs. Bending over me, he tugged one of my nipples between his teeth. The feeling, between a tweak and a pinch, along with the relentless pounding of his cock, sent me over the edge. As my world exploded into a kaleidoscope of color and sensation, I clutched his head against me and called out his name. He released my nipple and bit me right above my chest, sending me into another orgasm immediately. After a long drink, he pushed up on his hands, and thrust high and deep a few more times before achieving his own release and collapsing on top of me.

Only then did I become aware again of my other two husbands still in the room, their breaths heightened as they watched us. In a flash, Thane was beside us, pushing Derrial off of me. "My turn, brother," he growled, and Derrial reluctantly slid off the bed and settled in another chair nearby.

Thane's mouth descended on mine in a highly charged kiss, shooting my arousal sky high again in a matter of seconds, even though I'd just had several orgasms already. The kiss reverberated throughout my entire body, my inner walls clenching tightly. It didn't matter that I'd just had Derrial. I wanted Thane inside of me just as badly.

Pushing past the emotions strangling me, I whispered, "Make love to me."

He growled again in response. Without a word, he flipped me over onto my stomach and pulled my hips up until I was on my knees, spread wide. His large hand pressed on my back until my face met the pillow that smelled like all three of my men. I inhaled deeply, the scent flooding me with even more moisture. A shudder roared through me as his warm tongue took a long, slow swipe. He groaned, like I was the best thing he'd ever tasted, before gripping my hips tightly and plunging into me.

We moaned in unison. After holding still for a minute, as if he was savoring the sensation, he began to move. He pulled out so only the tip of his cock remained inside me, and then he pushed slowly until he was all the way inside, as far as he could go. His fingers on my hips held me in place, keeping me from pushing back and accelerating the rhythm. Then he began alternating long slow glides with short fast ones. Nine long, one short, eight long, two short... It was my new favorite pattern. In only a few more cycles, he'd be pounding into me.

With each deep stroke, the sensations intensified and my anticipation ratcheted up a few notches. Fuck. I wasn't sure I'd make it to the ten short, fast strokes. Thane was giving me everything I wanted.

Gritting my teeth, I braced my arms and held on for the ride. It didn't matter that I couldn't catch my breath - I'd already gone to heaven. His strokes changed, deepening, filling me.

"You feel how deep I am? Do you feel how you're mine?"

I gasped at his delicious words. I sure felt owned in this moment. He placed a stinging smack on my butt. At the same instant, he plunged deep inside me, deeper than ever before. The momentary flash of heat and the full-body pleasure of his penetration flung me over the edge. As wave after wave of sensation reverberated throughout my entire body, he continued to hold me tight, pounding into me, never letting up on the speed or power of his strokes. Even before the contractions inside me completely subsided, his teeth sinking into my shoulder sent me over the edge again.

This time he joined me. With a loud groan and a final tremendous push that sent me sprawling, he came too, collapsing on top of me, his lips pressed against my shoulder as he took one last sip of my blood before finally releasing me.

Looking up, I saw Corran standing there, his cheeks flushed with desire. "Do you need a break?" he asked in a hoarse voice as Thane pulled out of me and got out of the bed. I shook my head and held out my hand to him. "I want you," I said in a throaty whisper, and it was the truth. No matter what had just happened with Thane and Derrial, I would always need Corran. I would always want him.

And my wedding night would not be complete until I felt each one of my husbands deep inside me. This was a night I never wanted to forget.

I curled a finger and called Corran to me. Just seeing him stare at me like I was his world left me shivering with excitement.

He gave me a dangerous smirk as his hands slid down the front of his chest seductively. My insides thrummed, and I drew my lower lip between my teeth, gnawing on the flesh. This man was breathtaking.

Thane rolled off the bed, his cock still hard, glistening with our slick. Derrial was on the other side of the bed, his hand on his erection. These men were insatiable and all mine.

Corran unbuttoned his shirt in slow motion as I propped myself to lean back on my elbows., my legs crossed at my ankles.

"Take it all off," I teased, and blew him a kiss.

He shouldered the shirt down his strong arms, and all I saw was muscles. The perfect specimen of a man with angles and lines that left me weak with desire. The way his torso narrowed down to a lean waist that led down to a thatch of dark hair and... my mouth was parched. His cock stood so stiff and tall, the tip glistening with pre-cum. Corran was hot.

A quick shuffle, and he'd kicked off the pants that had sat low on his legs.

Everything about him had me burning, and the liquid fire between my thighs dripped.

"Fuck!" Corran growled. Then he spun and walked out of the room.

I jolted to sit up in bed. 'Umm, Corran, are you coming back?" I glanced over at Derrial and Thane, who both shrugged their shoulders.

Just as fast, Corran whipped back into the room and shut the door behind him with finality. Then he smirked at me.

"What did you do?" I asked, looking him up and down, scanning his open hands for a clue, anything.

Suddenly, a strange weightlessness flared over my body, like I was effortlessly floating. My heart started accelerating at the weird feeling. The whole room was lowering around me, and a whimper fell from my lips.

"Corran?"

But his whole body was lifting up off the floor.

"It's okay, gorgeous," he said.

I went to push myself backward as unease clung to me. But my hands pushed through the bed... I jerked to glance down and found myself floating too. "Oh, crap. What's happening?"

My insides leapt with the sensation of falling, like I was on a rollercoaster at Six Flags. I cried out as I lost complete orientation. I reached out frantically to catch myself, arms and legs flailing. All I saw were Derrial and Thane levitating near the bed, watching me.

Strong hands grasped my waist and drew me. "Ella, I got you. I've just switched off the gravity in this room. Your brain is telling you that you're falling but we're all just floating.

I clung onto his arms, breathing heavily, trying to tell my head to calm down. "Scared the hell out of me."

"Sorry, angel, thought it might be a nice surprise."

I laughed. "It's a surprise all right."

"Think of it as floating in a pool without the water on your skin," he explained, and when I imagined myself that way, I found my calm. I still wasn't letting go of Corran's arm, but now I felt like I was inside the Fizzy Lifting Room from *Charlie and the Chocolate Factory*. Except, the four of us were all naked, and I was likely about to have my first mid-air sex.

When I glanced over to the other two, Derrial winked, and Thane's hand was still somehow gripped around his cock eagerly.

Corran's lips were on my neck, and my skin rippled. Then he swung me around to face him by my shoulders. The ability to just float and move with such grace was exhilarating. Corran kissed me, his tongue pushed past my lips, dancing with mine. My body pulsed against his, sending wave after wave of heat through me. It didn't matter that I'd just been with two of my husbands. Hot liquid still built in my core.

He dragged me close, our chests mashed together, my body on fire. Gently, he slid a hand down the back of one of my thighs and guided my leg around his hip, then did the same with my other leg. His mouth brushed over my neck, finding the soft skin beneath my ear and nibbling on me.

I relinquished control to Corran, wanting him to take me. And as if sensing my decision, he pulled back from my neck with a devilish smile on his lips.

"You ready, gorgeous?"

"Fuck yeah, she's ready," Thane responded on my behalf, and I laughed as I looked over to him and saw he wore the sexiest expression ever. He loved seeing me with the other men.

"Do you even know what you do to us?" he groaned, his eyes glazed over with lust.

Derrial wore the same look.

"I'm the luckiest girl in the whole freaking universe, because if this is what our sex nights are going to be like, I won't be seeing much of the outdoors."

"Outdoors is overrated," Derrial added, chuckling, and I basked in the sound.

I loved seeing my husbands so playful and flirty.

"She's mine right now." Corran grabbed my ass and squeezed it as he pressed the tip of his cock to my opening.

I gasped at first from feeling him... Corran was not just medium or large, he packed an incredible size. "You alright, beautiful?"

"Yes." I stared into his stunning hazel eyes as my whole body purred beneath him. "Don't make me wait," I teased, running my hands over his shoulders, and held onto him as I adjusted myself over his cock.

He unleashed a panty-wetting roar before pushing a bit deeper into me. "Love it when you try to boss me around."

"Hey -- Ahh..." I cried out as he then drove into me unceremoniously. My fingernails dug into his skin. He held me tight.

Each time he thrust into me, the momentum sent us gliding across the room. It was the strangest feeling to be suspended while Corran held me locked to him. When my back kissed the wall, he pinned me in place and fucked me.

I moaned as my body exploded with my building desire. I felt every stroke as he adored me with his cock, his mouth on my neck before he tipped his lower and found the top of my breast, licking me.

We danced in each others' arms, lost in the moment. My body tightened as his fingers gripped my ass cheeks.

"Things I want to do you...that I want you to do!"

I melted to hear that gravelly dominating voice.

Sharpness pierced my breast as he bit down into my flesh with sharp canines.

My heart raced at double time while he drew my blood, drinking from me while bringing me closer and closer to the edge of arousal.

He swept his tongue over my bouncing breasts as he rocked in and out of me. "You're so fucking wet and tight."

I wanted to reply to say that he was so fucking big, but all I managed were moans. Heavy breaths.

"You are so perfect. Come for me, babe. Squeeze my cock with that sweet pussy."

Hearing those words ignited a trigger inside me...and holding anything back now was ridiculously impossible. He thrust that hard, thick dick into me.

"Fill me, please." I broke into screams as the orgasm broke through me. I shuddered as my sex quivered around him, squeezing him.

"Fuck! You're strangling my dick. Don't you dare stop."

I convulsed in his arms with the most insane orgasm.

Corran pushed us off the wall right then. He howled with his own release, pulsing inside me.

Connected, we stayed locked together and floated around the room as if we were one. Fluidly, we glided, our bodies rocking in unity. And all I could think was how perfect we were wrapped in each other's bodies.

My body trembled as Corran held me as close as he possibly could. I looked up at his face and asked, "How do we get down?"

It was Thane who chuckled as he floated just over the bed, tugging himself.

"Who said anything about being finished?" Corran teased, and leaned in to kiss me.

And I knew this was exactly where I needed to be...where I wanted to be.

3

I supposed with the planet of Veon in chaos mode, I really should be terrified. And I was when I thought about it, no question about it. People were scared to leave their homes. A virus was spreading, and zombie-like Vepar roamed the streets. The council remained broken and corrupt.

But amid all that jumbled mess, I had just married three of the most incredible Vepar. I had to keep reminding myself because it felt so surreal. Coupled with being pregnant, my life itself had morphed into a movie. A crazy, alien one where I had no idea what exactly was growing in my stomach, but I'd love the baby regardless.

Truth was, I wouldn't change a thing about my situation for the simple reason that if this insanity hadn't happened, I wouldn't have met my husbands. After everything we went through I understood that now.

We found my father, and next we'd find my mother. Good vibes had me rolling out of bed, even in a world breaking apart at the seams. The fact that my entire body was sore was just another sign of how good the last couple of days had been for me.

Sunlight poured through the window, and the smell of something savory like eggs wafted on the air. The bed lay empty of my men. Not finding my clothes anywhere, I picked up Thane's shirt from the floor and dragged it over my head. His masculine scent covered me, and I embraced it, loving how much his scent alone put me at ease.

I stepped into the kitchen, the floor cold under my feet. The three of them stood around the kitchen counter. Corran was placing eggs into a machine on the counter that resembled a microwave, and seconds later, he opened the door and the plate was filled with fluffy scrambled eggs. I still hadn't gotten used to how incredible the technology was on this planet, but I wasn't sure I could go back to the hassle of cooking from scratch.

The table in the middle of the room was filled with eggs, bacon, and waffles. I salivated at the sight.

Derrial turned to me first, his smile intoxicating, those green eyes to die for. With all three now staring at me, all I could remember was the most incredible night of my life. Their affection, their hunger for me, the insane sex marathon. They were my soul matches, my protectors, my lovers.

"Morning, my husbands." It felt so strange and dorky saying that, but also weirdly comforting.

"Hey, babe," Corran said.

"You look gorgeous," Derrial added.

Thane strode over, wearing only blue pajama pants that sat dangerously low on his chiseled hips. He was incredible to look at, and just staring at his bare chest had warmth searing my insides. Add to that his infectious smile, and no wonder I lost myself to them. His lips brushed over mine, and it was heaven. My skin prickled, instantly reacting to his touch.

"Morning, my pet. Are you hungry?"

I laughed at his question. "How much food did you all make?"

"We did some research and tried to make every human breakfast dish for you. We hope everything tastes the same."

My heart sang. I reached up and cupped his face, raising myself on tippy-toes before kissing him back. I melted against him, wishing I could have eternity to spend in their arms. "I love this so much."

It wasn't long before we all sat around the table to eat. I took a mouthful of the eggs, which surprisingly tasted similar as they would back home. The bagel turned out more like sweet bread, and the waffles more savory than I was used to. But I didn't care and ate them, suddenly starved. Between the four of us, we nearly finished everything on the table.

I sipped the lukewarm coffee, then said, "With everything happening, I think we need to find my mother. We found my father, so maybe she's still in one of the Khonsu female camps."

"Exactly what we were discussing this morning," Derrial murmured before taking another bite of the bacon. "There had been rumors that the Khonsu used a nearby moon to hold their females."

I immediately started imagining my mother trapped at a Khonsu camp on some remote moon... I pictured her inside a cage with other females. Similar to the state we found my father in. My stomach tightened with worry that we wouldn't find her. That somehow, I was too late. My heart gave a hard thump at that thought.

Stop it, I thought to myself. I couldn't let myself think like that, or I'd paralyze myself with dread.

Corran, who sat next to me, must have sensed my tension as he placed his hand on my thigh. "We'll turn this universe inside out to find her. I give you my word."

I leaned against him, and he wrapped an arm around my back as he kissed my brow.

"You three search the local moons, while I'm going to try to sneak into a few labs and see what I can find on the antidote for the virus."

I swallowed hard as reality pushed everything else aside. "Are you sure you should return there alone?" That honeymoon feeling dissolved into the background when there were so many more pressing issues.

Corran nodded, his eyes glinting as he tried to smile to ease my worry, but the smile was forced. "It will be easier to sneak around on my own."

The last few times we went to a lab, I was kidnapped by the feral, invading Khonsu race, then impregnated by the council, and then attacked by the virus inflicted Vepar. I hated those labs.

Thane tapped the comms on his wrist, and a holograph of a television screen appeared at the end of the table. We all turned to the new broadcast of a street view of the city. Three homeless men and a female stood near a storefront together. Torn clothes, dirty faces…something I didn't think existed on this planet. They huddled close, the wind tugging on their clothes. The view was patchy and grainy, and from the angle, it seemed this was filmed from a permanent street camera.

Unease slid through me, and I breathed out shakily as I watched them talking casually.

Next minute, they looked over to the street, and their eyes flew open. A small group of infected Vepar rushed toward them at lightning speed.

I flinched, and Corran held me tight.

The virus ridden had pale faces, clothes ripped and hanging off their dirty and injured bodies.

They attacked those poor people where they sat, the savagery ripping me to shreds. I was going to be sick. I squeezed my eyes shut, unable to view the attack anymore.

"It's okay," Corran cooed in my ear. "That scene is over."

I opened my eyes to a screen listing the number of expected infected per region. The numbers were staggering, and suddenly, the earlier peace I felt vanished. Fear slid into its place.

"See what you can find, but no heroic shit," Derrial muttered to Corran. "Call us if you need backup."

I sat there, still in Corran's arms, trying to smile and hide the trepidation rippling over me. That news footage freaked me out, as it reminded me how horrific the situation was getting. I slid a hand over my stomach, thinking about the little life inside me coming into this world. Around me were three Vepar who could make a difference, so I couldn't be in better company.

After we finished breakfast, I went to get dressed. I stood in front of the full-body mirror in the bathroom, looking at myself sideways, pushing my stomach out, trying to picture myself with a huge belly. The deep blue dress I wore drew in tight around my waist and chest, pushing my breasts up, the rest falling loosely to my knees. I'd lost quite a bit of weight since coming to Veon with all the stress and lack of eating as a result. But if I kept eating meals like I did this morning, being too skinny wouldn't be a problem for long. Especially with a baby bump coming on. I looked at my reflection again, and swore that I saw a bump still. I guess it was from the large breakfast.

Part of me was beyond ecstatic to have a family of my own, to meet the little angel inside me. I didn't want to think too much about things like what they would look like and get myself overthinking. There was no turning back now, right?

It was hard enough pushing aside the worry that I didn't know who the real father of my baby was... If my men were truly okay with it potentially not being one of theirs, then I was okay too.

I ran my shaky hands through my loose hair, still slightly damp, and pouted my rosy lips.

I could do this. Today was all about finding my mom.

"You look spectacular," Corran said.

He met my gaze in the mirror. He was standing in the doorway to the bathroom, arms deep into the pockets of his black pants. He wore a matching, long-sleeve top.

"And you look ready to go all ninja on someone." I laughed at his confused expression and sauntered over to him before wrapping my arms around his middle. Pressing myself to his chest, I listened to his beating heart. His body radiated heat, and I drank it in since most of the time, I felt so cold.

"I'm about to head off, gorgeous."

Glancing up, I locked eyes with him. He tilted his head forward to brush his lips against mine. He held me tight, kissing me deeply, his tongue sweeping into my mouth. Everything about him made me feel even more intoxicated. I loved the way my body reacted, how incredibly sweet he tasted, how his hands always roamed over my body like he couldn't get enough either.

"You are everything to me," he breathed into my mouth.

"I love you. Please be careful. I can't lose you."

He kissed my face while my stomach somersaulted with a sudden flare of panic that he'd get caught by the council, or attacked by the infected like those poor people on the news.

Air. I suddenly needed fresh air, as so many emotions came at me like a raging storm. Tears pricked my eyes at the thought that somehow, with this world going to chaos, I'd lose the men I'd fought so long to keep.

Corran pulled back from me while I ducked down the hall and opened the balcony door. A breeze swished over my face, and I inhaled deep. My heart raced in my chest, my head slightly dizzy.

"You alright?" Corran stood behind me, his hands wrapping around my waist. His breath was on my ear, gentle and soft, comforting me.

I nodded. "Think everything just hit me at once."

He rubbed my arms and held me close, encasing me in his love. "Nothing will harm you. And we have too much at stake to let anything happen to us." His large hands swept over my stomach.

"We ready?" Thane called out from the kitchen.

"What do you think?" Corran whispered in my ear. "Are we ready to do this?"

I turned around in his arms, searching his eyes for a sign that he was confident that he would return back to me. What I saw filled me with hope and belief that everything would turn out well.

My mouth tugged upward at the corners. "You're right. No more panic."

"That's my girl." He kissed my lips and then collected my hand into his before we returned to the kitchen.

Derrial and Thane were both dressed as if they were headed out to battle. Black heavy leather pants. Thane's had straps across the thighs, and he wore it with a red fitted jacket, zipped up to his neck. He reminded me of Star Lord in *Guardians of the Galaxy*. Derrial wore a long black coat with a matching top underneath. Simple, but they both looked deadly and sexy as hell.

"I feel like I'm underdressed," I said, staring down at my dress and black combat boots.

"You look perfect." Derrial closed the distance between us and slid his hand in mine. "Are you ready to go?"

The first thing I learned since coming to Veon was that things were unpredictable, and the best approach was to be alert and expect the worse. So, I nodded and glanced at my three husbands. "I'm ready. Let's go find my mom."

4

From up in space, everything looked tiny and beautiful. I glued myself to the window of our small cruiser as we approached the moon, Vetov. Cloud-blurred contours and a mottling of oranges and purples covered its surface. I assumed they represented oceans and continents. Nothing near as beautiful as I remember Earth from space with all those spectacular blues, but it still left me in awe.

With an utter lack of motion from our ship, we descended to the moon's surface.

So many emotions jumbled into a heap inside me, tugging me in every direction. Derrial and Thane didn't say a word, but left me alone with my thoughts. My heart raced while my knees bounced in my seat.

An urgency pulsed through me that I had to hurry to find my mother, that I was running late. Fear brought on darker thoughts.

Derrial murmured something into his ear piece about us coming in for a landing. And it didn't take long before we descended. I could make out a landscape of orange and green meadows and bright yellow trees. Mountains in the distance crowned the area. One thing about these alien planets were how spectacular they were with the bright colors.

There were no docks to pull into here, but open territory, which meant lots of walking to reach nearby settlements.

My heart skipped a beat as we hurried down. The moment we landed, I unbuckled myself and leapt to my feet, too restless to sit a second longer.

"Slow down, my pet," Derrial said, his brow furrowed as he studied the comms screen on the dashboard of the ship. "I need to get locations of all settlements first."

I grunted and stepped into the back of the cruiser where Thane grinned at me. He snatched me by the hips as I passed and drew me toward him. I fell onto his lap, my arms reached for his shoulders out of instinct.

"It could be dangerous out there, so you stay with us at all times. No running off, understand?"

A few months ago, I would have disagreed. Except now, I nodded because it wasn't just my husbands or myself I might put in danger anymore. But our baby. "I know, I'm just excited and nervous, and feel like I might explode from all the waiting."

He cradled me in his arms, holding me close against his chest, and kissed my brow, my nose, then my lips. "I know how you're feeling. I'm hoping this is the place, and we find your mother quickly."

"Me too." I leaned against him and tucked my head against the curve of his neck. He ran his hand over my hair, which calmed my nerves.

"Alright, I've got it all," Derrial announced the moment I finally relaxed.

We stepped outside into a cold atmosphere, despite the lack of clouds and the sun out in full force. The air smelled fresh with a hint of pine...except there were no pine trees in sight.

Derrial stood at the rear of the vessel where a latch opened up. Thane went to join him, while I looked around. It didn't look anything like Earth's moon. This place was lush and inhabited.

The door to the cruiser slid shut and the whole thing shimmered to an invisible finish. Corran explained to me once that the effect was created with a reflective mirror technology and a bit of illusion.

I looked around and found no sign of my two husbands, so I assumed they were still behind the cruiser.

The crunch of grass sounded behind me, and I spun around.

An invisible window rolled down in front of me to reveal the inside of a car. Derrial sat in the driver's seat of a vehicle also with invisibility shields that reminded me of a 4WD in height. "Get in," he said.

I approached the back and stretched my hand out through the air until my fingers brushed a metal finish. Running my hand down the surface, I found a latch and flicked it. The door opened in front of me.

Not wasting a moment, I jumped in and shut the door. Black leather seats, dark upholstery, this car reminded me of a limousine. "This is a very fancy ride." I leaned toward the front where the men sat. Thane stretched his hand between their two seats to reach me and took mine in his. "The vehicle is a bit run down, but it does the trick."

"Run down? This looks fancier than my whole apartment." I laughed as I settled down and Thane turned back to face the front.

And we were moving. Just like the cruiser, the drive was smooth, with what I imagined was the universe's best suspension.

An array of buttons covered the door offering various drink choices, each filled with different colors, from blues, oranges, and greens. I pressed the clear one. A panel instantly popped out, and I flinched. A glass slid out, filled with what looked like water. I picked it up and smelled it. No real scent, so I sipped it. Refreshing water ran down my throat. Then I gulped the rest of it down in one go.

When I set the glass back down on the panel, it drew back into the door and the panel shut. The technology in this world astonished me.

As I sat back in my seat, I noticed Derrial looking at me through the rear-view mirror, his gorgeous eyes smiling.

We kept driving, and I looked out at the open landscape of rolling hills, then we drove around an enormous purple river. The surface was pristine, the sun glinting like jewels against the water.

How could something so beautiful be home to the vicious Khonsu? Last time I encountered them I'd been kidnapped, then I was forced to participate in an insane Mating hunt. So the idea of going anywhere near these aliens again terrified me.

"How much farther?" I asked.

"First settlement isn't far," Derrial explained. "This must remind you of road trips humans take often."

I shrugged. "Sort of. Guess there are some similarities, like we're in a car and driving."

"So, what's missing?" Thane asked, glancing at me over his shoulder.

"Music, snacks, lame jokes...a fun destination. But to be fair I've only ever been on one road trip with my old friend." Cherry came to mind, the only close friend I thought I had, except turned out she was only using me. In truth, I was too scared to do anything about it, as I didn't want to be alone after losing my parents. I sighed heavily, remembering life before I left Earth. That girl who was timid and scared was no longer me. I'd come so far since arriving on Veon, since falling in love, since surviving so many almost deaths. And... I lowered my attention as I rubbed my stomach, which almost felt like a little bump. Or it could be all those waffles I ate for breakfast.

A sudden explosion of fast beat music burst from the car speakers. I jumped in my seat as Thane rapidly pressed buttons on the front dashboard of the car.

Derrial was saying something, but it was too loud to make it out.

"That's very loud," I called out.

The panels on the doors flipped open and threw out green crispy packets at me. I flinched back at the sudden commotion. I snatched one from my lap to see an image of a snapple on the front, so I ripped it open to find fresh slices of the fruit.

"Sorry," Thane yelled, just as the music flatlined.

"Oh, that's better," I said, and pushed a piece of snapple in my mouth. It was crisp and moist.

"The music only has one volume level, and well, at least you got some snacks."

I nodded and swallowed the food. "Not exactly road trip food, but it's good."

Thane's smile was contagious, and I loved seeing him proud. "Do you still miss Earth a lot?"

His question threw me off guard. "Parts of it. Like the places where I hold the fondest memories. The botanical gardens. The zoo where Dad would take me. Feeling safe most of the time... I miss that part a lot." I shrugged. "I used to miss it a lot, but lately, I've hardly given it thought. My home now is where the three of you are."

Thane blew me a kiss, and my heart beat a bit faster.

I leaned forward in my seat and stared out through the front window at the path we drove alongside a lofty stone mountain without anyone in sight.

"Why couldn't we just fly here if you have an invisible aircraft?" I asked.

"Space cruisers are easily detected, so we can't risk being seen near any villages to avoid an all out attack. They will shoot before asking questions."

Suddenly, I lost my appetite, and I pushed my third packet of snapple slices on the seat next to mine.

Up ahead, a crowd of trees clustered together. We slowed down as we approached and parked on the outskirts.

Panic skittered down my spine. "What now?"

"You stay here," Derrial explained. "And we go and scope out the area and make sure this is a camp."

I frowned and sighed loudly.

"We want to know you are safe," Thane added. "Even if this vehicle is detected, which is highly unlikely, the locks are impenetrable."

My muscles tightened, but I nodded as both of them stared at me expectantly.

"Good. We won't be long."

"Be safe," I said.

They shut the doors, and I watched them sprint into the woods, vanishing into the shadows. I slumped back in the seat and reached for my half uneaten packet of snapple, suddenly hungry again.

The car still ran, as it pumped out cool air, and I kept looking out to see if they had returned, even though they'd just left.

Anxiety stretched through me as I sat there and waited. And waited. And waited.

When I caught movement from up ahead, I shuffled forward in my seat. Derrial and Thane strolled back almost casually, which told me this settlement wasn't a camp. Now fear gripped my spine at the possibility that the rumor they heard about this moon having female camps was just that - a rumor.

The next two locations on the map proved just as useless. We reached the fourth place, which consisted of a group of over-sized warehouse buildings huddled in a large circle. We pulled up toward the rear of a shed, when the car made a strange clunking sound. Then it stopped suddenly. I lurched forward from the movement, and fear shot to my heart.

"What the hell was that?" I asked, glancing out to the metal buildings not too far from our position. I didn't see anyone walking around.

"Fuck," Derrial growled. "We don't need this now."

Goosebumps swept down my arms.

"Engine failure? How the fuck?" Thane muttered.

"I don't know, unless I check the motor, and that means standing out there in plain sight."

"Are we still invisible?" I asked, gripping onto the door handle.

"Unfortunately, no. And if we can't fix the motor with no tools or parts, we have no choice but to go on foot."

A terrible feeling sank through my gut.

Derrial tapped his comm on his wrist and raised it to his mouth. "Corran, we need urgent extraction. I'll send you coordinates."

Corran was probably too busy sneaking about a lab right now to hear our call.

"So, what do we do?" My brain stuttered, and I felt vulnerable out here. We were sitting targets. "Wait for Corran to come get us?"

"We need to move on foot and fast," Thane answered, and I didn't like his answer at all. Us out there with nowhere to go.

"And pray to the universe no one finds the vehicle before Corran arrives." Dread wove through their words, and now fear coiled tighter in my chest.

We were trapped. This couldn't be happening.

5

We peered out from the edge of the forest toward the open yard. Long grass and blue weeds smothered the land. Six similar warehouse structures surrounded the area, each facing each other in a semi-circle. Why else would they have these out in the middle of nowhere, but to hide something...to hide the females they kidnapped. My gut clenched at the idea that maybe my mom was in this settlement.

A place run by Khonsu, alien creatures who infiltrated the Vepar's homeland and kidnapped their females for breeding. Add to that, the Khonsu used a type of glamor technology to conceal their real appearance to look like my Vepars. So detecting them wasn't always easy.

With a flick of Derrial's hand, we ran from the woods to behind a stone building the size of a large shed...perfect for keeping prisoners.

Another hand signal, and Derrial pivoted around the opposite side of the building. Thane and I inched forward on this side.

The silence grew heavier, and I was certain the next planet over could hear how hard my heart hammered.

Thane twisted his head to look at me and whispered, "Let me check the front, then when I give the signal, you join us."

Before I could even nod, he darted forward and slipped around the corner. Crap, he hadn't even told me what his signal was, so I rushed forward and stuck my head around the building to watch.

He and Derrial both fiddled with a lock to the door into the place.

I looked around the area, surveying the location, when my sights fell on someone sitting on a bench in front of the next building near us. He wore gray clothes, which easily blended him in with his surroundings. He had to be a Khonsu.

The Khonsu shot me a venomous glance, his nostrils flaring as he sniffed the air for our scents. He looked normal...like one of the Vepar. Short gray hair, tiny horns over his temples with a burley build. Khonsu were primal and wild and I could see the wildness in this creature's eyes. He didn't say anything, but slowly rose to his feet.

Shit! Panic launched to the back of my throat. "Thane, Derrial," I whispered loudly, but they didn't hear me.

I ran to them just as the Konshu darted across the field toward the black warehouse across the field.

"Fuck, he's spotted us," I blurted, pointing.

Both men snapped around and saw where I showed them.

Thane's face blanched and he leapt into a run, moving faster than I'd ever seen anyone move, closing in on the alien in seconds.

The Khonsu yelled out just as Thane lunged into him, bringing him to the ground with a thud.

They rolled on the ground, fighting, the thump of dull punches from Thane, who straddled the alien. In seconds, he leapt up and snatched the creature's legs before dragging him our way. I couldn't take my gaze off the Khonsu who no longer resembled a Vepar, but took his own form - pale skin and hair, and dead eyes black as the night. I remembered well the fact that these monsters had a mouth filled with razor sharp teeth. I wanted nowhere near it.

My skin rippled with fear, but I refused to panic. I wasn't the one trapped by these things and prepared for breeding. And just the thought had me scolding myself that I'd have such a thought. I kept fidgeting with my hair, unable to stand still. I struggled to keep it all together as fear coiled in my chest, and all I could think was that an army of Khonsu was about to come racing out of the sheds any second now. We had no car to escape, and who knew how long before Corran arrived.

I didn't want to panic. I'd been through so much since arriving in this universe, but it wasn't just me anymore... there was a little innocent baby inside me that I had to care for. Maybe I'd made a mistake by coming out here with them.

Thane dragged the Khonsu into the bushes in the woods.

As if sensing my unease, Derrial slid an arm around my waist and drew me against him. I wrapped my arms around him and pressed myself to the warmth of his body.

"We won't let anything happen to you."

Thane heaved for breath. "Okay, new plan. We need to check what's inside each of these sheds damn fast." He raised his hand with what looked like a laser pointer.

"Is that a key?" I asked.

He leaned closer and kissed me on the lips. "You bet it's a key, pet. We stick together and do this quickly."

I pulled free from Derrial and shuffled to face the building to our back. "Let's start here," I said.

Derrial pointed the pencil-shaped object at the padlock surface, emitting an orange beam of light. In two seconds, the lock clicked open.

I bounced on my toes, eager to get inside. Thane took the lead and opened the door. He peered inside and sighed loudly. He glanced back and shook his head. But I needed to know what he saw, and as he moved out of the way, I stuck my head inside to a huge enormous empty room. Broken crates and a few blankets lay in a heap to indicate there were living beings here at some point.

"Babe," Derrial murmured, and took my hand. "We need to go."

I nodded and followed him to the next shed, which was exactly what the Khonsu had been guarding, so my hopes sky rocketed we'd find something.

Thane opened the door hastily, and shut it quickly behind him.

Dread collided into me, and I exchanged worried glances with him. "He's found something, hasn't he?" I whispered.

Derrial nodded and leaned closer. "If he doesn't come out in a minute, I'm in there. Otherwise, he's scoping for guards and danger and he'll be right out."

I kept glancing over my shoulder, staring at the other buildings. Our saving grace was that they didn't have windows, so unless more Khonsu emerged from the building, they wouldn't see us.

My head was spinning. Derrial was deadly quiet, not breathing heavy or sweating like me. The breeze picked up, bringing with it the scent of forest and animals. The utterly agonizing silence sat on my chest, and to be honest, when we spoke about coming out here, I'd assumed we'd find a small camp and women huddled somewhere near in a cage. Delusional hope on my end.

"Has it been a minute?" I trembled, my gaze flipping between the door and the rest of the field.

When the door to the shed opened, I flinched backward and bumped into Derrial who caught me in his arms.

Thane stuck his head out. "All safe. You gotta come in here."

He opened the door, and we both hurried inside as Thane closed us in.

It took my mind a moment to work out what I was looking at. On the three walls in front of me were metal cages stacked on top of each other, four cages tall. Each was easily six-foot high and wide, except there were people inside them.

Something in my gut twisted at the sight. Only females filled the cages... maybe half a dozen in total.

Derrial and Thane rushed forward and started to release them from their imprisonment, starting with those higher up. Together they helped each other climb the top, then used the laser key to open the doors.

I couldn't move, couldn't breath as I selfishly scanned the faces for my mother. It had been so long since I had seen her, and she looked like me everyone said, so I searched the cages. The room was dimly lit with the only shards of light slicing the dark through holes and cracks in the ceiling and walls. The first woman I found appeared about my age. Blond hair and wild blue eyes, and human. She lacked horns or a tail or those stunning colorful eyes Vepar were known for.

She pressed herself to the metal bars. "Please let us out before they return. Please." Her voice trembled, her face stained with dirt and dried blood. "The things they do to us if we don't behave. I don't want to die." She lashed out a hand through the bar and snatched my wrist. Her grip was weak. She looked thin and so exhausted. Tears rolled down her cheeks. She stared at me blankly, like she's seen so many horrible things, she was completely stunned.

"We're going to get you out, I promise."

Her fingers uncurled from my wrist, and she withdrew back into her cage, sitting in a corner, rocking herself.

The ache in my chest as seeing her agony carved me in half. Why hadn't the Vepar council demolished these camps if they suspected they existed? Or were they too busy lining their pockets and creating a new virus strain to care about fixing the existing problems?

Quickly, I moved to the next cage, which sat one higher, and a woman with golden curls and short white horns stared down at me with desperation in her eyes.

What surprised me was how quiet everyone was, and I suspected they knew noise meant the chance of them not being rescued. Whispers drew my attention to Thane, who hopped down, carrying a young girl who wore a tattered yellow dress. She had to be fifteen, maybe sixteen.

I wanted to murder these Khonsu, rip out their spines for destroying these people's lives. The more cages I searched, the more my hope dissolved at finding my mom.

The next cage I stepped in front of left me breathless. I dropped to my knees and watched a young mother with black horns and red eyes cradling a tiny baby in her arms. They were both fragile and my eyes pricked with tears. I wanted to scream at the cruelty, but it was heartbreak that climbed up and over my body, icing every cell in my body.

"You're going to be free," I promised, and she lifted her gaze to meet mine. The fabric from around the baby's head slid down to reveal a tiny bundle with tiny pointy horns running in a line across the top of his brow. It did so all around his face, and that was when I noticed a long white tail flicking over the mom's lap.

The woman didn't say anything, her expression stoic like she'd forgotten how to feel, then quickly covered her sleeping baby.

"He's beautiful," I said, my breath hiccuping. "What's his name?"

"Jihl. She's a girl."

"I'm so sorry, I-I..."

"It's hard to tell at this age. Who are you?" she asked bluntly, her eyes squinting my way, studying me as if trying to see right through me.

"I'm Ella, and I'm looking for my mom who was taken from Earth. I'm hoping she was brought here and I can find her."

The woman studied me for a long pause. "They used to bring and take females from the other buildings, but then they consolidated everyone who remained in here. I've been in this cage for three weeks, and seen enough death to last me a lifetime."

"You've been stuck in here for three weeks?" My heart bled, and trying to keep my head straight seemed impossible when I just wanted to burst out crying for these prisoners, for this woman and her child, for my mother going through this.

"I've been hoping my husband will come and find me, but he hasn't." Her voice trembled.

"He's been trying, I'm sure of that. Not many know the Khonsu keep female camps on this moon though."

I turned around and waved down Thane while wiping the escaping tears. The heavy burden of this place clung to me like boulders, weighing me down. I'd never be able to unsee this.

I wiped away the unstoppable tears as an ugly pain clogged in my throat.

When Thane looked at me, his face paled. "Are you alright?"

I shook my head, dying on the inside at seeing the suffering.

He kissed my brow and held me tight for a few moments. His breaths were on my ear. "Trick is to focus on the act of rescuing and nothing else."

I shook my head, except it was too late... I was thinking about everything but the rescue. I was thinking about how a child ended up in here, about how I'd feel if it was me in that cage with my newborn.

"Remember how much I love you." He then broke away and hurried to release the woman and her child. I quickly turned and helped her out as she clasped onto her baby, ready to fight to the end if anyone touched her.

My baby was still unborn, but I already felt that same protectiveness of him or her. I'd give my life to protect my baby. And that meant destroying every last one of these camps.

"Is your name Ella?" the woman asked with the softest voice, drawing my attention. I snuck in a quick wipe of my eyes and smiled at her, trying to put on a brave face.

"I thought you looked familiar. I may have seen your mom in one of the other buildings." She rocked her baby in her arms, staring at the child as she hummed a soft song.

Her words cut through me, and suddenly the room tilted. My heart pounded in my chest. I was too afraid to ask the question. Each inhale grew shorter, and my insides were a chaotic mess of panic and sorrow. All these years later, and it felt like I'd just lost Mom. Like I stood over her empty grave long after everyone left. It was the only way to give myself closure without going crazy.

"So she's still alive?" I gasped, more to myself. "What building is she in?"

When the woman glanced up at me, grief swept over her expression. Then she gave me a heartbreaking shake of her head. "There was an explosion in that building, and no one survived. I'm so sorry, Ella." Her eyes glistened at delivering the news.

Suddenly, my whole world shattered like glass.

My soul darkened.

I no longer felt my body... it wavered and my legs fell out from under me. I hit the floor, falling to my knees. Tears welled in my eyes and drenched my cheeks as I choked on my breaths. I clenched my fists to my chest, fingernails digging into flesh, breaking skin. Nothing took away the pain. Nothing ever would.

Long ago, I grieved the loss of my mom, said my farewells. But since finding my dad, I grasped onto the hope that my mother was still alive too, that somehow, I'd find both my parents and be a happy reunited family again.

Except now, my heart was splintering into thousands of shards.

"She can't be dead." The whispered words escaped past my lips.

6

T hane crouched next to me having overheard the Vepar's news about my mother. "Oh, baby, I'm so sorry." He drew me into his arms and held me tight, and I couldn't hold it together anymore. I just broke down and ugly cried against his chest. The cries shredded through me like a storm, unleashing the years of grief I'd held onto.

He clasped a hand to the back of my head when I finally quieted down and kissed my brow. "I love you," he whispered.

I finally drew back and wiped my tears. Derrial approached me while others neared as well. All these prisoners who were terrified and shocked at how close they had come to death.

Derrial drew me to my feet by my hand and embraced me, his strong arms like belts around me, holding me, reminding me I was no longer alone in this universe. I had my three husbands and Father.

The ache in my heart deepened, but I wiped my eyes and put on a brave face in front of everyone else. "I'm okay. Let's find a way to get everyone out of here."

"What we need is one of the Khonsu ships," Thane explained.

The Vepar female with golden curls and short white horns cleared her throat, and we all turned to her. She wore a tattered dress that hung loosely around her thin frame. "I saw one of their cruisers. They keep it in the building right on the edge across the field." She pointed toward the door in that direction.

Just as Derrial's mouth parted with a response, a loud boom from outside stole his words.

I flinched and bumped back into Thane. He clasped my hips, drawing me closer, protectively. Everyone stared toward the door and silence fell over us.

"Quickly, get down in the corner and stay low," Derrial ordered. With a flick of his hand to Thane, both of them darted across the enormous room, then shoved their backs to the wall on either side of the door, their laser guns drawn.

I ushered everyone to crouch together in a corner where the shadows were the darkest. Bending down, I waited shoulder to shoulder with the mother and her child.

My heart beat so fast. The silence strangled me, and sweat dripped down my back.

Voices streamed from outside, growing louder as if they stood just outside the door. I stiffened at realizing we didn't lock the door, and they'd know someone was in here.

My pulse raced in my veins, and we were here in the open, making us an easy target. I choked down every breath, trying to calm myself.

When the door swung open, four Khonsu charged inside. Huge brutes as big as bears.

My blood turned cold at the sight.

Their gaze all swung in our direction as if they could see in the dark. Maybe they could. My body numbed and I felt completely paralyzed with fear. All I could think about was my last encounter with them and I wanted to run for my life.

A sharp, shrill sound reverberated against the walls just as one of the aliens fell face first, smoke wafting upward from his back.

They turned on Derrial and Thane, guns raised. The horrific sound of the shooting had me flinching. Everyone around me murmured, and the baby broke into a scared wail.

Derrial shot one man in the gut, then threw himself into a forward roll to miss a fired laser. Thane slammed the back of his gun into another man's face, and in seconds, the two had disposed of the Khonsu.

My heart leapt at how swiftly they fought, how strong and fast they eliminated the enemy. I couldn't possibly love them more if I tried as there was something exhilarating at seeing my protectors battle. They were my everything.

Thane stuck his head outside, while Derrial crossed the room in seconds. "We all need to go now."

"Are you sure we're safe?" a younger girl asked, her face so pale, I was worried she might pass out.

"We'll all be safer trying to make a break than stay in here," I said. "Take my hand, you can run with me, alright?"

She didn't move at first, and I understood the feeling of panic being so heavy that even the thought of running became too daunting.

"Raemy, you know we can't stay here," the mother said, rocking her crying baby to a soothing gurgling sound. "You'll end up as a breeder, or we'll die if we stay. We need to leave."

Raemy nodded and tears slid down her face.

I offered her my hand, and she took it, her touch trembling against mine. "Just run, no matter what. We are getting out."

She wiped her tears and gave me a crooked smile. Raemy had the thinnest horns I'd seen on any Vepar. And the palest hazel eyes, reminding me of a deer.

"Let's go," Derrial instructed, and we rushed toward the door. Then we stepped outside where the wind was icy, and ran for our lives.

I felt anything but cold as adrenaline drove me. Hand in hand with Raemy, we cut across the field with everyone else. Thane in front, Derrial behind us, all making for the shed and praying to god the cruiser was there. Otherwise we'd need a plan B, and I couldn't for the life of me think of a plan B right now.

I sucked in each breath, terror clinging to my ribs.

Thane shot the lock to the door on the last building from a distance. Then he sprinted forward faster, his boots hitting the ground hard. He ripped open the door and his shoulders sagged.

No, no. Please, no!

The closer we got, the more the empty building came into view. My stomach sank right through me, and now panic came at me in waves. To run. To scream. To do something other than stand out here, vulnerable on enemy territory.

Thane's face blanched when he turned toward us, but he didn't show the panic, but held himself strong and in control. "Everyone inside, now!" He was always two steps ahead.

I released Raemy's hand as she darted inside, and I stopped near my husband, sidling up to him, my arm grazing his. "What do we do now?"

He clutched my waist and held me close, and I felt the quiver in his touch. He was scared too. "I'm going to go find the ship, because they might have it in a different location. Derrial will stay here and guard you all."

"Please be safe."

When he met my gaze, a softness swept over his expression. "I'm sorry we brought you with us. We never should have put you in danger." A hardness crept into those spectacular blue eyes, and the pain in his voice touched me. I saw the ache in his expression and how much this upset him.

"I wouldn't have let you go without me. How would you know who my mother was?"

His frown deepened, and I saw the sorrow and pain in his eyes. "I love you so much. I'll die before I let anything happen to you and our baby." He kissed my face, then ushered me into the building and shut the door.

Our baby.

The words whirled in my mind. We still had no idea who the father was, yet these gorgeous Vepar in my life loved us just the same.

I moved quickly into the building with the other women. Derrial stayed at the door, and opened it an inch so he could spy outside.

The other women huddled together, and I pressed my spine against the wall, then we all waited.

So many emotions battled inside me. My whole body shook, muscles tensed. Derrial looked over to me with so much devotion in his eyes, it softened the worry gripping me.

We just had to get these people to safety, that was priority. Focus on the job, not my emotions. Not that my mother died in this camp. A tear escaped from the corners of my eyes, and I blinked to push them away. If I started crying again, I'd never stop. I couldn't let myself picture Mom's last days, the terror she felt, the helplessness.

Tears fell faster now, my chest splintering, and I abruptly pushed myself away from the wall.

Stop it, I scolded myself.

I walked over to Derrial, needing something other than being inside my own head. "Anything?" I asked.

"No one's come out yet."

"Maybe there's no one else here. Just the four Khonsu you and Thane finished off," I whispered hopefully.

"That would be ideal, but I doubt it. If Thane comes back with no news on a cruiser, and I hear nothing from Corran, we will need to get everyone away from this camp. We're sitting targets right now."

Fear slid down my spine at his words.

He reached over and cupped the side of my face, and something shifted. Gone was the warrior, and in its place, my husband appeared. He spoke with a heavy sigh. "I'm so sorry about your mother."

I nodded, unsure what to say because the situation sucked so hard. I wished for anything that I didn't come to this moon. Then I could still grasp onto the hope that Mom was still alive, rather than feeling like my insides were utterly broken like glass. My hand instinctively fell to my stomach. How was I meant to be a mother without having my mom to help me?

A great bang sounded at the back of the building we were in. I flinched around in response, along with everyone else. No one moved or dared to make a sound.

My heart pummeled in my chest as I imagined dozens of Khonsu coming for us.

The front door pushed open, and a shadow fell on us. I spun, a small cry escaping from my lips.

Thane pushed the door open wider, and I breathed a sigh of relief, wanting to scream at him for scaring the hell out of us.

"Out the back, fast!" he commanded, his voice terrified.

No one argued. Thane took the lead, and we all followed. It was only when Derrial and I reached the side corner that a terrifying war-cry came from behind us.

We both twisted around.

A handful of Khonsu poured out of a building all the way at the end of the field.

I rocked on my heels and terror slammed into me.

"Oh, shit!" I whimpered.

Derrial snatched my hand, and we ran around the corner for our lives.

Quickly catching up with everyone farther from the camp and in an open area surrounded by woods, I gasped at the sight.

An enormous black spaceship sat in the field. The surface glinted in the sun, oval in shape, it had arched windows around the vessel. It was easily the size of two of the warehouse buildings, so that was why it was parked here... no way it would fit indoors.

A door slid open and stairs slid out.

"Everyone on now!" Derrial hollered, dragging me and pushing me onboard. We scrambled together, my skin crawling as I kept looking over my shoulder.

Black walls and nothing else in this room of the space cruiser.

Thane sprinted to my right and lasered the wall where a door slid open to reveal a huge flight deck.

A shot hit the side of the doorway.

One of the women screamed, and I scrambled deeper into the cruiser just as the river of Khonsu rushed toward us. Derrial dove inside. I threw myself to the panel near the door and hit the button, just like on Corran's vessel.

Stairs withdrew into the side of the ship as our ship began ascending. A Khonsu hurled himself upward, his hands on the entrance ledge, snarling.

Derrial stomped down on his fingers, and the alien screeched before releasing his grip. The door zipped shut.

My heart beat so fast, that was all I could hear. I turned to find all the women huddled against the back wall, terrified.

And as the realization finally hit that we had actually escaped, they all cheered and threw their fists into the air.

Derrial embraced me and kissed the side of my head. "Go join Thane, I'll find everyone somewhere more comfortable to stay for the flight. I'm guessing this cruiser is used to transport a lot of prisoners.

"That was so close, I still can't believe we got away," I said as the woman with the baby approached. Without a word, she simply gave me a side hug as she still held onto her bundle.

"Thank you for everything," she whispered, and then smiled as she went to join the others, who walked through an open door that led to a wide corridor.

My chest clenched with her words. I took a deep breath and made my way to Thane, who sat in the huge flight deck, taking us off this damn moon.

I couldn't help but watch out the back window of the bedroom I'd eventually hid away in, scared that the Khonsu were suddenly going to send out a fleet after us. But as the moon faded from sight and we flew to the other side of Veon, and we appeared to still be alone in space, I gradually relaxed.

But with that relaxation came sorrow, sharp and intense. The chaos of our rescue mission had distracted me from the full brunt of finding out that my mother was dead. Now, safe on the ship, there was nothing to block me from experiencing the full range of emotions that the news of her passing had brought. I had mourned my mother for years, but that mourning was always laced with the possibility that I would somehow see her again.

My mourning had almost been frozen in place at the time that I had lost her as a younger girl. And now, even though I was a grown woman about to have a child of my own, I felt like a young girl again that had just been abandoned by her mother.

I let out a hiccupped sob as I stared out into space, feeling so alone, even though I knew that wasn't the case.

I idly rubbed my belly, the movement already becoming a habit, even though there wasn't much to rub.

I felt guilty at what I was feeling. I wasn't the one who had died in a Khonsu camp. Although my experience with the Khonsu camp wasn't something I would forget any time soon, because of my breeding capabilities, I'd been relatively protected compared to what other prisoners would have experienced. But my mother...she must have felt so alone in the end, trapped in a small cage, the cries of the other prisoners around her. My mother had always been a gentle soul. She hadn't been able to watch the news because most of the stories made her too sad. She would stop by every beggar on the street and give them whatever she had in her wallet, even though my dad always told her they were just going to buy booze with it. She spent hours in her garden, lost in her own pretty world, and her whole life's goal was to make my father's and my life the best it could be. What it must have felt like for a soul like that to be trapped in such a brutal, ugly place.

Had she been terrified in the end? Or did she welcome death as a chance to escape the hell she'd found herself in?

My thoughts haunted me. I could still picture her face as clear as day, the loving way she would look at me, the sweet words that she would speak to me. I understood heartbreak now. I'd thought I'd experienced it before when I first lost them, and after I thought that my men had betrayed me...but this was something else. This was my heart actually aching inside of me. This was my heart beating so out of control that it felt like my chest was going to explode.

This was the heartache that they sang about in country songs, the kind of pain that artists spent their whole lives trying to put into words and into pictures.

Having to say goodbye unwillingly was a monster like none other. Especially when that goodbye was permanent.

And I wept. I wept like never before. It was a full-body kind of cry, the kind where your whole body shakes and you can't breathe because you're crying so hard.

I'd lost myself in my sorrow, and it was only the feel of Thane's arms around me that brought me back.

"Baby," he whispered in a voice as soft as a sigh. I turned so that I was facing him and melted against him, wanting him to somehow take this pain away from me. I couldn't stop crying and my tears soaked his uniform. He didn't say a word about it though. He just stroked my hair softly as my pain continued to flow out of me.

"Tell me it gets better," I begged him in a hiccupped voice. Although Thane's mother was still alive, who she had really been...his actual mother had died a long time ago. I know Thane understood grief and had somehow managed to live with it. I needed his strength right now more than ever.

I suddenly couldn't deal with what I was feeling. I was certain that if it continued, I was going to die right then and there. It might have sounded dramatic, but anyone who has experienced true pain would know what I was talking about.

I pulled on his uniform frantically. "I need you to make me forget. Just for a little while. I can't breathe," I explained to him as Thane looked at me concerned.

I tried to kiss him and he let me, but he prevented it from going any deeper than a light brush of lips.

"Please," I begged him.

"Pet. I don't think you're in an okay state of mind right now. I don't think that will help," he tried to tell me, gently trying to keep some distance between us. But I wasn't having any of that.

"Make me forget. Do it," I ordered, and Thane stared at me, torn.

"Promise you won't hate me later," he whispered in a throaty voice. I just pulled him towards me without answering. I locked eyes with him. Thane's sapphire eyes sweltered as they gazed deeply into mine, and I could see a longing in them. Despite what he said, Thane wanted this.

Desperate to feel better, I leaned in and placed my lips on his. There was nothing cordial about this kiss as I crushed against him with hopeless need. I almost expected him to pull away from me again, but he didn't. His arms rested on my hips, drawing me close. As my lips pressed against his, he began to kiss me back, gentle at first, but then more intensely. Thane's tongue parted my mouth open, and the tip slid inside, making me sigh softly. His hands moved from my waist to my back and then lower, squeezing my ass to pull me even nearer to him.

I could feel his need pressing through his uniform. It sent a wave of desire coursing through me. Thane lifted me up, and I wrapped my legs around his waist, gripping him like a vice as he pinned me against the wall. Thane carried me to the king bed, laying me gently on the silk cover, his lips never leaving mine. I felt his weight as he hovered above me. Though he was a large, muscular man, his heaviness wasn't uncomfortable, it never would be. Having him on top of me felt like the most natural thing in the world. It was the comfort I needed right now, to feel like I wasn't alone.

His hand slipped past the waistline of my pants, moving downward inch by inch, sending tantalizing chills down my spine. After what felt like an eternity, he finally cupped my sex in his hand. I groaned, my body swollen and sensitive with need. He inserted two fingers inside of me, air hissing through his teeth when he felt how wet I perversely was, despite the situation.

I closed my eyes and basked in pleasure as his fingers continued moving in and out, almost to the tune of my heart as it thumped against my chest. Soon my back arched off of the bed, and my toes began to curl. I was getting close, so close, when suddenly, he stopped.

I looked up to see the uncertainty still in his eyes.

I narrowed my gaze, annoyed that he wasn't giving me what I needed, even as I knew in the back of my mind that everything about this situation was wrong.

My agitation quelled when Thane quickly began to take off his clothes.

I stared at his naked body, appreciating the curve of every muscle, knowing that I would never get used to such perfection. His abs rippled as he moved, making him look more like a god than man. My eyes moved down slowly, taking in his tantalizing body and letting it distract me from every-thing else. My eyes flicked to his again, and this time I saw a burning plea within their depths.

Unable to wait any longer, I grabbed Thane's bicep and pulled him toward me. I let out a sigh of relief as he eased inside of me, the pleasant pressure filling me to the brim. I ran my hands over his flexed muscles, a coating of sweat making them gleam in the starlight that streamed in through the windows. Thane's hips moved against mine as we synced our tempos, the two of us getting lost in a familiar dance that got better every time.

I forgot everything else and focused on the pleasure building up inside of me. Thane's breathing accelerated as he picked up speed.

"Are you close?" Thane asked, a tinge of desperation in his voice that I knew meant he was doing everything he could to stop himself from coming before I did.

Belatedly, I realized that although the sex felt phenomenal as usual, I wasn't even close to coming. My sorrow was making sure of that. "I'm about to come," I assured him, wanting him to finish even if I couldn't. Thane let out a moan of frustration, and then he let out a loud groan as he finally came. Staying inside of me, he rolled us gently so that he was beside me instead of on top of me.

"Fuck," he muttered. "I'm sorry. I couldn't stop myself."

"I love you," I told him, not caring in the least bit that I hadn't orgasmed. I knew what we'd just done was a very unhealthy way to cope, but connected to him like this, I felt a little less broken.

As long as Thane, Derrial, and Corran were around...I would never be alone.

We stayed entwined for a long time, and the pain eased enough in my heart so that breathing was a little less painful.

Thane's comm on his wrist vibrated suddenly, and Derrial's voice came through the speaker barking at Thane to get his ass to the deck and help him.

"I can tell him to fuck off," Thane whispered, stroking my hair softly as we continued to stare at one another.

"No, this was selfish of me. You need to go help. I need to go help," I told him, pulling away from him reluctantly.

I got off the bed and began putting my clothes back on, missing his comforting touch already.

"It won't ever stop hurting," he told me as he laid there still watching me. "But one day, you'll wake up and realize that you can think more about the good times with her instead of thinking about the fact that she's gone."

I pursed my lips, trying to prevent myself from crying again. Who was I to have the luxury of grieving, when the twelve women out there had been to hell and back in a way that couldn't be fixed?

Thane got out of bed and hurriedly put on his clothes as well. "Can you help the women and see if there's anything I need while I find out what Derrial needs?" he asked hesitantly.

I tried to look tougher than I was, giving him a resolute nod, determined to pull my weight and help these women. At least in that way, I could honor my mother's memory.

Thane gave me a long kiss, and then he was gone.

I took a deep breath and followed him out into the hallway, going the opposite way to where I knew the women had set up shop. Although there were several bedrooms on the ship, much nicer than I would have assumed the Khonsu capable of possessing, the women had chosen to stay together. I think after so many years of being locked up in cages side by side, they needed the comfort that only their close proximity to each other would bring.

As I walked, I felt a strange twinge in my stomach, almost as if little butterflies had taken up flight. Stopping in the hallway, I rubbed my stomach, wondering if I'd eaten something strange. It was disconcerting. I knew you didn't really feel anything with your first baby until around eighteen weeks, and I was far off from that. I'd have to ask Thane and

Derrial if they had anything for stomach issues that was safe to take when pregnant.

I walked into the large common room where pillows and blankets had been laid out on the floor. The sofa-like seats in the room had been dismantled and the cushions laid out as makeshift beds. While some of the women were sleeping, most of the others were talking softly, their eyes flitting around the room like they still couldn't believe where they were.

I found the Vepar and her child, and automatically gravitated closer to her. I was intrigued by the baby's horns and tail, really realizing for the first time what having a baby with alien DNA inside of me could actually entail.

She gave me a smile as I sank to the floor next to her, and continued to softly sing to her baby that was struggling to keep her eyes open. My stomach did the strange twitching again, and I rubbed it absentmindedly as I stared avidly at the baby.

"How far along are you?" she asked me as the little darling finally succumbed to sleep.

"How did you know?" I asked.

"I overheard your men at the prison camp," she softly explained. "And it's a pregnancy thing, the constant rubbing of your belly. I did it too."

"Not far along," I answered, smiling at her as I caught myself rubbing my stomach once again. "Just a month or so."

She pursed her lips, like she was trying to hold back a smile. "Oh dear," she said.

"What?" I asked, alarmed.

"Your baby is part Vepar, is it not?" she asked.

"Yes," I answered, leaving out the fact that I didn't know what part Vepar the baby actually was.

"At a month along, you're already a quarter of the way done," she explained matter-of-factly as if she was trying to deliver the news quickly like you would tear off a band-aid.

My mouth dropped open, panic rising up and overcoming the steady drum of sorry that was constantly pulsing through me.

"You're just joking, right?" I whispered, the small bulge under my fingertips taking on new meaning.

"No," she said slowly now, her face a little wary in reaction to the panic that flooded my features at the news that I was going to be a mother in under three months.

"Oh," I responded lamely, my eyes widening as I absorbed the news. A rush of irritation passed over me that none of the guys had bothered to tell me that. But they'd probably been waiting for an ideal time...like not during a wedding. I didn't have the best track record of handling major surprises well.

My eyes flicked to the baby, and I got the awful realization that she most likely didn't know who the father of it was either.

She saw my look, and pulled the baby closer to her protectively. "It's from their experiments, but she's not a monster," she exclaimed vehemently.

"I would never think that," I responded honestly. I had always believed that monsters weren't born...they were made. It was the only way that I could deal with the fact that my baby was half stranger.

"She's some species that I'm not sure of. The Khonsu transfers all failed, killing the female host immediately. I was lucky that they had switched to other transfers when it was my turn," she explained in a hollow voice. "I never thought I would get the chance to have a child. It's been so long since any Vepar woman has succeeded. I'll never regret what I've been through," she whispered.

"My baby is from an experiment too," I told her haltingly, my voice choked up from witnessing this woman's strength. "I'm the first Vepar/human transfer they've done."

Her eyes swam with tears as she reached out and softly touched my hand. "Then you know that loving them was the only option you ever had."

I nodded, cradling my tiny bump protectively as the butterfly type feeling started up again.

"You said that I'm a quarter of the way through...Would I be able to feel the baby already?" I asked.

She smiled. "Yes. I felt her within two weeks. It's incredible isn't it?"

I nodded, unable to form words. I was awestruck that I was actually feeling my baby. The woman yawned just then, and I realized that I needed to stop bugging her so that she could get some sleep. They had all been through so much.

Just then, it hit me that I hadn't gotten her name yet. "What's your name?" I asked, feeling stupid that I hadn't asked her for it yet.

"Hasso," she responded with a smile, and I nodded as I stood up.

"Please let me know if you need anything. I'm going to go check on the guys on the flight deck, but I'll be back."

"Thank you, Ella," she said sweetly as she laid the baby down next to her and curled up on the cushion that she'd laid out.

I was smiling as I left the room, something that I hadn't thought possible under the circumstances. But every slight twinge in my stomach signaling that my baby was in there brought another me another spark of joy.

Thane and Derrial were pouring over a map when I reached the flight deck. The Khonsu technology on the ship was more primitive than the Vepar, but still far exceeded that of Earth's.

They both looked at me concerned when I came in, but I waved them on to keep doing whatever they were doing. I huddled in a chair in the corner and stroked my stomach softly, lost in thought about everything that had happened over the last forty-eight hours. I wouldn't ever be able to say that my life was boring. After all of this was over, that's what I wanted. Boring. Everyday. Forever.

Just then, the comm came to life on Derrial and Thane's wrist. The one on their wrist held the ability to see the person you were talking to, so they had started using it instead of the earpiece one.

Corran's voice came through the comm, and then a second later a holographic image of him appeared. He was frantic looking, hurrying through some kind of hallway it looked like at a rapid run.

"I'm on my way. Your message just came through," he said frantically. "Where's Ella? Is she okay? Our comms have never failed before. The council must have had some kind of block in this lab that prevented messages from getting in or out. I only got your message when I snuck back out."

He ran a hand through his hair and then pulled at it, looking like he was going to have a nervous breakdown.

I got off my chair and darted over to the table so he could see me. I hated how panicked Corran's voice was.

"I'm right here," I said reassuringly. "And we're fine. We got out of there. You don't need to come."

He held up a hand, almost as if he was tracing the image of my face. "What aren't you telling me?" he asked, his voice a little calmer. "How much danger were you in?"

I cast a guilty look at the guys, not wanting to give Corran the full picture of how bad it got when he was on his own important mission. I went for diversion.

"We were able to rescue twelve female prisoners," I told him, my voice not as happy as it should have been when delivering the news, because it made me think of my mother again.

Derrial saw how much I was struggling and pulled me towards him. "Ella found out her mother had passed," he said somberly, and Corran's face dropped at the news.

"Shit," he said as he put a hand across his eyes as his face wrinkled with pain. "I'm so sorry, baby."

"It's not okay. But eventually, it will be," I told him. "But we shouldn't even be talking about this right now. Are you safe? Did you find anything?"

Corran frowned. "This wasn't the site the mutated virus originated from," he said annoyed. "But I did find a document that had the location of some of the other labs. I just can't believe that the council had all of these operating right under my nose."

"We were a little distracted when we went to Earth," Thane said jestingly.

A hint of a smile appeared on Corran's face as his gaze flicked over to me once again. "That we were."

There was a loud noise in the background of Corran's comm, and he looked behind him and cursed. "I've got to go. I'll send the coordinates of the labs to you just in case you need one. I'll just be going down the list."

There was another loud boom, and he started running, throwing glances behind him every couple of seconds like someone was chasing him. My heart raced, and a scream was caught in my throat as I watched him. This was the definition of true helplessness.

"I'll send a message when I'm back on the ship, but I've got to go," he said, before his image disappeared.

I grabbed Derrial's wrist and began to press on the comm. "Get him back on," I begged before Thane gently grabbed me and pulled me away.

"Corran knows how to handle himself, but he needs to be able to concentrate," he told me, but I could see the fear that lingered in his eyes.

I don't think I would survive if something happened to him.

I had already lost so much.

We waited tensely for Corran to alert us that he had made it back on the ship. I paced the room, every sound that I heard made me look hopefully at Derrial and Thane that it was Corran trying to send us an update.

But so far, it never was.

I had just made what seemed like my hundredth circle of the room when all of a sudden, sharp pains started to shoot through my stomach. I sunk to my knees and held it protectively.

"Ella," Derrial and Thane both cried, dropping what they were doing and running to my side. "What's going on?"

"It hurts," I gasped. "I think something is wrong with the baby."

I let out a hiss when another sharp pain darted through me. The guys looked at me in panic, obviously having no idea what to do. This was Corran's territory, and he wasn't reachable at the moment.

"Maybe some of the females have medical training," Derrial exclaimed, hoisting me up into his arms and racing out the door of the flight deck and down the hallway to the room I had visited earlier.

"Do any of you have medical training with pregnancy?" Derrial shouted as we made it into the room. He startled the females, and several of them lunged for cover, obviously thinking we were under attack. I'm sure our panic wasn't great for their already fractured nerves.

Hasso was at my side in a flash, another Vepar holding her baby. She knelt by my side. "I have a little bit of training. When I was in school, I thought I would learn what I could just in case I ever did get pregnant," she explained as she softly started pressing on my stomach.

The pains continued. The only thing that comforted me at all was the fact that I could still feel the little butterflies every couple of minutes, signaling that the baby was moving.

"Do you have anything I could use to listen?" Hasso asked.

"I'll go check what Corran left with us," Thane answered as he jumped up and sprinted out of the room.

"Lay her down," Hasso ordered Derrial, and he quickly obeyed. Thane returned a few minutes later with something that resembled a human stethoscope. Hasso grabbed it and pressed it against my stomach as she listened from the other end.

"The baby's heartbeat sounds strong, but obviously without imaging capabilities, it's hard to know for sure," she said somberly.

Everyone was silent for a minute as they watched me grit my teeth as pain ripped through me.

Hasso suddenly jumped up, startling all of us. "Wait. Has she done the Arcathian ritual yet?" she exclaimed.

Thane and Derrial looked confused. "What are you talking about?"

Hasso rolled her eyes, looking decidedly less like she thought I was in mortal danger, and more like she was angry with the guys.

"Every pregnant Vepar must bathe in the Arcathian waters at the start of her pregnancy. The flowers in the water give off some kind of compound that is necessary to the vitality of the baby. Ella might be human, but that baby is part Vepar, and she must complete the ritual in order for this pregnancy to make it."

"How did your baby...?" Thane began, closing his mouth when he realized how sensitive his question was.

"My baby does not have Vepar blood, so there was no need to complete the ritual," she explained fiercely, protectiveness over her baby springing forward again. Hasso was the exemplification of a mother, her love for her child practically bled out of her.

"How do we get to these waters? I've never heard of them." Derrial asked a bit suspiciously like he didn't believe that it actually existed.

"It's something that's passed down from mother to daughter. It's why you haven't been told of it," Hasso responded as she sent a sympathetic glance my way. Not that my mother would have known about these waters either. *She would have been able to help me decorate the nursery though*, I randomly thought as another streak of pain hit me.

She fired off a set of strange words that evidently were the coordinates in Veon. Derrial looked like he had a million questions, but he hustled out of the room to steer us to our new destination.

Evidently, I was about to take a swim.

7

Luckily, the Arcathian waters were only a few hours away, because the pain I experienced was almost unbearable. If pregnancy could feel like this already...what was labor going to feel like? I sure hoped that Corran had some alien version of an epidural, because I was not prepared to have a natural pregnancy after this.

I told Thane this, and he barely repressed his grin. He obviously didn't realize how serious I was.

I felt a small shake as Derrial landed the ship, and a minute later he was back in the room. Thane already had me in his arms though.

I wasn't going to complain about being carried everywhere. The pain was enough that it would knock me to my knees every time.

Hasso followed us as I was carried off the ship, but the rest of the females chose to remain on the ship. Which I was grateful for. I'd gotten the impression from Hasso's description that this was usually a private event. I'd already been impregnated with a room full of scientists, a fact that I couldn't think about. It would be nice to have some relative privacy for some parts of this pregnancy.

We stepped off the ship, and I gasped as I looked around. The area looked completely different from the other parts of Veon that I'd seen. I was quickly learning that Veon had just as many different terrains as Earth. I wasn't sure why it surprised me still every time. We were surrounded by what looked like sand. Except it was the whitest sand that I'd ever seen. A more brilliant white than even the beaches I'd visited once as a child in Orange Beach, Alabama. The sand was so bright that it hurt my eyes after being in the relative dimness of the ship and my eyes watered as I adjusted. I had expected the water to be lavender-colored like the sea in the area we'd been in before. But this water was more like water you would find on Earth, with the exception that it was far clearer than any water you would find there. The clarity of the water allowed me to see that there didn't seem to be any creatures around at least this part of the water. At least I would be able to see if a predator was about to attack me.

Besides its remarkable opacity, what made the water even more unique were the giant gold flowers that covered every inch of the sea's floor. The petals were at least three feet long, and they shimmered as if they'd been sprinkled with gold pixie dust.

Without realizing it, I had started to push away from Thane. It was like my body knew that it needed whatever power was waiting in those waters.

The pain I'd been experiencing seemed to be abating a bit already as well.

Thane reluctantly put me down as he eyed the water distrustfully. It was true that some of the most dangerous things on this planet were also the most beautiful. But something told me that water wasn't one of those dangerous things.

I walked towards it, taking off my shoes as I did so. I stepped into the water and immediately, a tingling sensation started to spread from my toes up towards my head. Without thinking about any modesty, I began stripping out of my outfit until I was left in nothing but my underwear and bra. I continued walking into the water until I was covered up to my chin.

The tingling sensation continued to spread and with it now came a soft heat that made me feel like I was bathing in a warm bath. I was aware that Thane and Derrial were watching me, a quick glance around told me that Hasso must have returned back to the ship, because I couldn't see her.

I floated on my back, enjoying the sensations. The pain in my stomach had completely disappeared. The fluttering of my baby had picked up though. The water seemed to have excited it.

"Are you going to join me?" I asked the guys. "I'm feeling much better. The water is incredible." I closed my eyes again as I heard the sounds of the guys stripping. Light splashing told me they were in the water, but I didn't bother opening my eyes. I was too comfortable.

Derrial and Thane both softly stroked my stomach as I floated. I opened my eyes and smiled at them. "Doesn't it feel wonderful?" I asked.

"What does it feel like for you?" Thane asked, cocking his head as he studied my surely euphoric expression.

"There's tingling all over and a warmth, almost like I'm having a hot stone massage or something," I explained.

"It doesn't feel like that for me," responded Thane with a fake pout.

"Nor for me," added Derrial. "It must have special properties that only affect women...or pregnant women.

"Mmmmh. Regardless, it's amazing. I wish Corran was here. His science mind would be exploding right now." No sooner had the words left my mouth than I stupidly realized that I shouldn't be enjoying myself right now. Corran was in trouble still.

"Relax, pet," soothed Thane. "Derrial heard from him while he was flying here. Corran's safe on his ship and headed to the next laboratory."

"You promise?" I prodded, wanting to make sure he wasn't just saying that to try and make me feel better, like they'd been prone to do in the past.

"I swear," Thane answered, and I let myself relax again.

Finally, after at least an hour had passed, I stopped floating and stood back up. "Did Hasso say I was supposed to do anything special besides swim?" I asked, dunking myself for good measure, just in case I had to get completely covered by the water for the ritual to work.

"She said that you needed to eat a petal from one of the flowers," Derrial said, diving down under the water and plucking one of the large petals from the luminous flowers.

"Is she sure?" I asked, eyeing the flower.

"She hasn't let us down yet," said Thane. Agreeing with that, I tore off a small piece of the petal and placed it in my mouth. Immediately a sweet flavor exploded in my mouth, the taste exceeding even the best food that I'd ever had. I devoured the rest of the petal, unable to stop myself as Thane and Derrial watched me, amused.

"This is the best thing I've ever tasted," I tried to say with a full mouth. This time, both Derrial and Thane flat out laughed at me. But I didn't care, I was too busy stuffing my face.

It was so delicious that as soon as I was done, I took a deep breath, preparing to dive under and get another petal to eat.

Thane stopped me before I could dive under. "Sorry pet, Hasso specifically said you were only to eat one petal. More than that can be addictive."

I did feel like a druggie desperate for a fix at the news that I could only have one. "I need it," I whined, realizing how crazy I sounded as soon as the words came out of my mouth.

Derrial just kissed me in response.

"Do you think I've stayed in the water long enough?" I asked as I realized that as many healing properties as the water seemed to have, it also held a bit of danger as well that I wasn't in the mood to test. "I could stay here forever, but I don't think that's wise."

"I think we are good to go whenever," answered Thane, and I closed my eyes and soaked in the warm, tingling sensation one more time before I started to swim towards the shore when I spotted another smaller flower. And I couldn't help myself but take it with me, figuring it might be something I could have when I was alone. The temptation to not put it all in my mouth now was almost unbearable. I immediately missed the water the second I got out, and it took all I had to drag myself back to where the ship was waiting for us.

But the pain was gone, and my little baby's kicks felt stronger than ever.

Veon was a strange but magical place.

When we got back on board, the women were all in the same place we had left them and Hasso was rocking her sleeping child. I mouthed thank you and blew her a kiss, not wanting to wake up the baby. I would need to do something else to show her my appreciation when all of this was over.

I went to a room to change out of my wet undergarments. Corran, ever prepared, had attached compartments of our clothes when we left the other day that although appeared to be as thin as an envelope, held several changes of clothes along with other supplies. I was never going to get used to Vepar technology, but I was grateful for it now that we had lost our ship that held the rest of our supplies.

After I'd changed, I placed the tiny flower in a small paper and wrapped it up before placing it into my pocket as I didn't want the guys to think I was weak and couldn't resist the plant. Which clearly, I couldn't, but I'd keep that to myself. The flower made me feel incredible, and I was doing this for my baby.

Then I headed to the flight deck where Thane and Derrial had gone as soon as we'd returned to the ship. They'd already taken off by the time I got there, and they were discussing the best place to drop off the rescued women before we went to meet up with Corran.

There didn't seem to be any good options besides Derrial's parents for where to leave the women, but we'd already asked a lot of them by taking on and nursing my father back to health. Twelve women plus a baby was too much.

"What if we took them to one of the safe houses for the time being?" I asked, and Derrial put a hand to his head in frustration.

"I obviously haven't been sleeping enough. Of course, that's the best option. There are unlimited food and clothes at our safe houses, and they can always camp out on the floor like they have been on the ship."

I nodded eagerly, glad we'd come up with a solution.

Derrial typed in the coordinates for one of the safehouses and away we went.

We'd been traveling for about an hour when the ship seemed to hit something. The whole vessel rocked and shook, throwing us out of our seats. I managed to grab on to a handle on the console in front of me and prevented myself from flying across the room with the impact.

The ship righted itself and we all got unsteadily to our feet. Thane and Derrial flew to the controls, pressing buttons and trying to read on the scanner what had happened.

All of a sudden, the screen flicked on in front of us and one of the council members appeared, armed with a cocky smirk.

"Distracted on the job?" he sang as he looked at Derrial and Thane glee-fully. "The old you would never have missed a council ship tracking you down."

My guys looked like they wanted to jump through the screen and choke the council member. Fear gripped me like a vice.

We were never going to be safe.

8

THANE

Fuck! I seethed as the Councilman smiled at us through the screen. He was right. We had been distracted, and I was furious that they'd managed to track us down.

"Surrender," he ordered.

All I could think about was how much I wanted to shove my fist into his face. Instead, I jabbed a finger at the off button on the screen and just growled under my breath.

"They're going to shoot us down?" Ella's panicked voice melted my heart. Getting caught by the council wasn't an option. Not when we'd be locked up for life...if they didn't kill us first. And what would they do to Ella and our unborn baby? The council was behind the virus spreading through Vepar, taking so many lives. Their experiments led to this disaster, and suddenly I knew what they were going to do. Frame everything on us.

I checked the radar with a wide radius to another ship speeding up behind us from a fair distance. Even in this cloud cover, he'd track us down with ease.

"They're not going to get a chance," Derrial murmured, and I realized belatedly I'd been speaking out loud.

I glanced back to see him holding Ella tight and looking at me with fear in his eyes. Hell, we were fucked, alright.

"So, what are we going to do?" Ella asked, her voice shaky as her gaze drifted to the coms screen. "What about all the women in this ship? The baby? We can't endanger them." The worry on her face twisted an invisible blade in my heart. She was right. Of course she was, but our choices were limited.

"We're going to jump out of ship," Derrial announced.

Ella's mouth dropped open as she stared at him incredulously. "Are you crazy? How is that woman's baby going to survive a jump?" She pulled out of Derrial's arms and started pacing back and forth.

I met Derrial's gaze and nodded. "I think it can work. We leave the women on the ship."

"Exactly my thoughts," he responded.

"What are you talking about?" Ella asked.

"Pet." Derrial reached out and took her hand before taking it to his mouth to kiss her fingertips. I adored seeing the affection she received, because she deserved so much more.

"Thane is going to set the cruiser on auto-pilot with a destined landing position, which he'll give to the council. There's heavy cloud cover farther ahead, and the ship's got exactly three parachutes with non-detection shielding. It's how those bastard Khonsu have been sneaking into cities to steal women."

Ella was shaking her head. "I've never jumped out of a plane and I don't know what to expect." Her words were running into one another. She was so adorable when she got nervous.

Derrial held her tight, covering her face with kisses. "You won't be alone. But it's the only way for us to escape, and the women to survive. If the council gets ahold of us, I'm worried what they'll do to you. We need to leap to safety right under their noses."

Derrial gave me a nod, and I turned in my seat to the controls, sending the council coordinates of where I'd be landing. A perfect spot right in the middle of a park near residential homes to draw just enough attention from locals to see the terrified women emerge from the cruiser. For one main reason - the women's presence would gain a lot of attention, and meant more time before the council sent a search party for us. By then, we'd be long gone.

I shot the message to the council and waited for their confirmation. Moments later, a word flashed up on my screen.

Agreed.

I set the coordinates in auto-pilot, then shot Corran a message of our change of plans and where to come and meet us next. I hoped he wasn't caught but just distracted. Then I sprung to my feet.

My heart thumped in my chest as I marched across the flight deck. I approached Ella and cupped the sides of her face. "Hey, gorgeous. I need you to do something while Derrial and I prepare our jumps."

"What is it?"

She looked at me with those heartfelt eyes that gripped my very soul. I would do anything she asked, anything that kept her safe. My heart hammered and gut twisted at the idea of her and our baby hurt. I'd kill before I let anything happen to her. She was mine to protect, because if anything happened to my beautiful Ella, I'd never forgive myself.

"I need you to speak to the women and explain to them the ship is taking them to safety. That they are to tell everyone that we saved them from the Khonsu, in particular the media."

"So, you want them to give everyone our names?" She arched a brow, as if questioning my decision.

I nodded. "Their arrival will gain media attention, and we might as well use the opportunity to show people we aren't as evil as the council paints us."

"That's a good idea," she said. "Don't think it will change their minds, but we've got nothing to lose, right?"

"Exactly." I leaned in for a quick kiss on the mouth, but the moment our lips touched, I lost myself.

The way she mewled from my kiss went straight to my head, along with the heat and growing arousal. I gripped her waist and drew her closer, then really kissed her. Tongue plunging into her mouth, her gorgeous breasts pressed against my chest. Blood rushed to my dick as she nibbled on my lower lip and moaned. And we kissed until the room spun with me. Until nothing remained but the primal need between us.

She breathed just as fast as me, and if were anywhere else, I'd carry her to a room to strip her down before fucking her.

Derrial cleared his throat. We broke apart, our heads touching, her long lashes blinking as if she'd just awoken from a dream.

"Later, gorgeous." I leaned in closer to her ear. "Later, I'm going to lick you all over and fuck you real slow."

She gasped in my arms, and my cock punched at her reaction. Every sound she made was like nectar to me.

"We need to move fast, now," Derrial reminded me, and he was right.

Ella slipped out of my arms, her full lips red and raw from our kiss, and already I wanted them back.

"I'll speak to the women and be back in five minutes."

Derrial and I nodded, then we set on getting everything ready for our jump.

By the time Ella returned, Derrial and I were strapped in our parachutes. I turned to her. She was studying the straps, fingering the harnesses.

"Is everything alright?" I asked.

"Are you sure this will hold me? It just doesn't look sturdy enough."

"You and I are jumping together, baby," Derrial stated, taking her hand in his.

"You're going to be fine," I reassured her, cupping the side of her face. She meant the world to me. "Priority is jumping out now that we're in cloud cover." I pressed the button on her strap sitting just below her left shoulder to activate the invisibility device to any sensors once she exited the plane. I lowered my hand to the rip cord dangling from the strap across her chest. "Once you're outside, follow Derrial's instructions. This cord will spring open the parachute." Underneath she wore a full body suit the color of the clouds to help protect her against the cold.

She nodded, but fear shone in her eyes.

"We need to go," Derrial said urgently.

"Let's do this," she said.

I was so proud of her at that moment, and I slammed a hand to the sensor on the door. It swished open in a heartbeat, and a gush of cold wind burst inside, freezing my cheeks. I tapped the sensor built into the head gear. A transparent mask slid over my face, and the other two did the same.

Derrial drew Ella closer to the entrance. And without hesitation, they leapt out hand in hand without a single sound. Wasting no time, I tapped my invisibility shield button, then I hit the sensor on the wall, then lunged outside as the door shut behind me.

Cold air slammed into me and tugged at my hair and jumpsuit. I fell through the clouds fast, until I came out and saw the other two not far below. Falling from such a great height felt much like flying. Down below, the land was a tapestry of country fields, and farther in the distance, lay the heart of the city.

I leaned my body forward in Derrial's directions, my arms tight by my side and I accelerated faster and faster. They grew closer, and before reaching them, I pulled up, muscles taut to not lose my balance.

Ella's head twisted in my direction, and her expression surprised me. She was beaming a smile and waved to me. My little vixen loved skydiving. I tucked that piece of information into my mind for later.

Derrial was pointing to an open landscape slightly to our right then back at me, instructing our destination. I nodded. The landscape came closer to use, looking larger now.

He and Ella tugged on their rip cords, and their parachutes blossomed overhead, hauling them away from me.

I followed suit, and my whole body jerked upward, the hardness cutting into my armpits and sides. I tugged lightly on the toggle on the left and glided toward to the left. Adrenaline pumped through me, and I fucking loved the feeling of falling and seeing the ground rush up to me. That sensation of almost dying tugged at my heart.

When I finally touched the ground, I stumbled forward a few steps before stopping. Without wasting time, I unbuckled the harnesses and let them drop down around me as I looked up to see Ella coming down. Her face was panicked as she came in ahead of me.

I threw myself into a run after her and caught up fast. Her feet dangled, the toes of her shoes almost touching the ground. The moment her feet touched the ground, she was still running forward from the momentum, her body tilting forward. I swooped in and collected her, holding her still.

"I got you."

She was breathing so hard, her mask fogged up. The parachute fell around us, and I quickly unlatched her. She tapped her temple and the mask vanished. I did the same, and she burst into laughter.

"That was incredible! Oh my gosh, why haven't I done it before?"

I held her close, even if she was shivering uncontrollably from the adrenaline rush. "If Veon is ever back to normal, I will take you skydiving every weekend," I promised her. "But for now, we need to move and fast."

Derrial had already unbuckled from his parachute and ran toward us. "Corran is here!"

Just as the words left his mouth, a searing heat grazed over my back, and I turned as Corran's ship appeared out from under the invisibility shield, and winked in the sunlight.

The panel slid open to the doorway into the side of a cruiser, and Corran stood there. Eyes strained, shadows underneath, hair messy as though he'd been running his hand through it over and over. His heaved for each breath, his posture curled forward enough to tell me he'd been working tirelessly. I'd seen him this way before when he worked himself to the bone to find a solution in his experiments. I studied his face for any indication that he found a cure, except he gave none. Fear speared me like lightning. I took a tentative look at Ella who studied Corran just as closely as me.

"Get inside," he ordered tersely, and the three of us rushed inside.

The door shut behind us, and I needed answers.

Ella was at Corran's side, concern flashing over her expression as she studied him and took his hand in hers. Her care and love for each of us was endless, and my heart beat a bit harder at the reminder of how lucky I was to call her my wife. How lucky all three of us were.

"What did you uncover?" she asked, her voice choking as she waited for good news like all of us. A solution to our problems.

"The city is almost overrun, but I found the location of a laboratory in the middle of the city that might be the source to all the chaos with the infected. So, that means that's the one place that is most likely to have some information on an antidote."

"Then we go to the city," Derrial agreed, his voice firm and determined to eradicate the spreading sickness. Just like we all were...all I wanted was to spend time with my new wife away from danger and prepare for our newborn. I had no doubt Derrial and Corran were the same. So, we needed to find this damn antidote, then clear our names.

I gritted my teeth just thinking about how much was still unknown for us.

Corran kissed Ella on the brow, then pulled back and returned to the driver's seat. "Let's head off. We'll break in and see what we can find."

I took Ella's hand and drew her with me to a seat and made sure she was buckled in.

"I'll drive," Derrial said, to which Corran didn't object but slumped in the front passenger seat.

We ascended in no time, and I glanced over to see Ella rubbing her stomach. She had definitely started to show a bit already. Reaching over, I stole a quick kiss.

"You look beautiful," I whispered.

She looked up at me with a sweet smile, one that told me her mind was miles away and she was trying to hide her emotions. I was certain they had everything to do with the loss of her mom. I wanted nothing more than to hold her in my arms, inhale her into me so nothing could ever touch her. Nothing could hurt her.

"I'll be alright," she said, as if reading my mind, then reached over and smoothed out the crease at the bridge of my nose.

I loved how strong she was after everything she'd gone through. And after so much, I'd give up everything to keep her safe.

The rest of the trip went by quick and we descended in what looked like a small park in the city. With chaos running amuck, we could easily leave our concealed ship here without detection.

When the cruiser gave a small jolt from our landing, I unbuckled my belt and was on my feet. Staring out the front, there was nothing but trees and a small kids' swing set. In the distance, lofty buildings surrounded us.

"We move fast," Derrial said, already on his feet and heading to the door before looking at us. "And we stick together no matter what."

"How far is the lab?" I asked as Ella pressed up against my side and I slid my arm around her waist.

"Just a few blocks. Not far at all. We just shoot any infected on sight and don't make too much sound to draw any attention."

"Then, we'd better hurry," Ella said.

Derrial opened the door and hopped out. He checked the perimeter around the ship. Once we returned and waved a hand, we all followed as a close group. I quickly took the lead, my tactical training making me the best person to help us avoid detection. I knew this city like the back of my hand. At one point, my team had been in charge of putting a security system in place to protect it. Looking around, it didn't seem that the council had bothered using it to protect the city from the infected.

We moved down a side street and kept to the sidewalk before taking another backstreet.

The place was barren and empty. Storefronts smashed in, rubbish rolling across the road in the howling wind. There was a sadness to see our home in such decay. If nothing was done, the place would turn to wastelands. So many lives and homes and memories lost. This wasn't how I wanted to see my home planet end up. My heart clenched, but I swallowed back the boulder in my throat and kept going. This wasn't the time to get sentimental or let anything get in my way.

Movement caught my attention from an old building up ahead. It was only three stories tall and looked like it had been used as an information storage center before it had been destroyed. I stopped and the others did the same. "Infected just ahead," I whispered, my heart pounding.

"Go round the building then." Derrial pointed to a side road just ahead.

If we moved quickly enough without sound, then we wouldn't grab any attention.

Corran held onto Ella and they rushed forward.

In their rush, Ella accidently kicked a loose rock from a broken wall and it skittered right across the road like a rocket and smacked into the old building near the infected.

In that exact moment, the building exploded and ignited into a fiery ball of yellow flames and stones, billowing outward. The booming sound reverberating over the city with such ferocity, it shook me to the bones.

We all flinched backward.

"Oh fuck!"

Ella screamed and we all darted for our lives down the side street.

"What the fuck was that?" growled Derrial as we stared at the smoldering wreckage of the building behind us that we'd passed. The air was thick with smoke, and the only reason I wasn't on the ground was thanks to Thane grabbing me at the last second and taking the brunt of the aftershocks of the explosion when it went off.

I was trembling with shock. If I hadn't been clumsy and kicked that rock...we would be nothing but cinders right now because we would have been too close to the blast.

Thane let me go and then hunched over, his body slightly shaking. He looked like he was about to be sick. He suddenly straightened up, and I knew by the look on his face that I wasn't going to like whatever else came out of his mouth. "You need to stay here, Ella. There's no way we're bringing you with us," he said firmly.

I didn't want any of us to go, but I knew we needed to get in that laboratory. But there was no way that I was going to let them leave me behind. I had already made a vow that we weren't going to be separated again. Crazy or not, our separation from Corran had about done me in. I had promised these men an eternity. I wasn't going to let them leave me prematurely.

"That's not happening," I told him quietly, but resolutely.

His face fell. He looked to Derrial and Corran for help. They all looked like they wanted to agree with Thane, but knew that it would be a losing endeavor. "You don't understand. They've triggered the traps," Thane said fervently. "If they've changed things from when I designed them, we'll all be dead."

"Traps?" I asked, my voice rising with a bit of hysteria.

"The Battalion Project?" asked Derrial sharply. "That was you? I thought that was just a myth. Fuck."

Thane nodded, ashamed. "I was head of that project." He turned to me. "Pet, if you remember, I was once upon a time head of security for the council and all of Veon. One of my projects was to protect one of the important government buildings located in the center of this city. They told me it was an archive for our world's history. But evidently they were lying. My team and I set traps throughout the city that could be triggered in the case of a Khonsu attack-" His voice broke off. "I never imagined they would be used against me."

We were all quiet for one shocked moment before Derrial took control. "Do you still remember where all the traps are?" he asked.

Thane seemed to respond to the authority in Derrial's voice, and he squared his shoulders, a determined look appearing on his beautiful face. "I do, but if they've changed anything-"

"We'll just have to take that risk," said Derrial, cutting him off. "There's little risk that they did that though. The council has never been one to get their own hands dirty with hard work. I'm sure they didn't think they'd be using it against the person who designed it. We've been good foot soldiers for a long time now."

"I can't put Ella's life in danger like that," said Thane, sounding desperate.

"We're not leaving her," said Corran all of a sudden, sounding exhausted. He looked like he was about to fall over. "I'm not willing to leave her behind and I'm also not willing for the three of us to be separated. I'm going to need help once we get to the lab. It's been..." His voice broke. "It's been a rough few days," he finished quietly.

"Let's get started," I announced, trying to keep my voice level, despite the fact that the baby had chosen that moment to give me a choice kick.

At some point in this pregnancy, I needed to rest. Which reminded me...

"We have less than three months to figure all this shit out. Let's go," I ordered, finally letting them know I'd found out the kind of a big thing they'd neglected to tell me about Vepar pregnancies.

The three of them all looked guilty. "Sweetheart-" Corran began, but I made a slicing motion with my arm.

"We can talk about that little detail you left out later."

They nodded, and then Thane took a deep breath. "The first layer consisted of bombs. We had it triggered that every twelve steps or so, there would be a crack that if stepped on would trigger the explosion. So long as we don't step on any of the cracks..."

This put a whole new meaning on the nursery rhyme "don't step on a crack or you'll break your mother's back."

Derrial grabbed my hand. "Stay close to me," he ordered and we all began walking. We all followed Thane who was counting the steps we took. The walk was tedious, as it quickly became apparent that twelve steps was not a lot in between traps. I'd decided very early on that I wasn't going to step on any cracks...just in case. This only made us slower going. It took us three hours to get through two layers of the city, something that we usually could have walked in less than fifteen minutes.

But as we stepped over the last crack, we were all still alive, so I guess it was three hours well spent. It was eerie to see a city so deserted, but with this laboratory being the epicenter of the infection, it made sense that the city's inhabitants had run. Many of them not making it very far, based on the large amount camped outside the walls still.

I had never seen Thane look so on edge. I wanted to soothe him, but now wasn't the time.

"Fuck, Fuck, Fuck," he said, and then he took few deep breaths as if to calm himself down.

"What's next?" asked Derrial, who only seemed to be getting calmer as Thane fell apart.

"As soon as we step onto the next street, a gas will start to pour out of the buildings. It's a hallucinogenic gas. It creates illusions similar to what the Khonsu can do. The effects will fade as soon as you get past the layer, but it's designed to be a hell of a trip on the way."

"What kind of hallucinations will it be?" I asked in a trembling voice as I thought about the torture I'd gone through with that first Khonsu.

"Bad ones, pet," Thane said apologetically. "Every fear you've ever had, magnified."

We were all somber with that knowledge.

"Will it hurt the baby?" I asked. We had just survived potentially being blown up, but somehow subjecting the baby to potentially poisonous gas seemed like a pretty big deal. I was definitely not following what the pregnancy books said. I wish there was a pregnancy handbook on how to survive your pregnancy in an alien world.

"It's *compru gas*," Corran explained. "Besides the hallucinations, there aren't any adverse effects. The council's used it on prisoners for years to get information out of them." He shook his head and I knew what he wasn't saying was his role in creating it. I'm sure all of my Vepar were really regretting their early lives right now. "We have to go," said Corran tiredly, and I knew he was thinking about all the people he'd left beyond the city's walls that still needed help.

We all seemed to take a collective breath as we stepped into the next row of buildings.

Thane was correct. As soon as we stepped out from beyond the building we'd been hiding behind, little holes opened up at the bottom of the domed structures and a fluorescent looking green gas started pouring out.

At first, I didn't notice anything besides the fact that the gas seemed to be making me a little bit tired.

But that changed quickly.

I screamed as a horde of Khonsu began running towards me, each of them holding their whips. I crouched down in the street with my hands out in front of me, but when a moment passed and I felt nothing, I opened my eyes to see that the Khonsu were gone. It had just been an illusion.

The rest of the guys were struggling just as much. Derrial was actually sobbing at whatever he saw. Corran disappeared right in front of my eyes, replaced by a corpse of him that was bleeding from large cuts all over his body.

"It's not real. It's not real. It's not real," I chanted as great sobs wracked my body. I couldn't stop myself from leaning forward to try and touch it. As soon as I did so, of course, Corran's dead body disappeared, and I became aware of his live body standing in front of me once again.

By this time, Thane was screaming, shouting my name over and over again as he looked all around me as if he had lost me. I tried to go to him, but I was stopped when my mother appeared in front of me. She was on her knees, begging to be spared.

"Mom," I called out, running towards her.

It continued like that for what felt like an infinite period of time. Every bad thought I'd ever had, every dream I'd woken up from in a cold sweat, every fear that I'd internalized...they were all there. Appearing before me over and over again, until I was sure that the world had ended and there was no happiness to be found anywhere. The air was filled with the screams of my hallucinations and that of my lovers.

I would never be the same after this. Never.

I had just convinced myself that we had somehow died and were now trapped in hell where we were being tortured, when it was like a haze seemed to clear around me and suddenly I found myself and my three husbands standing back in the street, completely alone, and completely hallucination free.

All four of us were ashen, shaking, and soaked in sweat. Corran was the first to move. He grabbed me and hauled me into his chest. "You're here, you're here," he repeated over and over again as he assured himself of my existence. Derrial and Thane didn't try to take me from Corran. Instead, they crowded around until we were all in one big embrace, locked in each other's arms.

We stood there for at least fifteen minutes, just trying to reassure ourselves that we were all alive and together. Derrial tried to shift away at one point, and I made a savage squeaking sound before yanking him back towards me. We only were able to move again if they all stayed close enough for me to touch them.

"What's next?" asked Derrial hoarsely. And I knew we were all wondering whether we could survive whatever was "next" after the nightmare we'd just made it through.

"The next layer is designed to flood and drown any intruders if you step in certain spots. Just follow behind me and we should be fine."

We arranged ourselves in a line, me right behind Thane with Derrial behind me, and Corran at the end. As in the first layer, we walked slowly. I made sure to step exactly where Thane stepped.

We'd made it three-fourths of the way through the rows of buildings that made up this layer when I heard a panicked grunt from behind me. I looked back and saw that Derrial was holding up an exhausted-looking Corran, who must have stumbled.

That was all it took. A roar shook the street as water started to flood in from all directions. The water was immediately up to my shins and it was quickly rising. I couldn't even tell where it was coming from, because it was like the area had transformed into a lake with how much water was coming in from every direction.

"Run," yelled Thane as he grabbed me and hauled me forward. A quick look at Derrial and Corran showed me that Derrial had his arm around Corran's waist and was attempting to drag him forward. Corran looked dead on his feet, like he was going to pass out at any minute.

The water was quickly rising, making it harder and harder to run as we sloshed through the street.

"We need to get to higher ground," Thane yelled back at us as he continued to drag me along. Derrial and Corran were losing steam as Corran was barely helping Derrial at all at this point to move them both along. "The flooding is designed to rise to the level of the roofs and dissipate after a few hours. We figured that most threats wouldn't be able to make it to safety in time."

No kidding. Like right now.

Thane kicked open a door, and water started to flow in after us as we darted inside. Since the city had been shut down, the technology that would regularly have flown us to the next level wasn't working. There was obviously something to be said for old-school things...like actual stairs.

"Stay here," Thane ordered, like I was somehow tempted to go off on my own. He ran to the far wall where a beam led up to the second floor. He started to climb the beam, his muscles flexing with the effort. I hoped he had a plan once he got up there, because there was no way that I was going to be able to climb that. And neither was Corran. Another look at him showed me that his face was even paler than before. I wasn't sure if he was sick or just exhausted. How were we going to get him through the city if the rest of the levels were like this?

Thane somehow leaped from the pole to the balcony of the second floor. He then pulled a rope from the satchel around his waist, tied one end around himself, and then threw the other side down to us.

"Climb up," he hollered. Derrial was by my side in a flash, leaving Corran to sit on a chair that had floated by. The water was still rising, and it was above his waist in the chair.

"Hop on my back, Ella," Derrial ordered, and I hoisted myself upon his back, trying not to choke him as I threw my arms around his neck.

Derrial then began to climb up the rope. I was so happy for the Vepar's superior strength, even if it had been used against humans from the beginning. I didn't think there were very many human men or women that could climb a rope with someone on their back.

Derrial was breathing heavily when we finally made it to the top. Thane had been straining to hold up our weight as we climbed, but there was no time to rest. Corran was still down there, and he'd had to stand up as the water was too high. I could see him rocking back and forth unsteadily as he tried to stay standing as the water pushed against him.

Derrial quickly tied the rope around his waist and held onto it as Thane scrambled down the rope, a bit slower this time as his muscles had to be burning. Corran was a lot larger than me, and it was painful to watch how slow Thane's progression was up the rope with Corran on his back. Corran was trying to help. I knew that if he was at full strength he would have no issue getting up the rope. But that was not the case now.

Looking down, the water was high enough that it would have completely enveloped us if we were still standing on the ground floor.

Thane had to stop several times and I let out a small scream when Corran almost slipped off. Thane managed to stop him just in time, almost at the expense of one of his arms getting ripped out of its socket as he held onto the rope with one hand and held onto Corran with the other.

He groaned as he pulled Corran back up so that he was steady on his back once again.

I think I held my breath until they got to our floor, because I was feeling light-headed as the three of them all collapsed to the ground breathing heavily.

I ran over to them and hovered, needing to be close to them. I glanced down at the floor below and the rapidly rising water. We couldn't afford to try and recover. The water was rising faster and it would soon be to our floor.

How were we going to get to the roof though? There was no way the three of them could handle another rope climb.

Thane staggered to his feet and jogged to the far wall. "There's an escape hatch that leads to the roof on every building, and there should be some kind of emergency ladder here somewhere," he explained as he began to run his hands all over the wall. "Found it," he exclaimed triumphantly, and I watched open-mouthed as a ladder seemed to just appear out of the wall. I'm sure they could explain the technology to me later but a lot of what I saw on this planet appeared to be magic.

"You first, pet," Thane called as he all but pushed me onto the ladder. I realized his hurry when I felt water rush over my foot, it had reached our level.

I hurried clumsily up the ladder, my feet only slipping once. "Now what?" I called down.

"Just push up on the ceiling right above you," called up Thane.

I was expecting it to give me trouble, but as soon as I pushed on the ceiling, it flew open, showering me with fading sunlight.

I pulled myself out onto the roof and gazed down the opening as the guys began to climb up.

Derrial pulled himself up first, and I moved aside to make room for him. The roof was domed but it was such a large building that there was plenty of room for us all to be on a relatively flat part of the roof.

Thane was last up. He'd had to help Corran up again. As soon as Corran fell onto the roof he was out, passed out from sheer exhaustion. He still hadn't told us all that had happened while we'd been separated, and I was scared to find out. The fact that he'd had to experience it all alone...I never wanted that to have to happen again.

Thane and Derrial sat on either side of me as Corran slept behind us. We stared out at the still-rising water. I hoped Thane was right that it was designed to stay below the rooftops. Some of the smaller buildings were almost completely covered, but the building we were on was one of the highest in the city.

"How did I get here?" I whispered as I watched the water rise. The baby chose that moment to give me a sharp kick, and it just reminded me what a dangerous world I was about to bring it into.

"It will all work out, Pet," Thane said softly to me as he put an arm around me. I realized that he had been watching me instead of the water.

I smiled at him sadly. I wasn't sure he could say that.

"So what's next?" Derrial tried to joke. "Fire, earthquakes, rabid dogs?"

Thane sighed. "There's a few more traps. One opens holes in the ground that the intruder falls through if they step on specific spots. Another is a pack of *rabins*..."

Derrial took a huge inhale when he heard that.

"What is that?" I asked anxiously, scared of Derrial's reaction.

"It's similar to a cat on your planet. Except its bite creates excruciating pain that can lead to heart failure," Derrial explained reluctantly.

"Of course it does," I sighed.

"Let's get some rest. We can talk about everything tomorrow," said Thane. "Corran won't be able to go anywhere for awhile anyway."

I nodded, glad for the rest, even if I was anxious to get to the lab and start actually solving all the problems we were facing.

Despite my fear of the water and what we were going to face tomorrow, I fell into a deep sleep filled with images of the hallucinations I'd suffered from earlier in the day.

It wasn't a peaceful sleep, to say the least.

orran was already up when Derrial woke me up, and my heart clenched with how much better he looked after a good night's sleep. I was afraid that he'd been sick or worse...was beginning to be infected. But there was no sign of any symptoms today in the bright morning light. Corran evidently had just been extremely tired.

I next looked out to see how the water was looking, and I was shocked that there was no sign of it. The ground and all the domed buildings looked completely dry. I knew Thane had told us it was going to subside, but actually seeing that happen was something else.

After eating some crackers that Thane explained were from the military, evidently packing quite the caloric punch, it was time to set off. We made our way down the ladder to the second floor, and then used the rope to get to the ground floor. Derrial carried me down the rope this time. Thane and Corran both used the same beam that Thane had climbed up first yesterday to get down.

And then we were off to whatever hell waited for us.

I just knew as Corran gave me a kiss and grabbed my hand, that despite everything, I was where I was supposed to be.

10

It was too quiet in this section of the city. After the constant booby traps of the last few layers, it didn't make much sense that now that we were so close to the laboratory that it would now be a walk in the park. Thane and his team hadn't put anything in this section of the city, stating that this was where the soldiers were supposed to be stationed to protect the building. But the street we were walking down was completely deserted. There were no signs of any soldiers.

We stayed in the shadows, close up to the buildings still, but the chaos of the rest of our trip was nowhere to be found.

"What do you think is going on?" I whispered to Derrial. He shook his head, reminding me to stay quiet. One of the traps we'd gone through had been triggered by any sound. That hadn't been fun.

I wouldn't risk testing it, but the silence was almost more unnerving than the death traps had been...almost.

We turned the corner, and that's when I realized why there didn't seem to be any traps or soldiers in this section of the city...because they weren't necessary, due to the hundreds upon hundreds of infected Vepar we'd just stumbled across in the road surrounding the building that housed the lab.

The infected Vepar at the hospital where we'd been visiting Thane's mother had been crazed. They'd been desperate to attack us.

These infected Vepar were decidedly not crazed...at least at the moment. They were walking slowly, as if they were all in a trance. It was impossible to miss that they were infected though. Nearly all of them held ghastly wounds where they had been attacked in the near past. If the council's infection didn't finish them off, the infection that was growing in their wounds certainly would.

As terrified as I was of them, I also felt immense anger on their behalf that their own government had done this to them. I just hoped that Corran could figure out an antidote, and that all of these poor Vepar wouldn't remember what they did while they were infected. That would probably be hard to deal with, if you could remember tearing another Vepar's flesh off their bone with your mouth.

We were frozen in place as we watched them. "Is there another way into the facility you think?" I asked hopefully, even though I knew the answer would be no.

"We need some kind of diversion," said Derrial, ignoring my question. "If we could blow something up down the street and get them moving that way, we could hopefully make it in before they saw us."

"It will take a little time to figure out the code to get in. Every lab we have has a complicated set of security protocols. I'm sure that this one would be no different from the others. Especially if they were working on so many things they weren't supposed to."

"Alright. Create a big enough explosion to get us through the next few streets and allow us to crack a few codes. Sounds simple enough," said Thane sarcastically. But I could tell that my soldier was already working through the logistics of everything. If there was a way to do it, he would figure it out.

"Aha," said Corran quietly as he pulled two small vials out of his waist satchel and handed them to Thane. "Shellum and Wenciom," he explained.

Thane's eyes lit up, but Derrial just shot Corran a look. "What are you doing with Shellum and Wenciom? And how do you have big enough balls to carry those things around your balls?" he whispered with wide eyes.

"What are they?" I asked confused.

"Two powders that if combined, create quite the chemical explosion," Corran answered me matter-of-factly. Derrial was still looking at him like he was crazy...or he had big balls. I really couldn't tell.

"I'm going to circle around and blow up that eating hall down the street," Thane told us, pointing at a small, silver-colored domed building a few blocks down, or at least, what would be blocks if the Vepar did things that way.

"Wait," I whispered urgently, grabbing his arm before he left. Fear was coursing through my body at what would happen if he separated from me right now.

"Pet, I'll be right back," Thane reassured me as Derrial tried to pull me away from him.

"Okay," I answered, but I was still holding onto his arm tightly.

"Ella," Thane said again, and I finally pried my fingers off his arm. He was gone before I even blinked.

I paced back and forth beside the building we were hiding behind, practically gnawing my fingernails off. Derrial was keeping watch, and Corran was fiddling on a device, trying to see if he could hack into the council's information database in order to find blueprints of the lab. Unfortunately, the guys had been the ones responsible for setting up the security for the council's database, which meant the job had been well done and it was almost impossible to get in.

Derrial suddenly grabbed me and gently took us both to the ground as he covered my body with his. "Thane's almost to the building. The explosion will knock us down," he explained. Corran crouched down beside us, also trying to shield my body with his. It said a lot about how bad the situation we were in was that I didn't even feel a tingle of lust at their close proximity to me. They were just that incredible.

The explosion went off. The ground rattled under us, and the two buildings we were in between shuddered. I would have definitely gone flying if Derrial hadn't had the foresight to get me on the ground first. Debris went flying everywhere, and I couldn't believe that two tiny vials could create an explosion that large. I couldn't even comprehend the damage that large amounts of those compounds could create. I just hoped that Thane had managed to find something to get behind. I didn't know how he could have set off the explosion and gotten to safety in time. My heart was thudding painfully fast, and the baby gave me another kick, evidently not liking the weight of Derrial and Thane in its space.

I really needed to get an ultrasound of this baby - if they did that on Veon - so that I could stop calling my baby an "it."

In the aftermath of the explosion, the eerie silence came back, somehow quieter than before. Derrial and Corran slid off of me, and Derrial darted to the edge of the building to see if the infected Vepar had taken the bait. He pumped a fist as we watched. I assumed that meant that Thane had been successful. We needed to run to the lab...but where was Thane?

I got my answer when there was the sound of running feet coming from behind us and then Thane was there, swooping me up into his arms as he slowed down to a jog and began heading towards the lab. "We don't have much time," he exclaimed.

Derrial and Corran were right behind us as we left the safety of the building. I let out a sharp inhale as I looked down the street and saw the horde of infected gathering at the explosion site.

Where the restaurant had once stood, there was now nothing but a small crater. The infected were pouring in from other streets, and I shivered at the sight. There was even more of them than I'd thought. And they'd definitely picked up speed. That desperation that I'd seen in the infected Vepar was definitely there now as they pushed each other to get to the explosion. Corran was going to have to explain the science behind what the council's failed experiments did to the Vepar's brain to make them behave like this. The Vepar hadn't allowed our schools to teach us about their genetic makeup, so I had no clue if their brains were similar to ours or had different parts. Would humans be similarly infected?

I remembered that I needed to pay attention when an infected suddenly darted out a side street and came flying towards us. Derrial met it before it could reach us, slinging what looked like silver string towards the Vepar, who was frothing at the mouth and had a particularly nasty looking neck wound. This wasn't like any string I'd seen before however, because it sliced the Vepar's head off like it was cutting through butter and not muscle and bone.

Thane and Corran continued to jog towards the lab like nothing had happened, and I was once again aware of the fact that the three of them were predators. I was a bit lucky that I wasn't their prey anymore.

We got to the entrance of the lab without any more Vepar appearing and Corran went to work on his device trying to crack the code that was required for initial entry into the lab. Corran had explained that there would no doubt be eye scans and other security systems in place as we went in, but if we couldn't figure out this initial code, it wouldn't matter. Once again thanks to the systems that Derrial, Corran, and Thane had created together under the council's direction.

The three of them started brainstorming possible things to try after Corran's initial attempts failed. I took a step away from them to check on the status of the infected. The entrance to the lab was set in from the outside walls of the lab, providing us somewhat of a buffer, but it wasn't enough to make me feel safe in the least bit.

I'd no sooner had that thought when an infected Vepar woman appeared in the entryway and charged towards me, running as fast as she could.

The guys weren't quick enough since they were behind me, and she was on me before they could stop her. She managed to take a bite out of my arm that had me screaming in agony. Thane tore her off of me while Derrial once again used his silver string weapon to end her life.

But the damage had been done.

I was trying to be quiet as I moaned, but the pain was so intense that it was hard to do that.

"Fuck," Thane all but roared, causing Derrial to push him against the wall and cover his mouth in warning.

Corran tore off my top and was examining my wound with frantic eyes. It was bleeding furiously, and I was lightheaded just from the sight of all the blood flowing down my chest and over Corran's hands as he tried to slow the blood. He looked frantic, devastated. I could see it in his eyes how bad this was. Somehow, I'd never allowed myself to comprehend what would happen if I became infected. Would the baby automatically become infected too? Or could Corran somehow pull it out now and just use their technology to help its development outside my womb. I started crying, and I threw a hand over my mouth to dampen the sound.

"Put your hand here," Corran ordered Thane and Derrial. "I have to get us in this building."

Derrial released a still struggling Thane and flew over to me, replacing Corran's hand with his own. Corran continued working on his tablet although I knew I wasn't imagining that he was working at a much more intense pace than before.

There was a slight tremor to Derrial's hand as he held it against my bite. "I'm so sorry, baby. So fucking sorry," he kept chanting as I tried to control my tears that were caused by a mixture of fear and pain. Thane had recovered enough to help Corran, and they were both muttering feverishly about different options.

"I'm in," Corran suddenly said excitedly as he tapped on the screen a few more times. "I just needed to insert a virus in the central nebulium of the program." I had no idea what that meant but I didn't really care since the door to the lab had just opened.

Derrial gently picked me up, still keeping pressure on my bite with one hand, and ran me inside followed closely by Thane and Corran.

The blood kept pouring out from underneath Derrial's hand and the panic was growing in Derrial's eyes. The opening slid shut behind us and we were in a small box of a room. The walls, ceiling, and floor were all the same bronze color, and I felt a little bit suffocated even as the world started to spin around me. I couldn't tell if it was from the bite or the blood loss but either way it didn't seem like a good sign.

Derrial laid me down gently on the floor, still putting pressure on my bite. Thane knelt down beside us while Corran went to the wall opposite where we'd come in and started to type on his tablet, presumably to try and get us to the next section of the lab.

Cursing when it didn't immediately open, Corran ran over to us to inspect my wound. Derrial moved his hand so that Corran could see the damage and I saw them all flinch as the blood flow increased. Derrial quickly put his hand back.

"We need to get the wound cleaned and get it sewn up," said Corran as he began to grab supplies from his pack. Thane also grabbed things out of his pack and Derrial's, since Derrial only had one hand at the moment.

"When I say three, move your hand, and I'm going to replace yours with my own and this cloth that should disinfect the wound. It can't do anything-" He stuttered over his words. "It can't do anything about the virus, but it can prevent another type of infection from growing. Who knows what that woman has bitten lately?"

I shivered just thinking about it, and Derrial glared at Corran. "Sorry," Corran responded, his cheeks flushing.

"Focus," Thane ordered gruffly, his voice sounding choked. Corran nodded and grabbed the cloth that was supposed to disinfect me.

"This is going to hurt at first, Ella. But there's no other way for me to do this with the supplies we have," Corran told me apologetically.

I nodded stiffly and gritted my teeth. At least the pain might help distract me from the fact that a virus could be spreading inside of me right this very minute about to turn me into a mindless savage. At least I could console myself that we had made it to the lab, and even if I was infected, Corran would hopefully soon have access to something that could eventually cure me. If I didn't infect the guys first...

"Fudgeeeee," I squealed as Corran doused my wound with the cloth and began to apply pressure. Evidently I had missed the countdown with my dour thoughts. The pain was ten times worse than the peroxide or alcohol we would use on Earth to clean a wound. Why was it again that everything on this forsaken planet had to be a million times more extreme than its counterpart on Earth?

A bubbling sound was coming from underneath the cloth and it was strange, but it was almost like I could feel it making its way into my muscles, cleaning everything out. It was also leaving a numbing sensation in its wake, so although the initial pain hurt like a bitch, it was almost worth it to get some relief.

"Still hurting badly, angel?" Corran asked, and I realized how avidly the three of them were watching me. I shook my head, weakly.

"It's numbing the area now," I explained, and he nodded satisfactorily.

"Unfortunately, it's not as much numbing as we would need so you don't feel this next part at all, but it will help to make it tolerable," he explained as he held up a small red device that had an extremely sharp needle protruding from the bottom of it.

"What is that?" I asked with widening eyes.

"It's similar to a needle and thread I suppose," answered Corran, pressing something on the device.

"You're going to use that to sew my arm?" I asked, horrified. It was all I could do not to try and move away from it. I'd never been fond of needles, and the one on that device looked particularly unappealing.

"It's alright, pet," said Thane as he ran a soothing hand down my cheek.

"Ready?" asked Corran, holding the device over the cloth as he prepared to take it off.

I nodded and looked away. Even as a child I couldn't watch them giving me shots at the doctor. I didn't think this experience was going to help cure me of that fear.

Corran pulled the cloth away and immediately replaced the cloth with the device. Immediately, I felt a sting around my wound and a low buzzing sound filled the room. Corran was right, it did still hurt. It kind of felt like being stung by a bee over and over again, not a fun feeling at all. But I had to admit, it was more preferable than bleeding out in this tiny room that was beginning to give me claustrophobia.

"That will take a minute to sew all that up, and then we'll run my healing device over it for good measure," said Corran, pulling on his lip as he watched the little machine continue to work. "I'm going to work on getting us out of here." He moved to stand up and then hesitated. "How are you feeling, love?" he asked, his eyes worried and searching.

"Weak," I responded honestly.

"Anything else?"

"Not yet," I answered, and he nodded, taking a deep breath before standing up all the way this time and walking over to the wall. "Do you think our baby will be alright?" I called after him in a broken voice. The three of them froze at my question.

Corran turned and rushed back to me. "I promise I'll do everything I can to help you and our baby, Ella."

I brushed a tired kiss across his lips. I knew that already. But I hadn't missed that he couldn't give me a yes or no about the effects the virus could have on our child.

A tear trickled out of my eye, and my fear was reflected in the eyes of my three men.

Corran stood up, suspiciously wiping at his eyes as he walked back towards the wall and got to work.

We sat in silence, nothing but the sound of the small machine and Corran's occasional curses as his attempts to hack into the system failed.

The buzzing went on for a while, and then stopped suddenly. Derrial and Thane came closer to me to inspect the bite, nodding satisfactorily when they saw the job it had done. I glanced down the best that I could at my wound. It was just another reminder how amazing Vepar technology was. The stitching was so small that you could barely see it. An injury like this would have left a hideous scar on Earth. I doubted I would even have one even though the bite had gone down into my muscle.

If only a scar was what I had to worry about.

Corran came over with the small silver device that I had seen work miracles on other injuries. "Why didn't we just start with that?" I asked curiously.

"With injury to the muscle like that...and the chance of infection, I like to do a bit of old school medicine before using this. It's an amazing feat of technology, but it's not perfect."

"Corran admitting that something he created isn't perfect...it's a miracle," Derrial smirked and a tiny smile made its way onto my face.

Corran shot him an annoyed glare and then hovered the device over my skin, making the stitches disappear completely. My mouth parted in shock. It looked like I hadn't even been bit, with the exception that there was blood all over Derrial and me.

"How are you feeling?" Corran asked again.

"Tired, but not crazy?" I told him and he nodded seriously once again before getting back to work. This time Thane followed him over the wall to help him.

I yawned, and Derrial pulled out one of the blowup pillows from his pouch and set it up on the ground.

"Why don't you try to sleep? It looks like it might be a while for them to get past this set of security measures and your body needs as much sleep as it can get."

I didn't even try to argue, immediately laying down on the pillow and letting Derrial cover me with a foil looking blanket that I had discovered was actually the warmest blanket I'd ever experienced.

I was asleep before I took my next breath.

When I woke up, Derrial was passed out on the floor next to me, Thane was sitting against the far wall - watching me like he was standing guard in case I woke up and tried to attack everyone - and Corran was still working. It didn't seem like he'd made any progress while I was sleeping, based on the small tick in his cheek, his hair that was all over the place, and the stressed shadows under his eyes.

"You're awake!" Thane exclaimed, jumping up and stalking towards me. Corran stopped what he was doing to come over to me as well. I was still groggy from sleeping so heavily so it took me a moment to remember where we were and what we had been doing. It hit me then - I had been bitten by an infected Vepar. I immediately took stock of my body.

I felt sick, but it was the kind of feeling that came from needing more sleep and from going through something traumatic and painful, like having your shoulder ripped open. I didn't seem to have any urges to go after anyone in the room, and I still seemed to have a clear head. The baby gave me a sharp kick just then, and I rubbed my stomach carefully. It would seem that so far, so good.

"You're still you," Thane said as he examined me critically.

"I think so?" I responded, shrugging my shoulders.

"Corran, how long has it been taking for Vepar to get infected?"

Corran held a device to my forehead that I knew from past experience was taking my readings. "Within a few hours," he murmured in a distracted tone as he read whatever information was coming off the device.

"How long has it been?"

"Ten hours," answered Thane, his voice growing excited. "She's probably not going to get it if she hasn't already?"

Corran wasn't as quick to agree with that statement, but he looked like he was getting a little excited as well. There had been a general air of sorrow and despair in the room before, but that was quickly dissipating.

Belatedly, I realized what he'd just said. "I've been sleeping for ten hours just now? And you still haven't been able to get us into the main part of the lab." Corran flinched at my questions and I immediately felt bad. I knew he was trying as hard as he could to figure it out.

"How are you feeling?" he asked, choosing not to answer my question-which I didn't blame him for. "You have a low-grade fever."

"I feel achy," I admitted. "Like right before you get the cold or something."

Corran nodded like he'd expected that, but his mood seemed to improve even more.

Surprisingly, I yawned again. Thane was lowering me back to my pillow before I could say another word. "You should try and sleep more. Between carrying a Vepar baby and someone trying to eat you, you need to sleep as much as possible."

I wasn't quite as tired this time, but again, I didn't put up a fuss. And surprisingly, despite the fact that I'd just slept for an incredibly long amount of time, it didn't take me long to fall back asleep.

When I woke up the next time, it was because Thane had just picked me up and was about to carry me through the opening that had finally appeared on the far wall. Through it, I could see a large room that resembled some of the other Vepar labs I'd been in.

Corran had done it, we were in!

II

I felt like crap. Like I somehow contracted the worst flu in the world, and then compounded it with my head feeling like it might explode and my emotions blurring into one great heap.

But I pushed on, because we'd come this far. The answer to the infected had to exist in this laboratory. The bitemark on my arm still throbbed, and I was terrified I'd soon become one of the sick, and that included my baby.

We'd been through so much, fought so much, struggled so much. So I refused to let this thing beat me.

Thane held me tight and dragged me deeper into the lab. It was a large room that could easily fit fifty people standing. A large counter ran down the middle and another against the back wall, filled with all kinds of technology I couldn't begin to comprehend. But Corran smiled for the first time in days and raced up to the wall of glass refrigerators with shelves of vials of different serums and god knew what else kept in here. The place smelled sterile and like antiseptic. I assumed the scientists would have been horrified to see us in here without proper gear.

The room seemed to tilt around me, and Thane swept me off my feet and carried me across to where a medical bed lay near the refrigerated samples.

Derrial joined Corran in searching everything in this place while I lay there trying to steady the room from dancing so much in my head.

"See if you can get some rest or even sleep while I help Corran." He studied me all over like I was the experiment, but I knew he meant well. His hand touched the skin on my arm just below the bitemark. I flinched.

"It's so sensitive," I explained.

His fingers moved up and gently pressed on my shoulder, and I winced. He did the same across my collarbone, and the pain followed.

Worry pushed his thick eyebrows together, and he didn't need to say anything. I knew the look. "It's spreading, isn't it?" I couldn't bring myself to ask the question of how long I had before it really changed me and I became something other than myself.

He held my hand and pushed away the loose strands of hair caught on my eyebrows. "Don't worry. We are going to find a cure, and you will be the first to be healed."

As much as he tried to smile, I watched the crack in his demeanour. The terror behind his gaze. The slight shake of his hand against mine. He was terrified and wouldn't show it in front of me. Except, I was beyond scared now. My thoughts were so far beyond that.

I held onto his hand tight. "Please, you must do something for me."

"Of course." He ran his hand through my hair as I looked up at him from the medical bed. "Anything."

"If it looks like I'm not going to make it, you need to save the baby."

His face paled, and I tightened my grip. "Please, Thane. If it's too late for me, promise me you'll save the baby."

His eyes glistened, and he swallowed loudly, struggling to find his words. "Oh, Ella. Even if I have the strength to make such a promise, I don't know if the little one is infected or not. We haven't done enough tests to properly understand how this virus works."

The words were a blade to my soul, and I wanted to scream and cry. Except, I knew he was right. My throat thickened and a tear trickled down my face that he wiped away with a thumb.

"Ella, please don't cry. Don't give up hope. We made it this far. You have one of the best scientists in Vepar in this room working on it. If anyone can find the cure, it's Corran."

I nodded, not trusting my voice.

Thane leaned down and kissed me sweetly. "Just rest for now. I'm going to see what I can do to help."

"Thank you," I murmured and watched him head over to the other two. All three were whispering so low, I couldn't make out their words.

Then all three broke out into a frantic rush and began checking every single thing in the room. Cupboards. Vials. What looked like test tube bowls sitting on the counter inside a plastic transparent box. My head hurt too much to even try to make sense of everything here.

But I just watched them. My three husbands, who were working frantically for me, for our baby, for their planet.

All I could think about was how I first met Derrial at the nightclub back on Earth. How that one decision to go to a club had changed my entire life. Where would I be now if I didn't go out that night? Would the Khonsu have tracked me down, and I'd be one of those women trapped in the farms?

I felt a spark of appreciation that I had met these Vepar. Without them, I never would have found my father or discovered what happened to my mother. I never would have found love in a world ravaged and torn apart.

Looking up at the ceiling, the fluorescent lights shone with a blue tinge, and I squeezed my eyes shut, trying to push all thoughts out of my mind. To calm my racing heart. To stop feeling like I might pass out from the panic strangling me.

I had no idea what was going to happen, but Thane was right about Corran, and I had every faith in them.

Unsure how much time had passed, it was Corran's strong voice that lured me out of my half sleep state.

"It's the contaminated blood samples," he explained as Derrial and Thane approached him. I pushed myself up on my elbow and stared out toward them, listening to them.

"This proves they have been testing the virus here, and we're going to continue their experiments until we find that cure."

I trembled at hearing both the fear and excitement in his voice. This was a step forward as he'd found some progress, except what if he didn't uncover the antidote in time for me? In time before the council arrived and arrested them?

Laying back down, I tried not to overthink and trusted my three husbands could do this. I lay in bed and tried to fight the wave of exhaustion pulsing over me. I shut my eyes once again and tried to drift off.

I didn't remember falling asleep, but when I groggily opened my eyes, the three Vepar were still working frantically in the lab, Corran calling out instructions. He sounded frustrated and roared at one stage.

I stared at the frustration and anger on his face.

"Fuck. That's the sixth trial and none of them are fighting the virus." He dragged a hand through his hair, shadows dancing under his eyes. My heart hurt to see his struggle, how he would never stop until it killed him.

"Keep going," Derrial barked.

"I've tried every technique to eliminate everything the scientists could have used to create the virus. It comes down to a chromosomal level, as the scientists have manipulated nature. They removed DNA, replaced it, changed it so much that it mutated into the infection taking over Veon. So maybe I was wrong, and there was no cure after all. All I have are the samples of Vepar blood they experimented on to develop this pathogen, but not how to undo the mess they created."

"We need some of those samples," Derrial stated, his voice stoic and authoritative. "That shows the council has used these labs to test on Vepars. And right now, I'll take any fucking bit of evidence against them that I can get."

"Yes, but I still haven't found a cure." His voice shook and I knew what he was thinking...he thought of me as he glanced my way with dread in his gaze.

Fear settled heavily in my heart.

"Maybe we need to come at this from another angle," Thane suggested. "You're trying elements already used in the creation of this plague... What if it needs a different element to counteract it?"

Corran huffed. "There is a very slim chance anything like that exists in this lab they haven't already tested. I don't even know where to begin." He clasped his hands behind his head as a strained expression washed over his face. "Nothing I've tried has created any impact on the virus."

"Then we test again," Derrial muttered. "We keep going, in case we missed something."

I lay back down, feeling hollow. Corran's fear affected me. If the best scientist couldn't find a solution, what hope was there for me and everyone else? The bite mark on my arm pulsed as if it had its own heartbeat. The strange thing was, that I didn't feel much pain now at all, but more like numbness. And that terrified me because it meant one thing... my body was getting closer to assimilating and changing.

The shock of that realization jolted through me. I hugged my stomach. I didn't want anything to happen to the innocent baby inside me. I felt like screaming.

Corran was using sophisticated equipment, and he still had no luck.

Their conversation kept playing over in my mind about his failed tests. My hand remained on my small belly that churned as I thought back to the Arcathian waters. At how easily they eased my pain and gave my baby energy. What I needed was to bathe in those rejuvenating waters, as they would make me feel better. I knew they would. The tingling over my body from the experience drew away the pain. With that memory came the gorgeous gold petals that I'd eaten that had tasted like the nectar from the gods.

My hand instinctively went to my pocket where I had taken one of the flowers. It would be completely squashed now, but I pushed myself to a sitting position. Slowly, I pulled out the flower and unwrapped the crinkled paper where inside lay a broken and bent stem. Somehow the long petals survived unblemished. The golden color was as vibrant as I remembered it, shimmering under the lights in the lab. And just looking at it had my mouth salivating as I remembered the sweet taste that lay somewhere between honey and the sweetest melon.

Thane's words came to mind again, and my words fell from my lips before I could give them enough thought. "What if we try experimenting with the properties from the Arcathian flower?"

All three looked over to me, confusion pulling at their features.

"Those waters were miraculous and helped with the vitality of the baby, right? And my pain disappeared completely. So these flowers have healing properties. Isn't that what we need? Something to help heal the mutated cells? I'm probably saying it wrong as I don't know the technical words, but what if Thane is right and something like this can help?"

I lifted the paper with the flower in my other hand. "What do you think?"

"You snuck out a flower?" Thane asked. "You were going to eat it, weren't you?" He smiled as he shook his head.

"Lucky I didn't."

Derrial crossed the room in a few long strides to reach my side. He took the flower and smiled at me. "Smart thinking." He turned to the others. "I agree with Ella. We try out the healing properties of this plant."

Corran studied the flower in my hand, his brow pinching.

"You said it yourself, we've exhausted all other options," Derrial continued.

Corran nodded. "Fine. We have nothing to lose. I'll add that to the tests as I do another round of the previous tests in case I missed something. Let's move fast."

The three were back at it, and I lowered myself back down, feeling strange all over like I wasn't quite in my own body. It was a hard sensation to comprehend.

I glanced up at the white ceiling, tired of being inside laboratories. If we ever survived this and escaped, I wanted freedom and to enjoy the outdoors as much as possible.

The baby kicked. I smiled, then placed a hand over my belly and felt the small movements. Despite all the darkness burrowing through, joy pushed to the surface to feel a life inside me. To hold my baby for the first time would be the most precious thing to me. Tears slipped out from the corners of my eyes, thinking that such a chance might be ripped away from me.

I wiped my eyes and shut them, trying to forget everything, to somehow fall asleep again as I waited. For so long, nothing happened, but when someone touched my arm gingerly, I fluttered my eyes open.

Corran stood over me. "I need to take some of your blood, beautiful."

I quickly nodded and stuck out my hand. "Take what you need." He wasted no time in finding the vein on the inside of my elbow and I turned away as he used a syringe to extract blood. After all this time in labs, I'd think I would be used to needles, but I still hated them just as much.

I stared at the white wall next to me, blinking away the tears, hating how emotional I was getting. "Do you think the plant will work?" The words escaped my lips.

"We're about to find out." Moments later, he whispered, "And I'm done, gorgeous." Then he folded my arm over my stomach.

I turned as he stole a kiss and lit up my insides. He was gone just like that, and the three of them busied with testing my blood. I didn't want to overthink if we would succeed, because I wasn't sure I could take anymore bad news. My gut roiled at the thought.

I pushed myself up to sit on the edge of the bed, unable to lie down another moment. I had no clue how long this part would take. Derrial and Thane crowded around Corran, and they all stared into the glass-like incubator. I shifted to the side to see robotic hands placing a drop of the serum Corran created into a small round dish that had something red inside...I assumed it was my blood.

Then Corran turned to the computer screen on the counter, and frantically typed something. Seconds later, the screen was filled with numbers and symbols along with a line chart. None of it made sense to me.

A startled sound came from Corran as he turned to me. Derrial and Thane studied the screen results closer.

But Corran crossed the room. "Ella, I don't know how you knew that the flower would work, but its properties are reversing the virus. It's killing the infection in your cells at such a rapid rate, I can't believe it." His smile was infectious and the most amazing thing I'd seen in days.

He cupped my face and kissed me. "I think we did it!" He beamed an explosive smile.

My response came out as a hiccupped cry because I still couldn't believe it. "You found the cure? Holy mother of all things, you did it. I'll be cured and so will all those people out there?" I clung onto his arms, happy tears rolling down my cheeks.

"It should work," he admitted. "I mean I would need more time to test this out, especially for side effects."

"Use it on me," I interrupted. "I can feel myself changing, and I don't want it to be too late for the baby."

He stared at me as if ready to argue, but I didn't give him the chance.

"If you don't, you might lose me. For our baby, I need it. Please, Corran. We don't have much time."

I watched the pain cross his face at his decision.

"I think we should," Thane added. "Those results are spectacular. And her body responded so well in the Arcathian waters."

"Agreed," Derria murmured as he approached me.

"Are you sure about this?" Corran asked me.

As if his question lured the sickness in me, that strange pain swept over my chest. I shut my eyes for a moment as the sharp pain flared over me.

"Yes," I finally gasped. "Please yes."

"Alright, get her ready," he ordered and rushed back to the test as Derrial helped me back on the bed. He pushed the sleeve of my other arm up and found a vein easily. "We want to put it straight into your bloodstream for fast results."

Another wave of pain rolled over me, feeling like dozens of knives raking over my skin. I nodded my response, biting down on my lower lip to fight the ache. Thane was there and wiped a small tissue that smelled of alcohol over the skin.

I looked into both of their gazes. At their love, their worry, their hope.

"Everything will be okay, I know it will," I reassured their fear more than mine.

As Corran returned, holding a very large syringe, my mouth dried.

I cringed and looked away, every inch of me tense.

A sharp prick pierced the skin, and I clenched my teeth as the sting lasted for the whole duration. Once done, Thane wiped the tissue over the spot once again.

"And done," Corran said, returning to the counter where he worked.

I felt nothing at first, then small tingles started up my arm that quickly spread over my body... not too different to what I felt in the waters.

A sudden explosion boomed somewhere in the building.

I flinched upright, my heart pounding into my ribcage. My three Vepar froze, the blood draining from their faces. Then voices sounded just outside the door to the lab.

"Fuck!" Derrial murmured. "The council found us!"

I blinked in bewilderment, too terrified to move or make sense of what was happening.

A shudder ran through my body. We finally found a cure and now we were going to get caught!

12

An explosive bang hit the door to the lab.

A small cry slipped past my lips as panic curled around my chest. I couldn't breathe as I backed away.

"We're trapped!" I whispered, my hands pressed to my chest. I wanted to scream and run, except I had nowhere to go.

Corran snatched a small cooler bag and placed a handful of blood vials inside, then rapidly typed like a maniac on the computer. I had no clue what he was doing, but he had to hurry.

Derrial took my arm and pushed me behind him.

"Corran," Thane roared. "Is there another way out of here?"

Corran spun to face us, his face pale as snow. "At the back," was all he said as he darted to the rear of the room. Fiddling with something on the wall, the next thing we knew, a door slid open before my eyes and led to a dark passage.

We didn't wait another second and ran just as the lab doors burst open, slamming into the wall with a resonating boom.

I dove through the secret doorway, as did Derrial and Thane on my heels. My heart banged so hard in my ears. I frantically turned around to see Corran slapping a hand to the wall inside the dark passage, and the door slid shut. We were thrown into darkness.

In seconds, a small beam of light ignited from the pen Corran held, streaming light like a flashlight.

Without a word we followed him, traveling down a dark tunnel. Cemental walls and ceiling guided our path, and we descended down a set of circular escape steps. I held onto the cold, metal railing for dear life and rushed down the three flights of stairs.

My heart thundered when explosions detonated upstairs and the stink of smoke reached up. They were burning down the lab. So how long would it be before they discovered our escape route?

Corran led us left just as overhead, a boom shook the whole building. Voices came so loud now that I knew they had found our passage.

My feet moved faster down a passage, until Corran stopped and I bumped into him.

He fiddled with the control panel, and next thing, the door slid open to a back alley behind the building.

Behind us, the rush of feet pounded the stairs.

The hairs on the back of my neck lifted.

Feeling intense fear in my chest, I moved quickly outside, and we all ran like the devil chased us down the sidewalk. I didn't remember ever running this fast in my whole life, but nothing was stopping me.

I moved on pure adrenaline. It wasn't long before Corran soon had us careening back toward the quiet park. No one was around, just the trees swaying from the wind. We scrambled inside the cruiser, and I collapsed into a seat, gasping for air. I couldn't keep doing this...running for my life. I was so tired of being terrified.

Derrial dove for the driver's seat and had us ascending in record time. Thane rode shot-gun, while Corran stood nearby, staring outside as if expecting the worst. When he turned to me, his face was ashen, his thick hair the color of mahogany messy, and caramel eyes wild and filled with fear. Much like my own.

Once we had flown so high that we were practically in space, all I could see was a huge portion of the planet. It looked gorgeous from up here...lots of greens and yellows and purples like moving swirls covered the planet's surface.

"What now?" I asked.

"Now, we need to hide out and make sure there are no side effects to you," Corran explained. "To keep you safe because you are the most important thing to us."

"Right now, I feel incredible," I replied.

He half smiled at me. "Because you are still high on adrenaline from the chase. What you need is to take a hot shower and let your body relax so I can keep track of how you're responding to the serum."

"And your body is changing as it prepares for the baby," Thane said. "We can't risk you getting hurt now."

I fought back the emotions that this ordeal still haunted me with. "You're scaring me a bit. Is there something I should know about the upcoming birth?" I got to my feet.

Thane and Corran exchanged looks before glancing at me with soft smiles.

"Tell me," I demand. "I have to know what to expect."

Corran shook his head. "Not yet, kitten. First, you heal and nurture your body. That is most important right now."

I hated not knowing, but I also knew how stubborn these Vepar were when it came to getting them to reveal a secret. I had time until the birth of my baby, so I'd keep working on convincing them.

"Have a shower and rest. Leave the rest with us for now, please." Corran was at my side and he kissed my nose and my cheeks and chin, and finally my lips. "We need to see how your body reacts to the serum."

When he nodded, I did the same, parroting him because I knew he was right.

"Shower sounds perfect." I headed into the rear of the cruiser where our living quarters were. I had spent so much time on spaceships that they felt like a home, which was a strange thing to think.

By the time I showered and dressed in fresh clothes, I felt somewhat normal. What just happened came crashing down on me as I entered my shared bedroom with my husbands. A large bed in the middle of the room waited. Deep blue bed sheets looked crisp and so inviting. Except I found myself returning to the built in wardrobe behind me. There, I pushed my head inside and inhaled the faint smell of my Vepar, even the slightest smell of them calming me. Derrial's woodsy and musky scent stood out the most, and I savored the way the smell made me melt with comfort.

I couldn't explain it, but I needed my Vepar next to me. But they had to work out where we were going and our next steps. I'd join them as soon as I had a small break. So, I grabbed an arm full of their clothes and tossed them onto the bed. Then I climbed into the bed and curled myself in the middle of them, drawing the shirts and pants and jackets closer to me like a cocoon. In my head, I knew this was crazy behavior I couldn't explain, but something about having their clothes around me put me at ease.

As exhaustion wracked my body and mind, I refused to make sense of it all and just closed my eyes.

Six Weeks Later

The antidote Corran created with the healing flowers from the Arcathian waters worked. They more than worked... they cured me of everything from the ache I'd always had in my elbow, to the sore neck pain I got when I didn't sleep well, and even the spider veins on my thigh vanished. Most importantly, the bite I got never infected me.

I rubbed my now huge belly as the baby kicked, restlessly. The pregnancy moved so quickly that I still couldn't believe how large my stomach had grown in such a short time. Both excitement and fear sat on my mind, and I was left unsure exactly what to expect for the birth. And none of my men would elaborate on what I was to expect, which only made my mind go wild with ideas on what would happen.

After escaping from the lab, we'd been hiding out in a safe house away from the city to keep a fair distance from the council. Just us four in a small undetectable house while my baby belly grew bigger and the three Vepar worked tirelessly on mass producing the antidote serum. Along with figuring out how to best distribute it to the greater population. The process of mass production had taken them longer than expected due to the constant trips back and forth to the beach to collect the healing flowers and remain undetected. Then they ran across problems in making larger batches.

Recently, they had sent squads of a small handful of family and friends they trusted to administer the antidote. To themselves first, and then everyone they knew. It was a small start, but it meant the serum in their bloodstream made them immune to a bite. All this under the nose of the council. They'd been slowly building a team of supporters with the hope they would spread the word once they were ready with more serum.

From what they'd told me, and what I'd seen on the news, Veon was wrecked and would need to be rebuilt. It was horrible to see the planet fall apart at the seams.

I let the three of them focus on the solutions while I dealt with my growing belly.

The baby was coming in two weeks...according to Corran, though by my size, I somehow doubted there was any more space for the baby to grow inside me.

Fear built in my chest as I still had no clue what to expect, and they always changed the topic when I asked questions. Which of course, made me worry a million times worse.

I stepped in front of the mirror in the bedroom, standing sideways, looking at how large I looked.

"You look more beautiful today than I've ever seen you," Derrial said as he stood in the doorway, admiring me. Just having his eyes on me heated me instantly. Since settling in this house, our sex life had intensified, and the majority of the time, I instigated it. I felt constantly horny lately in their company, as if their presence alone ignited my arousal.

"You have to say that as you're my husband," I teased him as I looked at my reflection once more. My long dark hair had grown so much longer since I left Earth, and I looked so puffy, I sighed. "Gosh, I look like a giant marshmallow."

Derrial stepped close and stood behind me in the mirror, his arms looped around my wide stomach. His lips found the tender curve of my neck and kissed me up to my ear.

"All I see when I look at you is an incomparable beauty. My heart beats faster. And..." He pressed his groin against my ass, and I gasped at the hardness of his cock.

"That's what you do to me, my pet, from just looking at you. You are the love of my life, Ella."

I adored the way he stared at me with such admiration, but underneath lay a sliver of fear for me. I couldn't help but love how much he struggled to rein in his emotions around me. My heart squeezed. I shouldn't have expected that reaction, but it still took me by surprise.

His mouth dragged across my neck as his hands swept to my shoulders and pulled down the straps of my dress. He pushed the fabric down my arms, and the material shivered all the way down to my feet. I wore nothing underneath as I had just come out of a shower.

Derrial swiftly grasped my breasts and squeezed, his fingers pinching my hardened pebbles. I moaned against him, heat already pooling between my thighs at his touch.

His breath hitched as he rocked his hard-on against the ass. Next thing, he took my wrist and turned me around before guiding me to the bed. He swept me off my feet and into his arms, then he lay me down on the mattress, my ass still to the edge of the bed.

"Spread your legs for me, my pet."

I quivered when Derrial spoke to me with such authority. I pried open my knees. His gaze lowered down my body, and the way he stared at me with such primal, intense hunger that it sent a flame of heat through me. He dropped to his knees between my legs, and his mouth was on my heat in seconds.

I arched my back, a moan streaming past my mouth. Fuck. Damn. The flat of his tongue rubbed over my clit, and desire overflowed over every inch of me. I couldn't breath as he devoured me, my mind whirling with desire, my heart racing.

My head grew dizzy from the building climax. I writhed, loving every velvety lick. My heart thundered. I was on the verge of exploding when he pulled back, as if sensing my build up.

He rose before me, already peeling off his shirt up and over his head. He was so muscular, from his strong jaw, clean and shaven, to those angles cutting across from his chest and powerful biceps. My body reacted, nipples hardening.

"Shuffle farther up on the bed," he asked as he unbuckled his pants and dropped them before stepping out.

I pushed myself up but never looked away from the stiffness of his large cock. I inhaled and exhaled forcefully at the sight.

"I want you so damn much," he murmured as he climbed onto the bed, crawling toward me with his hands and needs. He gently rolled me onto my side as he positioned himself behind me. His chest plastered against my back. His hand reached down to lift my leg as he slid his thigh between mine. His fingers found my drenched heat while his mouth kissed my neck.

"It feels amazing," I purred.

His hand moved up to the curve of my hip and maneuvered himself for easier access. I felt the thickness of his cock sliding between my ass cheeks and to my slick heat.

I gasped, my body responding instantly, liquid fire coating the insides of my thighs. I was breathing harder and faster.

Derrial guided the tip of his cock to my opening. My whole body tensed, anticipating, craving him. "I want to be balls-deep in you. I can't get enough of how delicious your taste and smell, how your soaked pussy sucks on my cock. I dream about fucking you most nights."

A shiver coiled tight in the pit of my gut. Derrial's words completely undid me. I shook with need. "Please take me," I said. "I can't stand it any longer."

His hot breath skated over the burning flesh of my neck. He leaned in close and ran the tip of his tongue around the outside of my ear. Then he pushed into me. I cried out from the pleasure it brought to have him stretch me. All thoughts dissolved as only the two of us existed at that moment. He thrust into me, in and out, faster, the friction igniting a fire inside me. He fucked me like he'd been holding out for months. It had only been days.

His body grew so hard and tense against my back.

The groaning sounds that came from him drove me insane with need.

His fingers found my nipples and pinched them as he fucked me from behind. I grew wetter the deeper he drove into me, my body completely at his mercy.

He pulled out of me then slammed back in, his fingers deftly flicking and tugging at my nipples. I moaned, dying for more as I rose to a peak. The harder he took me, the quicker I escalated, and he pushed me over the edge.

I cried out as I shuddered with the orgasm rocking my body. In that same moment he groaned loudly and pulsed inside me, filling me. He held me tight as we both floated on pleasure. Our bodies pressed together, covered in sweat.

"You are so perfect, Ella. You are everything I want."

I opened my mouth to respond when I spotted Corran and Thane near the doorway, watching us. Their hands were on their cocks, and I loved the way they stared at me.

Today wouldn't be an overly productive day for me, but what a day it would be.

13

I was enormous. There was no other way to describe me. Looking at the black and white dress I was trying to squeeze myself in, I was reminded of Kim Kardashian's unfortunate "killer whale" dress during her first pregnancy. This was not a flattering look for someone who resembled an enormous whale.

It was amazing to me how fast my body had changed. Three and a half months ago, I'd been a tiny thing, half-starved and rail-thin from everything I'd been through on this planet. Not saying that was a good look at all, but it was incredible that my body could go from that...to this, in that amount of time.

Maybe I was just forgetting what human pregnancies were like, but I couldn't recall any of the pregnant people that I'd seen on Earth ever getting this big. I turned to the side and examined my belly. Corran had assured me that there was only one baby in there, but I wasn't sure that he was telling the truth. This better not be one of those things that they decided was better that I found out at birth than before. We'd done an ultrasound, but the image had been suspiciously blurry. Somehow I didn't think that Vepar technology - which was always leagues ahead of Earth on everything else - would somehow be lacking in the ultrasound department.

I guess it didn't really matter, there was nothing more that I wanted from life than this baby, healthy and here in my arms.

After some prodding, I'd finally convinced the guys to get me information on a Vepar birth. Of course, there wasn't anything out there about how it would go for a human who was carrying a Vepar, but the information was still useful just the same. It at least explained some of the odd things that I'd found myself doing.

For example, I'd begun nesting. Now I knew that on Earth, it was called nesting when a human mother began cleaning her house, organizing, and putting the nursery together in preparation for the birth. But my version of nesting had been nothing like that.

I was literally creating a nest that consisted of every piece of clothing from my husbands, blankets, and pillows that the safe house had, along with all sorts of other things. The instinct to create this "nest" was so strong that at first, I hadn't even realized I was doing anything strange. That is until the guys asked where all their clothes had gone, and we realized that they all had ended up in the giant pile of things that I'd put together.

I'd started hoarding snacks as well. I would get sealed packages of snacks from the blessed Vepar machine in the kitchen that gave you whatever food you wanted, and I would hide the snacks in various places in my nest. Apparently, my subconscious was very worried about being hungry while giving birth.

I'd also made Corran get rid of the feature that allowed you to see outside. I needed my nest to be dark and cozy. I had the guys bring in pieces of furniture to put around the bed so that the room didn't seem as big, since my limited supply of blankets and pillows limited how large the nest could get.

I spent most of my time in the nest at this point, adding little things here and there. This safe house also had the machine that could make you clothes, and I'd been having fun getting it to create little baby outfits. Since we'd decided right before Corran did the ultrasound that we weren't going to find out the baby's sex until he or she was born, I was having the machine create clothes for both genders. Those found their way into the nest as well.

I'd seen the guys exchanging amused glances, but I didn't care. Besides, the information that Corran had given me said this was totally normal. I'd checked a few times to confirm that, since I felt like I'd been going crazy.

There were some other odd things that I knew were not normal for a human pregnancy. For example, besides the ever-present feel of the baby pummeling the hell out of my insides, every once in a while, I would feel something sharper jab into me. The first time that it had happened, I'd shrieked, sending the guys hurtling into the room. I'd thought that it was just a sharp kick until it happened again, and I realized that there was no way that was a foot unless that foot had a sharp set of claws attached to it...

Luckily, the book assured me that my baby was not going to be born with claws. But it would most likely be born with horns...and maybe a tail. Vepar didn't learn to hide those traits until they were at least ten years old. At first, I'd been a little disoriented about the extras my baby would come with, but then I'd thought of Hasso's sweet child, and it no longer scared me. Horns or not, I was going to love the hell out of this baby and think it was the cutest thing on Veon.

Another strange thing, I could actually hear the baby inside of me. And I didn't mean that I could hear its heartbeat with a stethoscope. I could actually hear the baby, clear as day, every time it cooed, gurgled, and cried inside of me. It was like my stomach had been stretched so thin that there was nothing in between the baby and me but skin.

Corran assured me this was not the case, and the baby information confirmed that, but it was exceptionally strange to be trying to have sex with one of your husbands and for the baby to begin crying.

I guess it was good preparation for after the birth.

Most of the rest of my symptoms were pretty normal for humans. I wanted to eat everything in sight, but the baby had gotten so big that I could only eat a few bites at a time before having to take a break. Of course, then I would be hungry again half an hour later. Keeping myself fed was a full-time job.

My swelling was also terrible. My feet could barely fit into shoes since my legs and ankles were so large so I spent most of the time barefoot. Since walking on cankles wasn't the most fun, and I was beyond tired anyway, I spent most of my time curled up in my nest, reading up on the baby. Whenever I wasn't in my nest I was either eating, cleaning, or setting up for the baby, even though I knew we would have to leave the safe house soon after the baby's birth.

The thought of leaving our little home filled me with dread. Alone in the middle of nowhere, it was hard to remember how terrible the rest of Veon actually was. The temptation was enormous for me to just forget about all the problems that existed out there. But I knew we couldn't do that. I wanted a world where my child would be safe. And that wouldn't happen without us, that much was clear based on the news that continued to stream in every day.

"Owwww," I all of a sudden hissed as a contraction hit me. I'd been having Braxton Hicks the last two months, but over the last week, the contractions had been getting heavier and heavier. Corran hadn't needed to tell me that it was almost time for the baby to get here. My body was making that part clear.

I'd just caught my breath when another contraction hit. There'd barely been a couple of minutes between the two of them, and my heart began to race.

Was today going to be the day?

Panic coursed through me. *I couldn't be a mom, especially a mom of an alien baby. I didn't know the first thing about motherhood. I was going to mess everything up. And how was I going to keep my baby safe with everything going on? Its parents were the most wanted beings on Veon.*

"Fuckkkk," I all but screamed as another contraction hit, cutting off the doomsday road I'd been heading down.

Derrial popped his head into the room, a concerned look on his face.

"Everything alright, love?"

"Nooo. Everything is not alright. I think the baby is coming," I wailed as I struggled to get off my nest. I had to pee and eat and make sure the baby's room was ready.

"The baby's coming...today?" Derrial asked in a panic.

I screamed as another contraction hit me. Weren't these supposed to build in intensity? How was I possibly going to survive if they were already this bad? Corran had better have figured out the right dose of epidural to give me because....fuckkkkkk.

My knees buckled from the pain, and Derrial barely made it in time to catch me.

"I'm not ready," I sobbed.

"Let's get you back in bed, baby," he soothed. He pressed his comm. "Get in here," he barked into it before sweeping me into his arms and walking me to the bed.

He had just set me down right in front of my nest when I felt something wet and warm trickling down my leg.

We both stared at the floor in astonishment as a small puddle collected under me. "Did I just pee?" I asked in horror. I needed to go to the bathroom but...

"Your water just broke," said Corran as he rushed in. "Clean that up," he barked at Derrial before gathering me into his arms and helping me into the nest. "Bring me some towels," he ordered Thane, who'd just rushed in as well.

"Ahhhhhh," I yelled out as another contraction hit. Thane handed Corran a wet towel and a dry towel, and Corran wiped me down, helping me out of my undergarments so I was just in the comfortable nightgown type clothing that the machine had created for me earlier that morning.

"Spread your legs, I'm going to check you," he commanded me gently, and I took a deep breath before spreading my legs wide. Corran inserted a finger to check me, and I flinched from the pain. "Your cervix is still as tight as a rock," he explained. "And you're only dilated to a one. It's going to be a while yet."

"How is it hurting this bad at a one?" I sobbed as another contraction ripped through me. I knew I had an above-average pain tolerance so this wasn't about me being a wimp.

"We don't have anything to compare your symptoms to, Ella. You're the first..."

"I know I'm the first," I screamed as tears rushed down my face. I knew I was out of control...but this seriously hurt. It was like my insides were being forcibly ripped apart. "Is there anything you can give me?" I whimpered, not sure how I was going to make it.

Corran was already shaking his head though. "If I give you anything for the pain right now it could delay the labor, basically freezing you at this point which could be dangerous for you and the baby. We're going to have to wait until you're at least at five before we can do it."

Derrial had settled in beside me and was holding my hand while I cried. Thane was pacing behind Corran as he ran his hands frustratedly through his hair.

The next hours were literal hell. I'd tried to imagine what labor was like, tried to remember what people I'd talked to back on Earth had mentioned about it, but nothing could have prepared me for this. I'd been crying the entire time, unable to stop since the contractions were coming in one after the other, barely giving me a breath to recover before the next one hit.

The worst thing was, in all of that time, I had only progressed to a four.

I started to sob harder at the news, and Derrial started yelling at Corran that there had to be something they could do.

"I'm going to start the epidural. It's a little different process on Veon, but it's still a needle in your spine," he explained, and I nodded gratefully, up for anything if it could mean that there would soon be relief.

I remembered that one of my mom's friends had said she loved delivery day. She and her husband got a break from her other kids, she would get the epidural early, and then they would spend the day watching movies and reading as she progressed.

"Loving" delivery day was probably the last thing I would say at this moment. Thane had tried to put up a movie for me at one point, trying to help me take a mind off what was happening, but after I threw one of the books I'd hid in my nest at the screen when the female actress looked a little too pretty and skinny for my current pregnant self to take, we'd all quickly decided that movies weren't going to work.

Derrial helped me set up as I tried to breathe through the almost constant pain. Corran cleared off the area with the cleansing solution and then he picked up a shot looking object that seemed closer in size to a sword than any shot needle I'd seen on Earth.

"What the hell is that?" Thane asked in horror. I was right there with him, trying to decide if I really could live through the pain I was dealing with because that thing was going to slice through my spinal cord.

"I know it looks a little menacing, but you will barely feel anything after the skin numbing solution kicks in," he explained as he applied said solution with his other hand.

"There's no way that can go in me," I squeaked, and Corran moved it out of my eyesight. Thane could still see the needle from his vantage point and he looked like he was about to pass out.

"Take a deep breath," he said. "You'll be thanking me for this later."

I nodded, tears squeezing out of my eyes as I took my deep breath right after a contraction had stopped.

Sure enough, somehow I only felt a small pinch as the needle went in. Corran talked me through the whole process and within five minutes, my contractions felt like light period cramps instead of the soul-shattering contractions they'd been prior.

My whole body shook as I laid back down in my nest. The adrenaline rush from hours of extreme pain was hard to recover from and Corran frowned as he examined my vitals. "Your heart rate is a little low," he muttered as he concentrated on listening to my chest.

"How is that possible?" I whispered, feeling light-headed. "It feels like my heart is going a million miles a minute."

"How are you feeling?"

"There's barely any pain...but - " My voice broke off as my lungs seemed to close up. It was hard to breathe and I felt so freaking tired.

"Ella!" Corran yelled sharply. "Stay awake!"

"She's having a reaction to the epidural," he explained as I faintly saw him reach to unhook the device in my back from the medicine that had been flowing into it. He then grabbed another bag of fluid and attached it to my IV.

A few minutes later and the fuzziness that had built up in my head, and the pressure in my chest...they both eased, and I was able to start breathing again.

Unfortunately, with those changes came the return of my contractions.

"You're going to have to do this unmedicated, baby," Corran explained softly. "We can't risk that reaction happening again."

I cried as I nodded. There was no other choice, and screaming and protesting wasn't going to change the fact.

Pain. That's all I was conscious of for the next few hours. Hours that seemed like days. Everything was pain.

I was only faintly aware of the others' presence in the room. All of my concentration was on surviving the next contraction. I'd begun to progress, thank heavens. So I lived for the checks that would get me closer and closer to it all being over.

"It's time to push," Corran announced triumphantly and I mustered a small smile right before I almost broke Derrial's hand that I was holding as another contraction rolled through.

Corran pressed a button, and a small table suddenly rose up from the ground at the bottom of my nest. Derrial and Thane helped me scoot so that I was right up against it.

"Ok, I want you to take a deep breath and then push as hard as you can," Corran explained and I nodded hesitantly. It hit me once again that I was about to meet my baby. Everything had hurt so much that I hadn't really been able to think about it much.

Taking my deep breath, I began to push. And I pushed, and I pushed, and I pushed.

And the baby didn't budge.

"Fuck," Corran muttered as he brought up the complicated ultrasound type system to the side of my nest and held it over my stomach.

"What?" Thane asked anxiously. He hadn't stopped looking nauseous.

"The horns are preventing the baby from coming out," he said quietly. "Ella's vagina doesn't have quite the stretching capability as a Vepar mother's would to accommodate them."

"The horns?" I gasped out. "Our baby is stuck inside me because of its horns?"

Corran nodded, not making eye contact with me. They thought I was freaked out because our baby had horns, but I was actually way more freaked out over the fact that the baby was stuck inside of me because of the horns."

Corran began gathering supplies. "What are we going to do?" I groaned as another contraction hit. They were basically constant now, maybe fifteen seconds in between each one.

"I'm going to perform a cesarean," he said calmly, despite the fact that I knew Corran had never done one before.

Thane looked like he was about to pass out, and Derrial's hand was probably broken from me holding onto it so tightly.

"Is that really necessary?" I asked, knowing it was a stupid question.

Corran stopped what he was doing and knelt next to me. "Ella, you are doing so well. And I know it hurts, and I know you're scared. But we're about to meet our little baby. And then all of this is just going to be a faint memory. Because it's going to be here." There were little tears gathering in his eyes at his little speech. Hell, everyone had tears in their eyes at his little speech.

I nodded determinedly, until he brought another bag to my IV. "What's that for?"

"I can't just use an epidural for this because of your reaction. I'm going to have to knock you out. But luckily, our drugs are much more concise than you're used to and I'll be able to wake you up as soon as you're sewn up."

I cringed at the thought of being knocked out with my insides splayed out, but a quick glance at the heart rate monitor showed that the baby's heart rate was showing it was starting to be stressed.

No sooner had I said, "Ok," then everything faded to black.

The sound of a baby crying was the first thing I heard when I woke up. It took me a minute to open my eyes, but when I did, everything hit me at once. That was *my* baby I was hearing.

"You did so good, love. She's the most beautiful thing I've ever seen," whispered Corran as he handed her to me.

A girl. We had a girl. I started sobbing as I examined our baby who was wriggling in my arms. She'd stopped crying as soon as he laid her in my arms. She had dark hair, so dark it was almost black, and almond-shaped, hazel eyes that looked the same shade as Corran's. I knew that human babies were usually all born with blue eyes, but Vepar babies must come out with their eye color already in place because the proof was right in front of me. She had bow-shaped lips and a tiny nose. And...she had two tiny white horns.

She was the most beautiful thing I'd ever seen and I immediately burst into tears as I looked at her.

Looking up at my men who were all gathered around me, they were all openly sobbing as well. My heart felt like it had expanded in size by a million somehow. I'd never known I could love something so much, so immediately.

She let out a little cry that sounded like a dove cooing and we all laughed through our tears. "She's probably hungry, my darling," said Corran in a choked voice, and he helped me take off my top so that I could bring her to my breast.

To my surprise, she immediately latched and started sucking, her eyes closed and her tiny fist clenched on top of my breast.

I had been wrong before at feeling like home. We'd always been missing something before this. Only now, with her, were we truly complete, were we truly home.

"I'm so proud of you, my pet," Thane cooed and pressed a kiss against my forehead.

I smiled tremulously at him.

"Thank you for giving us a family," added Derrial, blinking furiously as he tried to control his emotions.

"I love you," added Corran.

Despite all the pain and agony, this was the best day of my life.

We'd been parents for a few days now. We'd all instantly agreed that we should name her Rory, short for Aurora, after my mother's name. We were all exhausted, but the happiest we'd ever been. I spent every second in my nest with Rory, while the guys took turns in the room with me while the others would work on the antidote and keep up to date with what was going on around us.

Despite my fears that I wouldn't be able to be a mother, I realized quickly that most of being a mother was just loving your baby. She kept us awake most of the night, and even with the fancy Vepar diaper technology, I was pooped on at least twice a day. And sometimes I cried when she refused to latch. And I still just loved every second of it.

Vepar babies advanced faster than human babies, but because Rory was half-human, she developed at a speed more advanced than a human, but less advanced than a Vepar baby. It was fascinating to see her change almost every day though. She smiled constantly. And because of how advanced she was, you couldn't even say it was gas. Everything the guys did was funny to her, but she was a momma's girl through and through. She liked to be holding on to some part of me at all times and her upper lip would quiver if I left the room for even a minute. I didn't mind it one bit. She laughed at two weeks old, and I wanted to bottle up the sound and keep it forever. It sounded like a tinkling of bells, very different from a human laugh. And it was the most amazing thing I'd ever heard.

We were in heaven.

A couple of weeks passed like this and as much as I tried to block it out, I knew that we had stayed away for about as long as we possibly could. The guys were getting more and more concerned with what was going on, and with what the reports were saying, it wouldn't be too long anyway before the trouble out there would find our safe house.

We had no other choice.

Our babymoon was about to end.

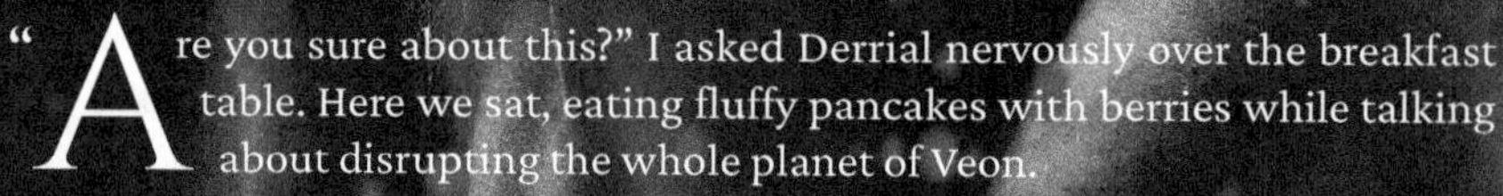

14

"Are you sure about this?" I asked Derrial nervously over the breakfast table. Here we sat, eating fluffy pancakes with berries while talking about disrupting the whole planet of Veon.

Derrial nodded and took a mouthful of pancakes, as if we casually talked about what we'd do with our day. "We're good to go. The serum is ready to be dispatched worldwide to everyone needing it. And the only way to get distribution is to let everyone know what the council has been up to. To show them evidence of their corruption. To cause distrust so that when we offer our serum, more people will be inclined to accept it and see the truth."

"We'll need to overpower the council," Thane added, supporting this decision. "It's the only way to derail their plans and save everyone."

I pushed my plate away, my stomach feeling queasy. "So, you're going head to head with them?"

"Not quite," Corran answered. "If our plan works, we won't be alone in this battle."

I shifted in my seat uncomfortably. "I'm just scared this will backfire. The council will never go down without a fight."

"And that's what we are counting on. No one will stand up to them alone, but as a collective, people will stand up and fight," Thane explained.

Derrial and Corran nodded.

All three looked at me and smiled like I had nothing in the world to worry about.

I bit on my lower lip, thinking it over, praying this plan worked. "I know you're right. It's just me being worried. We are a family now, and we have Rory to care for."

Derrial leaned closer and took my hand in his. "This is why we have to stand up to them. They'll continue to walk over anyone in their way and they'll continue to destroy our people. If we don't fight, what sort of future will we be leaving for our precious little girl?"

My heart clenched at hearing the ache in his voice, at what was at stake. I looked at each of my three husbands, loving each one of them with everything I had. If it wasn't for them, I never would have found this new future. And that was a future worth saving beyond anything.

"Okay, we do this, but we'll just be super vigilant," I said, knowing even as I said it what I was asking for wouldn't be possible.

Derrial got up. He was the leader, the Vepar with the strongest political position in Veon besides the council. The Vepar knew him and the hard work he'd done for their kind over the last hundred years.

"It's time," Derrial said strongly as he got to his feet. "Thane, prepare the media channels to ensure we tap into every single airwave. Corran, you're with me during the talk." Derrial looked over at me. "This will work, pet. You will see."

I loved his confidence and believed in him. Everyone had left the table to get ready so I checked on my angel who was still fast asleep in her crib, then had a shower and dressed. Next, I packed a bag with baby clothes, formula, diapers, and everything else our parents would need to care for Rory. She would be safe with them while this went down. I couldn't have her with us in case something went wrong. That wasn't a risk I was willing to take.

My stomach churned with worry about what we were about to do, but if we did nothing, then what? We kept running while the planet of Veon became a wasteland?

The sound of voices drew my attention, and I slipped out of the nursery and moved quickly down the long hall with white halls and to the far room where the three of them had started the broadcast.

Pressing my back into the wall just outside the room where Derrial and Corran were broadcasting themselves, I remained silent and listened as Derrial finished introducing themselves.

"Veon is devastated. Our futures are in jeopardy, and the infected fill our streets. The council is doing nothing to help because they don't know how. They are responsible for the virus that has taken your loved ones, yet they do nothing to help you. For years, our council has been experimenting for a way to aid our women in becoming fertile again. But they haven't been experimenting just on humans. They also have been experimenting with Vepar. They've treated our kind like animals." There was a pause, and I heard a small electronic click.

"The images you are seeing on your screen," Derrial continued, "are the test papers of the subjects from the council's laboratories. It clearly shows they are Vepar and being experimented on. These are the same tests that resulted in the virus outbreak that now plagues our lives and devastates our planet."

Derrial swallowed loudly. "This is our chance to stop the council's destruction and bring back the Veon we once loved. They must be stopped. I invite you to join us to finally make the council responsible for their actions. The coordinates flashing across your screen is where we will be meeting today at 16:00 hours. Show up and show your support to save our planet before it is too late."

A loud click sounded of the broadcast ending, and both of them sighed heavily.

"Fuck!" Derrial announced. "That has to work. Did that broadcast reach all the various council airwave channels too?"

"It sure fucking did. And I'm sending them a copy just to ensure they don't miss it. We need them there."

"We're finally doing this," Corran added, and they cheered. But I sensed the fear in their voices. This was a massive gamble and could just as easily turn against us. So having as many supporters turn up as possible was the key to success.

I stepped into the doorway, unsure how to feel. Scared. Excited. Worried. Still, I smiled. "I may need another quick rundown on using a huge laser gun."

Thane smiled. "Kitten, I've got just the weapon for you. It will fit perfectly in your tiny hand, but will blast someone's face off."

"Now you're talking." After everything we'd been through, I was ready to eradicate the council and help Veon rebuild itself into a strong world where people didn't live in fear. I was tired of being scared, and I wanted a bright future for Rory.

"First, we need to drop off our angel at our parents," I added. "Then I'm ready to kick ass."

"That's my girl." Derrial stretched out his arm toward me, and I accepted his hand. He drew me closer and my husbands all closed in around me. We huddled closer, and I bathed in their warmth and love. Their presence alone encouraged me to stand tall and not back down. We were in this together, and it reminded me why I fought so hard to survive. When I left Earth, I thought I lost everything, but I'd been wrong. That was the moment that I finally started to find myself.

"Today is going to go down in history," Corran said. "It has to be the start of a new beginning. Otherwise, we'll all need to move to a planet as far away as possible because if the council survives today, they'll hunt us down across the universe."

On that foreboding note, we separated to complete our tasks.

"Do you think anyone will come?" I asked Thane who stood next me in Farilion Park. These were the coordinates they blasted over the airwaves for a final stand off between the Vepar and the council, to finally put an end to their tyranny.

"I pray to the universe they do," Thane responded. " I sent out requests to all our allies and friends. They should also join our forces."

Except, right now the forces were four of us and an empty field. Had the broadcast worked? I couldn't stop shaking from the trepidation. What if the people didn't believe us despite the evidence Derrial showed them? What if they preferred better the devil they knew, then actually standing up and fighting back?

The longer we waited, the more the trepidation dug its claws into my chest. I felt vulnerable standing at one end of the field. Our ship was shielded in the trees not far in case things went to hell and we needed a fast escape. But I hoped it didn't come to that.

The laser gun at my side felt heavy on my belt. The wind blew past, rustling the brightly colored leaves of the nearby trees.

We waited.

The place remained empty of allies.

Empty of our supporters.

Empty of the enemy.

I turned to Derrial when movement across the field caught our attention. I jerked around, my heart in my throat, my fingers grazing the hilt of my gun on my belt.

A river of soldiers suddenly poured out from behind the trees, streaming across the field in front of us. All I saw were their black uniforms, the once brightly colored greens and purples swallowed by darkness.

Any hope I'd held onto now dissolved around my feet. My three Vepar closed in to my sides, weapons raised, except we were out-matched. I knew that. They had to know that.

Fear gripped my chest and squeezed the life out of me.

Breaths caught in my lungs, and a scream rose through me. The council had arrived with the full power of their army against just us four. There was no sign of the council members, but they were near, hiding like gutless rats on their ships.

There were dozens of soldiers...hundreds. More coming out from the tree lines ahead of us.

I gripped my gun, and my muscles tensed.

We'd made a mistake... a terrible mistake. My arms trembled as terror flashed over my thoughts. We had to turn and run.

And all I could think about was never seeing my little angel ever again.

15

I embraced every sliver of emotion I felt - all the fear and rage - taking it into me as I readied for the unknown.

The four of us faced a monstrous council army. There was no way we could win, no matter how many weapons we had. Not alone. Our gathering in this park was meant to be more about a power play, to show the council the people of Veon had had enough, all under the watchful eye of the media, but not even they turned up.

This was supposed to be an event for everyone to finally see the council's devious actions.

What it was, was a failure.

No one had come but the enemy. How could no one else have come? Did no one care about their futures, about their leaders' deceitfulness, about the virus wreaking havoc across Veon?

"We need to get out of here." My words trembled as my feet slid backward. I gripped Derrial's arm. "Please, this is suicide."

"Derrial," a deep male voice called out over the field, seeming to come from the sky itself, almost god-like. Except it belonged to one of the councilmen I disliked the most. His voice was deep and nasally.

It was Chloped. He'd been the one who ordered blood tests on me when I first arrived on Veon and stared at me like I was a science experiment. Just thinking of him had my skin crawling. I loathed him then and I detested him even more now.

"You started a war today," Chloped growled, his voice screaming over the open field as if the place was hooked up with speakers.

"A war you will regret," another council member added, while another two voices in the background mumbled something.

Derrial stood tall, his chin high, never showing fear. And I admired him so much at that moment. The odds were against us, but he didn't panic or lose his head.

There were four councilmen ruling over Veon. I pictured all four of the weasels hiding in their ship nearby, watching us, too scared to show their faces.

My blood boiled.

Derrial lifted the comm on his wrist to his mouth, and snarled, "You killed so many innocents." His voice roared as though he spoke through a microphone. "You unleashed the virus killing our people and now you hide from the mess you've made." Derrial turned his attention to the army a good fifty feet away, yelling, "How can you support a council who is killing your families? Who is destroying our planet?"

The river of soldiers never moved or responded. They were trained to be nothing more than mindless fighting machines.

I swallowed hard, and sweat dripped down my spine. They were too far away for me to see the reactions on their faces or if they even cared. Were they so far gone that they did as they were told, not even concerned with the repercussions?

"Enough! Do not spread such lies." Chloped hollered. "You have once last chance, Derrial, Corran, and Thane. Admit to being instrumental to the spread of the infection on Veon and I will let your human survive. It's too late for you three."

"No," I gasped. "He'll kill me and our..." I couldn't bring myself to even say her name in case anyone heard us. I didn't want anyone to know we had a baby girl... me, a human birthing a Vepar baby. My baby girl and I would be hunted for eternity. I wanted to help the Vepar be able to bear children again, but not at the expense of my own life and future. Which was why councilmen like Chloped could never be left in charge.

Thane's arms wrapped around me, standing behind me and holding me against his chest in a protective manner.

"You have no other choice," Chloped reprimanded. "Do the right thing for once."

I seethed at his arrogance. Thane breathed heavily behind me, Corran's face twisted into pure fury, while Derrial held himself composed. But I knew him well enough to know he was a bomb on the inside ready to go off.

An icy wind shrieked past.

Derrial glanced over his shoulder at me, the blood drained from his face. He'd run out of options. With no backup, our hope disintegrated. No one else would know the truth of what really happened, what the council covered, and we... we'd be a distant memory. My three husbands would be murdered. I'd be chained in a laboratory and tested on... and what about Rory? How long before they found out about her? What would they do with the first half-human, half-Vepar child?

I couldn't think about that because already my chest splintered at the thought.

Stepping out of Thane's arms and closer to Derrial, I took his hand in mine and held his gaze. "We have to run for our lives. We need something to distract them to give us a chance to escape."

The sorrow on his face speared in my heart. "Listen baby," I said. "I think the council did something to stop everyone from coming to find us. That's the only explanation I can think of for why they wouldn't come. So we need to escape and find another way to let the world know. Otherwise, the council wins here today, and they'll lie through their teeth. We'll be blamed for everything."

"I know," he muttered, his gaze lowered for a moment before turning to Thane. "Do you still have that trial drone you were testing for weapon use?"

"Yeah, but it's back at home. I'll activate it now to come here for the perfect distraction. But we need close to ten minutes before it arrives."

Corran stepped forward. "Let me try." With the comm to his mouth, he lifted his chin and addressed the council, wherever they were hiding.

"Councilman, Chloped," he began. "We all came into this with one mission. To help Vepar females fall pregnant again. What if I said I found the solution that could help millions of Vepars? Release the rest of them and you can take me. I'll give you everything you need and so much more."

My heart dropped through me. I reached out to grab him. "No, you can't do--"

Derrial snatched my arm and drew me back against him, his hand over mine. "Shhh. He knows what he's doing. We need the time."

Silence followed, while Thane frantically tapped the comm on his watch, calling his drone. In truth, I was worried it wouldn't get here in time.

"I don't negotiate with terrorists, you should know this, Corran," the councilman's voice boomed.

"After how much our people have gone through, I would have thought someone like yourself would embrace such a discovery."

No response for a long while, and my body trembled. "What if they just shot at us?" My muscles tensed as I stiffened. Derrial held me close to him, an arm around my waist.

"Chloped needs you alive, and he'll never accept Corran's offer. He'll take you both, but he won't openly shoot us in case you get injured."

That small bit of information made me stand up strong in front of my men as their shield.

"I want the human! The rest can die!" Chloped growled.

The soldiers lunged toward us, and just as Derrial said, they didn't shoot when I stayed near my men.

My blood ran cold, and a strangled cry escaped past my lips.

And just like that, my world fell into absolute chaos. This was what everything had come down to.

Death.

Derrial's hand locked with mine tightly. The four of us violently snapped around and ran toward our hidden ship to our right to the side of the cluster of trees. Time felt like it stood still as terror squeezed my heart.

Adrenaline punched my gut, driving me faster. I no longer felt my limbs or any pain. Just the pure need to escape. My brain felt numb. All I could think about was my angel and never seeing her again. Having her grow up without her mom.

A blur of shadows slid out from the woodland ahead of us. A heartbeat later, and more soldiers emerged, coming right for us. Blocking our path.

We halted, and I frantically scanned for another escape. My heart thumped so hard, my knees were so weak from the terror gripping me.

Fear twisted my gut. I cried out with pure shock, with the dread of what was coming for us. I couldn't let them take my men from me. I couldn't. Tears drenched my cheeks as I shoved forward and in front of my husbands so they couldn't dare try to take a shot at them.

Derrial grabbed my wrist and we were running, away from both swarms of soldiers. I looked over to Corran, his eyes darkening and bathing with fear. Thane was the same...we all were because it was clear we were trapped. How far could we really get?

I couldn't stop crying as I pictured losing everything. I finally found my own family, gained what I thought I lost, and now... now these monsters were going to rip it away from me.

Thundering footfalls pounded behind us, closing in fast.

We ran but we weren't fast enough. When my heel caught on a rock, I slipped out of Derrial's grasp and fell to my knees.

Panic wrapped around me. I jumped to my feet quickly as the army closed in.

I screamed out of pure terror. Everything was too late. We'd lost... we'd fucking lost and I wanted to just cry as my insides shredded to nothing.

Thane had his arms on my waist, dragging me backward, and I spun and ran with them.

My body wracked with sorrow, and desperation clung to my ribs.

A sudden explosion of voices came from behind us, booming like a thunderous storm.

I twisted my head back. The skies behind us were dotted with cruisers, dozens and dozens of them all descending onto the field.

My heart beat too fast, my brain too terrified to make sense of what was going on.

An explosion of Vepar appeared from all around us... rushing toward us with weapons raised. But the closer I looked, the more I realized these weren't soldiers. They were civilians, rushing toward the army, not us. They shouted and roared with fury as they turned vicious on the soldiers.

Those chasing us forgot us and soon turned to those attacking them.

We stopped and I gasped for air as I stared out at the sheer mass of Vepar coming to our rescue. They were easily ten Vepar to every soldier.

"They've come!" Thane cheered. "Everyone has arrived."

I hiccuped a cry because somehow the universe brought in the cavalry, saving us by the skin of our teeth.

In front of us, the once calm field was now a war zone. The Vepar were angry, and I didn't blame them. They'd been lied to, cheated, mistreated and infected. And now they fought, finally able to express their rage with understanding about what really happened.

Soldiers ran in every direction, knowing when they'd been outnumbered. Others fought but were quickly taken down by so many Vepar males mostly, fighting ferociously. Punching and ripping apart any soldier who fought back.

Thane held me tight, Corran and Derrial on either side of me. I suspected they would have loved to join the battle, but they also didn't want to leave my side. And I didn't want them to leave either.

"We need to track down the council," Derrial finally said.

Without a word, we all darted past the chaos, the yelling men, the pleading soldiers on their knees.

But we ran through the mass fight, following Derrial as if he sensed exactly where the Councilmen hid.

I didn't hesitate or question him. Or any of my men. They were spectacular, intelligent, and I trusted their instincts.

Just as we burst out of the battle, a silver oval shaped cruiser ascended out of the pocket of trees up ahead.

"Fuck!" Derrial raised his laser and shot, but they were too high up now. He growled. "Sonofabitch! No fucking way are they surviving."

A small beep sounded on Thane's comm. He looked down at it and smirked. A few taps and he lifted his gaze.

"They aren't going anywhere," Thane happily explained. "Now, watch for the fireworks."

We all looked up as a black drone appeared, a fraction of the ship's size. That little thing zipped across the sky and rushed up right for the silver cruiser.

The drone slammed into the ship, exploding on impact. And in that thread of a heartbeat, the whole cruiser burst into flames, blasting apart in the sky.

Boom! The sound deafened me at first. The flames blotting out the sun, smoke and dust rising from the broken bits of ship that remained dropping out of the sky.

I couldn't help but cheer. I never thought I'd ever celebrate the death of someone… but these four nasty pieces of work didn't deserve life after all the ones they stole.

While the world would soon find out what happened here today, I couldn't believe how close we came to losing everything. How lucky the planet now was to be rid of four monsters who led Veon to ruins.

Derrial turned to me and lifted me into his arms, then kissed me. He smiled brightly. Corran and Thane stood closer, holding onto me. Around us the battle ended. Soldiers fell to their knees, accepting defeat. There was so much to fix and get right.

But those things could wait a little longer. I met my husbands' gazes as a silent heartfelt moment passed between us. A reminder of the lifelong commitment we made to each other on our marriage day that we'd be together for life.

"I love you Derrial. I love you Corran. I love you Thane. I have no idea how we got so lucky and survived today. But let's make a promise to never try to save the world again?"

Thane burst out laughing first, followed by the others. I couldn't help it and joined in as their smiles and cheers were contagious.

I was ready for a new start in our lives together. A new beginning on Veon.

16

Three Months Later...

The aftermath of war was never the happily ever after that people thought it would be. It was wishful thinking to believe that everything could instantly go back to normal. Despite the serum and the fact that the council was gone, the council's actions had left a dark mark on the Vepar people that would take a very long time to disappear. Many of the infected had died in the initial months before we'd discovered the cure, and all those that we had saved carried memories that would never go away. I had hoped that they wouldn't be able to remember their actions after the serum was administered. But of course, that would be too easy. Counseling centers had been built all over the world to help out the previously infected to come to terms that the raging monsters they'd become weren't really them.

Veon as a whole needed to be almost completely rebuilt.

There was no government in place, but as my husbands were the de facto leaders of the rebellion, most of the responsibility fell on their shoulders to help try and put it back together. They left first thing in the morning and came home late at night, exhausted and overwhelmed. I tried to help where I could, but I still had a newborn to take care of, so I could only go with them for a few hours each day when their parents would watch Rory. I spent most of my time trying to help the women who were still being retrieved from the secret camps that the council had set up to perform experiments and the Khonsu camps where women were also imprisoned. There was not a moment of the day that I wasn't tired, but after a lifetime of not really knowing what my purpose was in life, it felt like maybe I'd finally figured it out.

The Khonsu remained a threat, they always would be, but without the resources that the council had been sending to them - something that set off world-wide horror throughout the Vepar people after it was discovered - the Khonsu would never be the threat that they were.

I'd decided to stay home today, needing a break due to the sleep regression that Rory was currently going through. I was rocking her in her bedroom when Derrial popped his head in, immediately gravitating towards Rory.

"Can I finish up?" he asked eagerly, already reaching for her. I nodded, giving him a soft kiss and leaving him to put Rory to bed.

Thane and Corran walked in the front entrance just as I was grabbing a glass of water.

"Pet," Thane murmured exhaustedly, scooping me up in his arms and spinning me around as he kissed me fervently. Corran grumpily pulled me out of Thane's arms and leveled me with another kiss that had me seeing stars.

What we felt for each other only seemed to intensify each day, and it was hard to believe that I was actually loved so completely by three different men...aliens.

After Corran set me down, they both eagerly got dinner from the kitchen and then settled down at the table to eat. I noticed right away that they were quieter than usual. Derrial was eating as well now, and although they were tired every night, they still always kept up conversation with me. Tonight, there was only pensive silence.

"What's going on?" I finally asked. And it was like the three of them took a collective breath.

"Today was an interesting day," Derrial finally answered. "The three of us were asked to take over the council and become the leaders for our people."

I wasn't that shocked. They'd basically been in that role since the council fell. They all seemed very weird about it though.

"What aren't you telling me?" I pushed.

"That would mean that we would have to stay on Veon," said Corran carefully. And I nodded with a frown. I wouldn't have expected anything else.

"We want you to make the decision," added Thane. "If you want to go home, we'll say no."

And there it was. The issue that was obviously tearing them up. If they were appointed as the head of Vepar society, then my dreams of returning to Earth...they would remain just that...nothing but dreams.

Except...I couldn't remember the last time I'd thought of Earth. I tried to look inside of me for that longing that I'd constantly felt in the beginning when I'd come to Veon.

And I couldn't find it.

How could that be?

It was like it didn't matter anymore.

It took me a few minutes. A few minutes where I knew the guys were waiting desperately for my response. In the beginning, I would never have believed them that they would actually give up on ruling to return to Earth with me. But now...I didn't doubt it for a second.

And it just reinforced it for me that I didn't need to travel back to Earth to be home. They were my home. Rory was my home.

I was home.

"I don't want to be anywhere but here with you," I finally said truthfully.

"You don't need to lie to us," said Derrial exasperatedly, and I went up to him and grabbed his face with both hands.

"I've learned that home is a person...and not a place. I've told you this before, and I'll tell you again. I would go anywhere if it was with the three of you and Rory. And I would be happy there. My love for you has no regrets."

There was a long silence, and then the three of them were on me at once. My happy cries filled the air as the three of them let me know just how happy my words had made them.

Corran
Eight Months Later...

It didn't matter, I told myself, even as I performed the test. Rory was ours no matter who her father was. And that really was how I felt, how we all felt. But as she grew more every day...there were just so many things about her that I recognized that I was beginning to think wasn't just a coincidence. Because they were all things that I did.

Like the fact that she was already talking in almost complete sentences despite being just a little over one years old. And the fact that she could already recognize and identify numbers and words. Her IQ was off the charts, as mine had been. And although she had the sweetness and personality of her mother, the rest of her, including her eyes...they seemed to be just like me.

And that's why I was here, even though the others would kill me, performing this paternity test.

I placed the lock of Rory's hair into the machine and waited with bated breath. The machine made a small *whirring* sound as it analyzed the data.

And then it was done. I pressed the button that would show me the results with trembling hands. I was really regretting doing this, because there was no way I could be her biological father.

But Melba Cryon had been the scientist that did the transfer. We had always gotten along, and I'd frankly been shocked to find out that she was working with the council. I'd always considered her a friend before that.

I shook my head. No, it was better to keep low expectations. It didn't matter. This was just for science's sake that I was even doing this.

And then I looked at the results.

I sunk to my knees, something I'd never done before Ella had come into my life. And now it was something I found myself doing often.

I was Rory's biological father. Melba had used *my* sample that I'd submitted.

My love didn't feel any different, I felt more complete somehow. Rory had been mine in all the ways that counted, but now I could say that she was my blood as well.

I had originally decided I wasn't going to mention it either way. Ella would be disappointed in me that I even tested it, but I think she would understand. She knew the way my mind worked, the questions that always burned inside. But now that I knew the results, I was burning to tell the others.

I flew my craft to our home. Ella had loved our safehouse by the Cardian sea. She'd loved looking out and seeing the colorful forest and the lavender sea right outside of our door. We'd expanded it, making it an actual home instead of a temporary safehouse and now it was a strange mix of an Earth home and a Vepar home. But then again, maybe it wasn't so strange. We were a mix of Earth and Vepar, after all.

I heard giggling as I walked in the door, and I immediately headed to the living room area where I knew my family was gathered. If we were home, we were all together, always.

Rory was riding around on Thane's shoulders, giggling wildly, as he galloped around the living room floor like he was that Earth creature, a horse I think they called it. I snorted at watching the fierce Thane, former captain of all of Veon's special forces, pretending to be a horse of all things. Derrial was wrapped around Ella on the couch. He was whispering in her ear, I'm sure trying to convince her to sneak off with him while Thane kept Rory busy. She was laughing and pretending to say no, but I knew that if I wasn't coming in with my news, he would have her in the bedroom sooner rather than later. We couldn't keep our hands off of her.

She held a gentle beauty that only grew more attractive to me every day. The Vepar people had unanimously called for her to be the first human placed on the Veon Council, and she was now overseeing Veon-Earth relations. She of course immediately made substantive changes to the way the Vepar treated her planet, namely that we weren't in charge anymore. We were working together. And there were no women being kidnapped any longer for fertility experiments. She had unwittingly been the factor for changing the fate of her world. And I knew that she would never recognize how truly remarkable she was.

Ella's face lit up when she saw me, and Rory struggled to jump off Thane's back to toddle towards me. Her brain was far ahead of her age, but things like walking were still about average for others her age. Similar to how I'd been.

"Dad!" she screeched, and I picked her up and swung her around, savoring the sound of her little laugh. She yawned just then, signaling it was time for a nap.

"I'll go put her down and be right back," I told Ella, Thane, and Derrial. Ella blew Rory a kiss and then gave her own giggle when Thane took advantage of the empty spot on the other side of her.

"I love you, Daddy," Rory cooed as I laid her down. "When I get up from my nap, can we go over prime numbers again?"

I laughed, throwing my head back. I had never laughed before Ella had come in my life. Now with her and Rory, I found myself doing it all the time.

"We'll do prime numbers, and I'll teach you all about what happens when a black hole swallows a star."

Her eyes lit up, and she snuggled into her blankets, eager to go to sleep so she could wake up again. She was a little ball of energy. And all mine.

I left her room and walked to the living room, where my family had not so mysteriously disappeared from. Smirking, I walked to the bedroom where I knew Thane and Derrial would have dragged Ella to take advantage of Rory's nap. It's what I would have done.

Ella was already half undressed when I walked in. Derrial and Thane were eying her like they were going to eat her.

"I have some news," I said carefully. Ella sat up and looked at me.

"What is it?" she asked nervously.

"I did a paternity test," I blurted out.

"You did what?" gasped Ella, her face filled with hurt. "I thought you said it didn't matter?" Thane and Derrial looked like they wanted to punch me.

"It doesn't...it didn't. But surely you've seen things about Rory that have made you wonder?" I hurriedly explained.

Ella hesitated, and I could see that she'd had the same thoughts as I did. She hadn't known me as a child obviously, but Rory's thirst for knowledge and her gold-hazel eyes couldn't be missed.

"What did it say?" asked Derrial carefully.

"I'm her biological father," I told them, unable to keep the smile from beaming out of my face.

"What!" the others exclaimed at once. "Melba must have used my sample for the implantation. Not sure how she could have done it accidentally, so it must have been her way of trying to apologize for what the council was making her do."

Ella was softly crying, and I knelt down in front of her. "Why are you crying? This should be happy news," I whispered to her softly.

"I just don't know how I ended up getting everything I wanted, when I didn't even know how badly I did want it," she said.

And my grin grew even wider.

"Lucky bastard," hissed Thane, clearly jealous. He pulled her down to the bed and tore off his shirt.

"What are you doing?" Ella asked through her happy tears.

"Trying to make a baby, of course," he smirked at her.

"But we already know we can't do this the natural way," commented Ella, and Thane's smirk only spread.

"But we can certainly try our hardest," he told her as Derrial came up beside them.

"I'm in," added Derrial, stripping off his shirt.

I had a feeling that I'd be having to get the lab ready sooner rather than later for another transfer.

"Are you coming?" asked Ella throatily as Derrial kissed his way down her neck while Thane finished undressing her.

"Always," I said as I walked toward them, beginning to strip as well.

We couldn't have babies the natural way, but I would always be up for trying.

Any other thoughts soon disappeared as the three of us took turns with our mate. Our Ella. Our everything.

Three Years Later...

I was exhausted as Corran laid the little bundle in my arms. Caspian let out a little growl that had the four of us in the room laughing. He was definitely Thane's child. After Corran's announcement, Derrial and Thane had quickly gotten to work convincing me to do a few more transfers so they could have biological children with me as well. Derrial's sperm had proved to be of the superhero status, and I'd ended up with identical twin boys during the transfer. It was the first set of twins in Veon history, and Derrial was as proud as could be. Dalton and Titus were energetic, balls of fire that could only be tamed by their brilliant older sister.

I knew I'd been missing something however, and so when Thane had asked for it to be his turn, I hadn't argued. Now, with Caspian in my arms, I knew we were complete.

"Give me an hour, and then we can let our families in," I told the guys, who all looked like they were in heaven right now as they watched me hold Caspian.

"Lela is going to go crazy when she sees him," said Derrial with a laugh, commenting on my dad's new Vepar wife, who happened to be in love with my kids like they were her own. Everyone had been shocked when Lela and Dad had fallen in love. I wasn't sure that he would ever find love again after losing my mom. But Lela had fallen head over heels for my dad, despite the fact that he was a human. She had lost her husband during the first few weeks of the virus outbreak, and she and my dad had been able to grieve together. And then fall in love.

I was so happy for both of them.

"They all will," I said softly, stroking Caspian's soft little cheek.

"I'm going to let the rest of our babies in to see their new brother," said Thane, striding towards the door.

A minute later, our three children were rushing into the room, eager to see the new addition. It was exhausting having three kids under four, but every second was worth it.

As I looked around the room at my little happily ever after, I was reminded once again how far I'd come from that lonely girl, just trying to get by on Earth.

I'd somehow found a place to belong.

I'd finally found my home.

ABOUT C.R. JANE

A Texas girl living in Utah now, I'm a wife, mother, lawyer, and now author. My stories have been floating around in my head for years, and it has been a relief to finally get them down on paper. I'm a huge Dallas Cowboys fan and I primarily listen to Beyonce and Taylor Swift...don't lie and say you don't too.

My love of reading started probably when I was three and with a faster than normal ability to read, I've devoured hundreds of thousands of books in my life. It only made sense that I would start to create my own worlds since I was always getting lost in others'.

I like heroines who have to grow in order to become badasses, happy endings, and swoon-worthy, devoted, (and hot) male characters. If this sounds like you, I'm pretty sure we'll be friends.

I'm so glad to have you on my team...check out the links below for ways to hang out with me and more of my books you can read!

www.crjanebooks.com

About Mila Young

**Find all Mila young books at
www.milayoungbooks.com**

Best-selling author, Mila Young tackles everything with the zeal and bravado
of the fairytale heroes she grew up reading about. She slays monsters, real
and imaginary, like there's no tomorrow. By day she rocks a keyboard as a
marketing extraordinaire. At night she battles with her mighty pen-sword,
creating fairytale retellings, and sexy ever after tales. In her spare time, she
loves pretending she's a mighty warrior, walks on the beach with her dogs,
cuddling up with her cats, and devouring every fantasy tale she can get her
pinkies on.

Ready to read more and more from Mila Young?
www.subscribepage.com/milayoung

Join Mila's **Wicked Readers group** for exclusive content, latest news, and
giveaway.
www.facebook.com/groups/milayoungwickedreaders

For more information...
mila@milayoungbooks.com